Raves

"Readers will be grateful for the extensive appendixes, which include a cast list, a glossary and a brief history. While the pace can be leisurely at times, Farrell continues to shine as one of the strongest voices in the Celtic fantasy subgenre." —*Publishers Weekly*

"Farrell's smashing series outdoes itself with each new volume. This one constitutes a wonderful tale of transformations, personal for Sevei and Kayne, global for the evolving consciousness of two species in conflict. Good enough to be cast in gold." —*Booklist* (Starred Review)

"An atmosphere of ancient Celtic magic is effortlessly brought to life by Farrell's colorful and fast-paced style. In classic sword-and-sorcery style, plots and intrigue abound and danger and dark magic lurk at every turn." —*Locus*

"This spirited and vivid fantasy continues a compelling saga that will appeal to fantasy fans, particularly those who enjoy strong female heroines and Celtic lore. This book is perfect for teens who enjoy well-crafted fantasies with lots of battles and magic." —*VOYA*

Heir of Stone

The Cloudmages

**HOLDER OF LIGHTNING
MAGE OF CLOUDS
HEIR OF STONE**

Heir of Stone

The Cloudmages #3

S. L. Farrell

DAW BOOKS, INC.

DONALD A. WOLLHEIM, FOUNDER

375 Hudson Street, New York, NY 10014

ELIZABETH R. WOLLHEIM

SHEILA E. GILBERT

PUBLISHERS

http://www.dawbooks.com

First Paperback printing, January 2005
1 2 3 4 5 6 7 8 9 10

DAW TRADEMARK REGISTERED
U.S. PAT. OFF. AND FOREIGN COUNTRIES
—MARCA REGISTRADA
HECHO EN U.S.A.

PRINTED IN THE U.S.A.

This one's for Denise, alone, who is my Lámh Shábhála: my strength and my love

ACKNOWLEDGMENTS

Sonic inspiration this time around: Capercaillie still found lots of play in iTunes. A new group this time around is Gaelic Storm (also known as the "Steerage Band" from the movie *Titanic*); I've enjoyed listening to their CDs that I've picked up and also put in iTunes. I've also come across a local group called Roger Drawdy and the Firestarters who do Celtic-based rock and who are a riot to see in person. Dead Can Dance also spent some time being played, even though they're more Middle Eastern-influenced than northern Celtic—I think of them as my "Arruk" group. In honor of the passing of their harpist, I also put several of my Chieftains CDs on. And, as always, the Osna CD received a few plays, especially with Jenna's scenes. And Kate Bush, a long-time favorite, found some time in the rotation while I was writing—her evocative vocals seemed to fit.

The Celtic Way of Life by the Curriculum Development Unit (The O'Brien Press Ltd., 1998), is a small but interesting book giving an overview of daily life among the Celtic people of Ireland; it served as a quick source of inspiration for some of the aspects of life in the fictional Talamh an Ghlas.

For a more detailed and in-depth look, *The Course of Irish History* by Professors T. W. Moody and F.X. Martin (Roberts Rinehart Publishers, 1995) proved invaluable. The book is essential reading for anyone interested in a detailed and well-researched overview of the history of Ireland.

My apologies in advance to speakers of Irish Gaelic. Through the book, I have borrowed several terms from Irish and though I've made my best attempt, any mistakes in usage (and I'm sure there are many) are my own and are due to my limited understanding of the language.

I also need to express my gratitude to Sheila Gilbert: for seeing the initial story and loving it, and for invariably giving me fabulous editorial suggestions that made each of the novels thus far a better book. Sheila, thanks for making me part of the "family" at DAW.

If you're connected to the internet, my web site can be accessed from www.farrellworlds.com—you're always welcome to browse through.

CONTENTS

Part One: Betrayal

Part Two: Division

Part Three: Alliance

Part Four: Confrontation

Part Five: Decision

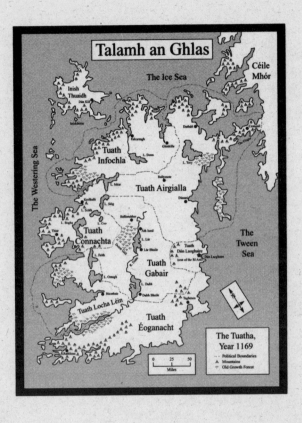

Talamh an Ghlas

Inish Thuaidh

Dún Kill

Hikkleén

The Ice Sea

Céile Mhór

Tuath Infochla

Falcarragh

L. Donn

Glenkille

Dúbhaill

L. Tory

Tuath Airgialla

Dúnmór

The Westering Sea

Mör

Keelballi

L. Síóg

L. Scáth

L. Cos

Ballintubber

Ballinasloe

Áth Iseal

L. Lár

Tuath Connachta

Thurn

L. Beiginn

Lár Bhaile

Tuath Gabair

L. Feith

L. Omagh

Bánrobán

L. Dubh

Dubh Bhaile

Tuath
Dún Laoghaire
(seat of the Rí Ard)

Dún Laoghias

The Tween Sea

Tuath Locha Léin

Tuath
Éoganacht

Taghmon

The Tuatha,
Year 1169

- - - Political Boundaries
▲ Mountains
🌳 Old Growth Forest

0   25   50
Miles

PART ONE:

BETRAYAL

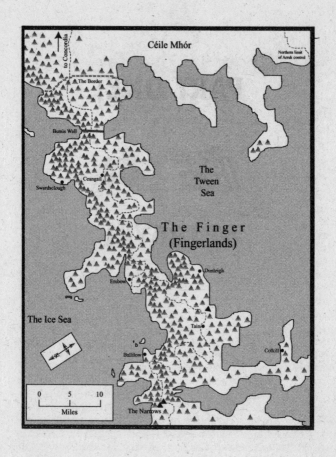

1

Crow in the Trees
(A Prologue)

THE PINES NEAREST TORIN Mallaghan sighed in the wind as if weary of holding up their branches. Underneath his boots, the ground was carpeted by a thick, soft covering of needles. The man kicked at a brown drift pooled around his toes: dry and pale on top, below the needles were wet and so dark as to be almost black. They clung to the slick, polished leather of his boots—he would have to have one of the servants clean them tonight. The wind gusted in the high branches, sending a momentary drizzle of green, fragrant needles down over his well-made, intricately-embroidered clóca. He brushed them away, looking up at the swaying branches fringing the overcast sky. A crow darted and swooped through the trees, coming to rest on a nearby branch. Torin scowled at the creature and kicked again at the well-needled ground, looking for a rock to throw at the bird, but his horse, tied to a nearby tree, nickered restlessly. Torin heard the sound of another horse approaching slowly on the road through the forest.

Torin's hand went to the jewel captured in a cage of silver and suspended from a gold-linked necklace around his neck, not to the sword in its scabbard. He caught sight of the rider; slowly, his fingers relaxed around the gem. He stepped out onto the rutted, muddy road, holding his hand up in greeting. "I was beginning to wonder whether you'd actually come today," he said. "But I should have known you would obey orders. Tell me, what news do you bring, Doyle?"

The rider pulled at the reins of his mount. He leaned forward in the saddle. His face was stained with travel, his eyes snagged in dark, puffy circles. Red hair spilled from under the hood of his clóca. "You're here alone, my Rí?" he asked with some surprise. "Is that wise?"

"How better to make sure there are no unwanted ears listening? You look . . . disappointed."

The rider shrugged underneath the clóca. "All I could think about the entire morning is reaching Lár Bhaile, where I could rest in comfort in the Order's common room, drinking a good mug of stout and sitting by the fire. We could ride there together, and talk while riding so we get there all the sooner."

Torin waited, arms crossed over his chest, and Doyle finally sighed. "All right, since it appears the stout and the fire will have to wait until you get your answer. I've spoken to the other Ríthe, as you requested; they're in agreement and they're willing to offer you their help as long as they're not seen to be directly involved." The man couldn't keep the disappointment from his voice, but then Doyle Mac Ard's emotions and ambitions had always been transparent to Torin—it was what made the man easy to manipulate.

"As long as they're not seen to be directly involved," Torin repeated, mimicking Doyle's tone. "But they're not willing to do all I asked for." Again, Torin's fingers brushed the stone at his chest. From the corner of his vision, he saw the crow flap heavily from its branch to one just above them. "I must admit I'm disappointed. To have Jenna MacEagan received in Dún Laoghaire, to have the Banrion Ard greet her as if she were one of *us* . . ."

"Even with the Mad Holder's impending arrival, the other Ríthe are still not willing to move directly against our Banrion Ard," Doyle answered. "But in truth, Rí Mallaghan, did you really expect them to do so? They're all afraid of the Banrion Ard's popularity with the tuathánach—and not just with the common folk, but even some of those among the Riocha."

Torin scoffed. "You mean that's what *you're* afraid of, Doyle."

Doyle nodded. "Aye, I am, Rí Mallaghan. That doesn't make it any different for the Ríthe. None of them want to be known as the one who brought down the beloved Healer Ard. But . . . they'll offer what help they can as long as they're not visible giving it, and they're more than willing to share in the vulture's feast once she's gone. Banrion Taafe, in particular, had a . . ." Doyle paused as if uneasy. ". . . specific recommendation," he said finally. "A person she knew, discreet and reliable though expensive. I've already hired the woman and sent her on to Dún Laoghaire, and she only awaits word from us to act. She's supposed to be excellent at what she does, and frankly, *I'd* rather that our hands aren't seen in this either. No mage from the Order of Gabair should be directly involved in the Banrion Ard's death, nor should you, my Rí. No clochs na thintrí should be used. This shouldn't look like the work of the Riocha."

Torin nodded. The crow hopped on its branch alongside the road. Its eyes stared down at them, a brighter black caught in jet, "Oh, I agree. You've done well, then. As well as I hoped for, anyway. And as for the rest of the Geraghty brood?"

"I let the Ríthe know what we had planned. Assuming all goes well in Dún Laoghaire, Rí Mac Baoill will take care of Owaine Geraghty and Kayne, and Rí Fearachan has a spy within the Mad Holder's retinue who will help us deal with Sevei and perhaps the Mad Holder herself." Doyle smiled grimly. "Though, if you've no objection, I'll deal with *her* myself." The harsh emphasis in Doyle's voice surprised Torin not at all; he smiled, hearing it. *It's that long hatred of Jenna MacEagan and his lust for what she holds that makes the man so malleable. When this is done, I may have to do something about Doyle, too. . . .*

Torin brought his attention back as Doyle sighed and continued. "As for Meriel and Owaine's other children . . ." Doyle shrugged. "They're too young at this point to be players in this; we'll only need to be certain that they're . . . *removed* so they can't be used as pawns by others."

"And Edana, back in Dún Laoghaire?"

Doyle laughed mirthlessly at that, shaking his head. "Oh, I'll say *nothing* to my dear wife about this, my Rí. Ever." Doyle let out a long breath. A squirrel chattered on the crow's branch, its tail flicking angrily, and the crow fluttered its wings. "After all these years, to think that the wait might actually be over . . ."

"You must feel pleased and vindicated, my friend."

"Honestly, Rí Mallaghan, I feel mostly tired. It's cold and I want to be somewhere familiar and comfortable. I'd like to see Edana and my children again. I'd like to see the end of this. Talamh an Ghlas needs a strong leader, now more than ever if we're to deal with the threats around us, and I'm glad you've made this decision. It's long past time to rectify the mistakes the Ríthe made in the wake of Falcarragh."

Torin's gaze moved from the man in the road to the crow. His eyes narrowed. He lifted his right hand, the white sleeve of his léine falling down to reveal a faint pattern of scars reaching to the wrist, and placed it over the jewel at his breast. He spoke a quick phrase as the crow, seeming to understand, cawed and started to fly away. The squirrel chirped and vanished behind the trunk of the tree. But as the bird's wings flapped and it started to rise, something unseen struck the bird. Black feathers exploded in a flurry at its chest as if an arrow had found its mark; the bird gave a startled *caw* and fell, landing in a dark, motionless heap at the side of the path.

"We're too close to Doire Coill to trust crows," Torin said.

Doyle nodded with a glance at the dead crow. "Then, my Rí, let us get to Lár Bhaile and see if I can find that fire in the Order's Keep . . ."

Torin unhitched his horse, swung up into the saddle, and the two rode off.

The squirrel reappeared on the branch and looked down at the crow. It scurried quickly along the branch, leaping from there to the branch of the nearest tree, and vanished among the needled crowns, hurrying in the opposite direction to that taken by the riders.

The wind stirred the pines, sending dry needles down to cover the body of the crow.

2

Arrivals

SEVEI STRODE OUT of the surf into the overcast day, the gray waves lapping around her knees as her body shifted from that of a seal back to human form. With the change, she shivered, the air suddenly cold and the water dripping as frigid as a winter rain down her bare back. She ran to the rock where she'd left her clothing and a towel. As she wrapped herself in the cloth and started to dry her matted hair, she heard someone clear his throat loudly from behind a screen of boulders green with moss and algae.

"It's about time, Bantiarna Geraghty," the voice said.

"Dillon?" Sevei said hopefully.

"If I were Dillon, then I'd have been absolutely remiss in my duties," the voice answered, and this time she heard the quaver of age, the rough gravel in the words. Sevei pressed the towel tightly to herself with a hissing intake of breath.

"Máister Kirwan?"

"This is the beach where your mam swam during her time here on Inishfeirm. If you thought I wouldn't know what you do on certain nights, then you're making the same mistake she did. And if you think I'd allow one of my male students to follow you down here, you're doomed to be forever disappointed." She heard the Máister clear his throat again with a rumble of phlegm, though he stayed discreetly behind the rocks. "I trust your swim was pleasant; my wait certainly wasn't. Damn this weather. Are you dressed yet, girl?"

"Not yet, Máister."

A sigh. "Then quickly. There's someone waiting for us up at the keep."

"Who?" Sevei asked, then the answer came to her. She saw the flash of a vision in her head, as she sometimes saw people in her family: *a slender, gray-haired woman, her face creased and folded with a life of cares and loss, and a small green stone caged in gold and silver at her breast. She sat in the chair in Máister Kirwan's office. She was drinking something from a steaming mug* . . . "Gram!" Sevei shouted gleefully. "Gram's here!"

"Aye," Máister Kirwan's voice answered gruffly. "The Banrion of Inish Thuaidh is here and she wants to see you. It's impolite to keep a Banrion waiting, not to mention that half my staff is acting as if they've never seen a Riocha before. I've been waiting here for half a stripe or more for you to show up, and every joint in my body is aching. So I'd suggest you hurry, Bantiarna Geraghty, or perhaps Siúr O'Halloran will get the notion that it's your turn for kitchen duty after supper."

"If your staff doesn't know how to act around Gram, then perhaps you should have sent one of them to fetch me and stayed there yourself to teach them, Máister," she answered teasingly. She tilted her head impishly even though she knew the man wasn't looking at her. "Or were you hoping to catch a glimpse as I came out of the water?"

Máister Kirwan sputtered once from behind the rocks, then sniffed. "You flatter yourself needlessly. Get dressed, child, or I'll mention to Jenna that you go swimming with the seals without permission," he said, though she could hear the amusement in his voice.

"And perhaps I'll mention that you refer to the Banrion in public by her given name," she answered with a laugh. She shrugged on her red léine and white clóca: the uniform of an acolyte of the Order of Inishfeirm. "I'm ready, Máister. You don't need to hide any longer."

Máister Kirwan stepped out from behind the rocks. His bald head was protected by the hood of his clóca. In the shadows cast by the rolled cloth, she could see his thin mouth pursed under the strands of a gray-white beard, but his dark eyes glittered kindly. He leaned on a staff of oak, and Snarl—one of the Clochs Mór, the great stones of magic—lay atop the white cloth of his léine. "Come on, then, Bantiarna Geraghty," he said. "Before your gram causes all the bráthairs and siúrs to go into apoplexy or my bones freeze up entirely."

He turned his back and started toward the long trail up the steep flanks of Inishfeirm to the White Keep, but Sevei suddenly gave a gasp. She stopped, putting her hand to her forehead. "What's the matter, Sevei?" Máister Kirwan asked, but she couldn't answer him through the welter of images flooding her vision.

An awful creature, scaled and horrible . . . the stench of carrion . . . her beloved twin brother Kayne's face, mouth open in mingled pain and fury . . . He was close, closer than he'd been in so long, but . . .

"It's Kayne," she answered finally. She clutched her side as if something had struck her, groaning. "Something's happening to him . . ."

The wind was cold in the Mountains of the Finger, and snow swirled down from low gray clouds shredded by the rocky peaks surrounding them. Kayne shivered in his furs, glowering as his da, Owaine Geraghty, raised his hand. The riders—now only a few hundred, though they'd ridden away a year ago with over a thousand mounted troops—halted. They were at a crossroads, the town of Ceangail nearby. "What's the matter?" Kayne asked his da, bringing his horse Gainmheach up alongside his da's dappled stallion.

"Nothing," Owaine replied. "I thought we should rest the horses for a moment."

"So close to the town, Da?"

His da's eyes narrowed at the question. For a moment Kayne thought that he wouldn't answer—Kayne knew *he* wouldn't have, if their positions had been reversed and Kayne had been the one giving the orders. He would expect his orders to be obeyed, unquestioned and immediately. But, of course, Da sighed and answered. "We have time to get there yet today, Kayne. Why risk hurting one of the animals? Besides, we should check the wagons before we start the descent into Ceangail. The road's rough and we don't want to lose one or hurt any of the injured."

Owaine's voice was calm enough, but Kayne could see

Harik MacCathaill—as Owaine's Hand the person responsible for the discipline of the gardai—scowl openly at
Kayne for daring to demand a reason. The gardai nearest
them looked carefully away. Most of them knew the tension that existed between Kayne and Owaine, a tension
which had only become worse over the last year. The campaign had begun badly before they even left Dún
Laoghaire: there was to have been an army five or perhaps
even ten thousand strong riding from the Tuatha into Céile
Mhór and ready to lend succor to the besieged lands of
Thane Aeric MagWolfagdh, but the usual squabbles and
disagreements had broken out; the Rí Connachta had been
openly irritated upon learning that Owaine would lead the
expedition. "The man's no more than a common tuathánach, no matter what titles the Mad Holder may have bestowed on him," he was reputed to have said. Not much
more than a third of the hoped-for number had finally assembled, mostly from Dún Laoghaire itself along with a
full squadron of clansfolk sent from Inish Thuaidh. Tuath
Infochla had sent nearly its full allotment, but there were
few from Tuath Airgialla, Tuath Connachta or Tuath Locha
Léin, and none at all from Tuath Gabair or Tuath Éoganacht. The only Cloch Mór among the group had been
Owaine's own, and there were few clochsmion.

The Thane of Céile Mhór had been hard-pressed to con-
ceal his severe disappointment upon their arrival. And
over the year, with few exceptions, the battles with the
Arruk had not gone well.

Some of the gardai had witnessed the heated confrontation between Kayne and Owaine after the battle at Lough
Scáthán. The memory of that day still burned in Kayne's
mind like witchfire. If *he* had been wielding Blaze, his da's
Cloch Mór, then the Arruk would have regretted their decision to attack the hill held by Thane MagWolfagdh.
Kayne would have ignored the Thane's orders to remain in
position on the flank; he would have disdained the signal
to retreat. No, *he* would have moved the gardai of the
Tuatha forward in support and driven the foul Arruk back
into the deep, shimmering waters of the lough.

There would have been no ignominious rout, had that
been done. Thane MagWolfagdh might still be alive and
sitting on the throne of Céile Mhór in Concordia and not

that incompetent, ungrateful first cousin of his. The slow advance of the Arruk might have been halted for a time. They might have been going home heroes rather than as simply a troop of weary, tired soldiers whose tour of duty was thankfully over.

Owaine, to Kayne's mind, had proved to be a cautious and too-obedient general, a careful one who loved and protected his troops too much. The cautious and obedient and careful are rarely heroes, Kayne had long ago decided. He wondered when Da had changed. After all, he'd heard many times the story of how nearsighted Owaine Geraghty had left Inishfeirm, alone and unarmed, in pursuit of the woman who would become both Kayne's mam and the Banrion Ard of all the Tuatha. At one time in his life, apparently, Owaine had been as reckless and impulsive as Kayne, uncaring of risks to himself.

No longer.

Kayne heaved a sigh as cold as the lines of snow whipping around the horses' hooves. *He's too cautious to even get out of this weather without first checking the wagons ...* "Fine," he said to his da and started to turn Gainmheach. But the wind shifted slightly, blowing for a moment from the northwest. They all smelled it in the same moment, the soldiers' weary heads lifting: woodsmoke, and with it a bitter tang they all remembered too well. "Da?" Kayne said.

Owaine shook his head. "No, son. It can't be," he insisted, but his face creased to match the landscape around them.

"It is," Kayne persisted. "You know it is. The Mother knows none of us can forget that stench."

Owaine grimaced. "Leave the wagons here," he called out. "Those who can ride, come with me." He led the gardai along the stony, ill-marked road: around a barren outcropping, up a steep slope to where they could look down through the gray-white haze of the flurries into the valley where the town of Ceangail lay. But Ceangail was obscured behind a screen of black smoke.

Several buildings within the walls of Ceangail burned.

Riding next to his da, Kayne could see the corded muscles on Owaine's neck, the flare of color on his cheeks, and the narrowing of his dark eyes. Owaine rose up in his stirrups, glaring down into the steep-sided valley. The figures they saw besieging the walls were all too familiar, as were the cries that echoed from the green-wrapped slopes around them.

Arruk. Here in Talamh an Ghlas. Here in our own lands.

"How in the Mother's name did they come to be here?" Owaine asked the wind, staring.

"That doesn't matter, Da . . ." Kayne began impatiently, but Owaine glared warningly at him and turned to his Hand.

"How many are there, Harik?" he asked. "I think we should come at them from two sides so we can cut off their lines of retreat. We don't want any of them escaping to—"

"Da!" Kayne shouted. "The town burns while you're sitting here talking. We have to ride!" He wheeled Gainmheach around and shouted to the others. "Ride!" Without waiting to see if anyone followed, Kayne plunged downward recklessly, Gainmheach's hooves skidding on the frozen ground. "Go, Gainmheach!" He dug his heels into the stallion's sides.

He risked a glance back.

"Go!" he heard Owaine say belatedly. As one, the riders stirred on the crest of the mountain road. Like a dark avalanche, they spilled downward with Kayne at the fore. The sound was enormous: hooves pounded the rock-strewn, wet earth like it was a vast drum; hoarse battle cries shrilled like the calls of fierce banshees; the air shivered with the high ring of armor and sword. Kayne held desperately to Gainmheach, urging the horse into a desperate downhill gallop as much from fear of being overtaken by the thunder behind him as from an urgency to reach the smoldering buildings ahead.

He'd worry afterward about what Da would say. Now, he only wanted to kill. He wanted revenge for the far too many dead they'd left behind, buried in foreign barrows. He wanted retribution for the Arruk's temerity in entering his land. *His*.

At nineteen, even after a year's experience, the onset of a battle was still exciting to Kayne, and he held the young person's belief that he was invincible. Scars he had, aye, but they were minor and he was, if anything, proud of what they represented. He wore them with honor. In the past several months he had seen death and grave injuries, had seen it happen to friends and foe alike, but Kayne had no sense that anything like that could happen to him. The son of the beloved Healer Ard never learned to fear injury; over the years, his mam had healed the broken bones he'd sustained in play, and he'd seen her call on the power of the mage-lights and bring back soldiers whose souls were already half in the grasp of the Black Haunts, restoring them to health. The men in the wagon, those too wounded to ride or walk, held onto life with the hope that the Healer Ard would aid them in the same way, once they were back in Dún Laoghaire.

Kayne didn't fear battles. He only feared losing them.

The cold wind threw Kayne's long, braided hair behind him and made him squint. He reached the foot of the mountain; the slope gentled as Gainmheach vaulted a scree of fallen rock and pounded over the soft, thick turf of the valley. The shouting of the gardai, tinged with a shared outrage, rose louder as they approached Ceangail. After the long campaign in Céile Mhór, the soldiers with them were—like Kayne—furious to find the Arruk within their borders. Kayne heard his da's voice, directing two of the squadrons to wheel left and attack from the flank.

Kayne wanted only direct confrontation. He was close enough to see their ugly faces now as the Arruk turned from their attack on the walls of Ceangail to peer at the charging riders. They howled, waving the huge, long pole weapons they called "jaka." He could see at least one of the Arruk mages—the Svarti—among them, raising his spell-stick. Kayne reached for his sword, pulling it loose from the scabbard lashed to his pack. He waved it high, screaming the caointeoireacht na cogadh—the terrifying war cry of the Inishlanders that Da had once taught him.

Kayne smelled the Arruk waiting in ambush before he actually saw it—a strong whiff of rotting meat and musk. Almost before the scent could register, the creature sprang up from a weed-choked hillock to Kayne's right as he galloped past: scaled skin in mottled yellow and brown, a snouted face with its spinal crest flared and erect. The Arruk's muscular legs—articulated backward like those of a goat—bent, then straightened as the creature launched itself at Kayne. Clawed hands grasped for him, missing Kayne but finding the rump of his horse. Gainmheach screamed in pain as the talons ripped long furrows in its flesh before digging firmly into muscle. The Arruk was flung sideways as the horse reared, falling, and Kayne went down with it, his breath leaving him as he hit the ground. Somehow he managed to keep his grip on his sword and pushed the point into the ground to help him rise. He nearly went down again when he took a breath—he'd slammed his ribs against rocks hidden in the grass. He forced himself to ignore the pain and stay upright, crouching and wheeling in a slow circle with his sword out as he looked for the Arruk. "Gainmheach! Here!" he called to his horse, but though Gainmheach had stopped several paces away, it only shook its mane and pawed the ground with its front hooves, its eyes and nostrils wide with fright and pain.

The Arruk rose up from the ground between Kayne and the horse. It was weaponless and young, but that hardly lessened the danger. Kayne had seen an Arruk disembowel a sword-bearing gardai in boiled leather armor with a single, ferocious kick. This one was clothed in a loin-rag with its tribal crest on the right hip, and on the left were three slashes of bright color: green, blue, and yellow—the sign of an Arruk mage, though this one must have been an apprentice, too young to be a full Svarti. It crouched down and snatched up a spell-stick lying in the grass.

Kayne scowled; if the spell-stick still had slow magic stored within it, then Kayne was dead.

The rest of the riders had swept on past, Kayne's da with them; he could hear—faintly—the shouting voices and the clash of steel as the line hit the Arruk attacking the village, and the smell and haze of woodsmoke was heavy around them. Bloody light flashed in the sky: Owaine's Cloch Mór, Blaze, raining fire down on the enemy.

Late, as usual. You should have used the cloch sooner, Da . . .

The Arruk snarled, its lipless snout curling over snaggled teeth. Kayne waved the tip of his sword in its direction. "Run away or make your move," he said to the creature, even though he knew it was unlikely the Arruk understand Daoine. "*Kapasti!*" he added in the Arruk's own tongue: *Castrated coward,* one of the few Arruk words he knew. The insult was enough: the Arruk howled, but he didn't lift the spell-stick and unleash magic; instead, he charged. Kayne screamed his own defiance and swung his blade.

The Arruk's attack was the same Kayne had witnessed a hundred times over the last year, one that Kayne himself could admire: direct and heedless of the creature's own safety. Kayne's stroke chopped deeply into the Arruk's neck and left shoulder, slicing down to bone, but the Arruk snarled and slashed at Kayne with its right hand even as Kayne—grunting with the effort—yanked his sword away from where it had caught in bone and scale. Kayne half stumbled, narrowly avoiding the Arruk's following kick. Thick blood drooled down the Arruk's chest and its left arm hung limp and useless. It snarled again and blood frothed in its mouth. It took a step toward Kayne, slashing again with its right hand, but the intended blow came nowhere near Kayne and the creature's deep-set eyes had gone cloudy. It took another step and went down on its knees, hissing at Kayne and speaking a phrase in its own language.

From the sound, it was almost certainly an insult.

The Arruk considered capture to be worse than death; the few wounded ones the Daoine forces had managed to take alive had refused food, water, or the ministrations of the healers and simply waited for their wounds to fester and kill them. From the soldiers of Céile Mhór, who had dealt with the advance of the Arruck for two decades, Kayne had learned that the Arruk themselves did not take prisoners or hold them for ransom as did the Daoine—any Daoine found wounded and still alive on the battlefield was always summarily executed.

The soldiers of Céile Mhór no longer took Arruk prisoners either. Kayne stepped carefully around the kneeling Arruk until he stood to one side. The head followed him, glaring, and the right hand was curled, the claws extended in defiance. Kayne brought his sword back once more; a moment later the Arruk's head rolled across the grass.

"If you'd stayed with me, Kayne, this wouldn't have happened. What you did was foolish."

Kayne leaned on his sword, panting and trying to ignore the pounding ache in his side as his da jumped from his horse and hurried over to Kayne. Owaine's Cloch Mór swung bright on his chest, and the clóca underneath was spattered with blood. He smelled of the Arruk.

Kayne ignored the rebuke. "The town?" he asked.

"The town will survive; the fires are already mostly out. A few houses burned and some townsfolk dead, but it could have been far worse. Our return was well-timed." The spark of anger faded in his dark brown eyes as he looked at Kayne. "Are you all right, son?"

"Aye," Kayne said, then groaned as he tried to straighten. "I think so. The damned thing took me off my horse and I probably cracked a few ribs. The rest of the Arruk . . . ?"

"There were only three double-hands of Arruk or so—considering how far they are from the current frontier, this must have been a group sent out to scout new territory. None of them will be reporting back." Owaine sighed and muscles jumped in his lean face along the jaw. "One of them was a Svarti with slow magic, and we lost Padraic O'Calhain and Harkin O Floinn. Here, on our own soil, where we thought we were finally safe. I was afraid . . . I was afraid we'd lost you as well, but I couldn't take the time to find you . . ."

You shouldn't be afraid, Da. You're the commander. You shouldn't think of fear at all . . .

Kayne's mouth pulled down in a frown. "Sorry, Da," Kayne said. "This one was waiting in the grass and surprised me."

Owaine glanced down at the body. "Young one. Mage-marked, too. Probably sent back to recover his spells for the final assault. Lucky for both of us that he never got the chance to finish, eh?" Owaine took a step toward his son and embraced Kayne, pulling him close. Kayne kept his arms at his side and a moment later, Owaine stepped back. "Thank the Mother," he husked. "I don't know how I could tell your mam if you'd been lost."

Is that why you've been so cautious, because I'm with you? That's not what I want, Da. That's not the way you should be. "I'm not afraid to die in battle, Da. If that's the Mother-Creator's will, nothing any of us can do will stop it from happening. I'd prefer to die with my sword blooded and as many of the enemy dead as I can manage."

"I'd prefer to win the battle with as few losses as possible. Maybe if you had to look the dying men in their faces, you'd feel differently." Owaine looked away. Back. "Can you ride, son?"

"Aye," Kayne told him. "I can manage. Gainmheach . . ."

The horse came this time at Kayne's call, limping visibly from the injuries caused by the Arruk. Blood soaked its rump. "Take my horse," Owaine said, but Kayne shook his head.

"I'll walk him back, Da. Go on. I'm fine—see to the others. Make sure we've got all the Arruk."

"Aye," Owaine said, but he didn't go. He regarded Kayne, watching as he wiped his blade on the grass and sheathed it. "Kayne." Kayne looked over at his da. "What you did just now . . . There's a difference between bravery and foolhardiness. You can't just rush into battle without a plan, not if you want to come back out again."

"The town was burning, Da. There were Arruk and we outnumbered them a good hand to one. Did you plan to wait until they'd taken Ceangail?"

The anger flashed again, Owaine's nostrils flaring. "After a year in the field, I would think you'd have gained some knowledge and wisdom, Kayne."

"I have, Da. I know that the Arruk think we Daoine are too weak to defeat them, and I'm wise enough to know why."

He thought that Owaine was going to scream at him. His da's face flushed and he sucked in a harsh breath, but Harik came riding up. "Tiarna Geraghty!" the Hand shouted to Owaine. "The Ald of Ceangail would like to speak with you, and the men are wondering where to make our encampment."

"I'm coming," Owaine said to Harik. With a final glare at Kayne, he stalked over to his horse and pulled himself up. He rode off without another word.

Harik stared hard at Kayne for a long moment before turning to follow.

3

Banrions

THE HAND OF THE HEART knocked once on the door of the Heart Chamber, a small room jutting from the main hall of the Banrion Ard's keep in Dún Laoghaire. Meriel, waiting inside, adjusted the heavy golden torc over her clóca and nodded to the garda standing at his station by the door. The garda reached over and pulled at the ornate bronze handles chased in swirls of gold and silver: a bejeweled imitation of the mage-lights.

The Hand of the Heart—Áine Martain, a Siúr of the Order of Inishfeirm, her own clóca and léine a pure, unadorned white—stepped inside, followed by a hand and more of supplicants: a man with a twisted leg who hobbled in leaning on a gnarled length of hickory; a well-dressed young woman who met Meriel's eyes unflinchingly and gave her a polite curtsey before entering the room; two men carrying a litter on which another man lay moaning softly. A pregnant woman walked alongside the latter group, holding the hand of the man on the litter. The litter bearers were all shabbily dressed, their hair and beards disheveled and matted, and with them came a faint stench of manure and sweat that wrinkled Meriel's nose. The woman's clothes were as ragged as her companions' and she looked as if she might drop the child at any moment.

They all formed a rough line in front of Meriel. "These are the chosen supplicants today, Banrion Ard," Siúr Martain said.

Three supplicants. She knew that there had been several more when the keep's gates had opened this morning—

she'd watched them enter from the window of her private chambers high up in the keep: the lame, the sick, the deformed, the broken; a crowd of perhaps three doublehands or more, all of whom Siúr Martain had interviewed. That was the Hand's task, each and every day that Meriel was in Dún Laoghaire as well as when she traveled throughout the Tuatha. Meriel was desperately glad such decisions were no longer hers.

She went first to the man with the crutch. She touched Treoraí's Heart, on its chain that was nearly as heavy as the torc around her neck. The Heart was a cloch na thintrí, one of the stones of magic—and at the same moment her fingers brushed its surface, she put her hand on the man's shoulder. She released a trickle of the energy that was captured within the pale blue cloch, letting it carry her awareness into the man. She could see the poorly-healed fracture in the lower leg and the knob of scar tissue where the break had healed crookedly. There was genuine pain there, but not so much that she recoiled. She released the Heart with a quiet sigh.

"Can you walk?" she asked him. "Without the stick?" The man's eyes widened. Siúr Martain came over to him and held out her hand to take the crude cane. He handed it to her and took a tentative step, then another. He smiled. "Thank you, Banrion Ard," he said. She could see tears welling in his eyes. Meriel returned the smile.

"Your thanks should be for the Mother-Creator, and for the Créneach Treoraí who gave us his own Heart," she told him. "Not for me. I'm just a vessel." She smiled again at him, patting his shoulder as she nodded to Siúr Martain— they both knew that Meriel had done nothing at all. The man's leg was still as crooked as ever; she had only given him a reason to ignore the pain. "Go on, then. One of the Hand's aides will see you out of the keep." He mumbled his thanks again and walked from the Heart Chamber, limping visibly but leaving the staff of hickory behind.

Meriel turned to the Riocha woman, who had sidled away from the litter beside her. She noted that though the woman was well-attired and bejeweled, she wore no ring or chain with a marriage signet. "This is the Bantiarna Fainche MacKeough," Suír Martain told Meriel as the woman curtsied again. "She suffers badly from lackbreath."

"Bantiarna," Meriel said. "I certainly know the Mac-Keough name. They've served the Tuatha well over the years."

"Thank you, Banrion Ard." Even with the initial greeting, Meriel could hear the wheezing from the woman's lungs. She was unable to get more than a few words out at a time before pausing for breath. Her face was pasty and gray, the eyes sunken and ringed with unhealthy brown. "My da is Tiarna Blake MacKeough. We have our land near Taghmon in Tuath Éoganacht."

"Aye. I was introduced to your da at the Festival of Méitha last year, as I recall." She took a step closer to the bantiarna, closing her hand quickly around Treoraí's Heart again as she took the woman's hand. Meriel found herself taking a breath as she let herself merge with the young woman. *Mother, it hurts to breathe* . . . Each breath was a struggle, and her chest muscles ached from the exertion, and yet she could gain little more than a sip of air. Her lungs felt as if a great weight were sitting on them, and she coughed—a barking, thin sound laced with thick phlegm. She felt also the despair inside the bantiarna: *All the nights where I lay there unable to sleep, fighting for every breath and wondering if this were the night I was going to die . . . The looks of sympathy from the men Da would bring to the house, but none of them would want a wife who would almost certainly die early, who would probably never give them an heir or even manage their house . . . the almost angry glare I'd sometimes catch on Da's face when he looked at me gasping for breath . . .*

Meriel released Treoraí's Heart with a gasp. Cool, sweet air filled her lungs. "It's so difficult for you, Bantiarna," she said quietly. "I know. I understand." She nodded to her, then turned to the man on the litter.

The two carriers stared at Meriel with wide, almost frightened eyes, stepping back from the litter as she approached; the pregnant woman stared also but stayed resolutely near the litter, though she looked like she wanted to bolt from the room. The man on the litter continued to groan, his eyes closed. He seemed oblivious to anything, lost in his pain. Meriel crouched down alongside the man, feeling the pull of Treoraí's Heart as it yearned to be used. Her fingers absently brushed the stone as she spoke.

"Who are these people, Siúr Martain?"

"The injured man's name is Cristóir Barróid, Banrion Ard," Áine told her. "The woman is his wife, and the men with him are cousins. His horse fell on him a week ago, and he's no longer able to be in the fields or keep his sheep."

"The work's hard enough, Banrion Ard," one of the men against the wall said, "an' we canna be there every day to work his land and our own besides. Marta's heavy with their first child, as you can see, an' besides Cristóir needs to be looked after all day. It would'a been more merciful if—" He stopped as Marta shot a venomous look at him.

Meriel nodded. She looked at Marta, cradling her heavy stomach with her hands. Her gaze was pleading and worried.

Meriel took Treoraí's Heart in her left hand, and there was an audible intake of breath from one of the cousins as they saw the white scars that lined that hand. Meriel smiled reassuringly at them and closed her fingers around the cloch. She let her mind fall into the linkage between herself and the jewel. She saw with doubled sight yet again, her own vision overlaid with the bright world of the cloch. There, in the cloch-vision, she could see the red-orange mass of this man's pain. She touched his arm, and the ruddy landscape rushed toward her, the tendrils of his agony lashing out toward her. She gasped at its touch but allowed herself to sink farther into him, to *be* him. Cristóir's thoughts rose in her head as if they were her own. He knew nothing about where he was now. The constant pain overlaid everything, and his thoughts rested nowhere— . . . *Mother, it hurts . . . the damned horse . . . when will this end . . . can't bear it can't bear it much longer* . . . She could hear him screaming inside, a wail of torment that racked every muscle in his body though he remained nearly silent. The scream drowned out nearly everything else, yet . . . the internal howl contained more than just pain: there was a terrible worry and concern for Marta, for his unborn child, for the work undone on his small piece of land. There was despair, a certainty that he would die or, far worse, be trapped like this forever.

Meriel sobbed with him, helpless, her own emotions tied to his. She let herself drift through him, examining the bloody wreck of his body as she fought to keep her own identity separate from his: the broken ribs, the internal bleeding, the torn and bruised muscles, the spine that had been fractured. He *would* live, she saw, but he would never walk again, would never be without great pain, would never be more than a burden to his family.

She forced her fingers to release Treoraí's Heart, though it ached to be used. She took a long, slow breath, closing her eyes. She could feel them all watching her.

This is the moment I hate. This is the hardest part: choosing. Treoraí's Heart could be used once before needing to be replenished with the mage-lights that came nearly every night. And each and every day there were more people who came here, with injuries and afflictions as bad or worse than these . . . She couldn't cure them all, only a bare few.

It's never easy. It's never fair . . .

"Bantiarna MacKeough," she said, opening her eyes again. The woman smiled at her expectantly, and Meriel hated the hopeful expression on the bantiarna's face. "My Hand will direct you to a healer here in Dún Laoghaire who has potions and herbs that should ease your breathing. I hope that will help you. Siúr Martain . . ." Áine came forward then, taking the bantiarna's arm before she fully realized what Meriel was saying and escorting her to the door. Áine beckoned to one of her aides in the corridor outside and gave him quick, whispered instructions as the bantiarna turned her head to stare back into the chamber. The look on the young woman's face was hurt and angry. Meriel had seen that look many times before. Too many times.

Áine came back into the room as Meriel turned to Marta. "The Heart will bring Cristóir back to you," she said.

The woman nodded, silent, her eyes shining, biting at her lower lip as if to stop from crying.

Meriel took Treoraí's Heart in her hand again, kneeling alongside Cristóir's litter and placing her free hand on his chest. Again the pain and madness and screaming rushed at her, slamming into her like a gigantic sea wave, threatening to pull her under and drown her. Meriel fought to hold onto herself as Cristóir's world merged with hers. . . . *let me die let me die . . .* Despair was sickly pus yellow; pain was fiery red. The colors lanced into her and she heard herself screaming as one with Cristóir. The part of her that was Meriel responded: this time she allowed the energy to flow out unrestrained from the cloch and she directed its path—where she let the power touch, the red heat subsided to yellow, fading through pale green, then blue to white before the false colors faded entirely. She took the broken bones in her mind, let Treoraí's Heart knit them back together whole and smooth. She closed the wounds inside him and healed them. She salved the bruises and repaired the torn muscles and tendons.

She felt herself shudder as Cristóir's eyes flew open, as the haze of pain receded like a morning fog. "Marta?" he said through dry and cracked lips, and Meriel spoke the woman's name at the same time.

"Banrion Ard," she heard Áine say as if from some great and vast distance. "It's done. You may come back now." Meriel sighed, letting her fingers relax around Treoraí's Heart. The mage-scars stood out prominently on her hand and arm, pure white and raised. As the cloch dropped from her grasp, the sense of being two people fell away, the shock of the release causing her to reel backward in Áine's waiting arms. The Hand helped Meriel to her feet as the final vestiges of Cristóir's thoughts fell away from her. Cristóir was sitting up on his litter, Marta crying on her knees alongside him as they embraced each other, and the two cousins were gaping in wonder at the scene. Meriel's left hand throbbed and ached, and she flexed stiff fingers, her whole arm trembling from the exertion of being a conduit for the mage-forces held within the now-emptied Treoraí's Heart.

Someone cleared their throat near the door, and Meriel saw one of the pages for the keep standing there, his head discreetly lowered so his gaze was on the brightly-tiled floor. "Aye?" she asked the boy, and his head lifted.

"Banrion Ard, the Banrion Mac Ard asks that you meet with her," the page said. His gaze flicked once over to Cristóir and Marta, still embracing tearfully without seeming to notice the others. Meriel grinned at Áine. "A good choice, I hope," Meriel said, and Áine smiled briefly. "Escort the Banrion to the south porch," Meriel told the page. "Tell her that I'll be there directly."

"Have you heard recently from the twins or Owaine?"

With the question, Meriel smiled. "Aye, all of them," she said. "Sevei's doing well at Inishfeirm, or so Máister Kirwan tells me. He thinks she might be ready for a cloch na thintrí of her own. Sevei wrote me a letter herself—she evidently has a beau there, someone named Dillon—one of the Ó'Baoill clan. She'll be coming back here with her gram, though she doesn't know it yet. And Owaine sent a message bird that arrived yesterday. He and Kayne should already have passed the Bunús Wall. I'll be glad to have them home again, finally, also. And safe, thank the Mother."

Edana, seated across a small table from Meriel, smiled in return. Meriel's hand, cupped now around a mug of kala bark tea, still ached from using Treoraí's Heart; Edana's hand stretched over the linen to touch Meriel's in mute sympathy. The keep servants had placed refreshments on the inner porch of Dún Laoghaire Keep. A quartet of gardai stood discreetly away from them on either side—with Edana as the Banrion of Dún Laoghaire and Meriel the Banrion Ard of all the Tuatha, they were rarely alone and unguarded outside their private chambers. On the grassy sward before them, Ennis, almost two double-hands of years of age and the youngest of Meriel's children, was examining a map of Talamh an Ghlas under the supervision of his attendant-tutor Isibéal, a woman of perhaps thirty. The boy's face was solemn and intent as he pressed his finger down on the parchment and asked Isibéal an unheard question. Ennis was always serious; sometimes, Meriel thought, too much so for such a young child. She wished he were playing with a ball or chasing butterflies rather than pressing his nose to a piece of yellowed, dusty paper.

"He should be out more," Edana said, as if guessing Meriel's thoughts. "I know a good family with holdings near Tuath Gabair who would be happy to take him in fosterage for a time—they have sons his age. Here in Dún Laoghaire, there's so little for him. I think that's why he's so quiet and intense. Born with the caul over his face . . . well, you know what they say about that."

Meriel smiled indulgently toward her son. *"What's the*

matter with him?" Meriel had said, worried and exhausted
after the long labor. The two midwives were glancing nerv-
ously at each other, but Keira, the old Bunús woman who
was also the Protector of the old forest Doire Coill, clucked
angrily at them and took the child, holding it up. Edana saw
the pale blue membrane over the infant's face, like a translu-
cent mask. Already, Keira was wiping it away with her hand
as the baby squalled its irritation.

"Give me a piece of blank parchment," Keira snapped at
one of the midwives. "Now! Go, woman." Then she turned
back to Meriel. "You have another son," Keira told her,
much more gently. "And born with a caul . . . He will be
gifted, Meriel."

"Gifted?"

"Those with the caul are often given second sight. And the
color of the caul and the size of it . . ." The midwife came
scurrying back with the parchment. Keira had laid the baby
down alongside Meriel. She took the membrane of the caul
and pulled it slowly away from the child, placing it on the
parchment. The Bunús studied it, biting at her lower lip. Her
rheumy eyes, already enfolded in deep wrinkles, seemed lost
as she frowned. "He'll be a strong one, this one. A natural
mage . . ."

"And Isibéal?" Edana said, the question taking Meriel
away from her reverie. "She seems to be working out well."

Meriel nodded. "Aye. I had misgivings, but with her references from Banrion Taafe . . . When Doyle comes back
from Lár Bhaile, thank him for me for suggesting her. But
you didn't come here to talk about Ennis."

Edana glanced away toward Ennis and Isibéal. "No," she
answered finally. "I'm . . . worried, Meriel."

"About?"

A hand lifted from the tablecloth and fell back. "Rumblings," Edana said. "Some of my ears among the Riocha
are telling me that there's been strong talk lately—about
you, and about your mam. About Jenna's visit here and
what it implies."

Meriel would have laughed at that in dismissal had
Edana's face not been so serious. "There have *always* been
rumblings like that," she said. "For how many years now?
Nothing's ever come of it."

"I know, but this is different. No Rí or Banrion of Inish

Thuaidh has come here in five centuries, and now your
mam is coming: the Mad Holder herself." Meriel blinked
and drew back at the term, and Edana pressed her lips together. "I'm sorry, Meriel, but you must know that's what
they're saying. One of my people in Tuath Connachta said
she overheard Rí Fearachan talking about a spy in Inish
Thuaidh and how some plan is to be put into action."
Edana hesitated, looking away toward Ennis and Isibéal,
and Meriel could sense that she was considering her next
words. "The discontent among the Riocha is higher now
than it has been since you became the Ard," she said finally. "It's been building for the last year, since you sent the
troops to Céile Mhór."

Meriel was already shaking her head. Sending out the
army hadn't been a choice she'd wanted to make. Sending
soldiers off to war was never a decision with which she
could be comfortable, especially since her husband and
oldest son were among them. But the reports from Céile
Mhór had been so dire and terrifying. The Arruk, vile creatures flooding into the peninsula from their homelands in
Thall Mór-roinn, had pushed their way relentlessly north,
killing and destroying as they went, and the Thane of Céile
Mhór had finally sent a desperate plea for help to Dún
Laoghaire. The discussion had raged for days when she'd
called the Comhairle of Ríthe together. "*Céile Mhór may
be far from the Tuatha, but those are our cousin Daoine
who the Arruk were killing and they are the buffer between
us and the Arruk. If they fall, then the Arruk will inevitably
come here and it will be our families who are slain and our
fields trampled underneath. We need to—no, we must—answer the Thane's call.*" To demonstrate the seriousness of
her belief, she had named Owaine as the commander for
the Tuathaian army that would be sent, though the decision
had made her tremble, and Kayne—full of youthful con-
viction and fervor—would not be left behind either. Yet
though they'd all finally agreed, when the troops had assembled, the Ríthe had sent far fewer soldiers to her than
promised. . . .

"The Arruk left us no choice," she said to Edana. "We
both know the arguments."

"I agree, but . . ."

Meriel raised an eyebrow. "But?"

"You complained at the lack of troops from some of the Tuatha, but while Inish Thuaidh sent clansfolk, they didn't offer any cloudmages at all, and Lámh Shábhála remained at home."

"It's that old complaint again? 'The First Holder doesn't do enough with her power. If *I* had it . . .' Did you really expect Mam to go riding off to war with Lámh Shábhála?"

"I wouldn't expect that at all," Edana answered, and there was a sharpness buried in her words that indicated she expected very little of the Banrion of Inish Thuaidh in any case. "Meriel, you know the affection I have for you, so forgive me when I say that in some ways I must agree with that complaint. The First Holder hasn't used Lámh Shábhála as much or as well as she could, and it's well past time for Inish Thuaidh to become part of the Tuatha and under the control of Dún Laoghaire. Now, your invitation for the First Holder to come here and your treatment of Inish Thuaidh as if it were an entirely independent land is causing the anger of the Riocha to boil."

Meriel felt her face flush with the criticism. "All the money and artisans Mam sent to rebuild Falcarragh, all the treaties she's signed, the trade we now have between us, the peace that has existed between the Tuatha and Inish Thuaidh since that time . . . over three hands of years now, there's been peace between the Tuatha. I would say that she's done all she need do, and perhaps more. What do they expect of her: to ride all over Talamh An Ghlas and use Lámh Shábhála to plant the fields or clear the bogs or create whole new towns of sparkling stone? Even if she did that, the Riocha would all be complaining that she was planting the wrong crops and stealing their peat and that the streets in the new towns were too narrow. They'd come here screaming about her trespassing on their lands and insisting that she go back home."

Meriel realized that Edana was waiting patiently and closed her mouth on the remainder of the tirade. "I'm sorry," she told Edana. "I know that you're giving me an honest evaluation of how you see things, and I appreciate that. It's just . . . well, she's my mam. Go on, say what you wanted to say."

Edana's hand brushed her again, the touch of a good and familiar friend. "I know she's your mam, Meriel. I know

you feel a need to defend her because of that. But . . ." Edana
shook her head as if she'd changed her mind about what she
wanted to say. "I look at what you've done with Treoraí's
Heart, and I wonder what you could have done if Lámh
Shábhála had been around your neck after Falcarragh."

Meriel remembered the Battle of Falcarragh all too well.
They were memories that would never fade: the terrible destruction, the death, the undeniable insanity of her mam at
that time and the sacrifice that had been required to save her.
Sometimes, she'd wondered herself at the cost. "Edana . . ."

The woman sighed quietly. "I know. You didn't want the
great cloch, and I understand that, too, even if Doyle never
will. But you need to understand that the voices against the
First Holder are rising again, especially since she chose not
to lend her aid to Céile Mhór. And the voices are rising
against you, because you did. The Ríthe see her arrival
here as a symbol—one that diminishes them and favors
her, and they hate her. They will always hate her."

"What you're saying is that there's no path I could follow that would appease them."

A shrug. "You have enemies: some of them old, some of
them newer. Some Ríthe who wouldn't mind being Ard
themselves, or Riocha who think that by bringing you
down they'll increase their own standing, or that they
might gain Lámh Shábhála or one of the Clochs Mór, or
those who simply are angry because you so often choose to
help the common folk over Riocha with Treoraí's Heart."

Meriel remembered the look on Bantiarna MacKeough's
face, just a few stripes of the candle ago—she could well
imagine that she had made another enemy there. "The Riocha have money and servants to help them. The tuathánach have only themselves."

Edana's hand rose and floated down again like an autumn leaf. "I know. I don't fault your choices, and I can
only imagine how difficult they must be for you. I'm only
saying that they gain you more enemies than friends
among those who have the most influence, and that those
Riocha you've passed over to help some sheepherder instead of them will resent your choice. I'm worried that the
voices are on the verge of being no longer just words, that
someone may attempt to do something more."

Meriel could see the true concern in Edana's eyes. She

wondered if there were more. "Would Doyle's be one of these voices you're hearing?" she asked, and the twist of Edana's mouth told her more than the woman's reply.

"I don't know. I hope not. He's said nothing to me, but in truth . . . Well, of late we spend more time apart than together. He's always in Lár Bhaile on some business of the Order of Gabair, or up in Infochla looking after his family's estate, or visiting one of the children. Dún Laoghaire doesn't interest him—or me, I'm afraid."

The recent estrangement between the two was no secret to Meriel; she and Edana had spoken of it often enough over the last months, but the open pain in Edana's voice made Meriel wonder. "Has something more happened . . ."

The woman shook her head. "No, there's nothing new there. Meriel, I just want you to be careful. I've also heard that Owaine's returning with less than a third of the soldiers who left and no victory—aye, I see the truth of that in your face, and if I know this, then so do others, and that's also going to cause a furor. You need to be careful."

"Don't worry. I'll protect you, Mam."

Ennis' voice startled both of them. The boy had crept up unnoticed close to the railing of the porch. He was looking at Meriel with a look of such utter seriousness that she wanted to laugh and cry at the same time. "If someone hurts you, I'll hurt them back," he told her. His small hands were clenched into fists. "I will. I know it."

Isibéal came hurrying up. The woman was a half Taisteal, with tightly-curled black hair and olive skin that reminded Meriel of Sevei, a Taisteal woman she had known years earlier, and for whom Meriel had named her own daughter—Sevei had saved Meriel's life, and in doing so, had died herself. "I'm sorry, Banrions," Isibéal said. "I was putting away the map and I looked up to see him over here."

"It's all right," Meriel told her. She leaned over the railing and tousled her son's hair. He grimaced, and she realized that the days were rapidly passing when she could treat him as a child. Already, she was beginning to see in his face the young man he would soon become. "Don't worry, Ennis," she told him. "No one's going to hurt me." She smiled at him as she said it.

"Aye, they will, Mam," he insisted, shaking his head. "The blue ghosts told me."

Meriel frowned. The "blue ghosts" were something Ennis had begun talking about not long after Owaine and Kayne had left for Céile Mhór a year ago. Her other children had indulged in imaginary friends as well, but most of them conveniently vanished after a few months while Ennis had been talking about seeing these creatures for a year now. *"They're what might be,"* he'd said, when she'd questioned him about them, and she'd remembered Keira's words: *"He will be gifted, Meriel . . ."*

"There aren't any blue ghosts here," she told him. "So they couldn't have told you anything."

Ennis shrugged. "Well, Aunt Edana thinks so, too."

"No, she doesn't," Edana told him. She pointed at the gardai around the porch. "See? Your mam has people watching out for her. They'll make sure she's safe." Edana's gaze found Meriel. "We all will," she said.

Ennis didn't look as if he was convinced, but when Meriel stood up and helped him over the railing, he hugged her fiercely, and when she tickled him, his laugh rang from the walls of the keep, making them all laugh with him.

4

A Gifting

"IS KAYNE badly injured?" Jenna asked Sevei, her voice trembling with worry. Sevei and Kayne, who had shared Meriel's womb together, had been Jenna's first grandchildren. They'd been the *only* grandchildren for several years before Meriel became pregnant again, and Sevei knew that though Gram loved Tara, Ionhar, and Ennis, it was Sevei and Kayne who would always be Gram's favorites.

Sevei shuddered at the memory of the vision she'd seen, but she shook her head. She'd seen worse; she'd seen *much* worse over the last year while Kayne had been in Céile Mhór—flashes of gory battles, of dead and dying men, of the grotesque creatures called the Arruk. This had been almost gentle in comparison. Though she could feel the pain in her brother's side, she knew he would recover. But she wondered at the vision: the last letter she'd received from Kayne had said they should be returning home by now and she had thought that he had felt closer than any time since he'd left with Da, but there were no Arruk here . . . Had they decided to stay in Céile Mhór a while longer?

"No, Gram," she told Jenna. "He's not badly hurt—nothing serious, anyway."

Gram looked uncertain and her fingers brushed the silver-caged facets of Lámh Shábhála, the stone which had opened the way for all the Clochs Mór and clochsmion, the major and minor stones which could hold the power of the mage-lights. With the gesture, the sleeve of her embroidered léine fell, displaying the white, swirling lines of the

scars curling on her stiff right arm, the legacy of the mage-
lights. "You're certain, child?"

"I'm certain, Gram, and I'm not a child. Not anymore.
Ask Máister Kirwan; he knows—he's always watching
me."

Máister Kirwan grunted at that, his eyes narrowing
under bushy white eyebrows. He sat on the ledge of one of
the windows of his office, like a beam of sunshine caught
and hardened. He glanced at Jenna, and Sevei thought she
saw more than simple respect for the Banrion in his eyes.
The two of them caught each other's gaze, holding it for a
moment . . . then Jenna was staring at Sevei, her mouth
twisted in a small half smile as if she were amused.

The Banrion sat in Máister Kirwan's padded leather
chair behind his desk; she looked tiny there, her body
hunched over with the inner pain Sevei knew bothered her
more and more with each year. Sevei's mam had tried to
ease Jenna's physical discomfort with Treoraí's Heart, her
own stone, a few years ago, but Jenna's affliction was beyond the scope of the Healer Ard's magic—*"It's Lámh
Shábhála, Mam," Meriel had said. "There's nothing I can do
for you."* A scent of spice lingered around Jenna, coming
from the mug of kala bark tea in front of her. In the four
years since Sevei had been fostered out—first to Dún Kiil
and then to Inishfeirm to learn the mage-craft—she'd
rarely seen her great-mam without some sign of discomfort
twisting the lines of her face, making her look far older
than her nearly five double-hands of age. Jenna used kala
bark often, and, it was rumored, other more powerful and
dangerous painkillers. Rumors also said that she rarely
used Lámh Shábhála at all anymore, because the agony of
wielding it was more than she could bear. Sevei only knew
that she'd never actually seen Gram use Lámh Shábhála.

Jenna took a swallow of the tea, grimaced, and set it
back down on the desk with a sharp *clack* that nearly made
Sevei jump.

"No, you're not a child," Jenna said, her voice still strong
and vital, even if her body was not. Her mouth tightened,
dozens of small lines appearing around it. "Mundy—that is,
Máister Kirwan—tells me that you've been swimming with
the seals since the month of Brightflower."

Sevei felt her face color. She heard Máister Kirwan shift

on his window ledge in a rustle of heavy cloth, but she didn't look at him. "Aye, Gram," she answered, knowing it was useless to lie. "It was just after the Festival of Fómhar. I thought . . . I mean I know about you . . ." She ducked her head. ". . . about our family, and I wondered, and I heard the seals one night and went down to the beach . . ."

"I allowed her to go, Jenna," Máister Kirwan interrupted. "I could have warded the doors, but that didn't stop your daughter when she was here, and I know it wouldn't have stopped you. You Aoires are extraordinarily stubborn." He sniffed loudly.

Jenna's mouth relaxed and she laughed, a crystalline sound that made Sevei relax slightly. "I knew you held the Saimhóir blood when I first saw you, child. I knew the sea would call you as it did me and your mam, even as I knew it would never call to Kayne. Was it the Saimhóir you swam with?" Jenna asked, and Sevei shook her head.

She had always imagined swimming with the Saimhóir whose lineage flowed in her veins: the great blue seals who could speak and use magic, whose fur sparked in the sun, but she'd never seen them, though families of them were reputed to come to the shore of Inishfeirm from time to time. Sometimes she even saw them, in the way that she sometimes saw Kayne or her mam. The whispers were that both Jenna and her own mam had once had lovers among the Saimhóir, and Sevei wondered at what that must be like. She'd wondered about that quite a lot, especially since she and Dillon had become intimate. "No, not the blues, Gram, just the normal browns."

Jenna closed her eyes. Whatever was in her mind pursed her mouth again, as if she tasted something sour. "The Saimhóir don't trust the earth-snared changelings, not anymore," she said, and her eyes opened. "They certainly don't trust our family." Sevei nodded solemnly at that and Jenna seemed amused. "So you know that tale also? Not one of my finer moments, I have to say." By the window ledge, Máister Kirwan coughed, drawing Sevei's gaze. He was watching Jenna, his eyes soft and gentle, his mouth seeming to smile under the beard.

"Mam always told me that what happened at Falcarragh wasn't your fault, Gram," Sevei said. "She said that the madness came because you'd lost Lámh Shábhála and because of the andúilleaf you were taking. She's never blamed you, Gram. I've never once heard her say anything that would make me think that you did any of it deliberately."

"Your mam is too gentle to say such things," Jenna answered. "But *I've* blamed myself. And so have many others. I daresay that the Riocha are pleased that I've stayed in Inish Thuaidh ever since, and just as angry that I've finally accepted Meriel's invitation to go to Dún Laoghaire. But I do miss my old homeland from time to time, and I wonder at the changes that have taken place there." She took another sip of the tea. "I'm going to Dún Laoghaire," Jenna said suddenly. "You'll be going with me, Sevei."

Sevei blinked in surprise and dropped her head again, but she could feel Jenna's gaze probing her. "You don't seem particularly overjoyed with that news," Jenna said.

Sevei hesitated. "It's not that I don't want to go back," she said finally. "It's been so long since I've seen Mam, and Kayne should be heading back there with Da, and I haven't seen the little ones in forever. Why, Ennis must be two double-hands now. It's just . . . leaving right now . . ."

"What's the young man's name to whom you're so attached?" Jenna asked. That brought Sevei's head back up. "Oh, don't look so surprised, child. I haven't *completely* forgotten what it's like to be your age."

"Dillon Ó'Baoill," Máister Kirwan interjected, "one of our young bráthairs." When Sevei, blushing as she remembered her brief hope on the beach, glanced at the Máister, he lifted an eyebrow but said nothing more.

"So he's an Ó'Baoill," Jenna repeated. "From Tuath Airgialla, then?"

Máister Kirwan shook his head. "His branch of the family is from Tuath Connachta. Dillon's da is a third cousin to the Rí. Most of our acolytes from the Tuatha are from Connachta or Infochla now; the others go to the Order of Gabair for training."

Jenna's face crumpled into a quick scowl at the mention of Gabair. She shook her head and turned back to Sevei. "So, is it serious?" Jenna asked her. "I hope you're not considering marriage—that's for politics, not love."

"Gram!"

Jenna sniffed. "Oh, don't be so dramatic, Sevei. You're

old enough to know love and smart enough to understand the consequences. I don't know that I'd trust a Connachtan too far. Your loyalty is to Dún Laoghaire and Inish Thuaidh, equally."

"To you and Mam, you mean," Sevei answered evenly. "You don't know Dillon, Gram. I do."

"Is it love, then, or just infatuation?"

"More than infatuation," Sevei answered. "And maybe love." She felt her cheeks color. "Or, aye, I'd think it's love, Gram."

Jenna shook her head, but there was a faint smile on her lips as she leaned back in the chair. For a moment, her face twisted as if with some inner pain and her lips tightened, then relaxed again. "I should meet this young man while I'm here, then. Bring him to supper tonight in my chambers." She took a long drink of the kala bark tea and pushed herself up from the chair. She moved like a woman much older than her true age. "Now, I have business to tend to. I think half the court of Dún Kiil traveled with me, and the Comhairle insists that all this session's proposals have to be settled before I can leave for Dún Laoghaire. So . . ." She glanced at Máister Kirwan, and again Sevei saw a look almost of affection pass between them. "Mundy has something for you, Sevei. You'll go with him, and I'll meet you tonight for supper—with this Dillon Ó'Baoill of yours. We'll leave Inishfeirm within the week."

"Is Greada going with us also?"

"No," Jenna answered shortly, without elaboration. Sevei wasn't surprised at that: Sevei's great-da Kyle MacEagan and Jenna seemed to have a placid if passionless marriage and were rarely together except for court occasions. Though Sevei loved her great-da and enjoyed his company, he lived most of the year attending to his duties in his clan's ancestral keep in Dún Madadh, in his townland of Be an Mhuilinn rather than in the capital of Dún Kiil.

Jenna came around the desk and Sevei went to her, hugging the smaller woman and kissing her cheeks. "It's good to see you again, Gram," she said.

"And you, Sevei. You've become a young woman without my realizing it." Jenna's arms tightened around Sevei again for a moment before loosening. Sevei saw her glance again at Máister Kirwan. "That makes this visit all the more important," she said. "We'll talk later."

Máister Kirwan had come over to Jenna; she took his arm as she walked to the door. Outside, Mahon MacBreen, the captain of the Banrion's personal gardai, waited for her. He nodded to Máister Kirwan as Jenna transferred her arm to his. "I'll talk with you later, also, Mundy," Jenna said. "Perhaps I can convince you to come to Dún Laoghaire with us."

With that, she turned to walk slowly down the ancient stone corridor of the White Keep. Acolytes passing in the hall stepped aside to let her pass, their heads bowed respectfully, then chattered in bright excitement as they moved on.

Máister Kirwan still held the door open. He inclined his head to Sevei. "Come with me," he said.

Sevei followed Máister Kirwan through the twisting hallways. The stones under their feet had been polished to a slick patina by countless soles, a visible double groove eroded in the thick granite flags. They walked in silence, their footsteps echoing hollowly. The acolytes rarely came here; the few bráthairs and siúrs they passed nodded to Máister Kirwan and went silently about their business. The White Keep had been built in slow stages over centuries, and Máister Kirwan now led Sevei to the most ancient section of the rambling building which held the Order's library, with its history of Talamh an Ghlas and the clochs na thintrí, the stones of power. But he didn't take the stairs leading up to the library; he continued on into the dark bowels of the building.

Máister Kirwan brought her to a closed door. He put his hand on the door and whispered a ward-word she couldn't hear; the door swung open with a groan of hinges. He lifted his hand and spoke a phrase of slow magic—in response, witchfire pots burst into flame down the passage beyond, illuminating a long staircase winding downward. Cold air spilled out from the doorway, bearing the scent of must and dampness. "Where are we going, Máister?" Sevei asked, her voice a whisper.

"Just stay close," he answered; he led the way down, the door closing sharply behind them, the bolt of the lock clanging into its hole without being touched. Sevei followed Máister Kirwan down the stairs, which ended near another door. Máister Kirwan again put his hand on the door, and a disembodied voice spoke as if coming from the thick planks of iron-banded oak. "Máister Kirwan . . ." The door's lock clicked and it opened.

The chamber inside was small and dark. Máister Kirwan took a few steps inside, and witchfire brightened. She could see that the room's furnishings were few and plain: a small table with a few chairs pulled up to it, the witchfire guttering in a glazed pottery bowl in the center. "Come in," he told Sevei, his face seemingly amused in the ruddy glow of the witchfire. "You needn't hang out there in the damp." Sevei stepped inside; the door shut behind her, untouched.

The walls, ceiling, and floor of the chamber had been cut from the stone of the mountain on which the White Keep sat. Though the floor had been polished so that it reflected the light from the witchfire, the walls were rough, still showing the grooves of chisel marks. Máister Kirwan's head nearly brushed the low ceiling, also roughly cut. Sevei felt a moment of slight panic at being enclosed in the space. She took a long, slow breath, trying to calm herself. "Máister?"

"Don't worry," he said. "There's nothing sinister about to happen. In fact, you should find it rewarding. Sit, sit . . ." He gestured to one of the chairs. As Sevei sat, Máister Kirwan paced to the back wall of the room, ducking his head as the roof above brushed the few wisps of hair left on the crown of his head. "Do you know why your great-mam is going to Dún Laoghaire?"

Sevei shrugged. "I assumed it was to see my mam," she said. "And to see some of the land she came from."

"That, aye," Máister Kirwan answered, "and more. Mostly, she's going because your mam invited her to come for the political impact it would make. It's time that Inish Thuaidh was acknowledged as its own domain by the Tuatha. But there's more." He paused, exhaling a long breath. "Your great-mam doesn't believe she will live much longer," he said abruptly. He raised his hand against Sevei's protest. "That is something we can only say here, and I pray to the Mother-Creator that she's wrong."

"Why would she believe that?" Sevei asked. A suspicion came to her suddenly and she felt coldness grip her throat. "Is it something she's *seen* with Lámh Shábhála?"

Máister Kirwan shook his head. "No, it's not a foretelling. At least, none that she's shared with me." The way he said it, so proprietarily, as if he and Jenna regularly shared confidences, made Sevei look at him with sudden curiosity. *Just how close are they?* she wondered, and then quickly banished the image from her mind. "But that's what she believes," Máister Kirwan continued, "and I see how the years have taken their toll on her. Lámh Shábhála weighs heaviest on the First Holder, and she's borne that burden for many years. Let's see how well you've paid attention in your studies—how long did Caenneth Mac Noll hold Lámh Shábhála?"

Sevei blinked, trying to recall the long list of Holders she'd been forced to memorize in her first year on Inishfeirm. "Umm . . . nine years?" she answered.

Máister Kirwan nodded. "Aye, though Caenneth was the only other Daoine First Holder. However, the Bunús Muintir lore says that their First Holders' lives were also short. I can see how frail Jenna's become over the years, especially since Falcarragh. I hope she's mistaken, aye, but I'm afraid that she may be right. What weighs on her mind now is who will hold Lámh Shábhála after her. She wants it to go to the heir of her choice, not to whomever can claim it after her death. She wants Lámh Shábhála to go to someone loyal to her, and to have the chance to pass it on herself."

"Then she wants to go to Dún Laoghaire to give it to Mam," Sevei said firmly, but Máister Kirwan's head moved slowly from side to side.

"No. Your mam's already refused Lámh Shábhála once, years ago. She has no interest in clochs beyond Treoraí's Heart. She would have been a good Holder, perhaps as competent as Jenna, but . . ." A shoulder lifted under the white robe. "I don't think that is what she wants, even now."

"Then Da?" Sevei ventured but the look on his face told her she was wrong. "Or you, Máister?"

Again the headshake, this time with a wan smile. "Not Owaine, and my own time has passed, I'm afraid, though

I'd certainly take Lámh Shábhála rather than allow certain others to have it."

Sevei sat silent, realizing what Máister Kirwan was implying. *Then it is Kayne or me, and I was the one sent to the Order to learn the art of the cloudmages* . . . She felt fear grip her chest, making it hard to breathe. "Máister," she began, but Máister Kirwan lifted a hand. He went to the rear wall of the room, speaking a word she could not overhear. A section of the stone swiveled outward: a tiny door at shoulder height to Máister Kirwan. He reached inside; when he withdrew his hand, the door closed again, leaving no indication that it had ever been there at all. He came over to the table and laid down a small pale yellow stone on a necklace in front of Sevei. "This is a clochmion," he said. "It was once your da's, when he was here. Jenna gave it to him and he kept it until your mam gifted him with the Cloch Mór Blaze."

She knew, but she asked anyway. "Why are you showing me this?"

A faint smile touched his lips under the beard. "It's yours now. If you want it. Your great-mam wants you to have it and it's time to see if you can truly handle the mage-lights."

Sevei imagined the glowing curtains and tendrils of power that came nearly every night. She'd watched—all the acolytes often did—as the cloudmages with their clochs filled them with snarling, vibrant energy. She'd watched Jenna do the same with Lámh Shábhála. The lights gleamed brightest around Gram, around the great cloch that had opened the way for all the rest. Jenna would stand there, seemingly snared in brilliant colors, the deep scars on her arm glowing also. Sevei had often wondered what that must feel like. Her fingers started to move toward the clochmion. She stopped them before they touched the gleaming facets. "Do *you* think I'm ready, Máister?"

"Aye, I do. I think you've *been* ready, Sevei. You're already older than Jenna was when she first took up the stone. I think you have the same kind of strength both your great-mam and your mam have."

Her fingertips came close to the stone and hovered over it, nearly touching. "What does it do?"

"For your da Owaine, it was a finder of lost things. But

clochsmion are different than the Clochs Mór. It takes an exceptionally strong and well-trained mind to turn a Cloch Mór from the manifestation that has been worn into it by centuries of use; few Holders even try. A Cloch Mór has great power and carves a deep path and only rarely can someone force it to a new road. But a clochmion . . . often a person can turn it to what is in their own mind. Someone with your training and strength will almost *certainly* change it, but I don't know what this one will do for you until you take it." He smiled again. "Go ahead," he said.

Sevei closed her hands around the small jewel in its cage of silver. With the touch, she drew in a breath. The clochmion was a presence, a brilliant spark in her mind. Her vision was doubled for a moment: she saw her hand holding the clochmion yet at the same time she saw the light rushing toward her, growing larger until it held her whole body in its glow. It closed around her, *became* her. The sparking energy filled her, as warm as blood and as vital. Her entire body sang with it.

Sevei gasped.

"Aye," she heard Máister Kirwan say. "It quickly becomes part of you."

"How will I choose what it does?"

"You don't know?"

Sevei shook her head as Máister Kirwan shrugged. "Your mam, with Treoraí's Heart, knew right away. But it doesn't matter. You—or you and the clochmion together—have already chosen, in the moment you became one. Exactly what it is . . . well, if you don't know now, you'll know when it happens. The clochmion will call you."

The cloch was part of her already. She could feel the clochmion as if it were an organ of her body, a second heart or a set of eyes—and she could sense how terrible it would be if it were ever taken away. "I knew what it was like to hold one of the stones, even the clochsmion," she said wonderingly. "I mean, you and the bráthairs and siúrs all taught us what it was like, but I could never have imagined what it would actually *feel* like. This is only a clochmion; a Cloch Mór, or Lámh Shábhála . . ."

"Aye, their presences are more powerful still," Máister Kirwan finished for her. "You really can't imagine the connection, not unless you actually hold them." He moved to the door. "One day, I suspect, you *will* know." He spoke the opening word and the door swung open, the cold and damp air of the corridor sweeping inside with the movement. "Come on," he said. "Put the clochmion around your neck, and we'll go to Siúr Cullinane—it's time to change your red léine for a white one."

5

Caught in Mage-Light

KAYNE ENDURED the feast and the speechmaking in Ceangail's town hall. The fire pit in the middle of the hall radiated a suffocating heat through the packed room and the drone of voices made Kayne simultaneously sleepy, irritable, and nauseous. ". . . and it was only by the providence of the Mother-Creator that we came here at this crucial moment," his da said, his voice stentorian as he stood at the head of the massive long table down the center of the room. "We of the Tuatha must stand together with our cousins in Céile Mhór to stop the menace of the Arruk, which Ceangail has now experienced firsthand. We'll report the bravery of the citizens here to the Rí Airgialla and the Banrion Ard . . ."

The speech didn't seem to be having the effect Kayne thought it might have. Some were listening intently, but there were frowns and bored looks among the Fingerlanders present in the hall.

Kayne pushed away from the table. His da glared at him, but Kayne ignored the silent rebuke, striding down the long table toward the entrance as Owaine cleared his throat and picked up the shards of his interrupted speech. ". . . so that they know that Ceangail has made certain that these Arruk, at least, will never return to their homes to tell of what they saw here, in our green land . . ."

Owaine's voice trailed into silence as Kayne left the building. A crowd of the townsfolk, unable to find seats inside, moved aside from the doorway as he came out. He thought their demeanor and stares too arrogant, almost as if they were judging him, but as he came close, they ducked their heads respectfully and mumbled in their rolling, thick, Fingerlander accents: "Excuse me, Tiarna." "A good evening to you, Tiarna." "We're grateful to you, Tiarna."

Kayne grunted in answer and stalked away as the on-lookers closed in again behind him. The western gates of the town loomed dark against the sky, still touched with the dying gleam of the sun, already below the western mountain ridges. The mage-lights would come in the next stripe or two, and Da would come out to fill Blaze along with Harik, who held a clochmion that could strengthen his voice so it could be heard a hundred strides away as if he were standing next to you—a useful trick for a Hand who often needed to address large groups. In Dún Laoghaire, his mam would be standing on a balcony of the keep with Treoraí's Heart, and in Lár Bhaile, the mages of the Order of Gabair would gather under the mage-lights with their clochs. Away beyond the far coast of Talamh an Ghlas in Inish Thuaidh, his great-mam Jenna would be doing the same with Lámh Shábhála, and it was to her that the great-est power would flow.

Kayne went to the open gates, nodding to the gardai placed there, and walked out a few paces, gazing at the mountains around them, now wrapped in deepening shadow. He wondered what it would be like to hold Lámh Shábhála, to have the power of the sky-magic at his beck and call. If the stories he'd been told over the years were even half-true—how the great cloch had defeated the armies of the Tuatha at Dún Kiil, how Gram had nearly de-stroyed the city of Falcarragh against the massed power of the Clochs Mór . . .

If *he* held Lámh Shábhála, its power would not be wasted. Its strength would not be languishing in Inish Thuaidh. No, he would use it to unite the Tuatha and ride with its power to Céile Mhór and drive the Arruk all the way back to Thall Mór-roinn, and if the Thane seemed un-grateful afterward, then Céile Mhór itself could become a dominion of Dún Laoghaire.

He would be remembered as a Rí Ard who was truly the Ard. The One.

"A son should be more respectful of his da."

The voice came from behind him, dissolving the vision of

Rí Ard Kayne Geraghty. Kayne didn't turn; he continued to
stare out at the crumpled landscape before him. "What's between me and Da isn't your business, Hand MacCathaill."

Without looking, he could imagine the scowl twisting the
garda's face, the thick white scar that ran from the corner
of his left eye to his chin standing out against flushed skin.
"Oh, it's my business," Harik answered. "I may not be Ríocha, Tiarna Kayne, but I *am* your da's Hand, as you say,
and what concerns your da's relationship with the troops
also concerns me. The way you question Tiarna Owaine's
decisions—that hurts the morale of everyone with us. Gardai shouldn't be going into battle with doubt in their
minds—if they do that, they hesitate, and that's when we
lose battles and lives."

"Are you accusing *me* of being responsible for the loss of
our men, Harik? Are you saying that I'm disloyal to the
Tuatha or to my parents?" Kayne asked in fury, wheeling
around with his fists balled. The man's impertinence
burned at him.

"No," Harik answered placidly. He stood his ground in
the face of Kayne's anger and his hand stayed carefully
away from the hilt of his sword. "I'm just telling you what
you need to know, because one day it will be *you* at the
head of the gardai and then you can't afford to be as igno-
rant as you are right now."

"You *dare*!" Kayne exploded and stopped at the look on
Harik's face.

"Aye, I dare: out here where it's only the two of us to
hear. You're a man, Kayne Geraghty, but you're still a boy,
too. I'm not a Riocha who has to be concerned with my
holdings and keeping my place with the Ríthe. I've spent
my whole life with the gardai, Tiarna, and I *know* how to
handle troops. You know it, too, if you'd listen to your head
instead of your heart and your wounded pride. You think
we're slinking home defeated and broken. You think that
your da didn't do all he could have done. But I tell you this:
none of the men with him believe that. They saw that all
the great armies of Céile Mhór haven't been able to stop
the Arruk. They saw that they had a commander who cared
about them, who wouldn't throw them needlessly into a
hopeless situation for his own glory. *They* are coming home
proud, because they've kept their word and their honor

when others chose not to answer the Banrion Ard's call. So, aye, I dare. And don't *you* dare to dishonor the soldiers you've served with because you wanted your da to be some legendary hero, and you to be one, too. Tiarna Owaine's a good man and a decent one, the best of the Riocha, as far as I'm concerned. I'm honored to have served with him; you should feel the same. I don't care whether you're his son or not, or whether you're Riocha or not; you'll be as respectful to him as any garda with us or you'll answer to me the next time."

Kayne blinked. Harik was a man of few and simple words; he'd never heard him utter more than a few sentences at a time before. He wondered how long he'd been composing this speech in his mind. The presumption and unfairness of it made Kayne clamp his mouth shut. "Have you said everything you've come to say, Hand MacCathaill?" he asked.

The man's eyes glittered. The muscles in his neck flexed and the scar on his face pulled at his skin. "Aye, Tiarna Kayne. I've spoken my piece."

"Good. Know that if you ever speak to me that way again, you *will* need to defend your words. I tolerate your impudence only because of the service you've given Da. Do you understand?"

Harik's eyes narrowed, nostrils flared. "Aye, Tiarna. I understand very well."

"Then this conversation's over. I'd suggest you return to the hall and your commander."

Harik's mouth snapped shut and he turned. Without another word, he strode quickly back toward the town gate, leaving Kayne in his cold wake.

Kayne stood outside, watching the sky darken and the first stars appear to the east. He stayed there for a halfstripe until the mage-lights came—earlier than usual, just before the last of the sun's light left the western sky—snarling their bright tendrils around the zenith and touching the few clouds with color.

The wind sprites lifted from the grass, drifting in a stream of glowing light around the keep and past the balcony where Meriel stood. She heard their high, thin voices calling and felt the plucking of tiny fingers and the brush of small wings. She laughed and brushed at the sprites with a hand, and they went spiraling off in a chattering of high protest, the wavering lines of them sliding down to flow along the slope of the twilight-wrapped mountainsides that bordered the harbor of Dún Laoghaire, their summits still brushed with the dying sun's light. The wind sprites wound among the green hillocks that were the barrows of the most ancient Ríthe, back in the time when Talamh an Ghlas was broken into hands upon hands of tiny warring Tuatha, each controlled by a single clan. The barrows now were nothing more than shapes in the grass, the deeds and the names of those who slumbered there long forgotten. The flickering lines of the wind sprites flowed down the flanks of Cnocareilig, the Grave Hill, where the tombs of the more recent Ards lay—where, Meriel knew, her own body would one day rest.

"See," Meriel said to Ennis. He was staring, wide-eyed, at the last of the wind sprites as Meriel lifted him a bit so he could see past the balcony's rail. As she looked at him, smiling, she saw again the lines of Owaine's own face in Ennis'. Like his older siblings Tara and Ionhar—both of them currently away in fosterage with relatives—Ennis was undeniably Owaine's child. He had the same hair: wavy, and so dark brown that it was nearly black, and pupils the color of the richest soil.

Sevei and Kayne, though, they were red-haired and green-eyed like Meriel, and the shape of their faces . . . They were not like Owaine at all.

She smiled again and kissed Ennis' brow, brushing back the hair from his forehead. Ennis was all the more precious for being so much younger than all the rest of his brothers and sisters, coming to her when she thought that perhaps she would have no more children.

"They're pretty, Mam," Ennis said, "but I want to know how they fly." He reached out with a hand as if he could touch them. Together, they watched the sprites vanish around the headland at the edge of the harbor. Ennis' attention slid to the flickering lights of the city below them as it prepared for night, then to the sky's drapery of sunset-touched clouds. *Serious. His face is always so serious, like he's trying to make sense of everything, like he sees something none of the rest of us can see . . .*

The sky brightened, a wash of red and searing orange flickering from the west and snaking overhead. "Mam, the mage-lights are coming."

"Aye, I see them," she said to him, surprised. *So early tonight . . .* "Do you want to watch while Mam catches them?" Ennis nodded solemnly and she put him down near the doors to her chambers. "Stay there, then," she told him and lifted Treoraí's Heart on its necklace, sliding it from under the torc of the Ard. She closed her hand around the stone and lifted hand and stone toward the sky.

Instantly, she felt the connection with the crackling energy contained within the mage-lights. She saw not only with her eyes but with the perception of Treoraí's Heart. She was encased within its rough facets; she could feel its yearning and need to be filled with the mage-lights, and she and the stone called to them. A tendril of purest yellow light shot through with blue sparks responded, curling down from the sheets and flares of color overhead and wrapping around her upraised arm, touching the faint pattern of scars around her wrist. "Oh, Mam, they're so bright tonight . . ." she heard Ennis say in wonderment behind her, and she laughed.

"Aye," she told him, gasping with the cold touch of the mage-lights, barely able to hear him through the hum of the mage-lights in her body. "Maybe one day you'll do this, too."

"Will you send me to Gram, like you did with Sevei?"

"Maybe." *He'll be a strong one, this one . . .* Meriel could believe that. She would be surprised if Ennis weren't well suited to being a cloudmage. But not yet . . . He was still her baby, even if he were looking older with each passing day, even if she knew that the time was fast approaching when he'd be sent out to fosterage like his siblings.

"When will Sevei and Gram be here? I want to see them."

"Not too long now, Ennis. The message bird your gram sent just came yesterday, and the note with it said that they would be leaving in another few days, but we're still a long sail from Inish Thuaidh."

"Do you think Sevei will remember me? I don't remember her, not really. What does Gram look like?"

"You'll know what Gram looks like when she gets here. And aye, your sister will remember you, I'm certain, though she'll be surprised at how much you've grown. Now be quiet, darling, and let me do this . . ."

It was difficult to concentrate on the boy's conversation; the rush of energy swept into and through her, warm and comforting, nearly sexual in intensity and as insistent. She held the power, embracing it with her mind, letting it seep into every part of her and the stone. She sighed, holding the mage-lights. She'd used Treoraí's Heart again today—it was a rare day when she did not—this time to cure a woman from Tuath Locha Léin with a growth in her belly, a fetus that was not a child but her own tissue gone mad. There were always far more supplicants every day than there was power in the stone to cure them: Dún Laoghaire sometimes seemed full of no one else. Over the past several years, Meriel had added a staff of a dozen retainers to the Hand of the Heart's staff, whose task it was to help Siúr Martain evaluate those who came here to be cured of illness or injury, of defects physical and mental. Once filled with the mage-energy, Treoraí's Heart burned to be used, filling her with an aching need to empty it once more.

Sometimes it seemed that her only role was that of Healer Ard, that she neglected the rest of her duties as Banrion Ard. She knew that many of the Riocha felt exactly that way, especially since she made little distinction between Riocha, the half-blooded céili giallnai, or the common tuathánach when she used Treoraí's Heart. At least, that was what she told herself, but she sometimes wondered if she *did* make distinctions, if she wasn't more likely to help the tuathánach because they had so few chances to help themselves. She had to admit the truth of what Edana had said to her yesterday—she'd felt it without being told. Much of the progress made following the debacle of Falcarragh had been unmade in recent years.

The common folk might call her the "Healer Ard" with affection, but it was becoming a term of derision among the Riocha.

She knew it. She knew that she should pay less attention to Treoraí's Heart and more to the politics in which she was necessarily embroiled, but it was difficult. The cloch didn't want that, and the stone was more a part of her every day.

She forced her thoughts away from politics, concentrating instead on the web of energy that flowed above her, letting her awareness drift upward through the mage-lights and outward, searching. She could feel Jenna with Lámh Shábhála—still far distant, her great cloch sucking greedily at the power above. Meriel let her mind drift eastward and smiled. Aye, there was Owaine with Blaze, and closer than she could have hoped. She felt the touch of his mind through the mage-lights, faintly, and for a moment the image of his face came to her. *My love,* she thought, wishing he could hear the words, wishing she could hear him . . .

"Look, Mam—over there at the other tower."

Treoraí's Heart was nearly full now. Meriel opened her eyes, allowing herself to withdraw from the cloch-sight. Ennis was pointing to where two more tendrils of mage-light snaked down to a balcony on the tower across the courtyard, snarling and fuming around each other. The mage-lights there were exceptionally luminous, far brighter than the remaining sunset glow, and Meriel knew they replenished Clochs Mór. One of the clochs would be Demon-Caller, held by Edana as the Banrion Dún Laoghaire. The second cloch with Edana must be Snapdragon in the hands of her husband Doyle. *Her husband . . .* Meriel always thought of Doyle that way: as Edana's husband, not as Meriel's half uncle—the latter wasn't a relationship she cared to contemplate often. So Doyle had returned from the Order of Gabair in Lár Bhaile.

"That's Auntie Edana and Uncle Doyle," Ennis burst out with the same realization. "Can we see Auntie Edana tomorrow, Mam? She promised me that Enean would show me what his Weapons Máister has been teaching him." Ennis clenched both hands around the hilt of an imaginary sword and chopped earnestly at a foe only he could see.

"You're too young for that yet," Meriel told him.

"The blue ghosts show me that I'll need to know how to fight," Ennis replied.

Meriel frowned at that—*blue ghosts again*—but Ennis pouted, his lower lip sticking out dramatically, and she finally had to laugh. "All right, I'll have Isibéal take you over there tomorrow, if you like. But you mustn't bother Enean if he's busy with his studies or doesn't want to see you. He's a young man now, not a child."

"He's not as old as Kayne," Ennis insisted. "He still plays with me. Well, sometimes. Not as often as he used to," he amended. *Always serious. Always wanting to be right . . .*

"That's good. But still . . ."

The door to Meriel's bedchamber opened and Isibéal peered in, her gray-streaked black hair caught in a colorful scarf. "Isibéal," Meriel said, waving to her. "Please, come out here."

The Taisteal woman nodded, moving with unconscious grace and ease across the bedchamber toward the balcony. She stopped at the open doors and gazed up at the fading mage-lights. Her eyes, even in the starlight, were an odd light blue in her dusky face. "I came for Ennis, Banrion Ard," she said. "It's time he finished his studies for the day and then got to bed. I hated to bother you, but the hall garda said the boy was with you . . ."

"Thank you, Isibéal. You're right, of course. Ennis . . ."

"Mam!" Ennis protested automatically, but Isibéal laughed and took three lithe and quick steps onto the balcony, sweeping the child up in her arms and spinning him around twice so that he finally laughed and squealed in delight. Meriel noted that Isibéal's feet, as always, were bare.

"It's how I grew up," she'd said to Meriel when they'd first met. *"My soul feels trapped when my feet are all bound in leather."* Meriel had found herself more interested in the woman's Taisteal background, remembering her own times with the itinerant folk. *"My father was some handsome, smooth-talking clan wanderer, who came to my mam's village and left a day or two later. One of the things he left behind was me in her belly, and I think I have more of him in me than her . . ."*

Isibéal had been sent by the Mother-Creator, in Meriel's view. Theneva, the matron who had been in charge of the staff for Meriel and her children, had vanished not long after the Festival of Méitha, without notice or so much as a word of warning. The other servants, one of whom Meriel had hoped would take over Theneva's role, seemed helpless and overwhelmed by the responsibilities of tutoring and caring for the Banrion Ard's son. The head of Edana's household staff had sent Isibéal to Meriel. Isibéal had references from Banrion Taafe of Tuath Éoganacht and was seeking employment; the serendipity had been compelling, as if Fiodóir, the Weaver of Fate Himself, had arranged things. And Ennis . . . when Ennis had been introduced to her, he'd fixed Meriel with that strange and serious look. "You need to hire her, Mam," he'd said solemnly. "It's important."

"How do you know that?" she'd asked him, laughing.

"The blue ghosts told me," he'd answered, then frowned when he saw that the response caused Meriel to clench her jaws in irritation. "I *know*, Mam," he said then. "I just do."

That had been but a month ago. Already Meriel couldn't imagine her household without Isibéal's presence. "Now you come with me, young Tiarna," Isibéal told Ennis, "and I'll tell you a tale. What would you like to hear?"

"Tell me about the haunts in the barrows!" Ennis answered. "I liked that one."

Isibéal glanced at Meriel with a grin and a sidewise roll of her eyes. "And have the wights chased you in your sleep?" she asked.

"I'll kill them with my sword," Ennis declared, and he held out his imaginary weapon again. "See!"

The women both laughed at his fierce scowl. "Even warriors must have their sleep," Isibéal told him. "Let's go and leave your mam to her duties." Isibéal cuddled Ennis to her and caught Meriel's gaze. "Banrion Mac Ard asked if you would care to take some refreshment with her and the Tiarna Mac Ard, and there was a rider from Tuath Airgialla just come in who has a message for you, also."

"From Airgialla?" *Perhaps there's word of Owaine and Kayne. They should be returning from Céile Mhór by now, and I feel Owaine so much closer . . .* She went to Ennis and kissed him on the forehead, ruffling his hair. "Go on with Isibéal, darling. I'll come see you later, and make sure those wights aren't bothering your dreams." Isibéal's gaze was on her, those odd light eyes. "Airgialla. It would be so wonderful to be with Owaine again after so long."

Isibéal's smile widened. "I'm sure you will be," she told Meriel. "Very soon."

"I hope you're right, Isibéal."

Isibéal shifted Ennis' weight on her hip. She kissed the boy where Meriel's lips had touched him a moment before. "I'm certain of it," she answered. "We Taisteal know these things."

6

A Clochmion's Use

DILLON'S LIPS were warm and incredibly soft, and tasted slightly of the sweet milarán cakes that had been served for dessert. Sevei pulled back reluctantly from the long and lingering kiss, leaning her head on Dillon's shoulder and enjoying the comfort of his arms around her.

They were pressed into the corner of one of the small courtyards of the White Keep—the First Holder's Wing. Sevei's gram had created this section herself over the space of a week several years ago, crafting the rooms and corridors and sweeping great halls with the power of Lámh Shábhála. The stone was gleaming white, so pure that it seemed to capture the light of the sun and release it in a soft glow for hours after sunset. In the mage-lights, the smooth and slick walls glittered with the captured colors of the sky. Sevei thought that the First Holder's Wing was the most delightful of all the spaces within the White Keep; the fact that it was her gram's design only made it more special.

Though there was still light in the western sky, she and Dillon cuddled in relative darkness, with Sevei's back against the cold curve of a tower's base. The fireworks display of the mage-lights had come far earlier than usual, just as they'd finished their supper, with the edge of the sun still visible over the horizon of the Westering Sea. For the first time, Sevei had lifted her own cloch to the lights, standing between Gram with Lámh Shábhála and Máister Kirwan with Snarl, both of them instructing her as the intense colors of the sky inundated them, banishing even the dying sun's light. The brilliant multicolored shadows had swept around the White Keep and the First Holder's Wing, and Sevei had gasped with the wonder of it all, marveling at the feeling of holding the mage-lights within herself, within the clochmion.

Though she still didn't know what her stone could do. It had yet to tell her.

"Was it awful for you tonight, my love?" she whispered into Dillon's ear. "I know Gram can be . . . intimidating."

"Well, that's certainly one word for her," Dillon answered and she felt him shiver once in her arms. "She seemed . . . I don't know, a bit distant all evening."

"She's not feeling well," Sevei answered, "and she's taking medication for the pain. Kala bark."

Dillon nodded. "The rumors I've heard among the students are that she uses andúilleaf, too."

Sevei shook her head at that. It was gossip she'd heard as well, a tale she hoped wasn't true. Andúilleaf addiction had driven Jenna mad twice already, with disastrous consequences both times. "I don't think so. I don't think she'd be that foolish."

Holding him, she felt Dillon's shrug. His breath tickled her ear, warm. "Maybe not. But when she finally started talking during dinner, I thought she was going to interrogate me about every last person in my family down to the fourth cousins. I swear that she knew family members *I* didn't know I had."

"I'm sure Gram had her staff doing research all day before you arrived. She's thorough that way. I don't blame her for wanting to know, though. A little suspicion is a survival trait in our family, I'm afraid."

"I understand." He gave a quick chuckle. "And then watching all three of you, with the mage-lights . . . well, I'm amazed that I'm allowed to be near you at all." His lips sought hers again, and she lifted her face to his.

For several long breaths, they said nothing. Sevei let herself fall into him, as if they were one body. She'd had infatuations before, some serious, some not. Before she'd been sent out to fosterage, she and Padraic Mac Ard—Banrion Edana and Doyle Mac Ard's oldest son—had become close enough that she knew Mam and Auntie Edana had whispered about a possible marriage in the future.

But Dillon . . . Dillon was an even more intense attraction than Padraic: handsome, intelligent, a talented Bráthair of the Order even if he held no cloch na thintrí yet, and a gifted musician with the harp. She could sometimes feel as close to him as she could her twin Kayne. She wondered if she could feel his thoughts as she did her twin's, if she tried hard enough. They'd been together for half a year now; a time that felt simultaneously like forever and but a few days. When at last she reluctantly pulled her head back, she put her mouth next to his ear.

"I suppose you'll do," she husked.

They both laughed—that had been Jenna's comment to Sevei as they left her chambers hand in hand: *"I suppose he'll do. As long as he's what you want right now . . ."* They kissed again, shorter this time but more urgently, and when Dillon's fingers slid down her side to her waist, she caught his hand with hers. "I should be getting back to my room. Máister Kirwan said he was going to be following along in a few minutes, and you know what that means."

"Aye, I know. Though . . ." He stopped. "Maybe he'll spend the evening with your gram instead."

"Dillon!" Sevei exclaimed in mock horror, then chuckled. "So you noticed, too."

"Aye. It was obvious. Our Máister likes the First Holder, and she seems to like him as well." He kissed the nape of her neck and she lifted her chin with a sigh, feeling the kiss all the way to her core. "I wonder if your great-da knows?" he continued.

"I don't think he would care, actually. They hardly spend much time toge—" Dillon stopped her words with his mouth, but she gave a gasp, feeling a stabbing of something almost like pain in her chest; Dillon pulled back, looking at her quizzically.

"What's the matter?"

"I don't know . . ." Sevei felt as if a knife point had been pressed between her breasts, heated to a white-hot glow. She reached for the spot and felt the clochmion there. Her fingers went around it, almost involuntarily, and with the touch, she felt her awareness double: part of her was standing there in the courtyard in Dillon's arms, and another part of her went sweeping outward over the Westering Sea. She could feel . . . out there . . . something . . .

. . . the beating of huge wings, slow and steady and com-

*forting ... the waves rushing below cold and gray, the wave
tops tipped with red from the sunset, the wind lifting phos-
phorescent whitecaps from the tops ... off to the left, the island rising from the sea ... and there the touch of
recognition ... the rumble of heat in your belly and the urge
to be with another of your kind, but the pull of recognition
brings your head around on your long neck ...*

*helpless to ignore the summons, your wings tilt, and the
ocean looms close and clouds wheel overhead with the
turn ...*

"Sevei, what is it?"

"Shh ..." she told Dillon. "There's something close to us,
out to sea."

Letting go of Dillon's hand, Sevei hurried to the entrance of the courtyard and the bars of the gate. She
pushed open the gate open and stepped out from the keep
wall, peered down the steep slopes of Inishfeirm to where
the Westering Sea could be seen through the trees fringing
the cliffs of the island. To her right, the main wing of the
keep loomed. "I don't see anything," Dillon called behind
her, still inside the gateway of the courtyard. "Maybe if we
went up into the tower ..."

"We don't need to do that," Sevei answered. "I can feel
it with the clochmion." She lifted the chain over her head,
holding the stone in her hand. It was glowing now, as if in
response.

*... the island coming near ... an anger roaring in the belly
at being forced to respond this way ... wanting to turn and
go seek out the nest of your own kind, but you can't because
of the call ...*

"No, wait," Sevei said. "There *is* something. Look. Is that
a bird, maybe?"

She tried to point so that Dillon could see, though it was
difficult with the doubled vision in her head: she saw both
herself looking out but also staring inward at the island
where she stood. The form *did* seem like a large bird—a
shape seen against the stars—but suddenly the perspective
shifted on her and she realized that the creature was much
farther away than either of them thought, and that the
beast was far, far too large to be a bird. The creature
rushed toward her, or she rushed toward it—with the twin
visions in her head, it was difficult for Sevei to tell which.

"By the Mother . . ." Dillon husked behind her. "Sevei . . ."

"I know," she answered, not looking back at him but at the creature, her voice full of awe. "Dillon, I think I brought it here."

Majestic and terrible, the dragon swelled in size as it came over the island, the tops of the very trees bending with its passage. It hovered above the library tower flanking the main gate of the keep: leathery wings catching the cold air, brown-and-gold scales glinting in the last light of the day, though with the moonglow from the east and the twilight to the west, the tail stretched out behind the dragon seemed to be blood-red. The wings flapped once with a boom like thunder and clawed, muscular feet grasped the top of the tower as it perched there, far down the main wing from Sevei. Claws clenched and mage-stones fell, cracked and broken. The creature stared at her down the length of the White Keep: at Sevei and the stone in her hand. Even at this distance she knew the creature's attention was on her, because she could see herself through the dragon's eyes. Its mouth opened and it screeched as alarm bells rang throughout the keep, heat shimmering from the tooth-lined cavern of its mouth. Then the wings flapped again and it pushed away from the library tower, sending a portion of the wall falling. Now it came toward the First Holder's Wing and her.

Sevei was frozen; she could only watch.

Dillon darted out and pulled Sevei under cover of the archway as the dragon half landed, half crashed into one of the guard towers above them. A milk-white block smashed to the ground a dozen strides from them, burying itself in one of the garden beds as it crushed pansies and herbs. The beast's frilled head lowered on its long neck and eyes the size of a man's head glared at them under thick ridges, no more than an arm's span away. It opened its mouth once more and there was a glow inside, while heat wavered and steamed in the night air. They could feel the warmth of the air and smell the scent of carrion.

The dragon spoke, sounds Sevei could not understand with her ears, but which formed into dark and low words in her head.

"Why do you call me, Soft-flesh?" it asked.

Sevei almost staggered. "Call . . . you?" she stammered, her voice seeming impossibly small against the roar and presence of the dragon. "I didn't . . . I mean . . ."

"You called me here and now you hold me," the dragon intoned. "If there is nothing you want of me, then let me go."

"Let you go?" Sevei repeated, then saw the dragon's gaze lower from her face to her hand (and seeing its viewpoint in her mind), and she realized that she was still clutching the clochmion, that the energy of the mage-lights was pouring out from it. She also realized that it was emptying quickly of the power she'd placed in it just a stripe ago.

So that's *what it does . . .*

One of the bráthairs emerged from the doorway of the opposite tower, gaped in astonishment at the dragon perched above, and fled shouting for help. Close by, Sevei felt a Cloch Mór open, and then—like the sun rising again—Lámh Shábhála also wakened. Sevei wasn't sure how she knew this: she could feel the impact on the net of energy flowing outward from her clochmion. *Dragoncaller* . . . She thought the name involuntarily and knew that would be the name for her stone. *Dragoncaller* . . .

"Let me go," the dragon said again, "or wait, if you prefer." Its face seemed to leer at her and she could hear amusement in its voice. There was sharp intelligence behind those eyes, but also a strong malevolence that made Sevei shudder. She realized that the creature cared nothing about or for her or the world of humans—there was no common ground between them. She stared into the cold eyes of Otherness. She knew—somehow, inside—that the dragons called themselves the *Earc Tine,* and that this one's name was Kekeri the Bloodtail, and that . . . "You can't hold me much longer," it said, guessing her thoughts, and she knew it was right—already the clochmion was nearly drained and once its power was gone . . .

If she had called the dragon, if she held it here with the clochmion, then once the cloch's energy was drained, the creature would be free to do whatever it wished. As if to underscore her thoughts, the dragon's claws clutched hard at the lip of the tower and more stones fell.

Gram would emerge in a moment, and Máister Kirwan, and she could imagine what they would do with the beast perched on the ramparts of the White Keep, and she could also imagine what the dragon might do in response. An image flashed before her of the White Keep caught in dragon flame and the lightnings of the clochs na thintrí. She could smell the fire and hear the screams.

She could see people dying. People she knew and cared about.

"Go!" she told it loudly. She waved her free hand at it as if shooing away a persistent fly. "Go back to your journey!"

The dragon lifted its head. "I will meet you again," it said. "Another time . . ." It lifted its head away as the great jaws opened and it screamed: a deep mournful howl that shivered with the sound of hissing flame. The wings flapped once, sending a blast of summer-hot air over the courtyard that raised dust from the flagstones. Its massive legs pushed hard against the tower, cracking the stones and showering the courtyard with a final cascade of rock. The scarlet tail slapped at a crenellated wall and it fell. The dragon's shadow flitted over the court as Sevei heard shouts of alarm from around the keep. Sevei and Dillon rushed out from their shelter to see the dragon wheel high above the keep and then flash downward over the cliffs of the island toward the sea. In a moment, it was gone behind the screen of trees.

Sevei released the clochmion. There was but a bare breath of power left within it. *When it was gone, what would have happened?* Sevei found herself shivering from more than just the cold.

"Sevei! Sevei, where are you!"

"Here, Gram!" Sevei stepped out into the open with Dillon beside her. Jenna was standing at the balcony of her room overlooking the courtyard, clutching Lámh Shábhála, and Máister Kirwan stood there with her.

"The dragon—"

"It's gone, Gram. I—"

Jenna peered down at them. "I know what you did. I felt it." The light had nearly vanished in the west and in the gloom and with the distance, Sevei could not read the expression on the older woman's face. "You'll come up here," Jenna said, and it wasn't the voice of Gram but the command of a Banrion who expected obedience. "Both of you. Up here. Now."

"You called that creature with the clochmion." The way Gram said the words made it a statement, not a question.

"Aye, Gram," Sevei answered. "I didn't know . . . I felt the clochmion, and when I touched the stone, it was like I *was* the dragon. I know exactly how the beast felt: the stone called and it *had* to come even though it didn't want to. The clochmion could hold it as long as there was still power in the stone, and I think if I had ordered the dragon to do something, it would have, though with a great reluctance. The dragons don't really like or understand us, or us them . . ."

"It talked to you . . . You could understand dragon-speech . . ." Sevei saw her gram glance at Máister Kirwan. "All her da could do with the same stone was find lost items," she said to him, "and *this* child brings down half the library and one of my towers the first night she fills it. Dragons, of all things!"

"She's an Aoire," Máister Kirwan answered. "Look what Meriel has done with Treoraí's Heart. It's your bloodline, Jenna. Don't act so surprised."

Jenna sighed at that, but Sevei thought she looked secretly pleased. Next to Sevei, Dillon stirred uncomfortably and Sevei took his hand. Jenna's eyes followed the motion and she scowled. Sevei hurried into the silence before her gram could speak again.

"Da always said he was fascinated by dragons, Gram, and he'd even seen them three times in his life," she said, "the first time when he was looking for Mam after she was taken from here and he was still holding this cloch. Maybe that's why the stone took that ability—because of Da's interest in dragons."

"*Why* doesn't matter," Jenna snapped. "What matters is whether you can control the clochmion, rather than the reverse."

"I can, Gram," Sevei said, her voice taking on an edge to match Jenna's. "I didn't know what I was doing or even what I had called just now—I was only responding to the cloch. Now I *do* know—and I'd remind you that I also knew enough to release the beast before Dragoncaller had spent all its energy, or we might not be talking together.

The way the thing looked at me . . . it would have crushed me in its jaws."

"It would have had to take me first," Dillon interjected, and Jenna made a sound of rude disdain in her throat.

"*Phah!* Brave words are easy when you don't have to back them up, Bráthair Ó'Baoill. And you, child," she said, turning her gaze on Sevei. "So now you *name* the stone, too? It's a simple clochmion, not a Cloch Mór. You don't need to be so overdramatic, Sevei.'

"And you needn't be so condescending, Gram," Sevei retorted.

"*Sevei* . . ." Dillon whispered, squeezing her hand warningly, but she ignored him. She sat forward in her chair, ready to answer heatedly, but Máister Kirwan interrupted the tirade she might have unleashed.

"I think," he said, stepping forward to stand between Jenna and Sevei, "that if a mirror could show the soul of a person and not just the body it inhabits, the two of you would see that there's not a whit of difference between you. Which is why you'll get nowhere arguing with each other, and why you *will* argue. Sevei, I'll spend the time between now and your departure for Dún Laoghaire working with you and the clochmion. That way we'll *all* be certain that there aren't any more, ah, unfortunate accidents with it. And that should satisfy Banrion MacEagan, also." He looked more at Jenna than Sevei. Jenna frowned, refusing to meet Máister Kirwan's eyes, but she finally gave a huff of exasperation and waved a hand at Sevei.

"I've never been good at acknowledging when someone tells me the unflattering truths about myself," Jenna said. Her face softened then. "But . . . Mundy, as usual, you're right—even if I don't want to admit it. Sevei, I'm sorry. I just . . . worry, that's all. For you to do this . . ." She shook her head. "You're stronger than most cloudmages, that's for certain. You'll need to be careful because of that. Do you understand?"

"No," Sevei answered truthfully. Jenna laughed at the bald starkness of the answer.

"Good. That's the most intelligent thing anyone has said here tonight." She waved her hand again. "You've exhausted that stone and can't fill it again until tomorrow night, so we're safe for the evening. Go on with you, then. I'm tired."

Sevei rose and went to Jenna. She kissed her on the forehead. "I love you, Gram," she said. "You know that, don't you? I'm sorry I argued with you. You're a Banrion and the First Holder besides, but you're my gram and that matters the most."

"Aye, I know," Jenna said quietly and patted Sevei on the cheek. "And I love you as well, daughter-child. I . . . I just don't want you to be hurt. I'll need you. I know that for certain now. I'll need you soon." She put an odd stress on the last word, and Sevei nodded. Dillon had come up alongside her; he bowed to the Banrion, who inclined her head in response silently, watching as Sevei took Dillon's arm and went to the door. Máister Kirwan followed after them.

"Mundy," Jenna called out. "Can you stay for a bit? I'd like you to fix some of the tea you talked about earlier . . ."

Máister Kirwan halted. "Certainly, Banrion. Bráthair, if you'll go on ahead with Sevei and escort her *directly*—" he paused to emphasize the word, "—to the women's wing . . . and see that this time she doesn't feel a need to use her clochmion."

"She won't, Máister," Dillon said. Sevei saw him start to grin, then his face went serious as he glanced back at Jenna.

"Tea," Dillon said to Sevei as Máister Kirwan shut the door behind them. The grin was back on his face. "I'll bet she just wants him for tea."

She kissed his grin away, and then raised an eyebrow at him. "Tea," she said firmly. "Or are you calling my gram a liar?"

"Never," he answered, his hands out in mock surrender.

"It's a good thing," she told him, "because she and I *are* alike, and what you say and think about her you also say and think about me."

She smiled at Dillon, but the way his eyes narrowed told her that he heard the bones within the words.

7

Morning Affairs

THE ARRUK SNARLED and hissed, raising its long-bladed jaka and swinging it toward Kayne. He brought his sword up to block, but the blade seemed impossibly heavy. Iron rang, and Kayne's sword went spinning out of his nerveless hands to land in the mud three strides away. Everything seemed to stop and shift into underwater motion. He had forever to notice that his feet were mired to the ankle in the muck of the bog, that his armor and clothing were spattered with blood, that a storm was beginning to blow in from the west and that the battle around him was eerily silent.

Da was standing at the top of a rise just behind the Arruk, and he held a bow in his hand with an arrow fitted to the string. His Cloch Mór sat untouched and gleaming on his gray léine. Owaine watched, but though the Arruk lifted his jaka again with a roar, swinging it back to make the strike that would kill Kayne, Da didn't move, didn't draw back the bowstring and send the arrow into the Arruk's unprotected back, didn't bring his hand to his cloch to send the terrible lightning of Blaze down on the creature.

He just watched. Waiting.

"Da!" Kayne screamed, but Owaine's dark eyes only stared, impassive. Desperate now, Kayne tried to leap to one side to regain his sword, but the swampy ground held him fast. He could hear the mud squelching under him, could smell the ripeness of the bog and the rotting flesh odor of the Arruk's breath. Kayne raised his hand in a useless, hopeless gesture of defense, knowing that the leather wrapping around his arms couldn't hold back the bite of the notched blade, that his next few breaths would be his last. "Da!" he screamed again.

Owaine shook his head, mute.

"Da! Help me!" The blade was sweeping down, as inevitable and bright as the sun . . .

"Tiarna!" A hand shook him. "Tiarna, wake up!"

Kayne fluttered his eyes open to find a young woman's face framed in unruly, long red locks staring at him. Dawn light streamed in through the painted slats of shutters and the remnants of a fire glowed dully in the hearth. Kayne was sweating and tangled in the sheets of the bed; the young woman, sitting up alongside him, was naked. She seemed to realize it belatedly, reaching to bring up the sheet and holding it before her with a tentative smile. "You were shouting in your sleep, Tiarna," she said. Her voice held the thick Fingerlander accent.

Kayne blinked, rubbing at his eyes. His head throbbed with the fumes of too much ale. His stomach was sour; his mouth was caked with foul-tasting gunk. He remembered only fragments of the night before: leaving the hall while his da had been speaking, arguing with Harik, and then going back to the hall and drinking until the building seemed to dance a reel about him. He remembered once looking across the room to see Da glaring at him reproachfully, but Kayne ignored him and continued drinking with a group of the gardai. Then, sometime not long before sunrise, he staggered up here with the village lass on his arm. He didn't know her name; she'd told him, but he hadn't bothered to remember it—that wasn't important. She wasn't the first lowborn tuathánach lass he'd lain with, and he'd made her no promises. He was certain they both knew the boundaries.

Kayne was well aware of the double standards at work between the classes. He'd learned early on that while he had to be very careful of any dalliance with Riocha women, it didn't matter if a girl without the proper pedigree turned up big-bellied. It didn't matter if she claimed the child was that of a Tiarna—any unwed lass might do the same and none could prove it. For all Kayne knew, there might be a half dozen bastard children of his born or swelling the womb of a mam-to-be between here and the plains of Mid Céile Mhór. It would be different for Sevei, for instance, or any Riocha woman. Sevei would be carefully watched, especially with young men of lesser standing. And if Sevei ended up pregnant from such an encounter, it would mean a hasty negotiation between the respective families and almost certainly a marriage.

There'd be a marriage or Kayne would have the man's head, no matter what Sevei said.

"Tiarna?" The girl was staring at him. "You look so fierce. Was it the dream?"

"Aye," he told her. "The dream . . ." The reminder brought back the images and he shuddered once, muscles rippling in sinewy forearms. *The Arruk's blade coming down to him; Da watching, just watching* . . . His breathing, in response, quickened and he forced it to slow once more, swallowing hard. Someone seemed to be pounding a drumbeat on his temples, and his stomach lurched like a sour sea. "I need to get up . . ."

Kayne threw back the blankets and stood in the cold of the room, reaching for his clothing. Her hand trailed his spine; he ignored it. "We'll be mustering in less than a stripe. I have to go. You can stay here as long as you want—I'll pay the innkeeper for another day and night, if you like."

He stood, turning to look down at her. Her face was that of a stranger, her features plain and unremarkable in the dawn light, her cheeks pocked with the scars of some childhood disease, her bright hair tangled and unkempt. There was hurt in her eyes. "If . . . if I come to Dún Laoghaire, Tiarna, you said . . ." She sniffed, rubbing her nose with her hand and wiping it on the bedsheet she held around herself. ". . . you said you would find me a position . . ." Her lower lip was trembling; he thought she would cry in a moment.

"Come there and I will, lass," he told her, forcing a smile to his face. It didn't matter, he told himself. The likelihood was that she would never leave the Finger or come within a week's journey of Dún Laoghaire. And if by some fluke she did, well, Mam's staff would take care of it, as they'd taken care of the two local indiscretions Kayne had committed a few years previously: find the girl a lowly position in the household where she wouldn't come into contact with Kayne or the rest of his family at all. A few mórceints in her purse and she'd be satisfied and properly silent. "I promise."

He reached down and let his fingers graze the length of her cheek. She smiled shyly at him and let the sheet drop. "Stay a bit longer?" she asked.

There was no lust in him, looking at her. He was hungry, he was tired, he wanted desperately to empty his bladder. Looking at her reminded him of the nightmare. Looking at her reminded him how furiously he wanted to be home again. He wondered if Sevei would be there, or if she was still away at Inishfeirm learning the ways of the cloud-mage . . . "No," he told her. "I wish I could stay longer, but no."

He turned from her to slide on his clóca so he wouldn't have to look at her disappointment. He turned his back to her to use the chamber pot, sighing with relief at the bright tinkling. Finally, he picked up his weapons and overcloak from where they lay, the equipment heavy in his hands. "I have to leave now . . ." he said, his voice trailing off.

"Róise," she said. "My name is Róise Toibin."

He nodded. He didn't want the name, didn't want to have to remember it. He *wouldn't* remember it; his head hurt too much to make the effort. He fumbled with the leather purse on his belt and slipped out a few mórceints. "Thank you," he said. "There's . . . something for you here." He smiled again at her—a brief, empty lifting of his lips— and left the room before she could speak again. Outside, he leaned against the closed door, taking a long breath. Shaking his head, he went down the corridor to the short stairs and down into the main room of the tavern. The sergeants of the gardai were already there, breaking their fast with biscuits and sausage. A few of them grinned, lifting their mugs of tea in his direction. The innkeeper, his wife, and children bustled around the tables, serving.

Da and Harik were there also, at the table nearest the stairs. Owaine glanced at Kayne, his gaze shadowed and careful. "You're ready to ride, Kayne?"

"Aye, Da," Kayne answered, and the pain that Owaine allowed to show in his face made Kayne want to apologize for his rudeness of the night before. *That's what the dream was telling you—that you poison the relationship between your da and yourself.* Sevei had warned him of that, before she'd gone off to Inishfeirm.

"Da loves you more than life, Kayne, but he doesn't understand you. He never will, not the way I do or Mam does. He wants to, but he can't, and you can't let yourself blame him for that." She'd smiled at him then and hugged him. *"I know you don't understand him either,"* she'd whispered into his ear. *"But you should try. He's a good man. He has to be, for both Gram and Mam to love him so much."*

"And you understand Da completely?" he'd wanted to retort, but he'd held the words back. She did have a rapport with their da that he had never been able to manage. Twins, he and Sevei might be, aye, but though they loved each other, the two of them were more different than they were alike. . . .

"Did you hear me, son?" Owaine was saying. "I said Harik's going to stay here with five double-hands of the gardai—those who don't have family to return to—until Rí Airgialla can send troops to watch the border. Harik's going to go back to the ruins of the Bunús Wall. I want him to see if perhaps we could rebuild it as a defense work against the Arruk."

Kayne almost smiled. "I'll stay, also," he said. If the Arruk were coming, then he would stay here—he would lead the defense. He would lead the men as his da never had: without timidity and with raw courage.

"No." It was Harik who answered. "Tiarna Geraghty has already decided that you'll return to Dún Laoghaire with him."

Kayne drew back, surprised at the temerity of the Hand answering before his da. Harik held Kayne's gaze, his face carefully unexpressive. Owaine hurried into the tension. "This will be Harik's command," Owaine said. "To have you here, Kayne . . ." He shook his head. They all knew what he was saying: Harik MacCathaill might be the Hand but he was only a céili giallnai, one of the minor nobility, and a Riocha couldn't serve under him, especially not the Banrion Ard's own son.

"Then give me the command, Da, and let Harik be my Hand as he's been yours. I want to stay. There isn't anything more important that I can do than to protect the border from the Arruk."

"No," Owaine answered. "We've already discussed this and the decision's been made. You'll come with me; your mam would never forgive me if I left you behind when you were so close."

Kayne saw the truth then, coming to him in a flash as it sometimes did, and he spoke it rashly, as he also sometimes did. "Harik has already told you that he wouldn't serve as my Hand, hasn't he, Da?" He glared again at Harik, who looked back at him blandly.

"Harik is the best man to stay here," Owaine said, and all of them knew that he hadn't answered the question. "He knows the Arruk and the men trust him. He's loyal to Dún Laoghaire and the Tuatha and I trust him utterly."

"And you wouldn't trust me."

Owaine frowned, and his voice lowered in both volume and tone. "After yesterday, Kayne? After all that you've said to me and Harik?" Owaine's dark eyes held quiet reproach. Then he did answer, and the word was a blade slicing between Kayne's ribs. "No."

"The gardai trust me," Kayne said, a little too loudly—a few of them glanced over toward their table. "They would follow me—they *did* follow me. Just yesterday. Or have you forgotten?"

"They admire your bravery, aye." Again it was Harik who responded, and Kayne glared at the man's temerity. "And they smile and tell you what they know you want to hear when you're in their presence. They give you sweet little flatteries because you're Riocha and they're not. When you're just a garda and a tuathánach, you hide your real thoughts from the Riocha. But do they *trust* you? Would they give you their lives?" Harik shook his head before Kayne could respond. "I know them, and the answer is 'no,' Tiarna. I don't think they would. They've seen your bravery on the field and they admire it, but they also see how reckless it is. The kind of trust a commander needs you haven't earned yet. Maybe one day you will. But not yet. Not now."

Kayne could feel the heat on his face. He wanted desperately to shout at Harik, to demand satisfaction for his harsh words, but Da's face was steel and he could hear the sudden silence in the tavern as everyone pretended not to watch the three of them talking. He wanted to strike at

Harik, to slap the man across the face and bury his words in blood. Every muscle in Kayne's body felt as taut as a bowstring; he could hear his heart pounding against chest and temple.

"Kayne!" It was Da's voice, sharp. "I think you should see to the horses, if you're not going to sit down and break bread with us. My decision's made and it's the right one. If you're going to be a soldier, then right now you need to act like one and obey your orders."

Kayne trembled, his hands clenched. He was taller than his da by half a head, and younger and stronger. He ached to defy him. He clenched his teeth, hearing them grate against each other. Owaine stared and Harik watched: Kayne knew that if he moved, so would the Hand. "Aye, Tiarna Geraghty, Hand MacCathaill," Kayne answered finally, almost spitting the words. "I'll go see to the horses, then. I'll be glad to put my back to this filthy shite-hole of a village and those who will be staying anywhere near it."

With that, he stalked out of the tavern. "Let him go, Tiarna," he heard Harik say as he left. As he pushed open the door, he heard the talk begin behind him.

You don't want to like these people. You don't want to admire them . . .

Isibéal and Ennis watched through the grillwork at the end of the Heart Chamber, masked behind a screen of plants and draperies. There were five supplicants this morning in the Chamber, standing just behind Siúr Martain, the Hand of the Heart. Banrion Edana and Tiarna Doyle Mac Ard had also joined the Banrion Ard in the Chamber. Isibéal shivered: two Clochs Mór and Treoraí's Heart all in the same room; two Banrions and a cloud-mage—so much power was concentrated here.

And one of them was Doyle Mac Ard, brushing back his long, fiery red locks. Seeing Tiarna Mac Ard here, so close, made her suck in her breath harshly enough that Ennis looked up at her.

"We have to be very quiet," Ennis told Isibéal with an overserious expression on his face. "Sevei showed me how to get back here before she left, but she said that Mam would be angry if she ever knew we were watching her, and the blue ghosts have shown me what would happen then."

"Then let's not talk," she whispered back to Ennis. "Just watch . . ."

Isibéal cradled the boy on her lap and leaned in closer to the grille. The stone flags of the little alcove behind the chamber were cold on her bare feet. She could hear the voices faintly from the other end of the Heart Chamber.

"Thank you, Siúr Martain," the Banrion Ard said. "I appreciate all you've done today." Through the grille, Isibéal saw the woman bow to Meriel. The Banrion Ard, holding Treoraí's Heart in her left hand, walked over to the supplicants. Most of them lowered their heads as she approached, not daring to look at her directly; two of them, standing slightly apart from the others and, from their dress, obviously Riocha, did not; they met Meriel's gaze. The Banrion Ard moved slowly down the line, pausing in front of each one. There was conversation between the supplicants and Meriel, though it was so soft and garbled by the echoes in the hall that Isibéal couldn't hear it. One of the supplicants, a woman with a bandage holding a greasy poultice of some sort to her head, gasped as Meriel spoke to her. She gave a shout of glee, ripping the poultice from her head, and the Banrion Edana and Tiarna Mac Ard applauded softly. The woman sank to her knees in front of Meriel, kissing the hand clutching Treorai's Heart.

"She's not really the one," Ennis whispered to Isibéal. "Mam says that many of those who come to her fix themselves somehow. She said maybe it's just the Mother-Creator working on Her own. She'll use the cloch with the lady who has the black hair."

"Why do you say that, Ennis?" Isibéal saw nothing special about the woman. The others all seemed to suffer from obvious physical deformities: a withered arm; a leg whose bandage seemed to be seeping some dark pus; the wrinkled, shiny scars of horrible burns on flesh. The black-haired woman—dressed in a ragged, torn léine and soiled woolen clóca—appeared healthy enough compared to the others, with no visible problem.

"I just *know*," he answered, snuggling up against her. "Can't you see the blue ghosts?" Isibéal clasped her arm tighter around him, the movement instinctive and maternal. She remembered the child she'd lost—he'd been Ennis' age, almost exactly, and sometimes when she held Ennis, she leaned in and smelled him, and he smelled like Adimu had. She could imagine she was holding her own son again . . . *You don't want to feel sympathy for these people . . .*

Meriel had stopped in front of the black-haired woman. She spoke, and the woman answered so softly that Isibéal could hear nothing. "Her sickness is inside," Ennis said with a certainty that was curiously adult. "Mam says that's the hardest thing to heal with her stone. She says it's hard, too, because no one else can see it, and they sometimes wonder why she chose that person."

"People don't believe miracles they can't see," Isibéal told the boy. "That's just our nature. Do you understand what I mean?"

He nodded, his large eyes wide. "Mam could heal the sickness inside you," he said. "If you let her."

Isibéal found herself holding her breath, staring at the boy. "What . . ." She had to stop and swallow. "What do you mean, Ennis? I'm not sick."

"You don't think so," Ennis answered with the same dry solemnity, as if he were reciting his lessons. "But you are." Before she could reply to that, he wriggled in her arms and pointed. "Look!" he said breathily.

Meriel had dismissed all the other supplicants except for the dark-haired woman. The poor ones left quickly with downcast eyes. The two Riocha also bowed and gave polite thanks, but Isibéal could see the frustration and distaste in their eyes at realizing the Banrion Ard had again chosen a tuathánach over them. When they'd gone, Meriel motioned to the woman, who came and stood nervously in front of the Banrion Ard. Meriel's hand tightened visibly around the clochmion she held, and she reached out to cup the woman's head with her other hand. Meriel stiffened at the touch, as if it pained her to make the contact. Her chin lifted, the torc of the Banrion Ard gleaming on her léine, and her eyes closed. She groaned loudly, a keening low wail almost like the grieving of the sochraideach, the professional mourners who attended the Riocha funerals. A blue glow surrounded the two of them, the illumination flaring quickly to white and then vanishing as Meriel lifted her hand from the woman. The woman gasped as Meriel sank backward, her knees gone limp. Siúr Martain rushed to the Banrion, but it was Doyle Mac Ard who caught her, holding her until Meriel's eyes flickered open again and she stood. "Thank you, Uncle," she said to Mac Ard. "And you?" she asked the woman, who only shook her head mutely.

"I don't know what to say, Banrion Ard," she answered finally. "I've never . . . The pain, it's gone."

"Aye, gone forever," Meriel told her with a gentle smile. "Go on now, back to your family. You'll live long, the Mother willing." The woman hesitated, and when Meriel opened her arms, the woman rushed forward to embrace the Banrion Ard. Edana smiled indulgently at the display, but Doyle's smile seemed more smirk to Isibéal.

With another bow, the woman left the room. Edana stroked Meriel's long hair. "They love you, Meriel," she said. "Every time I watch you do this, I realize how well-chosen you were."

"The common folk certainly love you, all those unwashed tuathánach that parade through the keep every day," Doyle interjected.

"Doyle . . ." Edana pressed her lips together, and Doyle shrugged.

Meriel sighed as if she hadn't noticed Doyle's comment. "I'm tired and dreadfully hungry—will the two of you join me? I want to hear all about the children. Doyle, I haven't seen Padraic since he went to the Order of Gabair, and you were just there. I hear that Alastríona is going to be coming back from fosterage this summer. I'm sure you can't wait to see her again and see how she's bloomed . . ."

They moved toward the door, still talking, and the hall garda opened it for them. As they were leaving, Doyle stopped, allowing the Banrion and Banrion Ard to pass out into the corridor before him. Slowly, he turned, looking directly back at the lacy grillwork where Isibéal and Ennis were huddled. His eyes seemed to find Isibéal's and—very deliberately—he nodded once.

Then he turned and followed the two women from the room.

"You're shaking, Isibéal," Ennis said, looking up at her solemnly. He said it as if it were a reaction he'd expected.

"It's nothing," she told the child. "Nothing at all. Come, it's time for you to eat."

Taking the boy in hand, she led him away from the Heart Chamber.

8

Preparations

"**Y**OU'RE GOING TO MAKE dinner for us?" Ennis asked Isibéal, and she nodded.

"Tomorrow night, for both you and your mam. Just for us."

"Why?"

"It's a special day for the Taisteal, when we honor the god Fiodóir who is the son of the Mother-Creator, and who weaves the tapestry of Fate. I wanted to make a special meal to celebrate."

Isibéal and Ennis were walking through Oldtown, the narrow, crowded streets of Dún Laoghaire near the north end of the harbor: a boil of grimy, close-packed buildings set in a chaotic whirl of tiny lanes. There were always shadows here, not only those in the narrow gaps between houses or beyond the depths of ancient archways leading into musty catacombs, but the human kind who dealt in illegal goods and other activities on the fringe of society. A quartet of solemn-faced gardai walked with them, a few respectful steps behind but ready to intervene if anyone in the crowded lanes tried to bother them. Isibéal had no illusions as to whose aid they'd come to first—she was just a hired servant; it was Ennis they were there to protect. The people who passed them glanced carefully at Ennis, dressed in a fine, pale gray léine and clóca, his hair freshly cut and oiled. Even if they didn't know he was the Banrion Ard's son, they knew he was Riocha. If they wondered what such rich folk might be doing in this neighborhood, they knew better than to wonder aloud.

Isibéal took Ennis' hand, steering him around a pile of nightsoil in the foul central gutter of the lane. Ennis wrinkled his nose at the smell and looked up at Isibéal.

"The Mother-Creator doesn't have a son, just a daughter," he said. He seemed to find the sights around him more fascinating than disgusting. He looked about wide-eyed and eager.

"That's what you Daoine believe, aye, but the Taisteal believe differently."

"Which one is right?"

"I don't know," Isibéal answered. "Perhaps both. Perhaps neither."

"Then I'll ask the Mother-Creator, after I die."

Isibéal shivered at that. "Here—this is where we're going." She pointed to a sign painted with fanciful leaves and red-berried plants, the colors now chipped and faded and partially lost under a green beard of mildew. Isibéal opened the door to the shop and the pungent smell of spices wafted out to them. They walked into the fragrant atmosphere, the shop as dark and poorly lit as the rest of Oldtown—two of the gardai came with them, the other two remained outside.

"There's no one here," Ennis started to say, then visibly jumped as a net of shadows shifted in the rear of the shop. A cackling laugh emerged from the darkness and an old woman hobbled into the flickering light of tapers, tapping along the uneven flooring with a thick cane. She was white-haired and as wrinkled as an old apple, stooped over with a dowager's hump.

"One day soon enough, you'll be right, boy," she said, laughing again to reveal a mouth with only a few remaining teeth. She tapped her way forward, stopping near a table piled with racks of drying herbs. "Ah, Isibéal. Here to pick up your order?"

"Aye, Asthora. You were able to get everything I asked for?"

A nod. "'Tis not easy to get all you wanted this time of year, but I managed. All of it. Here." Groaning, the old woman reached under the table and brought out a large packet of thick, folded paper sealed with a wax seal. Eyes with whites gone the color of egg yolks flicked over at the gardai. She lifted the package to her hooked nose and took a long, appreciative sniff. "Ah, the very aroma makes me hungry. Do you want to see?"

Isibéal shook her head quickly. "I trust you, Cousin. How much?"

Asthora set the packet down on the table. "Two mórceints."

"Two mórceints," one of the gardai muttered. "Are those spices made of gold, woman?"

Asthora only chuckled. "Not gold. There are herbs and spices far rarer than mere gold. And to those who need them, worth more. Would you like to buy some of my herbs, perhaps? Why, I have something that would put steel in the weapon you young men like to brandish the most. The ladies would like that, eh?" She grinned at him. The garda shook his head while his companion snickered.

Isibéal handed Asthora the coins. "Thank you," Isibéal said as she took the parcel.

"I'm sure it will be a fine meal. One to remember," Asthora answered. "Cousin."

Isibéal glanced at the gardai. "I hope so," she answered. "Come, Ennis. It's time we got back to the keep."

"Is she really your cousin?" Ennis asked as they left the shop, the gardai falling in behind them again.

"Possibly," Isibéal told him. Outside, the air seemed colder than usual, and Isibéal placed the packet under her clóca. The paper seemed strangely heavy and she could smell the herbs in the movement of the air. "On my da's side; the Taisteal side. All Taisteal call themselves cousins, even if they're not sure."

"Mam stayed with the Taisteal once. She liked them a lot, she said. One of them once saved her life, she said. My sister Sevei was named after the Taisteal woman, but Kayne was named after my great-da on my da's side."

Isibéal forced herself to smile at him. "I'm glad your mam likes the Taisteal. But they're just people, like any others. Some are good, others . . ." She lifted her shoulders.

"Was your son a Taisteal?" he asked. "The one who died?"

"Adimu?" Isibéal frowned. "How did you know . . . ?" The boy just looked at her innocently. Isibéal shook her head; she must have mentioned having a son, though she didn't remember doing so—Ennis seemed to remember everything that anyone told him. "Aye, Adimu's da was Taisteal, too."

"I like you, Isibéal," Ennis said. "No matter what."

Isibéal looked away. Above the houses of Oldtown, the keep loomed against a gray sky. "Let's get you home," she told Ennis, "before your mam begins to worry."

Sevei came out of the crashing surf a moment after Jenna, allowing the touch of the wind to start the change and shift her from seal to human form. She shivered in the air, and the pummeling waves nearly knocked her over as she walked out onto the rocky shingle of the beach. Jenna was waiting for her, watching, and Sevei saw the gleam of Lámh Shábhála between her gram's breasts. "Here," Jenna said, handing Sevei a towel. "I'm always amazed at how cold the air and water are once I've changed back."

Gratefully, Sevei took the cloth, though Jenna remained naked despite the goose bumps prickling her arms and shoulders, standing on the beach and staring out at the water. "Thank you," Jenna said. "That was delightful, having someone to swim with and share the experience. Swimming alone isn't the same."

"Was it wonderful, Gram, being with the Saimhóir?" Sevei asked her, and Jenna turned to smile.

"It was. I had good friends among them, though they're all gone now. The Saimhóir don't live as long as we do, and for several years now they've actively avoided us." The smile went quiet and sad. "Or perhaps it's only me and our family they avoid. It's my fault and I can't blame them." The smile evaporated and her hand went to Lámh Shábhála. "I wasn't all I could or should have been . . ." Her voice descended to a whisper before she smiled again, the fine lines around her mouth deepening. "Now I'm cold, too. Let's get dressed and go back up to the White Keep. Mundy will be waiting and there's much to do tonight if we leave in the morning for Dún Laoghaire."

"I hear that Máister Kirwan will be coming with us."

"You get to bring the Ó'Baoill boy; I get to bring Mundy," Jenna answered. Sevei had been happily surprised when Gram had announced that Dillon would accompany them to Dún Laoghaire, but now she raised her eyebrows in surprise that was only half-feigned.

"Gram!" Sevei laughed in shocked bemusement at what Jenna's comment seemed to imply.

"What?" Jenna asked. "Don't act as if you're offended. I love your great-da and respect him for all he's done for me, but both of us also have other . . . friends. Kyle knows Mundy will sail with us, and he knows what that means. He's comfortable with that."

"I don't think I want to hear this, Gram."

"Then don't listen," Jenna chuckled. "And for the Mother's sake, don't tell anyone." Jenna reached down for their clothing and stopped. She groaned, clutching herself around the waist.

"Gram?" Sevei went to her, putting a hand on her shoulder. Jenna was trembling under her touch and her skin felt as warm as if she had a fever.

"It's nothing," Jenna said, straightening carefully, her eyes closed against the pain. "Or everything. The change takes away the pain for a time, or at least shifts it around, and I forget . . ." Her eyes opened and she sighed. "There, it's easing a bit."

"The cloch?"

Jenna nodded. "The years of holding it. Of being the First."

"The First Holder bears the most pain. I remember Siúr Caomhánach teaching us that in class." Jenna picked up the clothing and handed her great-mam her léine. "She also said that you've held Lámh Shábhála longer than any known First Holder."

Jenna grimaced, lifting her arms to let the folds of the tunic fall over her body. She pulled water-heavy hair out of the neck opening. "I won't hold it much longer." She held up her hand against Sevei's automatic protest. "No, don't tell me how I have years yet. I'm tired, girl, and the pain . . . I can't stand it much longer. I'm already using . . ." She stopped, pressing her lips together; when she continued, Sevei could hear a tinge of bitterness in her voice. "I would have given Lámh Shábhála to Meriel, but your mam didn't want it. Treoraí's Heart was enough for her—even if it's a mere toy in comparison."

"Mam's done a lot of good with that mere toy, Gram," Sevei answered, sharply enough that Jenna's eyes narrowed. *Maybe more than you've done with Lámh Sháb-hála*... Sevei thought the words but didn't dare say them. She put on her léine slowly, letting the cloth hide her face. When her head emerged, Jenna was still staring at her.

"Will the ability to call a dragon if one just happens to blunder nearby be enough for you?" Jenna asked.

Sevei's hand went to her own stone. She could feel its power: comforting and familiar even though she'd had the clochmion for just two short days. Touching it, she could feel her awareness sweep outward across the sea and over Inishfeirm, but there was no answering call within the clochmion's small range. Like most clochmions, this one's gift was limited—and actually, she had to admit, potentially dangerous; the damage to the keep just from the dragon's presence had been extensive and though Gram had re-paired much of it with Lámh Shábhála, some of the scrolls in the library had been lost forever and they'd been fortu-nate no one had been seriously injured. Still, Treoraí's Heart had always seemed more like a Cloch Mór to Sevei, with its skill at healing. But perhaps that was also her mam's gift, augmented by the stone.

"I don't think so," Sevei answered honestly. "If I have the chance to hold a Cloch Mór ... Aye, I would take it."

"Mundy's talked with you about my being weary of the burden of Lámh Shábhála." Sevei glanced at her, wonder-ing whether that was something she should admit to know-ing, and Gram smiled. "I told him to tell you," she said. "Don't worry."

Sevei nodded. "Aye, Gram, he told me when he gave me Da's clochmion." She looked at Lámh Shábhála, resting now against the brocaded edging of Jenna's clóca. "But I don't know ..."

"Neither do I," Jenna said, her voice almost harsh. "Nei-ther do I. Not yet." She glanced back at the gray waves in which they'd been swimming. The wind was tearing at the tops of the waves, the salt spray stinging their faces. "But there's still time. I'm not ready to pass the stone on. Not yet. There's still time."

Sevei wondered who Gram was trying to convince.

Two days from Ceangail, Owaine, Kayne, and the gardai who hadn't remained behind with Harik were still in the mountains of the Finger, moving in the highlands through the snowy Narrows, the pass that led down into the plains in front of Lough Tory. They were riding slowly so that the wagons carrying the wounded and ill rolled as smoothly as the badly-maintained High Road allowed. Now and again, they caught a glimpse of the land before them: a cove of Lough Tory twinkling in the far distance, or the gray-green expanse of the old forest Tory Coill that spread along the lough's southern shore. Even a double-hand of years ago, there would have been no question as to their route. They would have followed the High Road north to Dathúil and Glenkille, taking the circuitous northern route around Lough Tory rather than attempting to pass through Tory Coill. But Kayne's mam and his gram both had forged alliances with the Bunús Muintir, the ancient folk who lived in the oak forests, and now one could travel through the Coills with a reasonable expectation of emerging safe on the other side. There were no guarantees—but there were no guarantees even if one traveled the High Road. The Bunús Muintir would allow travelers to pass through unmolested as long as they stayed to paths the Protectors of the Woods had marked.

Kayne had been pushing his da to take the southern route once they descended from the pass. As they ascended into the last high valley before the final long slope to the lowland plain, Kayne flicked Gainmheach's reins to move closer to Owaine, riding at the head of the column. "Have you thought more about what I suggested, Da? The men are tired and want to be home. Going through Tory Coill would save us days, if not a week or more."

Owaine's glance at Kayne was sour. "Aye, I've thought about it, but no, Kayne. We'll follow the High Road."

"Why?" Kayne asked, unable to keep his exasperation from showing in his voice. "Da, if we go through the forest, we'll be in Dúnani in a hand of days, and Dún Laoghaire in another hand. Less."

"Kayne—" Owaine gave a *huff* of frustration or irritation; Kayne couldn't tell which. He looked around as if seeing who might be listening, but they were a little ways ahead of the column and out of easy earshot. "Why do you question every decision I make?" Owaine said, his voice pitched low. "I'm your da, aye, but I'm also in command of these gardai, and you are one of my officers. Your duty is to obey. That's all." Kayne didn't immediately reply, and finally Owaine spoke again. "The High Road is the better road, and with our wounded men in the wagons, that's important. Tory Coill has bogs and swamps, and the trail through the wood is narrow and overgrown. The High Road's also well patrolled; no common thieves are going to attack a force as large as ours . . . but dire wolves in Tory Coill might smell the blood and sickness of our wounded, or there may be other, worse things there who wouldn't fear us at all. I want to get home as quickly as we can, but I also want to get my men there safely. I'm responsible for the well-being of my soldiers, and that's my first loyalty. That's something you need to realize if you're ever going to be in a command position yourself. You always think of yourself first, Kayne."

The accusation brought blood to Kayne's face. "That's not true, Da. You don't understand. You're still thinking about Ceangail."

"Aye, I am," Owaine answered, "and the way you spoke out after the battle at Lough Scáthán, and the dozen other times you acted as if you wanted to be a dead hero rather than a live soldier. A hero doesn't do things for his own glory. A hero doesn't get to choose his time or even to know whether he was successful. For all he knows, he's just another nameless dead garda . . . and that's all you would have been."

"Da, I'm talking about taking less time to get home. That's all. You're making this much more than it is."

"You're talking about your own comfort over those who have given their own blood in our service. I think—"

Owaine stopped. He peered up at the lip of the pass ahead of them, dark against the lowering sun. Kayne saw nothing, but he also knew that Owaine's sight was keener than most. Then he saw it: the glint of sunlight on a banner and the cloud of dust raised by riders. Kayne could see no colors or insignia on the banner; it was simply a piece of cloth. "Who are they, Da?"

"Red and white," he answered, though Kayne could see no colors at all. "They're from Tuath Airgialla. I'll bet the

Rí has heard of what happened at Ceangail and has sent gardai to reinforce the borders. Good. Then Harik and the others can return home, too." Owaine waved to the rest of their group, pointing to the summit of the pass where the riders could now be seen cresting the lip. There were already at least three double hands of gardai visible, and more kept coming: it seemed to Kayne that the Rí Airgialla had sent out a small army and he frowned at that, wondering why.

"Let's go meet them," Owaine said to Kayne. "It'll be good to get some news from the Tuatha."

9

The Coming Storm

UAIGNEAS ROLLED IN a heavy, restless sea. Sevei tried to ignore the freezing rain that found every crack in her reed coat, soaking her hair and *clóca* underneath. The wind smashed into the rising waves and tore streaks of white from their crests. The captain had ordered the sails furled and the crew were struggling with the long oars, keeping the ship's bow into the wind so that *Uaigneas* laboriously climbed the slope of each wave and then streaked down the other side into a new green-foamed valley. The storm had roared in from the Ice Sea, driving them rapidly south. They'd been planning to skirt Talamh an Ghlas' west coast and thus come around to Dún Loaghaire, but the storm had risen the second day out. Before the clouds and rain had closed around them, they'd glimpsed the rocky humps of the Stepping Stones, a chain of islands that curved from the southern borders of Tuath Infochla northward toward Inish Thuaidh. Now they could see nothing, and the captain had ordered them to turn back north, not wanting to be driven unwittingly onto the rocks of one of the islands.

There had been fright in the eyes of the servants who accompanied them, but Sevei thought of it more as an adventure, conjured up for her enjoyment.

The sea could not harm her. She loved it too much.

"You shouldn't be out here." She felt arms go around her even as she heard the voice, and she leaned back into the welcome embrace.

"At least I'd have a chance of survival if I fell over the

side," she told Dillon. "You wouldn't." He sniffed at that, or perhaps it was only the wind, and his arms tightened around her. "I thought you were staying in the cabin, love."

"The Banrion's come out, too," Dillon told her. "Said she'd had enough of being tossed about and was going to do something about it. I wanted to watch." He pointed to the bow of the ship near the small, roofed cabin. Sevei saw Jenna there, with Máister Kirwan at her side and the captain of *Uaigneas* looking concerned near them. Jenna appeared to be frail and in more pain than usual, and Mundy held her left arm carefully. But Jenna reached under her clóca for Lámh Shábhála, and as she lifted the cloch, her demeanor and attitude changed: in Sevei's vision, she seemed to grow larger, her back straighter, all her pain banished under the caress of the power within the stone as the years fell away from her. Sevei glimpsed Jenna as she must have appeared when she was Sevei's age: young and vibrant. Her hair whipped about in the wind as she held Lámh Shábhála high, displaying it defiantly to the storm. Light flared as if Jenna held a small sun in her hand and shadows dashed madly over the ship as the vessel lurched in the waves. Coruscations of bright, saturated color flickered, ribboning northward and up into the mist and cloud, spreading outward. Sevei could see the reflections of the power, glimmering in the gray expanse above and before them.

Jenna cried out, words that Sevei couldn't hear in the gale. The ribbons of color brightened, steadied, and then seemed to explode, sparks flying away above them as if the gods had struck a hammer to molten steel. Sevei and Dillon both lifted hands to eyes to shield them from the glare. Sevei couldn't see well even after she let her hands drop again as spots of wild hues chased themselves in her vision. But she could hear the difference immediately: the wind had eased and the rain had stopped; as her vision cleared, Sevei could see blue sky overhead and the evening sun sent shafts of light through shredded clouds near the horizon. The storm still raged a few leagues or so away all around them and the waves were still huge, but *Uaigneas* rode in a clear, circular space within the storm.

A cheer went up from the sailors, and the captain barked the order to raise sails again. "Come on," Sevei said to Dillon. Taking his hand, she went to where Jenna leaned into Máister Kirwan's embrace, her face now sallow and old, the pain etched again in the lines around her eyes, mouth, and forehead. "Gram," Sevei said, "that was amazing. I knew Stormbringer could control weather, but—"

"Lámh Shábhála can do anything any of the other Clochs Mór can do, and more," Jenna told her. "Stormbringer couldn't have done all this." She nodded to the open sky above them. "But storms are larger than even Lámh Shábhála's power. I gave us a respite, that's all. A chance for the captain to find a harbor and a place to anchor so we can ride out the rest of it."

Uaigneas was already turning around, heading south once more. They could see two large islands close by, both with high cliff walls against which the waves were breaking in furious white spray—they'd been blown even farther south despite their attempts to make headway north. Wisps of darkness were fraying the edges of the clouds lining the clear space around the ship, promising that the storm would return in a stripe or less. A ring fort perched on the promontory of the larger of the islands, and a wind-torn banner fluttered there: green and gold—so these were islands owned by Tuath Infochla. "Can we reach them?" Sevei asked.

Jenna shrugged. "Only the Mother knows. At least we might be able to put one of them between us and the storm waves." She stood away from Máister Kirwan, glaring up at the sky. "You see, Sevei?" she said. "What does it matter if you hold Lámh Shábhála? The world is still stronger than you are. Nothing is permanent. Nothing. Even the walls of the White Keep will fall one day. Nothing lasts—nothing we create." She glanced at Sevei's hand, still holding Dillon's. "And certainly nothing we feel." Jenna grimaced, her eyes closing as she clutched at her soaked clóca. "I need that special tea, Mundy," she said. "I need it now."

"I'll make it for you, Banrion," Máister Kirwan told her. Jenna grunted and started walking toward the cabin, but Máister Kirwan lingered. "She's not feeling well," he told them, "and draining Lámh Shábhála this way is a strain and makes her feel vulnerable. She'll be better once the mage-lights come again."

"I know, Máister."

He nodded. "You ought to get into some dry clothes—you wouldn't want to catch a chill or worse."

"I know that, too," Sevei told him. "Despite what Gram says, death, at least, is permanent." The words seemed to come to her without thinking.

Máister Kirwan's mouth turned down under the beard and he cocked his head quizzically. "Why would you talk of death?"

Sevei shook her head. "I don't know . . ." She looked at the sky again. The storm was clutching at the open sky with fingers of gray-black. A sense of dread had wrapped itself around her and yet she didn't know why. She thought of her family: her mam, her da, Kayne, her brothers and sister, and the feeling of dread increased, yet no images came to her.

"I don't know," she said again. She let go of Dillon's hand. "I should go change," she said. "Why don't you get your harp out and sing us something cheerful? We could all use that, I think."

10

Fiodóir's Meal

"HERE," Isibéal said to Ennis. "Eat this."

"What is it?"

"A treat," Isibéal told him. She held out the small ball covered with honey and spices toward him. She held up another in her other hand. "See, I have one, also." She placed it in her mouth, chewing the confection. It was perfect, the honey camouflaging the sharp, bitter taste of the nugget at the center. Ennis took the piece from her hand and put it in his own mouth.

" 'S good," he said, the words obscured by his chewing. He swallowed and she smiled. "Do you have more, Isibéal?"

"No, I'm afraid I only had those two. One for you, one for me."

"Too bad Mam can't have one."

Isibéal forced herself to smile at that. "Aye, 'tis indeed. Ah, here's your mam now. Shh, we'll let the treat be our little secret, eh?" Ennis smiled at Isibéal as she moved to greet the Banrion, just stepping into Isibéal's small chamber. Meriel stopped and looked at the table. "It looks wonderful," she said. "And smells wonderful, also."

"Thank you, Banrion." Isibéal had spent the day preparing the meal and arranging her chambers. The keep's kitchens had supplied her with fillets of plaice and white pollack from the cold waters of the Inner Sea and allowed Isibéal to prepare and cook the fish herself, though the cooks had watched her suspiciously and warily when she brought out the packet of spices. They'd wanted to know the names of each, and Isibéal had told them what they were and where they were from: Taisteal spices that had originated from Thall Mór-roinn, though the Taisteal had been planting small patches of the herbs in secret here and there through the Tuatha for decades. She'd also made a salad of sea campion, wildflowers, pepperroot and young stonecrop, tossing the leaves gently with oil she'd purchased from Asthora on her first visit to the herbalist's shop. She allowed the cooks to prepare two vegetable dishes under her supervision—in Isibéal's opinion, the cooks for the keep, like most cooks in the Tuatha, tended to boil everything into bland mush. There was cold soup and warm bread of specially milled flour, and for dessert a cake drizzled with molasses and berries. For drinking, she'd chosen a new mead, sweet and strong.

And she'd prepared the two pieces of honeyed confection: one for herself, and one—for reasons she could not even explain to herself because it went against both her judgment and her true employer's orders—for Ennis. The piece for Ennis had slightly different ingredients than the one Isibéal herself ate. *It's because he's so much like Adimu. Too much like him . . .*

She'd draped the chamber, attached to Ennis' rooms by a back stairs, with blue cloth—"That's Fiodóir's color," she told Ennis, "because he lives in the sky"—and made the air fragrant with pots of burning incense. She'd laced circles of pine branches in the center of the table with butterwort and sundew flowers as decoration. Each of the plates held a single stalk of lady's bedstraw as accent. Isibéal had been pleased with the look herself—she could imagine that a Taisteal table at festival time might look like this, back in the homeland, though she'd never been there herself. "Please, sit," she told the Banrion Ard, gesturing to the chair at one end of the table.

"I wish Owaine and our other children could be here for this," Meriel said as she sat.

"I do also," Isibéal responded, "and I'm sure Ennis feels the same way, don't you?"

"I do, Mam," Ennis said energetically, bounding into his seat. "Can we eat now? It looks *so* good and I'm *so* hungry," he said with exaggerated impatience, and both women laughed.

"We can eat now," Isibéal told him. "Just make sure you leave room for the cake. And you, too, Banrion. On Fiodór's Feast, you must eat the cake."

"Oh, I will," Ennis promised solemnly. Then, as Isibéal, sitting alongside him, placed some of the fish on his plate, he turned to his mam. "When are Da and Kayne going to be back? And what about Sevei and Gram? They should be here by now. What about Tara and Ionhar? Are they coming here, too?"

Meriel laughed again. "So many questions . . . Let's see . . . I don't know when your da and Kayne will be back, but it should be soon. And aye, Sevei and Gram are due here in a hand of days now, though you never know about the weather at sea. Tara and Ionhar won't be here, though. Now, will you pass me that fish, Ennis—it smells delightful, Isibéal."

Ennis reached for the plate and handed it to his mam. As she reached for it, he held it for a moment too long. "Mam, you'll always be with me, won't you?"

Meriel's eyes widened slightly and Isibéal felt the breath catch in her throat. "Why, what a question, Ennis," Meriel said. "I'll always love you, aye, but as you grow older, you won't *want* to be around me. You'll go to foster-age, like your brothers and sisters, and probably to Inishfeirm like Sevei or maybe you'll learn to command the gardai like Kayne, and you'll be married and living somewhere else, in time—"

"No, Mam," Ennis interrupted. "I mean, no matter where you are, will you think of me?"

Meriel took the dish from Ennis and placed a fillet of the plaice on her plate. Isibeal watched, her breath shallow. "Of course I will, Ennis. Always. I promise. No matter where I am."

Ennis nodded quietly at that. "Good," he said. He looked at Isibéal. "We can eat now," he said.

". . . I remember Fio . . . Fiodóir from when I . . . when Sevei . . . the old Sevei, I mean, not . . . my daughter . . ." Meriel stopped. Blinked. Her voice had become increasingly slurred over the last half a stripe. ". . . when I was . . .

with the Taisteal," she finished. "The God of Fate," she said, and giggled. "Had too much . . . mead, I think."

She looked at Ennis, curled up in one of the stuffed chairs in the corner of the room, asleep. "He must have been . . ." Her eyes seemed to roll upward, showing Isibéal the whites. Meriel started as if jerking from sleep. "I'm sleepy," she said, her voice barely understandable.

Her eyes widened, her breathing became ragged. She collapsed sideways to the carpeted floor, dragging her plate down with her. The remnants of the meal spilled over the Banrion Ard's clothing. For a moment, Isibéal held her breath, afraid that the noise would bring one of the hall gardai to the door, that they would open the door—in the keep, only the Banrion's private chambers were allowed to be locked. But no one came. In the silence, she could hear the stuttering of rain starting to fall on the flagstones of the keep.

Isibéal rose from her chair. She stooped down alongside Meriel, listening. The woman's breathing was labored and thin. As Isibéal touched Meriel's neck, she felt the pulse there flutter and stop. Meriel's eyes were open—she stared blindly at the woven fibers of the carpet and the scattered leaves of the salad. The goblet of mead, tipped over, dripped golden droplets in front of her nose.

"I'm sorry," Isibéal whispered to her. "Go now to the Mother." Reaching down, she closed Meriel's eyes. She slipped her hand down farther until her fingers touched Treorai's Heart on its chain of fine gold. The cloch, her employer had told her, was to remain behind. But she had already disobeyed him by leaving Ennis alive, for reasons she still didn't entirely understand. She pulled hard at the chain and the clasp broke. She held the stone in her hand for a moment. She gasped at the touch, as the stone seemed to reach deep into her and she into it. Suddenly, she wanted the stone more than anything else, and she could not imagine anyone else having it. *So that's what it feels like . . . Well, it's mine now . . .* She placed it, reluctantly, in a pocket of her clóca, knowing she had to hurry now.

Straightening, Isibéal took a long breath. Going to Ennis, she picked up the child, cradling him in her arms. He stirred slightly, his eyelids fluttering.

"Mam?"

"Shh," Isibéal told him. "Your mam's asleep. It's all right."

Ennis' eyes had already closed again. He nodded against Isibéal's shoulder, his breath deepening, his legs dangling below her waist. He was heavier than she'd thought. She hurried away from the table in the outer chamber to the rear stairs. She'd placed a bag there, filled with a few essentials and a change of clothing. She set Ennis down long enough to place the bag around her shoulders, then took him again, swaddling him in a blanket pulled from the bed. She took a candle from the mantle, opened the door and hurried down the stairs in the warm yellow circle of light.

She figured she had another half-stripe at the most before someone would wonder where the Banrion Ard was and discover the murder. Isibéal would be doing well to be out of Dún Laoghaire before the alarm was raised. Even though her employer would try to protect her, she also knew that he wouldn't hesitate to let her be killed to protect his own identity—and he had the power to have that happen, especially when he discovered how she'd disobeyed him with Ennis and now with the Heart.

If your preparations have gone as they should have, if no one has betrayed you, you will survive this . . .

She passed the next landing, which would lead out into the Banrion's own chamber, and continued down. She heard footsteps ascending and the chatter of a few of the maidservants. She let them pass; they looked at her curiously but said little beyond a quick greeting. They patted the sleeping Ennis on the head and went on. Isibéal hurried down the stairs to the bottom, coming out of the keep into an interior courtyard. She pulled her cloak up against the rain, bringing the edge of the blanket over Ennis' face.

Isibéal felt relief surge through her: she *would* get out of here. The stable hand she'd bribed was standing there holding the reins of a brown mare, his wet hair plastered to his skull. She handed him the rest of the coins she'd promised him; he grinned and weighed them in his hand, then helped her up, handing her the still-sleeping child. She'd told him that this was simply a kidnapping—that she was taking the child to hold him for ransom. Such things happened often enough among the Riocha. He knew nothing about the rest. Isibéal suspected that he wouldn't live long enough to enjoy his bribe.

*Now, if the garda has left the southern door through the
wall open as he said he would* . . .

The stable hand backed away, still grinning, and Isibéal
kicked the horse toward the bailey wall. She saw light play
on the glossy hair of the mare; she looked up to see the first
tendrils of the mage-lights curling under the clouds, the
streaks of rain illuminated by them: even a storm could not
keep away the mage-lights.

Early again tonight . . . that was a bad omen. There was
little time. Very soon, too soon, someone would wonder
why the Banrion Ard hadn't come out to fill Treorai's
Heart. Worse, she could feel the pull of Treora 's Heart in
her own mind, yearning to be filled, and she could not afford to do that. Not now. And if the southern door was
shut, if she had to try to talk her way past the gardai at the
main gates and then ride all the way through Dún
Laoghaire . . .

But the gate *was* open and the gardai were inside out of
the weather, and she was able to resist the temptation to
take out the Heart and lift it to the mage-lights. Isibéal
ducked her head, maneuvering the horse through the low,
thick-walled gap and out beyond the wall. There were few
houses here and no town wall, only the shoulder of Cnocareilig and the dark hills beyond, swaddled in mist, beckoned with the promise of escape.

Isibéal clutched Ennis tighter and kicked the horse into
a gallop.

11

The Battle of the Narrows

KAYNE WASN'T sure when he realized that something was wrong. As their small troop approached the larger Airgialla force between the craggy, fissured walls of the Narrows pass, he could feel a prickling unease lift the hairs on the back of his neck and on his arms. He wasn't sure what it was. Perhaps it was the fact that the Airgiallaians stopped as soon as they caught sight of his da's gardai, or the fact that the troops were set in battle formation even here in their own Tuath, or maybe it was the stiff way the Riocha riders nearest the banner sat on their horses. Perhaps it was the oppressive feel of the sky, the clouds gathering in twilight.

Owaine waved to the riders.

"Ho, Airgialla! Tiarna Geraghty of Dún Laoghaire greets you," Owaine called. "Kayne, unfurl your mam's banner."

Kayne saw the lifting of bows behind the front ranks then, and the warning he shouted—"*Da!*"—was a breath too late. Arrows hissed and fell in a deadly, hard rain. Kayne heard a grunt alongside him and the rider to his right toppled from his horse with an arrow feathering his chest. Horses and men screamed—a hand of gardai and as many horses were down as Kayne whipped his head around to look. "Take cover!" Kayne shouted. "Shields!" He ripped his own shield from where it hung on his livery as bowstrings sang the deadly note once more. Kayne brought his shield up to protect his and Gainmheach's heads.

A Cloch Mór opened: Da with Blaze. The second flight
of arrows vanished in flame as a sheet of fire rippled before the Airgiallaians. "Stop!" he heard his da shout to
them. "We are friends, going to the Banrion Ard—" but the
riders brought their lances down and charged as another
flight of arrows darkened the sky.

Kayne saw his da's hesitation. "Da!"

Owaine seemed to shake himself. He held Blaze high.
Arrows vanished to ash and lightning arced out to meet
the riders, striking the front ranks. Kayne shielded his eyes
from the awful flash and roar of the Cloch Mór. Kayne
could hear the riders scream, as he'd heard the Arruk
scream when Owaine had used the cloch on them, but
more riders were coming and foot soldiers charged behind
them. The attackers poured down the slope of the pass
toward them, a deadly wave of leather and steel.

Too many. Too many to face with the few gardai they had
and the wounded.

"Retreat!" he heard his da shout, waving at Kayne and
the others. "Kayne, lead them! I'll hold them back!"

"I'm staying with you."

"*Do* it!"

Scowling, Kayne yanked at Gainmheach's reins and gestured to the other gardai. "Back!" he shouted. "Get the wagons turned; riders, stay with them." He glanced at the
landscape around them; there was a narrow cleft in the
rocks to the south, leading into the broken slopes where
riders and wagons couldn't go—if they could get there,
perhaps they could hide on foot . . . "There!" Kayne cried,
pointing. "Make for the opening."

He heard the crackle of Blaze's energy behind him, and
this time an answer came from where a tiarna sat astride
his horse next to the banner holder. Where Owaine
wielded fire, the rider hurled ice: a cold wall that to
Kayne's eyes surrounded his da, encasing him in shimmering glacial blue. Kayne knew that name of that cloch: Winter. And he also knew who must then be wielding it: Mal
Mac Baoill, the son of Morven Mac Baoill who was the
current Rí Airgialla and great-son of old Mal Mac Baoill,
also once Rí Airgialla and only three years dead. The im-
plication struck Kayne as it must have come to his da: this
was a deliberate betrayal, a planned ambush from which

neither Owaine, Kayne, nor the men with them were intended to come through alive.

Blaze gleamed red inside the ice, a dying sun that flared suddenly, melting away rime and frost. Owaine shouted in true fury now, as angry as Kayne had ever seen him. A flare of blood-red arced toward Mac Baoill; it was met by ice halfway, the forces exploding above the onrushing gardai. They screamed and wailed in surprise and pain; several went down, but there were far too many more behind and the momentary gap in the line was filled.

The Airgiallaian riders reached Owaine. He sent searing waves of fire at them and those closest to him went down, but more rushed past him toward Kayne, his companions, and the wagons. They were nearly at the cleft, but Kayne knew they wouldn't make it. "Turn!" he shouted to the gardai. "Turn and stand!" As one, the soldiers with him gave up all thought of retreat and drew weapons to fight, the wounded rising from their beds to grab swords and hobble from the wagons.

It was slaughter, not battle.

There was no orderly lines here, only a roaring chaos. Kayne blocked a notched sword and hacked at the nameless, grimacing face behind it. He didn't know if he struck the person or not—perhaps he did, because the rider was gone, but there was another to take his place, and another on the other side. He knocked down a thrust from a lance, shouting in rage as the blade he blocked gouged his thigh rather than running through his abdomen. He could smell the blood; so could Gainmheach, who wickered nervously. Kayne heaved his sword back up in a quick arc and was rewarded with a gurgling cry as his attacker toppled from his mount.

But the garda on the other side of Kayne leaned over, his weapon slicing deep into one of Gainmheach's rear legs, severing tendons and ripping. The horse screamed, an awful sound that Kayne remembered from other battles, and went down, bearing Kayne to the ground with it. Gainmheach's body slammed sideways to the rocky ground, Kayne's leg trapped underneath; he screamed with Gainmheach at the rush of pain. "Up!" he called to the horse, but though Gainmheach tried to rise at the command, it couldn't. Kayne was pinned. Helpless.

On the ground, Kayne looked up to see another rider in the colors of Airgialla over him, a long lance in his hand. He raised it, ready to plunge it down in Kayne's body. Kayne tried to roll, but Gainmheach's weight held him fast.

He looked up at his death, wondering what it would feel like.

It reminded him too much of the dream he'd had at Ceangail.

Crackling lines of fire tore the garda from his seat atop the horse even as the horse went down, the lance's shaft withering to ash and the steel blade dropping to the ground alongside Kayne's head. Kayne felt the heat of the blast and the horrible smell of charred horse-and-man-flesh. Boots stomped grass near him as someone dismounted. Hands pushed at Gainmheach, helping the horse roll away from Kayne's leg. Kayne, hissing at the pain of moving the bruised and battered limb, sat up.

Another hand reached down to him; he took it. The Airgiallaian riders had passed beyond them and were wheeling back, and now the foot gardai also approached. They stood in a momentary open space in the battlefield, but it would not last long.

"Thanks, Da."

Owaine nodded without answer. He held no weapon other than Blaze. "Give me your sword," he said. When Kayne hesitated, he barked angrily, "*Now!*" Kayne handed him the sword, and Owaine remounted his horse. "Here," he said, taking Blaze and its chain from around his neck. "You take this." He tossed the Cloch Mór down to Kayne; as it left his hand, an expression of horrible pain came over Owaine's face and he swayed, nearly falling from the back of his horse.

"Da?" Kayne looked at the stone. He could *feel* the Cloch Mór in his mind: a compelling presence, an aching emptiness that yearned to be filled again with the mage-lights.

Owaine straightened with a visible effort. The setting sun had vanished behind the rank of spreading clouds, but even in the twilight, his face was pale. He seemed to be barely able to hold the sword. "Take any wounded who can walk and leave here," he said. He was staring at Blaze rather than Kayne as he nodded to the cleft and its inviting screen of brush and trees. "The rest of us will give you time, and darkness will give you cover." Owaine's face was a rictus of pain and fury, of loss and betrayal. He looked already dead. "For once, Kayne, obey me without question. For once, be a soldier. *Go!*"

Owaine didn't wait for an answer. He gave another longing glance to Blaze in Kayne's hand, then yanked hard at the reins and dug his boot heels into the horse's side. As he rode away, he screamed: the eerie, frightening warble of the *caointeoireacht na cogadh,* the war cry of the Inishlanders. Seeing their commander, those of the troop still able to ride or run joined him in the charge, rushing directly into the oncoming line of the Airgiallaian foot soldiers. Clutching the emptied Blaze, Kayne almost turned to join them, but his leg collapsed underneath him and he nearly fell.

He saw the two lines meet. He saw Owaine disappear into the mass of shouting troops. He saw blue mage-fury erupt where Owaine had been.

He couldn't get there. Couldn't get to them. Couldn't help his da.

A hero doesn't get to choose his time or even to know whether he was successful. Kayne knew what Owaine meant by that, now.

For once, obey me without question . . .

And if he did not, his da's sacrifice would be for nothing.

Groaning, Kayne pushed himself up. He patted Gainmheach, whose eyes rolled white with pain at him as it thrashed on its side. "I'm sorry, old friend," he whispered to the horse, then reached for his boot dagger, slashing deep into the horse's neck. Blood gushed and pulsed as Gainmheach lurched up, nearly knocking Kayne to the ground again before falling back quiet, its lifeblood staining its coat and dripping onto the ground.

Kayne put his back to the sounds of battle. He heard someone call his name from beside the wreckage of one of the wagons: Bartel, one of those who had been in the wagons with one leg gone at the knee from an Arruk jaka. Bartel clutched a sword whose edge ran with blood, and a garda in red-and-white colors lay on the ground before him.

"Come with me," Kayne told Bartel, putting the man's arm around his shoulder. "We have to leave. Quickly!"

Kayne glanced back one last time. He couldn't see his da, could see nothing but a roil of bodies further up the pass, murky in the growing darkness. He placed Blaze's chain around his neck and took Bartel's weight on his good leg.

They limped toward the cleft and cover. Behind them, the sound of steel against steel battered the gray clouds lowering over the pass and shook rain from them. Kayne was glad for the drops, which mingled with the salt from his eyes.

12

The Wreck of the *Uaigneas*

"**N**O! NO-NO-NO!**"**

Dillon scrambled away from Sevei, his hands leaving her. "I'm sorry," he said automatically. Sevei didn't answer. She stared outward without seeing Dillon's face in the careening light of the lantern hung on one of the beams. What she saw was inside, and it had torn her away from Dillon's embrace.

The two simultaneous images warred with each other in her mind: her mam, falling lifeless from her chair; Kayne surrounded by fighting men, with the fury of Clochs Mór crackling around him. Pain and loss and grief welled outward from the vision, and she cried aloud again with the grief and loss, sobbing.

"Sevei?" Dillon's hands touched her cheeks. She looked up at him, her voice trembling with the tears. "Sevei, what's the matter?"

"Mam . . . Mam's dead and Kayne's badly hurt," she told him. Her voice sounded like someone else's, high and fast. "By the Mother . . . I felt Mam die, felt her breath leave her. And Kayne—I can feel everything." Her breath was so fast, her heart hammering inside her chest so that she could barely talk. She was clutching her leg as if it pained her. "They're killing my family, Dillon. They're killing them all!" She sobbed, screaming the words. "Gram! I have to see Gram!"

"That can't be," Dillon said. "Sevei, you're just worried, what with the storm and being away so long. I'll bet they're both fine . . ."

"No!" she shouted at him, pushing him away. She was sobbing, unable to stop the welling of grief. "It's true. I *know* it." She sat up, pulling her léine down and wrapping her clóca around her. She could hear voices on deck, among them her gram and Máister Kirwan. "I have to go to Gram," she said again. She wanted to sob against Gram's shoulder, wanted her strength and her familiar presence, wanted her to use Lámh Shábhála and take it all away.

Sevei hurried from the tiny cabin, Dillon following in her wake. Her breath was caught low in her throat and the terror inside her threatened to rip through her body and leave her broken and wailing. Outside, the cold wind whipped her hair around her neck; a few spatters of returning rain were already touching the deck. The circle of clear sky around them was nearly gone, the blue sky hazed with high, thin clouds and the storm clouds dark all around them. Gram and Máister Kirwan were huddled with the captain near the bow. They were passing the jutting headland of the nearest island and gliding into the more sheltered bay beyond. Waiting for them there were three other ships; though they were obviously warships from the navy of one of the Tuatha, none of them flew a banner of allegiance. Sevei could already see that they had flanked *Uaigneas,* using oars and sails.

The dread that had struck Sevei in the cabin now filled her entirely. She knew, knew without Gram or Máister Kirwan saying anything, that the ships were not there to aid them, that they had come deliberately expecting them to pass near here. Her vision and this reality before her were connected, she was certain.

"Gram?" she said, but Jenna didn't turn. Máister Kirwan glanced over his shoulder at Sevei and Dillon, then turned back.

"There are Clochs Mór aboard each ship," Máister Kirwan said, but he was talking to Jenna, not them. "I can feel them."

"They knew they would be facing Lámh Shábhála—and they must also know now that it's been nearly drained," Jenna agreed. "They'll have seen what I did to the storm, and they'll figure it's safe to attack us." She seemed oddly calm. Sevei moved toward them and noticed that Jenna's eyes were half-closed and almost sleepy, and a strange herbal smell clung to her. She blinked heavily, her shoulders slumping. She looked at Sevei. "I didn't know you well or long enough, daughter-child," she said. "I failed you." Her gaze went to Mundy. "And you, too, my good friend."

Mundy shook his head. "Not yet," he answered. "You're assuming they're hostile."

"They are, Máister," Sevei told him. Her throat convulsed, making it hard to talk. The tears were hot on her cheeks. "I know . . . it's already . . . already . . ." She couldn't continue. Jenna took Sevei's face in her hands, kissing her forehead gently.

"Go on," Jenna whispered. "Tell us."

"It's Mam . . ." Sevei managed to say. "And Kayne . . ."

"You saw them?"

"Aye, Gram. Mam's . . . dead." The word seemed impossibly heavy and leaden. Unreal. "Kayne's hurt and in terrible trouble, and I think . . . I think . . ."

Jenna took a breath. "Ah, my poor child . . ." She kissed Sevei again and her hands dropped to her sides. Jenna was weeping, or perhaps it was the first drops of rain from the closing ring of clouds. "There's no hope here either," Jenna told all of them. "It's over."

"There's still this," Máister Kirwan said, his hand seeking his own cloch.

Jenna smiled sadly at him. "You're one against many, Mundy. Those are no odds at all." She lifted her scarred right hand and closed it around Lámh Shábhála. At the same time, her gaze went distant, as if she were listening to voices only she could hear.

"It begins now," Jenna said.

"And it can end as quickly," a voice answered, "if you'll let it, my sister."

Sevei whirled around to see a red-haired man in the dark green clóca and léine of the Order of Gabair, in age close to her own parents. She recognized him even as Jenna gave a cough of wry surprise—Sevei had seen him often, talked with him many, many times over the years. *Uncle Doyle* . . .

"I should have known you'd be involved in this, Doyle Mac Ard," Jenna said. "And that false Máister O Blaca's out there with his cloch, too, to send you over here. I'm

surprised you'd expose yourself this way—it's not your
style to be in front of the troops."

"I'm only part of it this time, my dear sister," Doyle said.
"This wasn't my plan—well, not entirely. I'm only following orders."

"And whose plan would that be? O Blaca's? No ... One
of the Ríthe, then, or all of them?"

Doyle shook his head in answer. "It's over this time,
Jenna. You know what I want. Give it to me and we can still
avoid bloodshed. You have Máister Kirwan here and my
great-niece; I should think you wouldn't want them hurt."

Jenna laughed. "If the Order of Gabair thinks it can take
Lámh Shábhála with just a few Clochs Mór, then you
haven't learned any of the lessons from your past."

Sevei saw a brief smile drift over Doyle's lips. "That's a
poor bluff, Sister, but it's one I would have made also, in
your place. I know the clochs na thintri as well as any
cloudmage of Inishfeirm and that wasn't Stormbringer that
cleared away the squall. You've used up most of Lámh
Shábhála's power and the mage-lights won't come for a
stripe or more yet. There's no hope here, Jenna."

Sevei heard the rustle of cloth behind her, and Doyle's
gaze went to Máister Kirwan. Doyle's hand rose immediately to the red-and-gold stone around his neck. "Don't,
Máister. I remember from Falcarragh the skill you have
with that cloch, but even if you could defeat Snapdragon,
there are two full hands of Clochs Mór out there waiting."
Doyle gestured at the ships, now very close to *Uaigneas*,
close enough that Sevei could see the gardai crowding the
rails and the grim faces of the Riocha mages beyond. One
of them was familiar to her: Padraic Mac Ard, who she'd
once imagined might be her future husband, now wearing
the green clóca of the Order of Gabair. He saw her too,
and his face tightened.

Sevei clutched Dillon's hand tightly. "That many
clochs . . ." Sevei breathed. She didn't realize she'd said it
aloud until Doyle's grass-green gaze went to her.

"Aye, Sevei," he said to her. "That many. Enough even if
Lámh Shábhála were full. Enough for Máister Kirwan's
Snarl and whatever that clochmion you're wearing might
do. And we've spent a week preparing slow magics as well.

Jenna, don't be a fool. You know what I want. Give it to me so we can end this."

The grief and fear washed over Sevei as Doyle stared at her gram. Sevei was trembling, and her fingers stroked the cage of her clochmion. She opened the stone with her mind, letting the power slide out, searching. *I could bring a dragon. I could have it smash their ships and send them to the bottom, and I wouldn't care if it took me down with them. . . .*

But there was no answering call. The energy of the clochmion spread out to its limits and found nothing. *Why did you give me this useless thing?* she raged to the Mother-Creator. *Why are you allowing this to happen to me? To us?*

"Am I wrong?" Doyle was saying. "Go on, Sister. Open Lámh Shábhála and strike me down—you know you could do that much before the other clochs retaliated." When Jenna didn't move, Doyle nodded. He held out his hand. "I'll take it now," he said. "I'll take what should have been my da's."

Jenna looked at the hand without moving. "You killed Meriel. My daughter and your niece. And Owaine, too. And no doubt all the rest of my great-children. Sevei's already told me."

Doyle's gaze rested for a moment on Sevei again. "Ah, so the rumors are true—she can sense what happens to her mam and her twin." He took a breath. "Dead they might be, but *I* didn't kill them, Sister. I'm here, across the Tuatha from them. Nor is it what I wanted. I argued strongly against that, but I was only one voice . . ."

"The blood's on your hands, Doyle Mac Ard, however far away you are. You've committed fingal—you've slain your own kin. The Mother-Creator will never forgive you."

"An odd accusation, coming from you," Doyle retorted. "And I'm tired of the chatter, Sister. I want my cloch. Now."

Sevei saw a strange expression come over Jenna's face, one of almost frightening calm. Jenna took a step backward from Doyle, then another, until her back was to the railing of the *Uaigneas.* The waves rose green and frothing behind her. "What makes you think I would ever give the stone to you, Doyle? I'd rather it was lost at the bottom of the ocean for the rest of eternity than see it in your hand."

With that, before any of them could move, Jenna took the necklace from around her neck and flung it into the waves. She started to dive after it—Sevei knew what she intended, even as Jenna crouched: Jenna would turn into seal form and find the cloch once again as it drifted down, with eyes that saw much better than Daoine ones and a form that could stay submerged for long minutes. Doyle must have known it as well: as Jenna started to jump, Sevei felt the prickling of magical energy being released. A golden dragon shimmered in the air just alongside the ship; the long neck arced back and it vomited fire that enveloped Jenna. She heard her gram scream, a wail of torment that made Sevei open her mouth to cry out in sympathy. The dragon's claws raked over Jenna's body, sending her bloody and broken to the deck, her clothes smoldering. Sevei launched herself at Doyle even as Máister Kirwan opened his cloch, as the energy of the Clochs Mór erupted all around them.

She would never be entirely certain what happened in the next few chaotic breaths. She saw the dragon reach down with its gaping, dagger-jawed mouth and snatch up her gram, but then Máister Kirwan's cloch attacked, its power snarling the dragon in blue-white ropes that hissed and crackled like mad things. Doyle's mage-dragon reared back, roaring in pain, and as its mouth opened, Jenna's body went tumbling into the roiling sea.

"Gram!" Sevei cried out, struggling to reach the rail on that side even though Dillon held her arm to stop her. She could feel the tingling pressure of magical energy all around her. The air above them wavered like the air above sun-heated metal; Sevei caught the faint outlines of a great hand hovering there for just an instant, and then a giant fist slammed itself into the deck of *Uaigneas* just in front of them, shattering the oaken planks and tearing Sevei away from Dillon. She half-fell, half-flew across a deck that was no longer level.

Sevei crashed hard against the railing on the seaward side of the ship, the breath going out of her with the impact, and she heard ribs pop and crack under her clóca. *Uaigneas* groaned like a wounded beast, sluggishly righting itself. Not far away, Sevei glimpsed Doyle, somehow still on his feet and unhurt. Her great-uncle's gaze found her, and she saw in his eyes a raw, unpitying anger. She started to try to rise, to run, but he called out to someone she couldn't see, pointing to her. "Don't let the girl reach the water! Make sure she's dead! All the Aoire spawn must be dead."

She saw a thicket of bright yellow spears appear in the air, rushing toward her. Sevei threw herself between the broken uprights of the ship's rail, but even as she fell into the air, she felt the stunning impact of a spear point in the back, and another ripping through the muscles of her arm.

She heard Dillon call for her, saw him fling himself toward her and then the fist came down again, smashing her lover to the deck.

Sevei didn't remember anything after that: not the pain, not the fall, not the final cold embrace of the sea.

13

In the Bracken

A HAND AND ONE of them managed to stagger away from the carnage into the brush-laden darkness of the hillsides. Kayne, Bartel, Garvan, Sean, Uilliam, and Flynn. Garvan had taken arrows in his right arm and left leg; Sean and Uilliam were both so badly wounded that Kayne knew they might as easily die as live; Flynn was only barely alive. Kayne managed to pull the unconscious Flynn from under the carcass of his horse and that of an Airgiallaian rider, who lay dead beside him. With the help of the others, he half-dragged, half-carried the man away from the scene of the battle.

Limping, sometimes crawling, they managed to slide and careen down the muddy hillside of the path and into a bracken-infested ravine. They could hear the sounds of the battle above them subside; not long after, Kayne saw a hand of gardai in red and white make their way slowly down the hillside, obviously searching in the darkness for survivors. Flynn was moaning in his delirium, and Kayne gestured to the others to keep him silent. The gardai stopped several strides upslope of the ravine. "Nothing here but mud and bramble," he heard one of them say. "I don't fancy getting myself all scratched up or having a leg broken looking for poor bastards who might or might not be out here. Let the damn Riocha come look if they want them."

The others grunted agreement, and the group went back up to the road, sheathing their swords and grumbling all the while as they climbed.

"They'll be back, Tiarna," Bartel said, lifting his hand from over Flynn's mouth. They were all looking at Kayne. "When the sun comes. They'll see the marks where we slid down here. They'll find us if we stay, if we aren't frozen or already dead by then."

None of the others spoke. They only looked at Kayne, waiting for him—waiting, he realized, for his orders. He stared upward through the thicket toward the terrible silence above them, the quiet of the dead. He imagined his da's corpse there among the others, his once-keen eyes open and staring out at nothing, his body mutilated and bloody. He felt rage surge through him and a keen desire to rush back up there, to cry the *caointeoireacht na cogadh* and charge at the mass of Airgiallaians with waving sword, to take with him to the Mother-Creator as many of their blood-bonded souls as he could.

And if he did that, then what did Owaine's death matter? If he did, then those here who looked to him for answers in this night, would also die.

The mage-lights would come, not too long from now, and he could take Blaze as his own. The Cloch Mór Owaine had given him felt heavy around his neck, a burden more weighty than lead.

"We need to move as far from here as we can during the night," he said to them. "No use going west, not with the Airgiallaians holding the pass. We'll try to head east, back toward the Wall, Harik, and the rest of our people. How is Flynn?"

Garvan glanced down, then placed his ear near the man's mouth. "Dead," he answered. He glanced at Bartel, who shrugged.

"Then we'll put his body there, in the open." Kayne pointed to the lip of the ravine above them. "With the sun, they won't miss that someone came down from the pass this way. Maybe they won't look farther than poor Flynn's body." He doubted the subterfuge would work, but the other men stirred and he glimpsed the first signs of a faint hope in their faces: despite the rain that poured down on them, despite the cold and the darkness. With the sight, he also felt the same hope kindle in himself. "I don't know why we were attacked by our own, but I do know that our companions gave their lives so we'd have a chance to escape and avenge them, and we won't fail them."

He scowled up into the storm. "We won't fail, we won't forget, and we'll make certain that no one else forgets either," he said. "But for now, let's leave here."

They moved eastward as well as they could given the difficult terrain and their injuries. They clung together in a group, each helping the other. Kayne found that his leg grew worse, not better, and he began to wonder if it hadn't been fractured. His ribs gave him sharp, angry pains any time he tried to draw a deep breath. Bartel and Garvan each found a stout limb to use as a crutch, hobbling one-legged as best they could. Sean staggered along with them; he and Uilliam had been in the wagons, both previously wounded during the campaign, and now again. An Airgiallaian arrow had caught Sean in the belly. Uilliam had the most trouble, with a leg broken two weeks before during a battle with the Arruk and now his sword arm dangling useless and dead from a cut that gaped open to the bone in his shoulder. They'd bound Uilliam's wound as well as they could, but the bandage was soaked with blood and Uilliam's face, even in the fleeting moments of moonlight through the fast-moving rain clouds above, was pale and drawn. Kayne tried to keep them to a path that involved the least climbing, but the mountains flung jagged feet in front of them, forcing them to either trek north or south around them or drag themselves over sharp inclines slick with rain.

Less than a stripe into their retreat, the mage-lights came, illuminating the banks of clouds with multicolored light. Kayne could feel Blaze pulling at his mind with its yearning to be filled with them, and he couldn't ignore it. "We'll rest here," he told the others, who sank down gratefully. Kayne pulled Blaze out from under his léine. It seemed to nearly leap into his hand with eagerness, and Kayne gasped—his ribs protesting—at the sensations as his fingers closed around the gem. It was like being with a lover, a needy lover who demanded your full presence and insisted on being the center of your world. Kayne had wondered whether he would know how to fill a cloch na thintrí with the power of the mage-lights; he knew now that the stone itself would show him the way. He could feel it guiding his clumsy mind, showing him the way to open the cloch to the lights. Above him, tendrils of orange fire and yellow flame circled, then leaped toward his upraised hand, wrapping around him. He gasped again, this time because of the fiery touch that was at once painful and wonderful.

The contact with the mage-lights seemed to take but a few minutes, though he knew from having watched his da that it might have been as long as a half a stripe. He could feel Blaze drinking in the power, and at the same time he felt the connection with all the other clochs na thintrí throughout Talamh an Ghlas. His da had told him that he could always feel the presence of Kayne's gram and Lámh Shábhála, "like the sun through a thin haze of clouds" was the way he described it. But though Kayne could sense the other Clochs Mór—and especially the one called Winter all too near to him—he didn't feel anything that could have been the overriding presence of his gram. He wondered at that even as the mage-lights reluctantly left him and faded from sight.

Blaze was full and seething under his touch. He wondered how he could handle that power. He had no idea how to actually use the cloch; his da had rarely spoken of it. He knew that there was indeed mental skill involved in the wielding of Clochs Mór, and that inexperienced mages inevitably lost the battle should they be pitted against a trained mage from the Order of Inishfeirm or the Order of Gabair.

He hoped he wouldn't need to learn that lesson firsthand, and soon. Regretfully, he released Blaze and placed it back under his léine. "We need to move on," he told the others. "They'll be looking for us, and the mage that's with them knows I'm here now. They'll be moving this way, if they weren't before."

He limped over to them, feeling even more exhausted now than he had before and trying not to show it to them. He reached down to help Uilliam to his feet, but the man shook his head. "Leave me, Tiarna. I'm just slowing down the rest of you."

Garvan, Bartel, and Sean said nothing. Kayne realized that if he nodded his acceptance of Uilliam's sacrifice, they wouldn't protest. He was the leader of their bedraggled troop; the guilt of any decision would be his to bear. Uilliam was right—if they left him behind, the four of them could travel somewhat faster, despite their own injuries.

Kayne found himself thinking about his da. He knew what Owaine would have done in the same circumstances. There was no question in his mind about that. Even a day ago, Kayne might not have believed that his da's choice would be the right one. But now . . .

Kayne reached down with his hand again. "We're slow enough on our own, Uillliam," he said to the man. "I'm not leaving a companion behind to be killed, not when he can still walk and fight if he has to. We're going to make it, and you're going to be with us when we do. Now, take my hand . . ."

Uilliam, grimacing, clasped his finger around Kayne's wrist and allowed himself to be helped up. "Put your arm around my shoulder," Kayne told him. "I'll take your weight for a bit. Once the sun starts to rise, we might be able to find shelter . . ."

In the light of false dawn, they came across a small river chattering white-watered and fast through a valley. The walls of two great hills pressed in on either side, green-covered, with hidden rivulets cascading down under ferns, bushes, and small trees. A meadow of tall grass spread out along one side of the stream and they heard the dull clanging of bells, the *baa*ing of sheep, and the barking of a dog. Someone was singing—a decent baritone, the song touched with the accent of the Fingerland—and as they came to a bend in the river, they saw a cottage in a copse of trees beyond. Peat smoke curled from the stone chimney to the rear, and the thatch roof looked old and in need of repair, the walls retaining only clinging fragments of the whitewash that had once brightened them. A fieldstone fence marked the outline of a tiny planted field, and sheep roamed in the grass near the water, with a black-and-white dog watching the herd from the top of the low wall. The dog noticed them at the same moment, barking loudly, and Kayne saw a gray-bearded man in a dirty clóca and furs rise from a stump in the yard, trailing tendrils of pipeweed. The man stared in their direction, then walked slowly toward them.

He stopped several strides away, his bushy eyebrows raised, one hand brushing back the straggling long locks of white on the sides of his bald skull, the other still holding the smoldering pipe. "We need help," Kayne, still holding Uilliam, called to him. "Come here, and help me get this man to your cottage."

"Aye, I would say you need help," the man answered thoughtfully, without moving. "The question is whether I should be giving it or not."

"Do you know to whom you're talking?" Garvan snapped at the old man. "This is Kayne Geraghty, the son of the Banríon Ard herself, and we've been attacked."

The eyebrows climbed a little higher, but the man still didn't move. "That may be. Or maybe not—people can say they're whoever they want and the Mother won't stop them, will She? One name's no more impressive than another, anyway—out here in the Finger, we don't much care for the doings of the Riocha." Kayne felt anger starting to build in him as the man slowly looked from one to another of them without moving. He thought of drawing his sword and striking the man down where he stood for his insolence—let him complain to the Mother directly if he wanted.

But the man shrugged even as Kayne's hand started to move. "But you're hurt and soaked through, and the Mother helps those who helps others. Come along—there's a fire, food, and tea enough for all." With that, he came up to Kayne and took Uilliam's arm under his own shoulder. "You have the hospitality of my poor house," he said to Kayne, "especially if you are truly the son of the Healer Ard."

A half-stripe later, they were sitting in the warm single room of the farmer's house, munching on hard bread, cheese, and cold sliced mutton and drinking lukewarm tea. Caolán O Leathlobhair ("The family name means 'half-leper,'" the man told them. "My great-da had the affliction, and the name stuck to my own da") bustled about the room, tearing sheets of old fabric for bandages, bringing water from the well, and talking incessantly. Kayne wondered if the old man talked this much when no one was there.

". . . I lost three sons, two daughters, and a wife," O Leathlobhair was saying. He poured a half-glass of clear poteen into the seeping arrow wound in Sean's belly, ignoring the man's moaning as the liquid seared the tissue, then packed the wound and bound it up with the firm hands of someone used to the work. "The Bloody Cough took a son and daughter before they were even old even to be named; lost my last son and wife both while she was trying to birth him. My first son, Kyeil, reached two hands and two of age before he went climbing Tundaer Cliff with a friend and they both fell. Then Aighna, my last daughter and my pride, who looked so much like her mam that it hurt me sometimes to look at her, got caught in the eyes of a Taisteal boy who passed by here a hand of years ago and I haven't seen her since."

Kayne thought that if the Taisteal happened to be a mute it might explain the daughter's choice, but he said nothing. He stood by the door, staring out through the cracks between the planks at the meadow.

O Leathlobhair didn't seem to care whether anyone seemed to be listening or not. "Those were Airgiallaian arrows we took from your friends, Tiarna. I could be wondering how it is that the Banrion Ard's son was attacked by the Rí Mac Baoill's troops, and why he's watching as if they were still chasing him."

"It's none of your business."

"Aye. We agree on that. As I said, those here in the Fingerlands don't much care for the Rí who sits in Dathúil. Morven Mac Baoill is no better than his da Mal—the Mac Baoills are all lowlanders and lake people, and they don't know the Finger or the clans here at all. All we're good for is the paltry bóruma we pay him every year and for the young men he presses into service because he knows Fingerlanders make fierce fighters. We don't like Riocha business. We have our own ways here in the mountains and our own laws, whether the Rí of Airgialla likes it or not." O Leathlobhair lifted his head as if hearing something, and a moment later the dog began barking and Kayne heard the low pounding of horses on wet earth. "It seems, though, that the Rí wants to know what happened to the Banrion Ard's son."

Kayne put his hand to the stone under his léine as the riders—two hands or more of them—came into view near the river. One of them pointed to the cottage and they turned to approach. O Leathlobhair put his hand on Kayne's shoulder. "Not yet, young Tiarna," he said quietly. "Only at need. Stay here with your men."

With that, O Leathlobhair opened the door and slid out, walking toward the riders with a loud greeting. Kayne watched him through the cracks in the door. The rider stopped near the fence, the dog barking at them and the sheep looking nervous with the commotion. O Leathlobhair spoke to the leader, a Riocha with brown hair and a scarred face, the old man grinning and babbling as volubly as he had inside. The tiarna seemed as annoyed as Kayne had been with the man. O Leathlobhair gestured toward the house a few times, as if inviting the riders to look inside, and actually started to the door once. ". . . come in and let me show you some of the hospitality of the Fingerlands," Kayne heard him say. "It's been so long since I've had people here. Oh, there's so much I could tell you about the Finger and the people here . . ."

"That won't be necessary," the tiarna replied with a visible eye roll. "You've seen no strangers about?"

"No, Tiarna. But the dog was barking early at something across the river, just before the sun rose. There's a ford, just east of here, where someone could cross . . ."

The tiarna nodded, waved at O Leathlobhair, and the group rode off, the dog growling and running after them for a bit. O Leathlobhair came back into the cottage. "Now," he said to Kayne, "don't you think that was easier than fighting them?"

Kayne, despite himself, chuckled. "Aye, that it was."

O Leathlobhair grinned. "Good. Now, take some rest here for the morning, sleep a bit, and this evening when the shadows are long, I'll take you to Liam O'Blathmhaic— he's the clan-laird hereabouts. If you're to survive here, you'll need his protection and his help."

O Leathlobhair started to move past Kayne, going back

to the hearth, but Kayne stopped him. "When I get back to Dún Laoghaire," he said to the man, "I'll make certain that you're well rewarded for this. I promise."

The old man smiled sadly at Kayne. "I know this much about Rí Morven Mac Baoill: he's not a man for bold moves. If Tuath Airgialla dares to march openly against the Banrion Ard's husband and son, then I don't think you're going to find Dún Laoghaire the same if you go back there."

14

An Ard's Funeral

EDANA DIDN'T LOOK up as Doyle approached, though he knew his wife had to have heard his approaching footsteps. At his entrance, the servants in the Great Hall judiciously scattered for the exits and other tasks. Edana continued to stare down at the body on the bier before her, but he saw her body tense under the ornate clóca she wore, the cloth dyed the dark gray of Dún Laoghaire, the same color worn by the body before her. A golden weaving of interlaced knots and curlicues shifted at the hem and collar.

"How is Padraic?" Edana asked without turning to Doyle. "If you've gotten him injured or killed with this business, I will never forgive you. Never."

The question momentarily shocked him. He'd underestimated Edana in the past; it was a lesson he'd thought he'd learned, but if she knew that Padraic had been with him and where, then it was obvious that her network of informants was larger and more capable than he'd believed. *So she knows at least some of it.* He'd have to do some hard questioning of the staff at the Order of Gabair.

And if she knew, there was no sense in maintaining the lie. "Our son's fine, Edana," Doyle answered. "Padraic's unhurt. Unbloodied, even. There was . . ." He sighed, remembering. ". . . no fighting at all with weapons, and only a little with the clochs."

Her shoulders relaxed slightly, but she didn't question his response, which told him that she knew where they'd been, and probably why. "Is he with you?"

"No. Shay O Blaca sent me back with Quickship just now—Padraic will return with the others in a week or so. To Lár Bhaile. I told him to send you a letter, at least."

Edana nodded, still staring. Doyle came up behind her, standing there without touching her. He glanced over Edana's shoulder at the body. Meriel lay behind a screen of filmy gauze, a pair of golden mórceints over her eyes, the string of an embroidered cap tied tightly under her chin to keep the mouth closed, her hands resting at her sides. He told himself he felt no guilt. He told himself that there was nothing he could have done that would have avoided this. He told himself . . .

He sucked in his breath. He'd expected to see a smaller body lying in the bier next to Meriel, and she was alone. Worse, around Meriel's neck there was a chain and a pendant with a jewel, but the stone wasn't one that Doyle recognized. He felt a quick stabbing of worry and panic. Too much had gone wrong already—if this had been another failure, Rí Mallaghan would be furious, and Doyle knew who would ultimately be blamed. *It doesn't matter that this was all his plan, that I told him that I was uncomfortable with it all, that I thought we should wait, that I worried about what could so easily go wrong* . . . "Where's Treoraí's Heart? Has someone taken it?"

Edana took a breath and finally turned to face him, and there was ice and scorn in her gaze. "What's the matter, Husband?" she asked. "Weren't your orders followed? Did you really hate poor Meriel that much? Were you that jealous that she was Ard?" The muscles in her face were tight and there were dark hollows under her reddened eyes. "Riders came to me today, one from Tuath Éoganacht and the other from Tuath Locha Léin. Meriel's other two children, Tara and Ionhar, seem to both have met unfortunate accidents in the last few days, despite the best care of their relatives. And there's been talk that the gardai of Tuath Airgialla are out riding near the Finger, where Owaine and Kayne are expected. I suppose there have been 'accidents' there, as well. Can't have any of the immediate family left to cause problems of succession, can you?"

This wasn't my idea, he wanted to tell her, as he'd told Jenna. *I argued with the Ríthe against this, but Rí Mallaghan was adamant* . . . He knew none of it would convince her or make her change the way she looked at him. He knew, also, that word would already have been sent to Rí Mallaghan about what had transpired here. They still did not have Lámh Shábhála; if they'd failed here also . . . "What of Ennis?" Doyle asked, and Edana's gaze narrowed.

"No one's seen Ennis or the woman who was watching him—Meriel had supper with Isibéal and Ennis the night she died. My aides tells me that the dessert was poisoned—they fed a piece to a dog and it died within a few hours. The herbalist I consulted tells me that the poison was almost certainly a Taisteal concoction." She cocked her head at Doyle, as if judging him. "Poison's a coward's tool, Doyle. I'm surprised even you would stoop to that. Perhaps I should hire someone to taste my own food in the future?"

The scorn and disgust in her face was shocking, if not surprising. For the last year, perhaps a bit more, he and Edana been husband and wife in name only, no longer sharing the large bed in their inner chamber—ever since Rí Mallaghan had approached him with the concerns he and many of the other Ríthe had about the growing influence of Inish Thuaidh and the Mad Holder with the Ard, with her popularity with the tuathánach and the increasing dissatisfaction among the Riocha, with her concern over the Arruk who had yet to threaten the Tuatha. As the talk and planning became more serious, Doyle gradually found himself spending more days in his private cell in the Order's tower in Lár Bhaile than in Dún Laoghaire. The more he had to keep hidden from Edana, whose friendship with Meriel had only grown deeper over the years, the more he felt her pulling away from him. They had always disagreed on politics; now the disagreements ignited into shouting arguments.

He still loved her. He knew that. He'd even told himself, before he'd had Shay send him back here, that with Lámh Shábhála lost he needed her love more than ever. But if he'd wondered whether there were any remnants left in her of the affection they'd once shared, he saw Edana's answer to that in her face now. The realization didn't hurt anywhere near as much as he thought it should, but there was enough of the memory of their relationship left that he wanted her to understand.

"My love—" he began and saw the muscles of her face

tighten with that. "No one intends you any harm, Edana," he told her. "You may think what you want about the assassination of the Banrion Ard, but this wasn't done at my instigation. My hand's not the one that started this, nor was I a willing part of it. You have to believe me." That was a half-truth and an evasion—aye, Rí Mallaghan had made it clear that Doyle's cooperation was required if he didn't want his family harmed, but Doyle's lust for Lámh Shábhála and knowing that Jenna would also die had made that cooperation easy. He suspected she knew that also.

"No?" She stepped away from him, looking at his chest where Snapdragon, his Cloch Mór, lay. "Where's Lámh Shábhála, Doyle? Aren't you wearing it yet? Isn't that why the Order sent so many mages west, and Padraic among them? If you're going to assassinate the Banrion Ard, you couldn't leave the Mad Holder alive to avenge her, could you?"

Doyle scowled inwardly, only lifting his eyebrows at Edana's questions. "I apologize, Edana. You're much better informed than I expected. But you've known all along how much I loathed Jenna, and why."

Edana pointed to Meriel's body. "Look at her, Doyle. She was my dear friend, and she was Banrion Ard because of me. She thought of herself as *your* friend, also—or, at least, she didn't think of you as an enemy. She loved our children as much as we did. Do you remember when Padraic was ill with the Bloody Cough and she took Treoraí's Heart and cured him? Do you remember? He'd be *dead* if Meriel hadn't been here, Doyle." Tears of grief and anger were spilling down her cheeks, and Doyle saw her wipe them away angrily and unashamedly. "Do you remember the last Feast, how the people of the city cheered her when she rode out to the temple? The common folk loved her, even if the Riocha didn't. And so did I." Edana sank to her knees alongside the bier.

"Edana . . ." In years past, he might have gone to her, might have crouched down alongside her and taken her in his arms and let her sob her grief against his shoulder. He wanted to do that now, wanted it more than anything he could imagine, but he could not. Instead, he stood with his arms crossed, watching her as she lifted the gauze around the bier and clutched Meriel's lifeless hand. "How can I make you understand? It was the other Ríthe who wanted this, not me; they kept it from you because they knew how you felt about Meriel."

"Then we could have stopped it, Doyle," she said through her weeping. "With Lámh Shábhála, the Inish-landers and their clochs, with Snapdragon and Demon-Caller, with those who were loyal to her, we could have stood against them. The two of us, together. But *you* didn't say anything. You didn't say anything because part of this, at least, was what you wanted, too. No, maybe you didn't start this, maybe you didn't do anything actively against Meriel or Owaine or their children, but you also didn't stop it. You didn't *want* to stop it."

The accusations lanced deep inside him, piercing all the way to his troubled soul. "Once I knew, I had to cooperate or they would have killed me, too, Edana—and you and our children as well, perhaps. You can't hate me for that. I . . . I cooperated to protect you."

"I'm sure they had to go to great lengths to convince you," she said, the sarcasm lashing at him. "Did Torin Mal-laghan—oh, I know it must have been him—offer Lámh Shábhála to you as payment, or did you tell them that Jenna's cloch must be your reward for planning all this? All this has your feel to it, Husband."

If her voice had been a sword, it would have gutted him and laid his entrails open on the floor. He gave her, for the first time in years, the bare truth. "Lámh Shábhála is lost in the sea," he told her, and he saw her gasp in surprise.

"I wondered, last night when the mage-lights came . . . Then Jenna—"

"—is also dead," he finished for her. He hoped it was true. It *must* be true.

"And Sevei, too?"

Doyle nodded. Neither of their bodies had been found, but Jenna had been grievously wounded and the storm waves terrible and unrelenting. They'd watched for most of the day: for either the two of them or for Saimhóir, the blue seals. They'd glimpsed neither. Doyle found it difficult to believe that either Jenna or Sevei could have survived. And that night, when the mage-lights had come, they had all noticed the absence of Lámh Shábhála.

If Jenna *were* somehow alive, she didn't have the Great

Stone. That at least was some comfort; he could bear not having Lámh Shábhála himself as long as no one else held it. And now Treoraí's Heart was missing also. The Ríthes' victory, already bittersweet, soured a little further. If that half-breed woman Isibéal had taken the Heart and left Ennis alive against all the arrangements they'd made, he would personally kill her. Slowly.

"Padraic saw this? Padraic saw the Mad Holder and Sevei die?"

A nod.

"You bastard," she said.

He said nothing. Edana sobbed for a few breaths, then drew up, sniffing. "They're all gone, then," Edana said, her voice hoarse and quiet. "The Mother-Creator will never forgive you, Doyle. No treachery before matches this. Will you be the new Rí Ard, Doyle, the new puppet for the Ríthe? Is that what they promised you for your part in this?"

He might have been Rí Ard, had he been able to take Lámh Shábhála. Even though Torin Mallaghan yearned to be Ard, Doyle had thought that once Lámh Shábhála was around his own neck, he would have a piece on the board so powerful that even Rí Mallaghan would have to bend before him. Now . . . he was no longer sure. "I was just a player, not the instigator, Edana," he said again. "There were no promises made to me. I tell you again; I had no choice. I was afraid that those I love would be hurt."

"I'm sure that eases your conscience." She kissed Meriel's hand, then pushed herself to her feet, confronting Doyle. "I've set the funeral for tomorrow—especially given what you've told me, I don't want or expect the other Ríthe to be here personally; their representatives here in Dún Laoghaire will have to suffice. I expect you to be beside me as my husband. Once we've given Meriel to the flames and the Mother-Creator and the Draíodóiri have finished their work, you'll leave Dún Laoghaire."

"Edana—"

She cut him off with a wave of her hand. "I don't care where you go, Doyle. Go to Lár Bhaile and celebrate with Rí Mallaghan and the Order. I don't care. Just don't come back to Dún Laoghaire. This is *my* Tuath, and I am still Banrion here. I expect you'll be returning for the Óenach to elect the new Rí Ard, but from now and forever, no matter what, you and I will be as strangers. I'm disgusted that I ever thought I could love you."

Doyle found that a righteous anger could manage to dull the hurt and mask the guilt. "If that's your wish, Banrion," Doyle answered, emphasizing the title. He gave her a mock bow. "You think too simply, Edana. That's always been your problem. I don't like what's happened, but I couldn't keep Meriel alive by myself. I made a choice for the good of *both* of us. I'll tell you now that if I *hadn't* made that choice, you wouldn't be Banrion Dún Laoghaire; you'd be lying there alongside Meriel. You're alive because I was willing to help those who wanted Meriel deposed. And if you don't watch your words carefully in the future . . ." He stopped.

"Sometimes, Doyle, things *are* simple. If I'd known what was planned, I'd have been willing to die with Meriel, if that was what was necessary. I'm loyal to those I truly love, Doyle, loyal enough that I will stand with them no matter the consequences. You, of all people, should remember that." She glared at him; he held her gaze. She didn't understand. She would never understand. Doyle stared back at her as he might at a stranger. "I don't know if you came to gloat or just to make certain that Meriel was truly dead, but now you know," Edana continued. "Leave, Doyle. Leave me alone with her to grieve. At least I have genuine sorrow for the loss of a friend."

"I have the same sorrow and the same grief, Edana, whether you'll believe it or not," he answered. He looked again at the bier. Emotions warred inside. Aye, he was truly sorry that Meriel was dead. She had been an innocent caught up in this. But other thoughts intruded on the sorrow. *Where is Ennis? Where is the Heart?*

Edana scoffed mockingly at him as he gazed down at Meriel's face, and Doyle shrugged. "I'll go, then," he said. He nodded to her, glanced a final time at Meriel's body, and spun on the balls of his feet, his clóca swirling with the motion. As he reached the doors and knocked for the hall garda to open them, he heard her call out behind him.

"I grieve most of all for you, Doyle," she said. "All Meriel lost was her life."

He had no answer for that, or rather, too many. The door

opened, the garda in the corridor bowing his head. Doyle
stepped through the doors as he heard Edana begin to sob
once more.

The Draíodóiri were attired in their most ornate robes,
with gilded torcs engraved with the Mother's sign around
their necks. The priests droned on and on, their voices as
thick as honey syrup. Doyle shifted uncomfortably from
foot to foot, standing next to Edana alongside Meriel's
bier, now placed atop a pile of oil-drenched logs. The smell
of the oil was strong and even the salt breeze off the bay
did little to ease the stench. The odor combined with the
over-strong perfume on Meriel's corpse and churned the
stomachs of those closest to the bier. Many of the Riocha
held cloths up to their noses and mouths; Edana's face was
pale, though that might simply have been grief. Doyle tried
to lose himself in the vista from high on Temple Hill, but
the sun glancing off the waters of Dún Laoghaire Bay
threatened to add to the internal sledgehammer blows that
slammed into his forehead with every beat of his heart. He
tried to massage the headache away with his fingers; it did
little to help. Edana glanced at him: cold and unsympa-
thetic and distant.

The Draíodóiri continued to chant.

The burning ground near the temple was packed; the
city of Dún Laoghaire seemed to have been emptied of its
inhabitants, all of them out here to watch the Healer Ard's
body be given back to the Mother. Afterward, the ashes
and bones would move in procession to the waiting
barrow-grave on Cnocareilig. The mood was solemn but
also tense. It was obvious to Doyle that the rumors of how
Meriel had died and who might have been responsible had
spread farther and deeper into the populace than any of
them had expected. There was submerged anger on the
faces of the watching multitudes, and the Riocha in their
fine clóca shifted uneasily near the bier, seeing how large
the crowd had grown. All the gardai in the city had been
put on alert and the ranks near the temple watched carefully, ready to intervene. Doyle noticed that those of the
Riocha who had clochs na thintrí kept their hands close to

the gems. Swords were forbidden by custom, but there were more "ornamental" daggers on the belts around Doyle than usual.

Doyle knew what the people saw and the conclusions they might draw from it. Even if the news of the Mad Holder's evident demise and the other deaths within her family hadn't yet become common knowledge, the absence of Meriel's husband Owaine or any of her children was conspicuous, as well as the lack of any of the Ríthe except Edana.

They knew. They knew that their beloved Healer Ard hadn't died accidentally: choking on her food while dining privately. That had been the official story Doyle had circulated, but too many servants on the Ard's staff suspected or knew the truth, and while Edana hadn't refuted the official story, neither had she echoed it. And Ennis—the pretense that he and his nursemaid had gone to relatives for a month was belied by the gardai out searching for them and the questions they asked—and Doyle knew that Edana had her personal gardai out looking for the boy, a fact that Doyle wasn't going to relay to Rí Mallaghan or the others. By now, no doubt, the rumors of the deaths of Meriel's other children were probably swirling around the town, and soon would come word of the Mad Holder's death, and of the battle in the Narrows of the Finger.

They knew; the tuathánach, the commoners. They knew that this had been a coup, that the Banrion Ard they'd come to love had been killed by her political enemies, at least some of whom were now standing next to her body pretending to grieve. Such assassinations had happened often enough in the history of Dún Loaghaire and the Ards, but not in the lifetime of those here now.

They'd let Meriel live too long, rule too long. Doyle had never wanted this to happen at all, but if it *must* happen, it should have been a double hand of years ago, not now. Every healing Meriel had performed had made her more popular with the tuathánach, had made them love her and identify with her just a little more.

He closed his eyes against the headache.

The Draíodóiri finished their chanting. The head of the group, an old woman with a prominent hump between her shoulder blades, lit several pots of incense around the bier with a torch brought out from the sacred fire within the temple. The incense only added to the stench, and several of those closest coughed loudly as fragrant streams of smoke rose in the still air. The old Draíodóir came up to Edana and handed her the torch. "Banrion . . ." Her rheumy eyes glanced over to Doyle as she stepped back. Doyle thought he saw disgust in her gaze.

Edana took the torch and approached the bier. Where each of the pots of incense were set, she touched the flames of the torch to the wood. Flames licked at the oil and by the time Edana had gone around the pyre, the logs were already burning furiously. The Riocha stepped back, away from the furious heat and smoke. The flames had reached the bier, the curling heat whipping the gauze curtains around the body, then they caught, revealing the body just as the first tongues of fire reached it.

A sigh went up from the massed throats of the crowd.

Something struck Doyle in the back of the head, so hard an impact that his vision blurred, the new pain momentarily banishing his headache. He gave a cry and brought his hand up reflexively; his fingers came away stained with blood. He blinked, the headache redoubling in intensity and roaring now in his head. Another rock struck his shoulder as he turned; at the same time, a bantiarna went to her knees just to Doyle's right, clutching the side of her face as blood poured between her fingers. The moan of the crowd became an angry howl, and more rocks rained down on the Riocha. The gardai surged forward with pikes to force the crowd away, but they resisted as the press of the mob impaled themselves on the front ranks of the pikes and brought them down. The line of gardai broke and the crowd pushed forward once more. Doyle could hear the shouts as the rocks continue to pelt them: "The Riocha killed her! Revenge the Healer Ard! Give her justice!"

The mob charged up the slope, so close he could see their faces.

A Cloch Mór was unleashed: a false wind howled and flung a section of the crowd back. Doyle grasped Snapdragon as another rock thudded to the ground in front of him. The golden dragon rose, snarling, in the narrowing space between the crowd and the Riocha. "Edana!" he shouted. "Your cloch—use it now!"

From the corner of his vision, he saw her shake her head. Her forehead was bloodied from a rock, and there were spatters of red on the torc of Dún Laoghaire that she wore. "I won't," she told. "I won't use my cloch against them, not when *she* only used hers for them."

"Edana, don't be stupid," Doyle said, taking his attention away from the crowd for a moment. Another rock hit him in the side as he turned and the dragon roared with his pain. The crowd surged uneasily around the beast. "We could all die here!"

Edana shook her head. She folded her arms, giving her back to both Doyle and crowd and staring at the pyre that was rapidly consuming Meriel's body. Black, thick smoke drifted over them, hiding the sky. Doyle uttered a wordless shout of frustration. He scowled and the mage-dragon reared back, spitting fire at the scant open ground between the Riocha and the mob. The crowd gave way at that, and retreated farther when the dragon's barbed tail lashed out at the front ranks, taking several of them down. More rocks were arcing toward them, but the mage-wind caught them and hurled them back into the crowd. A clochmion opened: tiny fireballs rained down at the front ranks of the mob just past the gardai. There were screams, but the mob was no longer moving forward.

The crowd's mood shifted suddenly from rage to panic. The front ranks of the tuathánach closest to the pyre turned and tried to retreat, colliding with those still pushing forward from behind. The gardai, heartened by the support of their leaders, charged at the crowd once more.

"Clear the hilltop!" Doyle shouted to them. The barrage of rocks had stopped; the crowd had turned entirely from the twin threats of the gardai and the Riocha with their clochs, fleeing down Temple Hill toward the warrens of Dún Laoghaire. Those few who stood their ground were trampled by their own or clubbed down by the gardai. Doyle sent the mage-dragon rushing through the air at the rear of the retreat—people screamed and fell to the ground as the great wings brushed close to them, then picked themselves up again and ran.

The retreat became a rout.

Doyle released Snapdragon. The yellow dragon snarled one last time and vanished into wind and vapor. His headache was gone, banished with the adrenaline of the attack. "They'll think twice about doing anything like that again," Doyle said. "We'll have the gardai take those responsible and we'll make an example of them—" He stopped; Edana wasn't listening to him.

She was watching the pyre. The logs groaned and hissed, collapsing into a gout of smoke and bright sparks. The bier tilted and fell into the center of glowing ash and coals, surrounded by flame.

He heard Edana sigh.

"This is how it all will end," she said.

PART TWO:

DIVISION

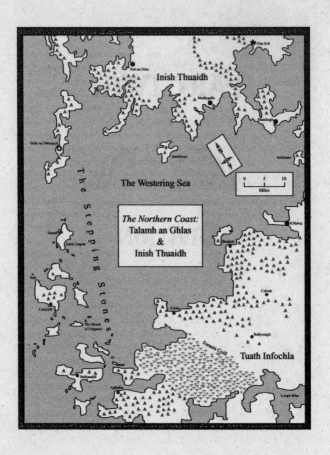

The Northern Coast:
Talamh an Ghlas
&
Inish Thuaidh

Inish Thuaidh

Dún Kiil

Port an Dúin

Maithgalla

Skadmagh

Inishfeirm

Inishlolar

The Westering Sea

0   5   10
Miles

Killyleg

Brádach

Do001

Inish Caoga

Colraic

Carrykill

The Wreck of Onisenis

Cloim

Ballycraigh

Fearais Geill

Ballymákil

Aghadoe

Tuath Infochla

Lough Mór

The Stepping Stones

15

On the Stepping Stones

THE SEA WAS BITTER cold and rough, then quickly warm and quiet. Salt water poured like liquid fire into the open wounds on her back and arm. She opened her mouth to scream, but water entered her throat and she was losing consciousness, drifting down, down into the heavy embrace of the sea and drowning. A strange calm came over her and she closed her eyes, accepting this death and wondering at the dark shapes that came and hovered around her. "Are you the black haunts, come to take me to the Mother?" she asked, but they didn't answer . . .

Sevei awoke with a gasp. Her body flopped strangely, and she realized that she wasn't in human form but that of a seal, though she could feel the comforting weight of the clochmion Dragoncaller still around her neck. A half dozen other seals lay on the rocks around her, but these weren't the common brown harbor seals she'd seen before. These were far larger: magnificent creatures with fur so black that the light reflecting from their coats seemed to strike blue highlights. She realized what they were even as their large, intelligent and coal-black eyes turned to her: Saimhóir. The blue seals.

The largest of them, a bull, waddled awkwardly over to her. His flipper touched her body.

"So you're awake at last," he said, but as she heard his deep voice speaking in her language in her head, she realized that her ears were hearing the grunts and moans of a seal. As if he guessed at her thoughts, she heard him chuckle. "You can understand me because I speak through

Bradán an Chumhacht, which is for the Saimhóir what Lámh Shabhála is for you stone-walkers. I am Bhralhg, who swallowed Bradán an Chumhacht after Challa released it, many cycles ago now."

"Challa . . ." The name seemed familiar to Sevei, but as she spoke the name, the syllables were slurred and unrecognizable coming from her mouth. Bhralhg chuckled again.

"Just think what you wish to say," he said/thought to her. "With Bradán an Chumhacht, I can understand you. You knew Challa?" His voice sounded puzzled or surprised. "She hated stone-walkers, and avoided all contact with them."

"I know her name, that's all," Sevei said. "My mam . . . she told me about Dhegli and Challa. And my gram—"

"We know your great-mam," Bhralhg answered, his voice turning grim. "She was the Holder of Lámh Shábhála, the stone-walker called Jenna. Challa hated her most of all."

With the mention of Jenna, the memories flooded back to Sevei: her great-uncle's confrontation, the golden mage-dragon, and the sight of her gram toppling over the rail of the ship. Bhralhg moaned and grumbled next to her, as if he saw those images himself. "We'd come out from the Nesting Land to see what brought so many sky-stones together," he said to her. "That's why we were there. When we saw the two of you, we thought you were two Saimhóir, lost and battered in the storm, so we took you to the surface and brought you here. It wasn't until later that we realized . . ." He stopped. "The Holder is here also, but she is badly injured in both body and mind, and she no longer has Lámh Shábhála. Whether she will live or not will be the WaterMother's choice alone."

"Gram is here? Where? I need to see her." Sevei willed herself to change so that she could stand and run to her, but Bhralhg touched her again and his voice sounded in her head.

"No," he said, almost gruffly. "You have none of the dead things that stone-walkers wear against the cold and you're still injured. Stay in this form; it will be most comfortable for you. Come, follow me . . ." His flipper moved away from her and his voice faded into the grunting of a seal. He laboriously dragged himself across the rocky shore to the water, splashing into the waves and vanishing with a flip of his tail. Sevei followed him—she could feel the scabbed wounds from the mage-spears pulling at her back as she moved—and dove into the embrace of the waves.

In the shifting light under the waves, she saw Bhralhg waiting for her, resting on kelp-draped stones farther out. She went to him, luxuriating in the feel of the water even though the salt burned in her wounds. She followed Bhralhg around a small outthrust foot of the land. He paused, waiting for the surge of the next wave, then let it carry him in a wash of foam to the shore as he hauled out on a flat rock. Sevei paused, then followed him with the next wave, striking the rocks harder than she wanted and mewling as her already-savaged body scraped over stone. As the wave slid reluctantly away, she saw her gram.

"She wouldn't stay in our form, even though we told her to," Bhralhg said, leaning his body against hers so that their bodies touched and his voice entered her mind again. "We could have helped her more that way, though we did what we could. The Holder is stubborn, even in her pain. None of us were surprised by that; the Holder Jenna has figured large in the tales we've told since Bradán an Chumhacht awakened again."

"No, I'm not surprised either," Sevei told him. Jenna lay huddled in the lee of several large gray boulders. The Saimhóir had draped kelp over her body so that only her head was exposed, her graying hair wild and crusted with salt. Even so, Sevei could see her shivering, the kelp blanket trembling over her. "How long ago did you bring us here?"

"One brightness ago. Not long after the warmlight came to the sky, other stone-walkers came here searching for you—the ones from the wooden islands that move, not the ones who live nearest here—but I used Bradán an Chumhacht to hide you and us from their eyes."

Sevei nodded. Jenna moaned softly, her eyes fluttering open, and Sevei let herself fall back into human form. Shivering and naked, she moved quickly to Jenna. Crouching next to the woman, she stroked her cheek—distressingly hot to Sevei's touch—and whispered to the bloodshot, swollen eyes that peered at her. "I'm here, Gram."

"Sevei?" Her voice was as cracked as her lips. Flies droned around her, lifting in irritation before landing again out of reach as Sevei brushed at them. "You survived, then . . ." Jenna tried to laugh, but it turned to a cough and Sevei saw flecks of blood spray from her mouth.

"Aye, I survived," she told Jenna, lifting the strands of kelp to look at her body then letting them drop down again with a grimace. Her great-mam's body was a mass of seeping, open sores, much of the skin burned and dead, the deep wounds from the mage-dragon's teeth and claws filled with yellow pus. Maggots already writhed along the edges of the worst wounds. Sevei fought the urge to vomit, pressing her lips together and swallowing bile. "We have to get you to a healer, Gram," she said. She looked to Bhralhg, who remained where he was, his expressionless black eyes regarding them. "There may be a village nearby, or I could swim to find someone. The Saimhóir might know . . ."

"No." Jenna raised her hand: the one swirled with the scarred patterns of the mage-lights. The marks were an angry red now, as if infected, and the burns had ravaged the arm above the elbow. "What I need most is nothing any healer can give me."

"Lámh Shábhála," Sevei said well before Jenna's faint nod.

"I knew I might be killing myself when I threw it in the sea. But I was willing to accept that rather than let Doyle have it." She laughed again. "My poor half brother. He'll never hold it. Never." Jenna's hand reached up and found Sevei's face, stroking it gently. "You could find it," she said. "Not in this form, but the other." Her hand, so stiff that it was more claw than hand, tangled in Sevei's hair, pulling it sharply. "Find it, Sevei. Find it and it might be yours one day, when I'm gone." Jenna's voice was a desperate hiss, her eyes wild.

"Gram, you're hurting me—"

"*Find* it, Sevei," Jenna spat. "Do you hear me, child?" Then, with a groan, she fell back, her eyes closing and her body hunching into a fetal ball. "Mother, you can't imagine how this hurts. I can't bear this. I can't."

"Maybe the Saimhóir have something that can help, some medicine."

"The Saimhóir?" Jenna snorted bitterly. "They love to see me like this. It gives them pleasure. They think that this is my proper punishment for Thraisha and Dhegli. They dragged me here so they could watch me suffer and die."

Sevei glanced again at Bhralhg, whose whiskers twitched as he grunted something in his own language that she could not understand. "You're wrong, Gram."

Jenna snorted again. "Are you going to talk to me to death, child? Is that what you want?" For a few breaths, the pain washed over her, her face a mask of lines and her eyes closed tightly shut as she huddled under the kelp. Then her eyes opened again as she panted. "You can stay and here and watch me die with the damned seals, or you can help me. You need to choose, Sevei."

Sevei started to answer, but a spray of rocks cascaded down from the steep hillside above them, bouncing over the rocks and into the water. Bhralhg was still moaning, his snout lifted upward toward the land, and Sevei followed his gaze.

Three men stood above them, not fifty strides away, looking down at the little cove where they were huddled: a blue seal, a naked young woman, and the injured Banrion Holder. Two of the men were dressed as gardai; the other was a young tiarna with bright red hair, clad in the green clóca of the Order of Gabair. A stone dangled from a chain around his neck—certainly a Cloch Mór or a clochmion. She recognized him immediately: Padraic Mac Ard.

He was looking directly down to where Sevei stood. He could not have missed her, staring up at him with her mouth half-open in surprise and fear. She was frozen in place, not certain what to do—she could dive back into the water, become a seal and perhaps escape Padraic, but her gram couldn't do that. She reached for the clochmion, closing her hand around its comforting facets, but there was no answering dragon call. Yet . . . Holding Dragoncaller, she could feel another power active close by, one that tasted of salt and water . . .

Through the noise of the surf, she could hear one of the gardai with Padraic talking. ". . . all day walking around this Mother-cursed island and we're seeing nothing but rocks, grass, birds, and sheep. Not to complain, but this cold and damp is hard on my bones."

"You're just getting old, soft, and tired," the other garda said. "Why, I don't think—"

"Shut up, both of you," Padraic said. "Neither one of you is out here to think." The younger garda snapped his mouth shut. She could see the older one roll his eyes at his companion behind Padraic's back. "We're here to look for the Mad Holder and Bantiarna Geraghty, either them or Saimhóir, and unless you idiots want to be the next ones that dangerous old bitch kills, I'd suggest you use your eyes more than your mouths."

All the time he was talking, Padraic's gaze was sweeping back and forth over the beach below. Sevei saw his regard pass directly over her twice and yet he said nothing, gave no indication that he saw her at all. She could hear Bhralhg moaning softly behind her, large and conspicuous on the rocks, and it was impossible that they did not see or hear him.

Yet they did not. "Nothing there," Padraic said after a few moments. "All right—we'll finish up this island, then move on to the next one. We can eat when we get back to the ship. Come on . . ."

Sevei watched them walk away, vanishing quickly over the brim of the hillside. The low keening from Bhralhg stopped. "You did that," she said to him. He could not have understood her words, but the amazement on her face communicated enough. He gave the toss of the head that she knew was a Saimhóir nod. Jenna seemed to have lapsed into unconsciousness or uneasy sleep. Sevei shivered, the wind and spray whipping around her. With the touch of the water, she let herself slip back into Saimhóir form and waddled over to Bhralhg. "Thank you," she told him when their bodies touched.

His voice came to her head, amused. "I know what the Holder thinks of me. Do you think the same?"

"No." She watched Jenna, shivering in her sleep and whimpering like a child. "Can you help her, with the power that you have?"

Bhralhg gave a shake of his broad head. "I've done what I can. I can't give her what she is missing."

Sevei sighed. "I need to go to where the ships—the wooden islands that move—were when you found us. Can you take me there?"

His large eyes regarded her thoughtfully. "I can," he said.

The part of her that was Saimhóir was comfortable out
here, but the human part felt lost and frail. The sea was
huge, featureless and eternally shifting, and the spot to
which Bhralhg guided her could have been anywhere.
Even the islands that she glimpsed as they bobbed up and
down in the long, low swells were no help; she hadn't been
able to see them very well in the storm that night. Her
body, even in seal form, ached where the wounds were still
healing, and she wondered whether she would have the
strength to search and still make it back to shore. She let
the next wave take her sideways until her body brushed
Bhralhg's fur. "You're certain?" she thought to him, and
she heard laughter in her head overlaid with the bark of a
seal.

"This is where we found you," he answered with a firm
confidence. "And I know what you're looking for. You
won't find it."

"What do you mean?" she asked him suspiciously.

Bhralhg swam away for a moment, then returned. His
voice came to her as they touched. "I know how it is with
Bradán an Chumhacht," he said. "You don't always choose
the power. Often—most often—it chooses you. When
Challa died and gave up Bradán an Chumhacht, there
were others who were closer to it as it came from her
mouth. They chased the Great Salmon, many of Challa's
milk-sons and -daughters, all of them ready to swallow and
take it in. But Bradán an Chumhacht swam to me and
away from them, and all I had to do was open my mouth.
It wanted me, for reasons I don't know. I think it may be
the same for you stone-walkers and Lámh Shábhála. The
cloch will find whom it wants, now that it is free."

"It's *not* free," Sevei insisted. "Gram is still alive and it
belongs to her. She needs it."

"She needs *it*," Bhralhg agreed. "But does Lámh Shábhála still need her?"

Sevei felt herself shiver at that. She rolled away from
him so she couldn't hear his voice anymore. He grunted
something at her in the Saimhóir tongue; she took a long
breath and dove.

The water quickly turned dark as she descended, and she

could feel the pressure flatten her body and push against
her ears. Twenty feet down, she could barely feel the pull of
the waves. Instead, she could taste a salty current washing
in from the west, warmer than the surface water and laden
with clouds of tiny plankton. The bottom here, another
twenty feet down, was rocky with stands of kelp waving
lazily back and forth like trees in a fitful wind. Sevei despaired, seeing that. The stone on its necklace could be
anywhere here. It could be right under her and she
wouldn't see it; the chain could have been caught in the
strands of kelp above or the stone might have drifted far
away in the strong currents. It could have been swallowed
by some sea creature. Bhralhg could be mistaken about the
location and Lámh Shábhála might be laying on the bottom a half-stripe's swim from here. The sea floor was as
vast as an unexplored continent, and Sevei needed to find
one singular pebble on it. It was an impossible task.

She noticed that Bhralhg stayed on the surface, waiting
for her. When she looked up, she could his dark form as a
shadow on the bright top of the water.

She searched, with increasing pessimism, until her need
to breathe drove her to the surface again. Bhralhg came
over to her as she panted. "You won't find it, Sevei. You've
done what you needed to do, and you've seen how futile it
is. Let Lámh Shábhála find who it wants. We should return
to the dry stones so you can rest in your own form."

"I can't. Not until I find the cloch."

The sun sparked blue on his wet fur. "Don't you think
that if Lámh Shábhála wished to stay with the First Holder
that it wouldn't have allowed her to throw it away so easily, or that it would have been there for her when she dove
after it?"

Sevei hesitated, Bhralhg's words feeding the unease inside her. She swam a few strokes away from him and took
several quick breaths, filling her lungs, and dove again. She
returned to the sea floor, searching in an ever-widening circle among the crannies of the rocks and the sandy floor
under them until she could stay down no longer. Her injured body trembled with the threat to return to human
form, but she sought the air once more, then again returned to the calm infinity underneath.

And this time she found the *Uaigneas*. The ship was

canted over on its side, its masts broken, the tattered sails
shredded and fluttering in the currents. Sevei swam over a
field of debris scattered on the ocean floor near the ship:
trunks, dishes from the galley, ropes, pulleys, an ax, furni-
ture she recognized from the small passenger chamber in
the ship. . . .

No stone on a bright golden chain. No Lámh Shábhála.

She swam closer, feeling the remembered terror welling
up inside her. Much of the decking was charred as if a
fierce fire had burned there before it sank, and as she approached, she could see worse: bodies, arms outstretched
as if waving to her. The sea creatures had already come to
dine on the feast sent down from above: starfish, crabs, lob-
sters, a bright welter of fish. The scavenger fish fled at the
sight of her seal form. She swam along what had once been
the ship's deck. There, that was the railing where Gram had
stood as she threw Lámh Shábhála into the sea. That body
there, in clothing she recognized, must be the captain. She
veered away, not wanting to see him closely.

And there . . .

. . . there . . .

It was the white clóca first, and the shape of his head,
turned in profile to her and ghostly against the burned tim-
bers behind him.

Dillon. Her snouted mouth opened with his name: a
plea, a prayer, a curse.

His leg was snared in a coil of rope and his left hand
gripped the railing that was now the top of the wreckage as
if he'd been trying to climb up to the surface as the ship
heeled over as it sank. His body was bloated, his hair
drifted like smoke, his mouth was open in a final water-
stoppered shout; as she stared, a tiny fish darted out from
the tooth-lined cavern. The full shock rippled through her
body then. She felt her awareness shifting, felt the hammer
blow of seeing Dillon start to send her body back to its
human form. She wanted to scream, wanted to wail,
wanted to do anything to stop the pain that threatened to
tear her open from the inside.

Something, someone struck her hard from underneath,
pushing her, nudging her upward, and she realized that
Bhralhg was there, guiding her up toward the surface and
away from the wreckage of the ship. She reached down for

Dillon, and the hand that stretched out before her eyes was furred like a Saimhóir but had her own fingers. Then, in a rush, they broke the surface of the water and Sevei gasped at the cold bite of the air. She struggled, trying to dive back underneath the surging waves, but Bhralhg's head butted against her, driving her back up.

"You must stop." Bhralhg's body was warm against the freezing cold of the water. "If you change out here, you will die. There is nothing you can do for those down there. You must stay in Saimhóir form." His voice was sympathetic and understanding. She felt a prickling of the fur that encased her and she knew he had loosed some of the energy of Bradán an Chumhacht. Against her own will, she felt herself calming. Seeing Dillon seemed somehow distant and long ago . . . She fought against the imposed tranquillity.

"Why?" she railed at him, though now she could hold back the change that threatened her. "At least I'd join the rest of my family with the Mother. We'd all be there together: Kayne, Gram, my mam, my da . . ."

"Not your da. Your da died long cycles ago."

The waves lifted them, dropped them again. His words banished the horrible image of Dillon, replacing it with confusion and uncertainty. Despite the serenity he'd forced on her, she felt as if her entire world had shifted. "What do you mean? I felt the attack, I felt Kayne's despair. Da was there; I could feel him through Kayne."

"You feel those of your blood, Sevei. You dream of them."

"Aye," Sevei admitted. "But I never told you that."

"Bradán an Chumhacht knows," he answered. "You dream of your mam and of your brother Kayne with whom you shared a womb. You see them the most, and sometimes you can even glimpse your gram and your other brothers and sisters. But the one you call your da—do you ever dream of him?"

Sevei gave a wriggle of her head. "No."

"Are there ever Saimhóir in your dreams?"

She remembered the times that images of the Saimhóir drifted through the images in her head. "Aye, but . . ."

Bhralhg gave her no chance to continue. She realized what he was going to say then, before he spoke the words and she shook her head as if she could stop them with the denial. "Your mam was a changeling like you. Meriel swam with Dhegli, who carried Bradán an Chumhacht before me and before Challa. And Dhegli, unlike Challa and me, was also a changeling." He hesitated as a wave pushed them momentarily apart. "Like you," he finished when he swam back to her. "Can your brother change, Sevei? Does the WaterMother call to him? The two of you are really so different, so unlike each other ..."

Even Bradán an Chumhacht couldn't hold back the turmoil in her mind at the implications. Again she struggled to retain the shape of a Saimhóir. She swam away from Bhralhg.

"No," she said.

She heard the word come from her mouth as a seal's grunt.

16

The Voice of Vengeance

LIAM O'Blathmhaic wasn't what Kayne had expected in a clan-laird. He seemed no more well off than O Leathlobhair: his house was in a state of eternal disrepair, the stone fences around his pastureland half-falling down the steep slopes on which they were set. Sheep stared placidly at them as they approached, and Laird O'Blathmhaic came from his house bearing a large cudgel that he waved at O Leathlobhair. A black-and-white herding dog which looked to be almost as old as O'Blathmhaic himself growled at them from his side.

"What is it now, O Leathlobhair, you crazy old man?" the laird shouted down at them. "I told you the last time: the ewe was more than enough in payment for the trampling of your field and that settles it between you and young Odhougnal. That was my judgment and I've not changed my mind. I don't care who you bring to argue with me . . ."

The tirade broke off in mid-sentence as Laird O'Blathmhaic stopped and squinted down the worn dirt path up which Kayne and O Leathlobhair were laboring. He brought the cudgel down and leaned against it as a cane. The dog sat. "The red-hair with you is no one I know. I see blood on his fine clothes, and he has a warrior's bearing."

"I am Kayne Geraghty, son of Meriel MacEagan and Owaine Geraghty," Kayne answered, giving his name. Behind him, O Leathlobhair hissed quietly: "Careful, boy . . ."

"I saw a great fire sending smoke from up on the Narrows earlier today, and crows gathering there," O'Blathmhaic said, nodding. "They were feasting on your companions, I would guess, from what I see in front of me."

Kayne grimaced. An image came to him: a huge black bird sitting on his da's chest, the beak open as it lowered its head to peck at his open eyes . . . He forced the thought away. "Aye, Laird O'Blathmhaic," he said. "We were cowardly attacked as we were riding in peace back to Dún Laoghaire from the wars in Céile Mhór. My da was the commander."

"And your attackers?" His massive, ancient face folded into a bearded scowl. "If you're accusing Fingerlanders, then you'd better be quicker with that sword than you look, boy. Old I may be, but my stick here has beaten the heads of stronger men than you, even if they don't bear fancy names and titles."

Kayne drew himself up at the insult and threat, but O Leathlobhair touched his shoulder and he held his temper with an effort. "The gardai wore red and white, Laird. There were Riocha from Dathúil with them, and at least one Cloch Mór."

O'Blathmhaic spat at that, sending a massive globule splashing against the stones of the path. "Come inside," he grunted. "I'll hear more."

A stripe later, Kayne had finished relating his tale, his throat eased somewhat by a tankard of bitter dark ale O'Blathmhaic set in front of him. The steep-hilled landscape outside the window was cloaked in night's shadow by that time, and the peat fire in the hearth filled the small dwelling with its ruddy heat. The dog slumbered, snoring audibly, under the table. O'Blathmhaic's pudgy fingers prowled his snarled and braided gray beard; his eyes glinted in the deep hollows of their sockets. In close proximity, the man smelled of peat and dirt and sheep, and the few teeth he had left were brown and tilted in the bed of his gums. "My companions and I need your help, Laird," Kayne finished, hating to say the words, hating the way the man seemed to leer at him with the statement. Liam O'Blathmhaic was the epitome of the tuathánach, the class of person that Kayne had always ignored when he rode past their hovels, had turned his head away at the sight and smell of them. Like most Riocha, he'd felt himself better than these common creatures; in truth, looking around the filth that this man called home, he still felt himself better. He longed for the keep at Dún Laoghaire: for its spacious chambers, its bright hangings and hordes of servants, its light and glory and majesty.

Here, in the dirt, he was begging a filthy graybeard for aid, because he had no other choice. The indignity of it made him scowl. "I need to warn Hand Harik of the treachery. Perhaps with the men we left at the Bunús Wall . . ."

"And why should we help?" O'Blathmhaic interrupted. "This is Tuath Airgialla, is it not?—the Rí Mac Baoill's land, not yours, even if you be who you claim to be."

"You don't believe me?" Kayne said, pushing his chair back as O Leathlobhair squawked in alarm and O'Blathmhaic watched with bland amusement in his gaze. "Then there's nothing to gain here." He rose to his feet, unable to stifle the groan as his ribs protested, as the deep wound in his thigh threatened to rip open again. His head brushed the low beams above him as he forced his body to straighten. He took a limping step toward the door as O'Blathmhaic's dog growled and nipped at his feet.

"And how are you going to find your way back in the dark, boy? You can barely walk as it is. We'll find your broken body in the morning after you fall over one of the cliffs. Sit, and listen to someone older and wiser than you— or is that something you Riocha canna do?"

Kayne glared at O'Blathmhaic, who gazed back at him placidly as he reached to the center of the table to tear off a piece of the bread loaf that sat there. The clan-laird pushed the wedge into his mouth, chewing noisily. Kayne looked at O Leathlobhair, who didn't seem inclined to leave with him. The dog sniffed at his boots.

Kayne sat again.

O'Blathmhaic chuckled softly to himself. He tipped back in his chair. "There now. You *can* think with that handsome head of yours." Now he leaned forward again, and Kayne could smell the man's breath: ale and bread and rotting teeth. "Listen to me now, and listen well. O Leathlobhair here has already told you that we Fingerlanders don't care for the Rí Airgialla. Mac Baoill can claim the Finger if he likes, but he also knows that he can't hold our land except in name. He can tithe us, but if he makes the tribute too burdensome, it won't come to him and he'll be forced to either look impotent in front of the other Riocha or start a war in the highlands that he can't win. Oh, he sends his gardai here when he has to, but they don't stay." O'Blathmhaic grinned gap-toothed at that. "Mind you, a few of 'em always *do* stay—or rather, their bones do. Help you? Maybe I can. It depends on what you're asking of us, and what the clans would get in return. The wars of the Riocha aren't our wars, Tiarna Geraghty. All we want here is to be left alone."

"Help me, and I make you this promise: the Finger will become its own Tuath, not under Rí Mac Baoill, but under whomever the clans wish to call Rí. Maybe even you, Clan-Laird."

O'Blathmhaic roared at that, pounding the table with his fist as the dog barked and O Leathlobhair grinned. "That's a good one, Tiarna. A good one. The likes of *me* as Rí. I'm sure you'd love having me visit your fancy chambers in Dún Laoghaire, eh?" The mirth seemed to die as quickly as it had come. He frowned, leaning forward toward Kayne. "A promise that can't be kept means nothing, boy. If Mac Baoill feels safe enough to attack the Banrion Ard's husband and son, then I doubt that Dún Laoghaire has enough power to take the Finger from him. You've been away, and everything has changed in that time. Why should I have any confidence in you and the few remnants of your troops?"

"Because I'm also the great-son of the First Holder. Because I hold a Cloch Mór myself." Kayne dragged Blaze from underneath his léine. The ruby facets glinted like rich wine in the firelight. "Because my mam is the Banrion Ard, the Healer Ard. Because, by the Mother, I *will* have vengeance for what happened here, whether you help me or not."

A trace of a smile touched O'Blathmhaic's lips and departed. "Brave words. But that's all. It still only concerns you Riocha."

"There's a war coming that *none* of us can avoid, Laird O'Blathmhaic," Kayne told him. "Not Riocha, not céili giallnai, not tuathánach. An enemy is coming from Céile Mhór, and they will affect everyone in their path. Everyone. They've already made their first strike here, in Ceangail."

O'Blathmhaic grunted. "Take my dog out to check the flock, would you, Caolán," he said abruptly to O Leathlobhair. The other man hesitated, then shrugged, rising from his seat and whistling to the dog, who padded out from under the table. O'Blathmhaic sat back, the rude chair creaking as he shifted his weight. "I heard the rumors about Ceangail, aye. So they're true?"

"They're true, and worse. It will take all of us, Riocha and Fingerlander, common or noble blood, to hold back this storm." Kayne felt the memories of the past year crease his face. "I've faced the Arruk, and I know how powerful they are. Laird O'Blathmhaic, all I ask now is that you help me and my friends reach Bunús Wall, where the rest of our people should be. Take us there, and you'll see the truth of Ceangail as we pass. Talk to the laird there."

O'Blathmhaic's fingers sought his bearded chin again. "I could do that, aye. Or I could tell Mac Baoill's gardai that I have the rabbit that slipped from their noose. I wonder what Mac Baoill would be willing to pay for a Cloch Mór?"

Kayne started to rise from his seat again, but he bumped into O Leathlobhair even as he stepped back, feeling a sharp and cold blade touch the side of his neck as the dog growled. "I wouldn't move your hand to that stone, Tiarna," the old man hissed in his ear.

As Kayne froze, O'Blathmhaic laughed and gestured. "Sit, boy! You think we'd give Mac Baoill a Cloch Mór when I could keep it for myself? Do you think I have any interest in doing a Riocha's dirty work for him? Sit, and be careful about it. Old O Leathlobhair's hand is none too steady, and I've seen the edge on that knife of his lay open a wolf's gut like it was a pie crust."

O'Blathmhaic watched Kayne ease himself back down, O Leathlobhair's blade remaining at his neck. "Now then, let me finish. I don't know if you're telling me the truth or not. Even if you are, helping you might not help us. But even here in the Finger we know the Healer Ard wasn't like the rest of the Riocha, and we've always had a certain sympathy with the Inishlanders for the way they've thumbed their noses at the Tuatha all these years. Taking you to Ceangail won't hurt, and I can as easily make up my mind there as here. So we'll go to Ceangail, and we'll talk to those there, and if I learn that what you say is true, then I'll take you to Bunús Wall and your men. Is that good enough for you?"

"Do I have a choice?"

O'Blathmhaic lifted a shoulder. "Aye. There's always a choice. You can accept the offer or I can let O Leathlobhair give you a second mouth." He took a sip of his ale and gave an appreciative smack of his lips. He stared hard at Kayne, his eyes unblinking and alert. "Here among the clans of the Finger, Tiarna, a person's word is taken as if it came from the Mother's lips, and when that word is broken or found to be false, the punishment is swift and harsh. Give me your word that you'll do nothing to harm any Fingerlander, and I'll have O Leathlobhair put his sheep-skinner away."

Kayne gazed steadily back at the man. "You have my word, Laird. I'll do no harm to those who might help me."

A nod. The blade was gone from Kayne's neck and he heard the whisper of steel in leather as O Leathlobhair sheathed the blade. Kayne rubbed at the side of his neck and looked at his fingers, half-expecting to see blood there. There was nothing.

"I'll meet you at O Leathlobhair's in two stripes of the candle," Laird O'Blathmhaic said. "And we'll take a bit of stroll in the dark."

It wasn't just O'Blathmhaic who arrived not long after the mage-lights had faded, but a quartet of clansfolk: two men and a woman with a long and ugly scar across her neck accompanied him. The group set out on sturdy and small highland ponies, with mounts for Kayne and each of his men. Garvan, Bartel, and Sean rode with Kayne, but they left Uilliam with O Leathlobhair, too injured to ride. "We'll be back for you," Kayne told him. "Get yourself better, Uilliam. I'll need you later."

They rode through the night by paths that Kayne could not discern, the ponies plodding slowly and surely through the gorse and heather that mantled the steep hillsides. They stayed mostly to the edges of the valleys and the shadows of the trees—stands of birch and elm and pines. Liam O'Blathmhaic said nothing once they were on the way, riding next to Kayne and content to let the scarred woman—who seemed to be the guide—lead the way. Watching the stars when he could glimpse them above,

Kayne could see that they moved sometimes north, some-times south, but always eastward as well. He wished he could see the land around them. Often, black cliffs reared on one side or the other, or there would be a yawning emptiness over a hidden ravine where water could be heard rushing. There were calls and cries from animals, and twice the shivering voicelike howl of dire wolves made Kayne sit up and peer about him.

O'Blathmhaic chuckled at that. "They're just letting us know that they see us," he said in a husky whisper. "They're no different than clansfolk—as long as you stay out of their territory and their business, they'll leave you alone. But bother them, and they don't like that a'tall."

Twice, they crossed the High Road, the woman always going ahead to make certain that the road was deserted be-fore they quickly crossed, moving swiftly down the rutted lane for a few breaths before leaving it once again.

They continued on for what seemed stripes. Kayne found himself nodding off even as they rode, lulled to sleep by the rocking motion of the pony and sheer exhaustion. He jerked alert suddenly, realizing that their little troop had stopped in the shadows of a copse of elms. O'Blath-mhaic raised a finger to his beard-masked lips, then pointed up a steep slope to where the wavering lights of campfires gleamed. "Some of your friends from Airgialla," he said in a low voice, "are camped alongside the High Road."

The woman guide had dismounted. She came back to O'Blathmhaic: she was perhaps the same age as Kayne, her face bearing the strain of a hard life, but there was also a pleasant handsomeness to her face, and her eyes were as large and dark as those of a fawn. Under her chin, the thick, twisted ridge of the scar pulled at her skin. She gazed up at O'Blathmhaic, lifting her head a bit though she said nothing at all. He seemed to understand. He nodded.

"Be quick about it, Séarlait," he told her. "We need to ride."

She turned in a single lithe movement, racing quietly off into the darkness. Kayne saw her pluck a bow from the pack on her pony before she scurried quietly up the brush-cloaked hillside toward the lights—she went alone, the other clansfolk remaining with the group. Kayne wondered at that. There was silence for several breaths. "Laird O'Blathmhaic . . ." Kayne began, but the old man's voice answered before he could phrase the question.

"Séarlait is my great-daughter," he said. "The daughter of my son. She was twelve when several of Rí Mac Baoill's gardai came here to collect the bóruma. The bastards decided they wanted to collect more than just our tribute. They raped her mam in front of Séarlait and my son, then they killed my son and his wife. When the gardai turned their attention to Séarlait, she fought back and bit one of them. After they were finished raping the girl, the garda she'd bitten cut her throat in repayment, leaving her for dead."

Kayne drew in his breath with a hiss. "Aye," O'Blathmhaic said. "That's why she canna talk." From up the hill came the twang of a bowstring, with two more quickly following, then shouts. Kayne could see the silhouettes of the roused gardai running in front of the fires. "At least not with her voice," O'Blathmhaic finished.

Not long after, a breathless Séarlait appeared out of the night, a tight-lipped smile on her face. She raised her hand toward the clan-laird, three fingers up, then unstrung her bow and shoved it back in the pack. She mounted her pony and led them deeper into the cover of the trees.

"You see, Tiarna," O'Blathmhaic told Kayne. "You can send an army here if you like, but only the clansfolk know the true paths in this land. You won't ever find us all, and clansfolk never forget who their enemies are. Never."

It had taken Kayne's troop days to get to the Narrows from Ceangail via the High Road, which had wriggled back and forth over the landscape, climbing ridges and descending again into valleys. When the sun peered over the tops of the mountains ahead of them, they stopped and the clansfolk passed around skins of water and hard biscuits. "Ah, Tiarna Geraghty, would you look at that!" Sean said suddenly, also nudging Garvan and Bartel—both of them half asleep sitting against a tree trunk—with an elbow. "Ain't that Ceangail already?"

Kayne blinked into the sunlight: though the valley into

which they were descending was still shadowed and foggy, what looked indeed to be the walls of Ceangail could be glimpsed among the trees several miles ahead, on the rise where they'd fought the Arruk—that battle seemed ages ago now. Another age. Another time.

"That can't be Ceangail," Kayne said. "It was nearly a three-day ride from Ceangail to the Narrows."

Nearby, O'Blathmhaic grinned into the yellow new light, shading his eyes against the glare and chuckling at Kayne's bemusement. "When the Ríocha brought their people in to mark out the High Road," he said, "they asked us where best to lay it. If they ignored what we told them and went somewhere else, they always had . . . accidents. Problems. Eventually, they followed the trails we Fingerlanders marked for them because that was easiest." He pointed to where the thread of the road could be seen behind them, a bare line through the green of the mountain. "Did you really think we'd show them our true paths? No, we made sure they'd move slow and be where we can keep an eye on them. Any Airgiallaians are a full day's journey behind us."

For the first time since the debacle at the Narrows, Kayne allowed himself to feel hope. Harik and the others should be out at the Bunús Wall, and if they could get word back to Dún Laoghaire . . . Kayne tightened his jaw, looking at the High Road.

Da, I will give you your vengeance for what they did. I promise that . . .

He hadn't realized that he'd fallen into reverie and that the others had remounted until Séarlait came up to him. She looked into Kayne's face, her head tilted slightly as if she were trying to see something that just eluded her gaze. Then she jerked her head sharply in the direction of Ceangail. Kayne found himself caught in her gaze, in the features of her face, in the pain and sorrow and loneliness he saw there. "Sorry," Kayne said. He smiled at her. "I was just—"

She didn't let him finish the phrase, walking off without waiting to hear the rest. Sean had helped the one-legged Bartel onto his pony and then mounted his own horse, Garvan was already astride his, and Kayne could feel the pressure of Laird O'Blathmhaic's regard on him as he went to the horse they'd given him. "Séarlait would tell you that revenge is a cold and jealous marriage that leaves you with no room for anything or anyone else," O'Blathmhaic said. "Are you looking to be betrothed, Tiarna?"

Kayne glanced back at the High Road as if he could see the Airgiallaian gardai approaching, with the Rí Mac Baoill's son Mal leading them with his Cloch Mór. Kayne's hand went to Blaze under the layers of the furs Laird O'Blathmhaic had provided. "Aye," he said finally. "'Tis a marriage I want very much."

O'Blathmhaic gave a laugh that was half grunt. "Then you're more like clansfolk than I thought, Tiarna."

Bunús Wall. Five miles long, the ruins of the wall undulated over the ridges and valleys of the Finger from the cliffs of the Ice Sea to the shore of the Tween. Most of the tall barrier of stone had tumbled down long ago, but some parts remained much as they had been: as thick as the outstretched hands of two men and as tall as three, the massive granite blocks carved from some quarry as yet unfound. The wall had been there, in nearly the same condition, since the Daoine had come to Talamh an Ghlas, almost 1200 years before. The legend was that the Bunús Muintir had built the wall as a buffer against some long-forgotten invaders, but even the Bunús Muintir who lived in Talamh an Ghlas didn't know if that was true or simply myth. Some said it had been raised by Bunús Muintir cloudmages, that even huge crews of slaves laboring away for centuries couldn't possibly have built it, that the Bunús lacked the technology to transport the immense carved blocks of stone so far from their source. Whatever the truth might be, the Bunús Wall was still magnificent even in half ruin. There were faces in the wall, leering gargoyles and fierce coiled dragons, snapping wolves and glaring demons—all of them carved in the stone, all of them glaring outward to the east and Céile Mhór. The faces were eroded now by time and weather, though once they must have presented a formidable scene, freshly carved and painted and snarling at any advancing force. Bunús Gate itself, where the High Road passed through it, was made in the form of a strange winged feline with scaled skin, its yawning mouth the opening through which the road passed, its clawed front feet the supports.

"Whoever it was the Old Ones fought, they defeated them, for the Bunús were still here when we came, eh?" Laird O'Blathmhaic patted a dragon's snout on a fallen stone. The dragon now stared defiantly at the sky and its mouth was stuffed with an old bird's nest. "I wonder if they didn't use their slow magic or their clochs na thintrí to make the dragons roar and the wolves howl, all the carvings writhing like they were alive. Now that would be a sight to make you piss in your boots, wouldn't it? We should be glad our ancestors didn't come then, or they might have gone running back to wherever they came from, eh?"

Kayne remembered how he'd shivered the first time he passed the Bunús Wall, riding through the magnificent remnants of Bunús Gate. He could well imagine how his long-dead ancestors must have felt seeing this for the first time. "The clansfolk all have Bunús blood in 'em. Most of us, anyway. That's where we get—" The old man stopped as Séarlait waved at him from farther down the wall. "She's found your people," he said. "Let's go meet them."

The men in the encampment Harik had established near Bunús Gate stared uneasily at the clansfolk even as they gathered around Garvan, Sean, and Bartel with cries of mingled greeting and alarm. Kayne led Harik away from the group toward the High Gate as Garvan began to relate their own tales of the ambush at the Narrows. Kayne found that it was difficult to even talk about that day, that when he spoke of his da the tears burned in his eyes, heated by the inferno of rage in his heart. Harik flushed, his hands making impotent fists as Kayne related the tale. He slammed one of those mailed fists against a gargoyle's skull, breaking off an ear flap as Kayne spoke of Owaine's last, futile charge into the Airgiallaian ranks.

"That is what I'd expect of Tiarna Owaine. He was always a man who thought of those around him first," Harik said, his voice oddly quiet. He took a long breath, his exhalation a cloud in the cold air of the mountain ridge. "I'll miss your da, Tiarna, and I will grieve a long time for him.

So will the rest of the men. Unfortunately, I think Laird O'Blathmhaic's right: if Rí Mac Baoill would send his gardai and his own son here to attack us, then I'm afraid the situation can't be good in Dún Laoghaire. The Ríthe couldn't move against us unless they also moved against the Banrion Ard herself, and probably the Mad—" Harik stopped. "I mean the Banrion Inish Thuaidh." He shook his head. "And we have a bare hand of double-hands of men here. That's all." He lifted his chin. "What now, Tiarna? You're now the commander in your da's place. You have my loyalty, as he did."

Kayne scoffed. "Do I deserve the gift of your loyalty, Harik?"

Harik started to answer, then stopped. He regarded Kayne for several breaths. "You're Riocha," he said. "You're the son of Owaine Geraghty, who was husband to the Banrion Ard. For all we know out here in this Mother-forsaken place, you may be the only one of the Geraghtys—" Again he snapped his mouth shut. Kayne felt the sense of loss and grief pounding at his chest. *The world has changed underneath me. The ground is no longer safe.*

"Riocha, Banrion Ard, Tiarna: those are just words and titles, Harik. Is that why you gave your loyalty to Da, for his title? Is that why you would take the chance and scold me like a misbehaving child not four days ago in Ceangail? Is that why Da loved you so much? Because of the titles he held?"

"You have my loyalty," Harik answered simply.

"Because of *me*, Harik," Kayne persisted, "or because of Da?"

Harik's gaze was fixed somewhere just above Kayne's eyes. "Because of your da."

Kayne snorted. He turned, looking back over the encampment of Harik's men, knowing that if—if—they would follow Kayne, it would be because Harik Mac-Cathaill the Hand ordered them to do so. Ahead of Kayne were the humped, blue spines of the Fingerlands, and beyond . . . Was there open war in the Tuatha, or had it all been settled already, with perhaps a new Ard sitting on the throne his mam had once occupied? Was the smoke from the pyres of his mam and his siblings already rising out there? For Sevei? For his gram?

Harik must have guessed at his thoughts. "We could go back to Concordia, Tiarna Geraghty," the man said. "The new Thane would give us refuge in Céile Mhór for the help we gave his father against the Arruk, no matter what has happened in Talamh an Ghlas. A life spent fighting the Arruk wouldn't be a wasted one."

The clouds, scudding over the sky, cast mesmerizing sun-shadows over the peaks. Kayne could glimpse the Tween Sea from here, where the Bunús Wall vanished to the south: a fragment of calm in a landscape where everything else was jumbled and broken.

"Tiarna?"

Kayne shivered.

"You and your men can make your own choices, Harik," Kayne said without turning. "Go back to Concordia if you want, or continue forward to Talamh An Ghlas if you think that you'll be safe—Rí Mac Baoill wants *me*, not you or the gardai. I won't ask anyone to risk themselves for me."

Behind him, Harik grunted. "And you, Tiarna?"

Kayne felt a leaden certainty settle around his shoulders. Blaze seemed to tug heavier on its chain. "I have questions I need to ask of the Ríthe who did this to my family," he said, "and I also have hard answers I intend to give them."

Kayne heard Harik turn to go back to the camp. The wall was a thick, cold presence on his left, but he hadn't followed it for more than a few strides when he saw Séarlait leaning there half-hidden in shadows. She was watching him. "You heard?" he asked.

A nod.

"It was none of your business," he told her, but he could not make the words sound as sharp as they should have been. Séarlait gave a shrug and continued to gaze at him, as if she were trying to judge him. He wondered what she saw, what she thought. He stared back at her, trying to imagine her as she could have been: a comely young woman, with a low, honeyed voice and a laugh that sparked with joy and delight . . .

She nodded again, as if he'd spoken. Leaning down quickly, she plucked two leaves of grass from the ground. She came closer to him, an arm's length away, and held one of the blades to her breast, placing the other against Kayne's chest. Her gaze never allowed his eyes to leave hers. Her lips relaxed into a brief, fleeting smile. She brought the two leaves together between them, tapping her hands together. She gestured at the grass below their feet, then pointed at him, then her. It came to him suddenly, what she was trying to say.

"We're alike, like two blades of grass? Is that what you mean?"

Séarlait nodded once, emphatically. The smile returned, vanished like the sun behind fast-moving clouds. She let the twinned leaves fall to the ground. She hesitated, as if she wanted him to say more, but he could only look at her: her face, the terrible scar across her neck showing above the top of her léine. She started to turn away, but he reached out and touched her arm. He felt her tense and he thought that she would slap his hand away. He looked down at his fingers instead, and he let his hand fall back to his side. She brushed hair back from her face and rubbed her hand on her arm where he'd touched her.

"You may be right," he told her. "More than we both realize."

17

Meeting the Taisteal

ENNIS SAID VERY LITTLE after he awoke.
Isibéal thought initially that it was because the boy
was understandably shocked by what had happened—she
hadn't yet told him that his mam was dead, but with their
frantic ride through the night away from Dún Laoghaire,
even at his age he must have known that he'd been kidnapped and spirited away. She'd expected tears or
tantrums or sobbing panic when the boy woke up from his
induced sleep. She'd expected disorientation and screaming accusations. She expected him to demand to be returned to Dún Laoghaire and his mam.

But Ennis did none of those. He woke during one of her
brief pauses to rest and determine where she was. He
blinked and looked around him with bright curiosity.
"When will we be there, Isibéal?" he asked, as if they were
out on some scheduled jaunt to one of his cousins' holdings. There was no accusation on his face, nor any fright;
he seemed older than his few years. He stared at her with
an intent curiosity, as he might some juggler's entertain-
ment and a songmaster's concert. His sober gaze unnerved
Isibéal.

"I don't know yet," she told him, and he nodded, accepting the answer and saying nothing more. That night, Isibéal
lifted the Heart to the mage-lights, and felt for the first
time the exhilarating and intoxicating pleasure of filling
the cloch. She also knew then that she could not ever willingly give up Treoraí's Heart. It would be hers until she
died—and she was afraid that would be far too soon. She

pushed the horse hard through the rest of the night, forcing herself to stay awake and touching the Heart over and over again.

As the sun started to rise the next day, she kicked the exhausted horse onto the willow-draped hummock. They were in a bog pooled in the hills south of Dún Laoghaire, not far enough away yet for Isibéal's comfort. Ennis sat quietly, watching as she struggled with the packs, as weary and battered as their mount. "Get over here and help me," she snapped at the boy.

He continued to stare, his eyes widening just a bit. "I mean it, Ennis. Out here, there's no one to hear you, and I don't have to answer to your mam. If I need to beat you, I will."

"No, you won't." He said it calmly, with a soft certainty. Annoyed and angry at his refusal, she lifted her hand, and finally shook her head.

She was too tired to argue. The ride during darkness had been tense and frightening. More than once she'd thought she'd heard pursuit behind them and she'd glanced back, terrified, knowing that it was not only the gardai who would be looking for her, but also those who had hired her.

I couldn't kill him. I know I should have, but I couldn't. That would have been too much like having Adimu die all over again. The Mother knows that I wouldn't even have killed the Banrion Ard if I thought I could have found any way to stay alive afterward—not after I knew her, not the Healer Ard. She didn't deserve that, and I wish I could have changed it. But I certainly couldn't kill poor Ennis. . . .

She knew the choice she'd made meant her death if she were captured now—by gardai or by those who had hired her. Those loyal to the Banrion Ard would want their vengeance; the Order of Gabair and the Ríthe would want the same. There was no place for her here. No place she could vanish, not even among the Taisteal. Her only hope was to leave Talamh an Ghlas entirely.

She felt a hand on the pack as she pulled it from the horse: Ennis had risen and come over to help her on his own. "I'm sorry, Ennis," she told him. "I'm just so tired . . ."

"I know," he said with that same unnerving seriousness. "I understand."

"You remind me so much of my own son . . . I couldn't . . ."

"I know that, too," he said, the words sounding too adult for the little boy's voice.

"How could you? I'm certain I never told you . . ."

"I just know," he answered confidently. "Get some sleep. The ones you're waiting for will be here soon. The Taisteal."

"The Taisteal . . . ?" she began, but he just stared at her as if watching a dragonfly on a rush. She shuddered; his gaze wouldn't leave her, but she was so tired, so tired. She quickly hobbled the horse and let it graze, then rolled up the blankets. She made a bed of them and snuggled down in the woolen folds. "Here," she said. "Sleep with me. We'll keep each other warm."

They lay together, cuddled in the early morning fog and light. She fell asleep quickly, drifting into dreams in which the Banrion Ard awoke from her death and pursued her and Ennis, her hands reaching out like claws, all the while with a strange smile on her face as if she knew exactly what Isibéal was thinking and what she had done. Her voice sounded like dull clanging bells as she shouted at Isibéal. The Banrion Ard reached out, and Isibéal felt the dead woman's hand close around her shoulder and the touch burned like fire.

"No!"

Isibéal sat up, gasping. Ennis stood beside her, his hand still raised from shaking her. She panted, blinking into the afternoon sunlight that dappled her clothing.

"They're here," Ennis said.

The old Bunús woman looked at him as if he were some strange insect she'd found. "Come away with me, Ennis," she said. "I want to talk with you. . . ."

He was four. Nearly five. They were taking Sevei to Keel-balli on the western coast of Tuath Connachta, where there was a ship waiting to take her to Inish Thuaidh. Sevei could have sailed from Dún Laoghaire, but Mam and Da had wanted to take them all to see Doire Coill. Ennis had thought it mostly boring—one forest looked like another,

*even ones that were reputedly haunted—but the Bunús
Muintir were at least interesting.* "Her name is Keira," Mam
had told him, "and she's the Protector of Doire Coill. She
even helped me give birth to you—if she hadn't been there,
I don't know how I would have gotten through it."

Ennis mostly thought Keira smelled funny, like the spices
in the kitchens.

In the fog-cloaked morning, Keira led Ennis away from
the cave where she lived, away from the others. She stopped,
finally, and sat down on the ground, motioning for him to sit
in front of her. She unfolded a piece of parchment she
plucked from a leather bag. On the paper, something shriv-
eled and dried-up clung, its edges hard and brown but showing a faint pale blue in the translucent center. Keira stretched
out a hand and placed a yellowed fingernail in the center of
the leathery thing. "You were born with that caul over your
face," Keira said in her shivery, old lady voice. "I took it
from you." She sat back again, leaving the paper between
them. Ennis stared at the caul. It smelled, too, but not good.
"Do you know what it means to be born with a blue caul?"
Keira asked him.

Ennis shook his head.

"It means you're different," Keira told him. "It means
you'll know things that no one else will know. You may
know what someone might do before they do it. You'll be
able to see the possible futures that are before you."

He must have looked confused, for Keira frowned and
sighed. She gestured at the misty landscape around them.
"It's a dangerous and tempting gift," she said to him. "The
more distant things are from you in time, the more vague
and confused they'll be until they all blend together, like
looking through the fog." She pointed to a path leading
down to a valley. "What if I told you that if you followed that
path, you'd find a lovely golden sword that you could keep,
a magical sword? Would you want to go that way?"

Ennis' eyes had widened. He nodded, imagining the
sword.

"Aye," Keira told him. "You'd go, because that way leads
you quickly to something you want. But you can't see far
enough ahead. Go that way, Ennis, and though you'd find
the sword, you'd also meet the Seanóir, the eldest trees of the
forest, and they would sing you their songs to draw you to

them, and then they would eat *you." With the last words,
Keira leaned forward so abruptly that Ennis startled and
began crying.*

*The old woman clucked in sympathy and pulled him into
her spice-laden embrace. She stroked his hair. "I'm sorry,
Ennis. I didn't mean to scare you . . . well, actually I did. I
want you to remember this, remember it when you're old
enough to understand what I'm telling you. You've had a
great gift bestowed on you, but it's also a dangerous one, and
it will be tempting for you to make the wrong choice."*

*Keira went silent. She pulled Ennis away from her and
pointed up the hill from where they'd come. He could see
figures in the mist walking toward them: his mam, his Da,
Sevei. "They're here," Keira said. . . .*

"They're here," Ennis said. He pointed through the over-
hanging curtain of the willows. Several strides away, a man
stood at the edge of the bog, staring in at the hummocks
rising from the black swamp. Behind him, on the road that
curved through the hills, were a quartet of horse-drawn
wagons around which Ennis could see several other people, dressed in bright, strange clothing. The breeze brought
the sound of pans clanking together as one of the thick-
bodied workhorses stirred in its traces. *Taisteal*, he realized.
He'd seen Isibéal's people in Dú Laoghaire, selling herbs
and spices and items from strange and distant lands, and
before his sister Tara had left for fosterage, she'd told
Ennis about Mam and the Taisteal woman that their older
sister Sevei had been named after, who died helping Mam.
Mam liked the Taisteal and always went to see their wares.
("And she always pays far too much for them, too," Da had
told Ennis once before he left with Kayne for the war. He'd
laughed, sharing the jest between them.)

Ennis watched Isibéal rise to her feet. He could see the
relief in her face as she noticed the Taisteal; she was ready
to hail the man, but Ennis was already moving, sliding
through the drooping branches of the willow to stand in
the high grass near the edge of the water. He waved.
"Hallo!"

It felt as if he'd done this before, like when Isibéal had

taught him one of the Taisteal dances: he'd practiced it every day for a week until he didn't have to think about the steps at all. His body fell into the motions, without his even knowing it. This felt the same though he'd never seen this man before. He just *knew,* the way he sometimes *knew* things back home.

He knew a lot. He knew more than Isibéal thought. The blue ghosts had shown him. They'd shown him the dance of what could be, the dance that would protect him.

The man waved back at Ennis and Isibéal, then turned his back and began walking back to the wagons. By the time Isibéal had unhobbled the horse and put the packs on the beast, the Taisteal had brought the wagons down toward the bog. An older woman stood a little apart from the wagons, waiting for them.

"Clannhra Ata! It's good to see you!" Isibéal called to her as they approached, the horse sloshing through the peat-blackened, opaque water, with Ennis seated in front of Isibéal. The old woman sniffed and spat once on the ground as the horse plodded from the swamp onto the drier ground of the meadow. She ground the spittle into the soft grass under her booted right foot. With the expectoration, Isibéal seemed to shudder at Ennis' back.

He knew why. He knew. He saw it.

"I have no doubt that you'd be glad," the Clannhra answered, her voice heavy with a distinct accent that sounded dark and sonorous to Ennis' ears. "Especially since you've managed to get yourself into so much difficulty. I won't say that we're happy to see you, Isibéal. I laid out the cards last night and they were ominous and angry, almost as if someone were interfering with them. Now I look at you and I see great trouble for Clan Kahlnik."

They had ridden up close enough that Ennis could see the Clannhra's face. It was brown like his mam had said the Bunús Muintir's faces were, but the shape of the face and the long nose were more like the Daoine. It was a face that had seen hard times and harsh judgments: her cheeks were mottled by long, pale scars, and her mouth was sunken around toothless gums; her hand were knobbed at the joints, trembling with a palsy; her legs were bowed as if carrying the weight of her stout torso was too much of a burden. The hair that escaped from under the patterned scarf she wore was as white as new-fallen snow, wispy and thin.

She seemed to be gauging Ennis at the same time; her lips tightened and the lines of her forehead became as deep as plowed furrows. "The news is already spreading," the old woman continued. "We heard it in the town we just came from when a troop of gardai came through. They were quite thorough in searching the town, and in searching our wagons also. They're looking for a half-Taisteal woman who may be with a young boy. A half-Taisteal who . . ." She stopped. "Have you told the boy yet?"

"No, Clannhra, I haven't. I intended to today, but we've just awakened from last night's ride." Ennis felt her hand brush his hair. He didn't say anything.

"I know what you're not saying," he wanted to tell them. *"I know Mam's dead."*

A nod. "The gardai came because of what's happened in Dún Laoghaire, and the description they gave of the person they were looking for was vague enough that they would have taken poor Unnisha if the village's healer hadn't sworn to them that she was with us for the last two days. I wonder how many other Taisteal women they *will* take, and what they'll do to them? The Riocha want you dead, Isibéal: the ones who hired you because you betrayed their orders; the ones who didn't for simple revenge, and they're all looking for the boy, and something else, too. I tell you this so you know why we can't take you in with us."

"Clannhra, you must," Isibéal pleaded. "I have nowhere else to go, no place where I could flee, no other allies. All I want is enough time to take ship away from here to Céile Mhór. That's all. We made an agreement, Clannhra—"

"The boy wasn't part of our agreement, Isibéal. You should never have taken him. You've been stupid and you're exposing us to that danger now." She spat again on the ground, this time using her left foot to smear the moisture into the grass. Ennis squirmed in his seat to see Isibéal staring at the Clannhra's foot.

"Clannhra . . ." Ennis heard Isibéal take a nervous breath as he turned back. "Please . . ."

"I'm a gift to the Taisteal, Clannhra," Ennis said before Isibéal could gather her wits to answer. "You'll keep me just like the Taisteal once kept my mam."

Ata's eyebrows sought the top of her forehead. "Children should remain quiet while adults are speaking, especially when it concerns them," she told him. Then, querulously: "What do you mean, boy?"

"Because I *know*," Ennis answered earnestly. *Follow the patterns of the blue ghosts, just like when you're dancing. The blue ghosts which show you all the things that could happen . . .* He could see them now, strong and gathering all around them: a hand or more images of himself, of Isibéal, of the Clannhra. "I'm supposed to be here. Didn't Unnisha just lose a boy my age yesterday because he got sick?"

"How do you know that?" the Clannhra asked suspiciously. She peered past him to Isibéal. "Did *you* know?"

Ennis felt Isibéal shake her head even though Isibéal remained silent. "Isibéal's afraid you're going to spit three times," Ennis said loudly and heard the gasping intake of breath from both women. "I know what that means, too. It means that Isibéal has to die."

Isibéal hissed behind Ennis.

Ata was staring at Ennis as if he were a dire wolf snarling in front of her. "What have you brought here?" Ata asked Isibéal, and there was fear in her voice. "What *is* this boy?"

Isibéal didn't answer and Ennis squirmed around on the horse's back to face Isibéal. "The Clannhra was going to spit again," he said to her. "I *know*. She doesn't think she has a choice." He shook his head, looking up at her. "You should have done what you were told to do. Too many people hate you now." He smiled at her: gently, innocently, like the child he was. *Patterns . . .*

"I hate you, too," he said. "Because of what you did." He felt Isibéal shift, felt her slip her hand into her pocket to touch the Heart. He knew that she opened the cloch, that she was taking the power from it and holding it, and that she would use it but not as Mam had.

Before Isibéal could release the mage-energy, Ennis moved. His small hand had slipped her boot knife from its sheath and brought the blade up to the side of her neck. The gleaming edge slipped easily into her skin before she could react, and he pulled back hard.

"This is because of my mam," he said as blood fountained, as Isibéal clapped a late and useless hand to the gaping wound, as she stared at him openmouthed. Isibéal tried to speak, but only a gurgle of frothing blood came out. Wild mage-light surged around her, as if she could no longer hold it. She took her hand from the pocket of her clóca, bringing out the Heart and clutching her hand tight around it. In the sea-colored image in his mind, Ennis saw her using the cloch as his mam had, the terrible wound he'd just given her closing impossibly, the power of Treoraí's Heart healing her. He grabbed at the stone himself with his free hand, tearing past her straining fingers. He felt the connection to the stone instantly, as if he struck his elbow on the edge of a table, but the prickling and tingling was a thousand times worse.

He gasped. There were voices in his head . . .

". . . this is my Heart, my gift . . ."

"Ennis, I'm here, my love . . ."

". . . let me have it! Let me save myself . . ."

The last voice, the strongest one because it was full of the mage-energy uncontrolled from the Heart, was that of Isibéal, but he didn't listen to her. The pattern he followed wouldn't let him, for in the shape of the future where Isibéal snatched the Heart back from him, he saw himself dead: out where the blue ghosts were still bright enough to be understood, no more than a few days distant. The horror of that vision gave him strength and he scrabbled for the Heart as the blood poured from her mutilated neck, as—connected to her through the Heart, the power of the mage-lights surging through both of them, the cloch caught between both of their minds—he felt her die.

"We're twined together now, Ennis . . . You did this. You have brought us together forever . . ."

Isibéal's mouth worked as if she wanted to speak, but she toppled to one side, her hand opening so that he was holding the Heart alone as her body fell with a thud to the soft earth, leaving a thick trail of blood splattered over the horse's back. Her body twitched once and lay still, a slow and thick pool of red staining the grass at her shoulder.

His clóca spattered with her gore, Ennis shifted again on the horse's back. He dropped the knife he still held. It landed softly near Isibéal's legs as he put the necklace holding Treoraí's Heart around his neck.

He heard the chuckle of Isibéal's voice. "*I'm still here, Ennis. Still here. I'll always be here for you . . .*"

The blue ghosts of patterns fell away then, leaving him alone and lost, and he finally began to cry like the child he was.

18

A Soul to the Mother

"**D**ID YOU FIND IT?" Jenna's voice was barely audible and the hope in Gram's eyes pained Sevei more than any of the wounds and bruises on her body. Gram's head lifted, the matted gray hair standing out stiffly as she stirred under the blanket of kelp. Then Sevei saw the hope die in her face as Sevei wondered what to say. Jenna's lips pressed together and the head dropped back down.

From a large rock at the edge of the lapping surf, Bhralhg and two of the Saimhóir cows watched.

"I'm sorry, Gram," Sevei said. She was shivering from more than the cold. "I looked, but . . ." The horror of the wreck came rushing back to her in the form of the bloated, dead-white face of Dillon. She shut her eyes, but it was still there. The tears came then—tears she could shed in human form but not as Saimhóir. She cried for grief and fright and the unknown. "I . . ." She had to stop, had to gasp for breath, had to force the heavy grief in her throat back down. "I couldn't find it, Gram. I'll try again, tomorrow."

She wondered whether that were true, whether she could dare to descend to the wreck once more. Even though her body ached and she longed to simply fall to the rocks and sleep despite the cold, she was afraid to close her eyes, afraid of what might haunt her dreams.

". . . I'm so cold . . ."

The whisper was so low that Sevei barely heard it. She went to Jenna, stroking her hair back. Her forehead burned to the touch. "You have a fever, Gram," Sevei said.

"We have to get you somewhere . . . If I could build a fire . . ." Sevei was still shivering herself, naked in the biting wind, hungry and worn out. The clochmion swung in her vision as she leaned over her gram again, and she touched it, feeling the cold power within it: mockingly useless. "What good is this when we need food and shelter?" she railed to the sky and the watching Saimhóir. She clutched the stone, taking the chain from around her neck. She drew her arm back, intending to throw the clochmion into the sea, but her hand would not open. Angrily, she placed it around her neck again. "Gram, I have to find us help. We're in the Stepping Stones, and some of them are sympathetic to Inish Thuaidh, so—"

"*No!*" The answer was strong and Jenna's eyes opened once more. "Just find Lámh Shábhála. Then it will all be fine." Her eyes closed again and the voice dropped to a whisper between cracked and broken lips. "Everything fine. Find . . . The voice trailed off.

Jenna's body convulsed under the blanketing kelp. Once. Then again. Then a quick series of contortions as Sevei—helpless—crouched alongside her great-mam, holding her as if by sheer force of will she could stop the jerking spasms. Jenna grunted as if someone were punching her and she spat clotted blood: brown-red globs that smeared her face and Sevei's body. "Gram!" Sevei screamed, clutching Jenna to herself. "Please . . ."

Jenna went still. "Gram?" She didn't dare look down. She relaxed her hold. Jenna's head lolled back: the mouth and eyes open, the body limp. *"Gram!"*

From his rock, Bhralhg gave a low, mournful cry, joined by the other Saimhóir with him. A few breaths later, Sevei heard the call taken up by the rest of the Saimhóir pod around the small headland.

"Gram, I'm so sorry I failed you," Sevei husked. "I'm sorry." She stroked Jenna's head, wanting to shake her but without the strength to do more than sit there and moan.

As the Saimhóir wailed, she cried.

"Sevei, you must come with me."

The voice sounded in her head, accompanied by the war-

bling coughs of the Saimhóir tongue. Bhralhg had come up
alongside her. Sevei could see his flipper covering her foot,
but she could not feel it. She could barely feel anything.
"You'll die here if you don't make the change to Saimhóir
form."

"She's cold. So cold," Sevei told him. Sevei had no idea
how much time had passed. She blinked; the sun had fallen
behind clouds and she was still holding Gram, the body
stiffening and as cold as the ground on which she sat. She
couldn't feel her hands or her feet. She must have fallen
asleep, and her eyes wanted to close again. She was too
tired to even shiver. "Cold," she said again.

"I know," Bhralhg said. "Put her down and come with
me, Sevei."

"No," Sevei said, as calmly as if she were back in the
White Keep. For a moment she thought she heard Máister
Kirwan's voice. *"Sevei, what are you doing?"*

"Sitting here, Máister," she answered. She thought that
she should somehow be embarrassed, talking with Máister
Kirwan in her nudity, but it seemed oddly normal. "Gram's
dead. I have to build a pyre to send her to the Mother, but
I don't have wood or oil or a fire. I don't know what to do."

"Then you must come with me," Máister Kirwan said.
He held out his hand. "Put Jenna down," he told Sevei,
looking sadly and lovingly at Gram. "You can't help her
now. None of us can. You must help yourself; that's what
she'd want."

"She wanted me to find Lámh Shábhála, and it's lost and
I couldn't find it," Sevei told him. "If I had, I could have
saved her. That's what killed her, Máister; losing the cloch
was too hard for her."

"I know," Máister Kirwan answered. "Lámh Shábhála
will return when it's time. When there's someone it wants
to take up the cloch again. Come with me," he repeated,
bending down to her. Reluctantly, she obeyed, laying Gram
back down on the bed of kelp and taking his hand. He led
her toward the shore.

"Is there a boat?" she asked, but the water was lapping
around her ankles and a wave crashed in cold and high, and
it seemed that Máister Kirwan was swimming with her, taking her down and her body was changing and the water was

warm now. A Saimhóir, dark and massive, swam in front of her and released a dead fish from his mouth, and it seemed to Sevei a feast. The realization of a deep hunger gnawed in her belly and she extended her head forward on her sleek neck and took the fish in her mouth, tasting its sweetness as she tore at it, gulping down the white, ragged flesh . . .

"Aye, that's it . . ." Máister Kirwan's voice came but it wasn't his any longer but Bhralhg's and she realized that she was swimming with the Saimhóir as one of them. "There's more of the sweetfish—follow me . . ." and he was darting away through the surging, powerful surf. Sevei hesitated, bobbing her head above the surface to look back at the little inlet where Gram lay.

"I'll be back," she called to her, though her words emerged slurred and unrecognizable from her seal's throat. "I promise you, Gram. I'll come back for you." She gulped air and dove, pursuing Bhralhg and the others.

She swam with them for a day, longer than she'd ever consciously stayed in that form before, eating and emerging from the water to rest on the land, all of them packed together and sharing their warmth during the night. When the sun rose again, she lifted her snout. A smell tickled the air, a smell she remembered: burning peat, carried on the breeze from the northwest and close. Bhralhg was beside her, his own head raised and his body touching her so that she could hear his words.

"Going to your people now is dangerous. You don't know who they are or what they might be after."

She gave a cough that might have been a bitter laugh. "I can't stay here," she told him. "I'm not Saimhóir."

He snorted. "No, you're not."

"I need to go back, Bhralhg. No matter what it means. Staying here . . . All I'm doing is running away, and all I accomplish is to give those who did this what they want. They wanted me dead; by now, they must believe that I am."

"So you want your revenge?"

She thought about that. "I don't know," she answered, but she did know. She felt it even as she denied it. Bhralhg stared at her. "Aye, I do," she said finally, "but . . . I don't know how I can do that yet. I just know that whatever it is I should do, it's not here."

He pointed with his head to the water. "Lámh Shábhála is here. If you stay, it may become yours."

"My mam could have held Lámh Shábhála," she said. "She refused to take it. Maybe she knew better than all of those who want it. Maybe even better than Gram. Máister Kirwan said that Gram wanted me to have it, but maybe Lámh Shábhála never wanted me." If she'd been in human form, she would have shrugged. "It's something I'll never know. All I know is that I can't stay here. I just . . . can't."

"Sevei, I don't know you well enough . . ." Bhralhg was saying, but she'd already slipped away from him and his voice became that of a seal as she slid from rock to water. She swam away hard, wondering if he would follow. She heard him enter the sea, but he stayed behind her, shadowing her as she swam around the curve of the tiny island, stopping a few times to lift her head above the waves and sniff the air. Around a rocky tongue, she saw the small currach pulled up between two rocks and the curl of black smoke higher up on the land.

She dropped back into the sea, wanting to at least say good-bye to Bhralhg, to thank him for all he'd done.

But he was gone.

"Da!"

Parlan MacMartain nearly sliced his hand open with his filleting knife at the cry. He dropped the fish he was gutting and glared at his son. "By the Rí's bollocks, Donal, what are you squawking abou—"

Parlan stopped in mid-word, his gaze following Donal's openmouthed stare. A naked young woman was limping up the slope from the water toward them, no older than his son, who was two double-hands of years. Her red hair was matted around her shoulders and water dripped from her body onto the stones and grass. She looked half-starved and hurt; she kept her left leg stiff so that the knee didn't bend, and her body was bruised, with the scabs of cuts and wounds on her shoulder and torso, though she seemed unaware of her nudity. Parlan rose to his feet, the knife still in his hand, and the apparition narrowed her eyes, seeing his motion. Her hand lifted from her side and Parlan saw the thin golden chain around her neck and the stone there. Her hand closed around the jewel, a gesture that he'd seen once before, when he'd been one of the conscripts in the army the Tuatha had intended to use to invade Inish Thuaidh—an invasion that had ended at the terrible Battle of Falcarragh.

He had seen that motion there, far too many times.

That had been a horrible experience, made worse by Parlan's unwillingness to be there. But the gardai who'd come to the village to enlist the young men had threatened the families if they didn't come peacefully. So he'd gone, and his brother with him. His brother hadn't survived Falcarragh.

A Riocha, with a cloch na thintrí . . .

Parlan threw the knife down near the fire and held out his open hands to her. "We have no weapons, Bantiarna," he said. She didn't reply, stopping a few paces away. "Donal," he called to his son. "Get one of the blankets, would you, boy? Bring it here . . ."

He took the woolen blanket his son hastily pulled from the tent they'd erected the night before. Staying out here on this miserable rock hadn't been their intention yesterday, but the currents had been against them and the sun had gone down too quickly. "Here," he told the seawoman, approaching her carefully. He stopped a step away from her, extending his hand. "You look cold, Bantiarna. Take it . . ."

Her right hand stayed around the cloch, but she snatched the blanket with her left. She was shivering, he saw, her lower lip quivering helplessly. "The fire," he said. "You need to get yourself warm . . ." She stared at him. Slowly, she let her right hand relax; she pulled the blanket tight around herself. Beads of salt water fell from the curled ends of her hair and rolled down the nap of the wool.

"Thank you," she said. Parlan nodded. Her accent was that of the Riocha, indeed, colored with a slight hint of the Inish.

"Get yourself warm, Bantiarna," he told her, "and we'll take you over to Inishlesch."

Inishlesch was a long and narrow island tilted in the water, the western side all high sea cliffs, the eastern side low. There was one village, placed on the low side next to a small notch of a harbor. Parlan's son's cottage was a two-room stone house on the windswept eastern shore, the village—no more than a dozen buildings—lay just around the curve of the shoreline to the north. Sevei could still hear the waves beating against the shore while, behind the house, the land climbed to the rocky, abrupt cliffs. Gulls cawed and wheeled above, and the wind whistled in the cracks of the small shuttered windows and under the door.

Sevei stared at it all dully. None of it seemed to touch her. She was numb everywhere, even in her head. She felt that she was floating outside her body, watching all of this as if it were happening to someone else. They could have taken her to her great-uncle Doyle and she would have sat there mute.

Donal's wife, Báirbre, cradled a baby in one arm while she filled the teakettle over the peat fire in the hearth. She was nearly the same age as Sevei, though life had already begun to carve defiant lines in her forehead and around the eyes and mouth. She kept glancing at Sevei, wrapped in Donal's blanket and seated at the only table in the house, and her glance was suspicious and wary. When the baby began to cry, she sat on the chair near the hearth and began to nurse her, rocking gently back and forth even as she glared at Donal and Parlan. "If I were fished from the sea, I might tell a tale of being Riocha, too," Báirbre said. "Especially if I thought those who saved me might be fool enough to believe it."

"Look at the lass," Parlan said to his marriage-daughter. "Look at her hands—those aren't the hands of someone who works. And she has a cloch—or at least a stone that looks like one. And if she *is* who she says she is, then that's hardly a tale I'd be telling right now."

Báirbre sniffed. "Well, she canna stay here," she said, her eyes accusingly on Donal. "There's no room. Donal, I don't know why you let your da bring her here. If she *is* the Banrion Ard's daughter as she says, then this isn't our affair. It's dangerous and you know it, and me with a new babe."

"Ah, leave my young man alone, Báirbre," Parlan an-

swered. He and Donal had strung some of the fish to
smoke in the little shed near the house; the rest would be
taken to the village to sell. "'Twas my boat and my decision
to make, not his. I couldn't leave the lass out there, now
could I?"

"She's the one the gardai came looking for the other
day, the one they said had betrayed the Rí Mas Sithig and
jumped overboard from one of their ships," Báirbre persisted.

"I thought you didn't believe her," Parlan said.

Báirbre frowned at him, twin lines deepening between
her eyes. She settled the baby at her breast with a quick
glance at Sevei. "If they find out we have her . . ."

"The gardai can go hang themselves," Parlan answered.
"I don't have any love for them or the Riocha or Rí Mas
Sithig. 'Twas his warring that killed my brother and he
wouldn't have cared a whit or even have known if I'd died
with him. As far as I'm concerned, that old bastard—"

"Aye," Báirbre interrupted sharply, "and we've all heard
that tale a thousand times before, Parlan MacMartain, and
don't need to hear it once more. That was then, and now
it's your son and me and your great-daughter who are at
risk. You should be thinking of us."

"Báirbre," Donal interjected. "I agree with Da. We
couldn't leave her there, and none of us have any love for
the Tuatha."

"You agree with the old fool, do you?" Báirbre sniffed
and shifted the baby to the other breast. Steam hissed at
the fireplace. "The water's boiling in the kettle."

"I'll get it," Parlan said. He fixed tea for all of them, driz-
zling honey into the brew and handing Sevei a wooden
mug full of the fragrant liquid. She tried to smile at him; he
smiled back at her. "Drink," he said. "Don't mind Báirbre;
she's only worried."

Reaching for the mug was more of an effort than Sevei
expected, and the ache in her shoulder snapped her back
to reality. She could see the tips of her fingers were still
tinged blue, and bending them through the handle of the
mug sent prickles to stab the skin of her hand and arm. She
cupped the mug gratefully. "I don't want to be a bother,"
Sevei said as Báirbre stared firmly at the fire. The child
suckled loudly, coming off the nipple once to look up at her

mam and then returning to the breast. "I could go to the village, see if I can find someone to take me to Inish Thuaidh . . ."

Sevei said it automatically, surprised to hear the words coming from her mouth. *Is that where I should go? Back to Inish Thuaidh? To Inishfeirm?* She found herself thinking about Inishfeirm and the White Keep and Máister Kirwan. She shook her head—just a few days ago, she'd been on her way to see her mam and sibs, hopefully even to see her da and Kayne again. Best of all, she'd been with Dillon . . . and thinking of him brought back to her his dead, bloated face and his hair waving in the sea currents, and she had to bite her lip to keep from crying out.

She realized that Parlan was saying something.

"You don't want to do that, Bantiarna. You wouldn't get that far; from what I hear, the Rí Infochla's ships are stopping every boat in the Stepping Stones, especially those heading out toward Inish Thuaidh. You'd never get there."

"Yet Báirbre's right," Sevei said, and saw the woman glance at her with the mention of her name. Sevei sipped at the sweet tea, grimacing at the heat but enjoying the feel as it spread through her stomach. She took a breath that shuddered with unshed tears. "I can't stay here either. I have no home."

"There's Dún Laoghaire," Donal said. "The Banrion Ard—"

"My mam's dead. They killed her, too, and my da. My whole family . . ." The tears threatened again; she hid them behind the mug, drinking without caring that the tea scalded her tongue. At least the pain reminded her that she was alive.

"How can you know that?" Donal responded. "No one here's heard such a thing. If that's true, then it is the worst news you could have brought. The Healer Ard, dead . . ."

"I *saw* it," Sevei told him. Donal grimaced, Báirbre gave a mocking exhalation; the baby stopped nursing and gave a vexed cry before settling back to feed.

"She sees visions, too," Báirbre said. "It must be wonderful to be a Riocha. And you *believe* her."

"She can stay with me," Parlan said. "You needn't deal with her."

"What, and have everyone in the village talking about how Parlan has taken a stripling young enough to be his daughter to his bed?" Báirbre told him. "I can hear it now: 'Old Parlan must have seen his son's reflection and thought it his own, and with his old gray-haired wife buried in back of the house, too. Her haunt will be howling in the wind and darkness. Taking up with some horrible lass he pulled from the water, who seduced the poor man . . .' And we'd be laughingstocks, too, for having a da who's gone daft." The baby was sleeping now; she put the child on her shoulder, patting its back softly, her dark eyes moving from Parlan to Donal but avoiding Sevei. "No good can come of this, whether she's who she says she is or just some waif washed overboard from a Riocha's ship. Take her to the village. Let the Aldman make the decision. That's the right thing to do. Think of us, if not yourself."

Parlan sipped his own tea, staring at the fire. Donal moved behind Báirbre and put his hand on her shoulder. Sevei felt depression and grief settle around her again. Bhralhg was right: going to her own people had done her no good. She could rise from the chair and run out of this house to the sea to change again, though her body rebelled at the thought, wanting to stay in this form. *Tired. You're so tired and so hurt . . .*

Parlan rose, the legs of his chair scraping against the stones near the hearth. He held out his hand toward Sevei. "Come with me, Bantiarna. We'll go to my house; you can rest there. Tonight's not the time to make decisions."

"Da . . ." Donal began.

"The Mother sent her to us," Parlan answered, "an' She didn't mean for us to just hand the lass to the Ald or the bloody Rí."

Báirbre's voice was gentle. "Athair Céile," she said, addressing him as her marriage-da for the first time, "she's only a lass taken by the sea and washed up, not a sign from the Mother-Creator. You're a good man who has raised a good son who I love. Don't let your goodness betray us. That's all I'm asking you."

"An' would I still be a good man if I abandoned the lass, no matter who she may be or who sent her here?" Parlan extended his hand to Sevei again. "My home's not much," he said to her. "'Tis smaller than this, but you can have the bed and a night's sleep at least, and we'll see what the morning brings."

Sevei stared at the hand. In the silence, she could hear the crackling of the fire and the soft snore of the baby.

She took Parlan's hand.

19

The Council of the Clans

KAYNE DIDN'T HEAR Séarlait approach. He only felt her presence suddenly at his side, and he turned from his contemplation of the mountains to look at her in the last fading light of the sun.

Séarlait was staring at him as she had near Ceangail, as if judging him with her oak-brown eyes. He still didn't know what she saw. Her bow, unstrung, was in its pack on her back: he realized then just how much longer her bow was than the shorter weapons he knew. "How many of them have you killed with that?" he asked her.

She showed him both her hands, fingers extended. She closed her fingers once and showed her hands again, with only two fingers and a thumb showing on her right: a double-hand plus a hand-and-three. "So many . . . When will it be enough?"

She seemed to chuckle at that, soundlessly and without mirth. They were standing atop the wall. She reached down and picked up one of the loose stones there. She showed the rock to him and showed him one finger on her other hand. She dropped the stone and gestured at the wall itself, its long length snaking over the land. "When you've killed as many as there are stones in the wall?"

A nod. She pointed toward him, tilting her head quizzically.

"For me? I don't know," he answered. He turned his attention back to the mountains, purpling with evening, the valleys shrouding themselves with a late fog. "I know the gardai—and I know that most of the soldiers from Airgialla were just doing what they were told they must do. So I can't really blame them. The ones I want are those who gave the orders to find my da and kill him. The others . . . I'd do what I need to do if they tried to stop me, but otherwise . . . I've seen too many of them die, just following orders. They're just people: some good, some not. Just people." He looked at her: at the determination in her thin face, at those expressive eyes whose gaze wouldn't leave his face. "What was done to you and your family—that was unforgivable and those who did it deserved death. But the others, the rest of them . . . I don't know. I'm sorry; I've no right to judge you. In your place, I might do the same, and you clansfolk have a different view of the Tuatha and the Riocha."

Her head tilted again. Her mouth opened slightly, as if she wanted to speak, then closed again. She stared at him and there was such desperation in her face that Kayne spread his hands. "Can you write, Séarlait?"

She shook her head.

"Teach me what you know about that long bow of yours, and I'll teach you to write. Then you could 'talk' to those who can read."

"Oh, she can talk, Tiarna. At least to me." Laird O'Blath-mhaic grunted as he climbed up onto the tumbled wall near them, though despite his age he climbed the broken rocks easier than Kayne had with his wounded thigh and bruises. His gray, braided beard swayed as he came over to them. "I can understand her with what she says with her hands and her face and her body. If you listen that way hard enough, you can understand. You can teach her to write if she wants, but there's few in the Fingerlands who could read it. Reading's for the Riocha, not the likes of us." O'Blathmhaic put his arm around his great-daughter, who hugged him in return, smiling. "She talked to me while you were off meeting with that grim captain of the gardai, she did."

With that, Séarlait scowled up at O'Blathmhaic and pushed his arm from around her. Her cheeks reddened, and the glare in her eyes was unmistakable.

O'Blathmhaic ignored her. "She said she thought you were like clansfolk, that you could understand us. That we should help you if we could. She told me that while I was talking with the Banlaird in Ceangail and Laird Woulfe of the Wall. She said that the Healer Ard hadn't been like the other Riocha, and that you were her true son and like her. She said you wouldn't betray us." Laird O'Blathmhaic stared hard at Kayne, his eyes unblinking and hard. Deep sunset gold played over his face, though the stones at his feet were in shadow. "Did I hear her right? Is that true, Tiarna? Can you look me in the eyes and tell me that you wouldn't betray the clansfolk once you're back in your splendid keeps and bright cities?"

"I keep my word, Clan-Laird," Kayne told him. "I said that if it were in my power, the Finger would be its own Tuath and belong to the clans and not Rí Airgialla. And I tell you this, too—if it were in my power, the Tuatha would come to defend the Fingerlanders with our Clochs Mór and our gardai, because that time is coming, too." Kayne pointed east toward Céile Mhór. "The creatures that attacked Ceangail will come here in all their numbers one day, perhaps sooner than we'd like to pretend. It's here, on the eastern side of the Bunús Wall, that we can best defend ourselves."

"And you'll accomplish all this with the few double-hands of men you have?"

Kayne laughed at that, bitterly. "If that's all I have, then that's what I'll have to use."

Laird O'Blathmhaic laughed then, a loud, hearty amusement that echoed from the nearest slopes. "Aye, spoken like a true clansman." He clapped Kayne on the back, the blow nearly making Kayne stagger on his bad leg. Then O'Blathmhaic leaned close, his forehead nearly touching Kayne's and his breath was warm on Kayne's face as he whispered. The man had been drinking. Kayne could smell the alcohol.

"Listen to me, boy. I've watched the way you look at Séarlait. More than that, I've seen the way she looks at you. The girl's old enough to make her own decisions, and the Greatness knows that I'm glad to see her finally looking at a man with something other than suspicion. But I won't see Séarlait hurt, do you hear? So you be careful that you keep any promises you make her, with your words *or* with your body. Are we understanding each other now?"

The man's gaze, close and hard, burrowed into Kayne.

Kayne forced himself to stare back, nodding once. "Aye, I understand," he said, "and if I were her great-da, I would be saying the same thing."

O'Blathmhaic grinned then, showing the few teeth left in his gums. His thick hand came up and slapped Kayne gently on the cheek. "I think it's time we call all the clan-lairds to Ceangail," he said, stepping back. "There's things they should know, and things we might do." The shadows had climbed to his waist, and he clambered down from the wall like a man half his age, into growing darkness. He was singing as he went away, a loud, off-key baritone.

"Scilidh leann fírinne," Kayne said to Séarlait: *Beer divulges truth.* She gave him a smile at that. She took the bow from her back; stepping across the stave, she strung it—as easily as any gardai—and handed it to Kayne. His hand touched hers, and the touch seemed to last for longer than necessary before she gave him the bow. She nodded to him, tapping herself and then mimicking drawing a bow-string.

Kayne frowned for a moment, not understanding, then realized. "You'll teach me? Is that what you said?" She nodded, then made a gesture as if she were writing in the air.

. . . be careful that you keep any promises you make her . . .

"All right," he said. "We'll teach each other."

"If I closed my eyes, I could be back in Dún Laoghaire, listening to the Riocha argue."

Harik and Séarlait, sitting on either side of Kayne, both responded with fleeting, tight-lipped grins. They were close to the door, at one of the several long tables placed in Ceangail's town hall. The hall was blue with smoke from pipeweed, hot with tight-packed bodies and a roaring wood fire in the massive hearth, and loud with contentious voices from the various lairds and banlairds and clansfolk. Kayne had been introduced to each of them, though he'd already forgotten half the names. The clansfolk, unlike the Riocha, seemed to have no rules of order to the meeting, and most already knew what was to be discussed when they arrived and walked in ready to shout their opinion to the others. Volume seemed to be the key to being heard, and even when the clansfolk paused in their several conversations to listen to one speaker, they constantly interrupted the person with comments, questions, and sometimes bald insults. There had already been two fights, quickly broken up, but with the amount of ale and stout being consumed, Kayne expected more would follow.

A few of the lairds, when they rose to speak, caused the others to at least moderate their noise. One was Laird O'Blathmhaic himself, and two others: an ancient man named Woulfe, so thin that he looked like a stick of dried, smoked meat, who was the clan-laird of the lands east of the Bunús Wall; and a woman named MacCanna who, except for the white color of the long hair tightly bound in a long rope down her back, appeared to be no more than Kayne's mam's age, and who led the clansfolk of the region of the lowering hills just beyond the Narrows.

". . . and the truth is that if we do as Laird O'Blathmhaic asks, then it will be my people who suffer the most, because we're closest to Airgialla," Banlaird MacCanna was saying, and the clansfolk at the table with her cheered and pounded the table with their fists in agreement.

"You hillfolk are half lowlanders anyway," a man called out from the clouds of pipeweed. "You've forgotten how to fight."

Shouts erupted all around, but in one swift motion MacCanna stood and slipped a throwing knife from its scabbard at her belt, flinging the weapon through the thick air. The blade landed quivering, embedded in the table a finger's width from the hand of the man who had just spoken. "Perhaps you're right," she said drolly into the silence, as the man stared at the knife. "I was aiming for that large gut of yours."

Loud laughter followed as MacCanna strode across the room to snatch back her knife. "I'm not saying that the clansfolk shouldn't fight to remove the foot of the Rí Airgialla from our necks," she said as she made her way back to her seat. "I just don't know that now is the time."

"What better time, when the Tuatha are all in a turmoil and fighting among themselves?" O'Blathmhaic answered. "We may not see a better time again."

"You don't know that, Liam," someone shouted back. "I was surprised the Healer Ard lasted as long as she did. My bet is that there's already a new Rí Ard on the throne, and one of the Ríthe holding Lámh Shábhála as well. If that's the case, we'll have the damned Great Stone against us."

Laird Woulfe stood, banging the head of his walking stick hard against the oaken table in front of him so that everyone turned to him. "An' if what the young Tiarna says is true, then we'll *want* the Great Stone here. Everyone here has seen the beasties that attacked Ceangail, and I remember how many gardai rode down the High Road to Céile Mhór a year ago and how few of them have returned."

Banlaird MacCanna rose again. "Then if we need the Great Stone to help us and not fight us, perhaps we'd best leave things as they are."

O'Blathmhaic scoffed. "Aye, and be begging the Tuatha and tugging our forelocks and asking them nicely to come to our rescue when those Arruk come snarling around our villages again."

With that, everyone started talking at once, the uproar seeming to shake dust from the ceiling. Séarlait tugged at Kayne's sleeve and inclined her head toward the door of the tavern. Harik saw the motion. "Go on if you want to," he told Kayne. "Stay close; if you're needed, I'll come for you. This is going to go on for another few stripes, at least." Kayne wondered what else Harik might be thinking, but there was nothing in his face to reveal it.

"I'll be just outside," Kayne told him, speaking loudly to be heard over the din of the clansfolks' discussion. Harik nodded. Séarlait was already at the door and Kayne went to her. He glanced back at the room just before he left and found both O'Blathmhaic's and Harik's gazes on him.

He let the door shut behind him.

Outside, the main street of Ceangail was quiet, and the West Gate of the town was open. Oil lamps had been lit on the poles of the gate and along the street. Séarlait was walking toward the gate, and Kayne hurried after her. He expected her to take his arm as he came alongside her, as any of the bantiarna back in Dún Laoghaire would have done. She did not, though she stayed close to his side. Several of the townsfolk were still out, and they nodded to

Séarlait as if they knew her before giving Kayne a more careful and guarded greeting.

"Tiarna Kayne!" He heard the woman's voice in the shadows of the street; a flicker of motion and she was embracing him, her long light-brown hair a glossy tangle at his chest. "I heard you'd returned, and I was so glad. I was hoping so much that I'd see you." Her face lifted, the features warm in lamplight, smiling, and she went to tiptoes to kiss him—a quick, almost shy kiss on the cheek. Her arm curled around Kayne's. "I've thought of you every night since."

He remembered her then, the lass he'd taken to his bed that night in Ceangail. Séarlait had taken a step away from the two of them, her expression carefully guarded. The young woman saw Séarlait also, and her arm tightened around Kayne's, possessively. "I could stay with you now," she said. "If you'd like . . ." She smiled up at him hopefully.

"No," Kayne said and the smile vanished slowly, like frost in the morning sun. He pulled his arm away from her and she released him reluctantly. "You can't."

"Oh," she said, and her gaze flicked angrily over to Séarlait. "You're part of what the lairds are talking about, I know . . . You probably have to speak with them . . . If, later . . ." The smile came and vanished once more. She shifted her weight. "If you're staying at the inn, I could . . ." One shoulder lifted.

"No," Kayne answered. "I'm staying with my men."

A nod. She blinked, and Kayne saw tears in the light of the lamps. "Perhaps later, then . . ." He didn't answer. She nodded again. Her gaze went once more to Séarlait, her lips tightening. "She's half-wild, that one," she said to Kayne. "Be careful she doesn't stab you in the middle of the night."

Séarlait hissed at that, taking a step toward the girl, who fled quickly away down the street. Kayne's hand had gone to Séarlait's arm as soon as she'd moved, but the gesture was unnecessary; Séarlait had stopped after the first step, watching the young woman's retreat. She looked down at Kayne's hand, then up to his face. Her stare was a challenge, and he released her.

Séarlait spun around and began walking. She didn't look at him at all, but strode out just past the West Gate and stopped there in the middle of the High Road, looking out over the night-shrouded mountains. Kayne walked over to her, stopping by the wooden frame of the gate. "I slept with her, when I was here. It was just a night. Nothing else."

Séarlait didn't move, didn't make any motion.

"It meant nothing. I don't . . . I don't even know her name."

Séarlait turned. There was fury in her eyes. She tapped herself hard on the chest with her forefinger, then swept her hands out wide as if she were casting something away. He shook his head. "I don't understand," he told her. She gave a moue of exasperation and repeated the gesture. She pointed to her damaged throat, to her body. This time he understood.

"You meant nothing, too," he said. "To the gardai who raped you."

A scowling nod.

"Are you saying I'm like the beasts who did that to you?" he asked her. He was answered with a brief lift of her shoulder as her head cocked defiantly. "I'm sorry for what happened to you," he told her. "I truly am. I would never do anything . . ."

He took a breath, unable to talk into her glowering, silent anger. Kayne remembered the last time he'd been here, when he and Harik had confronted each other. *So much has changed since that time . . .* He'd changed: he was no longer the arrogant young tiarna who had once been affronted by Harik's bluntness. His life had been shattered on the rocky ground of the Narrows and altered beyond recognition, had been catalyzed and fused in the crucible of grief and loss. Even the landscape to the west seemed to have changed for him: he'd once seen those mountains only as something through which he had to pass to go home. Beyond that, he'd given no thought to them or the people who lived there. Now he owed his very life to the clansfolk, and the mountains seemed a comforting bulwark. "I wish you could tell me everything you're thinking right now," he said to Séarlait.

She sniffed as if she found that somehow amusing. Séarlait went to one of the gate posts, taking the oil lamp set there from its iron ring and bringing it over to Kayne. Crouching down in the dirt of the High Road, she placed the lantern down and adjusted the shutters so that it threw a wedge of yellow light on the tight-packed dirt. She smoothed the ground with a hand, then handed Kayne a dagger from her belt. This time she was careful not to let her hand touch his.

She gestured at the ground, making a motion as if scribbling something.

"You want me to teach you writing now?" Kayne felt the heavy weight of the blade in his hand. She stared at him. "All right," he said. He plunged the tip of the dagger into the hard ground and made a mark. "There are eighteen letters in the alphabet . . ."

He taught her, crouching in the dirt of Ceangail until the mage-lights came and he had to fill Blaze.

20

The Blue Ghosts

"**Y**OU'RE SCARED OF ME," Ennis said to the Clannhra and Unnisha. He sniffed, the tears still wet on his cheeks. The Clannhra had taken him to the wagons, ushering him away from Isibéal's body even though he could see that the woman tried to avoid actually touching him. Unnisha had come at Clannhra Ata's call, and the two of them had taken Ennis into the Clannhra's wagon while others of the clan—making a warding motion with their fingers toward him when they thought he wasn't looking—had gone down to dispose of Isibéal's body. As Ennis sat in the nest of warm and brightly colored blankets in the wagon, huddling in the corner where only the fitful light of a lantern could find him, his fingers played with Treoraí's Heart. Both women's eyes were caught there. He knew it was because his hands were still sticky with Isibéal's blood, his léine and skin stained to the elbow. "It wasn't my fault. I saw the pattern, and I only followed it."

"The pattern?" Ata asked. Ennis nodded, his small head bobbing up and down. "I don't understand."

"The blue ghosts, Clannhra. Didn't you see them?"

Unnisha glanced at the Clannhra, who shrugged stiffly. Ennis started to cry again, knowing he couldn't explain.

The blue ghosts. The patterns . . .

Sometimes, when he looked just the right way, he could see them: glowing blue outlines that swirled around him. They surrounded him like a mist or a fog, but it wasn't a fog. He didn't have the words for the vision. The ghosts surrounded him in space, searingly bright close to him, and fading to nothingness the farther out they went, transparent and overlaying the more colorful world of reality and full of shadowy images of possibility. The blue ghosts also surrounded him in time: again, very bright if the moment were only a few breaths away and growing increasingly hazy and indistinct the further from Now it was.

He'd seen them long before he'd known what they were, beginning perhaps a year after his talk with Keira. Their appearances were rare, then, but even then he'd realized that if he could find a ghost that looked like himself, a ghost whose pattern in the time dance led to a place Ennis wanted to be, he could link himself to it. It was like Keira had told him: he could see what would happen, and if he did exactly what the blue ghost did, that future would come true. He could follow the dance of the blue ghost and he would be fine. He'd thought at first—like any child might—that everyone saw the blue ghosts at times, that they *all* saw the patterns, that all the strange things adults did was because they were tied to their own dances. It had been a long time before he realized that no one else could see the blue ghosts at all (and he sometimes still forgot), that this was the gift that Keira had said he would have. The gift of the blue caul.

But since he'd woken during Isibéal's flight from Dún Laoghaire, the ghosts had become more clear and sharp than they had ever been, so clear that they frightened him into silence. When he and Isibéal had come out from the hummock, when the Clannhra had started to speak . . .

He'd seen several images of himself, fading out to the future. In at least one, he was dead; in most of the others, he was captured and handed over to grim gardai. But in one, he saw Clannhra Ata helping him, and he'd followed that ghost, as he was supposed to. He put himself *in* that future's pattern and let the blue ghost speak for him, guide his actions.

It wasn't him who had killed Isibéal; it was the blue ghost. He had no choice; that was the path that would keep him safe.

Following the patterns. Like Isibéal's dances . . .

The ghosts and their haze were still around him, swirling, and now he was afraid of them. *Too many places, and so many of them awful* . . . "You wouldn't understand," he said to the Clannhra and Unnisha. "I'm sorry, I'm sorry . . . I miss my mam . . ." He began to sob, unable to stop himself. The blue ghosts of his mam had been the most horrible of all. He saw her dead in all of the images that surrounded her, every one, for the last hand of days. He'd searched everywhere for a blue ghost where she was alive and couldn't find one, and so he had chosen the pattern where she seemed to suffer the least. If Isibéal had not done what she'd done, someone else would have acted, so Ennis had blindly followed the pattern that bound Isibéal and himself, afraid that if he stepped out of it once or said the wrong thing, that one of the other patterns would sweep over them and Mam would die horribly, screaming in agony like some of the blue ghosts of her.

He was glad that hadn't happened. He was glad he had given Mam a quiet, peaceful death. His tears were as much of joy as sorrow.

He heard Unnisha give a long sigh and her arms came around him. He let himself sink into her embrace. She smelled strangely, but the embrace reminded him of his mam and he let himself sink into the embrace.

He didn't tell her that he'd seen this pattern, too, that when he'd taken the knife from Isibéal and let himself link with the ghost, he'd glimpsed Unnisha in the sea-fog, holding him well off in the azure distance of time, almost as far away as he could see clearly. He sniffed again, turning his head so he could see the Clannhra. A glowing outline of the Clannhra leaned back away from him; a breath later the Clannhra herself did the same, and he heard her words in the sapphire wash of sound before he heard it with his ears.

"What you did to Isibéal . . ." The Clannhra visibly shuddered. "I couldn't believe that a child . . ."

"She killed my mam," Ennis explained to her. "The patterns, the blue ghosts, told me. It was what I was supposed to do. I just let myself follow the pattern. I let it take me. It did it, not me." The Clannhra was shaking her head. The ghosts around the Clannhra shifted to bloody red, as they did rarely, and he knew somehow that he was seeing the past: a young woman who would be the Clannhra, standing weeping over the body of a man; a flash that made Ennis blink and gasp, and there was the Clannhra again, a few years older, her face stern and unforgiving as she watched another man clutching at his throat, the remnants of a meal before him, his eyes wide with fright and his mouth open as he gaped at the Clannhra.

Then the ghosts went blue again. The patterns of them in the near future whispered to him, and he spoke the words. "Isibéal killed my mam, and so I killed her. That's fair, isn't it?" He sniffed, wiping at his nose and looking up at her with wide, pleading eyes. "What if a person murdered someone *you* loved, Clannhra?" he asked her. "Wouldn't you kill that person if you could?"

The Clannhra drew her breath in with a sound like a boiling teakettle. Unnisha, stroking Ennis' head and cradling him, spoke. "He doesn't know, Clannhra. He can't."

"You weren't there this morning when he killed Isibéal," Ata answered. "He spoke your *name,* Unnisha. He knew you'd lost Kellsean. Who can guess what the boy knows, or how, or what he intends?"

"He's just a *child,* Clannhra," Unnisha protested. "Not much more than a baby." Her hand covered his head, pressing him against her breast. He put his arms around her, still snuffling. Now Unisha was crying with him; he could hear the tears within her and feel them throbbing in her body. "Maybe there's a reason the Mother-Creator made Isibéal bring him here."

"Isibéal was to—" Ennis heard her swallow the next word. "—leave him with his mam."

"But she chose not to. Clannhra, he's just a child who's been through a horrible experience—one we helped bring to him. Just a child . . ." She hugged him harder, rocking back and forth as they both cried.

"He can't stay with us. It's not safe, not with the gardai out scouring the land looking for him. And that cloch around his neck . . ."

Ennis heard the whispers of the blue ghosts, saw them moving. In the haze of the distance, he saw a moment he liked and he let himself fall into the pattern, sitting up in Unnisha's lap and wiping at the tears. "I want to stay with you," he told Unnisha, looking up at her. "I want to stay here and not go back." Voices whispered and he spoke the words. "I'm afraid to go back. They're all dead. All my fam-

ily. I don't have anyone else . . . My mam . . . I don't have a
mam . . ."

"Clannhra?" Unnisha whispered.

"It's too dangerous," the woman insisted.

"No, Clannhra," Ennis said earnestly. The ghosts shifted
around him; he listened to their voices and found the pat-
tern again. "You could change the way I look, couldn't you,
Unnisha?" The pattern lent his words a mournful pleading.
"Couldn't you give me a new name? You could call me . . ."
The blue ghosts spoke the name. ". . . Fiodóir."

Ata snorted. "You *know* that name?" she asked, and
Ennis nodded his head.

"Fiodóir is the son of the Mother-Creator, the one who
weaves the tapestry of Fate," he told her. "That's what Isibéal told me."

Clannhra Ata gave another snort, then sat back. She
pulled a pipe from her pocket, loaded it with pipeweed,
then leaned forward to light it over the lantern's flame. She
exhaled a cloud of fragrant smoke that drifted through the
blue ghosts. She blinked. He waited for her to say what he
heard the blue ghost around her say. "You have a cloch."

Ennis' hand closed around it. "This was my mam's, and
Isibéal stole it after she killed me. It's mine now," he said.
The pattern made him start crying again. "You can't take it
away, Clannhra. Please don't. It . . . it would hurt too
much . . ." He was weeping again, and Unnisha pulled him
against her once more.

"Hush," she whispered to him, though he knew she was
glaring at Clannhra Ata. "She won't take it. And you can
stay here. You'll stay with me."

"This isn't your decision to make, Unnisha."

"Aye, it is, Clannhra," Unnisha answered quickly. She
was one with the blue ghost of herself now, their words
coming at the same time. The haze of the future was dissolving, the patterns leaving his sight, their haunting fading
away. "We'll cut the boy's hair, dress him like us, and he can
keep the cloch under his clothing. And Isibéal . . . why not
leave her body in the bog? Even if the gardai find it before
the animals, they'll think she was killed by bandits or
someone else, and the boy either buried elsewhere in the
bog or carried off by scavengers, or not with her at all. We'll
be in some other town, far away." Clannhra Ata was puff-

ing furiously on the pipe, and Unnisha hurried to continue before she could answer. "Clannhra, the boy's meant to be here. Isibéal shouldn't have taken him in the first place, yet she did. I'm holding him the way I can't hold my Kellsean anymore. Don't take this little comfort away from me. Please. I'll make it work. I will."

Clannhra Ata didn't answer. In the silence, Ennis could hear Unnisha crying softly and he snuggled close against her. The blue ghosts had vanished entirely. He thought of Mam, of Da, of his siblings, and the terror of the last few days struck him fully. He gasped and the sobs began again, more awful than before, the tears hot and real against his cheeks, the grief he hadn't allowed himself to feel taking him, so hard that he could barely breathe through the sobbing. *Mam, I miss you so much . . . Mam, I want you back, want you . . .*

Unnisha kissed the top of his head, enfolding him.

"We need to leave here as soon as we can," Clannhra Ata said at last. "I'll have Isibéal's body put in the bog along with the horse." She sucked at the pipe and exhaled. "I hope you're right, Unnisha. For all of our sakes, I hope so."

Hearing that, Ennis allowed himself to drift off into an exhausted sleep in Unnisha's arms, a sleep that was haunted by ghosts the color of the deep sea.

Ennis woke in darkness. The bed on which he was lying swayed and jerked, the movement accompanied by the sound of hung pots banging together, and he realized that he was in one of the Taisteal wagons and that they were moving. "Pull over there," he heard Clannhra Ata say, and the wagon turned right and the bumping and swaying increased for a few breaths before it stopped. He heard the creaking of wagon wheels as the other wagons settled around them; the neighing of the horses and the low murmur of people talking as they settled the animals.

"Unnisha?" he called.

No one answered. He sat up, rubbing his eyes. That sent yellow afterimages fading into purple and dancing before him. He wondered how long he'd slept—it had been late afternoon when he'd talked with the Clannhra and Unnisha; now it was dark. As his eyes adjusted, he saw the light of a lamp filtering through the crack of the rear door of the wagon. He got out of the bed that smelled of Unnisha and padded toward the door. He pushed and the door swung open on well-oiled hinges. Outside, the Taisteal had gathered the wagons together in a small meadow just off the road. The west was still touched with fading red sunlight, but the rest of the sky was dark and the Seed-Daughter's Star was already bright above the horizon.

"Dobra vece, Fiodóir," Unnisha's voice said. For a moment, Ennis wondered who she was talking to, then he remembered. He saw her near the corner of the wagon, placing triangular pieces of wood under the wheels. "Did you have a good nap?"

He nodded and yawned helplessly. She laughed at that. "Are you hungry?"

This time the nod was more vigorous. "Oh, aye," he said. "Very."

She smiled at him. "I thought you might be. Tamara will be making a stew soon, but she'll give us a bit of bread and cheese to tide you over. Help me get the wagon set, and we'll go over to her . . ." She held her arms wide, and he jumped from the wagon door into her embrace. She kissed his forehead and placed him on the ground. "Here—we need to get the chucks under the wheels first, and then we'll help Estraven with the horses . . ."

A half-stripe later, he and Unnisha were seated with several of the other Taisteal around a fire, over which a black iron kettle had been hung. A thick stew simmered there, the smell making Ennis' stomach growl despite the small loaf of bread he'd already eaten. Unnisha sat next to him; across the fire, he could sense Clannhra Ata's gaze on him, though whenever he glanced at her, she was always looking somewhere else. This time, her eyes were lifted to the zenith where the curls of fragrant steam vanished. Ennis followed her gaze and saw curling green-and-blue lights crawling between the stars.

"Mage-lights," one of the Taisteal said. "They're late tonight."

The Clannhra nodded. Her gaze came down and this time found Ennis.

"Fiodóir?" he heard Unnisha say, and he realized that he

was standing. The hunger within him had shifted, no longer focused on his belly but now somewhere deeper inside him, frightening with its urgency. He found himself reaching for Treoraí's Heart, and he knew that the mage-lights were calling him as they'd called his mam every night. His tiny fingers found the stone. "Clannhra, he's far too young . . ." he heard Unnisha protest and saw the Clannhra wave her hand at the woman.

He took Treoraí's Heart in his hand as the mage-lights brightened above them. The swirls of light responded, coalescing above him and dancing down. As he'd seen his mam do, he lifted his hand toward the lights and several tendrils snaked down to wrap around his hand. He gave a sharp intake of breath at the first touch of them: like plunging his hand into an icy stream. Almost, he pulled away but the lights tightened about his wrist and he could feel Treoraí's Heart yearning to open to them. "I don't know how," he started to say, but he thought he heard his mam's voice: *"Here. Let me show you . . ."*

"Mam?" he said aloud, hopefully. "Mam, is that you?"

He thought he heard her start to answer, but there was a chuckle that overpowered his mam's voice: Isibéal's laugh, tinged with anger. *"Child, this was mine. It should have saved me . . ."*

"No!" he cried out. He wanted to release the cloch, but could not. The power of the mage-lights was burning him, searing the flesh of his hand. He heard another voice, a strange, deep one: *"Here. Let me show you . . ."*

Ennis felt the cloch open like a flower to the sun in his mind.

The energy poured into the receptive vessel of the cloch; at the same time Ennis' awareness drifted out so that he realized that all around Talamh An Ghlas others were doing the same. He could sense their connection through the mage-lights, a few of them—the Clochs Mór—immensely strong. Some of those he felt he knew: was that Uncle Doyle and Aunt Edana? And that distant tug at the lights . . . was it possible that was Kayne?

But Treoraí's Heart was already full and the lights were pulling away from him now, trailing upward and dimming once more. He sighed as they left him, in mingled relief and sadness. The stone pulsed cold in his hand.

"What does it do, that cloch? Will it do what your mam could do with it?"

Ennis blinked. In the time he'd been with the mage-lights, he'd forgotten where he was. The Taisteal were all staring at him, and the stew bubbled thick. Unnisha rushed over to him, enfolding him in her warm embrace, but Clannhra Ata's gaze on him was nearly as cold as the mage-lights.

"What does it do, Fiodóir?" she asked him again. Ennis heard the mocking laughter again in his mind. *"You set the pattern, boy, with the way you gained the Heart . . ."*

"I don't know," he told the Clannhra as he snuggled gratefully against Unnisha. "I don't know."

But he did. As his fingers opened around Treoraí's Heart and he let the stone fall on its chain against his chest, he knew.

21

Breath of Fire

THE SMOKE FROM the pyre drifted over the island
and out to the water where the wind finally tore it
apart. Sevei watched, the heat from the oil-fed flames making her face feel tight and hot. She wondered why she
wasn't crying, but the tears wouldn't come, even as the
small stack of logs collapsed in a fuming of sparks and the
smoke obscured what was left of her gram's body.

She could feel Parlan standing just behind her, his cap
off and in his hands as he watching the burning.

He'd brought her over in the little currach piled with
wood and flagons of scented oil. Jenna's body had been
where Sevei had last seen it two days before, strangely
undisturbed and untouched by corruption. For a moment, looking at her, Sevei had wondered whether she'd
made a mistake and Gram was merely sleeping, but no—
the chest was still, and her flesh as cold and hard as the
stones. She suspected that Bhralhg had used some spell
to protect Jenna; if so, she was grateful to him for that
small favor. The body seemed to weigh less than nothing
as she and Parlan lifted it from the niche near the beach
and brought it to where they'd constructed the pyre.
Sevei had said a silent prayer to the Mother, had kissed
her gram's forehead one last time, then Parlan handed
her the torch.

The flames had licked hungrily at the gift, roaring. She
watched until there was nothing left but black ash and
coals glowing a sullen red.

"The smoke . . ." Parlan said behind her. He whispered

as if he didn't want to break her reverie, but there was an urgency to the man's voice.

"I know," Sevei answered. "It may bring eyes that we don't want."

Parlan helped her pile stones on the remnants of the pyre until they had the mound of a cairn. Filthy and exhausted, her skin blackened with soot, Sevei knelt alongside it and kissed one of the stones. "Good-bye, Gram," she whispered. "I'm sorry I couldn't find Lámh Shábhála for you. One day, I'll bring you back to Inish Thuaidh. I promise that much."

Parlan put his hand on her shoulder. "We should go now," he said. She nodded. She touched her fingers to her lips and touched the stones.

The wind helped push them back to Inishlesch. A stripe later, they were in the single tavern in the village. Parlan's son Donal was there also, and motioned them over to his table.

The story they'd given the village was that Sevei was an orphaned cousin of theirs from Inish Cnapán, the northernmost island of the Stepping Stones. She could feel the stares of the other patrons in the inn and hear the muttering: *She's staying with old Parlan, is what I hear . . . Wonder what kind of cousin she really is . . . ?* but she did her best to ignore it. If the people of the island hadn't been welcoming, neither had they been hostile.

"What've you learned, boy?" Parlan said before they were even seated. "What's the word in Ballynakill?"

"Not good, Da," Donal answered. He kept his voice to a low, husky whisper. He wouldn't look at Sevei or talk directly to her. "They're still looking for the girl and the Banrion Holder. The gardai in Ballynakill are asking all the fisherfolk who are bringing in their catches if they've heard of any bodies washed up or of any unknown women showing up on the islands. I saw at least three of Infochla's warships on my way, and two of them sent boats over to talk to me and make certain I wasn't hiding anyone." He took a sip of the stout in front of him. His gaze never came close to Sevei.

Parlan grimaced. "They'll give it up soon enough," he insisted.

No, they won't, Sevei wanted to tell them. *Not as long as*

*Lámh Shábhála's still missing. Not as long as they don't
know for sure. They've made that mistake with my gram before; they won't make it again.* But Donal spoke before she
could stir herself.

"It's worse than that, Da. There are rumors all over Ballynakill about the Healer Ard being dead. They say the
Ríthe are already meeting to name a new Rí Ard, and
they're saying it may be one of the Order of Gabair's
mages."

"Was there news of Inish Thuaidh?" Sevei asked, and
Donal nodded.

"Aye. All sorts of talk: about the clans disagreeing about
who should be the new Ard there, though right now the
Banrion Holder's husband is acting as Ard." She noticed
that he wouldn't say "your greada" when he spoke of Kyle
MacEagan, as if he still didn't want to admit that Sevei
might be who she claimed to be. "There's talk and rumors
about the Tuatha sending an army over to take the island
now that the Mad . . ." He stopped. ". . . the Banrion Holder
and her cloch are gone."

"And the Order of Inishfeirm?"

"In disarray. I was talking to a drunken garda last night
who claimed that the Máister of Inishfeirm was a prisoner
in Lár Bhaile and that his Cloch Mór has been taken by the
Order of Gabair. One of the siúrs has been named
Máistreás in the meantime."

Sevei moaned. "Oh, poor Máister Kirwan . . ." She knew
now, holding the clochmion, how devastating it was to
cloudmages to have their cloch taken. To some, the pain
was impossible to endure: it could drive them to madness
or suicide. She thought she could see Máister Kirwan's
face, distorted by torment, screaming in darkness . . . She
shook away the image.

Donal was looking carefully away from her. His voice
was an urgent, harsh croak. "It's too dangerous for her to
be here, Da. You could bring the gardai down on all of us."

Parlan sniffed. "Is that my son speaking, or Báirbre?"

Donal flushed, his knuckles whitening around the mug
of stout. "We both think the same, Da, me and Báirbre."

"You do, eh?" Parlan answered. "Well, you can think all
you like, but I make up my own mind, and I do what I believe is right without worrying about what everyone else

might think. You might start doing the same." He rose, holding his hand out to Sevei. "We're going home," he told her.

"Da—" Donal shook his head.

"Parlan," Sevei protested, "I don't want to cause any trouble between you and your family."

"You're not," Parlan told her. "The trouble was always there. Donal prefers to let others do his thinking for him." Everyone in the tavern was watching them, the silence nearly deafening. "Come on. Suddenly it's gotten too cold in here."

She took his hand. His grip was warm and strong and she could feel the thick calluses on his palm. She let him pull her to her feet and toward the door. The world outside, full of the sound of the surf and gulls, the creaking of the wooden quay and the conversation of buyers and sellers at the market lining the harbor street, seemed an incredible din after the tavern's quiet. Parlan kept her hand in his as they walked; she made no attempt to pull away. She could sense the stares following them as they took the path away from the water toward the hills where Parlan's small plot of land lay. As they passed the last house of the village, he seemed to realize that he was still holding her. His hand opened.

"I'm sorry," he mumbled. "I shouldn't presume—"

She reached out and took his hand again. "It's fine," she told him. "I don't care."

"I don't mean nothing by it," he said. "You could be my daughter, and you're a bantiarna and I know . . ."

"Parlan, it doesn't matter." And it didn't. She felt numb, somehow, as if everything that had happened since the sinking of the *Uaigneas* had taken place to a Sevei who was somehow removed from her. The pain, the grief, the loss of Gram, of her mam, of Dillon, of all of those close to her: she couldn't quite feel the loss and sorrow, though she knew it was there. All of her senses were dulled, as if she viewed them through gauze. "It doesn't matter," she repeated. "Nothing matters." She could think of nothing else to say.

They were both silent the rest of the way home.

The dream had the clarity of life: she saw Kayne in the midst of a surging group of wild-looking folk. Kayne was alive and whole, and holding a Cloch Mór in his hand, his mouth open as if he were shouting to someone near him. "Kayne! You're alive!" she called to him. He seemed to look around as if searching for her, but she could feel a mingled fear and excitement in him, as if he were about to engage in some battle. "Kayne!" she called to him again, but then the dream shifted and he was gone.

"Kayne . . ." She was sitting upright on the straw-stuffed pallet she used for a bed. Her clochmion was throbbing underneath the léine of Parlan's that she wore as a nightshirt. She brushed her fingers against Dragoncaller and felt the shock of contact, as she'd felt it that day on Inishfeirm: *another mind, close by, feeling the pull of the call* . . . She let go of the cloch, getting to her feet and grabbing for her clóca and sandals. In the glow of the embers of the fireplace, she could see that Parlan wasn't in his bed against the far wall. Dressing quickly, she went to the door and pushed it open, shivering a bit at the touch of the cold air.

Parlan was there, staring down over the tiny, hard-won strips of field and the erratic lines of the bordering stone fences. His dog, an arthritic black-and-white mongrel, sat hunkered at his left side. The moon peered fitfully from between high, fast clouds, sending waves of slow light over the landscape. "Parlan," she called to him. "What's the matter?"

He didn't answer. He simply pointed down to where the village slumbered. Where the mouth of the small harbor opened to the sea, a dark shape moved on the water, pricked with the yellow light of torches: a ship. A banner flew from the single mast and when the moonlight touched it, Sevei thought she saw a flash of green and gold.

"Infochla," she breathed.

"Aye," Parlan answered. "And sailing at night through the Stepping Stones. Only one reason to do that—so the fewest eyes can see you, especially those of the Stones whose loyalty might be to Inish Thuaidh."

The clochmion burned underneath her léine and she had to resist the urge to grasp at it. *The feel of the wind lifting leathery wings, the smell of people wafting upward, seeking, seeking* . . . "Why would they be here at all?"

She heard more than saw Parlan sigh. "Ballynakill is part of Tuath Infochla still, and my Donal was just there and asking too many questions, perhaps. Or worse, he may have brought them here deliberately." He turned to her then, and his face was crumpled with guilt. "I'm sorry, Bantiarna," he said. "I'm sorry that it's one of my own family who has done this."

"You don't know that," she told him, but they both knew. They knew even as they saw the ship nudge up to the quay in the village below and tiny forms of the gardai swarm down the plank that was extended. A wedge of light emerged from the inn; a few minutes later, a line of torches swayed outward from the village.

Toward them.

The dog barked once, then more urgently. "Run," Parlan urged her. He pointed to the rising flank of the island behind them. "Up there, along the sea cliff, there are caves and hollows where they might not find you."

"I don't need the caves," Sevei told him. "All I need is to find the water . . ." A shadow swept over the moon. Sevei shivered; the clochmion screamed in her mind.

"Then go!" Parlan nearly shouted.

She could not. If Donal had indeed been the one to send word to the gardai, then they also knew that Parlan was sheltering her; if she wasn't here, they would take out their frustration on him when they couldn't find her. She might escape, but he would not.

A shrill, thin cry came from above. Dragoncaller screamed with it in her mind.

She brought it out, closed her hand around the facets.

She felt the other mind, high above, felt the compulsion the cloch put upon it. Reluctantly, the beast banked on its great, widespread wings, hearing the leathery skin between the flightbones snap in the changing wind. It brought the wings into its body, allowing itself to plummet down, down to the hard earth, down to the imperious, irresistible call of the stone.

Blackness covered the stars. Wings shuddered above, their beating sending hurricane gusts down at them. The creature landed in the field just below them and its great horned-and-scaled head craned upward on its long neck; its tail flashed red in the moonlight. The dog yelped and fled for the house. Parlan uttered a curse and made a motion with his hands as if warding off a spirit.

Low dragon-voice rumbled in the air and in Sevei's mind. "Soft-flesh," it said, the words growling in its own tongue while in her head Dragoncaller took the voice and transformed it so that she could understand. "We meet once more." *Kekeri* . . . Sevei remembered the name. *Kekeri the Bloodtail, of the Earc Tine* . . . Sevei could sense the amusement in the dragon's mind and also the intellect behind it; at the same time, she felt her own mind opening to the beast: through Dragoncaller, they were open to each other. The energy poured from the clochmion; Sevei could feel it draining away, more quickly than she thought. "Ah," Kekeri crooned. Its breath was like a burned charnel pit. "*They're* the worry . . ."

Its head snaked back, looking down to the line of torches. Claws raked the earth into furrows, the wings beat, the wind nearly knocking Sevei down and sending Parlan staggering back with his hands before his face. "No!" Sevei shouted at it, but it only laughed.

"This is what you want," Kekeri answered. "This is why I was sent . . ." and with the word she had an impression of someone else behind the words.

"Sent?" Sevei asked, but the dragon had already pushed off the ground on its muscular hind legs, sending one of the stone walls crashing down and gliding away. "Wait . . ."

It was gone. "It spoke to you? You understand dragon-speech?" Parlan was saying, but Sevei could only shake her head at him, still clutching Dragoncaller and feeling its energy being sucked toward the creature. A few breaths later, the night was sundered by light: a ragged gout of blue-and-yellow flame, an eruption that flared and died like thick, slow lightning. A moment later, they heard the screams, thin and high in the night air, and saw the dragon rise and fall, its tail lashing, the talons of its legs extended. It rose again, and Sevei saw the broken forms of soldiers tumble from the sky as it opened its claws. Kekeri stooped and rushed over the remaining soldiers, belching fire and death. Wings thrummed even as the last of the screams trailed off. A few breaths of time, that was all, and it was over.

In the cold moonlight, the beast descended again.

"Those you feared are gone," Kekeri said in her head, though she knew Parlan heard only the snarls and grumbles of its own language

"I didn't ask you to kill them," Sevei raged at the dragon. "That's not what I wanted."

"Isn't it?" Kekeri snorted, as if chuckling, sending heated air over them. "Then it's good I know your mind better than you do."

"You know nothing."

Another snort. "You soft-flesh ones are so arrogant and blind. You think the world exists only for you. Well, I tell you that there are more things in the vast lands than you can imagine, beings for whom your petty concerns mean nothing. And yet, you don't realize . . ." The dragon stopped, and Sevei again had the sense of something else behind the words, an unspoken sadness that was washed quickly away in scorn. "Look at you," it growled, "groveling in the dirt, cowering in fear. Why, a single blow from my tail would rip that old soft-flesh next to you in half." The dragon rose up slightly on its hind legs, the wings flaring out and the scarlet tail lashing to keep the dragon balanced. "Your clochmion is empty," Kekeri said. "You can hold me no longer."

Sevei felt the power within Dragoncaller flow from the stone even as the dragon spoke, leaving behind only a trace of energy, far too little to control Kekeri any longer. The dragon's jeweled eyes glinted in moonlight as it regarded her and she felt its satisfaction at being unfettered by the cloch, and its hunger.

"Parlan!" Sevei shouted. "Run! Now!"

The dragon's wings pulsed once, and again. Kekeri pounced, great stones scattering like tiny pebbles under its feet. Sevei was already scrambling away, not knowing where she could run. There was nothing here that the dragon could not destroy in a moment. It gave her no chance. She felt the rush of air as it arrowed toward her, saw the great claws open on the hind legs just before it struck her, a stunning blow that sent the breath from her and made new stars flare in her sight.

The dragon rose into the night sky with Sevei clutched in its talons.

22

The Battle of Ceangail Valley

THE ARMY FROM AIRGIALLA was spread out in a long double line on the High Road a few miles from Ceangail, the Riocha among them riding at the head of the column, the baggage train of supply wagons and soldiers wounded in the battle at the Narrows creaking well to the rear. The column had placed outriders ahead to scout out the road and send back word of any forces marshaled against them. To feed horses and men, raiding parties were deployed to plunder any of the farms or villages they passed as they moved deeper into the Finger.

The Airgiallaians were riding down from the spines of the mountains into the high valley where Ceangail sat. The High Road here was bordered on either side by flanking, steep slopes covered with greenery and striped with rushing white streams hurrying down to meet the small river that gave Ceangail its water supply, and Mal Mac Baoill gestured to the Hands to take advantage of the open space: two squadrons moving out on either side with their archers as flanking units, lancers on their horses and archers at the vanguard, the remaining mounted gardai and the infantry massed behind the vanguard in the middle, with their pikes ready against a mounted attack from the enemy, a small force sent as rearguard to protect the baggage train.

The tactics were the same Kayne had witnessed with his da's troops, as well as those of the Thane of Céile Mhór in the fight against the Arruk. The formation performed well on open ground and where the gardai were facing another force trained in the same general methods of warfare.

It wasn't necessarily a tactic that worked in the Finger or against the clansfolk.

Mac Baoill, with Winter gleaming against the red of his clóca, raised his hand as six riders in the colors of Airgialla approached them from the direction of Ceangail, which the outriders had been surveying. Mac Baoill called to them, his breath steaming in the cold early morning air. "What news? Have you seen the rest of the Banrion Ard's gardai?"

The outriders stopped abruptly several paces away from Mac Baoill, who leaned forward on his mount, peering quizzically at the silent riders.

He saw the bows they carried even as the nearest of the outriders threw her coat down, revealing the plain clothing of a clanswoman and a head of long, dark hair: even as the first arrows sang death; even as more arrows darkened the sky from either side of the slopes; even as a horde of clansfolk rushed toward the invaders from hidden places near the road.

As Harik also rose, screaming the *caointeoireacht na cogadh* with his men as they pulled swords from scabbards and attacked on foot.

As Kayne, from well above the scene, pulled his da's Cloch Mór from under his clóca and took it in his hand, hoping he would be strong enough to handle its power without training.

This wasn't battle as Kayne had experienced it in Céile Mhór. The Arruk moved like a well-disciplined plague on the land, burning and laying waste to any habitations they found and foraging from the herds of sheep and cows they captured, leaving behind them an empty plain of death. They asked for no mercy from their opponents and gave none in return. There, after a few days of open maneuvering for position by each of the armies, the horrifying masses of the Arruk would advance hissing and spitting their challenge at the waiting troops of the Thane arrayed before them, their war drums would begin to beat and the battle would commence: sword against jaka; clochs against the wild, erratic slow magic of the Arruk Svarti, their mages; the mounted forces of the Daoine smashing deep into the Arruk, who were all on foot. The Thane's armies and the armies of the Tuatha didn't engage in deception and ambush, but the Fingerlanders certainly did.

"You can have your honor and rules of engagement if you like," Laird O'Blathmhaic had answered when Kayne and Harik had protested the plan of the clan-lairds to ambush the Airgiallaians as they advanced toward Ceangail. "We don't have that luxury. Not if we want to live."

When Kayne had looked over the ragtag collection of clansfolk that had assembled for the attack—men and woman, old and young—he understood. The council had named Rodhlann O Morchoe, a middle-aged marriage-son of Banlaird MacCanna, to lead the Fingerlander fighters, and it was obvious from his bearing that he had training as a gardai, but the Fingerlanders were a motley bunch with erratic discipline. There were the five double-hands of Kayne's own gardai to add, but the Airgiallaians still outnumbered them easily two to one.

Yet they nearly evened the odds in those first few seconds, the Airgiallaian soldiers toppling from their horses or falling to their knees as Rodhlann directed the storm of arrows that hit their surprised flanks. A few hands of men to the rear of the main battle line broke and fled toward the baggage train as the clansfolk rushed out toward them.

The barrage of arrows and the surprising ferocity of the ambush alone might have been enough, if Mac Baoill and Winter had not been with them.

"Rodhlann will make certain that our arrows take out Mal Mac Baoill before he can use his damned cloch," Laird O'Blathmhaic had declared confidently. "Even a cloch can fall to surprise. And if not . . ." He'd shrugged. "Then you get to seek your revenge," he'd said to Kayne.

But Mac Baoill had managed to open his cloch despite the surprise of the attack, and the arrows had not found him: Winter sent a cold wall of blue ice rushing over the false outriders—Séarlait at the head of them—sweeping away the arrows the Fingerlanders had launched at the tiarna and sending their horses whinnying backward. Spears formed of frost struck around them; two of the riders were torn from their mounts and one of the horses went down with a terrible cry. As Kayne watched, closing his fingers around Blaze, the mage-ice formed again in front of Mac Baoill. He saw the man stare at Séarlait, saw

him scowl and wave his hand, saw the ice begin to coalesce
around her in a great, crushing block. "No!" Kayne
shouted as he opened Blaze, the red-hued energy of the
Cloch Mór filling his mind and overlaying his vision as he
sent a fireball hurtling outward.

Fire shattered ice. Séarlait fell from her horse, but Kayne
saw her stagger back up. He sent another fireball toward
Mac Baoill, but now the tiarna realized that a rival Cloch
Mór had entered the battle. Almost contemptuously, Mac
Baoill turned his horse away from the false outriders and
rode back to the vanguard; in his head, Kayne felt a shifting of attention in his suddenly-doubled vision as Mac
Baoill found him in the waves of cloch-energy. Directing
the energy within Blaze was more than Kayne had expected, even after practicing with the cloch the last few
days: the fireball that arced toward Mac Baoill was weak
and unfocused and poorly aimed; the tiarna deflected it
with a wall of arctic frost and the red fury struck earth
frighteningly near Séarlait: Kayne heard a scream from
one of the clansfolk—a man's voice, not Séarlait's. Then
the bitter cold wrapped around him, the deadly chill of it
making Kayne gasp in pain, a wall of blue cold gripping
his chest. He shouted, his voice a vapor torn away and lost
as he grasped with his mind for the power within Blaze.
He could barely handle the force of the captured mage-
lights; they burned at him as if he were handling molten
lava with his own hands, but it was at least warmth within
the frozen air around him and he threw it wildly in Mac
Baoill's direction.

The Mother-Creator was with him; he saw a fireball explode at the feet of the tiarna's horse just as he was about
to vanish within the milling vanguard. His stallion reared
in fright and pain. The cold wall around Kayne vanished
and he managed a grateful breath before more ice
slammed into him like a fist, throwing him backward. The
impact loosened Blaze from his grasp. For a moment
Kayne saw only with his eyes: the swirling chaos of the battle and the cries of mingled rage and pain. Even with Mac
Baoill's Cloch Mór engaged with Kayne, the battle was still
far too even. Rodhlann was screaming at the Fingerlanders; the gardai who had begun to retreat had stopped and
were returning. Kayne saw as many gardai in Airgiallaian

colors as clansfolk, and he knew that what might be an evenly matched battle otherwise would turn into a rout for Airgialla if the fury of Winter was turned against the Fingerlanders.

Mac Baoill was rising to his feet many strides away, his high forehead bloody under the shock of black hair, but with Winter still in his hand. As Kayne fumbled for Blaze, dangling on its chain, the ice formed around him again, crushing down on him, the cold burning his flesh. Kayne screamed with the pain of the assault against his already broken ribs and injured legs. He couldn't find his own cloch, and Mac Baoill was striding through the fray toward him, pushing everyone aside with fingers of blue ice, his ruddy and thin face a furious mask. Kayne could see that the false outriders nearest Mac Baoill were either dead or engaged in the struggle. And Séarlait; Mac Baoill passed her, her body draped over the gutted corpse of her horse, her bow still grasped in an unmoving hand. Mac Baoill's attention was focused on Kayne; Kayne could see it in his mage-vision: the two were locked together; there was nothing else around them for Mac Baoill, the battle constricting to their own duel.

Kayne knew what the man intended: Mac Baoill would kill Kayne, then shift his attention to the others. When that happened, the battle would be lost. Kayne could feel the man's strength, his skill, his concentration all now focused on Kayne. . . .

In the moment of that realization, Kayne heard Mac Baoill grunt and saw his eyes widen in shock. The ice melted around Kayne. As the man turned, Kayne glimpsed an arrow protruding from the folds of his clóca; another feathered shaft struck Mac Baoill in the throat even as he turned his head to look to his right, to where—from behind her downed horse, a bloodied Séarlait knelt with her bow in her hand. Mac Baoill gave a strangled cry; Winter dropped from his hand.

She watched him fall, and Kayne glimpsed a strange, sorrowful pleasure in her face. She had little chance to celebrate; two gardai had also seen Mac Baoill fall, and they rushed toward Séarlait with notched and stained weapons raised high as Séarlait belatedly plucked another arrow from the quiver on her back.

Kayne found the heavy weight of Blaze; there was still power within it, and he let himself touch it with his mind, to shape and hold the energy for an instant. The fireball rushed away from Kayne and enveloped Séarlait's attackers; he heard them scream, saw them fall blackened and dead to the ground even as his mind tore at Blaze again, taking the mage-energy and hurling it at a squadron of gardai in red and white. The fireball exploded in their midst: men ran with their clothing aflame, dropping their weapons as the mage-fire blistered and charred their flesh. With the explosion, loud even in the midst of the battle, the other gardai realized that their commander and his Cloch Mór had been lost. The mood of the battle shifted as Kayne emptied the cloch and Rodhlann and the clansfolk and Harik with his men pressed into the remaining gardai. The battle rapidly became a bloody slaughter.

Perhaps three or four double-hands of Airgiallaians managed to escape, turning their backs on the battle and running up the High Road toward the mountains and Airgialla. The clansfolk jeered at the gardai as they fled, waving red-stained weapons in the air.

Kayne watched only for a moment. He went to Séarlait, standing and staring down at the corpse of Mac Baoill. Deliberately, she spat on the man's body. "Séarlait, are you all right?"

A shrug. Blood had smeared across her face, but the long scratch on her forehead hadn't cut deep, and most of the blood on her appeared to be from her horse. She was still holding her bow. "I saw you on the ground, you with your horse. I thought you were dead, I thought I'd lost . . . we'd lost . . ." He stopped, the memory of that feeling sweeping back over him, surprising him with its intensity. "We would have had no victory here without you," he told her.

A smile curved her lips and vanished. She reached out and touched his hand: his right hand, where he could see faint, glowing swirls and curliques: mage-scars, which he'd seen on the hands of other cloudmages. Séarlait gestured at the field around them: the dead, the wounded moaning and crying out, the survivors walking through the battle-field exhausted and bloody, the remaining gardai retreating at a run. She touched Kayne's hand again, and nodded.

"None of them will make it home." Harik, Rodhlann,

and Laird O'Blathmhaic had come up to them, and it was O'Blathmhaic who had spoken. He glanced appraisingly at Séarlait, standing close to Kayne, before looking back at Kayne. "Without your cloch, Tiarna, it would have been different. It would have been us retreating back into our mountains. The clans will sing of this for generations."

"Your great-daughter made it possible," Kayne told the man. "Not me."

Kayne crouched down next to Mac Baoill's body and found Winter: sparkling crystalline facets with veins of pure ultramarine, caged in silver wire hanging from a hammered silver torc. Reaching down, Kayne took the jewel from the man's neck. "Aye," Harik said behind him. "Take the cloch, Tiarna. We'll hold it until we're back in Dún Laoghaire and can find a better holder for it than a Mac Baoill."

Kayne didn't answer. He straightened and went to Séarlait; he stood in front of her, silent. Her gaze stayed with his, and after a moment, he smiled. He placed Mac Baoill's torc around her neck; taking her hand, he closed it around the stone. "Winter is yours," he told her. "Tonight, you can fill it with the mage-lights."

She looked at the cloch wonderingly, turning it in her fingers, then at him. Laird O'Blathmhaic and Rodhlann chuckled.

And Harik . . . He gave no protest, but his gaze was hard and angry, and there was disappointment and contempt in his eyes when Kayne looked at him.

"Go on, Harik," Kayne said. "Tell me what you're thinking."

"You don't want to know, Tiarna," Harik answered.

"Tell me anyway."

They stood outside the town hall of Ceangail. Inside, they could hear the raucous and drunken celebration of the clansfolk and their own gardai. The main street of the small town was alive with people this night, walking in pairs and groups and laughing. For the second time in the last moon, Ceangail had escaped an attack, and they were rowdy and drunken and giddy. If the inhabitants seemed to think themselves blessed by the gods, that was something Kayne could understand.

Harik glanced back at the hall with disgust. "They act like they've won the war. This was just the first battle, and not the hardest. Rí Airgialla will send a full army the next time, with several clochs. He'll have the other Ríthe send troops to help. The Tuatha will be back, and next time these Fingerlanders won't have it so easy."

"That may be true, but it's not what you brought me out here to say," Kayne told him. "Say it. Talk to me the way you'd talk to my da."

"If you *were* your da, I wouldn't need to say anything," Harik retorted. The insult stung, but Kayne remained silent. "The girl doesn't deserve to hold a Cloch Mór," Harik spat out finally.

"Then it's good it wasn't your choice, isn't it?"

"Don't mock me," Harik answered. "You know what I mean."

"You mean that she's not Riocha. Well, my da wasn't born Riocha either, even if he ended up that way. And neither are you, Harik—but would you have complained if I'd given *you* the cloch?"

In the darkness, Kayne couldn't see the man's face flush, but he heard the controlled fury in his voice. "Aye, she's a tuathánach and that's part of it. I'm at least céili giallnai, with cousins who are Riocha. I was at least raised in the Tuatha and understand how our society works. I've served your da and your mam loyally, with every breath."

"And Séarlait served us today. Without her, it might have been Mac Baoill who had another Cloch Mór to give, and you and I would be out there moldering in the battle's barrow-grave."

"Aye, she served us. Today."

"Which means?" Kayne grunted the question between clenched teeth, trying to rein in the temper that wanted to flare, that made him want to strike at the man. *You asked for his honesty, and he was Da's friend as well as the Hand of his gardai. Listen to him. Control your anger.*

Harik's eyes narrowed, glittering like twin shards of glass. "This Séarlait's not trained to a cloch na thintrí and never will be. No, you haven't been trained either, but Tiarna Geraghty, the Banrion Ard, and your sister were.

You will be also, once we're back. This one . . . she'll be at best a wild talent; at worst, she'll be dangerous to everyone around her when she uses the cloch. Most importantly, she's clanfolk and her loyalty's only to them. I know the clansfolk better than you do. I was raised an Inishlander, where things aren't much different than here, and I was stationed in the Finger for a year when I was just a boy, in old Mal Mac Baoill's army during one of the constant clan insurrections. I know that if the situation changes, you may find Séarlait using the cloch against you. She'd do it, Tiarna. She would. That's where her loyalty lies: to her clan. To the Fingerlanders. She'd turn on you without even thinking about it if she perceived you as a threat to her people. You don't know her and her kind. You may think you do, but you don't."

"Is that all, Harik?"

"No," the man said. "You're becoming emotionally involved with her, Tiarna. I can see it, and so can everyone else. You'd know that if you were thinking with your head instead of—" Harik stopped at the sound of light footsteps behind them and a wash of lamplight from the doorway. Both men glanced toward the newcomer. Harik nodded, a barely perceptible motion of his head. "Séarlait," he said. He glanced at Kayne. "Are we done here, Tiarna?"

"Oh, we are," Kayne told him, keeping his voice tightly controlled. "Completely."

Harik's lips pressed together. He touched right fist to chest in a quick salute and strode swiftly away—not toward the hall and its drunken celebrants, but toward the gardai tents just inside the town wall. Séarlait watched him go. Her eyebrows were raised when she looked back at Kayne.

"It's nothing," he told her. "A little disagreement about tactics."

She nodded, but her expression looked decidedly unconvinced. She touched the Cloch Mór at her breast and pointed upward. Even as she made the gesture, Kayne felt Blaze awaken in his mind. Above, light crawled between the stars.

"Come on," he said to Séarlait, holding his hand out to her. "I'll show you how to call the mage-lights. We'll do it together."

He heard Séarlait's sigh as the last tendrils of the mage-lights left her upraised hand, climbing back toward the clouds even as they began to fade. He sighed also, Blaze full in his mind. Séarlait released Winter; as the cloch fell back on its chain, she wobbled on suddenly weak legs. Kayne steadied her, his arms around her waist as he came up behind her.

"It's all right," he whispered into her ear. "I nearly fell the first time, too."

She leaned back against him, and he was aware of the smell of her hair, the touch of her skin, the softness of her neck contrasting with the unexpected ridge of scar. He bent his head down to her, his lips brushing the cords of her neck as she inclined her head. Her breath shuddered as she breathed in, then rushed outward with a gasp as she pulled away, spinning around. He let her go. She stood in front of him, her eyes shining with moisture. She shook her head—slowly, back and forth—and he remembered what had happened to her.

"I'm sorry," he told her. "I don't want to hurt you . . ." She stared at him.

She held out her right hand, palm up.

He put his hand in hers. For a moment, she just held it there, staring at his fingers as if trying to read something there. Then she pulled him toward her with a gentle tug, releasing him. Her hands clasped his face and brought it down toward her.

Her lips on his were soft and warm and gentle. When he finally pulled back, he heard the breath catch in her throat and saw the tears on her face. He brushed them away with his thumbs.

You're becoming too involved with her, Harik had said.

You be careful that you keep any promises you make her, her great-da had warned him.

"If this isn't what you want . . ." he started, but she touched her finger to his lips, stopping him. She stared at him, and he saw the tears there even as her eyes challenged him. He knew what she would ask, if she could. He knew that this couldn't be a tumble into bed and a good-bye the next morning. He thought he might even understand how much courage this took on her part, to leave herself open and vulnerable to be emotionally wounded, to trust him this much.

"I won't ever hurt you," he said. "I promise that. Ever." He hoped it was a promise he could keep.

23

The Shape of a Future

CLANNHRA ATA AND UNNISHA had transformed
Ennis by the time they reached the first town. His hair
was cut in the short fashion of the Taisteal, his curls gone
and the hair turned coal black with an evil-smelling dye
that also blackened the leather gloves Unnisha wore while
rubbing it into his hair. An unguent darkened his skin, as if
he'd been days out in the sun. The last of the clothing he
had from Dún Laoghaire was burned, and Unnisha relentlessly schooled him on his accent. He learned quickly; even
Clannhra Ata seemed pleased.

He even seemed happy, laughing like any of the other
children and playing with them as the caravan slowly made
its way south along the rutted roads of Tuath Dún
Laoghaire toward Tuath Éoganacht, stopping occasionally
at farms and tiny settlements to trade and sell cloth and
spices, to tell fortunes, or to have their tinkers repair pots
and other metal implements. It was the nights that bothered Ennis, for at night he would find himself taking Treoraí's Heart in his hand, and listening for his mam's voice
inside it and weeping because he could not find it. He
heard her, faintly, a few times, as well as the low gruff voice
that seemed far older and more distant, but it was Isibéal
whose voice was dominant in the Heart, drowning out the
other two.

"*I won't let you have her,*" Isibéal crooned to him softly.
"*You can't have her, ever again. I told you that we're linked
together here. You killed me just as I took in the power, and
I used it to make me powerful in death. It's me you'll hear,*

Ennis. It's me who will whisper to you when you use the Heart. It's me you'll remember, every time . . ."

Yet, faintly and far away, he sometimes heard the whisper: *"Ennis, I love you. I miss you so, and I'm so sorry for you. So sorry . . ."*

He would cry afterward in the bed with Unnisha, and she would sometimes awaken crying herself for her own lost son.

They would hold each other, taking some comfort in their mutual grief.

And when the mage-lights came, Ennis would be there to take them in. Clannhra Ata would sometimes watch him with appraising and suspicious eyes, and he knew she wondered what the cloch did and why it needed to be filled again when he hadn't used it.

But except for Treoraí's Heart hidden under his clothing, Ennis was for all appearances simply another Taisteal child by the time the slow caravan rattled into Dúnwick, a small village on the coast south of Dún Laoghaire. In the few days since he'd taken Treoraí's Heart as his own, the blue ghosts had left him alone. Ennis thought they'd forgotten about him.

They hadn't. They were waiting for him in Dúnwick.

Dúnwick perched on a low shingle of rock, the Tween Sea opening its wide gray sweep to the horizon just beyond the rocky mouth of a tiny harbor. The smell of rotting fish and brine lay over the village like a transparent fog; the stones of the houses seemed to be imbued with the stench. The town slumbered, asleep, with its fishing boats laying tilted on muddy tidal flats, anchored to large stones that jutted out from the mire like an old man's teeth. Huge nets hung like torn lace curtains from long poles just onshore, with several villagers repairing the ragged holes in them; a nearby market was busy with inhabitants from nearby villages and farms buying the freshly-caught fish.

As seemed to be required, the Ald of Dúnwick scowled as if irritated by the appearance of the Taisteal caravan, accepted the usual bribe with as little good grace as she could muster, then directed them to a small field just north of the town, where the Taisteal set up their tents and tables. Ennis helped Unnisha bring the bolts of strange and exotic cloth out of their wagon and array it on the drop-down shelf on the side of the vehicle. By midafternoon, well before they'd finished, the first curious townsfolk had arrived in the meadow and were wandering around between the wagons.

The ghosts arrived with them.

"Where did this come from?" inquired a woman's voice, and Ennis turned to see an older woman fingering a bolt of red cloth on which darker swirls of near-black coiled like drifting smoke. Unnisha was in the wagon retrieving the last few bolts, and the woman was looking directly at Ennis. The bright outlines of blue ghosts accompanied her: the shifting glow of maybes and possibilities. Ennis blinked, staring at the landscape of the future she represented and seeing himself there. "Boy, did you hear me?" the woman asked, and a dozen of the ghosts echoed the same phrase with her. Her voice seemed more amused then annoyed, and Ennis shook himself.

"I'm sorry, Iníon," he said, addressing her politely. "The cloth is from Kallaigh in Thall Mór-roinn," he answered. He had no idea if that was true; it was a phrase he'd heard Unnisha use the day before when they'd stopped at a tiny crossroads hamlet. He mimicked her accent, sounding the hard consonants deep in his throat and rolling the "r's." *The truth doesn't matter, as long as they think it's something exotic,* Unnisha had told him that first time. *"In fact, all the cloth is from here in Talamh an Ghlas—traded for or bartered for what we brought over the Finger from Céile Mhór."*

"Ah," the woman said appreciatively. "So far away . . ." . . . *far away . . . far away . . .* the ghosts whispered. "It's very beautiful."

"Indeed it is," Unnisha said, stepping out from the wagon with more vivid bolts of cloth gathered under her arms. "That's an excellent choice. Not many people have such an instinctive flair. You obviously know quality when you see it, Iníon; this is rare cloth, indeed. It feels marvelous to the touch, doesn't it? So soft, and yet so strong."

The woman managed to look pleased and suspicious all at once, but she continued to finger the bolt. "But the color's not good for everyday use," she said.

"Perhaps not," Unnisha said, coming up beside her. She took the bolt and unwound a length of cloth from it, draping it around the woman's shoulders. "But a person wearing a léine from this cloth would stand out from everyone else's drab appearance. And that red would be so striking against your hair and your skin. Don't you think so, Fiodóir?"

Ennis nodded enthusiastically, as he knew he was supposed to. "Oh, aye, it does. Here, Iníon, look . . ." He took a disk of polished bronze from where it hung on the door of the wagon and brought it over, holding it before the woman. "See? I think it's very pretty."

"It is, isn't it?" the woman agreed. Then she seemed to realize that she was undermining her own position, and she shook her head. "It wouldn't be warm enough, though. Too thin. 'Twould probably tear through the first time it snagged on something. I couldn't possibly pay more than four coppers for the bolt, for all the trouble it would give me."

"Four coppers?" Unnisha repeated in an aggrieved and hurt tone, taking the bolt and wrapping the cloth again. She placed it back on the shelf. "Why, that would barely buy an arm's length of this. I sold a bolt exactly like this to the Banrion Ard's personal house servant for two gold mórceints, and . . ." Unnisha stopped, her cheeks flushing. Ennis was watching her. The blue ghosts moved strongly between them, and Ennis wondered which of them he should choose to follow. He tried to find his future self in their flow. Tried to find the pattern where he would be safest.

"Ah, the poor Banrion Ard," the woman said, noticing Unnisha's distress at her mention of Ennis' mam, but attributing her hesitation to recent events. "We just heard the news yesterday ourselves, from the gardai who came here. Such an awful thing: the Healer Ard murdered, and all her children but the one that was kidnapped were killed, too, they're saying. The ones who did it will be gutted alive and displayed when they're found, and it's less than they deserve. I don't mind saying to you that I think it's because the Healer Ard loved us tuathánach too much." She winked at Unnisha and nodded conspiratorially. "That's why they killed her. The rest of the Riocha didn't like her, didn't like that any of us common folk might go to Dún Laoghaire and be healed through that cloch of hers. Why, she cured a man just up the coast of the horrible boils he had all over his body . . ."

She stopped and leaned forward toward Unnisha. "I've

also heard that there have been riots in Dún Laoghaire," she whispered. "Some of the tuathánach rose up after the Healer Ard was murdered, but the Riocha used their damned sky-stones and killed those who dared to protest. It's bad times in the cities, they say. Bad times."

Neither of them was listening to her. Ennis touched Treoraí's Heart under his léine. *"You're destined for great things . . ."* Mam's voice whispered in his mind before Isibéal drove her away again, and at that moment he saw the blue ghost he wanted: the shade that would lead him to his future. He also saw what that pattern would mean for Unnisha, but it didn't matter. *"You're destined for great things . . ."*

He aligned himself with the ghost. Unnisha was looking at him with sorrowful eyes. He let himself fall into the new pattern: he smiled at her so that she knew he understood her slip and wasn't hurt by it; after a moment, she smiled back at him, pulling him to her and hugging him.

". . . and anyway, those gardai are staying in the village today. They've been traveling down the Coast Road in search of the Geraghty boy—Ennis, they said his name was . . ." the woman was saying. The blue ghosts merged into reality again with Ennis' decision, fading even as he watched. The woman stroked the cloth again. "The Riocha can afford to overpay for such things. For those like me, it's too dear."

The course was set. All he had to do was follow the pattern. He reached up to tug at the woman's sleeve. "My mam will sell it to you for but a single mórceint, Iníon, because you love the Banrion Ard as we do," he said, still cradled in Unnisha's arm and knowing that after a few more minutes of haggling with Unnisha, the woman would buy the bolt for a silver half-mórceint and four coppers. She would leave pleased with her "bargain" and Unnisha would pocket the coins, which were three times what she'd paid for the cloth in the first place.

Later that evening, when the sun was just leaving the sky, the two gardai the woman had mentioned would stroll into the Taisteal encampment.

That's what the blue ghosts had shown him, and Ennis waited for them.

They walked in their own clear space in the now crowded area between the wagons. They either didn't notice or didn't care that the villagers would lower their eyes and purse their mouths as they approached, and cast suspicious glances at their backs once they passed. Ennis thought he even recognized one of the two—a tall and thin man with curly red hair that verged on orange and a mouth that was set crooked on his sallow face—a keep garda that he'd glimpsed before, though he didn't know the man's name. The other, shorter and with hair the color of dry earth and eyes of the same bland color, was a stranger. They strolled slowly through the camp, glancing occasionally at the wares the Taisteal had out for sale or barter, but looking more closely at the people around them. They wore swords, dangling from wide leather belts under clóca dyed the dark gray of Dún Laoghaire, the color that Ennis' own small clóca had once been, and their chests were covered in leather vests that jingled with rings of steel.

Ennis had no experience of war, but he remembered his da play-fencing with him with wooden swords just before he left for Céile Mhór. "Why don't you wear your real sword, Da?" he'd asked afterward as they left the room. His da wore only his léine and clóca and the golden torc that matched the one around his mam's neck. Even Blaze was hidden, though Ennis already knew that no one who had a cloch could bear to be without it, and that Blaze was also around Owaine's neck even if he kept it from casual sight.

His da had shrugged at the question. "A true soldier carries his weapons when he expects he might need them or when it's required of him," he'd answered. "Only then." He'd grinned then. "Besides," he added, snatching Ennis up in his strong arms and clasping the boy to him, "how can I hug my son if I have a big, nasty sword in the way?"

They'd laughed, the two of them, and the sound had seemed to reverberate through the whole keep.

Ennis watched the two gardai make their way toward Unnisha's wagon, knowing that they, too, were part of the new pattern and all he had to do was follow it.

Unnisha saw the gardai at the same time; Ennis felt her

arm go around his shoulders as she drew him close. "Be careful with them," she whispered as they strode near, the crowd parting and then closing in behind them once more as they passed. Ennis saw them looking at him appraisingly, and the red-haired garda nodded to his companion. Unnisha smiled as they changed direction and strolled over toward them. "Good evening," she said to them, smiling, but Ennis could hear the slight tremor in her voice. "Can I interest you in some cloth? Something pretty to take back to your wives, perhaps? To the gardai, we always give our very best prices."

The short one sniffed at that. "Your very highest prices, most likely," he said. He was looking at neither the cloth nor Unnisha, but Ennis. Ennis ducked his head but he could feel their stares. "And no doubt you've also heard by now that the Banrion Ard was murdered by her Taisteal servant woman."

"No!" said Unnisha in feigned horror. "We knew about the assassination, but not that any Taisteal had been involved. Surely that's a mistake—we Taisteal are a peaceful folk."

"The mistake was for the Banrion to trust a Taisteal," the garda answered. "The woman's name was Isibéal—did you know her?"

Unnisha shook her head thoughtfully. "No . . . no. I never knew a Taisteal woman by that name. What was her clan?"

"She gave her family name as Gastiela."

"Ah. We're Clan Kahlnik. There are other clans traveling this land, but . . ." Unnisha raised a shoulder. "We might never see them their whole time here. The Taisteal are always traveling. Always moving. We've been in the south of your land for the last year; we're just now coming north."

The tall, orange-haired garda had been staring at Ennis through the exchange. "What's your name, boy?" he asked, abruptly.

"Fiodóir," Ennis answered, giving the answer the pattern demanded. He took the step to the left away from Unnisha, as he'd seen the blue ghost do. Her arm left him reluctantly. "I'm Unnisha's son. We sell cloth. I could show you some of it, if you'd like."

"Aye." The confirmation sounded more like a question. "What about you, do you know this Isibéal?"

He blinked, his mouth open for a distinct second of hesitation. "No," he said, shaking his head vigorously. "I don't."

The orange-haired garda cocked his head to one side, as if trying to straighten out his mouth. His hand drifted to the hilt of his sword. "Your accent, Fiodóir; to my ear it's different than your mam's."

Ennis heard the intake of Unnisha's breath. He pursed his lips, shaking his head. "I don't know what you mean ..." At the same time, he stepped directly into the last dying light of the sun, letting the light strike him full in the face. He knew what the gardai saw: the sun coaxing red highlights from his dyed hair. He scurried back to Unnisha, half-hiding himself behind her skirt and back. The orange-hair garda was smiling grimly. He glanced at his companion and nodded his head toward one of the other wagons. "We ought to talk with the Clannhra," he said. The two of them started to walk away, then the orange-hair stopped as if he'd forgotten something.

"Oh. Ennis, there was one more thing I wanted to ask you."

"What?" Ennis asked innocently, as the pattern demanded: even as he felt Unnisha's hand tighten on his shoulder in alarm, even as she started to interrupt and stop him from answering.

The gardai's swords flew from their sheaths. Ennis heard the alarm of the crowds, heard Unnisha's shrill, "No!" He felt the hand of the shorter garda on his arm as the soldier pulled him away from Unnisha, as the orange-haired one held Unnisha back with the point of his sword to her neck. "No! He's my son! My son!"

The other Taisteal came running, the men grim-faced. The Dúnwick residents moved back uneasily as the Taisteal gathered while Clannhra Ata pushed toward the front. "Back off!" the orange-haired garda said. "This is the Ard's business. Back off now!" The crowd obeyed; some scowling, but most simply openly curious.

"What is the matter here?" Clannhra Ata said, sounding both aggrieved and puzzled. "We've done nothing."

The orange-hair sniffed, still holding Unnisha against the side of the wagon with his sword. She was sobbing quietly, the tears tracking down her face, her gaze on Ennis.

Ennis stopped struggling in the shorter garda's grip. "You're the Clannhra here?"

"Aye."

"Then you'll be coming with us as well."

Clannhra Ata held her arms wide as if to show that she had no weapons. "We've done nothing," she repeated. "That boy is Unnisha's son Fiodóir. Tell them, Fiodóir. Tell these men your name."

"My name . . ." Ennis paused. The blue ghosts danced the outline of his future life around him.

They were all looking at him. He heard Unnisha's sob. He took a breath, drawing himself up and straightening his shoulders as he'd seen Kayne or his da do when they stood in front of the people they commanded. He lifted his chin, as if in defiance.

"My name is Ennis Geraghty," he said, "and my mam was the Banrion Ard who was also called the Healer Ard." He pulled Treoraí's Heart from under his léine. "And this was once my mam's."

He heard Unnisha's despairing wail. He saw the look of hatred and betrayal on the Clannhra's face. Inside the Heart, Isibéal chortled.

He would have smiled, but the pattern would not allow it.

24

The Dragon of Thall Coill

A T SOME POINT, Sevei stopped being afraid.

The dragon lifted her high among shredded ivory clouds and pale moonlight, but the claws that held her only clutched her tightly without crushing her. Sevei blinked into the lash of the wind, hearing the low, steady *thrump* of huge leathery wings above her and smelling the sulfurous stench of the creature. She looked down as Kekeri rose and banked in updrafts she could not sense, glimpsing far below the rolling wave tops of the sea, the white foam of the surf crashing into Parlan's island, and the humps of tiny specks of land farther out in the distance. The sight made Sevei wrap her arms around the scaled leg of the creature in fright, knowing that if it opened its claws now, she would plummet to her death.

She knew then that her fate was no longer in her own hands.

They seemed to be moving northward, following the long line of the Stepping Stones toward Inish Thuaidh. After a time, Sevei called out to Kekeri, but the wind caught her voice and made it seem like no more than a whisper against the rush of air in her face. The dragon didn't answer, either not hearing her, not understanding her now that they were no longer linked with Dragoncaller's energy, or simply not caring to reply. It seemed to be laboring with her weight, occasionally dipping so close to the water that it seemed that she could almost feel the salt spray, and then rising again with great, energetic flaps of its wings. Perhaps that was the way dragons always flew, though—there was no way for her to know.

They traveled on for what would have been stripe after stripe of a clock-candle. They passed an island, then another far larger one drifted by to the right, then another off to the left. For a time, there was only open sea, but as the moon lowered itself in the sky she glimpsed another headland moving toward them slowly, and they passed along a seemingly endless coastline as she watched below the jagged line of white foam: the sea flailing against stubborn rocks.

Then, for a time, she remembered nothing. She slept in Kekeri's grasp, a sleep that was punctuated by dreams of war and strife, of Saimhóir flying through blue water, of blood and murder haunted by the ghosts of her mam and great-mam.

The warm touch of the sun on her face woke her.

They were over water still, but rapidly approaching a high sea cliff beyond which she could see the green of dense treetops waving in the wind. The dragon was descending; she could hear its decidedly labored breath, huffing loudly with each stroke of the wings. The land approached, far too rapidly for Sevei's comfort, and she started to cry out in alarm as the cliffs rushed threateningly toward her. At the last moment, another beat of the dragon's wings took them just above the lip of the jagged rocks; the broken edges of stone flashed past no more than an arm's length from her dangling feet, so near that she drew up her legs afraid that they'd strike the rocks. They were passing over a high glade in front of the forest, the ground rushing by in a blur of green. Wings cupped air, hard: the dragon stopped, hovering for a moment, and then Kekeri's talons were no longer holding her. Sevei fell onto the soft ground, the breath going out of her as the dragon half-rolled to an awkward stop not far from her. It wriggled, squirming on the joints of its batlike wings like a man moving on his elbows. It turned to face her, and its breath smelled of soot, sulfur, and rotting meat, and the double rows of scything teeth glittered in the dawn. Sevei shivered in the cold, but she faced it defiantly.

"You brought me all the way here to eat me? You could have done that long ago."

A panting cough that might have been amusement erupted as it lifted its head above her. "You'd be nothing more than an unsatisfactory and dry snack. After this exertion, some farmer will find all his sheep gone tomorrow." The words rumbled around her in the thundering hisses of dragon language; in her head, Kekeri's voice spoke in Sevei's own language through the dregs of mage-lights left in Dragoncaller, in tones that were low and weary.

"Where am I? Why did you bring me here?"

"Questions. With you soft-flesh creatures, it's always questions. You should learn to accept your fates. You should learn patience, as we have. Perhaps it's because your lives are so short and pointless . . ."

"Shut up and answer, then."

The dragon hissed gray-black smoke from its nostrils. A stench like old eggs enveloped her. "I *could* have eaten you. Perhaps I should have."

"You didn't."

"I may still rectify the mistake."

"I certainly couldn't stop you if you wanted to. So either do it or answer." She fingered Dragoncaller, hoping that somehow, miraculously, the stone still had enough power in it so that she could control the dragon, but there were only wisps of mage-energy there. Kekeri saw the motion and snorted.

"You can command me for a few breaths with that, but a bound being resents enslavement and will turn on its captor when released. A slave will do what it's told; a friend will do what's needed." When Sevei didn't answer, the dragon gave another smoke-laden sniff of annoyance. "You're on *Krahl-Krok-Gral,* the land you soft-flesh folk call Inish Thuaidh, and the forest before you is the Old Woods of the north peninsula."

"Thall Coill? This is Thall Coill?"

"That may be what you call this place. It's not our name for it nor the name the first soft-flesh people here gave it."

"Why am I here?"

"Because this is where I was asked to bring you. By a friend."

"A friend? Who is your friend?"

The great scaled head lowered until the huge reptilian eyes were level with her own. "More questions? No 'thank you' for killing those who would have killed you or for carrying you safely all the way here?"

"I didn't ask for you to kill the gardai, who were at least my people. And I didn't ask to come here either—who told you to bring me?"

"It was Bhralhg who wanted you here, of the water-borne Aware."

"Bhralhg?" Sevei looked around, expecting to see the Saimhóir standing there near the cliff edge. "Is he here, then?"

"Another question. Is there no end to them?" The dragon stirred, pushing itself up on its rear legs. "I'm hungry and exhausted, and it's not safe for even Earc Tine to hunt near the Old Woods. I've done what I was asked to do, and your questions weary me." The dragon's wings flapped once and at the same time Kekeri pushed itself into the air with its enormous leg muscles. It hung above her for an instant, like a dark-scaled cloud.

"Wait! I don't know where I am or what to do."

"That's of no importance to me, and your cloch has no power to hold me," Kekeri answered. Its wings flapped twice more as the massive body rose. "Farewell," it said, and let itself fall over the edge of the cliff, its red tail slithering along the ground behind it, tearing at the grass. She heard the sails of its wings take the air, and a few moments later it reappeared, already well out over the water and flapping its wings energetically as it rose higher in morning sky. It wheeled around, flashing past her a hundred strides above and turning south, toward the unseen townland of An Ceann Ramhar and—Sevei assumed—its pastures dotted with sheep.

She watched until the dragon appeared to be no larger than a sparrow; a few breaths later, it vanished above the mountains.

For the first time, she looked around carefully. The closest of the trees were four or five strides away from the cliffs: huge and ancient, gnarled oaks looking like stooped-over old men with gray beards of moss and old bird's nests hanging from their limbs The trees quickly moved closer together until there was only a green-black darkness under their canopy, punctuated by infrequent shafts of yellow sun. The forest seemed to exhale a breath of earthy compost, and she could feel eyes watching her. At first, after the rumbling voice of the dragon, she thought the place was preternaturally quiet, but now she could hear that the forest was anything but silent: the groan of branches rubbing and cracking; the calls of songbirds; the croaking of argumentative crows; the calls of animals she could not identify and—once—the shivering, voicelike howl of a dire wolf. The wind howled in from off the Westering Sea, driving the waves that crashed in an endless susurration on the rock below the cliff.

Nowhere, though, was there any sign of her own kind. This was desolation.

Sevei sat, abruptly, on a nearby boulder. *Parlan . . .* She wondered what had happened to him. She wondered if she'd ever know.

Hunger gnawed at her belly, and her arms were goose bumped as she rubbed at them. She'd been taught the slow magic spell for fire-making during her time with the Order, but there was no dead wood here, and she'd heard enough tales of the old forest to be hesitant to cut greenwood from any of the trees. She remembered being in Doire Coill with her parents and Ennis and meeting the Protector Keira there before she'd taken ship for Inishfeirm—that seemed a lifetime ago. Other tales of the Bunús Muintir's oak forests came to her as well, tales she'd learned from Inishfeirm or from Gram and Mam and Da, and thinking of them brought back the grief and loss again. *All of them gone, all my family, and Dillon . . . Máister Kirwan . . .*

She wondered whether she might be better off going down to the sea and changing—at least then she would be warm, and she could chase the sweetfish for food. And if Bhralhg had, indeed, caused her to be brought here, maybe . . .

The feeling of being watched was stronger now than before. She lifted her head, peering around. Shadows stirred under the trees and resolved into a man's form. Sevei rose. "I see you there," she called out, ready to run for the sea at need. "Who are you?"

The man took a step forward into the light. She saw the flattened face, the skin the color of bark, the thick eye ridge below the high forehead, below which deep-set and dark eyes regarded her: a Bunús Muintir. He appeared to be as old as Jenna or Máister Kirwan—not yet a true ancient like Keira, but with hair rapidly graying, a beard that extended to the middle of his chest and a face that showed the carved lines of the years. In his right hand, as a staff, he clutched a long oaken branch stripped of its bark. The flaring top was carved with filigrees and knots. He had a leather bag draped over one shoulder and, like Keira, he wore furs rather than cloth, bound around him by leather strips.

"You saw me because I allowed it," he told her. He spoke in the Daoine language, in a pleasant alto voice that was colored with an odd accent. "And my name? I'm called Beryn. I am the Protector of Thall Coill. And I know you: you are Sevei, the great-daughter of the First Holder."

"How do you know me? Have we met?"

"We've never met, and I know because we Bunús speak to all those who can talk," he answered. "I also know the First Holder and the Holder of Treoraí's Heart are dead. I'm sorry for your loss, Sevei, more than you know."

Sevei blinked back sudden, unbidden tears, not wanting the man to see her cry. "Thank you. Did you know Gram or Mam? I know they knew Keira and I met her once myself, when . . ." She stopped. The man was smiling at her.

"I met your great-mam Jenna long ago, when I was pledged to Lomán, who was the Protector here before me. I was even younger then than you are now. The First Holder frightened me and I think Lomán as well, though he tried not to show it and wouldn't admit it. She was so powerful already . . ."

Sevei gave a short laugh that sent a tear tracking down her cheek. She smeared it away with a finger. "She scared many people, I'm afraid. Me, too, sometimes."

"She could have been more than she was," Beryn said.

Old anger and irritation flashed in Sevei. "What do you mean? She was the First Holder, and Máister Kirwan said that she held Lámh Shábhála far longer than most First Holders. I know those with the Clochs Mór feared her."

Beryn didn't answer. "You must be hungry and cold, Sevei. Come with me."

"Did you know I was coming?"

"I know everything that touches this place," he told her. He turned away from her, walking slowly back toward the darkness under the trees. He used the walking stick, she saw, leaning on it, and she could see that he limped as if with some old injury.

"Wait," she called after him, but he continued to walk. Sevei glanced back once at the sea and to the distant line of mountains across above which the dragon had vanished. Then she hurried after the Bunús Muintir, following him under the seemingly endless canopy of trees.

Under the trees, the sunlight turned cold and thin. The air she breathed tasted as ancient as the trees themselves, as if it had been trapped there for centuries, held in by the weight of the leaves and branches above. Beryn moved with surprising grace and ease, making almost no sound as he slid through the shadows, while Sevei stumbled along behind him, tripping over unseen roots, her booted feet cracking dead branches and scuffling the carpet of dead leaves. As they walked, Sevei became aware that something was padding along close behind her and off to her left. She turned to look and almost immediately fell to her knees as the toe of her boot caught under a hidden vine. At the same moment, there was motion to her right: gray fur dappled with brown, and a body larger and far more muscular than her own. The head, a toothy muzzle, leered at her, a red tongue panting over the teeth as yellow-shot eyes regarded her hungrily.

A dire wolf. "Beryn!" Sevei managed to call as the wolf slid with fluid, muscular grace to stand over her. Its breath smelled of raw meat. Beryn stopped, and the wolf's head swiveled to glance at him. It growled.

Beryn growled back and received a snarling response. Sevei realized that the two were conversing. The wolf's claws dug at the soft earth, digging deep furrows, and Sevei could all too well envision those claws tearing at her flesh the same way. If the wolf chose to attack, there would be no time for Beryn to respond. She would be dead with the first slash of talons or crush of teeth. She started to back away and the wolf glared at her with baleful eyes and slavering jaws; she stopped. Beryn snarled something to the wolf and it lowered its head. The creature sniffed once in Sevei's direction, then bounded away, vanishing into the forest's gloom.

Sevei began to breathe again. "How did you do that?"

Beryn laughed—she found the laugh as pleasant as his voice. "That was Kiraac, the current pack leader of the dire wolves who live here. He smelled you and wanted to

know whether you were under my protection or not."
Beryn grinned. "I told him you were."

"Thank the Mother for that."

Beryn nodded and the smile slowly melted away. "There
are things here that I *can't* protect you from. There are
more intelligences out there than either you or I realize,
and more continue to awake from long slumbers with each
turn of the seasons. I think that's what most Holders of
Lámh Shábhála have never realized—that the power they
wield is not only for Daoine or Bunús Muintir, but for all."

"Gram knew," Sevei protested, but Beryn shook his
head.

"No, she didn't. Not enough. But she might have, if . . ."
He stopped. "We're close now," he said finally. "Just several
double-hands of strides."

He turned and continued walking. Sevei wanted to ask
him more, but he gave her no chance, moving so quickly
that she had to hurry to keep up. He stopped at last before
what seemed to be an impenetrable screen of tangled,
snarled vines hung between two gigantic oaks. There,
Beryn raised his staff and called out a phrase in the Bunús
tongue. As Sevei watched in amazement, the vines began
to writhe like leafy snakes and an opening appeared.
Beryn stepped through, then gestured to Sevei. "Come," he
said. "This is my home."

She entered, marveling.

It was a house made entirely of living plants: the roof
overhead was like the doorway, a tightly-woven roof of
vines. The walls were three massive oak trunks with
saplings and vines filling the gaps between them, the floor
a deep carpet of soft green moss. A dead oak stood in the
center of the wide space, its branches hung with herbs and
drying meat. A pile of stone near the rear was a hearth, and
a thin, white strand of smoke curled upward and vanished
into the leaves overhead. Beryn's bed was a mound of soft
straw over which a woven blanket had been laid; another
bed was placed against the far corner of the room. "You
may have that bed tonight," Beryn said. "It belongs to my
pledge-daughter Saraigh, but she's away to the north for
the next few days on an errand."

Beryn set his staff against the oak tree and hobbled over
to the hearth, blowing on the coals to kindle the turf he

placed on the ashes. "I have a stew I started earlier," he said. "In that pot there by the roots. Would you bring it here?"

Sevei took the handle of the heavy black iron pot, the thick liquid in it sloshing and giving off a wonderful fragrance, redolent with spices she couldn't identify. Beryn set it on the hook of a tripod over the fire, stirred it once with a wooden spoon, and stood up with a groan and a crack of knees. "There. A half-stripe and you can eat, unless you want it cold. I have some bread and cheese until then . . ." He went to a cabinet near the hearth and brought out a loaf and a round of yellow cheese. He stuck a knife in the center of the cheese, broke off a bit of the loaf and handed the rest to Sevei. "Go on," he said. "I can see the hunger in your face."

She didn't hesitate, breaking off a large hunk of the hard-crusted bread and cutting a generous slice of the cheese. She sat on Saraigh's bed, eating and watching Beryn as he shuffled around the dwelling, taking herbs from the bag he carried and placing them on racks to dry, sniffing the herbs that were already hung up. He busied himself for a time without speaking, sometimes singing to himself as he worked: songs with words in the Bunús Muintir language and melodies that sounded discordant and strange to Sevei's ears. Finally, he stopped and came over to her.

"You don't seem frightened of me," he said. "I thought you might be."

"Both Gram and Mam considered the Bunús Muintir friends. They were both helped by your people more than once."

"Lomán had a pledge-son before he took me. The boy attacked the First Holder when she was weak and tried to take the cloch from her. And Lomán wasn't particularly helpful to the First Holder either, except under duress."

"I suspect that if you wanted to kill or hurt me, you could have done it easily. Am I wrong?"

A smile. "No. There are many ways to die here, and those who come to Thall Coill without being invited often find them."

"That implies I was invited."

"You're welcome here, aye." He went to the fire, stirred

the stew again, and tasted it. The spicy odor filled the room and Sevei's stomach growled in response. "It's ready. Would you like some?"

"Please," Sevei answered with such fervor that Beryn laughed. He filled a bowl, found a spoon and brought them over to her. She ate hungrily; he ate also, more slowly, sitting on his own bed and watching her. When she was done, she set the bowl down on the floor. "Thank you," she said. "That was very good." When he nodded, she held his gaze. "Are you going to tell me why I'm here?"

Beryn set down his bowl also. "You don't know?"

She shook her head.

"You're here to see whether you can succeed where your gram failed."

"I don't understand."

He gave her a quiet, almost shy smile. "You will. Tomorrow. For now, rest, and I will show you more of Thall Coill."

25

Choices Made

NOT MANY OF THOSE who weren't Fingerlanders
had ever heard of the Hall of the Clans, and even
fewer had ever glimpsed it. The first time he glimpsed the
hall, Kayne found himself gaping around him like a child
as he looked around, clutching at Séarlait's arm, wound
through his own.

The "hall" was a large cavern at the end of a long, twisting cave. "Once, ages ago, a river flowed through here,"
Laird O'Blathmhaic had told him as they entered the cavern. "Centuries ago, after carving out these tunnels, it
broke though the floor a few miles on the other side of the
hall; now it runs through caverns a hundred strides below
us. It left this behind . . ." He swept his arms around the
cavern.

The hall glimmered like a jewel in the glow from a hundred torches set around the chamber. The walls gleamed
with brightly-colored flowstone, polished and so smooth
that the rippling columns appeared to be liquid themselves. The cavern sloped sharply downward toward them,
so that they stood at the bottom of a natural amphitheater
with uneven rows of flowstone "seats," many of them covered with cloth pillows in the plaid colors of the various
clans. At the rim of the amphitheater, a quartet of pale
white stalactites and stalagmites had grown together to
create massive columns. The ceiling of the hall was studded
with snow-white, sparkling nodules like heavy frost.

For the last several stripes, the amphitheater had been
noisy and crowded as the clansfolk had discussed (though

Kayne felt that "argued" was perhaps the better description) their strategy in the wake of the Battle of Ceangail.
Kayne, Harik, and their gardai had been allowed to attend
the gathering but were not permitted to speak.

The clans had come away with a declaration, signed by
all the lairds and banlairds and to be delivered to the Rí
Morven Mac Baoill in Dathúil, a declaration that the Fingerlands no longer accepted the Rí's control of the Fingerlands, that henceforth the Fingerlands were free and
independent of Tuath Airgialla.

The declaration would be delivered to him in a box con-
taining the head of his son Mal.

Laird O'Blathmhaic had emerged as the political leader
of the nascent rebellion, not in little part because his great-
daughter now held a Cloch Mór. Rodhlann O Morchoe
would remain as commander of the Fingerlander forces
and be responsible for strategic matters.

Now, the hall was empty of clansfolk, even—reluctantly—Séarlait. Only Kayne and the rest of his gardai remained. Barely more than three double-hands now, with
nearly two double-hands of them falling during the Battle
of Ceangail, they looked insignificant against the natural
majesty and beauty of the Hall of Clans. Kayne stood and
walked down the broad stairs carved in the flowstone until
he stood at the bottom of the half bowl, looking up at them.

"We'll speak freely here," he said to them, though his
gaze stayed mostly on Harik's frown. "Not as commander
to gardai, not as Riocha to céili giallnai or tuathánach, but
as peers who have a common problem. You heard here
that the clans will go to war against Tuath Airgialla—
because that's certainly what their declaration will mean. It
may also mean that they will go to war against *all* the
Tuatha, not just Tuath Airgialla. It means that those who
stay here will be considered traitors and even if the clansfolk manage to win their independence, any of us who fight
with them may well never be able to return to our homes.
Back there, back home, everything has changed. I'm certain that the Banrion Ard, my mam, has fallen. The mage-
lights tell me that my gram the First Holder no longer has
Lámh Shábhála. Your Commander, my da, is now with
Mam in the arms of the Mother-Creator. You've all seen
how the Riocha will treat those who follow me. I brought

you here to say this: you have a choice before you now. If you leave, on your own, I have a promise from Laird O'Blathmhaic and Rodhlann O Morchoe that you will be allowed safe passage from the Finger as long as you take an oath never to reveal any of what you know of the clans. I can't be certain of what you'll find awaiting you in the Tuatha, but if you say to them that you renounced me because of your loyalty to your own Rí, I suspect you'll find forgiveness and mercy. If you stay, I can promise you nothing except more war and more battles and possibly exile here in the Finger for the rest of your life—*if* you survive. As for me . . . I'll stay here and fight with the clansfolk— I've already made that decision. I'm staying because I need to gain vengeance for those who murdered my parents. I'm staying because I saw my da and the men who trusted and followed him cut down by those we thought were friends. I'm staying because I am no longer Riocha and no longer Tiarna and those back in the Tuatha wish the same fate on me that they gave to my da. But you . . ."

Kayne lifted his hand, grimacing a bit as healing muscles pulled. "Each of you needs to make his own decision: to stay or to go. You need to make it now. Here. Today."

"I stay." The voice came from the midst of the gardai: Garvan, with Bartel nodding vigorously next to him in agreement—even one-legged, Bartel had insisted on being lashed to a horse so he could fight in the battle. "Bartel, Sean, Uilliam, and me already talked about it. You pulled us out when we would've died, Tiarna Kayne, and then the clansfolk helped us. We're staying."

"Those are brave words, Garvan," Harik said, and as the Hand rose, Garvan sat down abruptly. Harik glanced at Kayne, then to the others. "Since we're talking as peers, I'll be blunt," he said. "Kayne Geraghty might say that he's not Riocha, but that changes nothing. The blood of the First Holder and the Banrion Ard still flows in his veins, and he will always have that claim to the throne in Dún Laoghaire. If the clans should win—" the twist in his lips gave his opinion of that possibility, "—or if the political winds shift, who knows what that might mean? Tiarna Kayne also stays because he now has . . . *ties* with Laird O'Blathmhaic through his great-daughter—so he may become 'Riocha' here as well, for what that's worth." He scowled, and there was scorn in the glance he gave Kayne. "As to the Fingerlanders' promise of safe passage . . ." Harik sniffed. "Those are just words, and who will know that their vow wasn't kept if along the road those who leave all happen to die? I know that if *I* were laird here, I wouldn't care to have those who know some of my secrets walking into my enemy's camp, oath or not."

Kayne started to protest angrily, but Harik raised his hand with a glower and a shout. "No, Tiarna! You said we could speak openly and as peers, and I *will* speak. You had your say, now let me have mine. Let me tell them what you won't."

Kayne had to clench his jaw to keep from shouting back at the man. He took two long breaths, then nodded to Harik. "Say it, then." *And you will no longer be my Hand,* he thought.

"The clansfolk will be crushed like ants beneath a boot," Harik continued. "That's the reality. There are two Clochs Mór here, aye, but the Riocha have far more clochs and far more soldiers. They probably also have Lámh Shábhála, for they wouldn't have moved against the Banrion Ard unless they'd also made certain that the First Holder couldn't retaliate. The clansfolk have won a single, small battle against a tiny force, that's all, and now they're ready to piss in the face of a hurricane. What happens when the Riocha come in force? What happens when they bring a real army to crawl over the mountains in their thousands? What happens when a dozen Clochs Mór are arrayed against the Fingerlanders' paltry two, or when Lámh Shábhála itself takes the field under its new Holder? What happens? I'll tell you—the clansfolk will do as they've always done: several of them will be killed, but most of the rest will throw down their weapons and grovel, and the lairds and banlairds will take to their mountains and caves and hide like criminals for the rest of their lives. Those who are captured will be hung on gibbets as a warning to the others, the Clochs Mór will be back in the hands of the Riocha as they always have been, and in another generation this will all be just another failed, half-forgotten Fingerlander rebellion: the story of Kayne the Traitor and his all too brief time. Kayne, who looked to the west for his enemy when he should have been looking east."

Kayne wanted to rage. He wanted to launch himself at Harik and the man's undisguised scorn, wanted to vent the fury he felt with fists and blood. *Do as your da would have done. He was right—you can't simply rush into decisions based on your emotions* .... His eyebrows lowered, lines carving themselves in his forehead and he forced the muscles of his face to relax. The calm part of him knew that if he showed anger toward Harik now, most of the gardai would go with the Hand. Many them would do so anyway, but those who were still uncertain or afraid of the reception they might find back home ...

What he did next was nearly the hardest thing he'd ever done.

He inclined his head to Harik as he would to another Tiarna. "Then we know your decision, Harik MacCathaill," Kayne said, amazed that his voice could be calm when the anger still seethed inside him. "If that's the fate the Mother-Creator has for me, then fine. You served Da well as his Hand, but I never knew you were a seer as well." He forced himself to smile to cushion the bite in the statement, and a few of the men laughed softly in response. "Everything you said was true, Hand Harik, but I think you underestimate the clansfolk. I think you discount them because they fight using tricks and deception and ambush as well as force of arms. I know that wasn't the way we were taught to fight—but I think it's a way we can and should learn. Had Séarlait not done as she did . . ." He shuddered: *Mac Baoill's intense glare, the ice closing around him* ... "As to our enemies in the Tuatha ..." Kayne sniffed, the inhalation loud in the cavern. "They will be like crows squabbling over the remains of Mam's legacy and too busy fighting themselves to worry about us for a time." He gestured to Harik, who stared at him with the puzzled, uncertain look of a man who expected confrontation and found agreement.

"You served Da and me well and loyally, Harik. For that, I'll always be grateful. I'll sorely miss your counsel, your sword, and your honesty. But I'm staying here where I have allies with the clansfolk. I'll stay here and I'll fight and I *will* one day come out of the Finger to claim what is mine."

Kayne lifted his head, turning from Harik to sweep his gaze across each of the men in the cavern. "If any of you are thinking of staying here because of loyalty to the oaths you gave to my da and the Banrion Ard back in Dún Laoghaire, I release you from those oaths now. You're all free to stay or go, and no one, *no one* here will think less of you for following Harik back to your homes and your families. I'll leave the decision to you. Stay or go—you should do what your heart tells you to do."

With that, Kayne nodded again to Harik and turned abruptly, taking one of the torches from its sconce off the wall and striding toward the ragged arch that led into the hall and the long, twisting passageway that led down, and then up again to the outside. He heard the men begin to talk as he reached the arch. He hadn't gone more than a few dozen strides down the passage before he heard Harik's gruff voice. "Tiarna Geraghty!"

He stopped and half turned to look back over his shoulder. In the flickering, guttering light of the torch, Harik's battle-scarred face was as hard-edged as the rocks. "The decision's made," he said.

Kayne let his breath out in a quick exhalation; he could see the cloud emerge from his mouth in the cool dampness. His shoulders sagged. He nodded. "I'll tell Laird O'Blath-mhaic that you'll be leaving with the gardai this evening," he said. "May the Mother-Creator be with you, Harik. I hope all of you find safety. Truly."

"We're staying, Tiarna. Every man."

Kayne blinked. He could hear the crackling of the torch in the silence. He wanted to stutter his confusion, wanted to ask why. But he knew that wasn't what his da would have done. Owaine would have expected the obedience and accepted it. So Kayne nodded, though he was unable to keep a smile from his lips. "Then that's what I'll tell the laird," he said. More silence. The torch hissed and spat. "Thank you, Harik Hand."

Harik's face remained stonelike and solemn. "You've nothing to thank me for," he answered. "Today, for the first time, I saw the man and not the child. I don't follow children, nor all men. But Tiarna Geraghty . . ."

His chin lifted, his eyes glittered under dark eyebrows. "I would follow him wherever he asked."

26

The Pattern's Dance

THE BODIES OF UNNISHA and Clannhra Ata swung gently back and forth in their tight iron cages, the chains that suspended the cages from a wooden beam creaking and protesting as the wind pushed them. The gibbets had been set where the lane from Dúnwick met the High Road. The corpses appeared to be clothed in writhing black cloaks: the crows were at the bodies, pecking at them and tearing off bits of flesh, squabbling with each other as they fought over the choicest bits.

Ennis stared up at the cages, his eyes wide.

" 'Tain't a pretty sight, young Tiarna, an' I can understand your being upset by it," said the tall, red-haired garda, whose name Ennis had learned was Daighi. "But 'twill serve as a warning to others of what will happen if they try to hurt you."

Ennis nodded blandly. He stared at the crows, watching as one stabbed its beak into Unnisha's gaping mouth and ripped out a piece of gray flesh. He cocked his head to one side, wondering what it must be like to be a crow, wondering what they might be thinking as they ravaged the corpses. The sun peered momentarily from between the massed gray clouds and struck the gibbets, and the crows flapped their wings as if enjoying the sudden warmth. Ennis could barely recognize Unnisha or the Clannhra now, blood-streaked bone starting to show through the patches of skin on their faces.

There'd been a scuffle when Daighi tried to arrest the two women. Two of the Clannhra's sons and a few of her great-sons had resisted, and both gardai had been slightly

wounded. But when the villagers realized that the gardai
were accusing these Taisteal of being among the conspirators who had killed the Healer Ard, when they realized
that the boy was none other than the beloved Ard's son,
the inhabitants of Dúnwick had come to the gardai's aid.
The Clannhra's wagon had been torched and the residents
had been allowed to plunder the remainder of the Taisteal
wagons of whatever they wanted before the surviving Taisteal were ordered to take their now-empty wagons and
leave. But before they departed, the Taisteal had been
brought here to watch as Unnisha and Clannhra Ata were
stuffed screaming into the cages quickly prepared for them
by the local smithy, hung on the beams, and then dispatched with quick stabs from Daighi's spear. Ennis hadn't
witnessed the executions himself, but he'd heard them described by the Aldwoman of Dúnwick, in whose house
he'd slept that night, in a bed with a thick, soft blanket
bearing the colors and patterns of the Taisteal.

Now, Daighi and his companion—Brett—were to take
Ennis back to Dún Laoghaire. "The Banrion Mac Ard will
be most pleased to see you," Daighi said "It was she who
sent gardai out everywhere to find you. Come now, Tiarna
Geraghty; a boy your age shouldn't dwell on a sight like
this. You'll be back in Dún Laoghaire in two days."

Ennis forced his gaze away from the fascinating swarm
of crows. His face was solemn; his eyes were dry. "I'm
ready, Daighi," he said.

He walked over to where Daighi sat on his horse, his
shield arm bound and the bandages stained with blood;
Ennis' movement sent the crows into the air, cawing rau-
cously. Brett, wearing a wrapping of cloth over a long, ugly
cut on his forehead, helped Ennis up onto the pony they'd
taken from the Taisteal, then climbed onto his own horse.
They started northward along the High Road. As he followed along just behind the two gardai, Ennis glanced
backward at the gibbet where the crows had now settled
once more around the cages like a shroud. He touched the
Heart, and inside he heard Isibéal chuckling.

He smiled.

They rode for most of the day, through occasional curtains of soft rain interspersed with bright sunlight, keeping the horses to no more than a walk so that the pony would have no trouble. Ennis rode in silence for the most part, answering occasionally when one or the other of the men would ask him a question, but never initiating conversation himself. There was no need. He was locked into the pattern he'd chosen, the new dance, and he could allow himself no deviation from it, or the blue ghosts that guided him would vanish into the confusion of possibilities. "Poor child," he heard Daighi say once to Brett. "He's seen too much too young. They say that he was at the dinner when the damned Taisteal woman Isibéal poisoned the Healer Ard. To have watched his own mam die in front of him . . ."

I didn't see it, but I knew it would happen, he wanted to tell the man. But he couldn't say those words; the pattern wouldn't allow it. Instead, he watched the emerald hills of southern Dún Laoghaire slowly pass, looking always to the east where the Tween Sea glimmered occasionally between heather-clothed mounds, and waiting.

He waited until it was nearly evening.

They came to an intersecting lane that led off to the east. The smell of the sea was strong, even though Ennis couldn't see the ocean. There was a sign there, and Daighi peered wearily at the painted, fading words on the well-weathered plank. " 'Tis the road to Maithcuan—there'll be soft beds at the inn," Daighi said to Brett. "We can have a courier sent ahead to let the Banrion Mac Ard know that we've found the boy. If the gods are with us, we might even find one of the royal boats there and let them sail us back to the city. It's either that, or spend the night out here, which I don't want to do with the boy."

"Aye, and there's none better than the ale at The Laughing Heron," Brett agreed. Then he grimaced, stroking his bandaged forehead. "It's been a long ride today. What say you, young Tiarna?—the comforts of Maithcuan, or these rocks alongside the High Road?"

As Brett spoke, Ennis saw the blue ghosts appear around them, whispering of possibilities. He watched them, heard their whispers and their gestures, and saw himself among them. *No,* he wanted to tell the visions, though he knew that the blue ghosts couldn't hear him or respond to him. *I don't want to take this path . . .* But he saw where the other most likely path led, and in the hazy distance of the future, realized that if he continued on with Daighi back to Dún Laoghaire, it would mean his own death. Peering at the ghosts, he saw Aunt Edana pledging to keep him safe, but Ennis' existence was a threat to too many others. He saw the faint image of Uncle Doyle, glaring at him, and there was a knife and his own still body. . . .

His hand sought the Heart on the chain around his neck. *"Go back and they'll kill you as I was supposed to kill you,"* he heard Isibéal say. *"You're a threat to them and they can't let you live. But that doesn't have to be, does it? Not when you have the Heart. Not if you use the Heart in your own way."*

"Let me talk to Mam," he thought back to the voice, but Isibéal only laughed. The ghosts of all his futures surrounded him, and he had to choose. He let himself fall into the pattern.

"It's getting dark and the mage-lights will be coming," Ennis said. "You're both hurt and tired." He lifted Treoraí's Heart on its chain, showing the cloch to both of them. "I can make you better and fill the cloch again later. Let me do that for you."

Daighi looked at the caged jewel, then at Brett. "Our evening *would* be more enjoyable if we weren't injured. You can do that, Tiarna, young as you are?—you can heal with the stone as your mam did?"

"The Heart was my mam's; now it's mine," the blue ghost that was him said and Ennis let his own mouth echo the same words. The azure shape of the future slid down from the pony and Ennis did the same, as the other blue ghosts around him faded, the futures they represented now extinguished. The pattern smiled; he smiled—it was all part of the new dance. "I watched her, and she taught me. Here, I'll show you. Brett, come here . . ."

Both men dismounted, hitching the horses to the sign-post. Ennis took Treoraí's Heart in his right hand, closing his fingers around it as he'd seen his mam do a hundred times. The energy held within the stone surged through him and he nearly sighed with the delicious, comforting feel of it. He swayed on his small legs at the searing interior heat that welled outward from his right hand. "Here,

Brett. All I have to do is touch your head where you're hurting . . ." Brett knelt on the ground in front of him so that his head was level with Ennis'. Ennis reached out his left hand, laid it over Brett's bloodstained bandage, and released some of the power.

He was Brett. Ennis could feel the ache and soreness in the garda's head, the constant wash of pain. He could have stopped it, easily. But it was also just as easy to tear the injury open farther and deeper, to plunge deep into the man and rip him open from the inside, from here where the Heart had taken him. . . .

He saw Brett's eyes roll up until only the whites showed. The man's mouth opened in a soundless cry. He toppled to the ground. "Brett!" Daighi called in alarm, rushing over to kneel next to the man. "What happened here?" he asked Ennis. Ennis touched Daighi gently on the shoulder as the garda glanced at him. "Is Brett—?"

Power flowed from Ennis into the garda. Daighi's face convulsed, all the muscles going rigid. A moment later, he fell atop Brett.

The blue ghost vanished in a soundless pulse. Ennis looked down at the two men, releasing Treoraí's Heart as if it burned his hand. He sat abruptly on the ground, crying as any young boy might when confronted by death. He looked at Daighi and Brett, afraid now, afraid to touch them or look at them, afraid that he might see the Black Haunts gathering over them to take away their souls, afraid they might somehow stir, afraid that they might point at him accusingly. "I'm sorry, I'm sorry," he whispered to them. "I had to. Don't you see? I *had* to. I didn't have a choice."

He scrambled away from them, running to the signpost. He unhitched the gardai's horses and shouted at them so that both steeds bolted. Then, still sobbing, he pulled himself astride his pony. He moved carefully around the two men half-hidden in the grass alongside the road, and turned down the lane toward Maithcuan. He was shaking with fright and the tears were still running hot down his cheeks and Treoraí's Heart burned like a brand on his chest.

Maithcuan slumbered in a wide, shallow harbor sheltered by tall headlands. It lay in purpled shadow in the last light of the sun as Ennis looked down on it from a small rise. The town was far smaller than Dún Laoghaire, but he noticed that several ships were anchored in the harbor; one of them—one that he'd glimpsed in his visions of the future—flew a strange banner he'd seen once before.

"That's the banner of Céile Mhór, Son," Da had told him as he held him in his arm. They stood on the ramparts of the Banrion Ard's Keep, looking down at the harbor. "You remember when Mam introduced you to Toscaire Concordai Ghalai last night in the Great Hall? Well, that ship brought the Toscaire here, and Kayne and I are going to be going to his country ourselves very soon, to help them fight the Arruk. . . ."

After staring at the ship for a moment, Ennis slapped the reins of his pony and continued down the slope.

There were gates along the road and a low stone fence encircling the town. Ennis could see two men trudging slowly up the slope from town, both bearing lanterns in the growing gloom. He assumed they were gatekeepers like the gardai who patrolled the four passages through the great wall that girdled Dún Laoghaire, but these gates were just simple planks of board nailed to leather hinges. They hung askew and open; Ennis urged his pony through the opening before the men reached them. They looked at him curiously as he passed. "We're closing the town gate for the night, boy," one of them said as he came abreast them. "Do you know where you're going?"

Ennis nodded. "My da's down at the market buying fish. We're staying here tonight."

A nod. Ennis could already see the man's interest fading. "Good," he said. He gestured to his companion. "Let's get the gates shut, then. Don't know why the Ald insists on keeping 'em closed—the troubles in Dún Laoghaire ain't gonna come here. I heard that the Riocha executed a triple-hand of those who rioted when the Healer Ard was killed, just as an example. . . ."

Ennis let the pony find its own way into the town, moving through narrow streets toward the scent of brine. The blue ghosts rose up again around him: the city was full of possibilities and turns, but he could have walked through it with his eyes shut, following the path that he'd already chosen. *Stay with the pattern. Just follow it and you'll be where you want to be. You'll be safe. You'll stay alive* . . . He wouldn't let himself think about what he was doing or what he'd done. If he did that, he'd be lost. He could feel it all pushing inside him and he wanted to cry and wail and sob, wanted to let himself sink into Mam's arms or Isibéal's or Unnisha's and be comforted, but they were all gone now and he had no one.

Only the blue ghosts and the voices in the Heart.

Ennis let the pattern guide him through the streets, ignoring the woman who clutched at him as he passed, saying nothing to the merchants who called out, forcing himself not to look at the enticing bundles on the tables of the still-bustling market that ringed the harbor. Not thinking, just matching the steps of the pattern's dance. Above the houses of Maithcuan, he could see the masts of the larger ships at anchor out in the harbor. The banner of Céile Mhór still fluttered from the top of one.

By the time he came to the quays where the small fishing boats were tied up, it was full dark and the first hints of the mage-lights were beginning to glitter below and through the rain-heavy clouds. There, he let himself half-fall down from the pony and took the little pack that Daighi had made for him back in Dúnwick. Several of Maithcuan's inhabitants were watching him curiously—an obvious stranger and a very young one, dressed in plain but obviously fine clothes. Among those at the quays was a man who was bright with a blue ghost—Ennis knew that meant he was connected to Ennis' own dance. He was dressed in a léine cut from some cloth Ennis had never seen, and his clóca was shorter than those the Riocha wore and was trimmed in fox fur. His long, tanned features were subtly different from most of those around him, and he had a black tattoo curling down one side of his face: a fanciful bird with a wide, toothed beak that looked as if were about to close on his left eye. Ennis glanced at the man with the shy smile he knew the pattern required, then scampered off through the crowds toward one end of the harbor, leaving the pony behind. He knew without looking that the man would be following him.

At the edge of the town, he clambered up among the

rocks of the shore, sliding down into a small ravine where he could no longer see the light of Maithcuan. There, he pulled Treoraí's Heart from under his léine and lifted it to the brightening mage-lights. They danced toward his up-raised hand, curling around the stone and his clenched fist, and he gasped again at the cold wonder of the energy there as it filled the Heart.

When it was done, he reluctantly let go of the cloch and the mage-light slid upward toward the clouds. Ennis took a shuddering breath, waiting, and he heard the expected voice, echoed by the blue ghosts.

"You're taking chances doing that out here in the open, young Tiarna, with no one around."

Ennis let himself start as if surprised, his mouth open in fear, his eyes wide. He let himself speak the blue words. "Who . . . who are you? Stay back. I'm warning you . . ."

The tattooed man was on the rocks above him, his form dimly outlined in the watch fires along the harbor. His face was shadowed and dark, not even the eyes visible, but his voice was like the sound of a horn, rich and sonorous, and thick with an accent Ennis had never heard before. "No need to trouble yourself. I mean you no harm. I'm only sur-prised at seeing a boy, without his parents or guardians, holding a cloch na thintrí up to the sky. It's rare you see anyone with a cloch who's not a Riocha, even a clochmion. There'd be those who'd wonder how you came to have it, who'd wonder whether you stole it, for example, and from whom."

"I'm not a thief," Ennis said, the blue ghost giving his voice the heat of someone unjustly accused. "I'm not. I didn't take it from anyone. It was given to me. It's mine."

The man laughed gently at that. "From what I know, that's what anyone with a cloch would say. I understand that once you hold one, you can't willingly give it up. Is that true, young Tiarna?"

Ennis shrugged, a quick lift of the shoulders. He sniffed, as if he were cold and tired and scared. He heard a scrap-ing of rock as the man came down the rocks into the little ravine, moving with the grace of someone used to walking on rough terrain. "Where are the ones who should be watching you?" he said. "Back at the harbor? At the inn? They must be worried about you, especially with the mage-lights. Come; I'll take you back to them . . ." The man held out a hand.

Ennis sniffed again, and his voice trembled. "I don't . . . My parents are dead and so are my brothers and sisters. They're not here. I'm all . . . all alone."

"All alone?" The man's voice dripped with sympathy and concern. "Oh, young Tiarna, that's worse than I thought. You must be terrified."

Ennis nodded silently. The man's hand was still outstretched toward him. He reached out and took it, his small hand lost when the man closed his own fingers around it. His grip was tight and firm, though his voice was still gentle. "Come with me. I'll get you to a safe place, and then I'll find the gardai and have them come for you. A young Tiarna with a cloch . . ." He shook his head. "What's your name, so I may tell them?"

Ennis listened to the blue ghost and answered with it. "MacVahlg. Connail MacVahlg."

"Good. My name is Artol Jantsk. I'm a merchant from Céile Mhór—do you know where that is?"

"Aye. Far away."

"Aye, far away indeed," Jantsk laughed. "Are you hungry?"

With the question, Ennis heard his stomach growl. His head bobbed fervently, and Jantsk chuckled again. "Good. Then let's get you some food. You'd like that, Connail, wouldn't you?"

Still talking, he led Ennis out of the ravine, and—holding tightly to his hand—took him to where four men dressed in a similar fashion were talking near a long rowboat tied to the quay. He said something to them in another language, and the four got into the boat and unshipped the oars, placing them in their notches in the gunwales. "These are my friends, Connail," Jantsk said. "They'll take you out to that ship there. See?" He pointed to the ship flying the banner of Céile Mhór. "We'll go there first, and eat, and then I'll come back here and talk with the gardai. Here, let me help you in . . ."

Jantsk picked up Ennis and handed him to one of the other men, then untied the boat from the pier. He hopped down into it himself then, and pushed them away into the wavelets of the quiet harbor. He seemed to be watching the people nearest them as they rowed away, but if any of them had noticed the incident, none of them seemed concerned or particularly interested. The man sat next to Ennis on the wooden seat at the front of the boat.

"A young Tiarna with a cloch, and your parents dead," Jantsk said, shaking his head. In the light of a lantern hung at the front of the ship, Ennis could see the tattoo on the man's face leaping as he spoke, as if the bird were alive. He smiled, but in the lamplight there was greed in his eyes that he could not hide.

"A terrible thing," he said. "A terrible thing indeed."

27

The Rí Ard

DOYLE MAC ARD TRIED to keep the satisfaction from showing on his face as his carriage lurched to the crest of Halla Mount and stopped near the line of other royal coaches. His driver hopped down and opened the door. His son Padraic slid from the carriage immediately. Doyle glanced out at the stone ring of Tuatha Halla: the ancient edifice where the rulers of Talamh an Ghlas traditionally met, gleaming in whitewashed splendor in the sun. Tufts of ephemeral cloud drifted beneath a canopy of ultramarine, and Dún Laoghaire, spread out below them, shimmered in the warmth of the sun as the waters of the bay lapped at the shore.

There was a gathering of perhaps a hundred Riocha outside the massive oaken doors, representing most of the great families of the Tuatha. The Ríthe were already inside, but the mass of Riocha had paused to watch Doyle, Padraic and Shay O Blaca, the Máister of the Order of Gabair, arrive. Beyond them, standing under the watchful gaze of several pike-bearing gardai, a crowd of céili giallnai—the lower ranks of nobility—watched, and past them a large group of plainly-dressed tuathánach had also gathered.

It should have been an altogether beautiful day, Doyle decided. The decision of the Óenach—as the gathering of the Ríthe was called—was a foregone conclusion. Doyle knew who the new Rí Ard would be. Rí Mallaghan had already told him.

But the beauty was marred by the scowls and whispered taunts from the common folk and even some of the céili gi-

allnai who had come up to see the Riocha gather for the
election. The animosity of the commoners against the Riocha had reached fever pitch following the funeral of the
Banrion Ard Meriel—there had been attacks against Riocha in several of the towns along with some rioting and
looting. Riocha traveling the High Road had rocks and
vegetables hurled at their carriages, and there had been
clashes between gardai and groups of unruly youths. In the
moon cycle since Meriel's death, the overt violence had
ended, but it was obvious that those who the Riocha ruled
were angry and uneasy. Rumors abounded: there had been
sightings of the spirit of the Healer Ard in various locations, especially around her barrow on Cnocareilig, and
there were rumors that a group of Draíodóiri at the royal
temple were secretly praying to her spirit as one might to
a demigod.

His half niece a god ... Now that would be irony. Doyle
sniffed. Better a ruler here than a god in the afterlife Beyond.

Padraic was staring at the crowd, nervously fingering the
new Cloch Mór around his neck. O Blaca had seen the twin
crowds also. He sniffed and wrapped his clóca tightly
around him. "Let's get in, Doyle, Padraic. It won't do to
keep the Ríthe waiting, and I don't like the feeling out
here."

Doyle could already feel the weight of the torc of the
Ard around his neck. He imagined that somewhere in the
Beyond, Jenna, Meriel, and the rest of the damned Aoire
clan were screaming and weeping in frustration. He did
smile at that, causing some of the tuathánach watching
near the entrance of the Tuatha Halla to scowl and point.
Finally, Da, he thought, *I've given you your revenge.*

Doyle put his arm around his son's shoulders. "Come
on," he said. "The Máister's given us an order."

Unruly commoners could be dealt with—they would understand the whip and the noose well enough and bow
their heads. The only true flaw was that Lámh Shábhála remained lost under the waves. Every night when the mage-
lights came, Doyle lifted Snapdragon to the sky and he
followed the thread of power back toward the other clochs
na thintrí wondering if he would feel Lámh Shábhála
among them, sucking greedily at the power. But it had

been over a moon now, and the great cloch hadn't made its presence felt. Doyle felt certain that it was lost, but he was equally certain that it would appear again, washed up on some shore or lodged in the gullet of a fish. Lámh Shábhála would return to the world because it must; he would be there to take the stone when it did.

As it had always been his plan to take it.

Yet despite his satisfaction, the loss of Edana's affection cast a pall. *That is what you must fix now,* he reminded himself. *After today, you must do all you can to gain her back.*

She had fallen out of love for him, aye, but he had never stopped loving her. She was the other true constant in his life.

"Nothing's changed since your talk with the Ríthe last night?" Shay O Blaca asked as the trio walked from the carriage toward the doors of the Halla. The Máister of the Order of Gabair was moving slowly these days, troubled by gout in his right leg, a gout that Meriel had steadfastly refused to heal despite Doyle's suggestion to her—two years ago—that it might be a politically adroit move. *"I'm sorry, Doyle, but if I tried to cure all the gout in the Tuatha, I would do nothing else for the rest of my life,"* the great "Healer Ard" had answered. *"Treoraí's Heart should be reserved for better uses. Let the Máister live with it as do the others. There are salves and ointments he could try, and perhaps a better diet . . ."* Meriel had tried to soften the refusal with a smile and Doyle had smiled back at her, but neither of them had meant it.

"Nothing's changed, Shay," Doyle answered softly. "The only one whose mind I don't know is my wife's." He said it as gently as he could, but Padraic still glanced sharply at him. Doyle knew the boy was as torn as Doyle was himself, loving both Mam and Da when the two were at odds. Doyle and Edana had argued—again—this morning, and he was certain that Padraic had overheard at least some of it. "By my count, the vote will be a hand to one . . . with my wife abstaining; a hand to two if she doesn't."

O Blaca's eyes narrowed. "Edana would do that? She'd vote against you here? I don't like that. That will start whispers and dissension."

"The dregs of love are bitterness," Doyle answered, as much for Padraic as O Blaca. "I'm afraid that's all the two

of us have at the moment, though I have hope for better in
the future." He clapped Padraic on the back. "Aye, son?
Your mam's a person who stays with her convictions, and
that is part of why I have always loved her. We have to give
her time, but I have hope. I do."

He went silent then, smiling thinly as they reached the
first ranks of the Riocha, which parted to let the two of
them enter the Halla first. Clad in the dark green clóca of
the Order of Gabair, Doyle moved among the Riocha with
Snapdragon lying prominently on his chest. Among the
Riocha were several members of the Order, all there to
present a showing. He nodded to those he knew well, ex-
changing greetings and well-wishes as he and O Blaca entered Tuatha Halla, handing ritual knives to the quartet of
gardai at the entrance: long tradition dictated that no Riocha was allowed to enter Tuatha Halla bearing a
weapon—though that tradition did not extend to the
clochs na thintrí that many of them wore. Once through
the doors, they found themselves on a gallery overlooking
a great ring of stone thrones on the level below. In the center of the building, a large turf fire burned, the smoke
writhing upward in a coiling dance toward the opening in
the thatch roof. The Ríthe were seated around the fire: a
paltry hand and two in the circular arrangement of a hand
of double-hands of thrones. The painted visages of their
ancestors frowned down on them from the walls, stern and
forbidding.

The Ríthe were leaning toward each other, talking. As
Doyle and O Blaca entered the gallery, followed by the
flood of Riocha, they went silent. Doyle placed himself at
the rail where all the Ríthe could see him, at the stairs leading down to the ring. He glanced at Edana, already sitting
in her throne with the torc of Dún Laoghaire around her
neck. She saw his gaze and turned to her right to speak
with Rí Mas Sithig of Tuath Infochla. Doyle saw a flush
creep upward on her neck. When she glanced back he nodded to her; she looked away again, turning once more to
Mas Sithig and saying something. She did not look at him
again.

Rí Mas Sithig, as eldest of the Rí, nodded to Edana and
bestirred himself. He'd grown fat over the years, his strag-
gly beard looking like a dry autumn field, folds hanging

heavily over weary, yellow-rimmed eyes. Several of his teeth were missing, and Doyle knew from experience that the mint Rí Mas Sithig constantly chewed couldn't hide the scent of rot in those he had left. Every new season brought news that the Rí was ill and might die, but so far he had disappointed his heirs and fought off the Black Haunts. Doyle had been surprised that the man himself had come to the Óenach rather than sending one of his numerous offspring in his place. He spoke slowly and with slurred speech, but anyone who mistook his infirmities for an indication of a dull mind would have been surprised. No Rí could have survived this long without an innate political savvy. As was customary in the Óenach since the Riocha in the gallery were not permitted to speak, he addressed himself only to the other Ríthe.

"We are gathered here again to name an Ard. As First Speaker, I propose that we do so quickly. My old bones dislike the cold of the Halla and there are brighter fires and suppers waiting for all of us back at Dún Laoghaire Keep, thanks to the hospitality of Banrion Mac Ard and her husband." That was accompanied by a faint nod to Doyle in the gallery; Edana seemed interested only in the hands folded on her lap, though Doyle knew her well enough to see how the dimples at the corners of her mouth deepened as her lips tightened. "I know we've talked of little else in the last few days. As First Speaker, I also have the right to name a candidate for vote." He paused, wheezing a bit. "I place before the Ríthe the name of Doyle Mac Ard."

Rí Allister Fearachan of Tuath Connachta, youngest of the Rí, laughed scornfully at that. "Mac Ard?" he said without looking up at the gallery where Doyle watched. "My apologies to the Banrion of Dún Laoghaire for speaking so frankly about her husband, but Doyle Mac Ard's da was Riocha, aye, but his mam was entirely common born, a sheepherder. Not that this is unusual for the Mac Ards, a line that has gained most of its power through convenient marriages. Will we have a second half-breed set before us as Ard?"

Morven Mac Baoill of Tuath Airgialla interrupted with a loud expectoration in the direction of the fire in the center of the thrones. "That 'half-breed' to whom you refer was also the daughter of the First Holder. Perhaps the Rí Con-

nachta makes the mistake of thinking that 'common' also
means 'unimportant.' Seeing who has sprung from the
Aoire line, that's a dangerous assumption. And given the
mood of those common folk you so casually dismiss, I
would say that having an Ard who not only shared blood
with the Healer Ard but who also had some affinity with
the tuathánach would be an asset."

There were murmurs of agreement around the thrones.
Rí Fearachan scowled, sitting back and twirling a forefinger in his full red beard. Edana, Doyle noticed, said nothing. Her face might have been a carving. "There are other
considerations as well," Fearachan persisted. "Name Mac
Ard as Rí Ard, and we also elevate the Order of Gabair.
That's fine for Tuath Gabair, perhaps, but perhaps not for
other Tuatha."

"Did the Order of Inishfeirm rule the Tuatha while the
Healer Ard was on the throne?" Rí Torin Mallaghan shot
back—not surprisingly, since the Order of Gabair's Keep
stood next to his own in Lár Bhaile. "I don't recall seeing
white-robes writing laws for us. I didn't see gardai from
Inish Thuaidh protecting the Banrion Ard, and Lámh Shábhála never once came to Dún Laoghaire in all those years."

Though the Banrion Ard traveled to the First Holder sev-
eral times, and we all know that the Mad Holder was on her
way here, Doyle thought. He could see the same rejoinder
narrow the Rí Connachta's eyes. Fearachan started to answer, but Mas Sithig slammed the end of his walking stick
onto the stone flags. The Halla reverberated with the
sound and Fearachan closed his mouth.

"I've placed Tiarna Mac Ard's name in nomination,"
Mas Sithig said, "and I see no reason to withdraw it." He
groaned as he shifted the huge bulk of his body on the
granite seat of the throne. "And I see no reason to prolong
the agony of my backside here in this Óenach. I say we
vote and then return to the keep and supper." He lifted his
trebled chin with its thin gray hairs. "Infochla says 'Aye,' "
he said.

"Gabair says 'Aye,' " Torin Mallaghan spoke quickly, still
glaring at Fearachan.

"Connachta says 'Nay,' " Fearachan interjected immediately. "Not that it matters. It seems that this ascension was
planned from the start."

"Airgialla says 'Aye,' " Morven Mac Baoill spoke loudly. "And we believe that it matters very much who is Ard. We already have trouble on our borders with the damned Fingerlanders."

Caitrín Taafe, Banrion of Éoganacht, nodded agreement. "Éoganacht also says 'Aye.' The Tuatha will need to work together, not against each other."

Doyle's gaze was caught by movement. Edana had risen from her throne, even as the brown-haired, slight man to her left tugged at his clóca and cleared his throat. "And 'Aye' is also Locha Léin's vote," agreed Eóin O Treasigh, Rí of Tuath Locha Léin. He realized that no one was listening to him, that all of the Riocha in the gallery and the Ríthe on their thrones were staring at Edana.

Doyle saw Torin lean over to Mas Sithig and touch the old Rí's arm with a warning shake of his head, but Mas Sithig had already started to speak. "And Dún Laoghaire?" Mas Sithig asked Edana.

"The Óenach doesn't need Dún Laoghaire's vote," she answered. She looked up at Doyle, and he saw nothing but glacial ice in her eyes. "I can count as well as the rest of you, and you already have your Rí Ard. And I hope your lives with him end up happier than mine."

With that, her gaze dropped away from Doyle and she walked out of the Halla.

"I'm sorry, Mam. I truly am."

Edana turned from the window to find Padraic—dressed in the green clóca of the Order of Gabair, and with his new Cloch Mór lying there on its chain—standing at the door to her inner chamber. "Your maids tried to announce me, but I just came in," he continued. "Da's really upset, you know."

Edana lifted a shoulder. She made no attempt to hide the blotches of red on her cheeks or the trails of moisture from her eyes. "Your da is hardly the only one," she said.

"He wants what's best for the Tuatha, Mam," Padraic said. "He's also doing what he must do to protect us—you and me and the rest of our family. I believe that, even if you don't."

Edana tried to smile at her son. He sounded so much like Doyle. Looking at him, she could see a reflection of the Doyle with whom she'd fallen in love nearly two decades before. Padraic had the same brilliant red hair, the same intense eyes, the same way of standing with his weight shifted to one foot, the same unconscious presence. "I know you believe that, Padraic," she told him. "And I'm glad that you're so certain about your da's intentions. I truly hope you're right."

"But that's not what you believe."

"No." She said it more sharply than she intended and she saw him flinch. "I don't. Not anymore."

"Da cares very much about you, Mam. He loves you still." Padraic tilted his head slightly to the right, lifting his eyebrows as if inviting her to believe him. It was a gesture she'd seen Doyle make a thousand times over the years, and she found herself smiling softly in answer. "I've heard him say it," Padraic continued. "Just today at the Óenach, in fact. I've seen his face when he talks about you. It's just . . ." Padraic shrugged. "Da says that good rulers are married first to their Tuath. That's why they often have trouble in their other marriage."

So I'm to blame for us being apart, because I was Banrion and abandoned him . . . She thought it, but resisted saying it to her son. "You've grown up so much," she said instead. "Your voice, the way you stand and walk . . . Sometimes I forget that you're not the little boy who used to hold up a pebble to the mage-lights at night and pretend he was a Holder."

"Mam . . ."

"I'm sorry, Padraic. It's just . . ." She went to him, putting her arms around him. She felt him resist for a moment, then allow her to embrace him. Their clochs lay together, a hard barrier between them. "I always loved your da and our children first," she told him, whispering the words into his hair. "I always loved you. And your Aunt Meriel . . . I knew that it was the same with her, that she loved Owaine and her children ferociously, without any excuses or reservations." She stepped back slightly, holding his head in her hands so that they gazed in each other's eyes. "Aye, sometimes a ruler must put her duties first. But that doesn't mean she can't love or that any affection she feels toward someone else is doomed.

"Do you still love Da?"

"I don't know." She saw the hurt in his eyes at her honesty. She kissed his forehead and then hugged him once more before stepping back. "The truth is that your da has a jealous and demanding mistress."

Padraic shook his head. "No, Mam. I've never seen him with anyone else. Ever."

She smiled at his defense of Doyle. "She's not a person," Edana told him. "She's his Ambition, and once I thought that I was stronger than she was. Once I thought that I'd driven her away. I was wrong. I underestimated her determination and her influence and the lengths to which she would go, and because of that, Meriel and Owaine and Jenna and all the others are dead."

Padraic shook his head. "I don't like that either, Mam. Aunt Meriel was a good woman and I loved her also, and Kayne and Sevei . . ." He ran the tip of his tongue over his lips. "That act wasn't Da's doing, Mam. Aye, he attacked Aunt Meriel's mam, but in that there wasn't a choice. The Mad Holder would never have given up Lámh Shábhála voluntarily." If Edana had closed her eyes, it could have been Doyle speaking. "You know that. But even so, Da *didn't* kill them, Mam. I was there when he confronted the First Holder, remember? It was all so chaotic, with all the clochs fighting. The Holder threw *herself* into the sea, and then poor Sevei leaped after her . . ."

He stopped. She could see the pain and grief in his face, and she remembered, a few months before Sevei left for Inishfeirm, finding Padraic and Sevei laughing as they sat and talked with one another, their hands intertwined, and walking away softly before they noticed her. Edana could well imagine how conflicted and confused and hurt Padraic had been, being there when she'd been lost to the waves. "You can't blame Da for everything, Mam. You can't. This wasn't his doing or his plan. He had no choice."

Your da used the same words, and I didn't believe him either. He touched his cloch, and Edana realized that it was no longer a clochmion her son wore, but a Cloch Mór: the one named Snarl, which had once belonged to Máister Kirwan. So there was yet another casualty.

We always have a choice, she started to say to him, but swallowed the words instead. She lifted her hand to his cheek again, feeling the downy stubble there. "I don't entirely blame Doyle," she told him. "You can tell your da that. I don't blame him for all that happened."

She hoped it was true.

28

A Binding to Stone

"**I** KNOW THIS PLACE," Sevei said. She stared up at the gigantic statue perched on the edge of the sea cliff.

The trees of Thall Coill moved well away from the cliff here, as if the oaks themselves were somehow afraid to approach too closely to the statue of black, glossy stone, a material unlike any Sevei had ever seen. She couldn't quite decide what the huge carving was supposed to represent: the creature it depicted—four-legged and sitting like a cat perched on a sunlit ledge, contained feline elements but also seemed part dragon, part dog, or perhaps winged creature, since there were long broken ridges alongside its spine that might have been the remnants of long-lost wings. The stone was weathered and eroded from long centuries, the features blurred by time, and it looked as if the entire statue, rearing thirty or more feet above her head, had been ripped from the ground and then smashed down again at an angle. Its back legs were buried in the earth, the front paws resting on air, and a jagged crack stuttered along its haunches.

Far below, she could hear waves crashing in foam against the rocks and the barking cough of seals.

Whatever the statue was intended to be, it was impressive. Staring up at the distant head, Sevei shivered though the day was warm and the sun glinted on the polished stone. There was a sense of hidden power, something greater than mere mortality.

"I know this," Sevei repeated, her voice hushed with

awe. "Or rather, I've heard of it. This is Bethiochnead. This is the place of the Scrúdú, the test that Holders of Lámh Shábhála have taken. That my gram . . ." She blinked, unbidden tears rising at the name.

"That your gram underwent," Beryn finished for her. "And that she, like all the rest of you Daoine who have tried, failed."

Sevei's eyes narrowed in annoyance at Beryn's tone. "She didn't fail. She *passed* the Scrúdú. She must have. Those who fail the test die. That's what I was taught."

"Aye, all the others who failed perished here. I don't know why Jenna lived, but I know that she didn't succeed with the Scrúdú. I would know. We would *all* know if that had happened."

"But Máister Kirwan said—"

"Did the First Holder herself claim to have succeeded?" Beryn interrupted gently.

Sevei thought back to the conversations that she'd had with Jenna. Her gram rarely discussed the time surrounding her rise to Banrion of Inish Thuaidh, but on a few occasions, usually when she'd had more wine or ale than usual with her supper, Jenna had talked about those days. But even then, Jenna had remained reticent to talk about what had happened in Thall Coill. Sevei recalled the time that Máister Kirwan had spoken to one of her classes about the Scrúdú. *"Our First Holder underwent the Scrúdú, which few holders of Lámh Shábhála dare to even contemplate,"* he'd said. *"We don't truly know the histories of the Bunús Muintir holders, but we do know that of our Daoine ancestors. Caenneth Mac Noll in 241, Heremon O Laighin in 280, Ioseph MacCana in 333, Maitiú O'Doelan in 517, Garad Mhúllien in 662, Peria Ó Riain in 671: they all died undergoing this test. Only once has a Daoine survived the Scrúdú, whatever it might be—and that person was Jenna Aoire who is now Banrion Jenna MacEagan, the First Holder . . ."*

She realized now that Máister Kirwan had never said Jenna had passed the test, only that she, somehow, had managed to live through it.

"It was Jenna who broke the statue, years ago," Beryn said. "I was a young man, then, and I watched her lift Bethiochnead with the power of Lámh Shábhála and bring it crashing down again. I felt the ground shudder underneath me as it struck."

"That was the Scrúdú, then?" Sevei asked. "She would never tell us what it was. Even Máister Kirwan didn't know for certain."

But Beryn shook his head. "No. I know that wasn't the test. Whatever the Scrúdú might be, it's something that the holder of Lámh Shábhála faces inside. What they struggle against, we can't see with our eyes. And they die. They have always died. Except for Jenna. Your gram."

"Even the Bunús Muintir who have tried?"

Beryn gave a small smile at that, his brown, wide face creasing. "Most, aye," he said. "Bethiochnead—the statue—was here even when we Bunús Muintir first came to this land long, long generations before you Daoine arrived. We found Bethiochnead already here where we also found Lámh Shábhála, and it seemed immeasurably old even then. It's said that Carrohkai Treemaster, who was the third Holder of Lámh Shábhála, passed the Scrúdú though she lived only a few years more afterward. But in that short time, she performed wonders: it was she who brought the eldest trees to full life and gave them the voices that they keep even now today. It's her magic that allowed the old forests like Doire, Foraois, and Thall to remain alive and vital through the centuries when the mage-lights vanish, that keep them active even now. Who knows what she could have done had she lived longer. But she was old when she underwent the Scrúdú, and the ordeal weakened her body. She was buried here, where she could be near Bethiochnead. See—that faint rise there, near where the trees start? That's her barrow, though it looks hardly different now than the rest of the land."

"She was the only one?"

A shrug. "Not the only. But one of the very few."

When he didn't elaborate, Sevei stared back up at the blank, towering creature. "Bethiochnead," she whispered. She walked up to its enormous flank and placed her hand on a glassy paw, then withdrew it abruptly, sucking in her breath. "It's *cold*," she said, glancing up at the sun.

"Bethiochnead is always bitter cold, even on the warmest days," Beryn told her. "It always has been."

The mage-lights are always cold, and Gram always com-

plained at how frigid her poor scarred arm was. Sevei put her hand gingerly back on the stone. The coldness was deep and surprising, like plunging her hand into an ice-crusted stream in the mountains. And with the touch, she thought she heard laughter.

She snatched her hand back again, cradling it to her chest. She felt a touch of fur on the back of her leg.

"It wants *you* to take the Scrúdú."

She thought Beryn said it and turned around quizzically, but she realized that she heard the voice not through her ears but in her head. A blue seal lay on the grass behind her, startlingly close. Its dark fur was marked with the swirls of the mage-lights. "Bhralhg?" She remembered then. "Of course. You had me brought here. That's what Kekeri told me."

Bhralhg leaned his head forward again, brushing her side. "Aye." A cough came from the Saimhóir's throat though the voice sounded clear in her head. His head bobbed down and she saw the glint of silver as a chain slipped from his thick neck onto a bit of bare limestone at her feet. A hint of emerald glittered in the sunlight.

"Lámh Shábhála!" Sevei shouted. "You found it!" She started to lean down to pick it up, but Beryn raised his hand, palm toward her, shaking his head, and Bhralhg waddled forward so that his body shadowed the stone. She stopped. "Where was it? When did you find it?"

"I found the cloch the day before your gram died," Bhralhg told her.

"*Before* Gram died?" The excitement Sevei felt shifted to suspicion. "But that means . . ."

"Aye," Bralhg answered. "I had the cloch and I didn't tell you. I had the cloch and I chose not to give it back to her."

"Why?" She didn't trust herself to say more than the bare syllable.

"Because the First Holder was already broken and dying, and I didn't know that I wanted you to have it." The lack of hesitation in his answer indicated that hers was a question he'd expected. "Because I didn't know if you were the one who *should* have it."

Suspicion flowed into anger. "*You* didn't know? Lámh Shábhála belonged to Gram. What gives you the right to choose, one way or the other?"

Bhralhg lifted his snout, rising up on his front flippers. "If you think that Lámh Shábhála doesn't have some choice in the matter, then you're more foolish than I thought. The cloch came to me when it could have just as easily let you find it. That tells me that it wanted me to make the choice." His snout dropped back down, and his voice softened in her head. "If you'd found it while your gram was alive, what would you have done with it, Sevei?"

"Why, I would have—" She stopped. The seal's head lifted, the folds of thick fat around his neck smoothing, and she knew he'd seen the answer in her face.

"Aye, you'd have given it back to your gram—and that's why Lámh Shábhála hid itself. It was done with Jenna."

"You make the stone seem alive."

"Bradán an Chumhacht, the Salmon of Power that I swallowed, is definitely alive. Why wouldn't Lámh Shábhála also be alive?" The Saimhóir blinked heavily, the hairs at the end of his snout twitching. He snuffled, his nostrils flaring.

Beryn had been silent as he leaned on his staff and listened to the exchange, seeming to understand both the Saimhóir's language as well as Sevei's. He cleared his throat. "Your gram would have told you that it was alive, too," he said to Sevei. "It contains the voices of all the Holders. Your gram is there now, with the others."

That sent Sevei's gaze back to the cloch. "Why did you bring me here?" she asked them.

"To give you Lámh Shábhála," Bhralhg said. "To see you put it on *here*"— his gaze went to the statue whose color was that of his own eyes, "—where Bethiochnead will test you."

"Here is where I'll die, then." She said it scornfully, as if she were refusing the gift of Gram's cloch, but her gaze would not leave the gem. She wondered what it would feel like to put it on, to use it . . .

"Perhaps," Bhralhg answered placidly. "That's certainly possible. Even likely."

"Then why? Give it to Beryn—I'm sure the Bunús Muintir would love to have the cloch back again."

"We would," Beryn told her. "And we *will* have it if you refuse to take it or if you fail the Scrúdú. But I'd rather see it in your hand, and so would Bhralhg."

"Then I still don't understand."

"When the First Holder brought Lámh Shábhála back to life, we rejoiced." The voice was accompanied by the grunting tones of the Saimhóir: Bhralhg. "We were pleased because the First Holder was more than Daoine: she was Saimhóir also, and she was Bunús Muintir. The mingled blood of three races of the Aware flowed within her. Finally, we thought, here was someone who could pass the Scrúdú, who could take Lámh Shábhála's power and do more than just war with it, who would be a champion for all races already awake or yet to be awakened. In that, we were wrong."

"Gram loved the Bunús Muintir," Sevei said angrily. "And the Saimhóir. If you think she didn't, then you obviously didn't know her."

"Neither of us means any insult to Jenna," Beryn said. He used the tip of the oaken staff to prod the cloch. The chain clinked faintly. "She held Lámh Shábhála longer than most Holders could. She survived the Scrúdú when no other Daoine had."

When Beryn said nothing more, Sevei raised an eyebrow toward him. "But?"

"Jenna took the power of Lámh Shábhála and made herself a ruler who served your people well. I would like to see the next Holder make herself a ruler who serves *all* peoples well."

"And you'd do that, Beryn?" Sevei asked him. She could not keep the scorn from her voice. "Then why don't you take Lámh Shábhála without waiting for me? Since you and Bhralhg share the same concerns, I'm sure Bhralhg wouldn't stop you. Why, you can bring your people back to prominence with it—at least until the Riocha send an army and the rest of the Clochs Mór to stop you."

Eyes the color of stained, old oak regarded her sternly and she thought he was going to retort, but it was Bhralhg who answered. "I offered it to Beryn already. When I found it, after you left to go back with your people, I came here immediately. He convinced me that an Aoire was still the proper Holder." The Saimhóir hunkered down close to the cloch, as if tired. Glossy fur rippled as he shifted his weight "Jenna survived the Scrúdú. Beryn and I think that her progeny might be able to do more." He nudged the chain with his snout. "Take it. Take the legacy of your gram. She's there inside, waiting for you."

Bhralhg pushed himself awkwardly backward with his flippers. Lámh Shábhála gleamed on the limestone, snared in its cage. Sevei took a step toward it, feeling their gaze on her: watching, appraising. She crouched down in the sparse grass beside the jewel.

She'd never seen it anywhere but on Gram's breast, had certainly never touched it or held it. Her Da had said that once Gram offered it to Sevei's mam but that Meriel had refused it, preferring instead the healing ability of Treoraí's Heart despite the greater power that holding Lámh Shábhála would have given her. There was no such hesitation in Sevei; she knew that she would give up Dragoncaller without a qualm if it meant she could take Lámh Shábhála. But yet she paused, seeing in her mind the constant pain that had hounded Gram and turned her face into a twisted, angry mask. She saw the white pattern of mage-scars that reached from Gram's hand nearly all the way to the shoulder. She recalled the agony that Gram endured after Lámh Shábhála was lost. She wondered what Máister Kirwan, if he was still alive, would tell her. She could nearly hear his voice: *"You're not ready, Sevei. You've barely learned how to handle the clochmion. How can you possibly think you're capable not only of controlling Lámh Shábhála, but of meeting the challenge of the Scrúdú? It will consume you, girl. Look what it did to your gram."*

"It's not a gift. It's a burden," Beryn said, as if guessing her thoughts.

"Are you trying to convince me to take it or to leave it?"

Beryn's face creased into a smile. "Neither," he answered. "And both."

"And if I pick it up, will the Scrúdú start?"

"Not yet. Not until you've taken it as your own and filled it again with the mage-lights. Then . . . that's when it will start."

She looked up at the Bunús Muintir, unable to keep the apprehension from her voice. "What will it be like?"

"I don't know. But perhaps those inside Lámh Shábhála can tell you." He looked at her with sympathy. "You're right to be afraid, Sevei. In fact, that's the paradox: if you're not afraid to take up Lámh Shábhála, then you're not the right person to hold it."

"My great-uncle Doyle would disagree."

"Aye, he would." Beryn spoke with some satisfaction. "And you'll notice that he doesn't have the cloch."

From the woods, they heard a dire wolf howl. The shadow of Bethiochnead slid closer to them. Bhralhg grumbled low and guttural in his massive throat. "No one will think less of you if you make the same decision as your mam."

That brought her head up. "Mam's dead," she said to them. "Da, Gram, Ionhar, Tara, Ennis, Dillon, Máister Kirwan: they're all dead, those I loved, all of them but Kayne. I wonder—is revenge a good reason to want power?"

Doubts rose in her head like wisps of fog from a bog. Before they could overwhelm her, she pulled Dragoncaller from around her neck and in the same motion, reached down and plucked Lámh Shábhála from the ground. She closed her hand around the cloch.

"Oh . . ." she breathed, her eyes widening. "Oh . . ."

The world around her faded away, lost in a lattice of green crystal. Lámh Shábhála surrounded her, and it was alive with voices: a hand, two, a hundred, a thousand or more: all yammering at her. Sevei forced herself to concentrate, to find the one voice she wanted most to hear.

"*This one's too young . . .*"

"*She'll die, like all the others.*"

"*She's not even been adequately trained. She doesn't know . . .*"

Then: "*Sevei . . .*" The voice was simultaneously sad and pleased. "*I'm here, my dear. I'm here . . .*"

"Gram! Is that really you?"

A dozen different voices answered. "*Aye!*"

"*Lámh Shábhála holds the shape of all its Holders.*"

"*But a shape isn't the reality.*"

"*We're not real, only reflections caught forever.*"

"*Quiet!*" Jenna's voice shouted, and the other voices receded. "*So you hold Lámh Shábhála now . . . That means I'm dead. But at least the pain is gone, and I can think again. And you . . .*" Sevei felt something brush her mind, memories shuffling unbidden. When Jenna's voice returned, it was with a tone of sorrow. "*You mean to take the Scrúdú . . .*"

"Aye," Sevei told her. "Will you help me, Gram?"

There was a long hesitation and again the other voices intruded. *"You're too young and inexperienced . . ."*

"The First Holder failed the test herself . . ."

"Hope? There's no hope in this . . ."

"You'll be with us, very soon."

"Just another lost voice in the stone . . ."

Then Gram's voice banished the others. *"I can show you the place inside Lámh Shábhála that I found. Beyond that . . ."* Her voice faded and returned. *"Oh, Sevei. You don't know . . ."*

"You'll die . . ."

"Bethiochnead will crush you . . ."

". . . you'll be here with us . . ."

". . . with us . . ."

". . . dead . . ." the voices whispered.

Sevei forced them away, shoving them to the back of her mind. The emerald walls faded around her, and she was standing again next to the broken statue with Beryn and Bhralhg. The Bunús Muintir and the Saimhóir stared at her.

"I'll do it," she said. "As soon as the mage-lights come."

PART THREE

ALLIANCE

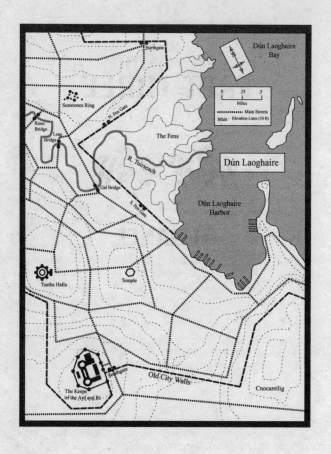

Dún Laoghaire Bay

Dún Laoghaire

0   .25   .5
Miles

••••••• Main Streets
Main · Elevation Lines (50 ft)

Northgate

Sunstones Ring

N. Fen Gate

The Fens

Riase
Bridge

Leac
Bridge

R. Tuirseach

Gal Bridge

S. Fen Gate

Dún Laoghaire
Harbor

Tuatha Halla

Temple

Southgate

Old City Walls

The Keeps
of the Ard and Rí

Cnocareilig

29

Another Binding

A TAP ON THE FOREHEAD, a fist touching her heart, and then a tap on Kayne's own forehead: Séarlait's gestures were accompanied by a kiss to the side of his neck. *I love you* . . . Kayne stirred—groaning as still-healing ribs pulled—and Séarlait took the opportunity to snuggle into the curve of his back, her arm around him. He could feel her fingers gently tracing the raised lines of the battle scars on his chest. He was warm under the fur that covered them, but the tent above drummed with the patter of rain and it was bright enough to see. Kayne watched the shadows of droplets hitting the fabric and washing away to join the small river that poured from the overhang. A steady drip plonked from a leak in the tent to form a small, dark pool in the carpet-covered grass just past their feet. Kayne yawned and kissed Séarlait, luxuriating in the feel of her.

"We have to get up," he said. "As much as I don't want to . . . It's an important day, eh?"

She grinned at him and yanked the fur away from him, grinning as she did so. She stared at his body, naked except for Blaze on its chain around his neck, but her gaze was directed lower than that. The grin widened.

Kayne shivered at the assault of cold air. "You're evil, you know that?" he told her, and tried to snatch the fur away from her also, She laughed and hugged it tighter to herself. "Maybe I should change my mind."

As Séarlait pouted overdramatically, boots squelched in mud outside their tent flap and they heard the careful clearing of a throat. "Tiarna?"

Séarlait made a face at Kayne. "Give us a moment, Harik," Kayne said, and the boots retreated a judicious distance. As Kayne quickly performed his morning ablutions and dressed himself, Séarlait grimaced and let the fur fall away from her. She smiled at him, seeing him watching her as she, too, started to dress. All around, they could hear the encampment coming to life. A cook fire sent fragrant smoke wafting through the rain, and a kettle whistled for attention.

When Séarlait was ready, Kayne lifted the tent flap, blinking at the gray morning.

They were camped high in the mountains of the Finger. The South Road, leading away from the High Road that ran down the length of the Finger until it reached the town of Colkill on the Tween Sea, curved in the valley below them through a thin stand of beeches and elms, following the twists and turns of a river thrashing furiously in its bed of dark stones. No one moved along the road in either direction as far as they could see. Yesterday, Kayne could look out to the south and see in the hazy distance the endless waves of the Tween; today he could barely see a mile before the rain and clouds turned everything to gray soup. "Lovely weather," Kayne said to Harik, pulling the hood of his oilcloth cape over his head. Harik stood bareheaded, the rain turning his thinning hair into straggling dark strands that dripped water from their curled ends.

"Bad for us; worse for them," Harik grunted. He nodded to Séarlait; if he was thinking anything, he kept it from his face. "One of the clan scouts has come back with word that there's a good-sized force on the High Road near Lough Tory, flying the colors of Tuath Airgialla: a thousand men or more, and several Riocha among them. She said she suspects at least some of them have clochs. We've had a moon of peace, now it looks like Ri Mac Baoill intends to have his vengeance for Mal's death. The Rí himself isn't with the column, though—he might want revenge, but he's not going to risk his own life to gain it."

"How's the response been to the clan-lairds' call?"

"We had another few hands of volunteers arrive overnight," Harik answered. "Boys, old men, a few women. That gives us maybe three hundred up in the Narrows, most armed with farm implements and rusty swords that belonged to their great-great-das." Harik kept his scarred face stern and noncommittal, but Kayne could hear the worry and pessimism underlying his voice.

"We don't need numbers, Harik," Kayne told him. "We need this land that the clansfolk know so well, we need to use the clansfolk's tactics, and we need to warm our hearts and our courage with the memory of those who have already died in this treachery. We'll harass them and whittle them down a hand at a time as they come through the passes and down the High Road and then slip away where they can't follow. They can't win here, not in the home of the clansfolk. Remember Ceangail."

"Aye, Tiarna." He didn't sound entirely convinced.

"Well said, young Tiarna," Laird O'Blathmhaic's voice boomed. He strode up to them, leaning heavily on his cane. He ignored the rain that muddied his boots, beaded on his furs, and plastered the few strands of hair to his age-spotted scalp. Séarlait ran to him and hugged him. " 'Morning, Séarlait, me darlin'. A glorious day, 'tis," he said, then laughed as Kayne involuntarily glanced up at the sky. "Ah, that?" he said. " 'Tis no bother at all. Another stripe and rain'll be gone and the sun'll be drying all." He pointed to the west, where indeed it seemed that the clouds were more broken, with a hint of blue behind them. He stared hard at Kayne, his bearded chin lifting as he blinked into the rain. "An' you, Tiarna—do you still intend to keep your word to me?"

Kayne took Séarlait's hand. "Aye, I do, Laird."

The man grinned and slapped Kayne on the shoulder, sending water flying. "Good!" he shouted. "Then let's make ready. The Draíodóir should be here by midday."

With that, O'Blathmhaic took Séarlait by the arm and walked toward the tent covering the main cook fire. Kayne started to follow him. "Tiarna," Harik said. When Kayne turned to look, he saw Harik watching Séarlait and her great-da. "Are you sure of this?" He spoke low enough that neither the clan-laird nor Séarlait could hear the question.

"Aye," Kayne told him. "I am."

Harik's lips moved as if he were about to speak, but he took a breath instead, looking down at the ground before returning his gaze to Kayne. "It's not my business to know, Tiarna, but I'd ask your da the same if he were here. Are you doing this because you love the woman, or because it's the best way to bind the clansfolk to us?"

You're right. It's not your business to know. Kayne nearly said the words aloud. But he looked at Harik's solemn face and saw the man who had been at his da's side for the last several years, who had kept the gardai here with Kayne. *He deserves more than that.* "You still worry that she's not my peer, Harik?"

The man's head moved in a brief and careful nod.

"I understand, Harik. But I'd remind you again to remember that my gram was nothing but a tuathánach."

Harik was already waving his hand. "I know all this and we've had the argument before. But I would ask you to consider this: if we do fight our way back to Dún Laoghaire, if we do prevail, then you will have a claim to the throne of the Ard. I may not be Riocha, but I know that marriage is more often an alliance than a romance. The one who will be Ard may need to make such an alliance, and not with the clans of the Finger."

"Mam married for love, not politics."

"Aye," Harik said. "And your da was a good man, and worthy. But—"

Kayne cut off Harik's response, holding out his hand palm up between them—like a Riocha gesturing to someone beneath his status, Kayne realized belatedly, but Harik closed his mouth. "I'm my da's son, and also my mam's," Kayne told him. "I'm tuathánach and céili giallnai and Riocha all, and I'll marry who I want and not worry about what others might think. I want my Hand to feel the same way. Does he?"

Slowly, Harik's face relaxed into a grudging smile. "Aye," he told Kayne finally. "He will, because he must."

The Draíodóir was there in a stripe and a half, by which time the rain had gone from downpour to drizzle to mist while the sun peered from behind wind-shredded clouds and sent rainbows scattering behind the eastern mountains. The priest was an old woman whose face was as deeply wrinkled as the bark on an old maple tree. She rode up to their encampment on a mule who looked to be similarly old and slow. When Laird O'Blathmhaic made as if to hurry her along, she simply glared at him through dark eyes nearly lost in the ruddy folds of her cheeks. She spat on the ground and handed Laird O'Blathmhaic her pack as if the man were a servant. "Take that up to the menhir," she said brusquely, though she gave Séarlait a quick smile and her eyes glittered as if amused. She slapped away Kayne's hand when he tried to help her dismount.

"I'm old, not dead," she snapped at him. "If you want to help, hold this miserable excuse for a beast still." With a sidelong glance at Séarlait, who was concealing a smile, Kayne held the mule's bridle while the old woman grunted and groaned and finally slid from the mule's back. The top of her head was no higher than the bottom of Kayne's rib cage as she stretched. Her hair was pure white and long, plaited in four strands tied together with a length of tartan cloth. She yawned, showing teeth still amazingly white and strong. "You're the tiarna?" she asked.

"Aye," he answered

"Bring the mule with you, then," she said. "You both probably have the same temperament." She went to Séarlait and took her arm, following Laird O'Blathmhaic up the mountainside and away from the encampment. The mule was gazing at Kayne with placid, large brown eyes. Kayne rubbed the gray muzzle. "Come on, then," he told the animal. "Only the Mother knows what she'll do if we're late."

A menhir loomed at the top of the hill, a standing stone nearly twice as tall as Kayne, its black sides carved with stylized animals. Kayne could recognize seals, wolves, eagles, and dragons, though there were also creatures he did not recognize at all. The creatures were entwined in vines and adorned with letters that he could not read: the Bunús Muintir language. The stone, O'Blathmhaic said, had been here since before the clansfolk came to the Fingerlands. In the center of the stone, about two arm spans up from where it met the earth, a large hole had been bored entirely through the stone, the arc of an eyebrow carved above it so that it seemed that the stone watched the valley below.

Most of the encampment had gathered near the stone: rudely-dressed clansfolk and the tattered remnants of the gardai, all forming a rough circle around the stone. Rodhlann O Morchoe nodded as Kayne passed, the Fingerlander commander's cheek lined with a jagged brown scab where an Airgiallaian sword had grazed him. Harik was there also—he touched his chest in salute to Kayne as he passed. The Draíodóir had taken her pack from O'Blathmhaic. From its leather mouth she produced two wide and shallow pewter bowls, into which she poured water from a wax-sealed flagon. She dropped a silver half-mórceint into each bowl.

"You first," she said to Kayne. "Take off your boots. Sit here." A long-fingered, arthritic hand waved toward a large boulder alongside the menhir.

Kayne did as directed, sitting on the boulder with his feet bare. The Draíodóir handed Séarlait one of the bowls along with a white cloth. Séarlait knelt in front of Kayne and washed his feet, smiling a bit as he grimaced at the touch of the cold water. She dried his feet with the towel, then stood facing the menhir and flung the dirty water over her left shoulder, the half-mórceint clinking as it struck rocks and bounced. There was a commotion as the nearest onlookers rushed to grab the coin, one of them finally holding it aloft in triumph. The Draíodóir grinned. "Good luck will follow both you and the lovers," he told the man, the words spoken with the cadence of a ritual. Then she looked at Kayne. "Your turn," she said.

Séarlait took off her own boots and sat on the boulder, and Kayne washed her feet as she'd done his. When he finished, Séarlait nodded to him and then the bowl, and he stood facing the menhir as she had, tossing water and coin over his left shoulder. Again, there was a scramble for the coin, this time from the women among the onlookers. When one of them held aloft the coin, the Draíodóir gave her the blessing and then looked at Kayne. "Do you have your bride-gift, Tiarna?"

Séarlait came to stand alongside Kayne. She lifted her Cloch Mór to the old woman, and the Draíodóir's eyes widened. "Ah," she breathed. She reached out with a trembling finger, stopping just short of touching the clear stone. She raised her eyebrows to Kayne. "Now that is a rare gift. And you, Séarlait? What is your husband-gift?"

Séarlait slipped a ring from her thumb. It was formed of

hard jet, polished and smooth and carved with the sigil of a bear. "That was her da's—my son's," Laird O'Blathmhaic said as Séarlait handed the ring to Kayne. "I gave it to him when he was married. She took it from his hand after he was killed."

Séarlait took Kayne's left hand. Her eyes were moist as she looked up at him. Her da's ring slipped easily onto his forefinger.

The Draíodóir grunted. "This way, then," she said.

She led them both to the menhir, placing Séarlait alongside the northern face and Kayne on the southern. "Clasp your hands through the Eye of the stone," she told them. Kayne slid his hand into the hole in the standing stone and found Séarlait's hand. They linked fingers as the Draíodóir put her hands on either side of the menhir. The old woman closed her eyes.

"The Mother sees this handfasting and smiles," she intoned. "Let it be so for a year and day, and more."

Still holding Séarlait's hand through the menhir, Kayne looked out at the crowd. Laird O'Blathmhaic and Rodhlann were smiling, as were the clansfolk and the gardai.

It was only Harik who frowned.

30

The Haunted Ship

HAUGHEY STOOD AT the wharf and stared out over the green waves toward the distant ship, wallowing near Oldman Head at the mouth of the harbor.

Haughey: I am bringing something that you won't believe. Something of great importance to the Thane considering our current troubles. Make sure you meet the ship at the dock.

That's what the message wrapped around the leg of the white pigeon had said, in Artol Jantsk's tiny, neat handwriting. The pigeon had arrived four days ago now, and Haughey had started worrying when the ship didn't arrive in the days following the pigeon's appearance. Yesterday, a fishing vessel had returned saying that they'd seen the ship approaching, and Haughey had waited most of the day today for it to dock.

Haughey: before the mess of the last several years, that's all anyone had ever called him. Haughey. Even he had forgotten whether that was his given name or surname. Now he was no longer just Haughey. Now he was the Ionadaí Haughey, His August Thane's representative in Cairnmor, not that Haughey had been to Concordia to report to the Thane in over three years, not since the blasted Arruk made their most recent push and effectively cut off the western coast of Mid Céile from its capital. Torness, the usual port for ships coming over from the Tuatha and the only large port in Upper Céile, had been overrun by the Arruk in '64. Before then, Cairnmor had been a slumbering harbor town where trading ships rarely came, the harbor clogged with fishing vessels that seined the banks of the Tween Sea for its abundant fish. Since the fall of Torness, Cairnmor had become the primary harbor for goods moving between Talamh an Ghlas and Céile Mhór, and Haughey had been transformed from a rather minor functionary to Ionadaí for the Thane. Haughey's position was now far more visible to Concordia and Thane MagWolfagdh.

In Haughey's mind, this was quite the opposite of an improvement. Haughey had been happy before. In the three years since his promotion, he was beginning to see gray hairs sprout at his temples and on his chin, and there was a constant burning in his stomach.

Among the multitude of new tasks which had been placed in Haughey's unwilling hands, a secondary function was to serve as the conduit for information regarding the Tuatha. Artol Jantsk was one of the Thane's multitude of eyes and ears in Talamh an Ghlas, and as such, was also Haughey's responsibility.

And now Jantsk was coming in bearing "something of great importance to the Thane," and there was a problem. A fire burned in Haughey's gut as he stared at the harbor.

"Why aren't they coming in?" Haughey asked querulously, glancing down again at Jantsk's cryptic note and wishing the man had been less mysterious about what he had. "It's after midday already."

Cairnmor's harbor master, a thin and harried little man, shook his head at Haughey's side. The lighthouse on Oldman Head had seen the ship the night before in the glow of the mage-lights, but they'd thought that the captain had decided to wait until morning and better light to avoid the shoals off Oldman Head. The keeper had also claimed that the mage-lights were swirling all around the ship, but everyone in town knew that the Oldman Keeper was a bit daft after too many years alone out on the Head.

"I don't know, Ionadaí," the harbor master answered. "We gave them the flag from Oldman Head to enter the harbor, but I've been watching them for half a stripe now and they're not making headway at all—see, the sails are down and the oars are unshipped. It's only the tide that's brought her closer, and that's due to change in the next stripe or so." The harbor master stroked his bearded chin. "I think you have a problem out there, Haughey."

Haughey didn't miss the emphasis on the word "you." He sighed. He hated problems. Problems meant more work. He stared at the paper the pigeon had brought once again and crumpled the sheet in his hand. He sighed. "Get me a boat," he said. "I'm going out."

A stripe and a half later, the currach was close enough to Jantsk's vessel to see that there was no one on deck at all. The young fisherman who'd been drafted to row Haughey out shivered visibly as he stared at the barnacle-encrusted wood and the ship rocking silently in the waves. "That ship's been taken by the Black Haunts, Ionadaí," he said. "Look at it. Canna you feel it?"

Haughey shivered himself at the man's words. "Hello!" he called loudly. "Jantsk! Are you there? Jantsk!"

There was no answer beyond the slapping of water against wood and the creaking of the masts. "I think we should go back," the fisherman said. "Only the Mother knows what's aboard that ship: fever or murder or worse. Let's leave it, Ionadaí."

Haughey wanted desperately to do exactly that. He wanted to go back to his house and pretend that the pigeon had never arrived, that Jantsk was still somewhere in Talamh an Ghlas or that the ship had been lost at sea. But he was the Ionadaí, and the Thane wasn't known to be particularly forgiving of those Ionadaí who failed him. With the current troubles in Céile Mhór, the Thane's mood was treacherous and foul. Haughey took a breath and tried to ignore the churning in his bowels. "Pull alongside," he told the man. "There—where that rope's hanging."

The fisherman obeyed with little grace, rowing the currach through the swells until it bumped against the side of the trading vessel with a hollow, ominous *dhoomp* that made both of them shudder. The wind died at the same moment, and they both inhaled the odor at the same moment: the scent of rotten meat, of corruption. The fisherman made a quick, furtive gesture to ward off evil. The burning in Haughey's gut reached white heat.

Haughey grabbed for the rope, grimacing at the slime-slick braids as he held them steady. He looked at the fisherman, whose eyes were wide enough to show whites entirely around the pupils. "Stay here," he told the man, afraid that as soon as he went aboard he'd see the currach rowing frantically for home. "Do you understand? You stay here until I get back." The man nodded, and Haughey grasped the rope and pulled himself up, managing to pull himself over the railing onto the deck.

"Oh, by the Mother . . . !" He wasn't able to stop the exclamation. He brought up the collar of his léine to cover his mouth and nose.

The ship had carried a crew of eight, including its captain. The deck was a charnel house; Haughey counted five bodies on the deck: one draped over the oaken tiller as if he he'd died at his post; two more huddled near the mast; the remaining two reclining against the overturned rowboat that served as an emergency ship and shuttle for the vessel. From the look of them, all had been dead for several days. The gulls, the sun and the rain had been at them. The rotting flesh had been peeled away in some places to expose the bones. They all wore plain ship's clothing: crewmen.

The smell of death pervaded the ship, and from the stench Haughey suspected that he'd find the rest of the bodies belowdecks.

The captain was in his cabin, in his bed. Also dead. The other two members of the crew Haughey found in their tiny bunks, their corpses drawn up in fetal positions with expressions of exquisite agony etched on their frozen faces. With his shirt still held over his nose and mouth, Haughey went to the door of the small passenger's cabin, which would have been Jantsk's. It was closed and he knocked, even though he knew there'd be no answer. He turned the latch and the door creaked open on rusted hinges. "Jantsk?" he called.

Jantsk didn't answer. Could *never* answer, Haughey saw as his eyes adjusted slowly to the dimness. In the light of the cabin's single, tiny window, he saw Jantsk lying on the bed, the same expression of awful pain distorting the tattoo of the bird on his face, his hands drawn in claws as they clutched the blanket that was half drawn over him. "Jantsk," he said to the staring body, "what in the name of the Mother happened here?"

A sound nearly made him jump. Haughey skittered backward, nearly falling over Jantsk's trunk and putting his back to the cabin wall. In the shadows of the corner of the room behind the door, something—someone—moved. "Help me," a small, high voice said. "Please help me. They're dead. They're all . . . dead."

The form shuffled forward: a boy, Haughey saw. The poor thing was no more than nine or ten years old: thin, scrawny, and dark-haired, with tears mottling his cheeks. "I'm so scared. So scared . . ." The voice had the accent of Talamh an Ghlas.

"I'm the only one left," the boy said. "The only one . . ."

Haughey's wife made a fuss over the boy as if he were one of their own sons found alive after he'd been feared lost. She crooned and clucked and mothered him, wrapping the boy in the blanket she'd knitted for their own youngest— just married now after the Festival of Fómhar—and setting more food on the table in front of him than he could have eaten in a week. "Brina, he's a boy, not a dire wolf."

Brina put hands on ample hips, standing behind the boy, and fixed a ferocious glare on Haughey, who sat across the table with a large mug of tea in front of him. "The poor thing's half starved, Haughey, and I won't have you badgering him while he eats either. Do you understand me?" She patted the boy's head. "Pay no attention to him, Connail. You eat all you want, and take your time. If there's anything else you want, just ask me. I'll be right back—that scullery maid has broken two dishes in the last week and I have to watch her . . ." With a final glare at her husband, she went back into the kitchen.

Haughey sighed soundlessly, his hands cupped around the warm, slick glaze of his mug. Connail—that was the name the boy had given him: Connail MacVahlg—wolfed down the eggs set in front of him and reached for the slices of boiled ham. Haughey watched him. "Where'd you say you were from, Connail?"

"Tuath Éoganacht, Ionadaí Haughey." The boy cut a piece of the ham, chewing and swallowing before he continued. "But we traveled a lot. My da; he was a Songmaster and knew all the old songs, and we were always traveling about from one Ríocha's estate to another and from town to town. That's why we were in Maithcuan."

Haughey *hmm*ed and let his fingers prowl the strands of his beard thoughtfully. The boy had given him the tale on the trip back to Cairnmor: how he'd been fascinated by the man with a bird on his face, how he'd wandered away from his parents and snuck aboard the trade ship in a bale of finished goods, how he'd been discovered when they were already a day out from Talamh an Ghlas, how the crew had gotten sick and died one at a time until only he and Jantsk were left, with Jantsk finally succumbing the night before. No, he didn't know anything about what Jantsk was supposedly bringing to Haughey, though he mentioned that Jantsk seemed very secretive and stayed in his cabin during most of the voyage.

Connail's earnest voice and tears seemed genuine enough, but . . . Something nagged at Haughey. The boy's accent—his clipped pronunciation and his vocabulary; if not for the blurred drawl of Talamh An Ghlas, he might have come from the Thane's court at Concordia. And the way he ate—he sat at a table and used his utensils as if he were at a banquet: not like a wandering minstrel's son, even that of a Songmaster.

Haughey wondered, but his puzzlement was tinged with exhaustion; it had been a long, tiring day.

The harbor master hadn't wanted the ship in Cairnmor port, not with the chance that it contained some plague. On Haughey's return to Cairnmor with the boy, both the harbor master and the fisherman who'd rowed him out to the ship stayed as far away from the poor child as possible, glancing at him with rolling eyes. Haughey had also noticed that they kept a judicious distance from him. *"Are you sure you want to take the boy to your house?"* the harbor master had said. *"I mean, after all, Ionadaí, if there's a sickness . . ."*

"Where else should he go?" Haughey had asked the man. *"Would you rather I'd left him out there?"*

"Everything *should* be left out there," the harbor master had replied. *"Everything. That ship is cursed, and I want nothing to do with it."*

The harbor master's opinion had been shared by the rest of Cairnmor. Haughey had been unable to find anyone to take him back out to the ship to search for whatever it was Jantsk had been bringing to him. Only Oldman Keeper, already known to be insane, had been willing to row the Ion-adaí back out to the death-ship. Haughey had searched for two stripes or more, first Jantsk's cabins and possessions and even (with extreme reluctance) the dead man's pockets, and then the ship's cargo hold full of pottery, ironwork, and fabrics. There was nothing unusual. Nothing that he could see that was worth the message the man had sent.

The strangest thing aboard, from what Haughey could see, had been Connail, who was only a frightened boy.

With Haughey's grudging permission, the harbor master had the ship towed out beyond Oldman Head that evening. He'd grounded it on the shoals to the south of the harbor mouth and torched the vessel. By nightfall there remained nothing more than a steaming hulk burned down to the waterline.

"You didn't by chance see Jantsk get one of the pigeons and send a message to me?" Haughey asked Connail.

"Oh, aye, Ionadaí," the boy answered. "He kept the birds in his cabin with me. One day, he wrote a message and took one of the birds out, then let it go."

"When he did that, he wasn't by chance already sick?"

Connail seemed to ponder that, then brightened, almost smiling. "Aye, Ionadaí. He was terribly sick by that time. He was talking strangely, too, and his skin was hot to touch."

"Ah, that explains much, then," Haughey said. Some of the doubt and worry dissolved. So Jantsk's note may have been—indeed probably was—the product of a fevered dream and not reality. That made the smoldering pile of peat that was Haghey's stomach subside just a bit. That gave him a reasonable and far safer summation for the report he'd be sending to Concordia. Haughey doubted that his monthly reports to Concordia were ever actually read by Thane MagWolfagdh himself, not with the far greater and immediate threat of the Arruk demanding his attention. No, they were probably scanned by some minor céili giallnai in the court's employ and filed away. Still, Haughey didn't want to take any chances that his competence might be examined, especially with what Jantsk had hinted at in the note he'd sent. Haughey was already forming the proper wording for the report in his mind: *"I have independent verification that Artol Jantsk was delusional with fever when he composed the message."* He nodded, folding his hands over his stomach. The boy had already gone through the ham and was attacking the bread, slathering it with the fruit jam that Brina had put away after the last harvest. "In a way, that's a shame. The damned Arruk . . ."

"Where are they?" Connail interrupted. "The Arruk, I mean? I've . . . we've all heard awful tales about them at home, and my da went . . ." He paused, looking confused momentarily. "Da said that he'd heard they were terrible, savage creatures that drink the blood of the people they kill."

Haughey chuckled at the obvious terror in the boy's face. "I don't know about that," he said, "but they are terrible and savage, and far too close, if you ask me—no more than a few days' ride to the east, not far past Lough Bogha."

For a moment, he thought he saw something almost eager in Connail's face, then it was gone. "That close?" the boy asked, and shivered. He looked around as if he might see one of the Arruk lurking in the corner of the room.

"Not to worry," Haughey told him. "The Arruk don't seem to much care for the sea, though I suppose them in Torness believed the same and thought themselves safe. And your Banrion Ard, the Healer—may the Mother bless her and keep her safe—well, she sent help from the Tuatha and with their troops and the Cloch Mór that came with the Banrion Ard's husband Tiarna Geraghty, we stopped the Arruk and even pushed them back some, even if we couldn't drive them entirely from our land."

As Haughey spoke, the boy's face clouded and seemed almost angry. He put down the bread; his knife clattered onto the table. "The Banrion Ard is dead," Connail said.

"What?" Haughey sat bolt upright. "Dead? The Healer Ard?"

"Aye," Connail told him. "And Tiarna Geraghty and her entire family. They're all dead."

"No . . ." Haughey realized that his report would now most definitely be seen by the Thane, that in fact he would need to compose it tonight and send it tomorrow by courier pigeon and fast ship both, to be certain that it arrived. "You're certain of this? It's not just gossip?"

"Aye, Ionadaí." The boy nodded solemnly. "It's all the talk of the Tuatha. They were assa . . . assass . . ." He blinked.

"Assassinated?" Haughey shook his head—if true, then this may have been what Jantsk had that was so important: the news of the Banrion Ard's death. "From what I'd heard, the Banrion Ard was well-loved by her people, but not necessarily by the Riocha. I suppose I'm not entirely surprised. Who is the Ard now?" Connail shrugged and shook his head at the same time in answer. As he did so, the léine he wore shifted, and Haughey caught the glimpse of a golden chain around the boy's neck under the cloth. He leaned forward. "What's that?" he asked. "You have something under there?"

Connail grimaced, a surprisingly adult look on the child's face. He placed his hand on the collar of his léine. "You shouldn't have seen that. It's not in the pattern. The blue ghosts . . ."

"Pattern? Ghosts? What are you talking about?" Haughey suddenly became suspicious. Why would an itinerant Songmaster's son have a chain of gold, and why would he hide it so carefully? "Let me see that, boy. Bring it out." Haughey reached forward and Connail sprang backward off his chair, the wooden leg scraping loudly across the flagstone. Brina and the scullery maid came from the kitchen at the noise. "What's going on here . . . ?"

Connail was shaking his head and holding something at the end of the chain in his hands.

"You weren't supposed to see this," he said. He was crying, sobbing, staring wildly around the room as if looking for something. "You *shouldn't* have seen. Now I don't have any choice."

"What are you talking about, child?" Brina asked. She leaned toward him, glancing from the boy to Haughey and back.

"I'm sorry. I'm so sorry, but I have to. I have to." It was the only answer Connail gave. He closed his hand more tightly, and touched Brina with his other hand.

Haughey would never forget the sound his wife made then, but fortunately he would have only a few breaths of life in which to remember it.

31

The Scrúdú of Bethiochnead

THE CLIFFSIDE OF THALL Coill was bright: with
the buttery light of the full moon; with the autumnal
flicker of the fire Beryn had built against the cold wind off
the Westering Sea; with the searing, cold beauty of the
mage-lights that looped in pale aquamarine and furious
emerald and eerie blood-red around Sevei's arm.

The riot of illumination was reflected in the glossy, utterly black sides of the statue of Bethiochnead.

"Oh . . ." The exhalation was all Sevei could manage as
the mage-lights curled away from her and snaked their way
back into star-pricked darkness. She opened her fingers
and let Lámh Shábhála drop to her breast, nearly falling at
the release. Beryn's arms came around her in support. "I'm
fine," she told him, almost angrily, and the Bunús Muintir
let her go, retreating a few steps as Dragoncaller, around
his neck, glittered in moonlight. She gave him a weak smile
in apology. "I'm sorry. I just didn't expect . . ." She took another slow breath, seeing it pulse cold and white from her
mouth in the evening chill. "This was nothing like it was
with Dragoncaller. I could feel every cloch na thintrí out
there: Dragoncaller, all of them . . . It was like they were all
part of Lámh Shábhála, all connected to it somehow. I
could feel the person behind each stone, and I could hear
all the voices of those who have ever held Lámh Shábhála,
and I could feel its power . . ."

She looked at her right arm. Curling white scars swirled
on her wrist. They seemed to glow, faintly, though it was
difficult to tell if that wasn't some trick of the full moon,

and her arm—it felt cold, stiff, and impossibly heavy. She forced protesting fingers to close again, and twinges of pain radiated out from her arm to her chest. *So this is what it was like for Gram, all the time,* she thought, and then: *This is what it will be like for me, from now on . . .* She moaned softly and Beryn looked at her anxiously.

"Can I help you? Some kala bark tea . . . ?"

She shook her head. "I'm . . . just a little overwhelmed, that's all. Those with Clochs Mór . . . They'll all know that Lámh Shábhála's been found, though they don't know by whom yet. I could feel Doyle and I know he felt my cloch. I felt Snarl, also, but it was Padraic wielding it, not Máister Kirwan and it was far away in the Tuatha . . ." Involuntary tears filled her eyes—for Máister Kirwan, for Dillon, for all those she'd lost, as well as with relief at knowing for certain now that Kayne still lived—and she wiped them away with the cold, dead right hand. It felt like ice against her skin. "And Treoraí's Heart, it was there, too, but even farther away and the person who had it kept his or her face hidden . . ." She closed her eyes, sighing.

"If you're tired, you could wait until morning for the Scrúdú; get some sleep first."

Sevei glanced sidewise at the statue looming above them, blotting out the stars like a darker night. She could see a muted reflection of the campfire in the great beast's flanks, and the moonlight glittered in the curve of its eyes. "No. If I wait . . ." *I might never do it at all,* she finished inside, but Beryn's nod showed that he'd guessed the thought. "How do I begin?" she asked.

"Open Lámh Shábhála," he told her. "That's all."

Grimacing, she brought her cold and stiff right hand over the gem at her breast. As her hand cupped it, it seemed to warm her so that her fingers could close again. The new scars at her wrist *did* gleam white, she noticed.

She closed her fingers around the stone. *"Hello, darling . . ."* her gram's voice whispered in her head. *"I will help you through this, as much as I can . . ."* But she heard the other voices as well.

". . . Fool . . . !"

". . . Stupid thing . . . !"

". . . How sad to hold the stone for but a few breaths . . ."

Her vision doubled, the emerald facets of Lámh Sháb-

hála overlaying what she saw before her like a new landscape, and she let herself fall into it . . .

. . . a black shape, gigantic as the shadow of a mountain,
stirred . . .

. . . she heard a purring growl that made the dirt tremble
at her feet, that shook pebbles loose from between the
rocks of the cliffside . . .

Bethiochnead *moved* and it was no longer a broken
eroded carving, but a living creature. The head shook itself
like a great cat waking from sleep, and there were wings on
its leonine back, and a barbed red tail thrashed the ground.
Claws gouged stone, digging furrows in the rock. "Ah," it
said, and eyes the color of summer grass stared at her from
an impossible height. "Welcome—I am An Phionós. I am
the First, and you are now in my world. I wondered when
the First Holder's whelp would want to try where she
failed."

"*I did* not *fail*," another voice protested—Jenna, speaking through Lámh Shábhála, and Bethiochnead laughed.

"But you also did not succeed," An Phionós answered
with the same mild, almost scornful, amusement. Sevei
could feel the beast's presence in her mind and though she
tried to shut it out, she could not. She realized that the very
landscape around them had changed: the cliff now ended
several feet farther away from the statue-creature, and the
forest seemed to have vanished. She could not see Beryn at
all. "You're not the one I expected," An Phionós rumbled.
"I had thought you would be the one who was in Jenna's
womb, but you're the daughter's daughter. Strange. But no
matter—you desire to pit yourself against the Scrúdú?"

Voices cascaded in her mind (*"No!" "Don't be foolish,
child!"*) and she had to force them down before she could
answer. "No," she told the creature. "I don't desire it. But I
gave my word that I'd attempt it."

The creature laughed. "A vow? Then I release you from
it, for you couldn't have known what you promised. The
Scrúdú is death—ask those inside your stone."

"I don't care if I live or if I die," Sevei told it, and voices
echoed from inside: "*That, at least, is the proper attitude . . .*"

"*Hush!*" her gram's voice scolded them. "*Be quiet and let
her listen . . . !*"

"That's what those who haven't yet died say," An

Phionós answered Sevei. "I thought the same until I was actually dead." Mage-lights were circling above the cliff, a banded whirlpool of them brighter than any Sevei had ever seen. They flashed like a lightning stroke and for a moment An Phionós was lit from within, as if its skin were black glass. *"Careful,"* Sevei heard Jenna say in her head. *"It's ready to attack. Shield yourself . . ."*

Sevei felt the frigid heat of the gathering mage-lights, and suddenly An Phionós roared, spitting out energy in a blast that nearly caught her despite the wall she suddenly imagined between them. The mage-lights struck the barrier in flares of awful primary colors. Sevei felt them pummeling at her, felt the shield bending and nearly cracking, but then the light was gone and she panted, blinking as her eyes readjusted.

"Now that was impressive for someone so new to Lámh Shábhála," An Phionós said grudgingly. "Even with Jenna helping you. So, as with your gram, this won't be simple. That's good. Good. Too many times it was just that easy for me. I enjoy a challenge after such a long wait. It keeps me awake longer."

An Phionós was pacing now, prowling from side to side of the open area before the cliffs, the barbed tail lashing and the feathered wings unfolding from its back. It seemed to be considering what it would do next, and Sevei watched the beast warily, her fist held so tightly to Lámh Shábhála that she could feel the silver wires caging it pressing deep into the skin of her palm. The end of the deadly tail flicked close to her once and Sevei flinched, ready to send the cloch's energy flooding out.

"You don't really know how to use Lámh Shábhála, do you?" An Phionós peered down at her, its huge eyes glimmering with moisture, its voice genuinely sad. "Not like your gram—when she came here, she'd been holding the cloch for many months and was fairly skilled with it. Or poor Peria; she'd had Lámh Shábhála for years. So had most of the others. You . . . You're only a fledgling. How could you hope to succeed here when they, who knew the depths of Lámh Shábhála so much better, failed?" An Phionós stopped and sat on its haunches as muscles corded in its powerful body. "I'm not without compassion. Let go," it told Sevei. "Let go and we will forget the Scrúdú."

"Do it!" the voices wailed inside her. *"Listen to the beast or you'll die!"* But Sevei listened only for one voice: Jenna's. *"An Phionós made me the same offer,"* she said. *"I refused. And I lived."*

"Your gram says that only to bring you in here with us," one of the ancient Holders said, a woman's voice, and Sevei knew it was Peria. *"Beware! You'll just be one of us, whispering to the next Holder."*

"I would never do that to you, Sevei," Gram answered, her voice louder than the others. *"I'll help you . . ."*

"Shut up!" Sevei shouted. "All of you but Gram! Let me think."

"Sevei . . ." She glanced up at the sound of her name. The huge body of An Phionós was gone; it was Dillon standing there, his face sad and full of longing. "Don't do this, my love," he said. "Let go of Lámh Shábhála. Stay with me."

"Dillon!"

He ran to her and she felt his arms go around her, felt the warmth of his body and the taste of his lips on hers. Her hand, holding the cloch, was nearly crushed between them, hard and uncomfortable. "I thought . . . I thought you were dead."

"What's death?" he asked her, laughing gently, and bent his head down to hers again. He kissed her long and deep, and afterward his breath burned hot on her ear. "I was dead," he whispered and pulled back from her. He cupped his hands around her right hand and Lámh Shábhála, the scars glowing in the dark. "Aye, I was dead but I've come back. If you want me to stay, let go of the stone. That's all you need do, I promise. Let go of the stone and I'll be alive again and with you. With you and loving you forever. It will be the life we wanted. I promise, Sevei."

His eyes were the color of summer grass . . .

"No," she said.

"I wouldn't lie to you, Sevei," he said, and she heard two voices speaking as one: Dillon overlaid with An Phionós. "It's not possible for me to lie; the gods won't allow it. You can have me back, forever, but you must give up the Scrúdú to have me. Do it, and we can be together."

"Why?" Sevei asked, her eyes narrowing. Dillon's form shifted, the hands becoming claws, the face elongating, the body swelling and turning dark. "Because you're afraid I might succeed?"

Now it was only An Phionós in front of her. "Ah," it said. "You have Jenna's arrogance, too." Then the creature was Dillon again, his face sad and mournful. "I'm not enough for you?"

Sevei was crying, the tears flowing down her cheeks. "Dillon, I miss you so much, and I wish . . . I wish I could truly have you back again."

"You *can*, " he insisted. "I'm here. Now."

She touched his cheek. It was warm and soft and she wanted to lose herself in his embrace. "No," she said.

He sighed, and his features ran like melting snow until he became An Phionós again. "So be it," An Phionós said. Its clawed forepaw slashed at her. Belatedly, Sevei drew power from the cloch—lightning arced and spat and thunder boomed and An Phionós hissed and drew back. Wielding Lámh Shábhála was like holding fire in her hands: the power throbbed and pulsed, difficult to contain. She might as well attempt to bridle a hurricane. An Phionós snarled and leaped toward her.

Clumsily, she formed the energy into a tangled wall of glowing vines. The obstruction slowed An Phionós only a moment, the creature snarling in the nest of clinging power before shredding it with claws and teeth, moving toward her step by step. Sevei felt each blow from the talons as if it struck her. She screamed in terror and anger, retreating backward under the assault.

"You think this will stop me?" An Phionós roared at her, its voice matching her fury. A forepaw snatched at a loop of energy around its neck and threw it aside; it vanished in a crash of thunder that reverberated inside Sevei's skull, pounding against her temples. "Can you do this forever, Sevei? I can. Don't you feel the power failing already? Can't you feel it draining from Lámh Shábhála? Once it's gone, what will you do then?"

Lámh Shábhála held the beast, but Sevei listened to An Phionós and despaired. The cloch had finite power, and she was wasting it with half measures. Desperate, weeping unashamedly, she emptied the power within Lámh Shábhála upon An Phionós, a great, flaring torrent of mage-energy in any shape she could imagine: flights of great spears as close together as blades of grass; shrieking winds that tore rocks from the cliffside and ripped the great oaks from the very ground; ferocious lightnings that crawled on the land like a spider's legs; gibbering armies of black nightmare creatures, shrieking madly and waving glowing swords as they charged. Sevei plunged ever deeper into the emerald depths of Lámh Shábhála, finding all the crevices with their pools of mage-energy and flinging them at An Phionós as if the creature contained all her pain and grief, her hatred and her sorrow. The landscape around them was ablaze: brighter than the moon, brighter than the mage-lights, a furious glare that rivaled the dawn. Sevei's assault was relentless, and now it was An Phionós who retreated, roaring and wailing. She pursued him, step by slow step, pushing him backward with the cloch, snarling like an animal herself, her lips drawn back from her teeth as she lifted Lámh Shábhála high.

An Phionós shrieked in pain and torment. A step, another . . . Her adversary backed grudgingly, its head low, the blood-colored tail tucked under the body, black blood pouring from its ravaged flanks. A rear leg tore rocks from the edge of the cliff to crash into the sea far below; the other dangled over open air. *"Aye! You can do this!"* she heard Jenna crow inside her. An Phionós reared up as Sevei plumbed the depths of Lámh Shábhála searching for the last reserves of its power. She took what was left and hurled it at her adversary. It screamed and fell backward, vanishing over the cliff edge. Sevei ran forward toward the lip of the precipice, expecting to see the creature's broken body on the jagged rocks below, hope rising up in her.

She stopped, hearing laughter.

An Phionós rose above her in the empty air, magnificent and terrible, its great wings thrusting. "I have not had an opponent like you in far too long," it said. "Not even Jenna was able to do so much." It landed gently a few feet from her as Sevei slumped to the ground, exhausted. The place of Bethiochnead was dark again, the moon struggling against the afterglow of the mage-power she'd expended. An Phionós was a black mountain, only its eyes aglow, and from its massive chest came a low purring. "You shouldn't have been able to do that," An Phionós continued, "not as inexperienced as you are. That was a work of true greatness and potential. A shame, then, that such talent is now to be wasted."

In her mind, desperate, Sevei searched the verdant facets of Lámh Shábhála, trying to find lingering remnants of the energy. *"There's nothing,"* the voices of the past Holders whispered. *"Nothing . . . nothing . . . nothing . . ."*

"Are you ready to die, Sevei?" An Phionós asked, almost gently, almost sadly. Its paw lifted, eclipsing stars. "I will be quick. You won't have time to scream or hear the crack of bones. Are you ready?"

"Go deeper . . ." a voice whispered: Gram. Jenna. *"Find the very heart of the stone . . . Let yourself fall . . ."*

"Aye," Sevei said, not knowing who she was answering. In her doubled vision, she let herself tumble into Lámh Shábhála even as she cowered below An Phionós.

The paw loomed over her, a final and eternal night, its cold skin just touching her . . .

. . . she plunged into green darkness, opening herself, letting Lámh Shábhála rip into her soul and her very being. Images flashed past her, and she felt as if she were falling not into some unimaginable void but into the past. She fell into herself. She heard the voices of the Holders, but they were no longer Daoine or even Bunús Muintir. They spoke in tongues older and stranger. Back, back, back . . . and here, here in the darkness there was an ending and a beginning and a light . . .

. . . time itself stopped.

"Oh, Mother," Sevei whispered. "Mother, I hadn't known . . ."

Lámh Shábhála filled her. She filled Lámh Shábhála. There was no difference. The necklace that held Lámh Shábhála burst into flame, the gold spattering and fuming; the cage of silver holding it running like bright water. Sevei released the stone as the molten metal burned her, but it didn't fall. It hung there before her, then turned and arrowed at her chest. The jewel struck above the heart and burrowed into her. Sevei screamed as Lámh Shábhála ripped into her, as it tore through muscle and bone. Then it stopped. She took a breath.

Time moved again. She saw An Phionós' great paw above her like a thundercloud, and she opened her arms to accept the blow. An Phionós' paw slammed down from above, but it could not crush her. The ground shuddered underneath, the very stones cracking, and yet she was whole. Coruscations of grass-green light flared, as if An Phionós' paw were a smithy's hammer striking molten steel.

Sevei blinked as the light failed. An Phionós was groveling before her, lying flat on the ground with its head lowered. Its wings fluttered and then folded on its great back. "Holder," it said. Its voice was full of sorrow and grief, full of the lives it had taken over the long centuries. "You have no idea how long I've waited."

It lifted its head, sitting up on its haunches again in the pose of the statue. As Sevei watched, the creature stiffened and turned to stone before her eyes, aging and weathering in a few moments: as the cliff edge seemed to melt toward her, as the trees of Thall Coill grew and marched in her direction.

And she was back where she had started. The statue of Bethiochnead loomed broken and tilted in front of her.

"Sevei?" Beryn rushed over to her. She felt him start to put a hand on her shoulder, then stop himself. "You're alive! I thought . . . I saw you fall, and the mage-lights were crackling all around you . . ." His voice changed then, to a tone of awe. "You've endured the Scrúdú and you're alive. But . . ."

He was staring at her: at her face, at her arms. Sevei looked down. Her hands were covered in a knotted pattern of white, swirling scars—scars that she remembered from Gram's right hand: the mark of the mage-lights. She pushed her léine back from her right arm, then her left. The scars ascended on both arms as far as she could see. She put her fingers to her cheeks and felt hard raised lines there. "My face . . . ?" she asked.

Beryn nodded. "Aye," he said softly. "Your face, too. And more." The way he averted his eyes told her how she must look, and she gave a cry of despair. She felt for the chain around her neck; it was gone, but with her probing fingers she could feel the nodule of Lámh Shábhála under her skin, on the inner slope of her right breast: hard and unyielding.

"You didn't tell me it would be this way!"

"I didn't know," he answered.

"No," she said. "No, this hasn't happened. It's another illusion like Dillon, still part of the Scrúdú." She was crying now, staring at him, pleading with him to tell her that, aye, she was right and this was only part of the test, and knowing that it wasn't. She moved, and the feel of her clothing was like the slashing of a hundred cats' claws on her skin, so unbearable that she cried out at the sensation. She tore at the cloth, ripping it from her body, not caring that Beryn saw her. The only thing that mattered was to take the pain away. She stood naked in the air, and even the touch of the wind hurt, and looking down at her body, she saw the mage-scars everywhere on too-white skin. "No . . ."

The answer came from inside, from the voices caught in Lámh Shábhála, Gram's among them.

"You've been marked," they said. *"Lámh Shábhála has claimed you. . . ."*

32

The Battle of the Narrows, Reprised

A MESSENGER RODE breathless into the Fingerlands through the Narrows Pass, his horse blown and
nearly dead. He was rushed to the laird's tent. After giving
his tidings of double ill news, the messenger was sent to his
well-deserved meal and bed, and Kayne was summoned.
He found Laird O'Blathmhaic huddled with Rodhlann O
Morchoe in a grim but strangely pleasant mood. "Here it
is," the man said without preamble. He tapped the table
placed on the soiled carpets under the tent's covering. The
table wobbled, mugs with the dregs of the previous night's
ale clashing. "The army of Rí Mac Baoill is on the move
toward the Fingerlands, coming fast up the High Road.
There were green-robes in the ranks of the Ríocha riding
with the army, mages of the Order of Gabair. The scouts
also are telling us that there are troops from Dún
Laoghaire and Gabair with the army, sent at the order of
the new Rí Ard to help put down the 'insurrection' in the
Finger."

"The new Rí Ard?"

Kayne could feel the grizzled old man's gaze on him.
Rodhlann, standing beside him, frowned tightly. "Aye,
Tiarna," Rodhlann told him. "A new Ard."

"Then it's certain. Mam is dead." He clamped his jaw
down against the cry that wanted to escape him. *This isn't
the time. You knew. You knew when they killed Da that they
couldn't move against him alone . . .* "Who is Ard?" he asked.

"The Óenach of the Ríthe has elected Doyle Mac Ard,"
O'Blathmhaic told him.

The name made Kayne grunt as if he'd been punched. "Uncle Doyle?" Kayne had never cared that much for Doyle Mac Ard, a man he'd always found glum and somewhat curt, though he'd loved Aunt Edana and had spent much of his childhood hours playing with their children Padraic, Alastríona, Ula, and Enean. Padraic, in particular, had been only a year younger, and he and Kayne had often played at cloudmage and gardai; Sevei had liked Padraic also—more than was good for her, Kayne had sometimes thought. And Alastríona . . . He knew that court gossip had often advanced Kayne and Alastríona as marriage partners; that had never occurred, but Kayne had once overheard his mam and Aunt Edana discussing a possible betrothal between Kayne's sister Tara and Enean Mac Ard when the two of them reached their hand of hands birthdays.

If everything that Kayne feared had come to pass, then little Tara's last birthday—a double hand and four—had been her last. Kayne shook his head, trying to fathom why Uncle Doyle would send an army against him. If Doyle Mac Ard was Rí Ard, then he must know what had happened. No, it was worse than that: if Doyle had the influence among the Ríthe to become Rí Ard, then he almost certainly had been involved in the machinations. Which meant that he would, at the very least, have known about the assassinations, if not been actively involved in planning them. And if Uncle Doyle was involved, then Aunt Edana most likely was too . . .

Kayne felt the beginnings of a sick headache.

"This changes everything," he said to O'Blathmhaic and Rodhlann. "If troops from three of the Tuatha have come here and the Order of Gabair's riding with the army, then Harik was right. Our two Clochs Mór won't be nearly enough. We stand no more of a chance than a sand castle against the tide."

"Not if we meet them openly," Laird O'Blathmhaic agreed. He tapped his forehead with a crooked finger.

"You're still thinking like a Riocha who makes war like a Riocha," Rodhlann agreed, nodding to the laird. "But that's not the only way. You saw what we did in Ceangail."

"There's no similarity," Kayne said, harshly enough that O'Blathmhaic's eyes narrowed and Rodhlann snapped his mouth shut. "That was a small troop of gardai. This is a true army. Those tactics won't work, not this time. In fact, they will get us killed."

O'Blathmhaic cleared his throat and started to spit, then glared at the carpets that covered the ground. He swallowed and gave Kayne a sour grimace. "You have a better way, then?"

Silently, Kayne shook his head.

His marriage-da snorted. "You forget that most of those troops are conscripts, and they won't be so eager to fight when they see their companions dying around them. They'll advance to the Narrows tomorrow, if I know them at all. Once they're in the pass, Rodhlann will start to whittle them down, and when they're *here*, in the Finger proper . . ." Laird O'Blathmhaic grinned evilly.

Kayne wanted to believe the man, but he knew it wouldn't happen that way. There were so many, and the mage-stones . . . "I don't mean any disrespect to Rodhlann, but you won't be able to whittle them down, Laird, not with the Clochs Mór they have, and you underestimate the morale of the conscripts—or maybe their fear of what will happen if they turn their backs on the battle. This will be slaughter, no matter how we try to fight them."

"You sound like a frightened old doe, Tiarna," O'Blathmhaic answered. "What does it matter? Then if we die, we die taking out as many as we can. Either way, the bastards will remember us."

"Are you Fingerlanders always so stubbornly optimistic?"

O'Blathmhaic and Rodhlann both chuckled grimly. "Are you Riocha always so stubbornly gloomy?" Rodhlann said. "We fight. Here. In the Narrows where we've fought a hundred times before."

"No," Kayne insisted. "We shouldn't meet them at all. We should retreat entirely. Go into the mountains and wait. Melt away so they can't find us. Maybe pick them off in ones and twos, but never confront them directly. We need to know more before we try to truly fight them: find out for certain what's happened to Lámh Shábhála, determine who is allied with whom back in the Tuatha. Maybe I can get help from some of the Riocha, those who aren't happy with what's happened . . ."

Both men were already shaking their heads, from the first word. "Boy, you don't understand," O'Blathmhaic roared, so loudly that Kayne was certain that the entire encampment must hear him. "If we send our people back to the clans to wait, it's over. They won't be coming back. The clan-lairds have made the decision to fight *now*. So now we fight." Laird O'Blathmhaic pointed a stubby finger at the carpets.

"If we fight against the force that you've just told me is coming for us, then we'll also die here."

"That doesn't bother me, boy. Does it bother you?"

"Aye, it does," Kayne insisted. He wondered if Harik would find this ironic, to hear Kayne advising caution when he'd spent so much time accusing his da of being overcautious, when he'd always been the one who wanted to plunge headlong into battle. *Da, I think I'm beginning to understand . . .* "This is needless death. There will be a better way, at another time and place."

O'Blathmhaic was still shaking his head. "I thought you half a Fingerlander when I let you marry my great-daughter. I'm guessing now that I was wrong."

"I love Séarlait, Laird. That's another reason not to make a stand here."

Rodhlann started to speak, but O'Blathmhaic raised a hand and the man went silent. "Listen to me with the heart of a Fingerlander, Tiarna," O'Blathmhaic said. "We've made our decision to resist now when we could have waited. We can't unmake that decision—not if you ever want the lairds and the clans to listen to you again. You can take your gardai and leave if you'd like, but then you leave Séarlait and your promises behind with you, and you and your descendants will be forever our enemy. The Fingerlanders *will* stand here," O'Blathmhaic insisted, "and Séarlait will stand here with us. If you love her . . ."

He left the rest unsaid. He waited.

Kayne sighed. "Then I stand here also," he said.

Kayne stared out over the sloping plain into a rare, clear night where it seemed he could have seen as far as Lough Tory. He found that he wished it were raining and cloudy, for the landscape in front of him was dotted with a thousand flickering motes: the campfires of the Airgiallaian army, all spread out along the High Road until they vanished into a blur on the horizon.

It was easy to feel gloom and despair, looking out on the campfires scattered like grounded stars on the plain. He heard Séarlait come up behind him but didn't turn. Her hand touched his shoulder and he heard her sigh. "I know," he said. "It doesn't do any good to sit out here and watch. It's depressing."

Her arms went around him, and he leaned back, reveling in the warmth and the closeness. She moved his hair aside and kissed the back of his neck.

"I love you, too. That's what scares me, too—I wonder how we'll both come out of this."

She turned him in her arms so he couldn't see the campfires. Her eyes held him, almost angry. She nodded once, harshly.

He smiled at her. "Aye, we will live, somehow," he told her, kissing her. He hoped he was right. He leaned in to kiss her, and for a moment lost his thoughts in the warmth of her mouth. But she pulled away after a few moment. "What?" he asked, but he already knew the answer by the multicolored lights that played over her face and glimmered in her hair. They both looked up: the mage-lights snaked between the stars, brightening faster than was usual for them. With the sight, Kayne felt the pull of Blaze, yearning to be filled with the energy above. Kayne and Séarlait stood, together, and both took their clochs in their hands, opening them to the sky. Last night . . . last night they'd felt Lámh Shábhála once more, even though the pull of it was distant and the Holder had seemed tentative and uncertain. Kayne—like every other cloudmage, he was certain—had tried to sense behind the Great Cloch's presence the person holding it, but whoever it was remained hidden. He wondered who held it: friend, enemy, or neither. The stone had felt far enough away that Kayne thought it might even be somewhere beyond Inish Thuaidh.

Perhaps you'll know more tonight . . . Kayne sighed at the feeling as snarling curls of light shot down to wrap around his hand and Séarlait's; as the clochs began to feed hungrily on the power of the lights.

The double landscape of the mage-stones opened in front of him, as if he were staring out from the center of Blaze through its ruby facets at another world. He could follow the path of the mage-lights out toward the other clochs: Séarlait, next to him; the Clochs Mór and clochmions out in the firelit landscape beyond. Doyle Mac Ard wasn't there—he could sense Snapdragon well off to the west and south, probably in Lár Bhaile or Dún Laoghaire—but several others were close by. He could not only feel them, but he could see with his own eyes the tendrils of mage-lights swirling down to them like brilliant tornadoes.

Then . . .

They must have all felt it, as strongly as Kayne. He heard Séarlait's intake of breath and he could sense the distress of the others. Out there, far to the west, Lámh Shábhála came again, a far more powerful presence tonight than the night before: an enormous maelstrom that sucked at the power of the mage-lights, that tugged at each of them. It was purest emerald, that aura, the rich, saturated green of the brightest mage-lights, and it was more potent than any hand of the Clochs Mór together.

Kayne let Lámh Shábhála pull him toward it. He searched for the mind behind the stone, searching for it within the blinding radiance of the stone itself. There was a familiarity there, someone . . .

"Sevei!"

An image rushed from the emerald light to him and suddenly he wasn't sure. It seemed to be Sevei but . . . Her face was changed, horribly scarred with raised white markings that reminded him of the patterns of the mage-lights themselves. Her eyes were the featureless black of a seal's, and her hair was the white of new-fallen snow. She seemed a fey thing, powerful and yet terribly dangerous. She was standing on a windy plateau, entirely naked, and every finger's breadth of her body was scarred with the same patterns. Behind her, he could glimpse a gloomy, murky statue of some creature. She reached for him, almost yearningly, or perhaps—Kayne thought—threateningly.

"Wait," her voice said. *"Wait two days, Kayne . . ."*

The surprise and shock of her appearance and her voice sent him reeling backward. The vision of her was lost. He thought he heard her voice calling to him again, but the mage-lights were already fading and with it the contact between the clochs. Kayne released Blaze and watched the last tendrils of light trailing a line of sparks as they receded into the sky. His vision returned to normal. He was staring out at the campfires of the army again.

He felt Séarlait's soft touch on his shoulder and turned to her.

"You felt that, too? You saw her?"

A nod. Her eyes were wide and frightened.

"Did she speak to you?"

A single shake of her head: left to right and back.

Wait two days . . .

"They'll also know." Kayne looked back at the camp-fires. Down there, the green-robes and the Riocha would be buzzing with wild speculation and, aye, probably the same fear he felt himself.

Lámh Shábhála had returned, and it was Sevei—who he thought was certainly dead like his parents and siblings—who wielded it. But this was a Sevei altered and changed, and he didn't know her.

He was afraid he might not know her at all.

The dawn brought news from a Fingerlander scout.

"There are troops quick-marching back down the High Road to the west," the scout said as he drank gratefully from the waterskin handed him by Séarlait. "At least a hand of the green-robes are with them, and a double-hand and more of Riocha in the colors of Gabair, Infochla, and Dún Laoghaire." He took another gulp of the water, then let the remainder drain over his sweating head. "There's confusion among the remainder of the army. They didn't break camp this morning as we expected. I crept down as close as I could, so I could see the officers' tents, and they're busy with people coming and going and looking grim."

"How many green-robes are left?" Kayne asked him, and the scout shook his head.

"I don't know if there are any left at all, Tiarna. Nor are there too many Riocha with mage-stones around their

necks either. Something seems to have happened last
night."

*The immense pull of the stone on the mage-lights, her
scarred face, her changed features . . .* Kayne exchanged
glances with the four other people in the tent: Séarlait,
Laird O'Blathmhaic, Harik, and Rodhlann. "Aye, that it
did," Kayne told the scout. He slapped the man on the
shoulder and opened the tent's flap for him. "Go get some
rest while you can."

Kayne could feel the others staring at him as the scout
left. "It would seem that the Riocha are rather concerned
about this new Holder," O'Blathmhaic said. "Séarlait tells
me that you believe it's your sister."

Kayne nodded. "I *know* it's Sevei. She opened herself to
me and I heard her voice and realized that it was her, but
just looking at the face she showed us all . . ." He shivered
with the memory. "I don't know that anyone else would
recognize her. It's not the new Holder that has the Riocha
concerned, though—it's Lámh Shábhála itself. The stone
was missing for over a moon; all of us with mage-stones felt
its absence. Now it's returned. I don't know what happened
to Gram, but she wouldn't have given up Lámh Shábhála
willingly. I'd wager that Uncle Doyle thought Lámh Shábhála was lost, or that he or some other green-robe would
acquire it. They expected it to end up in their hands or be
lost forever, and now they see a bigger threat at their back
than we represent. All the mages are rushing west to deal
with it."

"So . . ." Rodhlann pursed his lips. "Then we find a way
to use that. If they're looking the other way, then we can
strike at their backs."

Kayne's own thoughts drowned out the Fingerlander
commander's words; he heard none of it. "We expected to
fight today," Harik said, and Kayne started. "We still should.
But instead of waiting for them to come to us, let's go down
to them. Now. While they're still confused and disheartened.
Take the battle to them if they won't come to us."

"Ah, finally one of your flatlanders says something that
makes sense," Laird O'Blathmhaic grunted. "Aye, 'tis a
grand day to fight. Rodhlann, let's tell our own Hands . . ."
O'Blathmhaic started to move toward the tent flap with
Rodhlann; Harik, with a nod to Kayne, started after them.

Wait two days . . .

"Hold a moment," Kayne called out to them, and O'Blathmhaic spun about like a lumbering bear, his face flushed.

"You can't be saying no, Tiarna. Not now. We've already had that discussion, and all the arguments you gave us are dust. And don't be saying we should wait here for them— they may never come through the Narrows. Not now."

"I'm not saying no," Kayne answered. "You're right—if the green-robes and half the army have left, then there may not be a better time. But . . . everything changes now that Sevei has Lámh Shábhála. Think of what the Finger-landers could do if Lámh Shábhála were here. With us."

O'Blathmhaic laughed derisively. "It's *not* here, or haven't you noticed, man? Séarlait's already told me that Lámh Shábhála is probably in Inish Thuaidh or beyond. The Inishlanders have the stone and my guess is that they'll keep it. It'll stay there rotting on your sister's breast, as it did with the Mad Holder."

Kayne felt the insult to Jenna like a slap to the face. He could feel the heat rise to his face. Séarlait saw it, too; he felt her hand touch his arm as he took in a great breath. Harik watched him, the Hand's face impassive and un-readable.

"I give the orders here, not you, Tiarna," O'Blathmhaic continued. "Fingerlanders don't wait for possibilities when our homes and families are threatened. We fight so we can live. The Mother-Creator has gifted us with this opportu-nity and I'm not going to waste Her gift." O'Blathmhaic glared at Kayne.

"Even with their army in disarray, going down to them will cost lives. There are lives here I wouldn't care to sacri-fice," Kayne told them. He stroked Séarlait's face, and she smiled up at him. "Especially now."

Rodhlann, holding the tent flap behind O'Blathmhaic, shrugged. "I'd wait here in the Narrows for them if I had a choice, too, Tiarna," the man said. "It's better ground for us, and we know it. But they know it, too, and now they may not come to us until they're stronger again. That's what the laird is telling you: they may turn tail and go home, and they've been greatly weakened if the clochs are gone. This may be our best chance."

Kayne nodded. "I agree with you," he said. "But I still ask you to wait. Another day and night. No more. They won't break camp that quickly. A day and a night. *Then* we'll go down to them."

Laird O'Blathmhaic scowled. "You contradict your own words, then."

"No," he told them. "Listen . . ."

33

Arruk Encounter

ENNIS could feel the shift in the landscape.
Even though there were fields wrested away from
the pine-dominated forest on either side of the road he
walked, the farmland was knee high with weeds and grass,
unplowed and unsown. The houses he glimpsed up the
lanes were mere roofless shells, some of them with smoke-
blackened walls.

And even though the world was alive with birdcalls and
the sudden howls of wolves, and he glimpsed a herd of
huge storm deer grazing at the edge of one of the fields,
nothing of the Daoine moved here. He was alone walking
the road—itself half overgrown. There was no one in the
meadows, no fragrant cook smoke rising above thatched
roofs, no bright calls of children, no sheep or cows grazing,
no chickens or other tamed fowl in the yards. Haywagons
moldered in the fields. It was as if all the Daoine in the region had decided to leave one day.

Which they may well have done. The Arruk swarm had
swept through here only a few moons before. The last
Daoine travelers Ennis had seen—three days ago and well
to the west, before the land had become vacant and empty—
had been a hand of farmers carrying pigs and sheep to the
markets at Cairnmor. They'd been fearful and edgy when
Ennis had walked into the light of their campfire. They'd
brandished axes and scythes immediately, but then grew
more sympathetic as Ennis—listening to the blue ghosts—
told them a tale of being the lone survivor of a family
whose farm had been destroyed by a roving band of Arruk.

Ennis claimed to be trying to reach his uncle's house in Cairnmor.

"Aye, boy," one of them said as he finally laid down the cudgel he'd held. "You're indeed blessed by the Mother-Creator to have been spared. Them Arruk don't leave anyone alive if they can help it. I've seen that too many times out here."

"You've seen the Arruk?" Ennis asked with feigned horror. "Near us?"

"Near enough. Just two days ago, there was a group of the awful things near the lough to the east, near the old road to Dúnbarr—may all of those there rest in the Mother's arms." He made the spiral of the Mother over his heart. "We could smell them, we were that close, but luckily the wind was in our favor and they didn't notice us."

Ennis shuddered, and the man hugged him sympathetically. "Don't be afraid now, boy. We'll take you to Cairnmor and your uncle's house . . ."

He'd killed them before he left, of course, because the pattern insisted on it. He wasn't certain why that was and he was sorry to do so, but he didn't question the blue ghosts; he only followed in the dance they designed. He killed them, sniffing away tears as he did so, grieving for them and for himself.

Afterward, as the mage-lights gleamed above, he filled Treoraí's Heart . . .

. . . and he felt, for the first time, Lámh Shábhála, and with it a glimpse of a horribly disfigured woman with white hair and black eyes. He wondered who it was: she was far too young to be his gram, whose face he didn't know. The only time he'd met his gram, when Mam had gone to Dún Kiil to visit, he'd been only a babe in arms and remembered nothing of it. He could sense that this Holder also felt the Heart and was startled, that she let her awareness drift from Lámh Shábhála down the spider's web of the mage-lights toward him. Ennis saw the blue ghosts appear, and in their patterns he realized that he must not let this White Beast see him, realized that Treoraí's Heart was strong enough to hide from Lámh Shábhála. He created a barrier between them just before her mind touched his, and he felt her wonder at that, felt her probe and dig and

pry at the shield until the mage-lights failed and the feeling
of her vanished again.

He hid. He could not look out from behind the barrier,
couldn't see all the other wielders of clochs na thintrí, but
neither could they see him. He was safe, masked, as the
Heart fed on the mage-lights.

He was crying afterward, kneeling in the dirt with the
lifeless bodies of the farmers sprawled around the dying
campfire and the sheep and pigs grunting in their carts.

But now someone other than his gram held Lámh Shábhála. Mam had told him once that she thought Sevei might
be the next Holder, but Sevei must be dead too. Ennis
wondered why the blue ghosts hadn't shown him the new
Holder.

The corpses of the farmers stared at him with empty
eyes. There were no answers there. The only answer would
be at the end of the dance, the end of the pattern, which
was too far away for him to see. He would have to follow
the path to know.

He wiped the tears away from his eyes and went to one
of the corpses, grimacing as he pulled from it a short bow
and a quiver of arrows. Then he climbed into one of the
wagons to sleep until morning.

Now, three days later, Ennis was well into the empty land
between the Daoine and the Arruk. Once already, he'd
caught the scent of Arruk on the breeze, but the pattern
had told him it wasn't time yet, and so he'd hidden until the
troop of Arruk soldiers had passed. He watched them curiously from his hiding place off the side of the road: staring at their rude clothing—a simple loincloth around the
hips, at the reptilian skin and snouted faces, at the slime-
lathered nostrils and the great clawed hands, their flesh
painted with strange marks and sigils. He found himself
wondering whether the pattern was leading him to the
right place.

These were creatures from his nightmares. These were
the monsters from a Songmaster's tale. These were beasts
who were the grandchildren of the Seed-Daughter, the

spawn of the Miondia, the lesser gods who were the result
of the Seed-Daughter's rape by Darkness. Ennis had heard
the sinister tales of the Days of Creation, chanted by the
Draíodóiri during the gloomy Festival of Gheimhri. Some
of the older children sometimes laughed at the stories,
whispering that this was all they were: stories.

Now Ennis believed them. He shivered, not from the
cold, and wished he could go back the way he'd come: to
Cairnmor, to Talamh An Ghlas and Dún Laoghaire. But he
couldn't. The blue ghosts had sealed that way from him—
they showed him that if he tried to go that way, he would
certainly die. He could only go forward, following the steps
of the dance that he'd chosen.

When the Arruk passed, Ennis came out from the brush
and bramble. For a moment he stood in the road, as uncertain and scared and lonely as any child of his age would
have been. "Mam . . . Da . . . Gram . . . Kayne . . . Sevei . . .
Ionhar . . . Tara . . ." He whispered their names as if they
were incantations that could bring their ghosts to stand before him, but nothing happened. He touched Treoraí's
Heart on its chain, remembering how it would gleam on his
mam's clóca. *"You will wield the full power of the Heart,"*
Isibéal's voice whispered to him. *"You will be stronger than
your mam ever was, and no one will be able to kill you the
way they killed her and your da and your siblings. The
Heart might rival even Lámh Shábhála."*

That didn't comfort him. "Let me talk to Mam," he said.
"Let me hear her."

Isibéal only laughed in response.

Ennis wiped his nose. He sniffed.

He started walking east once more.

It was late afternoon when he smelled them again, and
this time the scenery around him was overlaid with the
traces of the blue ghosts. He knew that this was the moment. He hopped quickly over the stone fence bordering
the road, just to where it curved southward around a bare-
topped hill where sheep had once grazed, and whose lower
slopes were now blanketed with high, seed-topped grass.
He pulled the bow from his back and strung it as he'd seen
Kayne do in the practice yard of the keep. He heard the
Arruk talking as they loped down the road at a quick pace.
There were seven of them: four huge, naked Arruk with a

litter on their shoulders; two far more slender ones walking on either side of the litter with silken blue cloth wrapped around their waists and an orange crescent moon intersected by a jagged lightning bolt prominent at the front of their waistcloths—one of them also carried a long pole topped with a curved blade. The final Arruk was dressed in a tanned leather skirt dyed a bright blue with the same orange symbol embossed on it, and he reclined on the open litter. Ennis immediately recognized the attitude of the slender Arruk walking alongside the litter; he'd seen it in the servants who worked for his mam in Dún Laoghaire Keep.

Wait . . . the blue ghost told him. The Arruk passed the place where he crouched. Ennis fit one of the arrows to the bow and stood. *Now . . .*

"Hey!" Ennis shouted.

The servants jumped with twin squawks, looking back over their shoulders. The litter bearers came to a stumbling halt. But the Arruk on the litter hissed like a snake and, with one fluid motion, leaped down from the litter and snatched the pole arm from the Arruk carrying it. It snarled a challenge as it brandished the weapon, showing yellowed, pointed teeth. Ennis couldn't understand the words, but the intent was clear enough—the Arruk was daring Ennis to take his shot. His reptilian eyes seemed almost amused, staring at the tiny human accosting him alone. Ennis' arm shook with the strain of holding the arrow at full draw and the tip wavered. He wondered if, should he release the string, the arrow would even come close to its target.

Emerald outlines of possibilities danced all around the roadway, and Ennis looked for the correct one, letting himself mold to its pattern. The blue ghost of himself shook its head; he did the same.

"No," he said, knowing the creature couldn't understand the words but hoping that the intention came clear in the tone. "We're not enemies. I don't want to hurt you." Slowly, glad that the stone wall was between himself and the Arruk, he placed the bow down on the top of the wall and backed away a step from it. The Arruk growled quizzically. The litter bearers had set down their burden and were standing uncertainly in the road, looking horribly large but stupid, while the servants in their waistcloths hovered just behind their master. He waved them all back. The Arruk scythed the air with the pole arm, an ominous, low *whoomp* following the movement. Ennis, in lockstep with the blue ghost, stepped back again, pulling the chain with Treoraí's Heart from under his léine.

The Arruk slammed the end of his weapon onto the ground. He leaned forward and stared at the gem, his mouth half open as if in hunger, a red tongue slithering over ivory.

"Aye, I have a cloch," Ennis said an instant behind the blue ghost. Their two voices mingled in his head. "You know what this is, don't you?" He closed his tiny hand around it and the Arruk visibly flinched, a semitransparent membrane flicking over the eyes and then rolling back again. Ennis opened his fingers again and let the stone fall back. He spread his hands wide, showing his empty palms. "See?" he said. "Nothing. I don't want to hurt you. We're going to help each other."

The Arruk handed the pole arm back to the servant. Grabbing one of the litter bearers, he shoved the huge Arruk toward Ennis, gesturing to the creature at the same time as he stepped back. The invitation was obvious enough, even if Ennis didn't have the pattern of the blue ghosts to guide him.

Ennis climbed slowly over the stone wall and back onto the road. He put Treoraí's Heart in one hand as he approached the litter bearer. The stench of the creature made Ennis want to gag. The thing stared at him, snarling softly in the back of its throat, its mouth slightly open and exuding the odor of raw meat. Ennis touched the bearer's arm with his free hand—he could feel the Arruk trembling, the finely-scaled flesh slick with a sheen of oil. The blue ghosts wailed in his mind, making Ennis' head pound. He felt the surging power of the cloch rising up, and he took it, shaped it, sent it lancing forward into the Arruk.

. . . He felt mostly a compulsion to obey Kurhv Ruka. He felt hunger, and weariness from carrying the litter, and a fright he was struggling not to show. And then . . . then . . . the pain.

The thing gasped. It howled, lifting its head to the sky. As Ennis stepped back, gasping as he pulled himself out of the

Arruk's mind, the creature's body quivered, every muscle going tight and strained. It made a horrible, strangling sound and fell over. The other bearers and the two servants all scrambled back a few steps; the master—Kurhv Ruka, Ennis knew now—leaned forward curiously. He said something in a soft voice, looking at Ennis.

Ennis released the cloch, showing the Arruk master his empty hands again. "I can do this for you," he said. "I can do this to those who oppose you. Together, think of what we could do."

The Arruk was staring at Ennis thoughtfully. The blue ghosts were moving, and for a moment Ennis resisted, feeling himself fall out of the dance, but the fright of what might happen if he lost the pattern here made him move again. Without the pattern, anything might happen. Without the pattern, he would almost certainly die, alone. Without the pattern, he would not achieve the destiny he'd glimpsed.

He showed the Arruk his empty hands as he walked to him, stepping carefully around the body of the dead bearer. The stench filled his nostrils, and the top of his head was barely higher than the Arruk's waist. Ennis reached toward the Arruk, his breath fast and his heart pounding. He touched the scale-armored stomach—the Arruk staring down without moving—then his own chest. He looked beseechingly up at Kurhv Ruka. The blue ghost said nothing, but Ennis licked his lips and forced himself to speak. "Together, Kurhv Ruka? You and me? Do you understand?"

For a moment, Ennis thought that the Arruk did not. Kurhv Ruka went to his litter and sat down again. He gestured to the three remaining bearers, and then spoke to his servant, who placed the master's long weapon alongside him, then—looking distressed—stood beside the pole that had been the dead bearer's. The master's gesture to Ennis was unmistakable: *come sit here with me.*

Ennis went to him as the blue ghosts faded and the world returned in all its normal hues. He sat next to the master on the litter. The Arruk barked an order, and the bearers and servants reached down to pick up the litter as Ennis steadied himself on the cushions. He smiled up at the Arruk. "You really stink. Did you know that?" he said to

the master. "My name is Ennis Geraghty." He tapped his
own chest. "Ennis Geraghty." He touched the Arruk's
chest. "Kurhv Ruka?" he asked.

"Kurhv Ruka," the Arruk grunted in assent.

As the Arruck gave his answer to Ennis, the bearers set
off at a trot, the litter swaying and rocking gently with their
motions.

They left the body of their companion laying in the road,
unmourned.

The Arruk didn't have settlements—or rather, they
seemed content with the remnants of the towns they'd captured. Ennis and Kurhv Ruka were borne to a village that
might once have been picturesque and quaint, but was now
changed. There was a market in the town square, but the
booths seemed to sell only flyblown carcasses of unidenti-
fiable animals and drying sticks of what might have been
herbs. Only Arruk walked the streets now, and the lanes
were littered with droppings and foul-smelling puddles.
The Arruk seemed to have no domesticated animals—
Ennis saw several other litters carrying Arruck dressed in
leathers similar to Kurhv Ruka's, though with other de-
signs and insignia; other entirely naked Arruk—all
branded with a circle on their hips, Ennis noticed—acted
as beasts of burden, carrying huge bundles on their backs
or pushing wheeled carts that were obviously of Daoine
manufacture. The doors and shutters had been ripped
from all the houses, the entrances and windows open to
the air. The windowboxes, which had evidently once been
bright and alive with flowers, were overgrown with weeds
and filled with dead and brown stems, but brilliant colors
were splashed on the stone walls, adorned with what
Ennis assumed were words painted in an oddly curlicued
alphabet. The town shimmered in the sunlight, painted in
vivid hues.

Ennis could see immediately that other Arruk deferred
to Kurhv Ruka. He saw several of the warriors carrying
their pole arms, and their snouts wrinkled as the litter approached, as if they scented Ennis. They looked in Ennis'
direction to snarl threateningly until they saw that he was

seated beside Kurhv Ruka. Then their demeanor would change: the snarls faded from their snouts, and they stared, heads slightly lowered and their weapons pointed carefully away from the litter.

After a time, Ennis realized that all the Arruk he'd seen seemed to be adult males. There were no female Arruk here—either that or they were so much like the males that there was no discernible difference to Ennis' eyes—and no young.

They were carried through the center of the town to a temple on a hill just outside. This had once been consecrated to the Mother-Creator—the symbols carved on the lintel were similar to those on the temple in Dún Laoghaire. But there were no Draíodóiri here tending the temple or performing the services, though the pale brown stains that covered the walls near the archway looked suspiciously like old blood, and Ennis wondered if it might not be that of the priests who had once lived here.

Arruk guards stood near the temple's entrance, and as the litter was placed on the ground and Ennis and Kurhv Ruka dismounted and stood up, another Arruk, this one dressed in a warrior's leather marked with a sun half-covered with cloud, emerged from the dark interior. The Arruk blinked once at the sunlight, showing translucent eye coverings, then his snout wrinkled as he glared at Ennis. He snarled something to Kurhv Ruka that sounded decidedly aggressive. Kurhv Ruka spat back harsh syllables, his claws extending out from his fingers.

The blue ghosts came . . .

They appeared strongly here, surrounding Ennis and sliding over the confrontation between the two Arruk. With most of them, he saw the two Arruk leap at each other and begin to fight, and in each of those futures he saw that Kurhv Ruka would lose and that his own form would be lying on the ground dead immediately afterward. Ennis peered frantically around him toward the other blue ghosts, looking for the pattern that led to another conclusion, that would bring him closer to the future he'd glimpsed so long ago in Talamh an Ghlas. For a moment he despaired, for he was surrounded by images of his own death, so dominant that they obscured everything. Ennis shivered, frightened now as the two Arruk continued to

spit and growl at each other, as other Arruk warriors, seeing and hearing the conflict, started to gather around. He
was enclosed in a circle of them now, their scent overpowering and sour-sweet, their scaled bodies a forest around
him that blocked off sight of anything else.

The blue ghosts were starting to fade, and he still hadn't
found the pattern. Ennis started to sob, the sound of his
distress lost in the louder conflict near him. Kurhv Ruka
took a step toward the other Arruk, his claws slashing out
at the same time.

There . . .

Ennis saw the pattern finally. With a grateful sob, he let
himself fall into it, let himself merge with the blue ghost,
hoping the vision would last long enough for him to survive this . . .

"Wait!" the blue ghost called out, and Ennis let himself
shout with it. He pushed forward between the two Arruk.
He could hear the breathy gasp that was Arruk laughter at
the sight: a human boy, his head just reaching Kurhv
Ruka's abdomen, his skin pale and unprotected, no claws
on his hands or feet, no ripping incisors gleaming in his
mouth, no weapon at all in his hands. They laughed, including the warrior who had confronted them. It snarled
something at Kurhv Ruka, who backed away with a gesture toward Ennis. The warrior gave another laugh and
reached down, snatching at Ennis' clóca, the claws digging
into the cloth and drawing blood from Ennis' arm. He
gasped at the pain, but the blue ghost didn't cry out, so neither did he. The warrior held tightly to him, shaking him as
he ranted. Kurhv Ruka replied calmly. The gold-flecked
irises of his eyes watched Ennis.

Ennis saw the blue ghost that was himself touch Treoraí's Heart under his léine; he followed the motion and
opened the cloch . . .

Treoraí's Heart was growing stronger with every use, or
perhaps he was slowly learning how to use it. Through the
Heart, he slid himself into the body of the other person,
and there—an intruder—he simply released the wild energy inside them, letting it explode outward. There was no
careful guidance and no subtlety. Perhaps it was easier his
way—certainly where Mam could heal but one person a
day, he could take the life of more. Many more.

Once, he'd asked Mam how it felt to heal people, and she told him how with the Heart she *became* the person she touched, that she could find the hurt or injury and carefully direct the mage-energy to repair it. It was different for Ennis; he might hear the thoughts of those he touched or feel them, but there had never been the sense of merging with them. He was always separate, always himself, always held at a distance.

"It's because you're what you are," Isibéal whispered to him as he touched the cloch now. *"Your mam had true empathy. She thought of others first . . ."*

"You killed mam, and I killed you," Ennis answered. *"That's fair. I'll kill the ones who killed Da and Gram and everyone else, too. The blue ghosts showed me, but I have to do what they say. That's all. It's not me doing this. It's them."*

She responded, as always, only with mocking laughter. Below Isibéal, though, he thought he heard another voice sobbing.

In the cloch-vision, the warrior who held him was a radiant shell of yellow, a false sun. Ennis took a handful of the mage-energy and followed the connection of the Arruk's hand on his arm into the glowing shell of his body. He could feel the pounding of the creature's heart like the beating of a low, massive drum: *toom, toom, toom.* He was surrounded by the webbing of muscle and ligament, veins and arteries. With the connection came the creature's words, also: he still heard the hissing, spitting speech of the Arruk with his ears, but inside his head the words became ones he could understand. ". . . you think that this blunt-claw pup will take me more than a moment to kill, Kurhv Ruka? You're weak. You're deluded. You are less than the piss of the lowest."

He heard Kurhv Ruka's reply as if through the warrior's ears: "I told you, Noz Ruka." Ennis wondered whether the two Arruk were related, to have the same last name. If they were, there was no affection between them. "I accept your challenge, and this Perakli—this bluntclaw—will be my champion."

Noz Ruka coughed his derision. He shook Ennis as easily as if he were one of his sister's dolls, and Ennis clutched Treoraí's Heart harder. *Not yet . . .* The blue ghosts were unmoving around him. "You've finally gone mad, Kurhv

Ruka. No wonder the Kralj broke you to Ruka." With that, Ennis realized that what he'd thought of as Kurhv Ruka's family name was instead a title. He wondered what else he didn't understand, and that made him cling even tighter to the blue ghost. "Now I'll break you further. You'll take the brand of the lowest after I kill the pup."

"Then kill the pup, if you can," Kurhv Ruka answered. His golden eyes were on Ennis. The blue ghosts moved, taking Ennis with them.

He was still holding the mage-energy. Now, in the mage-vision, he opened his hands and let it blossom outward like an awful, deadly flower. He watched it rip through Noz Ruka's body, watched the power rip muscles from their attachments and shred organ and tissue, the blood boiling and erupting from torn vessels, bones shattering like a pottery mug hurled on rocks. Ennis could see the enormous agony rippling through the Arruk—a shell of blue sparks rising around him—and Ennis released the cloch as if it were a glowing coal, not wanting to share that pain the way his mam had.

"Killing is only healing gone mad . . ." Isibéal intoned. *"It's easier, so much easier . . ."*

Noz Ruka gasped and the talons that held Ennis opened; he tumbled away from the Arruk, sprawling in the mud. Noz Ruka's snout was lifted to the sky and he *howled,* keening like a maddened dog. He coughed, gulped, and then spat out an enormous clot of bright blood, spattering Ennis and the Arruk nearest him and causing the crowd around them to push hastily back. Noz Ruka shivered, his body frenzied, his clawed hands twitching and clutching at nothing. He howled again, spewing more blood; his bowels loosed at the same time.

He collapsed like a storm-felled tree, hitting the ground hard. His body convulsed, thrashing wildly at the earth.

He went still.

In the terrible silence that followed, Kurhv Ruka stepped forward. Lifting a flap of his leather loincloth, he carefully released a quick splash of urine on Noz Ruka's body. He came over to Ennis and lifted him the way his da had once lifted him, placing him effortlessly on his hip. The Arruk around them slid carefully back from the two of them as Kurhv Ruka stepped over the body and entered the temple.

Ennis could feel them staring at him, but the blue ghost simply held onto Kurhv Ruka and smiled gently and innocently back at them.

34

Movements

" . . . **A**ND THAT, MY RÍ ARD, is why we feel so strongly that Meriel Geraghty must be declared to be a Mionbandia. The declaration would mean so much coming from you, especially with all the troubles . . ."

Doyle stared from his balcony in the Ard's Keep out to Meriel's barrow on the Cnocareilig, the Hill of the Ards. Even at this distance, he could see the line of supplicants snaking down the road out of Dún Laoghaire toward the barrow. Where once they'd come to the Heart Chamber in the Ard's Keep to be cured of their afflictions, now they went to his niece's barrow to pray for her favor. Every day brought reports of more healings and transformations. Meriel had told Edana and Doyle, years ago, how some of those who came to her were hurt only in their own heads, and for that reason their own belief in the power of Treoraí's Heart sometimes healed them. Treoraí's Heart might be gone (and active again, too, far off and probably in the hands of that damned Taisteal woman Isibéal) but the belief in Meriel the Healer Ard still lingered, transferred now to Meriel's spirit.

"Meriel Geraghty must be declared as a Mionbandia. . . ." Meriel's Hand of the Heart, Áine Martain, had come to him yesterday and made that plea: "must be," not "should be." Doyle hadn't missed that distinction. The woman had gazed at Doyle and made the demand without flinching. Heart-Hand Martain claimed that Meriel's ghost had come and told her to remain at the barrow, and that is where she now lived: in the eyes of the populace, Martain the Heart-

Hand was now Meriel's Draíodóir, her priest, and she lived from the offerings the supplicants gave her.

Doyle believed none of it. But his skepticism did nothing to lessen the belief of the tuathánach. The tuathánach were restless everywhere, the Finger was in open revolt, his niece was a demigod, and now—worst of all—Lámh Shábhála had returned in the hands of some unknown Pale Witch, a Bán Cailleach with hair the color of snow and eyes like night, her face and arms and body scarred as if the mage-lights had burned themselves into her skin. All those with clochs na thintrí had seen that apparition in the mage-lights.

The burning in his stomach, the queasy fire that had been set alight the night Lámh Shábhála had reappeared with the Bán Cailleach, made him grimace. He touched the cold, smooth gold of the torc around his neck. After all the years, after all he'd sacrificed and all the loss in his own life it had taken to place the torc of the Ard around his neck, he should have felt triumphant, but it had all turned to ashes: first with the loss of Edana's love, and now again with the mage-lights.

"Da?" Doyle turned to see Padraic standing at the door to his chambers. "Rí Mallaghan is here."

The burning rose higher in his throat. He swallowed hard. "Send him in, Son."

Torin Mallaghan swept in before Padraic had even turned. "Thank you, Padraic," he said to the young man. "If you'd leave your da and me, and take the servants with you . . ." Padraic glanced once at Doyle; he nodded to Padraic, and his son gave a terse bow to Rí Mallaghan and left the room, gesturing to the attendants to follow. Torin waited until the door had closed behind them before he spoke. He brushed at the folds of his clóca, trimmed in gold and dyed in the green of Tuath Gabair; his own torc, well polished, lay under the chain of his Cloch Mór. Though his hair had long since gone gray, he still retained his full head of hair and the burly figure of a warrior. Torin Mallaghan, more than any of the Ríthe, gave the appearance of being regal. "I sent a messenger to give my regards to Banrion Mac Ard," he said, "but I'm told she's not in residence."

"Edana's at our estate in the Ceocnocs, along with her court. She says that the air here no longer agrees with her."

A single eyebrow raised itself. "The Ceocnoc hills are lovely this time of year, I have to admit, and the air sweet."

"My presence appears to be what spoils the air here," Doyle told him.

"I hope you don't expect me to tell you how sorry I am to hear that." Torin came out onto the balcony with Doyle; he sniffed at the line of supplicants shuffling toward Meriel's barrow. "I understand the Hand of the Heart wants a declaration from you. I think you should give it."

"My Rí . . ." After all the years, he couldn't call the man by his name. Not even when he was the Rí Ard and supposedly above the man. "I'm not sure that's wise."

"Why not?" Torin said. He smiled and waved down to the supplicants. None of them returned the gesture; none of them were looking at the keep at all. "After all, we Ríthe had nothing to do with the Banrion's death. That was the fault of that horrible Taisteal woman." He managed to say it without sarcasm. "Let's face reality, Doyle. The tuathánach will make Meriel MacEagan a Mionbandia whether you declare it so or not. By making the declaration, you make us look less . . . guilty, and perhaps throw some oil on the waters of the unrest. We have worse problems."

"Lámh Shábhála," Doyle said. The words burned in his throat.

"Aye, Lámh Shábhála," Torin agreed. "Which you should have had, eh?" That was accompanied by a sharp look of rebuke. Doyle pressed his lips together. He could feel a burning rising from his stomach to his chest. "And now we must wonder where will it go? Who is this Bán Cailleach who holds it and what is her alliance? Those are questions we must have answered, and quickly. Did you call back the Order's mages from the Finger, as I asked?"

"I did," Doyle told him, "but Rí Mac Baoill was incensed at the action, especially when several of the other Tuatha's troops went with them. I received a rather harsh message from him, especially after I gave him orders to advance his troops into the Finger anyway."

Torin frowned as though he'd eaten something disagreeable. "You did *what*? You were to wait until I came here to make any decision on the Finger." The acid burned all the way to the back of Doyle's throat. He touched the Ard's torc. Torin saw the gesture and shook his head. "Don't say it," he told Doyle. "You're Ard because I made you Ard, and for no other reason. You're still subject to me."

Doyle said it anyway. He couldn't hold the bile inside him; he was afraid it would kill him. "I obeyed you, Rí Mallaghan, and allowed my niece and her family to be killed. I obeyed you and I lost my wife's affection and respect. I obeyed you and we *still* don't have Lámh Shábhála—and that was not my fault. Well, I won't let you make me become the Puppet Ard. I've sent message birds to Mac Baoill, telling him that the Fingerlanders must be put down or we'll face Lámh Shábhála in the west and both the Fingerlanders and the Arruk in the east . . ."

Mallaghan's face had gone the color of the sunrise. "You don't know that."

"You saw the Bán Cailleach, my Rí. Whoever she is, *whatever* she is, she has no allegiance to the Tuatha, which means we must consider her a potential enemy. And the Arruk *are* coming; I've read the messages the Thane of Céile Mhór has sent over the Tween since Owaine Geraghty left, asking for more troops and clochs to return. The Thane's army aren't able to hold the Arruk. You made me Rí Ard; now I'm doing what that position demands—no matter who put me on the Ard's throne. Nothing more."

Torin still glared. He moved closer to Doyle, so that he stood a finger's distance from the younger man. "I don't care if it's the right thing to do. I made you Ard, aye. I made you Ard because that was the strategy that served me best, and here's what I expect in return. I expect to be consulted in the future before you make decisions that affect all the Tuatha. If I suspect that you ever again failed to do that . . ." He hesitated. Doyle saw his eyes narrow slightly. "Then Banrion Edana might find that no air anywhere in the Tuatha suits her, and Padraic and the rest of your children may find that they have no sponsors or support among the Riocha. As for yourself . . . Ards can be disposed of when they become liabilities; it's happened often enough in the past, eh? And rather recently, as well. We both know that, don't we?" Mallaghan smiled then, cocking his head slightly to one side and brushing the torc around Doyle's neck with a finger. "You understand me, don't you, Doyle? After all these years together, I'd hate to think that we misunderstood each other's place."

His gaze bored into Doyle's eyes. The burning in Doyle's throat touched the back of his tongue and he swallowed the sourness back down. "I understand you, my Rí."

"Good." The smile widened and Torin took a step back. "Then let's talk about the declaration you'll make tomorrow concerning your dear niece Meriel. . . ."

Laird Liam O'Blathmhaic might have been willing to give Kayne the two days, however grudgingly, but Rí Mac Baoill evidently was not. The word came in the late evening, not long before the mage-lights would begin sliding between the stars, as Kayne and Séarlait were preparing to fill their clochs outside their tent. There was a movement in the moonlight, and they heard a garda hail Harik. A few breaths later, the Hand appeared, nodding in Kayne's direction though his gaze never moved over to Séarlait at all. "The army's advancing toward the Narrows again, Tiarna," Harik said. Kayne could read nothing in the man's battle-scarred and weathered face, but he knew that his own face had to show his disappointment at the news. He scowled, his lips pressing together and he spat on the ground.

"Why would they do that after all their losses? I was certain they'd wait." *You needed them to wait. Two days, Sevei had said. And if she has Lámh Shábhála . . .*

"I'm surprised as well, Tiarna," Harik said, though Kayne thought he looked more pleased than disappointed. "I wouldn't have thought they'd risk the High Road in darkness, but the moon's bright enough tonight. Evidently their intention is to be close enough to come through the pass tomorrow and engage us by midafternoon."

"How many? Do we have a good count yet?"

"The scouts say they have five thousand or more, but that there are no mages from the Order of Gabair with them at all and nearly all the troops are from Airgialla. They'll have two or three Clochs Mór, at most." Harik gestured with his head toward the cleft of the pass, a darkness against the fabric of the star-speckled night. "You can see from the High Road . . ."

Kayne and Séarlait followed Harik out of the encampment and up to where the High Road lifted over the ridge of the last mountain and began its gradual descent toward Lough Tory. Laird O'Blathmhaic and Rodhlann were there with several of the Fingerlander Hands, O'Blathmhaic huddled in a sheepskin pelt against the cold wind that raked the stones. Seárlait's great-da pointed silently as they approached. Far below, the lights were moving in the darkness, a line of them snaking up the winding road. "We won't be waiting much longer, Tiarna," O'Blathmhaic said as Kayne stared down at the approaching army. "Tomorrow we'll fight rather than sitting here forever in the cold while our houses are warm behind us." The old Fingerlander sounded rather pleased with the prospect.

Kayne sighed. "We need to fall back, then," he said. "We can harry them from the hills after they come through the pass, but we can move our main force back down the High Road. Maybe to the high coast near Ballilow . . ."

O'Blathmhaic was already shaking his gray head, the strands of his beard waggling. "Have you gone daft and soft, man? Have you forgotten everything we said? We came here for battle, and first you ask us to wait. That was bad enough, but now they bring the battle to us, and you want us to turn like beaten cowards and show them our arses as we flee?" O'Blathmhaic glared at Kayne, then looked to Seárlait. "An' you, girl? Would you say the same as your husband here?"

Kayne looked at Seárlait. He could see the hesitation and uncertainty in her face. Her gaze flickered over to him, almost as if she were pleading, but she nodded firmly and emphatically. O'Blathmhaic spat on the ground, aiming carefully away from them. "And this Hand of yours? Harik?"

Harik shrugged. "I have no say at all in this, Laird," he said. "Tiarna Geraghty knows my thinking. I know my men and what they're capable of doing, but the decision isn't mine. My duty and my loyalty involves carrying out Tiarna Geraghty's commands to the best of my ability. And that's what I'll do." The words were correct, but they could all hear the unspoken criticism in them. O'Blathmhaic snorted, Rodhlann grinned.

"Well spoken," he said. "Well, I know the Fingerlanders. I know that once we've determined to do something, we do it. I know that there's already grumbling about the waiting we do up here when we can see our enemy below. I know that when I sent word to the other clan-lairds that we would wait here, they didn't like the thought of it and it took all that I could do to keep them here. I told them what you'd said, Tiarna: about your sister and Lámh Shábhála, and I don't know if they truly believed me or not. Most didn't, I'm sure, but I managed to convince them. I won't be able to do that again, not if you're telling them we're going to turn our tails without even drawing swords." He spat again, and this time the globule landed at Kayne's feet. Kayne stared at it for a moment.

"Laird," Kayne said slowly, trying not to match O'Blathmhaic's growing anger. "I ask this only because that will give us the time we need to see what my sister can do."

"And what *is* it she can do?"

Kayne had to shrug. "I don't know." O'Blathmhaic sniffed at that. The lines around Harik's eyes tightened. "I don't know," Kayne repeated, "but she asked me to wait. She has Lámh Shábhála. I know it."

"You say that, but you don't *know*," Rodhlann interjected. His hand stroked the hilt of the sword at his belt as if impatient to use it. "What if the person holding the cloch is trying to fool you, Tiarna Geraghty? Can you say that's not possible? Can you tell me that someone with Lámh Shábhála couldn't make you think it was your sister?"

"Aye . . ." Kayne started to say automatically. Stopped. "No," he admitted. "But I *feel* her. I'd know. I don't think someone would be able to fool me about that."

"Fine," O'Blathmhaic said. "I'll grant you that it may be your sister. But if it is, how soon can she be here? She's with the Inishlanders, and Inish Thuaidh is far from here."

"My gram could use Lámh Shábhála as Tiarna O Blaca uses Quickship," Kayne answered. "Distance isn't an issue." He decided not to mention that, like O Blaca, Gram could only take herself to places she'd personally been to and could envision in her mind, and Sevei had never been to the Narrows.

"So we're to wait for this person who may be your sister, who may be wielding Lámh Shábhála, and who may get here sometime." O'Blathmhaic's scorn rode the words like a garda on his horse. "It's obvious how little you know the

Fingerlanders, Tiarna, even if you're now married to one. We've managed to get the clans into fighting mood, and that's what they want to do. To fight. Now. Here." He jabbed a thick forefinger at the earth between them. "They—and I—don't care about odds. We'll take them ten to one if we must. We'll come at them from the hills and the rocks; we'll be demons they can't see until our swords pluck their heads from their shoulders like apples from the trees. We'll come down on them in a great roaring horde and the land—*this* land, *our* land—will roar with us and deafen them. We'll water the stones with their blood. And if, if they still defeat us, then we'll fight until the last one of us is no longer standing, and our children and our children's children will remember and tell the glorious story and one day *they* will rise up and finish what we could not." O'Blathmhaic took in a great breath though his nose.

Rodhlann hurried into the break. "Laird O'Blathmhaic is right. Send us back and the moment is gone, Tiarna Geraghty. Send us back and the clan-lairds will argue and disagree and finally take their people back to their homes, saying 'this is not the time' and how we must have been addled to become involved in a squabble among the Riocha."

Laird O'Blathmhaic grunted, lifting his chin. "Send us back, and I'll forever wonder what I saw in a cowardly tiarna from Dún Laoghaire that I would let him marry the great-daughter who I love best among all."

Kayne had no answer. Or rather, there was only one answer he knew he could give. He remembered standing with Da on a hill back in Céile Mhór, nearly a year ago, as a bright and glorious dawn shimmered from the dark scales of the Arruk horde before them and their war drums pounded the air. Da was alongside Aeric MagWolfagdh the Third, and he was counseling the Thane to pull their forces back to find better ground. The Thane shook his head into Owaine's argument. "No, we fight here," he insisted. "You're not from Céile Mhór, Tiarna. You can't understand what it means to see your lands overrun by these creatures. We fight them here. We must."

Back then, Kayne had found himself nodding in agreement with the Thane, eager for the battle to begin. He'd been as fervent as any of those from Céile Mhór. This was to be the largest battle yet; the others had been skirmishes and though Kayne had seen that the Arruk would fight fearlessly to the death, though he'd witnessed his own people struck down by the beasts' weapons and their slow magics, they'd eventually won the battles and Kayne was certain this would be no different. That it *could* be no different. Kayne's body trembled, his blood singing in his ear with the prebattle energy, and the sound of the Arruk drums, his fist closing again and again around his sword hilt in time to their beating, and it was all he could do not to speak up against his da. His cheeks burned with embarrassment that his own da would want to retreat when they could fight. Even more upsetting, Owaine continued to press the Thane, suggesting other fields of battle that he felt would be more advantageous, but the Thane had shaken his head to every suggestion.

Finally, Owaine had bowed to the Thane. "Then we fight here," he'd said. "But let me take my troops there; to that hill on the left flank." He'd pointed to a wooded mound well to the east of the advancing Arruk army, far from where the initial fighting would take place—not at the front of the battle but to the side. Kayne had been shamed at that, but the Thane had agreed. Kayne had argued with Da from the time they'd left the Thane to the time he gave his orders to Harik. All his protests had done no good: when the first roaring blows of the battle had been struck, the army of Talamh An Ghlas had been in a copse of trees to the left of the main force. The battle had not gone well in the first stripe of the candle, the Arruk pushing back the Thane's forces until Owaine's troops were actually somewhat behind the front lines. Kayne had been nearly bouncing in his saddle in his yearning to join the fray, but finally Blaze had opened and Harik gave the order for the riders to charge and they slammed into the Arruk in surprise from behind their unguarded flank, cutting their forces in half. In the confusion, they'd managed to reach the Arruk command—the Kralj—in the center of the force behind his wall of Arruk mages and field lieutenants and slay him. Kayne himself had struck that blow—and from that point, leaderless, the Arruk forces had dissolved into a chaos of isolated bands. Though the Arruk still fought viciously and defiantly to the death, the battle had quickly become a bloody and vicious rout for the Daoine forces.

Kayne remembered what Harik had said to him afterward, when Kayne had scornfully noted how Owaine had wanted to retreat from this victory. "Your da *saved* this battle," Harik had told him. "He was correct to criticize the Thane's plan—there'd be hundreds of men still alive this day if the Thane had listened to your da and delayed the battle until we were properly placed. But your da also knows when he can't change the decision, and he knows how to make the best of a bad situation. If we hadn't taken the flank, we would have lost this battle and if you were still alive you'd be slinking back to Concordia with the remnants, defeated. You should be *thanking* your da, young Tiarna. . . ."

Kayne hadn't understood then. Even a few months ago, he hadn't realized it.

He did now.

Kayne bowed to O'Blathmhaic, as he might have to his mam as Banrion Ard during one of the ceremonies back in Dún Laoghaire. "I'm sorry, Laird O'Blathmhaic," he said, and turned to the Fingerlander commander. "Rodhlann, if their Clochs Mór were gone or useless when their army reached the Narrows, what then?"

Rodhlann sniffed. "Then I think that we have enough good men here to prevail, especially with the Clochs Mór. We hold the pass and the heights around it and they have to come through the neck, which won't give them room to maneuver."

Kayne nodded. He stared down at the torches of the army coming toward them. "I agree. The mage-lights should come soon. And afterward . . . well, then afterward we'll make certain that their mages have used up what's in their clochs."

He felt them all staring: Séarlait, Harik, Rodhlann, Laird O'Blathmhaic. "They won't use their clochs except against another cloch," O'Blathmhaic said. "And neither you nor my great-daughter have held a cloch for more than a few days, nor have you been trained as they will have been. I would say that if you try that gambit, you won't return, and they'll have gained two Clochs Mór."

Kayne touched the stone around his neck and felt the surge of power that came from it: wild and grim and aching to be used. This was the way he'd felt himself until that awful day when his da had been killed: that he was invincible, that he couldn't be hurt or killed. That was the way the cloch made him feel now, yet it was a feeling that he could no longer believe.

"You're right, Laird," Kayne agreed. "We don't have the resources here to take out their clochs. At least, not if we follow the rules of war that they expect. You've already shown me how it could work once, and those people never returned to tell about it. So the same gambit may work again . . ."

Back in their tent, Séarlait pulled him around to face her. Silent, she regarded him, then pulled his head down to hers to kiss him. Here, alone with him, she allowed herself to cry, and he reached out to touch the salty drops on her cheeks. "Séarlait . . ."

She looked at him with a question in her eyes.

Kayne took a breath—it was a question he didn't know if he could answer. Everything was so tangled. "I have to do this," he began. "Your greada . . . my da . . . Everything that's happened . . ."

She put her finger on his lips, shaking her head. She pointed to the sky, and he saw then the colors that touched her face through the cloth of the tent. She took his hand to lead him outside. A finger of aquamarine curled around the moon, swelling and lengthening and spreading out like a writhing vine, sprouting new glowing roots and branches. Séarlait kissed Kayne again, insistently, uncaring that the Fingerlanders around them could see, her body pressing against him as she hugged him fiercely, and he heard her sob once. Then she sighed and released him. Still looking at him, she took the gem called Winter in her hand.

He took Blaze. The taste of her still in his mouth, he opened the cloch to the mage-lights.

He could feel the other Clochs Mór opening, too, and the smaller, fainter pinpricks of the clochsmion. So far distant that he wondered at it, he felt Treorái's Heart—in the hands of someone who cloaked himself or herself. Then, like a flash of emerald lightning in the interior landscape of the clochs na thintrí, Lámh Shábhála appeared. He could

feel the great stone pulling hungrily at the energy above.
As before, he could see the Holder behind Lámh Shábhála: the white hair and midnight eyes, the face scarred and
changed with the marks of the mage-lights. He also heard
the whispered name that ran through the snarled spider-
web that connected the clochs na thintrí to the power in
the sky, the name they'd given to the new Holder: Bán
Cailleach—the Pale Witch. *"Sevei . . ."* he thought toward
her, *"we can't wait. I'm sorry . . ."* but though he had a sense
that she was aware of him, this time she didn't open herself
to him; rather, there was a sense that she was using the
mage-lights even as they flowed into her—there was a
sense of movement, the hint of the cold wind of a passage,
and then she was gone entirely as the mage-lights died.

He felt a sense of loss and hopelessness as she departed.

Sevei followed the trail of energy down from the mage-
lights, and let their glow bring her back to reality. She took
in a breath of cool night air. The voices in her head yammered at her and she bid all of them to be quiet so she
could concentrate.

"Good evening, Greada Kyle," she said.

Her great-da had his back to her. He was dressed in a
rumpled clóca, his hair mussed as if from sleep as he stood
on a balcony of Dún Kiil Keep. His arm was lifted to the
night sky and the last fading tendrils of the mage-lights
were sparking and fuming as they lifted away from Firerock, the Cloch Mór clutched in his hand. She could see the
faint scars glowing on his wrist, a poor and pale imitation
of the ones on her body. Kyle started visibly at the sound
of her voice, and his eyes widened almost comically when
he turned to look at her. He tried to keep his voice calm,
but she could hear the shock in its faint trembling.

"How . . . No one realized who . . . Sevei? Sevei, is that
you . . . ?"

"Aye, Greada. I'm Sevei."

He gaped. "Oh, by the Mother," he breathed. "Did Lámh
Shábhála do that to you?"

"Aye," she told him, "and no." She knew what he saw: the
scars that covered her entire body glowing softly in the

night with the remnants of the energy she'd just taken in;
her hair white and flowing, her eyes twin pits of utter darkness, a tiny emerald sun alight under her breast. She must
look to be an apparition to him, a Black Haunt come to
steal his soul. She was naked: when the mage-lights came
and she took them in, even the softest touch of cloth to the
scars was an agony, and so she had abandoned modesty.
She took in a deep breath, letting the ice-cold of her mage-
passage from Thall Coill to Dún Kiil slowly fade from her
body.

She *was* Lámh Shábhála now—it was open and alive in
her all the time. When the mage-lights had come, she felt
the great mesh of power as each of the Clochs Mór and the
clochsmion connected themselves to that reservoir of
mage-energy above them, and she realized that she could
touch each of them, and follow any of them back to the
source. The voices in Lámh Shábhála had whispered to
her—especially that of Gram, telling her how to use the
cloch—and Sevei had touched the connection that was
Greada and thought of him . . .

. . . and she'd let the mage-lights take her here.

"He's a good man," Gram's voice whispered in her head.
For the first time since Sevei had known her, she sounded
free of pain, her voice young and vibrant. There was a joy
in her that had never been present when Sevei had known
her, a gentleness and empathy. *"Even if we couldn't love
each other as husband and wife, he was the best of my
friends, my support, and as good a da for Meriel as my
Ennis would have been . . ."*

Kyle was still staring. He seemed to realize it suddenly;
he turned so that she saw him in profile as he gazed down
at the town and the harbor caught in silvered moonlight. "I
wondered," he said. "I wondered when I felt Lámh Shábhála again a few nights ago who might be the new Holder.
All of us with clochs saw an image of you—Bán Cailleach,
some have named you. But no one saw the person clearly
enough to know who it was. I thought, hoped, that it was
Jenna somehow hiding herself." The corners of his mouth
turned in a soft smile touched with sadness and concern,
his lips closed. "So it's as I feared. Jenna . . . ?"

"Gram's dead, Greada. I'm sorry. But she's in here—"
Sevei touched her breast, where an emerald glow burned

under her skin, "—and she says to tell you that she loved
you, and will forever be grateful for what you did for her."
He gave a nod at that, and she saw his eyes shimmer with
sudden moisture. He touched the sleeve of his clóca to his
face. Sevei wondered why she wasn't crying herself in sympathy, but she was dry inside, all the grief burned away
leaving an arid void behind. "She's with me all the time,
Greada, in the cloch," she told him

He nodded without looking at her. The light of the oil
lamps on the wall of the balcony glittered in his eyes. "I
knew. I heard the rumors, and I knew she wouldn't have
given up Lámh Shábhála easily. When I couldn't feel the
Great Stone in the mage-lights for over a moon, when we
heard that *Uaigneas* had been sunk, when the horrible
news came out of Talamh An Ghlas about Meriel and
Owaine and all you children . . ." He gave a gasp and
leaned over his hands fisting around the rail of the balcony,
and she heard his voice break on a sob. "Oh, Mother, so
many of my family gone. I feel so sick . . ."

"At least some of the Ríthe were involved," Sevei told
him. "It was the Order of Gabair who came after us and
killed Gram. Uncle Doyle was there and so was Padraic,
along with a whole double-hand of the green-robes. The
Ríthe have named Uncle Doyle as the Rí Ard in payment.
I don't know who controlled it; maybe Rí Mallaghan; this
smells of him, and I know Mam never trusted him. I don't
think Aunt Edana was among the conspirators. At least I
hope not."

A nod. Kyle sniffed and wiped at his eyes again as he
straightened. "I suspected as much; the spies we have
among the Riocha said the same. My poor Meriel—the
long peace she brought us was only a lull . . ." He blinked
and wiped at his eyes again, and this time they remained
dry. After his first stare, he hadn't glanced at Sevei again—
his gaze kept slipping to one side or the other. "Are you . . .
cold?" he asked, and she remembered her nudity. The scars
were no longer glowing and the touch of the wind on her
skin raised goose bumps along her limbs.

"Aye," she told him. "I'm cold, Greada. And I hurt." *"Ah,
andúilleaf,"* more than one voice whispered that in her
head, but it was Gram's that scolded them and sent them
into silence. *"No, you must be stronger than I was, my dar-*

ling. *That path leads to madness, and I was mad—I know
that now. You must bear it. I'll help you as much as I can . . ."*
Sevei gave a short bark of a laugh; even to her ears, it
sounded like the cough of a seal. "I understand Gram better now than I ever did. Some kala bark . . . ?"

"Certainly," he said, his voice as formal as if he were addressing a stranger rather than his great-daughter. She
could sense that he wanted to hug and embrace her, but
that he was also afraid of this Bán Cailleach. He walked
past her carefully without touching her, avoiding looking
directly at her, and gestured to the arch of the balcony.
"Let's go inside, then."

A half-stripe later, Sevei sat gingerly in Greada's softest
chair, sipping the hot kala bark tea that Kyle's long-time attendant Alby brought. Alby's intake of breath was audible
when he first saw her, and he seemed to retreat gladly from
the chamber when Kyle asked him to leave the two of them
in private. Sevei told Kyle everything, from the attack on
the *Uaigneas* to the trial of the Scrúdú. Kyle shook his head.

"We Inishlanders will have our revenge for this," he said
grimly. He fingered Firerock. "Doyle Mac Ard and the
Ríthe will have to answer to the ghosts of those they murdered. You should be able to do that easily, Sevei. Follow
the path from the mage-lights to Snapdragon as you did to
Firerock, and strike Doyle Mac Ard before he even realizes that you're there. Or send me to do it, if you can."
Greada's face was set into what was almost a smile. "I
would make him pay for what he's done, gladly."

Voices screamed in agreement inside her, and she could
feel a sympathetic surge of anger in herself from their
emotions, but she shook her head. Her gram, though, easily overrode the others. *"Wait,"* she said. *"Wait until you're
certain who did what. Wait. Here, listen to someone else who
would tell you the same . . ."*

And now another voice rose alongside Gram's, a voice
she'd begun to hear since the Scrúdú, one that, like Jenna's,
she could easily pluck from among the others: Carrohkai
Treemaster. The ancient Bunús Muintir whispered to her:
*"Those who pass the Scrúdú have so little time. A few years,
no more and quite possibly much less, and you'll die. Yet the
changes you make will last for centuries. You will be remembered, but it's your choice as to how. . . ."*

"I've nothing to fear from one Cloch Mór, Greada," Sevei told him, fixing her pupilless gaze on Kyle. "If I were going to strike down Uncle Doyle, I'd make certain that he saw me. I'd want him to look into my face—*this* face, Greada, the Bán Cailleach's face, the one you have so much trouble looking at—and make him take that vision back to the Mother-Creator." With Sevei's rebuke, Kyle looked down at his hands folded on his lap, then lifted his chin until his eyes met Sevei's. He blinked heavily, but he kept his gaze there. She almost smiled; inside, Gram and Carrohkai Treemaster laughed with her. "I know what I look like, Greada. I saw it in Thall Coill. No one takes the Scrúdú untouched and unchanged, even those who survive. I know that now. That's why I won't go to Uncle Doyle and strike him down, even though he deserves less mercy than I'd give a mad dog."

"I don't understand."

Sevei shrugged. "I don't either. Not really. But when you can see the heart of your enemy, it's difficult to hate them. Uncle Doyle isn't so different from you or me. Well, maybe different from me, now." She laughed, and she could hear the bitterness that edged it. "I suspect he believed that what he was doing was right."

"Sevei, what's happened to you?" He leaned forward in his chair. He reached out toward her and placed his hand on her arm: gingerly. She could feel his fingers, as if a great stone had been placed on her arm, nearly crushing it. "Ah, my poor Sevei . . ."

She wanted to sob with his sympathy, wanted to let go of herself and collapse into his embrace as she had dozens of times over the years. She wanted to be a little child crying in his arms over a scraped knee or a cut, and have him kiss away the tears and reassure her that it would be all better soon. She wanted him to cocoon her against the world; she wanted him to take her back three months to when her world had been simple and free of this pain and grief, to when her world had been circumscribed by the routines of the White Keep and her love for Dillon, when she'd been looking forward to returning to Dún Laoghaire and Mam and Da and introducing Dillon to them, to when she'd seen her future as wife and lover and mage, with their own children. She wanted to rid herself of the voices that scolded

and mocked and screamed at her from behind Gram and
Carrohkai Treemaster.

Greada could do none of that, she knew. No one could.

"You are *Lámh Shábhála now, like us,"* Gram said. *"You
have no choice, my dear. No choice . . ."*

". . . great things. You can do great things . . ."

". . . you'll die in agony and terror . . ."

*". . . you're marked, and no one will ever know you or
love you or understand you . . ."*

". . . you'll be alone. Always alone . . ."

*". . . no, not alone. We'll always be with you. Always. You
can't ever be rid of us . . ."*

Gram's voice returned last. *". . . when you're here, when
you're with me again, the pain will be gone. I promise you
that much, my love. That's the gift of the Scrúdú: when
you're with those who have passed the Scrúdú, you'll be
whole again."*

Sevei bit at her lip, forcing back the cry she wanted to
make. "I don't know who I am right now," she said to him.
She could hear the tears trembling in her voice, but her
night-cloaked eyes remained dry. "I'm not Sevei—not the
Sevei I used to be. But I don't know what I am or what I'm
to do." She stopped herself then, taking a long, slow breath.
"Kayne's still alive, Greada," she said. "He's in the Fingerlands and he holds Blaze, so I know Da is dead. And Treoraí's Heart is in Céile Mhór."

"Who holds the Heart? Was the Thane part of the conspiracy against Meriel?"

Her shrug rubbed her stiff skin against the chair's cloth,
making her grimace. The kala bark was dulling the pain of
her scarred body, but she could still feel the throbbing, constant ache. She knew now how easy it must have been for
Jenna to have fallen into the terrible embrace of andúilleaf. *". . . the leaf, the leaf . . ."*

"I've felt Treoraí's Heart in the mage-lights," she said,
"but I can't see who's wielding it. Whoever it is pushes me
out and I can't break through the shield." She gave another
short, mirthless laugh. "Gram always seemed scornful of
Mam's choice, and Máister Kirwan always called the Heart
a clochmion, even though it scarred Mam's arm worse than
a Cloch Mór. I think they were both wrong, Greada. I think
the Heart is potentially a rival to Lámh Shábhála." She

frowned as her words brought Máister Kirwan's face into her memory, and that reminded her of another thing. "Greada, Padraic Mac Ard holds Snarl, so Máister Kirwan is dead, too."

"Perhaps not," Kyle told her. His hand tightened on her arm and she nearly screamed from the pain. He seemed to realize it and let go of her. "There are rumors that he's imprisoned in Lár Bhaile, in the Order of Gabair's Keep, though, without his cloch, he'll be in torment and may be wishing for death." Kyle let out a long, shuddering breath. His face seemed older and more lined than it had even half a stripe ago. "But I'm glad to hear about Kayne. All your other sibs are gone: Tara and Ionhar are dead—I've had confirmation of that from someone who saw the bodies. We've heard that Ennis was with Meriel when she died and was taken from Dún Laoghaire by the Taisteal woman who poisoned your mam, but no one knows what's happened to him. I don't have much hope for him, though, especially if Treoraí's Heart is in Céile Mhór. It would make sense for a Taisteal to go there, and from Céile Mhór all the way to Thall Mór-roinn, if she can get through the Arruk. We may have lost Treoraí's Heart forever." He stood and paced the room. "The Comhairle's in an uproar, Sevei. The Inish clans are concerned that the Ríthe might be sending an army here soon, and we have too few resources to resist them with the Order of Inishfeirm in disarray, Lámh Shábhála lost, and our Banrion dead. They'll be glad to know that you're here, that you have Lámh Shábhála . . ."

". . . war! Aye, let it be war! . . ."

". . . Aye! Bathe your misery in blood as I did . . ."

". . . it is what Lámh Shábhála has always done . . ."

". . . great things. . . . Great things . . ."

". . . war is not great," Gram and Carrohkai Treemaster scolded the voices in unison. "War is sadness and failure . . ."

"I only came here to see you again, Greada," Sevei interrupted. "So you'd know for certain what happened to Gram and me. I'm not staying here. I'm called elsewhere."

He spun about at that, his face limned in the glow of the hearth. It reflected dismay as well as heat. "You have to stay, Sevei," he said. "Inish Thuaidh needs you."

"The Comhairle and the clans don't want me, Greada.

They want Lámh Shábhála," she answered, touching her breast where the stone glowed. "In that, the Inishlanders aren't much different from Uncle Doyle."

She thought he might display outrage at that. His eyes widened, his mouth opened. But his voice was soft and gentle and understanding. "Jenna would never have understood or agreed with that," he told her. "But your mam . . . You sound like her, Sevei. How long will you stay? I should let the Comhairle know . . ."

"Until the mage-lights come tomorrow night," she told him. "No longer. But I'll go and talk to the Comhairle with you. . . ."

35

Arrows and Trees

HARIK ACCOMPANIED KAYNE as they rode through the pass and down toward the still-ascending army. The wind raked the slopes; the rocks of the mountains tore open the low clouds and tossed spatters of rain down on them; the horses skittered gingerly down the muddy slope until they reached a wide straight road well down from the Narrows where they could see for a long distance. Massive rocks tilted in the stony soil all around them, like the gravestones of giants. One of them had fallen recently, the torn ground at the base as black as old blood. Seeing it, Kayne stopped.

Glancing behind and up, Kayne could see the ragged jaws of the pass where the laird and the Fingerlanders waited. They could hear the clamor of the approaching vanguard. At Kayne's gesture, Harik unfurled the white banner; the advance riders of the Airgiallaian force saw them—they could hear the shouts of orders faint in the distance, and one of the riders below was given a hastily-made flag of parley. He rode quickly ahead to stop just out of easy arrow range—though, Kayne noted carefully, not out of range for the bows that Séarlait and the Fingerlanders used—and hailed them. "The Tiarna Maitiú O Contratha, commander of the Southern Army of Tuath Airgialla, demands to know who requests parley," the man called.

"I am Tiarna Kayne Geraghty of Dún Laoghaire, son of the Banríon Ard, Commander of the army of Dún Laoghaire and heir to the throne of the Ard," Kayne shouted back. "I would speak to Tiarna O Contratha."

The rider stared at Kayne for a long breath, then turned
his horse and rode back through the ranks of the gardai.
Not long after, the front row of the troops parted and two
horsemen rode forward under a white banner. Kayne recognized the man on the left, dressed in gold-stamped
leathers: Tiarna O Contratha of Airgialla, a nephew of Rí
Mac Baoill to whom Kayne had once been introduced. A
cloch hung around his neck on a golden chain. "The words
of a pretender mean nothing," O Contratha declared without preamble. "But I see you, Kayne Geraghty. You ride
with Fingerlanders who are traitors to their Rí—that
makes you a traitor also. There's no parley for traitors; you
know that law as well as I do."

"That's it, Tiarna? That's all you have to say?" Kayne
frowned, raising his voice so that his horse fidgeted nervously. He wanted the soldiers with the army to hear him,
though he had little enough hope that it would do any
good. "The Ríthe murdered the Healer Ard and the rest of
my family without warning or cause, and you dare, you
dare to call *me* traitor, Tiarna? My loyalty is to Talamh An
Ghlas and all the Tuatha. I am the heir to the Healer Ard,
and I name Rí Mac Baoill and the other Ríthe as true traitors. I've come to see if there is anyone here who will admit
the truth, who is willing to ride with me to Dún Laoghaire.
Ride with me, Tiarna O Contratha—ride because that
would be just and right, and the Mother-Creator and all
those who are honest realize it."

He could see that the gardai were listening, and that
there were stirrings in the ranks and a few nodding heads.
He could imagine their whispers even if he couldn't hear
the words. *"The Healer Ard's son . . . They say that she still
heals, even from the grave . . ."* For a moment, Kayne felt
hope rise within him—that he wouldn't have to do what
still struck him as somehow dishonorable, that the affection Mam had for all Daoine might reach out even in death
and end this peacefully.

But O Contratha glared back at his men, and the whis-
perings went silent. "You're deluded with grief, Tiarna
Geraghty," O Contratha answered coldly. "I'm sorry for
the Banrion Ard's death, but the murderer wasn't the
Ríthe, only her Taisteal nursemaid." O Contratha's gaze
went up to the pass above Kayne, pointing with his chin.

"Everyone knows that the Taisteal are as untrustworthy as Fingerlanders."

"I am married to a Fingerlander," Kayne told the man. "Insult them, and you insult her. Insult her, and you insult me."

"Then you've made yet another poor choice, Tiarna," O Contratha sniffed, "and we've nothing more to say to each other. Get out of my way and let me do what I must." He pulled at the reins of his horse, turning its head.

"We shouldn't be fighting each other, Tiarna," Kayne called out, caring more that the other soldiers heard him than O Contratha or the other Riocha, trying once more to end this. "Our true enemy is out there past the Fingerlands in Céile Mhór, and it's coming to us. The Arruk will laugh if they find we've slaughtered each other before they even arrive. The Banrion Ard knew that, which is why she sent my da to Céile Mhór. Yet we come back after fighting for Talamh An Ghlas, and find that our own cousins attack us—without warning. We find the Healer Ard assassinated. My mam *healed,* Tiarna. She healed anyone who came to her: tuathánach, céili giallnai, or Riocha, from the commonest to the most royal."

The whispers had begun again. *"Aye . . . She did that . . . My own cousin was healed by her . . ."*

This time Tiarna O Contratha turned and shouted back at his men. "Be silent in the ranks!" he barked. He gestured to the rider with him, and the man yanked on his reins and rode quickly back to the waiting army. Kayne heard him snarl at them.

"You want this battle to end without blood, Tiarna Geraghty?" O Contratha continued. "I'm willing to allow that. Tell the Fingerlanders to lay down their arms and go back to their hovels," O Contratha answered. "And surrender yourself to me to be taken back to Rí Mac Baoill."

"I've done nothing that deserves surrender, Tiarna. I'm the Healer Ard's son, and I served her well and loyally. She brought peace to Talamh An Ghlas for nearly two doublehands of years. I say that we should return to that. I say that we should heal rather than kill, and if you turn your army back now, *we* will let *you* go unharmed." Kayne pointed back to the Narrows above them. "There's nothing but death for you and your gardai there, Tiarna. The ghosts of the last

force Rí Mac Baoill sent to the Fingerlands are howling in
the air for you. If you listen, you can hear them."

The Airgiallaian soldiers nearest looked to where Kayne
pointed, but O Contratha laughed derisively and loudly.
His horse whickered in response, its front hooves tearing at
the ground. "Let them howl," he spat. "You'll soon be with
them. I'm done with you, Tiarna."

Kayne's faint hope faded and he realized that they must
do what they had planned to do all along. He frowned.
"No, you're not," he told O Contratha. He nodded to
Harik, who tossed the white banner aside. "The truce is
over. Take your cloch, Tiarna." As O Contratha scowled
and his hand flew to the chain around his neck, Kayne took
Blaze in his hand, opening the cloch.

Blaze tinged the world red, and in the midst of the
bloody wash was a blue star: the Cloch Mór known as
Bluefire. It bloomed and brightened even as Kayne took
Blaze and hurled its power toward O Contratha. Twin me-
teors belched smoke and flame, roaring away from Kayne
and arrowing toward O Contratha, but the cobalt star
flared also and the fireballs hissed and split to either side,
striking the ground to the right and left of O Contratha.
The tiarna laughed. "I was schooled by the green-robes of
the Order of Gabair, Geraghty," he said. "What are you?
Just an untrained Inishlander pup . . ." With that, the azure
radiance raced outward like the ripple on a pond. Kayne
pulled energy from Blaze, desperately throwing it between
the wave and his small group, but where the ring touched
the power that Kayne held, the impact was a physical blow
that tore Kayne from his horse's back and threw him to the
ground. Blue fire and red sparks exploded around him and
Kayne cried in surprise and pain. His ribs, not yet fully
healed, tore in his chest so that he could hardly breathe,
but he saw that Harik was still on his horse. "Go!" he managed to shout to Harik as he struggled to get to his feet.
"This is what we came for. Go!"

He saw Harik hesitate and then obey, turning his horse
and fleeing back up the road toward the Narrows. O Contratha saw him as well, and Kayne saw the blue sun bloom
again. In desperation, Kayne took the power of Blaze and
wrapped it around the sea of O Contratha's cloch. He
could feel the energy in the cloch yearning to break free,

but though the snarled energy crackled and hissed and
Kayne could feel each spark as if it were a flame touching
his own skin, he held. He screamed: he couldn't hold it back,
not with the agony of trying to contain the magic. He could
hold it only a few breaths, but even as he let it go, he pushed
it aside and the energy broke well to the side of the road.

Harik galloped on.

Kayne stood uneasily. He could see, with his true eyes, the
nearest soldiers readying bows, and the rider who had accompanied O Contratha riding hard back to his commander.

Kayne limped toward his own horse, his ribs stabbing at
his lungs with each jolting step, and he flung a firebolt
toward O Contratha as he ran. "Now!" he shouted to the
air, as if calling on ghosts that only he could see. "Now!"

Kayne held fire in his mind even as he took the reins of
his horse. He pushed it at O Contratha, not caring if he
managed to get through the man's shield, wanting only to
snare the man's attention and make him use more of the
power within the Cloch Mór. Blood met sky between them
in a fury, and it was all Kayne could do to continue to keep
his hand around his own cloch. He could feel the power
draining from it, too quickly, and he despaired, thinking
that it was too late, that he was lost.

Bowstrings sang the single note of their death song;
black darts arced in the sky from either side—the long
bows of the Fingerlanders, lying in ambush for O Contratha as they had for Mac Baoill. Belatedly, O Contratha
realized what was happening and he tried to pull the cloch-
power away from Kayne, but Kayne held him desperately,
sending more fire at him from Blaze. "Coward!" he
shouted at Kayne. "So you are indeed a Fingerlander!"

The other rider went down, arrows sprouting in his
chest, but blue fire consumed most of the bolts directed to
O Contratha. But not all. An arrow buried itself in his
thigh, another in his chest, and one arrow took him in the
throat. O Contratha's hand went to his neck, releasing
Bluefire, and Kayne saw blood spouting from between the
man's fingers. His eyes widened; his mouth opened as if he
were going to shout once more, but only blood emerged.

Harik had turned and come back at Kayne's call—now
he pounded past Kayne. Even as O Contratha started to
fall, Harik leaned over in his saddle and tore the chain of

Bluefire from around the man's neck. He lifted the Cloch
Mór high in triumph even as the shorter bows of the Airgiallaians loosed and a wave of riders came through the
ranks of the soldiers to be cut down in another storm from
the two double-hands of Fingerlander archers in the rocks
to either side of the road. Séarlait was among them—she
had insisted on coming, though Kayne had told her not to
use Winter unless there was no other choice: let them think
they faced only one Cloch Mór.

Despite the arrows, riders were still charging toward
them, and some of the foot soldiers had pulled swords and
were following them up the road. Worse, Kayne felt a new
Cloch Mór open somewhere close by, behind the ranks of
the army but moving forward.

"Back!" Kayne shouted. "We've done all we can do now.
Back!" Harik turned his mount hard at the command, glaring defiance at the onrushing Airgiallaians. The Fingerlander archers fired a last volley and melted back the way
they'd come, into the hidden paths that only they knew.

As he saw Harik turn, Kayne released Blaze and pulled
himself astride his own horse. As he did so, he felt something break inside and a terrible pain lanced through his
right side, so strong that he nearly fell backward to the
ground again. He managed to haul himself the rest of the
way up, but he couldn't straighten. He coughed in surprise
and pain, and flecks of blood spattered from his mouth to
dapple the neck of his horse. "Tiarna!" he heard Harik yell
from alongside him. "Can you ride?"

Kayne tried to speak and found that he had no voice—he
could barely draw a breath against the pain. He nodded, still
hunched over. He kicked feebly at his mount, who didn't
move. He felt Harik take the steed's bridle. "Hang on!" he
said to Kayne. "*Imigh!*" he shouted to the horse. "Go!"

Kayne clutched desperately at the reins and his mount's
neck as they galloped up the road in full retreat. Each
stride was like a knife in his side and the world slowly
darkened around him as they rode.

The news that Lámh Shábhála had returned to Dún Kiil
spread out like a spring flood, rushing everywhere that it

could possibly flow. The Comhairle—the council of thirteen, the heads of all the townlands of Inish Thuaidh—had
been in nearly daily session since word had come of the
sinking of *Uaigneas* and the death of the Banrion Ard.
From the point of view of the Inishlanders, until today the
news had gone rapidly from bad to worse. The initial report
that the Banrion Ard's death had been an accident in the
storm had quickly been debunked; like the rest of the
Tuatha, they soon realized that this had been a concerted
attack on the entire family. When Lámh Shábhála failed to
appear with the mage-lights in succeeding nights, when it
was apparent that Snarl, the Inishfeirm Máister's Cloch
Mór, was somewhere in Talamh An Ghlas under a new
holder, when it was learned that Doyle Mac Ard had been
named Rí Ard, the Comhairle had erupted into fearful and
accusatory arguments as old clan alliances—submerged
for long decades under Jenna's reign as Banrion Inish
Thuaidh—emerged once more.

   As the husband of the Banrion, Greada Kyle had been
named as Rí Inish Thuaidh in her absence, but where Jenna
had been able to command the Comhairle through a coali-
tion of clan heads among the Comhairle and because she
held Lámh Shábhála, Kyle MacEagan had neither advantage. The alliance had shattered under the pressure of the
current crisis, Kyle's cloch was but a Cloch Mór, and the
torc that Kyle MacEagan wore gave him little more than a
title. The Comhairle had been unable to even coordinate a
plan for defense. Half the clan leaders were ready to pull
back to their ancient mountain fastnesses and hiding
places should the Tuatha come with an army to take the island, as seemed likely.

   And now Lámh Shábhála returned around the neck of
Jenna's transformed great-daughter—the Bán Cailleach—
and the Comhairle was more confused and rancorous than
ever. Sevei was seated next to Greada Kyle, wearing a
clóca of the softest cloth that could be found, though it felt
as though she wore a robe of needles. Even clothed, they
stared at her as if she were something from a nightmare.
Whenever she caught someone looking at her, they quickly
turned their heads and would not meet her gaze. None of
them had yet addressed her directly.

   The Comhairle met, as it had met for generations, in the

Weeping Hall of Dún Kiil Keep. Even before this, in her
visits to Dún Kiil, Sevei had found the ancient chamber to
be depressing and cold, with the slow beat of water falling
from distant ceiling to stone floor like a wet heartbeat in
the background. Now the dripping was nearly unheard
through the passionate speeches punctuated by shouts of
agreement or objection from among the Comhairle.

". . . we can't stand against the Tuatha. Not this time, and
not even with Lámh Shábhála. The Order of Inishfeirm is
in shambles and utterly failed in its task to protect Inish
Thuaidh," proclaimed Ronat Ciomhsóg of An Cnocan to a
chorus of mingled support and disagreement. Siúr Alexia
Meagher of the Order of Inishfeirm, not a member of the
Comhairle but in attendance as the representative of the
Order in Mundy Kirwan's absence, rose immediately. Her
white clóca and léine swirled about her as she shouted
down the representative of Na Clocha Dubha who tried to
speak before her.

"The abilities of the Order of Inishfeirm have been damaged, aye, but we're not helpless," she snapped at Tiarna
Ciomhsóg. Sevei remembered that voice from her time as an
acolyte: searing and harsh, her head and her voice both qua-
vering from a palsy of age, but as strong as an ancient oak.

"What does Inishfeirm have now?" Ciomhsóg shouted
back at her across the chamber. "A few clochs and a bevy
of helpless acolytes? You stand here for the Order, and you
don't even have a Cloch Mór."

Siúr Meagher touched the clochmion around her neck.
"I have a stone of Truth-telling. Here in the Comhairle,
that's more powerful than any Cloch Mór." There was
laughter at that, and one of the tiarna near Sevei clapped
his hands. "The Order still has a few Clochs Mór and several clochsmion, and we have the slow magics that all the
cloudmages are taught, and if Máister Kirwan has indeed
been killed, we'll soon have a new Máister or Máistreás to
direct us."

Tiarna Ciomhsóg scowled. "The Tuatha are hardly going
to be frightened by a few slow magics."

"With those spells you ridicule, I could pull down your
keep around you while you cower inside," Siúr Meagher
scoffed. "I'd be happy to demonstrate for you, Tiarna, if
you'd like."

Both sympathetic laughter and disgruntled jeers answered Siúr Meagher, but Tiarna Ciomhsóg had no opportunity to respond. Bantiarna Aithne MacBrádaigh rose slowly to her feet, and the Comhairle went silent. Aithne MacBrádaigh was easily a hand and four of decades old, older by far than any of them here. A few scraps of white hair clung thinly to her spotted scalp, her spine was bent and her body slow, but the Cloch Mór called Scáil hung around her neck. She had been married to Ionhar MacBrádaigh, Rí of Inish Thuaidh before Jenna, and Aithne still ruled the townland of Rubha na Scarbh. Her voice was a rasp, a husk of what it had once been; her left eye was clouded by the white circle of a cataract and, unlike any of the others, her gaze rested unflinchingly on Sevei. "We can sit here and yowl at each other like cats squabbling over a dead mouse, but there's no decision we can make—not until the new Holder speaks," Aithne said. "Any action we take depends on what Lámh Shábhála does, and we all know that." The cataract-dimmed stare stayed on Sevei, and the old woman nodded at her, as if she understood what Sevei was thinking and was inviting her to speak.

"Aithne knows. She could have been a good Holder herself," Gram's voice said. *"I should have been a better friend to her . . ."*

"Lámh Shábhála belongs to Inish Thuaidh and it must protect us," a male voice interjected before Sevei could answer: Neale MacBreen, the son of Jenna's Hand Mahon MacBreen and the representative of the townland of Dún Kiil. Sevei had met the man many times; he was no more than a hand of years older than her, and she'd even flirted with Neale on one visit until Gram had scolded her. It all seemed so long ago: now he wouldn't look at her for more than a breath before his gaze went elsewhere. "The task of the new Holder is first to protect us, as my da served to protect the First Holder."

"So you'd name the Holder as Banrion, like her gram?" Tiarna Ciomhsóg grunted. He'd remained standing. "Well, that's not . . ."

"Speak . . ." Two voices called to her: Gram and Carrohkai Treemaster. *"Speak now, or they will argue forever . . ."* Sevei rose from her chair alongside Greada Kyle's, her hand placed over the glow of Lámh Shábhála

inside her, and allowing the barest tithe of the power within it to flow out to strengthen her voice.

"It doesn't matter what the Comhairle wants." Her statement boomed in the chamber, shaking more water down from the ceiling to splash behind the cold stone throne where Greada Kyle sat uncomfortably, the torc gleaming under the chain of his Cloch Mór. ". . . *my seat. For so long, I sat there . . .*"

Sevei sent Gram down in her mind, back into the babble of eternal voices. She cleared her throat. "Lámh Shábhála doesn't answer to the Comhairle, and Lámh Shábhála is not Inish Thuaidh's," she continued. She forced them to look at her, the horrible Bán Cailleach, turning their heads with the energy flowing from the cloch buried inside her. The scars on her arm glowed softly, and she could feel the angry, painful scratch of cloth against her skin, making her want to rip the clóca from her and stand naked before them. "*. . . so let them see you. Let them be truly afraid . . .*"

"I'm not my gram," she continued. "I'm an Inishlander, but I'm also a Riocha of the Tuatha. I'm tuathánach. I'm Saimhóir. I'm dragon and eagle, dire wolf and fia stoirm. I'm the Bán Cailleach. Look at me—I'm not what I once was."

"If you don't protect Inish Thuaidh, then you're also a traitor," Tiarna Ciomhsóg spat back. Kyle leaped to his feet at that, and Aithne glared at Ciomhsóg. Sevei waved her greada silent and fixed her gaze on Tiarna Ciomhsóg. He struggled to meet her eyes. "What would you do, Bantiarna Geraghty?" Ciomhsóg managed to continue. "Can the Bán Cailleach defeat all the Tuatha? Even the First Holder couldn't do that."

"I can do things that Gram could not. I can do the things Gram perhaps should have done."

Ciomhsóg scoffed loudly. Her greada's face reddened with anger, and he shouted at the man. "Insult my great-daughter and you insult me, Tiarna Ciomhsóg."

"*I will show you . . .*" Carrohkai Treemaster whispered, a stronger voice among all the others in Sevei's head. Sevei put her hand on Greada Kyle's arm. She gave him a brief shake of her head. "Follow me if you want to see what the Bán Cailleach is capable of doing," she said loudly to the Comhairle, and began walking from the hall. Slowly, they

obeyed her: passing through the great wooden doors, down
the flagged stone corridor hollowed with centuries of passing feet, out into the courtyard and across the north gates
of the Keep Wall. The courtiers and servants in the keep
stared as she passed—"Look! The Bán Cailleach . . ."—and
seeing the procession, several turned to follow.

The gardai opened the gates as Sevei, the Comhairle,
and the growing crowd approached. They walked out onto
Battle Heath, where two decades before Jenna had led the
forces of the Inishlanders and stormed Dún Kiil Keep, held
then by the forces of the Tuatha. The outer walls of Dún
Kiil Keep were still cracked where the Stone Folk, the
Créneach, had torn open the gates. The heath itself was a
rocky and windy plateau; sheep now grazed on the grasses
and the wildflowers growing between the rocks. Sevei
walked out onto the field for several long strides. She could
hear the Comhairle grumbling behind her as they walked,
accompanied now by the gardai at the gate as well. They
complained, but none of them stopped, not with ancient
Aithne MacBráidaigh hobbling determinedly behind the
Bán Cailleach and Rí MacEagan. Sevei finally stopped by
a menhir set well away from the keep: a standing stone
carved with battle scenes, a commemoration of those
whose blood had watered this earth. Panting, muttering,
the others closed in around her.

"... I'll help you. . . ." Carrohkai Treemaster whispered
again, and Sevei heard her gram's voice lift inside also. "I
planted Seancoim's gift here, under the stone, but nothing
sprouted. I thought it was dead," she said.

"Let me see, Gram ..." Sevei thought back to her gram's
voice, and she felt Jenna's memories open to her: an elderly
Bunús Muintir, handing a young girl an acorn from one of
the ancient oaks, the Seanóir who lived in the heart of the
old Coills. "Take this with you when you go, and plant this
where you find your new home," she heard the old man say.

Sevei crouched down and put her hand on the earth; she
could feel the acorn buried below: not dead at all, but alive
and filled with a slow vitality, still awakening from a
centuries-long sleep—awakened by Lámh Shábhála and
Jenna when the mage-lights had first returned.

"... I'll show you. . . ."

Still crouching, Sevei looked at them: Greada Kyle, Siúr

Meagher, Aithne, Ciomhsóg and the others. "It's different now," she said. "Gram could fill Lámh Shábhála with the mage-lights of a night, but there are crannies and wells within the cloch she couldn't see and they can be filled, too—night upon night upon night. And that power can be shaped in more ways than lightning and winds. Watch . . ."

She stood. Lámh Shábhála next to her heart, and the cloth of her clóca felt like knives on her skin. She loosed the clasp and let the clothing fall down her shoulders to pool on the ground; underneath, she wore nothing but the scars of the mage-lights. There were gasps and cries from the onlookers. "Sevei!" Greada Kyle called as the others reacted, but she listened to none of them. She placed her hand over Lámh Shábhála and closed her eyes, seeing the green landscape of cloch-vision open around her. The voices of the dead Holders filled her ears, and she listened for one among them.

". . . they're frightened of you and they'll kill you as they did me. . . ."

". . . you're no stronger than me and I couldn't handle the power after the Scrúdú. . . ."

". . . You're a fool! The only power they'll respect is that which destroys . . ."

"Here . . ." Sevei caught the husk of Carrohkai Treemaster's voice and followed it. Far, far down inside her, memories that weren't Sevei's opened: another time, another place. *"Shape the power this way. This is how I did it . . ."*

In her cloch-vision, Sevei reached deep into the well of Lámh Shábhála, filling herself with mage-energy that sparked like a false sun, hissing and fuming. The pain of gathering it radiated through her, and she quickly thrust the power into the ground in front of her, plunging it toward the acorn in its bed of earth. In her mind, she imagined the Seanóir breaking free of the shell, sending its first shoots thrusting skyward as hair-thin roots began to dig into the ground: years of growth passing in a moment. She let the sapling suckle itself on Lámh Shábhála rather than sun and earth. There was both satisfaction and urgency in the Seanóir's climb toward the surface, and Sevei shared it: the thickening of root and limb, the feel of rich soil sliding past living wood, and then, the exhilaration of finding the sun . . .

Sevei heard the Comhairle gasp once more. A writhing trunk emerged from behind the standing stone, coiling around it like a thick brown snake and ripping the menhir from the ground with the sound of cracking stone, bearing it upward. The Comhairle retreated, though Sevei stood there, her body caught in pale green light. The trunk split into new limbs and bloomed with dark green oak leaves, still rising toward the sky, entire decades passing in a few breaths. With the new oak now twice Sevei's height, the limbs shook as if in a heavy rain and acorns rained down. More trees sprouted where they fell, curling up from the ground a breath later. Sevei closed her eyes again, seeing only with the cloch-vision and letting the energy cascade like a nourishing rain from Lámh Shábhála's deep wells. Sevei could feel the sentient life within the oak: slow, bass thoughts in a language she could not understand. The Seanóir's awareness raced through the branches of the first tree, moving out from the tree holding the standing stone and receding away from them toward its children, which were now sprouting their own children. Sevei was dimly aware of the hubbub from the people watching, but she barely noticed it. Controlling the power in the cloch was like restraining an avalanche: it tore at her, it yearned to be break free and go where it wanted—*"Aye, using the power of the mage-lights to destroy is easier than using it to create . . ."*—and Sevei forced her concentration to stay on Lámh Shábhála, keeping the energy focused and gentle where it touched the Seanóir. The tree-mind was moving far from her now, crouching and settling in the center of the new wood, and she emptied Lámh Shábhála over it, thrusting the power deep into the ground underneath. She could feel the flow spreading, imbuing the soil with its potency, but as her mind pushed the energy ever deeper, the earth seemed to scrape over her body like sharp, broken rocks. *". . . let it go, let it go . . ."*

With a cry, Sevei released Lámh Shábhála, almost emptied now. She nearly collapsed, holding herself up only through sheer will. Greada Kyle rushed over to her, placing her clóca around her shoulders, and she gasped at the rasping touch of the cloth, unwilling tears starting from her eyes. She started to throw off the clóca, but realized that they were all staring at her. She bit back the tears, holding the cloth around herself and trying to see past the bloody veil in front of her eyes, beyond the hammer blows of her pulsing temples. On her hands, she could see the scars standing out like white ropes under her skin. Behind and around her loomed a forest, the trees the height of a dozen people, the green leaves flowing out onto the slope of the nearest mountain.

"This is what you brought us to see?" Tiarna Ciomhsóg. His voice sounded as if he wanted to scoff, but the mockery was frozen in his throat as he gaped at the trees. "So you can pull a few oaks from the ground . . ."

"You should think before you talk, Tiarna," she told him, "These are the Seanóir, the eldest trees, who can speak and think. This—" she gestured at the forest, "—this will be called Jenna Coill. My gram planted the seed; Lámh Shábhála has given it the start of untold hands of years. Aren't you awed by that, Tiarna? You should be. This forest will still be standing when the mage-lights fail again, it will survive through the darkness, and it will still be waiting when the mage-lights return once more. It will be here when we Daoine are nothing but whispers and legends and ghosts. You've just seen ages pass before your eyes and still you shrug? I'm sorry for you, Tiarna, if you're so blind."

"You play with your power," Tiarna Ciomhsóg's voice sputtered, "and you forget your family, your country, your loyalty, and your legacy."

Sevei saw her greada's eyes narrow at that as his hand reached for his cloch, and through the haze of pain she forced a laugh. "Tiarna, I know my legacy perfectly. I'm what the First Holder could have been. I don't ask or expect you to like that; in fact, I don't really care. Your mistake—the mistake all of you make—is thinking that Lámh Shábhála is only meant to do a Holder's bidding." The pain was growing worse and she wanted only to retreat to her chamber and gulp a mug of kala bark. ". . . *those who pass the Scrúdú don't have much time . . .*" Sevei heard Carrohkai Treemaster's voice and nodded. "Aye," she said as if conversing with the long-dead Holder. "Not much time." Then she shook her head, shivering as if cold. She looked at all of them: her greada, Siúr Meagher, Aithne, Tiarna Ciomhsóg, all of the Comhairle and those who had followed them out from the keep.

"I'm tired and I hurt," she said, "and words . . ." . . . *are useless,* she would have finished, but even as her mouth formed the words, she felt a great, ripping pain along the right side of her chest and her vision doubled again, as if she were still wielding Lámh Shábhála.

She gasped and stumbled; she felt more than saw Greada Kyle take her arm. She was herself, and she was, she realized, Kayne. She saw his hands before her and she could smell blood and see an army arrayed before him in the colors of Airgialla. The pain was intense and awful, different than the pain of Lámh Shábhála, and she knew he had been terribly injured. *"Kayne . . ."* she whispered to him in anguish and fear. She wanted to go to him, but Lámh Shábhála was empty now and even if it had been full, she could not go to him without the connecting web of the mage-lights. *"Kayne . . ."* she called again as if she could make herself heard, but he didn't answer. She felt the pounding of hooves on a broken, rocky path and the stern black rocks of the mountains, then the vision was gone. That terrified her more, for it was as if Kayne had closed his eyes.

"Sevei, are you all right?" she heard Greada ask. She took a breath, and this time there was no empathetic pain from her side. She straightened, frowning.

"I must leave," she said. "Tonight, when the mage-lights come." With that, she took her greada's arm and pushed through the crowd, walking back toward the keep, ignoring Tiarna Ciomhsóg's continuing protest and the murmuring speculation of the others.

Voices called to her in her head, her clóca tore at the scars on her body, and she could feel the cool breath of the forest at her back.

36

The Terrible One

ENNIS CRIED WHEN he was alone, nearly every
night.

He hadn't realized how horribly alone he would feel
here, the only one of his kind among all the Arruk. Surrounded, he had only the blue ghosts to keep him company, and they were silent, wraithlike companions of no
comfort at all: phantoms of what-might-be.

After the killing of Noz Ruka at the temple of the ruined
city, Ennis had been taken to a field where Kurhv Ruka's
troops were bivouacked. For his part, Ennis clung to the
pattern the blue ghosts had shown him, not daring—out
here and isolated—to deviate from the path on which he
was set. He saw the blue ghosts rarely; when he did, the
paths they offered often led visibly and quickly to his death
or mutilation. Ennis shivered and bound himself more
tightly to *his* ghost, *his* pattern, the one that showed him
safe.

He had learned several things in the intervening days, to
be certain. He learned that the Arruk, like dogs or wolves,
marked their personal territory with their urine, which
made their cities reek to his nose. He learned that in their
mythology the Arruk were descended from Macka, the
Cat-Father, who lay with a female dragon. He learned that
the Arruk ate few vegetables or fruits, and that they preferred their meat fresh and bloody. He knew that the title
of Ruka was similar to "Hand" or "Sergeant" among the
Daoine. He learned that only the higher-caste Arruk used
a birth name followed by a title, and that the lower castes

were referred to only by their birth name—there were no families among the Arruk as there with the Daoine.

He learned all this through a titleless Arruk named Cima, who had been ordered by Kurhv Ruka to teach Ennis the Arruk language. Cima was smaller than Kurhv Ruka, and his scales were less colorful, as if someone had scrubbed him too hard and worn off the hues and shades that touched most of the other Arruk Ennis had seen. From the fervor with which Cima threw himself into the task, Ennis suspected that Cima's life would be the penalty if Ennis failed to learn quickly or well enough. Luckily for Cima, Ennis was an apt pupil. Even if his accent and slowness still made Kurhv Ruka scowl whenever he came into the tent where Ennis stayed and tried to converse with him, Ennis quickly became able to understand a significant portion of what was being said around him.

Cima told Ennis more important things as well, things whispered only when Kurhv Ruka wasn't about to overhear. "Kurhv Ruka was once Kurhv Mairki, one of the four Mairki who lead the Arruk forces under the Kralj—and the Kralj rules all the Arruk lands in Céile Mhór." The Arruk's whisper sounded like a hissing teakettle, and Cima kept glancing out of the tent in which they sat to see if Kurhv Ruka were in sight. Ennis had decided that if a Daoine could ever like an Arruk, Cima was one he could learn to tolerate. There was something about him that reminded him of his older brothers; a rough attentiveness and a decided intelligence. He spoke the Daoine tongue with a distinct accent, but his words were perfectly understandable.

"That's terrible," Ennis said. "It must have been hard for Kurhv Ruka to be treated like that." Ennis remembered the scoldings he'd received from Mam, from Da, from his various nursemaids and how awful he felt afterward. "Will Kurhv Ruka become Kurhv Mairki again?" Ennis asked, and Cima hissed even louder and his already pale scales slid to nearly gray.

"Perhaps," Cima answered. "But a Ruka becomes Mairki only by killing his predecessor." Cima shuddered. "But you don't understand. The worst insult Kurhv Ruka endured was not that Grozan Kralj took his title, but that Kurhv Mairki wasn't allowed to kill himself rather than endure the shame of becoming Kurhv Ruka once more. That ... that is truly terrible. I know this." His snouted face wrinkled as if he scowled.

"Do you mean that the same thing happened to you, too? Were you with Kurhv Mairki then? How do you know?"

"I know," Cima spat. It was obvious he wasn't going to answer with any more detail than that, another mystery. The first day, he'd asked Cima how he'd come to understand and speak the Daoine language. Cima had only stared at Ennis and given him the same response then: "I know."

The two of them were startled as the tent flap was thrown back roughly and Kurhv Ruka strode into the room. Blue ghosts entered with him, leading to several futures; with them, he saw also himself and Cima as well. Cima seemed to draw down into himself as Kurhv Ruka approached, becoming even smaller and paler. That seemed to amuse Kurhv Ruka, who sniffed in their direction as he sat down on the bed in the tent. Ennis stared at the blue ghosts, glimpsing the dim visions they represented. *There. That one. In that one I'm safe for now* ... He shifted position so that he matched the ghost of himself and sank into it.

"We go north and west tomorrow," Kurhv Ruka told the two of them. "To the city your people called Torness before we took it from them."

Cima, huddled next to Ennis, started to whisper to him and help with the translation, but Ennis shook his head. Ennis had heard the question in the blue ghost, and he spoke a single word of Arruk back to Kurhv Ruka. "Why?"

A sniff. "Your accent is terrible. Cima, can you do no better than that with this bluntclaw? That is where we have been ordered to go by Lieve Mairki." Kurhv Ruka was speaking too fast for Ennis to understand easily. Cima translated, his voice unemotional. The way Kurhv Ruka had spat out the name told Ennis that Lieve Mairki must have been the one who took Kurhv Ruka's old position— the one Kurhv Ruka would have to kill to become Kurhv Mairki again. Kurhv Ruka pointed with his snout to the stone on Ennis' chest. " 'Gossip travels faster than feet.' Is that a saying with the bluntclaws?"

The blue ghost shook its head and Ennis did the same. "What does Lieve Mairki want?"

"To see you for himself, no doubt." Kurhv Ruka smiled, showing fangs. "Perhaps to see if he is stronger than a Perakli pup with a stone. If so, he'll have made the same mistake that Noz Ruka made." There was no mistaking the satisfaction and ambition in Kurhv Ruka's voice. Cima heard it, also; the smaller Arruk laughed with him, mirthlessly, the careful, protective chuckle of an underling laughing at his master's joke.

"I won't do it," Ennis wanted to say. *"I won't hurt this Lieve Mairki unless he tries to hurt me. I won't do it just because you want me to."* But he could see the blue ghost who did say that, and glimpsed the claw that raked across his face, and the blood and the way he cried out, and so Ennis only sat there, silent, until Kurhv Ruka nodded and walked out of the tent, and the smell of hands upon hands of Arruk flooded in from the encampment.

"Pay attention to me, young bluntclaw," Cima said. "Kurhv Ruka wants you to be able to understand everything by the time we get to Torness . . ."

Ennis nodded because the blue ghost nodded, and Cima started yet another lesson, but Ennis didn't listen. He gazed out from the still-open tent flap to the meadow where Kurhv Ruka's troops were settling down for the night, and he fingered Treoraí's Heart on its chain, waiting for the mage-lights to come.

The Arruk moved impossibly fast, loping over the emerald, sea-swell hills of Céile Mhór for stripes at a time and covering more ground in a day than Ennis believed possible. Ennis' own litter was borne by a quartet of stout and tireless bearers, following just behind Kurhv Ruka's own litter in the midst of the moving army. Ennis remembered taking a trip in a carriage the year before with his mam, traveling from Dún Laoghaire to Lár Bhaile in Tuath Gabair to see Uncle Doyle and Rí Mallaghan, and that journey had taken three days. Torness was easily twice as far, and yet they managed it in the same amount of time, moving swiftly day and night, pausing only for a few hours of sleep each night when the mage-lights swept over and through the clouds.

Torness . . . Torness was worse than anything Ennis could have imagined. It looked as if a great dragon had come and ravaged the city, tearing roofs apart with immense claws, knocking down walls with a huge, lashing tail and belching fire to blacken the stones. But there'd been no dragon, only the war machine that was the Arruk. Cima, riding in Ennis' litter with him, had told him what it had been like.

"It was a glorious four days, some of the most glorious since we came into these lands. Meidi Kralj led us then, who was killed by a bluntclaw soldier less than a cycle ago. Our army came full force on the trembling city. Often, the Kralj will move with only two Mairki around him, but here all four Mairki were in attendance, with all their Rukas and all their soldiers, something that we'd not done since Dúnbarr, nearly nine full cycles ago when Barat Kralj was still alive. The bluntclaw army arrayed themselves in the valley before the town in their thousands, clad in the false scales you bluntclaws use to protect your soft bodies and their little hand-stabbers that are so much shorter than our jaka. Some of them were riding four-legged beasts—very good to eat, afterward—and those bluntclaws used long poles with stabbers set on their ends for weapons, and the four-legs were also clad in false scales. There were a series of battles during those four days, and finally we had pushed them back and Meidi Kralj entered the city.

"Your bluntclaw cousins ran like scared furhoppers when we came. The injured ones they left behind completely dishonored themselves, cowardly begging for their lives. Kurhv Ruka, who was Kurhv Mairki then, didn't allow them to disgrace themselves. For their bravery in the long battle for the city, he rewarded them all with death so that they would find their place with Macka in the afterlife instead of forever wandering the world as meat-animals." Cima sighed at the memory. "We ate well that night. . . ."

Ennis decided that he didn't want to ask what they ate. "You were there, too, then."

Cima's head dropped at that. "I was," he said, as if admitting something shameful.

"Were you one of the soldiers?"

"No," Cima said, only that single word, and he would say no more.

Torness was an infinitely larger version of the ruined village they'd left. Though the Arruk used the buildings, they made little effort to repair them, seemingly satisfied with tumbledown walls and hastily erected thatch roofs braced with lumber from the rubble. Hands upon hands of naked Arruk, all of them with the circle brand on their hips, were hauling goods through the crowded streets or carrying the litters of the officers or serving as bearers. They passed a market square not far from the city gates. The gates to Torness were yawning open and unguarded, the iron-banded thick planks of oak blackened by fire, scored with blade marks and hanging askew from their hinges. In the square, Kurhv Ruka's soldiers had assembled, more Arruk than Ennis could count, filling the square so that the stalls were islands in a sea of leather, fur, and scales. Ennis had learned from Cima that Kurhv Ruka's troops had a blue chevron painted on the scales of their left forearm, blue being Kurhv Ruka's color; above that, near the elbow, was painted a yellow circle, which was Lieve Mairki's sigil. Other Ruka under Lieve Mairki's control would also have the yellow circle, though each Ruka's troops would have chevrons of different colors. Under the chevron were small multicolored squares which indicated the further subdivisions within the Ruka's command: the twelve Ured of the Ruka and then sixteen Nista under each Ured. Ennis found the arrangement strangely logical for such savage creatures as the Arruk: the Kralj with four Mairki under him, and eight Ruka reporting to each Mairki, twelve Ured under the command of each Ruka, and sixteen Nista under each Ured—the Daoine, too, counted in hands, after all, though they had one less finger than the Arruk.

The stench of them in the marketplace was incredible; the sight of them—fierce, battle-hardened, and ready— made Ennis shiver and want to hide. He found himself trying to make himself as small and inconspicuous as possible at Kurhv Ruka's side as the Arruk stepped up on a tumbled wall at one end of the square. *"Seiv oder Tog!"* he called to the troops, and they bellowed the words back at him, a roar that sent pigeons flapping from the broken rooftops around them. "Victory or Death," Cima translated for Ennis, and he shivered again. Kurhv Ruka gestured dismissal, and the Ured gave their commands to the Nista, who dispersed the titleless troops.

"Come with me," Kurhv Ruka said to Ennis. "We go to see Lieve Mairki." Ennis might have protested, but the blue ghost nodded its head and he had no choice.

Kurhv Ruka climbed into his litter and gestured to Ennis to climb up with him. He sat with Kurhv Ruka as Cima walked alongside the bearers in case he was needed. They moved away from the market square toward a tower set on a hill just outside the town's old walls. Through the open curtains of the litter, Ennis could see the Arruk everywhere, masses of them clogging the streets, and more in tent camps along the hillsides around Torness, all with the yellow circle of Lieve Mairki on their arm, and with chevrons of various colors underneath. Ennis remember how the soldiers had come to Dún Laoghaire before his da and Kayne had left for Céile Mhór, and how excited and awed he'd been by their presence: a thousand solders in their chain mail and with their weapons and horses. But that was a trickle against the flood of the Arruk army. Here there were Arruk beyond count, a plague horde that covered the land everywhere he looked. Kurhv Ruka must have noticed his gaze, for he leaned toward Ennis in their litter. "Your people cannot stop us," he said, speaking slowly like his mam had when he was younger. "We go to Cudak Zvati, and they cannot hold us back."

"Cudak Zvati?"

Kurhv Ruka glanced sidewise at Cima, and the smaller Arruk scurried over. "Cudak is the God who throws the net that covers the sky every night. He's awakened from his long sleep, and now he sits in Zvati, his lair to the north, calling for us to come to him. And so we come."

Ennis frowned. He imagined a giant Arruk the size of the Keep at Dún Laoghaire, casting a glowing net over the night sky. "Why does he call you?" he asked.

Cima glanced at Kurhv Ruka, who listened but said nothing. "Cudak has snared power and wrapped it up in his net," Cima answered. "That's what our Svarti are searching for—the gift that Cudak will give to us. We . . . I mean, the Svarti . . . they can feel the power that's in the glowing web, and Cudak . . . Cudak will teach us to take that power into the spell-sticks. Once, I thought—"

Kurhv Ruka grunted; Cima stopped, snapping his long jaw shut. He raised his head, as if looking at the sky.

"When I was Kurhv Mairki," Kurhv Ruka growled, now speaking too fast for Ennis to understand; Cima whispered along with Kurhv Ruka, translating, "I once saw Cudak's web come down to a hill where the bluntclaw army waited. The next morning, when they attacked, there was one with a great power among the bluntclaws, who threw fire and death from his hand, terrible flame that slew an entire front rank of our troops. The Svarti raised their spell-sticks and howled the release words, but Cudak's bluntclaw threw back their lightning and broke their sticks. They drove us back that day when I had promised Meidi Kralj a victory, but Meidi Kralj died himself in that battle to a bluntclaw rider, and Grozan Mairki became Kralj. After that, I was no longer Kurhv Mairki." Kurhv Ruka gave a wordless hiss, and seemed to glare at Cima. "That day, the bluntclaw pulled power down from Cudak's web and wielded it the way that had been promised to us . . . and now I've seen you do the same."

Kurhv Ruka stretched out a clawed finger and prodded the stone around Ennis' neck. His eyes glittered, and Ennis could smell the scent of decay in his breath. He lifted Treoraí's Heart, as if he might rip the stone from around Ennis' neck. The thought sent terror lancing through Ennis. Inside, he heard Isibéal laugh. *"I know that pain. I know it . . ."*

Ennis was more frightened than he'd been since Isibéal had taken him from Dún Laoghaire. He was certain he knew who the man was who held a Cloch Mór in that battle. *Da . . . Da had the Cloch Mór Blaze, and he said that none of the Thane's people have clochs na thintrí . . .*

Ennis trembled, and he did the only thing he could do: he remained locked in the blue ghost's shell even as Kurhv Ruka clutched at the chain of Treoraí's Heart. "I can give you Cudak's power," the ghost said in poor, halting Arruk and Ennis echoed the words. "I know how it works, but if you take the stone from me now, it will be dead. Only bluntclaws can use the stones. But . . . I can be your Svarti."

Kurhv Ruka hissed his assent: the Arruk "Aye." "You can, indeed," he said to Ennis. "And I will be Kurhv Kralj, and you will sit at my right hand, and we will find Cudak Zvati and take what is there."

He let Treoraí's Heart drop back to Ennis' chest. He hissed again. "Oh, we will do that, you and I. We will do that now."

37

Reunion

KAYNE THOUGHT that Séarlait might tear the head from the next person who dared to poke it into the tent. She hissed audibly and scowled when Harik and the laird entered, waving her arms as she strode toward them under the canopy. "Séarlait," he managed to husk out, not daring to move or speak too loudly because of the terrible pain that erupted in his left side when he moved. "Let them in, please . . ."

Still glaring, Séarlait stepped aside to let her greada and Harik into the tent. The healer who had been lurking alongside Kayne ever since he woke up to find himself back in the Fingerlanders' camp stepped back, busying himself with the pot over the cook fire, from which streamed the aroma of kala bark and other herbs. "How are you, Tiarna?" Harik asked, kneeling alongside the cot on which Kayne rested.

Kayne coughed before he could answer, and Séarlait rushed forward to blot his lips with a cloth as Kayne shuddered under the racking explosions of breath and the stabbing in his lungs. They could all see the blood that flecked the cloth as she brought it away; none of them mentioned it. "I feel . . ." . . . *like I was caught between a god's hammer and an anvil,* he wanted to continue, but had no breath. He lifted his hand instead, forcing himself to take a breath and ignoring the spear that jabbed his insides as he did so. "The Airgiallaians . . . ?"

You're dying. He knew it. *You're broken inside and there's nothing they can do.* He could feel it, had seen it in

the face of the healer when he'd examined Kayne, could
see it now in their faces and the soft, gentle way they spoke
to him, could sense it because the edges of his vision were
as dark and misty as if he were looking at the world
through the narrow end of a broken drinking horn. Only
Séarlait stubbornly refused to acknowledge it.

He must have been unconscious for several stripes. He
remembered nothing of the ride back from the confrontation with O Contratha. It was night outside; he glimpsed
the moon, and the tent was dark and shadowed except for
the flames of the cook fire.

"After we killed Tiarna O Contratha and took Bluefire,
they were in an uproar," Harik answered. "There was no
movement forward for stripes, and we saw the command-
ers meeting in a tent farther down the High Road. Our
watchers tell us that message birds were sent both north to
Dathúil and south, probably to Dún Laoghaire. But the Riocha gave orders to the troops to move; a stripe ago, they
started up toward the Narrows again."

"They still don't believe that mere Fingerlanders can
beat them," Laird O'Blathmhaic added. His normal roar
was strangely subdued here. "They'll find out differently
when they reach the Narrows. They won't even pass
through to the Finger. Not this time."

Kayne grimaced, as much from disappointment as from
pain. He'd hoped that the loss of the Cloch Mór would
have upset the odds enough that whoever had taken command of the army would retreat, or at least wait for new orders. Shay O Blaca of the Order of Gabair held Quickship,
the Cloch Mór that could send himself or another mage
long distances: perhaps one of the Order's mages had been
sent as reinforcement. He wondered if O Blaca might not
have transported Doyle Mac Ard himself.

The thoughts chased themselves through his head but he
didn't have the strength to speak them. "Bluefire . . . ?"

"I have the cloch, Tiarna," Harik said. He held out his
hand, the chain—broken—looped about his fingers but the
sapphire glittering below. Kayne was certain that Harik
had been careful not to touch the gem itself. Harik started
to give Bluefire to Kayne, but Kayne reached out and took
Harik's hand, turning it over and placing the gem in the

palm and folding his fingers around the facets. Harik gasped at the touch, his eyes widening.

"Now you'll keep it," Kayne husked. "Fill it with the mage-lights and use it."

"Tiarna—" Harik started to protest, "I'm not . . ." Kayne tightened his fingers around Harik's, trying to sit up.

"Aye, Harik the Hand," O'Blathmhaic muttered. Séarlait watched, a slow smile creasing her lips. "We'll need the cloch."

"I have no training," Harik insisted. "And I'm not Riocha." Though his head didn't move, Kayne saw his eyes flick toward the left where Séarlait stood.

"Neither was Da," Kayne managed to say. "Nor Séarlait. And training . . ." He ran out of breath then and shrugged.

"No one else here has the training either," Laird O'Blathmhaic told Harik. "And no Fingerlander is going to care whether you're Riocha or not if you use that stone against our enemies." He laughed at that, clapping Harik on the back. "You took it from that bastard of a tiarna," he said, as loudly as ever. "Now use it against them."

Harik did not look convinced, but he nodded, staring at Bluefire in his hand.

Kayne let himself fall back on the cot. "Good," he said. He could feel another bout of coughing coming on and desperately held it back. Séarlait moved alongside him; she stroked his hair, leaning over to kiss his forehead once. Her lips and hand felt cold against the heat of his skin. Twin waves of blue and red chased themselves over the fabric of the tent's canopy, and at the same moment Kayne felt the tug of the mage-lights. Séarlait felt it also, he noticed . . . and Harik. Kayne tried to sit up again. "The lights . . ."

Séarlait shook her head desperately, pushing him back down.

"I have to . . ." he insisted, though he didn't have the strength to move against her hands. "Séarlait, I must . . ." The mage-lights would make him feel better, and if the Airgiallaians were coming, if they brought more cloud-mages with them, then Blaze would need to be full even if in the end he was not the one who wielded it. He knew all that, but couldn't say it. He gazed up at Séarlait with desperation. Finally, she nodded her head as if she understood his thoughts, and when she blinked, moisture ran from the corners of her eyes.

She lifted a finger to him and left the tent, coming back with a quartet of his gardai. They picked up the cot and carried Kayne outside. Though they were careful and gentle, Kayne still felt as if he'd been dropped from the side of a mountain when they set him down again. Moving his hand to his cloch took nearly all the energy he had; opening Blaze in his mind to the mage-lights brought him to the edge of unconsciousness and nearly swept him under. He drifted there, feeling the energy of the lights pulsing in and around him, watching as a tendril undulated from the zenith to his hand, touching Blaze and wrapping about his arm. Kayne sighed. Around him, he knew, Séarlait and now Harik must be doing the same, but he couldn't see them, lost in the growing darkness at the periphery of his vision. He could only see above, and inside where the ruddy facets of Blaze opened to him, filling themselves with the fire above.

And there . . . there was Treoraí's Heart, with its hidden Holder . . . and there . . .

. . . there was the Presence: the Bán Cailleach. Sevei. Her horribly scarred face peered down at him with gentle sympathy in the unbroken blackness of her eyes. "Oh, Kayne. I didn't realize it was so bad . . ."

"Aye, it's that bad," he said. He wanted to laugh and dared not, knowing how it would hurt. "I'm dying, Sevei."

"You can't die," she said. "I need you too much." He wanted to believe her. The power of the mage-lights sang in her voice, an undertone like the roar of a wild sea, crashing and thundering. Her skin was so bright that it hurt his eyes to look at her. He closed them against the pain.

"Kayne, look at me," she said. "Stay with me," and it sounded as if her voice spoke in his ear. He opened his eyes, slowly, and saw her not floating in mage-light, but seemingly there beside him. She was naked, her white hair wild around her shoulders, her pale skin carved with the lines of power. He could feel the touch of her hand on his face. He wondered if he was already dead and this was a last vision granted to him by the Mother-Creator. He wondered when the pain would end, and he looked away from her to see if the Black Haunts had come.

"Mam could have saved me," he whispered to her. "With Treoraí's Heart."

"I have Lámh Shábhála," Sevei told him. "And I have my love for you. It will have to do." The mage-lights were still flowing, and it seemed to Kayne that she reached up and snatched a coil of them from the sky, bringing it down to him. She pressed the wild, snarling power against his chest: it burned and hissed and throbbed, pounding at his chest. Kayne cried out with the renewed pain and Sevei wailed with him as if she felt the pain herself, but she continued to press the mage-lights down against his body. He felt them break the skin and enter, the heat spreading through him, running through his blood and his sinews. The fury of it made him gasp ... and he realized with the intake of breath that he *could* breathe, that the knives which seemed to have been inserted in his lungs had vanished.

He took a long, shuddering breath. "Sevei?"

"I'm here, Kayne."

And she *was* there. The face he remembered was terribly changed and altered, but it *was* Sevei, and it was the Bán Cailleach at the same time. He could feel the power of Lámh Shábhála radiating from her, the mage-lights still pouring energy into the Great Cloch. He could see the others also, staring at her: Séarlait and Harik, their hands still entangled in bright threads; Laird O'Blathmhaic, the nearby gardai and the Fingerlanders. Sevei smiled at Kayne, and in response he lifted himself from his cot with a groan, his arms extended as if to enfold her in an embrace.

Sevei stepped back from him, her lips turning to a frown. "No," she said loudly, shaking her head. "The scars ... they hurt too much. I can't bear to be touched, not even to wear clothing ..."

Kayne could see the pain and discomfort in her face and the way she held her body, then. There was nothing sexual in her nudity; the intricate webbing of scars that covered her body glowed as if they were a silken coat reflecting the sun. He expected to see her holding Lámh Shábhála or to have the cloch dangling from a necklace around her neck, but it was not. The mage-light danced around her but rather than gathering around her hand, they seemed to lance directly into her chest. Through the radiance of the lights, he could see a pulsing emerald green buried within her, shimmering through her flesh and tinting her face, throat, and breasts with the hue of summer grass. Sevei sighed as the mage-lights continued to pour into the cloch, a twisting funnel of energy that coiled upward from her to the sky. She touched her hand to where Lámh Shábhála was trapped inside her, and the mage-lights curled reluctantly away like the touch of a jilted lover. The mage-lights began to fade, and he could hear the whispers all around them:

"The Bán Cailleach . . . The Pale Witch has come here. . . . The new Holder . . ."

Séarlait had watched as she fed her own cloch. Now she released Winter and came running to him. She hugged Kayne fiercely, then nodded to Sevei, her eyes filled with tears. Harik and the laird watched from where they stood.

Sevei's mouth lifted in a brief smile. She nodded to Séarlait. "So she's the one," she said to Kayne. "You need to introduce me, brother."

38

The Eyes of the Storm

THERE WAS A SOLITARY figure seated alone in the dust of the High Road as the vanguard of the army entered the Narrows.

It was a gloomy and overcast morning that promised a foul and wet afternoon, and there was an apparition in the road ahead of Tiarna Cairbre Kavanagh. The scouts for the vanguard had come back with the news, and the new commander of the Airgiallaian army, Tiarna Barra Rámonn, had ordered Cairbre out to see for himself, while Rámonn stayed well back with the main force. The person—whoever it was—was cloaked in a dark gray cloak that made it seem to be a piece of fallen cloud. The outriders pulled back on the reins of their horses, their sharp, suspicious gazes going from the lone person to the canyon walls around them. Cairbre, leading the group of two double-hands of riders, had heard how the cowardly Fingerlanders fought. He'd also seen vividly how they preferred ambush to honorable open combat, how their arrows could reach farther and strike deeper than those of the Tuatha, and so his group proceeded cautiously and slowly toward the person in the roadway.

The main force was yet several hundred strides down the torturous, winding path leading up to the sharp-spired crown of the Narrows. The wind shrieked through the confines of the pass, snapping at their clothing, and carried with it the clanking of armor and the groaning of the wagon wheels from the advancing army. Cairbre knew the waiting person could hear those sounds, too, yet whoever it was hadn't moved.

Cairbre gestured to the closest riders and they pulled already-strung bows from their holders and put arrows to the strings; the outriders on the flanks gave him their hand signals: *clear.* Cairbre touched the Cloch Mór around his neck: Darkness, which could cast a pall of impenetrable night in which only its Holder could see. But enough arrows can defeat even a cloch—as Tiarna O Contratha had unfortunately discovered—and Cairbre wasn't about to let himself fall prey to another of the Fingerlanders' dishonorable traps. The vision of Tiarna O Contratha falling under the assault of the traitor Kayne Geraghty's Blaze and the arrows of the Fingerlanders was all too present in his mind, and he wished that Tiarna Rámonn were also here. Had another Cloch Mór been with O Contratha, the former commander might well be alive.

Cairbre stayed well back, out of arrow range—even, he hoped, for the damned Fingerlander bows, and he was ready to throw false night around him and retreat behind the line at need.

The figure ahead appeared to be some ancient hag, but the scouts had told Tiarna Rámonn and Cairbre that she hadn't responded to their challenges. "Did you try to move her?" Tiarna Rámonn had asked, and the scouts had shaken their heads.

"Tiarna, there was something *about* her. I didn't want to get too near . . ."

Tiarna Rámonn had sighed as if disgusted at the scouts' cowardice, but he also didn't go himself. No, he sent Cairbre . . .

In the dim light, the wind flattened the dark clóca against the seated figure's body and Cairbre could see the curve of breasts; the wind also plucked a lock of long gray-white hair from under the cowl and pushed back the cowl enough that Cairbre could glimpse a shadowed face that looked to be covered with wrinkles. "Out of our way, Aldwoman," he called out loudly, his horse skittering nervously, "or today will be your last."

The woman lifted her head at that and the wind caught the cowl, sliding it entirely back from the face. Caibre sucked in his breath. What he had taken for wrinkles were the netted lines of white scars marring an otherwise young face, and the unbound, long hair was not the sad gray of

age but a pure white, and the eyes . . . The eyes were a horrible, unrelieved blackness in her face, darker than the
storm clouds above. Cairbre realized who he faced in that
instant, knew because he'd seen that face nearly every
night when he'd lifted Darkness to the mage-lights, knew it
because he'd felt her vast, awful presence sucking greedily
at the lights from afar. The breath he took in left him.

The Bán Cailleach . . . the Pale Witch . . .

The other riders heard his gasp, and several bowstrings
t-thunked angrily without his command. The Bán Cailleach
lifted one hand (the other clasped to her breast) and the
double-hand of arrows went to sudden flame and dissolved
to ash. The witch grimaced as if pained and let her clóca
slip entirely from her body, standing as she did so. She was
lithesome and might have been handsome but for the fact
that her entire body was covered in the same scars that
marred her face. A glow the color of swamp moss radiated
from her torso. The Bán Cailleach didn't seem to notice the
wind or the cold nor care about her nudity.

"Do you command the army, Tiarna, or is it another?"
she asked Caibre. Her eyes of starless night stared at him,
seemingly boring into his soul.

"Tiarna Barra Rámonn has taken command since Tiarna
O Contratha's murder," Caibre answered. *Had* to answer;
he felt as if the Bán Cailleach tore the words from his mind.

"I know his family, if not the man, and I would hate to
see them grieve," the Witch-Holder said. "Go back to
Tiarna Rámonn. Tell him that the war against the Fingerlands is over, and he is to take his army back to Dathúil."

"Over?" Caibre answered, the word coming out before
he could stop it. "After what the Fingerlanders have done,
this war has only started. The Rí Airgialla—"

The Bán Cailleach's right hand tightened to a fist at her
breast and the words died as if the fingers had gripped
Caibre's own throat. "The Ríthe have made a terrible mistake," she said. "They have slain the Healer Ard and the
First Holder; they've ignored the true threat in pursuit of
their own greed, and now they'll pay for that arrogance. I
won't let them make another mistake now. Tell them that.
Tell them that the Bán Cailleach refuses to allow them to
come here and war against the Fingerlanders and my
brother."

Caibre blinked. "Your brother . . . ?" It struck him then. "You . . . you claim to be Bantiarna Geraghty?"

"Aye," she said. "Not a claim, Tiarna, only the truth. I'm now the Holder of Lámh Shábhála and the one you call the Bán Cailleach. Tell them that also, Tiarna. Tell them that they needn't bring their armies here to find me, for I will come to them. I'll come to them very soon. Now—*Go!*"

Cairbre's companions had been struck dumb. They sat on their horses in a jangling of anxious livery and armor. "Tiarna . . ." one of them whispered, and the fright in his voice made it quaver like that of an old man. "Maybe we should go back . . ."

Cairbre wanted to do exactly that, very much. He wanted to turn his horse and flee to the main mass of the army at full gallop. But he could also imagine giving his report to Tiarna Rámonn: *We were turned back by a lone woman who claimed to be the Bán Cailleach. . . .*

The Bantiarna Geraghty—if that was who indeed she was—laughed as if she'd heard his thoughts. "Do you want proof to carry back with you?" she asked Cairbre, and her hand tightened again. Cairbre would have sworn that the scars on her body began to glow, radiating out from her center as if a fire had risen inside her. Aye, she *was* glowing, for he could see the shadows moving on the walls of the Narrows around him. Someone's horse nickered in fright. "Do you need to see what the Pale Witch can do?" she asked, and now her voice boomed like thunder, so intense that it pushed them back, the horses retreating before the sound, their eyes showing white and large. "I will show you, then. I'll show you so that they can all see it."

The Bán Cailleach's body was so bright now that it was like looking into the sun. Cairbre looked up and saw the storm clouds were rotating above her, two whirlpools of cloud that thickened and darkened until it seemed that two eddying, baleful eyes stared down from the heavens, storm-eyes as black as those of the Bán Cailleach. The moan of the wind had risen to a howl. The banner of Airgialla was torn from the hands of the young rider who carried it; the staff and banner went careening away, smashing against the cliff wall.

"I am Storm," the Bán Cailleach called out. The voice boomed so loudly that Cairbre was certain that Tiarna Rá-

monn and the army below could hear it. The eyes far above
suddenly wept: a torrent of rain lashing at them, a wind-
driven burst that left them drenched and blinking from the
fury of it. Cairbre wiped desperately at his face, trying to
see through the downpour. The Bán Cailleach was walking
forward toward them and Cairbre instinctively retreated
with the others, backing slowly toward the two spires that
marked the lip of the pass.

"I am Lightning," she called, and in response twin
flashes burst from the mage-eyes above, shattering the
walls of the Narrows and sending boulders the size of cottages hurtling down. One struck the ground not three
strides in front of Cairbre and just to the left of the Bán
Cailleach; so close that Cairbre wondered for a moment if
she'd been smashed. But no . . . she walked forward
through the rain and mud, an emerald sun below the
storm, and the storm-eyes above watched her.

"I am the Caller of the Filleadh," she shouted, the din of
her voice shaking more rocks from the walls of the pass,
and Cairbre heard an answering shriek in the storm. Below
the storm-eyes, two winged shapes fluttered down, seeming to be no bigger than birds at first but growing rapidly
larger as they descended until Cairbre saw that their batlike wings were like the great sails on a warship and
their scaled bodies—one red-black marbled with orange; the
other darkest blue swirled with deep yellow—would have
dwarfed the keep tower in Dathúil, and the claws on their
feet were blades longer than a man. Their shrieks sent the
blood in Cairbre's veins to ice, and they landed on the
spires of the Narrows, coiled snake heads glaring down
from either side. They reared up, and the passage of the
Narrows was roofed with an arch of awful fire from their
mouths that fell thick and bright to the ground behind the
Bán Cailleach. The horses whinnied in panic, a hand or
more of Cairbre's men turning their horses entirely and retreating at full speed.

"I am your Death," the Bán Cailleach roared, and the
wind became a hurricane and the rain a torrent, and the
dragons belched fire toward them. Caibre cried out in terror, his voice utterly lost in the clamor, and yanked at the
reins of his horse. He gave no thought to his Cloch Mór or
to challenging the Bán Cailleach—he fled from the pass

and the Pale Witch's presence toward the banner and front
ranks of the army just now approaching the Narrows, not
caring whether his men followed him or not. Fire, wind,
rain, and the Bán Cailleach's mocking laughter pursued
him.

"Tell them!" she shouted in a voice so loud that it nearly
tore Cairbre from his mount, hammering against his back.
"Tell them that I will not permit them to come here! Tell
them that they have created me, and now they must deal
with what they've made!"

Cairbre risked a glance back as he fled. Above him, the
dragons reared, their tails curled around the spires of the
Narrows. The eyes of the storm clouds, the Bán Cailleach's
eyes, turned in the sky, glaring down at them in defiance
and fury. Thunder boomed, the sound rolling over the
mountains and the land, and in it were the words of the
Bán Cailleach.

"Tell them!"

Grozan Kralj's palace was once the keep at Torness. Ennis,
comparing it to the keep at Dún Laoghaire, realized that
this place must be much changed from when the Thane's
Ionadaí had been installed here. The Arruk had torn down
the hangings that had adorned the stone walls; the ragged
weavings remained where they'd fallen, torn and dusty,
with mice prowling in their folds and chewing holes in the
once-bright fabrics. The stone flags were littered with the
refuse and excrement of the Arruk, so that there wasn't a
clear path for Ennis to walk without fouling his shoes.
Kurhv Ruka didn't seem to mind, striding barefoot through
the mess; the blue ghost of Ennis walked determinedly behind him, so Ennis did the same, shoving his distaste deep
in the back of his mind. He tried to ignore the stench, the
sight of the Arruk who glared at him as he passed, the sounds
that emanated from the bowels of the place, the taste of
the sour air in his mouth. He focused instead on the blue
ghost and Kurhv Ruka's back, and the promise that the
pattern he'd chosen had given him: the future that he'd
glimpsed at the end of the path.

In the dim, uncertain distance of the future, he saw himself on a throne, and around him the Arruk bowed down and the Daoine trembled. He saw himself in a place where no one could hurt him again, and where he could punish those who had wounded him in the past.

"Follow the path." He could hear Isibéal's voice speaking to him through Treoraí's Heart, and he listened. *"You will do to them what you did to me,"* Isibéal said. There were other voices in the Heart, too. He thought he heard Mam, crying far down, and that ancient, graveled voice was there, and the voices of the gardai and Artol Jantsk and the sailors and Haughey and his wife. . . . All of them that he had taken with the Heart.

"Let me talk to Mam. I want to talk to Mam."

"No," those he'd slain all shouted back to him. *"We won't allow it."*

He tried to shut his ears to them, but he could hear them still. *"Listen to the Taisteal,"* Noz Ruka howled, close by. *"Death. That is what we Arruk understand best. . . ."*

"Follow the path . . ." Isibéal admonished him. *"Follow the path of the blue ghost and perhaps we'll let you speak to your mam."* He nodded, though he wanted to cry, wanted to flee and run from here. He would do as Isibéal said. He had no choice.

The keep's throne room was worse than the corridors. The hall had evidently been the site of a battle during the capture of Torness, and the bodies of Daoine soldiers still lay there, desiccated and skeletal now, the bones and rusting armor and weapons shoved to one side of the hall near the door. The room smelled of their corruption, strong enough that it overpowered the Arruk reek and made Ennis gag and nearly vomit as he entered.

The room was crowded with Arruk. Ennis had certainly seen his own mam's throne room full with supplicants and officials and delegates, all clustering about waiting for their moment to approach; it seemed that the Arruk treated their rulers much the same. Many of the crowd had turned to look as Kurhv Ruka entered the hall—from the way their nostrils twitched in their reptilian faces, Ennis suspected that they smelled him as he could smell them. There were whispered comments and waving of taloned hands, but they gave way and made room for Kurhv Ruka as he strode forward.

Grozan Kralj sat on the dais, the once-embroidered cushion of the throne seat now torn, the stuffing falling from rips and tears in the cloth. The Kralj was not what Ennis expected: Ennis had thought that the Arruk ruler would be old and withered, like Rí Mas Sithig back in Talamh An Ghlas, whom he'd once met. But Grozan Kralj appeared to be hale and healthy and strong, as finely muscled a specimen as Kurhv Ruka. He realized then that it was probably a rare Kralj who lived to old age among the Arruk.

Another Arruk stood to the right of the dais: shorter by a head than Kurhv Ruka or Cima, his scales paler in color and smaller—more like Cima's—his entire frame slight and thin, rather than thickly padded with muscle. The creature held a knob-ended staff in his left hand, the wood carved with what seemed to be a snarl of animal forms, all curled about one another and painted bright colors. "That's Gyl Svarti," Cima whispered to Ennis, evidently noticing the boy's stare. "Watch him carefully. He's killed more people with his spell-stick than I can count, Arruk as well as you bluntclaws, and he's always at Grozan Kralj's side."

Grozan Kralj, slouching carelessly in the throne made for a Daoine occupant, watched them with hooded eyes as they approached through the mob of supplicants. Ennis could see the guards on their stations around the dais stiffen and tighten their grip on their jaka. Kurhv Ruka stopped a careful three strides from the dais. Gyl Svarti's slitted eyes narrowed and he tilted his spell-stick noticeably in their direction. Kurhv Ruka lifted his snout toward the dais, exposing the loose skin under his long chin— Cima had already told Ennis that showing the vulnerable throat was the proper sign of respect to a peer or higher-ranked person, rather than the Daoine bow of the head, which the Arruk would have interpreted as an insult.

"Ah, Kurhv Ruka," Grozan Kralj said, with a distinct emphasis on the title as Cima translated urgently in Ennis' ear. "So you've come to show us this bluntclaw pup we've heard about? I wonder, why did you come directly to me and not go to Lieve Mairki as would have been proper?" Grozan Kralj seemed to nearly smile at that; even Ennis could hear the taunting in his voice. Gyl Svarti snickered openly.

"Lieve Mairki wouldn't have understood the importance of this bluntclaw," Kurhv Ruka answered easily, and the undisguised scorn in Kurhv Ruka's face widened Grozan Kralj's eyes and pulled him upright in his chair. A ripple of quiet astonishment stirred the onlookers, and Ennis slid close to Kurhv Ruka, uneasy. Gyl Svarti leaned over to Grozan Kralj and whispered.

"Does Kurhv Ruka ask to challenge Lieve Mairki, then?" Grozan Kralj asked. "Interesting. I'll send for the Mairki . . ." He started to lift a hand to summon one of the guards, but Kurhv Ruka gave a cough of denial.

"I've no interest in Lieve Mairki," he said. "I will deal with him when he is under my command."

That brought twin hisses from both Grozan Kralj and Gyl Svarti. Grozan Kralj stood slowly, uncoiling from his easy posture in the seat. Ennis could see the muscles sliding under his scales and the scars from his previous battles. The Arruk was massive, half a head taller than Kurhv Ruka and wider by a hand. His legs looked like twin pillars, and the talons of his fingers and toes gleamed sharp and white. He leered, showing his teeth. "You've always been arrogant and rash, Kurhv Ruka, and always too forgetful of your place. I'd hoped that breaking you to Ruka would teach you humility and caution, but it has not. You've overreached yourself this time. I'll send your head back to your mates; I'll have the rats feed on your entrails."

Grozan Kralj yawned, stretching his arms out and flexing his hands so that the talons clashed with a sound like ivory daggers. The crowd in the throne room, sensing the conflict, stepped back. Cima slid away with them, leaving Kurhv Ruka and Ennis standing alone before the throne. Ennis wanted to go with Cima, to hide and lose himself in the crowd if he could, but the blue ghost would not move, and so he stayed where he was, trembling and terrified.

He knew what Kurhv Ruka wanted him to do. He knew. He could already feel Treoraí's Heart burning against his chest, a searing brand that linked his heart and his hand and made him want to close his fingers around the stone. *"Don't worry, Ennis,"* he thought he heard Isibéal whisper. *"It's your power and your destiny."* Or perhaps it was Haughey or Artol Jantsk or Noz Ruka talking; he couldn't tell. Ennis looked down at his left hand. The scarred flesh

there seemed to glow, the curled pattern rising well above
his wrist. He reached for Treoraí's Heart, fumbled with the
cloch under his clothing and brought it out.

Grozan Kralj took a step toward the edge of the dais,
looking as if he were about to launch himself at Kurhv
Ruka, but Gyl Svarti stirred, reaching out with his spell-
stick to stop Grozan Kralj. "My Kralj," the Svarti crooned.
"Wait . . ." That much Ennis understood without Cima. The
Arruk mage was smiling grimly, and his eyes were on
Ennis. Grozan Kralj's body remained tense and ready, but
he halted, glaring, and Gyl Svarti stepped down from the
dais. He walked slowly over to them, the spellstick tapping
loudly on the stone flags. He stopped a bare stride away
from them, glancing up once at Kurhv Ruka, whose gaze
was locked with that of Grozan Kralj, then down to Ennis.
Ennis cowered, trying to hide behind Kurhv Ruka's ar-
mored hip as he'd once hidden, shyly, behind his mam's
clóca. He waited for the blue ghost to respond so he would
know what to say or do, but the blue ghost had vanished as
if Gyl Svarti's presence had banished it.

Ennis was alone, and he had no guide. *"Isibéal!"* he
thought frantically. *"Mam!"*

There was no answer. He wanted to cry, but he sensed it
would be his death.

Gyl Svarti held out the knobbed end of the spell-stick
toward Ennis. He spoke, but Ennis could only understand
a few of the words: "Move . . . Noz Ruka . . . the Kralj." The
spell-stick jabbed toward him and Ennis cowered back.
The knurled wood seemed to glow, as if the Svarti were
about to release a spell. As Ennis retreated before Gyl
Svarti, Grozan Kralj snarled and leaped toward Kurhv
Ruka, who lunged forward to meet the Kralj in the same
breath.

Ennis gave a belated cry of alarm as the two Arruk collided before the dais. The crash of their scaled bodies was
as loud and percussive as the closing of the Dún Kiil gates
in the evening, accompanied by cheers from the onlookers.
Ennis saw the two of them roll on the floor, taloned
hands ripping and tearing at scales, and blood smearing on the
stones as they tumbled. He started forward, but Gyl Svarti
jabbed his spell-stick at Ennis' chest and the touch was as
if lightning had struck him: he was sent hurtling backward

into the ring of watching Arruk, his clóca smoldering
where the spell-stick had struck him and the smell of
charred flesh strong in his nostrils. Ennis screamed in pain
and surprise as the Arruk threw him rudely back toward
Gyl Svarti. He nearly stumbled and went down, but managed to keep his footing. His fingers were still around Treoraí's Heart, and he opened the cloch in his mind as Gyl
Svarti raised his spell-stick high. The Arruk mage's lipless
mouth moved. *"He's releasing a spell,"* Ennis heard Isi-
béal/Noz Ruka say. *"Go to him!"*

Ennis shouted, rushing toward Gyl Svarti. The mage
brought the spell-stick down, pointing it at Ennis, but
Ennis grasped the end of the staff with his free hand. He
could feel his awareness shift with the touch, traveling
through the wood to where Gyl Svarti's hand clutched it,
and snaking into the Arruk. He could *hear* the creature . . .

He *was* the creature. His lips moved with the strange, un-
familiar words of the spell—". . . *molim vas ponovite vrlo
vrlo sporo* . . ."—and he felt himself recoil at the intrusion
of Ennis' thoughts into his own: *". . . the bluntclaw is in
me . . ."* But it was already too late. Ennis released the
power of the Heart into Gyl Svarti even as he felt the
trapped slow magic begin to uncoil from the spell-stick.
Ennis held onto the staff desperately, thrusting with the vi-
olet spear of Treoraí's Heart, stabbing deep, deep into Gyl
Svarti's body, letting it rip and tear and rend what it found
there. Gyl Svarti's head reared back with a horrible, gar-
gling scream and Ennis did the same, feeling the mirrored
agony in himself. Gyl Svarti released the spell-stick from
hands struck nerveless and shattered; Ennis managed to
hold onto it as the mage fell backward to the flags. The
Arruk vomited black blood; his body twitched once . . .
again . . .

Everyone was shouting around him, the yowling din of
the Arruk deafening. The cloch-energy still filléd him and
he could hear Gyl Svarti in the roar of the Heart, still
moaning in terror and pain, but inside now, inside with
Mam and Isibéal and Noz Ruka and the others. Ennis
pushed into the creature's memories and plundered
them . . .

He reversed the spell-stick in his small hand. He brought
the end down sharply on the flags, though the sound was

lost in the roar of the crowd around him and the snarling of Kurhv Ruka and Grozan Kralj, still locked in combat. The spell Gyl Svarti had been about to release toward Ennis lingered in the staff, throbbing, only a few words needed to release it. Ennis found the words, stealing them from Gyl Svarti and speaking them.

He pointed the spell-stick toward the combat before him.

The fury he unleashed surprised even him.

Lightning crackled, and Treorái's Heart lent its own power to the bolt. The fury nearly blinded Ennis, the force almost taking the staff from his hand again, but his aim had been true enough.

Kurhv Ruka lay on the floor of Torness Keep and gaped at Ennis. He realized that he was still holding what was left of Kralj Grozan: a gory, open-jawed head and shoulders. The remainder of the Kralj was a mass of blood and tissue splattered in a gruesome spray away from Ennis, who stood with Svarti Gyl's spell-stick smoking in his hand. Svarti Gyl lay crumpled at Ennis' feet.

Kurhv Ruka flung the dripping remnants of the Kralj away from him and scrambled to his feet. Bits and pieces of the Kralj slid from his body in thick red streams. "Ka-pasti!" he cursed toward what was left of the Kralj. He roared in triumph.

The sound brought Ennis back to himself. He took a long, shuddering breath. He nearly threw away the spell-stick in disgust, then realized that he could feel other enchantments placed within it. The crowd of Arruk had been struck silent. They listened to Kurhv' Ruka's triumphal screams; they stared at Ennis brandishing the spell-stick and still clasping Treorái's Heart with his other hand.

"You have defeated me. You are stronger, and I will serve you in death . . ." The voice spoke in his head, in the language of the Arruk, and it was Gyl Svarti's voice. Ennis released Treorái's Heart and the voice stopped.

The pain returned then from the burns on his chest, but the blue ghost had returned and still wasn't crying, so he forced himself to stand there grim and glaring. Following the blue ghost, he turned slowly, pointing the end of the spell-stick at each of the watching Arruk in turn. The ring around them widened visibly.

Cima hurried back to Ennis as Kurhv Ruka stepped up on the dais recently occupied by Grozan Kralj. "I am now Kurhv Kralj," Kurhv Ruka declared as Cima spoke the words to Ennis in Daoine. "And Ennis Svarti will stand beside me. Does anyone here challenge me? Does anyone question my right to be Kralj?"

Silence answered him. Around them, Arruk lifted their snouted chins in submission. Kurhv Kralj snarled in satisfaction. "Stand here, Ennis Svarti," he said, pointing to the side of the throne. Ennis went to where he pointed, Cima following, and Kurhv Kralj sat on the throne. The Arruk were now crowding around, ignoring Gyl Svarti's body and trampling the bloody fragments that had once been Grozan Kralj.

"I am Kurhv Kralj," the former Ruka said again. "And you will follow me to Ennis Svarti's land, and we will trample the Perakli underneath us until we reach Cudak Zvati!"

The Arruk responded with a clash of fists on chest scales and a terrible shrieking roar of approval. Ennis wanted to do no more than clasp his hands over his ears at the uproar and run from the hall. But the pattern surrounded him in its sapphire cage, and he lifted the spell-stick in his hand and shouted with them. At the end of the pattern he saw himself on the throne where Kurhv Kralj now sat, and he saw all those who had hurt him and his family lying before him dead.

He found, seeing the vision, that he could smile even without the blue ghost.

39

Revenge

DOYLE MAC ARD NODDED to his son Padraic, and
together they lifted their clochs toward the swelling
veins of brilliant colors at the zenith, letting the draperies
of painted light dance down to envelop their hands in a
glorious embrace.

The mage-lights reflected from the stony flanks of Dún
Laoghaire Keep, and the rippling illumination swept over
the rooftops of the town spread below them, and lent their
hues to the slow, rolling swells of the harbor. It glinted
from the golden torc of the Rí Ard around his neck. It was
as entrancing a scene as Doyle had ever seen.

He wished, as he had nearly every night for the last few
months, that Edana was there to share it with him. He regretted much of what he'd done over the last year, regretted the decisions that, he told himself, had been forced on
him and the actions of which he'd been a part. Still, nothing wounded him more than the fact that this path—the
path of the Ríthe and Rí Mallaghan in particular, the path
that had made him Rí Ard but should have led him to
Lámh Shábhála as well—had lost Edana to him.

He should have been feeling pride at all he'd accomplished, far more than the bastard son of a tiarna could
ever have expected, but he felt an emptiness even as the
energy of the mage-lights filled him.

He could feel Edana close by in the opposite tower of
the keep, in the quarters they'd once shared along with
Padraic and their daughter Alastríona. Edana had returned to Dún Laoghaire to conduct Tuatha business as

well as to allow Doyle and Padraic to share in the celebration of Alastríona's birthday. Doyle had gifted his daughter with a clochmion from the Order of Gabair, but Edana had steadfastly and angrily refused to allow Alastríona to go to Lár Bhaile to learn how to use it, as Doyle had wanted. He could feel Alastríona's clochmion and Demon-Caller opening and calling the mage-lights to them in the far tower of the keep. He wondered if Edana felt his presence as well, and whether she, too, felt the emptiness.

Out there also was the Hidden One, distant but powerful with Treoraí's Heart, which nearly all the mages now realized must be more than a simple clochmion. As always, Doyle wondered if it was indeed Isibéal who held the Heart, and where she was.

He also wondered, as he must, about the Bán Cailleach. As the mage-lights reached their full brilliance, he felt Lámh Shábhála open and begin to feed—so did all of them caught in the netting of the lights over Talamh An Ghlas. He shuddered, as he had every night he'd felt her, at the vision of her scarred and awful face and the dead empty eyes. As always, he pushed at the wall she erected around herself and was rebuffed: she would not let him see her fully. Who was she? How had she come to have Lámh Shábhála, which he'd thought lost forever at sea. Mists wrapped around the Bán Cailleach, and even as he felt her push him back, the mists coiled and fled as if a great hurricane wind had taken them. Lámh Shabhála was gone. But yet . . .

"Greetings, Great-Uncle. It's a beautiful night, don't you think?"

Doyle heard Padraic gasp even as he turned, the golden-scaled dragon within his Cloch Mór already forming in front of him. An apparition had appeared at the open door of the balcony on which he and Padraic stood: a woman. For a moment, he wondered what she wore—a skin-tight wrapping covered with glowing white curliques that mimicked the mage-lights above them—then he realized that she was naked and that the lines over her body were scars. Her flesh was illuminated as if from inside, and the eyes in that marred face were an utter and complete void; mage-lights danced above and flowed down to her body, as if entering directly into her. *The Bán Cailleach* . . . The words she'd spoken puzzled him for a moment, then he saw the lines of the face under the scars and he understood. He knew who held Lámh Shábhála; he knew who had become the Bán Cailleach.

"Sevei . . ."

A harsh, bitter smile touched the corner of her lips. "Aye, Great-Uncle. I'm Sevei." She glanced at Padraic and the smile gentled momentarily. "Tráthnóna maith duit, Cousin." She paced at the open doors of the balcony, looking away from them into the Ard's bedchamber. "I barely recognize the room, Uncle. You've changed everything since this was Mam's. All the tapestries and draperies she used to love . . ." Then the smile collapsed entirely, and Doyle saw the scars on her body glow brighter, making the eyes two expressionless craters. "That seems like another life altogether. A long time ago. Why, I haven't seen either of you since you killed Gram Jenna."

"Padraic!" Doyle shouted. "Now!" Snapdragon hurled fire and the dragon's great muscular head snapped toward Sevei; in the same moment, he felt Padraic open Snarl, whipping lines of blinding, pure energy in Sevei's direction. Doyle felt despair even as he attacked: Jenna could have handled two Cloch Mórs with disdainful ease, and he suspected that whatever Sevei had become, the Bán Cailleach was more dangerous than the First Holder had been.

He found those fears quickly justified. Sevei moved not at all, yet the dragon's fire struck the air before her and splattered as if it had hit an invisible wall; when the dragon darted its head down in a snakelike strike, it howled in pain and recoiled as Sevei merely glanced at it. The scales at its chest ripped apart and blood poured out from under them. Doyle screamed with the dragon, caught in the mage-energy and feeling the terrible injury as if it had happened to himself. In his mage-vision, a fist of fire slammed into the dragon's chest, its blood boiling and steaming beneath the blow. The force of the strike sent the dragon howling into nothingness and Doyle went staggering backward, the stone railing striking him at the small of his back. The fire-fist caught the torc around his neck and the gold burned as if it had been thrown into a smithy's forge. Doyle caught himself on the railing's edge a bare breath before he would have fallen over; the Ard's torc tore itself from his neck and went hurtling into darkness. He heard the emblem of the Ard crash to the flags far below.

As he clutched at the rail in desperation, he saw the coils of Snarl touch the wall around Sevei; she turned her head to look at Padraic and the sea-blue power curved back to where it had come, snapping and hissing like lightning. Padraic wailed and went to his knees clutching his chest, making Doyle's heart freeze with terror for his son— Padraic was new to the Cloch Mór; she could smash him in an instant, as she would a mosquito.

"Sevei!" he shouted, regaining his balance and trying to push himself upright. He could not; Lámh Shábhála held him, easily. "I beg you. Do what you want with me, but leave Padraic alone. He had nothing to do with killing Jenna. If it had been his choice, he would not have been there at all." Sevei was still facing Padraic, but she turned her head slowly to stare at Doyle with that blank, terrible gaze. The remainder of Snarl's tendrils slashed skyward to the mage-lights, fading as they went, but they didn't touch Padraic. "I did it all," Doyle said softly. He touched his chest with the hand that still held Snapdragon. "I did it. Leave Padraic alone. Please."

Doyle glanced over at his son, desperate, realizing that he himself was already dead, that the best he could hope for now was that Padraic would survive this night. He could feel thick, fluid-filled blisters raising on his neck where the torc had once been. His head pounded and he fought to remain conscious, fought not to fall. "He'll release his cloch, Sevei. He's no threat to you." Doyle didn't dare look at Padraic, caught in the Bán Cailleach's baleful stare and afraid that if she glanced again at Padraic, she would kill him.

The Bán Cailleach sniffed. "Our dear Padraic has Máister Kirwan's cloch." Now she did look back at Padraic, glaring down at his panting, huddled form. He was moaning through clenched lips. "What did you do, Padraic? Did you take it from Mundy's body after you tortured him in Lár Bhaile? Did you laugh when he begged you not to do it, when he cried out with the loss of his cloch?"

Doyle could see the terror and fright in his son's face. "Sevei," Padraic began, "I didn't . . . I couldn't have . . ."

Sevei sniffed, her head swiveling to face Doyle again.

"You must have been pleased, Uncle, when you realized that you also had Snarl in your little trap. Aye, I know that Máister Kirwan was taken—and so does all of Inish Thuaidh. If you wished to make eternal enemies of the Inishlanders, you've taken the right course."

"Mundy's cloch was taken after the battle, after you and Jenna were . . . lost in the sea," Doyle gasped out. "The others—they wanted to kill him there, but I wouldn't let them. Instead, I had him brought to Lár Bhaile," Doyle told Sevei. "But there was no torture. I wouldn't allow that, even when some argued for it. I pleaded with Rí Mallaghan to send his healers to Máister Kirwan in the Order of Gabair's Keep, and he did."

Sevei gave a cough that was nearly a laugh. "No torture, Uncle? You took Mundy's cloch. You couldn't do more to torment him than that."

Doyle lifted a shoulder. "I *know* that pain, Sevei. I've experienced it myself, and yet I managed to survive it. I'd truly hoped Mundy could as well, but he was older and was badly wounded in the battle besides. He grew sicker every day, despite everything we tried to do. I didn't want him to die, but two days after we arrived . . ." Still caught in Lámh Shábhála's grasp, he shrugged again, licking his lips to get the words out, his hands clutching desperately at the railing of the balcony as his body was bent out over the night. "Tell me that I'm wrong, Sevei. Tell me that if our positions had been reversed, you wouldn't have taken Snapdragon from me to give to one of your allies—to Kayne, maybe, if you could. But don't blame Padraic, Sevei. He did no more than his da asked him to do. Don't punish him for loyalty to his family—you of all people should understand that."

"And he was well-rewarded for his loyalty, wasn't he?" Sevei paused, then pointed to the balcony entrance. "Leave us, Padraic. This is between your da and me."

Padraic shook his head, pushing himself to his feet with a groan. "I won't," he told her, still holding his chest as if it pained him to move. "He's my da, Sevei, and he's right— no matter what he's done, he has my love and my loyalty. I'm sorry."

The Bán Cailleach nodded. "So am I," she said. "For the friendship we once had, I'd spare you."

"Padraic, do as she asks," Doyle grunted, twisting in Lámh Shábhála's grip, feeling the cold emptiness of the fall beneath him. "Please, there's no need for this; Snarl alone can't stand against her. Go on."

"Would *you* leave, Da, if it were me or Mam that she wanted?" Padraic shook his head. He seemed to be looking past the Bán Cailleach at something else, and Doyle saw the movement in the Ard's chamber at the same time as a new voice intruded.

"If you intend to kill Doyle, it will be three clochs you face, and more." The voice came from behind Sevei, from the interior entrance to the Ard's bedchamber. Sevei spun about; beyond her, Doyle saw Edana and Alastríona as well as several gardai of the keep push into the room. "I felt the Bán Cailleach move with the mage-lights, and then I felt her here," Edana said. "I came as quickly as I could . . ." Doyle saw Edana stare at the naked apparition, saw her search the young woman's scarred face. Edana's voice softened then and became almost gentle. If there was any revulsion within Edana as she looked at the Bán Cailleach, Doyle could not see it. "Sevei . . . Oh, Sevei, I'm so sorry. For everything. I wish I'd known what was going to happen. I tried to warn your mam . . ."

Edana came forward toward Sevei, and the firelight of the bedchamber glistened in her eyes. She reached out a hand toward the Bán Cailleach as if Sevei were a Riocha coming to her for an audience, but Sevei extended a hand, palm outward, in warning. Edana stopped an arm's length from Sevei. "I don't expect you to believe this, but I loved your mam as much as I love any of my own sisters. She was my confidante, my best friend, my support." Edana's gaze flicked over Sevei's shoulder to Doyle and hardened. "Meriel didn't deserve to die. Of any of us here, the Healer Ard should have had a long life."

"She didn't." Sevei nearly spat the words, and Doyle felt Lámh Shábhála bend him farther backward as he clutched harder at the stone rail. "Mam died, and Gram, and my brothers and sisters. But not me. And not Kayne." She gave a grim smile as she turned away from Edana to look at Doyle again. Doyle felt his facial muscles tighten at the news. *Kayne is alive, also?* "The army you sent out from Airgialla to the Finger has been sent running back home,

Rí Ard." The title was a mockery on her lips. "Did you know that? Here, look . . ."

She released him; gasping for breath, Doyle scrambled away from the railing, but Sevei pointed out into the night, and he looked.

In the darkness beyond the balcony, the air shimmered as if a wind were stroking the surface of a still lake, the mage-lights sliding down at Sevei's gesture. A landscape wrought in perfect miniature and glowing as if illuminated by the sun appeared just beyond the rail, so close that Doyle could have reached out to touch it, though he dared not. He stared: it was as if he were a bird, circling high above the world. He saw the sharp spines of mountains and gleaming lakes and the winding silver threads of rivers. And there, on a lonely, desolate ribbon of a road, he saw the antlike specks of an army with its cavalry, the massive ranks of foot soldiers and the supply vans in the rear. The banners of the army were those of Tuath Airgialla. The mountains, he realized, were the jagged buttresses of the Finger, and the army was moving away from them toward the waters of Lough Tory.

"It's not real," Doyle said. "Just an enchantment. Why should I believe this?" But he knew, looking at it, he knew he was wrong. Sevei blinked, hiding her dark orbs for a moment, and the mage-landscape vanished with them.

"You may believe it or not, Uncle," she told him. "It doesn't matter." She waved an arm, and the scars on her flesh sent light sliding over the stones of the keep.

"Sevei," Edana said, and the Bán Cailleach's head turned sharply toward her. "I won't let you do this, Sevei," Edana said. "I can't." Doyle saw Edana came out onto the balcony, though Alastríona hung back with the gardai in the bedchamber. Edana placed herself, Doyle noted, between the Bán Cailleach and Padraic—a mam's instinctive, protective movement. "I can't just stand here and let you kill him. Doyle is my husband and my children's da, and I loved him once. If you strike at him . . ." Her lips pursed. "I will defend him, if only for what he once meant to me."

"He deserves death," Sevei interrupted. "Don't you believe I deserve my revenge, Aunt? For Gram, for Mam, for Da, for Ennis and Tara and Ionhar."

"Aye, you deserve it, Sevei," Edana replied, and Doyle

glanced at her sharply. "Many of us deserve better than we receive," Edana continued, "but the Mother-Creator and the webs of fate are fickle. Most of us have to endure what we're given. In death, Sevei, your mam has become one of the Mionbandia. People worship her: the tuathánach especially, but even some of the céili giallnai and the Riocha. I go and I pray at her barrow every day to ask her forgiveness, and I see more supplicants there with me each morning. They still ask her to cure their ailments and afflictions, as they did when she was alive, and every day someone walks away with her favor. I believe Meriel will be greater in death than she was in life. I know that's no comfort to you, and I'd rather have your mam here with me than anything else I can imagine, because I had no better friend in life. But I couldn't stop what happened, and so she's gone."

"Why do you tell me this, Aunt?"

"Because I want you to know that the Ríthe are finding that they made a mistake in murdering your mam and the rest of your family. They failed to gain anything they'd hoped to gain. I don't want you to make the same mistake, Sevei. Death can't be undone, not even by Lámh Shábhála."

Doyle saw the Bán Cailleach smile at that. "I've learned a lot about death recently, Aunt," she said. "I've witnessed it. I've caused it. I've had the Black Haunts circling around me and waiting. Please don't lecture me about death and its consequences. You have no idea what Lámh Shábhála is capable of doing; I'm not certain even I know yet."

"Then I'm sorry, Sevei. For both of us." Edana's hand went to Demon-Caller, her Cloch Mór, but Sevei's hand was already touching where Lámh Shábhála glowed under her skin.

"*Stop!*" Sevei's voice boomed and Edana's hand flew away from her cloch as if struck. Doyle had reached for Snapdragon in the same instant, and he cried out as green lightning arced between his hand and Sevei. The gardai in the chamber dropped their weapons with shouts of alarm and the clattering of steel on wood. Alastríona wailed, terrified.

The Bán Cailleach was no longer Sevei at all, but some larger being, a jewel inscribed in the curls and eddies of the mage-lights and encased in darkness. Doyle could see himself in the dark mirrors of her eyes. Her voice seemed to

come from the sky. "I ache for my revenge," the Bán Cailleach declared. "The old Holders call within me, Jenna
among them, and that's what their voices tell me. They—
I—want a death for a death and blood for blood." . . . *blood
for blood . . . blood for blood* . . . Doyle could hear the
words echoing from the keep walls, from the hillsides that
cradled it, from the rooftops of the city below. He heard
the alarm bells tolling at the keep gates; heard the clatter
of gardai being roused.

Then the glow faded, and the Bán Cailleach was only
Sevei again, scarred and fragile and naked. Her black eyes
found Doyle and held him. "Blood for blood is what they
tell me I should take. I came here to do exactly that,
but . . ." Her voice was barely a whisper and Doyle saw that
she was in pain, shivering and vulnerable. "I can't. I can't
kill you in front of Padraic and Alastríona, Uncle Doyle. I
can't when I might injure Aunt Edana. I can't when I see
there's still love within her for you despite all that you've
done."

Something golden flashed in front of Doyle: the torc of
the Ard. The sculpted end of the torc pulled apart and
came around his neck, cold and relentless. Doyle felt the
blisters on his neck break as the torc pressed against his
neck, spilling clear fluid onto the collar of his clóca. His
skin burned and the torc tightened around his throat, closing until it threatened to choke off his breath. He fought it
with his hands, but it continued to close. "I have other uses
for you first, Uncle," Sevei continued. "They made you
Ard, so you will be *my* Ard. You will be my mouth with the
Ríthe, and my hand among the Tuatha. You will be my dog,
not the Ríthe's, and you will give me your loyalty. Tell me
you'll do that, Uncle. Tell me that, and I'll let you live."

He was dying. He tried to pull in a breath and could not.
The edges of his vision sparked with lights that were not
the mage-lights and all he could see was the Bán Cailleach's face, Sevei's disfigured and horrible visage, before
him. He clawed at the torc, digging his own fingers into his
skin, but it continued to tighten like a relentless garrote.
He opened his mouth, trying to speak, but there was no air
for words. "You have two choices, Uncle. You'll do what I
ask you to do, or I'll show you the true end of the path
you've chosen." The torc tightened again, closing against

the sides of his neck. He felt himself losing consciousness. He wanted to cry out to Edana, to Padraic, to tell them to open their clochs and attack this creature before them, but they either would not or could not.

"Choose," the Bán Cailleach crooned. "Choose now."

Desperate, Doyle nodded his head. The torc loosened slightly, and he took in a shuddering gasp of air that burned his throat with its delicious coolness. "Tell me," the Ban Cailleach told him. "Tell me now that you'll do it."

"Aye," Doyle managed to husk out. "I will. Aye."

Suddenly, the torc was nothing more than a loose weight around his neck, cold and dead. "Good," Sevei said. "Then here's what I need you to do . . ."

"I won't kill him. . . . I promise . . ."

Sevei sent a tendril of Lámh Shábhála's power toward Edana, toward Padraic and Alastríona even as she slowly tightened the noose of the Ard's torc around Doyle's neck. She watched him scrabble desperately at the ring of metal; she watched his face go red and then pale, watched the eyes widen and bulge and the tongue begin to protrude from his mouth. *"I won't kill him, no matter what he says . . . I promise it on my mam's name . . . No matter how he answers . . ."*

She wondered herself if it was true.

Both Edana and Padraic put their hands on their Clochs Mór. Both opened the stones so that Sevei's mage-sight saw them bloom into sudden light, but neither did more than that. Sevei sighed inwardly with relief: had they attacked, she would have had to make the choice between destroying them or retreating—there would have been no time for subtlety, no space for finesse. Already the old Holders, including Jenna and Carrohkai Treemaster, were clamoring in her head, shouting contradictory warnings and imprecations.

". . . make no promises in my name, girl. As far as I'm concerned, he can die for what he's done to me and mine . . ."

". . . you can't ever trust him, even if he says 'aye' . . ."

". . . kill him . . . He'll only betray you later. Kill him and then kill the others . . ."

"... *take their clochs and give them to those you trust. You could make the Order of Inishfeirm all it was intended to be* ..."

Her body screamed with the power she had expended already this night. The scars seared her skin as if someone were pressing loops of red-hot metal to her. "Tell me," Sevei said to Doyle, hoping desperately that he would answer as she hoped he would, as he must if they were to avoid plunging the Tuatha into a hopeless war. "Tell me that you'll do it."

"Aye," Doyle managed to husk out. "I will. Aye."

Gratefully, Sevei pulled back the energy from Lámh Shábhála. The voices howled at her inside, nearly all of them angry. "Good," Sevei said. "Then here's what I need you to do ..."

Trying not to show the agony within her, she leaned forward and spoke into his ear, watching his eyes widen. Then, before he could protest or complain, she took the power of Lámh Shábhála within herself, opening the cloch fully. She looked out across the night landscape of Dún Laoghaire, at the hills she remembered so well, at Cnocareilig where her mam lay in her barrow. "Good-bye, Aunt Edana, Padraic, Alastríona. I wish ... I wish things could have been different. For all of us."

She wrapped herself in the clóca of the mage-lights and left.

40

On the Cnocareilig

THE SUPPLICANTS USUALLY began arriving in the early morning light, so Áine Martain usually arose before the dawn and walked up from the city toward Cnocareilig and the Healer Ard's barrow as the first light touched the cold waters of the bay. Today was no different. When she had been the Hand of the Heart and Meriel had still been alive, she had kept the same routine, though then she'd always awakened in her own comfortable chambers in the Ard's Keep and not in this tiny hovel just inside the city walls. Habit woke her in the predawn darkness, and Áine pushed herself from the bed, shivering in the cold. She went to the hearth and uncovered the coals, placing a brick of peat on them and blowing on the coals gently until the aromatic smoke began curling up and blue flames began to feed at the bottom of the peat. She placed water in the kettle and put it on the crane to boil, then took her chamber pot outside and emptied it into the street's central gutter. She fixed herself a cup of tea and nibbled at the berry muffins and potato stirabout that had been left as offerings to the Healer Ard yesterday. There was a light rain, and droplets pattered from the leak in the crown of the thatched roof. She placed a bucket under the leak, put on the clóca and léine of the Hand, pulled up the cowl against the damp, and left the cottage.

A gray dawn was just brightening a dull sky. The city was starting to awaken around her. She passed the market square near South Gate, where the sellers were just opening their stalls and shop owners were sweeping out the

floors of their shops. Many of them called out to her, smiling.

"Maidin maith, Hand Áine!"

"It's a fair day that starts gray, aye?"

"The favor of the Healer Ard be with you!"

She smiled back to them, nodding, walking through
South Gate and up the steep slope that led past the twin
keeps of the Ard and the Banrion. She scowled up at the
tower of the Ard as she passed it and the balcony she knew
led to the Ard's bedchamber, though she smiled at the gardai at their stations and received quick smiles in return.

Cnocareilig lay across a valley, then up and around several long bends, the approach to the Healer Ard's barrow
hidden behind the folded slopes. Áine walked with her
head down, still not yet fully awake. She turned the final
curve in the path as the drizzle stopped and the clouds
parted enough to let the sun peek out. A long morning
shadow that shouldn't have been there touched her.

She stopped. She felt her mouth fall open.

The Healer Ard gazed down at her, backlit in the dawn.

It took a moment for Áine to realize what she was seeing. It *was* Meriel: her features, her hair, her coloring, clad
in the clóca of the Ard with the torc around *her* neck and
not that of the traitorous Mac Ard. Treoraí's Heart lay on
its chain on her breast. Meriel was smiling and her hand
was lifted as if she were about to speak. Then the scale of
this vision struck Áine: the Healer Ard stood a good five
men tall in front of her barrow, perfectly formed but gigantic and still—not Meriel herself but an image of her
that dwarfed her own barrow and those of the dead Ards
around her. Áine thought she saw the vision—if that's
what it was—move slightly, but she blinked and stared and
no, the image was as unmoving as stone. If it was a statue,
it was like nothing that Áine had ever seen, far more real-
istic and convincing even in its enormous scale than the
carvings by the famous artisan MacBreanhg that adorned
the Dún Laoghaire's Sunstone Ring. Holding her breath
and gazing up at Meriel's distant face, Áine slowly approached. The eyes seemed to follow her. She knelt down
before the statue and touched the sandaled feet.

Áine drew her hand back with a cry. The skin was warm
and yielding to the touch: not stone at all, but amazingly

like flesh. The surface didn't appear to be painted, and the sandals looked not carved but genuine, as if Áine could remove them from the Healer Ard's feet, and the leather of those sandals pressed into the earth without a base, just as if the Healer Ard were standing there. She could see the pores of the skin and the hairs set there . . . "Healer Ard," she whispered, gazing up at Meriel's face. "Speak to me. Speak to your Hand of the Heart. Tell me what you want me to do." But there was no answer, and Meriel gazed serenely off to the west, unmoving.

Áine stood, her head at a level with Meriel's knees. She half expected to see the stone-sealed barrow opened, but the great stones were still there and still sealed with pitch, the sigils of the Draíodóiri unbroken.

This . . . this was a gift of the Mother-Creator, a sign that Meriel was indeed a Miondia and favored by the Mother-Creator, a sign that Áine's role as Hand of the Heart was indeed not over, that she had done the right thing continuing to serve the Healer Ard even in death. "Thank you," she whispered: to the Mother-Creator, to Meriel herself. She touched the statue again, marveling at its warmth and its feel, the clóca seeming to ripple slowly and yield under her touch.

She heard a gasp and a wail from the path. The first of the day's supplicants had arrived, an entourage carrying a litter on which an old woman rested. They had stopped, the litter on the ground as they all stared—half in fright, half in awe—at the apparition of the Healer Ard. Áine hurried forward, gesturing to them.

"Don't be afraid. Please, come forward. I'm the Hand of the Heart, and the Healer Ard is here to listen to you and perhaps to help. . . ."

41

Triple Hearts and Broken Walls

SOMEONE WAS CRYING in the darkness, an inconsolable, hopeless sobbing that welled up from the very center of the pain to touch every fiber of his existence.

Ennis realized that it was his own voice he heard.

He huddled in the farthest corner of the doorless room that Kurhv Kralj had given him, curled into a fetal ball with his body shaking from the force of his weeping. The blue ghosts had vanished into nothing. He couldn't see their dance and so he could be himself, but he was frightened and alone and terrified and he couldn't hold the emotions back any longer.

He wanted to be held. He wanted to be comforted. He wanted to be in his mam's or da's arms, or Sevei's, or even Gram's, who Kayne had said frightened him terribly the first time he'd met her. Ennis wanted to be with anyone who was like him and not one of the Arruk.

But he couldn't. Not even in this place, which the Daoine of Céile Mhór had built and then lost, and which reminded him too much of home.

He wept, because crying was all he could do.

Within the ball he'd made of himself, his fingers clutched at Treoraí's Heart, because he could hear the voices within it—Isibéal's voice, mostly, but at least she spoke Daoine and her tones reminded him of home, when Mam was still alive. The other voices—Daighi, Brett, Jantsk, Haughey, Brina, Noz Ruka, Svarti Gyl, all the ones he'd killed—clamored for his attention too, but he ignored them. *"Do you want me to feel sorry for you, Ennis?"* Isibéal crooned.

"Do you want me to tell you that it will be all right? Do you want me to say I forgive you for killing me and taking the Heart from me?"

"I want Mam," he told her. "Let me talk to Mam."

"Is that what you want?" Isibéal asked, and her voice shifted, took on the familiar tones he remembered so well. *"You can cry if you need to, my darling. It's all right."*

"But I'm . . . so scared . . . Mam," he said between choking sobs. "I'm . . . all a . . . a . . . *alone* . . ." The last word was a wail, and then he could say nothing more, shaking as the weeping overcame him again. He closed his eyes until they hurt, trying to shut out the world around him.

"I'm here, my darling boy. I'll always be here . . ."

"I've . . . I've done . . . bad . . . things . . . Mam . . ."

"You only did what you had to do, my dearest one. All the rest of us are dead, but you stayed alive. Now you have to stay alive for all of us." Her voice went deeper and huskier, and it was Isibéal speaking once more. *"You have to punish them, all of them. You've been given power; now use it. Hush, now. Hush . . ."*

"What is that sound you're making? Are you ill?"

It took a moment for Ennis to realize that the voice wasn't one of those in his head, but Cima, standing at the open doorway to the room and peering in at Ennis and speaking in his heavily-accented Daoine. Ennis sobbed again and sniffed, still huddled in his corner. He looked for the blue ghosts to tell him what to do, but there were none here and the voices in the Heart had gone quiet. He blinked, sniffing again and dragging the sleeve of his tattered, dirty clóca over his nose. "I'm not sick," he said. "Just . . . leave me alone."

"Can't," Cima told him. "Kurhv Kralj told me to find you." He paused a moment, his eyes narrowing as he stared at Ennis in the gloom. "Your face is leaking," he said. "Are you broken?"

"I'm just . . ." Ennis sniffed again, trying to control the sobs. ". . . crying," he finished. "Don't Arruk cry when you're hurt or sad?" Cima had never told him the Arruk word for the emotion. Looking at Cima, he wondered if perhaps there wasn't one.

Cima gave the yawning hiss that was an Arruk negative. "Do you know the story of the Three Hearts?" he asked.

Ennis shook his head, sniffling. "Then listen . . . It's said that in the Oldest Time, three gods came to the Arruk, and each gave us their heart. There is the heart that is in our mouths which is the one we show to others, and that heart will say whatever is best for us. With that heart we feel nothing and show nothing. Then there is the heart in our chests that we show only to those we trust and love: our mates, our families, our closest friends, and with that heart we *can* show our feelings—though I have to tell you, Ennis, that Arruk do not spill water from their eyes when they are sad."

Cima was silent for a time then, and Ennis thought he had finished. "What about the third heart?" he asked.

Cima gave a slow exhalation. "Ahh, the third heart. That heart is in the deepest part of ourselves, and it is open only to each Arruk alone, and that is where we keep our deepest feelings. That heart is the one we will take to the gods when we die, that They weigh on the scales of life to judge us. I can't show you that heart, Ennis, but I will open my second heart to you, because I know the Perakli have only one heart and I see yours in front of me now."

I have two hearts, Ennis nearly said. *I have my own, and I have Treoraí's Heart too.* But he said nothing as Cima came over and crouched in front of him. The Arruk reached out with one hand and stroked Ennis' face, his claws fully retracted so that Ennis felt only the brush of soft scales against his skin. "I understand," Cima said. "In my second heart, I am often sad, too. I wonder if we do the right thing here. I wonder if Cudak is really calling us to come to Him. Once, I was so sure. I believed He called to me personally."

Ennis wanted to cry again. He let Cima pull him in and cradle him in his strong, scaled arms. "I once held my own pups this way," Cima whispered into Ennis' ear. "My sons."

"You have sons?"

"Six sons from my first Hatching," he answered, "and one that my season-mate kept cool so that she would have a daughter to teach to bear more eggs, which is as it should be for the Arruk. My season-mate is far away in the place your people call Lower Céile, and should have borne a second Hatching by now to some other male. I enjoyed her company, that cycle, and I shared my second heart with her, too."

"I wish I could meet your sons."

"Maybe some day you will," Cima told him. "But for now, Kurhv Kralj has called the Mairki and their Svarti here, and he wants you in the Kralj's Hall by the time the Shadowlight rises. You're to bring Gyl Svarti's spell-stick with you."

The voices of the dead ones clamored in his head again, Gyl's most loudly, and Ennis held his hands over his ears, trying to stop the sound of them even as Cima's arms relaxed around him. "I don't want to go to Kurhv Kralj," Ennis said. "He'll make me use the Heart again, but there's too many of them inside already."

Cima blinked. His long throat pulsed under his snout. "This isn't the time for second hearts, Ennis, but our first. I'll tell Kurhv Kralj you'll be there," he said. He sat back, and touched his finger to Ennis' cheek, seeming to marvel at the wetness there. "Whether you're still leaking or not," he said.

Ennis knew that the other Svarti hated him. He could feel their enmity wash over him as he stood beside Kurhv Kralj. They glared at the spell-stick that he held, Gyl Svarti's spell-stick, and they clenched their own staffs all the tighter. Their spinal frills were erect and flared, displaying the colors of barely-subdued anger.

The four Mairki stood in a line before the dais, each with his chief Svarti arrayed behind him. The Mairki were naked except for the painted insignia of their divisions, but the Svarti all wore loin coverings with a tribal crest on the right hip, and the scales covering their left hips were marked with lines of brilliant green, blue, and yellow. Cima had told Ennis that each of the Svarti in turn had several Nesvarti, (who Ennis thought of as being like the Bráthairs and Siúrs of the Order of Inishfeirm) under them.

The Svarti of the Mairki were ostensibly under the control of the Svarti of the Kralj—who was now, supposedly, Ennis. They didn't look at him the way the gardai had looked at his da, or the way people had looked at his mam. There was no respect or even fear in the way they stared, only a sullen defiance. Even some of the Riocha who Ennis

knew didn't like his mam or da wouldn't have dared stand
in front of them this way; they would at least have pretended. In that, he thought, maybe even the Daoine have
more than one heart.

Ennis knew they all hated him: Svarti and Mairki. He
knew they hated that he was a Perakli, a bluntclaw who
was their enemy; they hated that he'd struck down Gyl
Svarti; they hated that Kurhv Kralj protected him; they
hated him because each of the Svarti wanted to stand
where he now stood.

Ennis shivered. He wanted to go back to the room and
huddle in the corner again. He wanted to cry. But he
couldn't. *"You can't show them weakness,"* Isibéal's voice
whispered as he brushed Treoraí's Heart with a shaking
hand. *"Cima said you must use your first heart, and he's
right. You must be brave, or else you'll die . . ."* Ennis looked
for the blue ghosts, but though there were wisps of them
around, everything was muddled, especially near the Svarti
and their spell-sticks. There was no pattern into which he
could fall. He wondered if he'd lost the future he'd
glimpsed.

"I am Kurhv Kralj," his protector was saying to the
Mairki and Svarti. Cima, crouching near the throne, translated for Ennis. Kurhv Kralj gestured to the head of
Grozan Kralj, now mounted on a Daoine spear to one side
of the stage. The stench in the room was foul and thick, but
only Ennis seemed to notice it. "I claim the title. The
Mairki will now show their throats to me or give me challenge."

Kurhv Kralj hissed after he spoke, extending his clawed
hand. Two of the Mairki had immediately raised their
snouts to expose the pale, unscaled folds of their throat. A
third followed, though the last in line did not move. "That
one is Lieve Mairki, who Grozan Kralj put in Kurhv Kralj's
place," Cima whispered. Ennis could hear the trepidation
in Cima's voice, but if Kurhv Kralj felt the same emotion,
he gave no indication. He leaped from the dais to stand before the first of the Mairki. He grasped the Arruk's throat,
his claws digging so deeply into the Mairki's skin that
Ennis saw it dimple and turn pale. Ennis knew that Kurhv
Kralj could kill the Mairki with a simple twist and pull of
his hand. The Mairki's eyes widened and he rose up on his

feet to relieve the pressure, but otherwise he didn't move. A breath later, Kurhv Kralj released him. He repeated the process with the other two Mairki until he stood at last in front of Lieve Mairki.

Lieve Mairki still had not shown his throat. He stared at Kurhv Kralj, their faces level. "Should we make space, then, Lieve Mairki?" Kralj Kurhv asked him. "Do you want your head displayed next to Grozan's?"

Lieve Mairki's eyes flicked over to the dead Kralj's skull. Ennis saw the Mairki's muscles flex in his arms, in his chest, and he was certain that the Arruk would hurl himself on Kurhv Kralj. But though his body trembled and his breath quickened, he held. Slowly, he raised his snout, and Kurhv Kralj's hand flashed forward, grasping Lieve Mairki's throat so hard and quickly that the Arruk stumbled backward. "How does it feel?" Kurhv Kralj asked him. "At least I gave you a choice, Lieve Mairki. I could have shamed you as Grozan Kralj did me. Look there . . ."

Kurhv Kralj turned the Mairki's head so that he was looking at Grozan Kralj's mounted head. Blood drooled down Lieve Mairki's throat to his chest. "That is what I do to my enemies. That is the fate of any who challenge my right to be Kralj." He shoved Lieve Mairki backward, releasing him at the same time so that he fell into his Svarti standing behind. The Svarti's spell-stick clattered to the ground and the Arruk mage pushed Lieve Mairki upright again as Kurhv Kralj strode back to the dais.

Kurhv Kralj's scales had brightened in satisfaction. Cima handed him his jaka and he slammed the end of the weapon against the dais three times. "I am Kurhv Kralj," he declared again, his voice booming in the hall. "And now it's the Svarti's time to show their throats." He pointed to Ennis. "This is Ennis Svarti of the Perakli, who defeated Gyl Svarti and who will stand beside me in battle. Svarti, step forward."

At Kurhv Kralj's gesture, the four Svarti moved forward as the Mairki slid back. The line of spell-casters stared at Ennis, radiating their hate like the heat from the bonfires of the Festival of Méitha. He clutched the spell-stick with one hand and Treoraí's Heart with the other. His clóca slid back, showing the scars of the mage-lights on his arm. *"Don't show them your fear . . ."* Isibéal whispered, but Gyl

Svarti's voice hissed even louder. *"They can* smell *the fear in you,"* he said. *"And it makes them hungry for your blood. But there's fear in them, too—look, you can see it. They know what you did to me; they know that it was* you *who killed Grozan Kralj, not Kurhv Kralj. They look at you and they see only a stupid, helpless Perakli pup standing there, but they're afraid to trust their eyes. They each want one of the others to challenge you so they can watch, but none of them are eager to be the one."*

The spell-stick was absurdly long in his child's grasp, and Ennis could see the end trembling as he held it; he hoped the Svarti couldn't see it. "Show your throats to Ennis Svarti or challenge him," Kurhv Kralj said. "Ennis Svarti . . ."

Ennis realized that Kurhv Kralj was waiting for him to step down from the dais and go to each of the Svarti in turn to receive their obeisance. "Go on!" Cima hissed in Daoine. "Quickly!"

The wisps of the blue ghosts shifted around him and he could see little of the patterns they made. He wished he'd never been born with a caul, even if that meant that he'd be dead now with Mam. He wanted to cry again, he wanted to hunker in the corner of his room again. He wanted to be home.

But he couldn't go home. That wasn't his future. His future, if the blue ghosts of the caul still had one to show him, was here.

He sucked in a breath that nearly sobbed and clutched harder at both Treoraí's Heart and the spell-stick in his hand. Kurhv Kralj wouldn't look at him. "Go!" Cima said. Ennis nearly jumped at the command, then stepped down from the dais. None of the Svarti had moved; not one of them had lifted their chins as the Mairki had to Kurhv Kralj. He went to the first of Svarti. Though the Arruk mages were smaller in stature than the muscular warriors, Ennis still barely came up to the bottom of the Arruk's rib cage. He could smell the musk, could see the colored striations in the creature's scales. The Svarti was looking down at him, an unblinking, unmoving glare. Ennis couldn't have reached the Arruk's throat with his hand as Kurhv Kralj had done; instead, he lifted the knobbed end of the spell-stick and held it toward the Svarti.

"You have to learn to control your gift," Isibéal whispered inside. *"Control it ..."*

They were all watching: Kurhv Kralj, the Mairki, the other Svarti. None of them said anything or moved to interfere. *"Kurhv Kralj has what he wants,"* Gyl said from the taunting welter inside Ennis, and there was no mistaking the satisfaction in the dead Svarti's voice. *"He'll let you die now, if that's to be, and take one of the others as his Svarti. He has become Kralj. He doesn't need you anymore."*

"Control your gift ..." Isibéal repeated, and he heard his Mam whisper the same words, far in the background over the welter of other voices in the Heart.

"I'll try, Mam," he told her. He saw the Arruk in front of him flinch slightly at the Daoine words. Wisps of blue ghosts slid around him and he tried to find the right one, tried to find the pattern that he'd lost. Through Treoraí's Heart, he could sense the magic stored in Gyl's spell-stick. He felt the spells as if he could touch them and he could see how they were set in the wood and how they were held ... "Cima," he called out over his shoulder. "Tell them I captured Gyl Svarti's spirit in the stone I hold. Through it, I can still talk to him." He touched his own forehead as Cima began to translate. "I can force him to tell me things. I know the magic of the Daoine sky-stones, and now I know the magic of the Arruk spell-sticks. I know it better than Gyl Svarti or any of them do."

There was a distinct snort of disbelief from the Svarti in front of him as Cima finished, and the creature raised his own spell-stick, holding it so close to Ennis' face that he could see the tool marks on the carvings that adorned it. "Tell the bluntclaw that I am Daj Svarti," he spat out as Cima translated, "and I challenge him. Tell him that I'll match my spell-stick and my skill with the pup's."

The Mairki and the other Svarti were already slipping back and away, and even Kurhv Kralj moved to the rear of the dais behind the comforting bulk of the throne. Daj Svarti took a step back from Ennis, slamming the end of his spell-stick down on the flags. The *crack* of wood on stone was like high thunder. Ennis saw the blue ghosts slide around him, most of them following a similar dance through the next few breaths. He realized that this was a ritual, like the ceremonies the Draíodóiri performed dur-

ing the festivals, that Daj Svarti was waiting for him to
mimic his motion and begin the challenge. But Ennis saw
the pale outline of another ghost, the one he'd sought, the
one where, at the end of this, his own ghost was still standing there alive.

He let himself fall into the blue ghost's embrace, locked
himself to its movements. Ennis lifted his spell-stick as if he
were about to bring it down hard, but instead he pointed
the knobbed end to the side, away from Daj Svarti and the
rest of the Arruk. He felt the magic caught in the carved
branch, the power trembling and seething. He could find in
Gyl Svarti's mind the words to release them one at a time,
but he didn't need them. Instead, he released a bit of the
power from Treoraí's Heart and let it enter the spell-stick.
"Let them all go," Isibéal whispered, and the energy of the
cloch leaped in response.

The spell-stick nearly burst apart in his hand. A wild coruscation flared, so bright that it tossed sharp-edged shadows about the sunlit room and left purple afterimages in
Ennis' sight. His ears were assaulted by a deafening, low
ka-rump and a smell like old eggs.

Where the mage-energy struck, the wall of the hall shattered, exploding outward in a dangerous, blinding shower
of broken stone and mortar. Through the blinding screen of
dust, there was the sound of an avalanche; as it slowly
cleared, Ennis could see that not only had the hall been
breached in a circle as wide as a hand of men walking
abreast, but the walls of the rooms beyond had also been
broken all the way through the corridor outside and an
outer room beyond it, all the way to the outside. Dust
swirled in a wedge of sunlight beyond three broken walls,
each hole large than the one before. Small stones continued
to fall in a harsh drizzle from around the yawning fissures.

The Arruk were staring dumbstruck at the destruction.
The blue ghost moved and Ennis swiveled quickly to face
Daj Svarti. He pointed the knob of the spell-stick, a wisp of
smoke still curling away from its blackened wood, toward
the Arruk, who scrambled almost comically backward
away from the sight. Daj Svarti's own spell-stick visibly
shivered in his clawed hand. "Ennis Svarti?" he heard
Cima call through the dust and the strange quiet.

"Tell the Svarti that's what I'll do to *all* of them if any one of them dares to challenge me," Ennis told Cima. He brandished the spell-stick in their direction, hoping the bluff would work. There was nothing left in the spell-stick now; it was just a piece of wood. Treoraí's Heart still held mage-energy, but to use the power in the Heart he would need to touch them; if the Svarti did use their spell-sticks, he could do nothing to stop them. He hoped he'd chosen the right ghost. The patterns had vanished, lost with the explosion.

Cima called out from the dais, speaking words in Arruk that made all the Svarti blink. Then, in Daoine, he said: "Ennis Svarti, take one step toward Daj Svarti. Keep your own head down. Don't look up at him."

Ennis obeyed. Daj Svarti stayed unmoving this time, but the Arruk's snout lifted quickly as Ennis approached, displaying the fold of softer skin underneath, pale blue and white. Ennis swiveled to face the other Svarti; they had all exposed their throats, their spell-sticks held carefully away from him. The Mairki, too, had lifted their snouts slightly. Ennis heard Kurhv Kralj's cry of satisfaction.

"Then it is settled," Kurhv Kralj bellowed. "You will follow me and Ennis Svarti, and we will go to the Perakli lands all the way to Cudak Zvati, and no one will stand before us."

He roared, and the Mairki and the Svarti all roared with him.

And so did Ennis.

42

Responses

THEY'D SEEN THE DRAGONS appear on the spires
of the Narrows, and watched the Bán Cailleach turn
away the army of the Tuatha. Kayne had been half terrified
himself; he knew and yet didn't know his sister at all.
They'd been so close as children, as if sharing the same
womb had forged an unbreakable bond between them.
They were very different, aye, with distinctive tempera-
ments and interests, but he had always been able to sense
what Sevei was thinking and feeling better than anyone.
He knew Sevei, he knew her moods and her dreams and
her thoughts. And she . . . Sometimes he thought she knew
him as well as he knew himself. More than once she'd come
running when he'd hurt himself, before anyone could have
known what had happened.

But the Bán Cailleach, the Pale Witch, the Dragon-
friend, the Scarred Woman, the Holder of Lámh Shábhála—he didn't know that Sevei at all. He was afraid that
he never would.

The dragons had sat roaring their defiance atop the
spires to the invading army all that day. In the fading light
of the day, with the Airgiallaian force in obvious retreat,
they'd uncoiled themselves and stretched batlike wings,
pushing off the crags of the summits to wheel dangerously
low over the Fingerlanders' encampment and fly away:
one to the west, the other—more interestingly to the Fingerlanders—to the east over the Finger. Kayne, with
Harik at his side, had watched them leave, and Laird
O'Blathmhaic had come up to them with Séarlait and

Rodhlann as they watched the dragon vanish into the haze to the east. "They say that there were once dragons in the deepest mountains of the Finger," Laird O'Blathmhaic said. "Clan Barrimaol has a skull in their Great Hall that they say is a dragon's, and some Fingerlanders have found bones and teeth that are too big to be a bear or dire wolf. If the Sleeping Ones are rising, then there will be dragons again in the Finger."

Kayne nodded. O'Blathmhaic said nothing for a few breaths, then stirred. "Some of the other lairds, they say it's time to return to their homes now that the army is gone."

Rodhlann nodded with O'Blathmhaic, patting the older man on the shoulder. "Aye, Tiarna," he said. "Liam's right. Banlaird MacCanna has sent word that I should return to the clan-home."

"It's not over," Kayne told them. "Not yet."

O'Blathmhaic chuckled at that. "Aye, with that, I agree. It's never over. Not here in the Finger. It started generations ago and will go on for generations more. But for the moment . . ."

Kayne stole a glance at Harik and saw the frown on his Hand's face. Séarlait, still standing alongside her greada, kept her face carefully neutral, though her gaze was on Kayne. "It's important that we stay together," Kayne said. "No, I'm not a Fingerlander, except by marriage—" Séarlait gave him a small smile at that, and he returned it, "—and aye, I don't understand how it is here as you do, Laird, but the Riocha may yet return with more Clochs Mór and more men."

"I thought the Bán Cailleach left to stop that," Rodhlann said.

"She did," Kayne admitted. "But if she's not successful, then they will come here again, and this time they will bring all the force the Tuatha can muster. We won't be able to stop them."

The laird sniffed skeptically. "Perhaps. But that's for then. Not now," O'Blathmhaic insisted. "For now, there is home and family, and the land and animals we've neglected."

"It's not just the Tuatha, Laird," Kayne insisted. "There are the Arruk to the east. We need men here, and we also need men at the Bunús Wall. The Finger may become like a snail caught between two stones. This is not the time to go home, Laird. That would be a fatal mistake."

O'Blathmhaic's face visibly reddened with that. "This isn't the Tuatha," he answered. "You may be Riocha and expect that because you say something that it must be so, but that means nothing here. We don't do the Riocha's bidding, and each clan-laird will make their own decision." The old man's grizzled face was set in hard lines, and he stared at Kayne without blinking, as if daring him to argue further. It was Rodhlann who continued.

"By the Mother, Tiarna," the Fingerlander said, "just a few days ago you were advising us to leave the Narrows. Now you're insisting we stay?"

"I wanted us to retreat before we were killed, aye, but I never wanted the force you've put together to dissolve," Kayne told Rodhlann, then turned to face O'Blathmhaic. "We need those who can fight to stay together now. And I'm not speaking as a Riocha, Laird. I gave that up when they killed my da. I'm saying this because I *know* them. Haven't I shown that?"

"Aye, you have. You may know them, but you don't know us well enough yet."

"I'm here. I married Séarlait, and I gave her my word that I won't leave her. My loyalty is to her and through her to all the clans. But returning to your homes . . . that *is* a mistake, Laird. If we can hold together for a just a month, or two . . ."

"It's not possible," O'Blathmhaic growled. "Another month, and the harvests will go rotten in the field. Flocks won't have been sheared, roofs thatched, hay put up for winter."

"Laird—" Kayne persisted.

Harik put his hand on Kayne's shoulder. "Don't bother, Tiarna," he said. "The Fingerlanders might be strong and fearless in a single battle, but they don't have the stomach for a war. That's why over all these generations they've never been able to cast away the yoke of Airgialla and the Tuatha. They're weak."

"Weak!" The word was a roar. Laird O'Blathmhaic straightened and his hand flew to his sword hilt, as did Rodhlann's. "You'll not be calling me weak when I've finished with you, Harik-Hand. Draw your sword, man, or put

the steel aside and let us use fists—I don't care. Come, and I'll show you how weak we Fingerlanders are, when even an old man can put an impertinent pup like you on the ground." Rodhlann and Séarlait both put their hands on O'Blathmhaic's arm, but the clan-laird shrugged them aside. He pulled his sword from its sheath, pointing the tip of it toward Harik. The heavy weight of water-hardened iron was firm in his hand. "Steel or fists? Choose, man, or be called a coward from this day on."

Séarlait moved to stand directly in front of her greada, shaking her head desperately at his anger. Kayne in his turn swiveled to confront Harik. "You won't insult those who have given us back our lives, Harik," he said, and Harik's face darkened with blood. "You'll apologize to the laird, or you'll fight me first."

"Apol . . ." Harik choked on the word. "My Tiarna, I only spoke what's obvious to all of us."

"You're my Hand, not my Mouth," Kayne told him. "You don't speak for me to the clan-lairds, or for our troops. I gave you the choice back in the caverns to go or stay. Are you saying that's a choice you regret now? Apologize to the laird, Harik-Hand, or you'll no longer *be* my Hand."

A movement caught his eye: Harik's hand sliding up his léine toward Bluefire around his neck. "You want that, Harik?" Kayne said to him in a whisper, so that only he and Harik could hear. "You want to use the gift I gave you against me? That would be a betrayal of all the trust my da and I have ever put in you."

"You're not your da," Harik said. "You're not anything close."

A few months ago, that would have brought a rush of anger from Kayne, and he would have flown at the man in a rage. Kayne was surprised at the calm he felt, at the way he bowed his head once into the accusation, accepting it. "No, I'm not," Kayne agreed. "I can only hope to one day be worthy of being called his son. But imagine Da here, now, in my place. What would he tell you, Harik? Would he have allowed you to speak that way? Would he have been pleased with his Hand? Would he have let you break apart the only alliance that gives us any hope at all?"

Harik's jaw clenched against unspoken words, but his

hand dropped from the cloch. He looked past Kayne to Laird O'Blathmhaic, still holding his sword, though he'd lowered it under Séarlait's pressure. "I apologize for my boldness, Laird," Harik said. "I spoke without thinking and because . . ." He stopped. His throat moved with a hard swallow. "The Fingerlanders have proven their worth in battle, many times over. I was wrong."

Laird O'Blathmhaic still glared, but he grunted and the skins around his shoulders moved with a shrug. "And for my part, I'll admit that you're at least partially right, Hand Harik," he said. "The clans have never been able to sustain a war against the Tuatha, and perhaps this is the time we must try." O'Blathmhaic turned to Kayne. "I'll do what I can. I can't hold them all—some of the clansfolk will be leaving. I need to leave myself. But I'll ask those who can to stay, and I'll send word to Banlaird MacCanna that Rodhlann should remain here as well, and we'll see. We'll see."

Séarlait moved aside, and the man shoved his sword back into its well-worn scabbard with a grunt. "Thank you, Laird," Kayne said. "Do what you can." O'Blathmhaic nodded and strode off with a final long stare in Harik's direction.

"I should go see to our own men, Tiarna," Harik said. Without waiting for Kayne to speak, he spun about and walked away in the opposite direction. Kayne started to call after him, but Séarlait touched his arm and he looked at her to see her shake her head once.

"I don't like it either," he told her. "I don't know if I can fully trust him. I don't know where his loyalty is."

She stroked his arm and he pulled her into him.

Sevei followed the thread of Blaze's connection to the mage-lights back to Kayne. In her mage-vision, she saw her brother and Séarlait standing together, still encamped in the high Narrows though many of the tents that had once dotted the landscape were gone. She let herself materialize a bit away from them, in the shadows of their tent. She looked at them, trying to ignore the racking pain and cold of her passage, shivering in the night air. They'd filled their clochs from the mage-lights, and as she watched, Kayne turned to Séarlait and gave her a soft, long kiss. There was such tenderness and love in the gesture that Sevei felt a stirring within herself, a deep regret that filled her with melancholy. She remembered Dillon, remembered holding him that way . . .

"I'm so sorry . . ." she heard a voice say in her head, rising above the constant low murmuring inside. *"You can't ever have that again yourself. It's not fair. I wish I could take the pain from you, darling. I wish I could bring Dillon back for you. All I can promise you is that when you're here with me, the pain will be gone and you'll be whole again . . ."*

"Be quiet, Gram," she snapped back almost angrily.

But another voice arose: Carrohkai Treemaster. *"The First Holder is right, you know. Physical love like that is something you'll never have, even if there was someone who could see past the scars. You are the Holder of Lámh Sháb-hála, you are the great-daughter of the Mad Holder and the daughter of the Healer Ard who was slain as an enemy of the Riocha, and you are the Bán Cailleach. Even if you could find someone, even if your body could manage to bear the touch of another person, you have too few years left to you."* Carrohkai Treemaster's voice was filled with a deep, sad empathy. *"I know. I know too well. You have little time and much to do, and that affection you're looking at now is the payment you've given for what you have."*

Kayne and Séarlait were holding each other tightly, Séarlait's head nestled against Kayne's chest, his hand caught in the strands of her hair. The mage-lights painted them with shifting blue and gold. Despite the lingering pain of her usage of Lámh Shábhála to return here, she found herself smiling, looking at them. She could feel tears at the corners of her eyes, and they burned like acid against her skin.

"I wish it were different for you . . ." Gram and Carrohkai Treemaster whispered together.

"So do I . . ." Sevei answered them silently, then stepped forward from the cover of the tents. "Brother," she said. "A beautiful night, isn't it?"

Kayne started, breaking apart from Séarlait and his hand going to the Cloch Mór reflexively. Then he smiled, though she noticed that he kept his eyes slightly averted

from her nakedness. "Sevei! I wondered, when you didn't
return last night . . ."

"After I spoke with Uncle Doyle, I went to Doire Coill
and spent the day there with Keira, telling her what has
happened. Do you remember Keira? We were so young
then, and Mam . . . Mam . . ."

Sevei stopped, her voice choking. The wound within her
that was her mam's death and the death of so many in her
family broke open again. She tried to take a breath and
couldn't. She thought of Meriel and the statue that now
stood before her grave. Sevei looked at the stars, at the fading mage-lights, and she saw Kayne start to reach out to
her, to touch her scarred, tormented skin. She nearly cried
out, snatching her arm away from him. ". . . *you can never
know love. Never again. . . .*"

"I know," Kayne whispered. "I know how you feel."

Séarlait stood next to Sevei, also, and the woman's face
was filled with sympathy, starlit tears on her cheeks. She
looked at Sevei, unafraid, her hands lifting as if she wanted
to touch her, but staying carefully away.

The tears in Sevei's eyes had evaporated. Sevei couldn't
cry, somehow, though she ached to do so. The changes
within her seemed to have dried up the tears and they
wouldn't come, though the ache in her throbbed with the
need. "Since . . . since this all happened, I haven't had time
to think about it," she told them. "I haven't *wanted* to think
about it." She looked at Kayne, stricken. "Oh, Kayne . . . I
miss them. I miss them all so much . . ."

Kayne nodded. Séarlait nodded also, and her hand came
up to touch the side of Sevei's face before she could react
or turn aside. Sevei felt the heat of the woman's hands, the
Fingerlander's fingertips feeling like a rasp against her
skin. Séarlait brushed Sevei's stark white hair; with the
touch, Sevei also felt a stirring within Lámh Shábhála, a
tugging that brought her hand to the glow under her skin.
She could nearly feel the hard facets of the stone. She let
the energy flow outward, and her awareness went with it.
Her eyes widened, as did those of Séarlait.

*Sevei found herself in a small one-room cottage, though
those in the room didn't seem to notice her. A girl—she was
no more than that, barely old enough to have had her first
moon-time—lay naked on the floor, blood between her*

*thighs and thick sheets of it falling down from the horrible
wound on her throat onto the buds of her breasts. Her eyes
were wild and staring, she was trying to scream or shout, but
no sound emerged. There was no sound at all in the small
cottage except for the fading laughter of a quartet of gardai
and the jangling of the livery of their horses as they rode off.
The girl pulled herself slowly up to a sitting position. She
rocked back and forth, so terrified and hurt she could not
even sob. The bodies of her parents were sprawled near her,
murdered, her mam raped beforehand, in front of both her
and her da. Séarlait had also been left for dead. Certainly the
wound on her throat had been intended to end her life.*

"Let me help you," Sevei said to her. "I can help you . . ."

*The girl shook her head, the terrible wound under her
chin gaping and closing again with the motion, causing
more blood to gush.* "I can't change what happened to you,"
Sevei told her. "I wish I could. If I could, I'd change what
happened to me, too. Neither of us can do that—we have to
live with what we've seen and what we've felt. I can't take
away the scars that are inside. But the others . . . perhaps . . .
If you'll let me touch you . . ."

*Sevei crouched down beside her, reaching toward the girl,
who pushed herself away with weak, trembling legs.* "I won't
hurt you," Sevei crooned. "I promise . . ." *The girl stopped
and Sevei put her hands to the girl's face. The blood was
sticky and wet and warm under her fingers, and she grimaced at the feel. Sevei remembered watching Mam in the
Heart Chamber and with the memory, the mage-lights
flowed through her and Lámh Shábhála . . .*

The contact was gone: Séarlait had taken her hand away.
Now it touched her own face, her throat: flawless, perfect,
smooth-skinned. Her mouth opened in a gasp, her eyes
went wide. *It's the look they would give Mam, after she had
touched them with Treoraí's Heart . . .*

"Thank you," Séarlait said. The words were hoarse and
ragged, but they were audible and understandable. She
sank to her knees in front of Sevei, grasping her hand. The
clasp was like fire and knives on Sevei's skin, but she endured it.

". . . aye, my love," Gram whispered. "I should have used
Lámh Shábhála in that way . . ."

Sevei shook her head, pulling the woman up. "I did it for

me, Séarlait," she told her, she told Gram. "I'll need your voice soon. I'll need everyone."

"Sevei says that none of the Ríthe are safe from her if we betray her, Rí Mallaghan. I believe that's true. When the mage-lights come, she can follow the lights down to any of us she wishes. We can't each of us have a half dozen Clochs Mór around us every night for protection, and frankly I don't know that a half dozen greater clochs would even be enough. She's *strong,* my Rí, as strong—nay, stronger— than the Mad Holder was at Falcarragh. I know all of us re- member that."

Doyle knew Rí Torin Mallaghan and Shay O Blaca re- membered Falcarragh all too well. None of them would ever forget it: *the tremendous glow of the mage-lights as the Mad Holder took them all on, Doyle's mage-vision bright with the aspects of a dozen or more Clochs Mór, all of them shattering against the wild defenses Jenna threw up against them, the booming of thunderous explosions and the rain of debris, the very ground shuddering underneath them as if the land itself were flailing in pain . . .* Doyle shuddered.

"The Bán Cailleach—Sevei, of all people; that damned Aoire family is infuriatingly resilient, isn't it?—is as mad as her great-mam, then," Rí Mallaghan said.

Doyle shook his head and shrugged at the same time. "Perhaps. I don't know, my Rí. I only know that with three of us there with Clochs Mór, trained and experienced, we could not have stood against her."

"Then you're fortunate that she took pity on Edana and decided to use the Rí Ard as a message boy," Mallaghan spat back. Doyle flinched at the rebuke, his eyes narrow- ing as if the Rí had slapped his cheek. Shay O Blaca, standing near the window, turned his head to look outside as if fascinated by the landscape he'd seen a thousand times before.

They were in Rí Mallaghan's chambers high in the keep of Lár Bhaile atop Goat Fell: Doyle, Rí Mallaghan, and Shay O Blaca, head of the Order of Gabair. Through the window, in the morning sun, Doyle could see the Tower of the Order, the stones painted a green as vibrant as the grass around it, gleaming nearby. The servants had set breakfast for them, obviously awed at having to serve not only their own Rí and the Order's head, but also the Rí Ard. They scurried gladly from the room at Rí Mallaghan's growl as soon as the table was set. The food sat untouched and the tea cooled in their mugs. Doyle was the only one still seated at the table. Rí Mallaghan had gone to one of the more comfortable chairs, while Shay O Blaca stayed by the window near the hearth, where—Doyle knew—the heat from a peat fire could warm joints that grew more painful with gout each year, the gout Meriel had refused to cure.

Rí Mallaghan scowled. "Lámh Shábhála can be taken," he said. "No matter how powerful this Bán Cailleach has become, she's not invulnerable."

"Labhrás Ó Riain took Lámh Shábhála from the Mad Holder only after I'd already defeated the Mad Holder on Knobtop," Doyle said. The memory was still as bitter as the day it had happened. "And Jenna took it back. I would have taken Lámh Shábhála from Jenna again this time, but she cast it into the sea. Aye, Rí, I know the Holder's vulnerabilities better than anyone." Doyle picked up the mug in front of him. In the dark glaze of the pottery, he could see his own dim reflection: a face older than he remembered, with the golden glint of the Ard's torc around his neck. He remembered it tightening around his throat, choking him as Sevei watched . . . "But Sevei has been through the Scrúdú. She isn't Jenna. She's . . . worse. All you need to do is look at her to know."

"She *says* she's been through the Scrúdú," O Blaca said from the window.

"Aye, and perhaps that's all it is: words," Rí Mallaghan agreed. "A bluff that's supposed to make us afraid to move against her."

"We've all felt her in the mage-lights, and I've *met* her in the flesh." Doyle shuddered at the memory and set the mug down on the table hard. Tea sloshed over the rim and pooled around it. "If it's a bluff, it's not one I'd be comfortable ignoring."

"Are you saying that she can't be brought down?" Rí Mallaghan asked. "I've known you since you were a boy, Doyle. I know that you've lusted after Lámh Shábhála

since the time you were old enough to understand what
had happened to your da. With my help, you've gone from
being a bastard half-Riocha child to a tiarna wearing the
Rí Ard's torc. Twice now, you've almost held Lámh Shábhála. Are you saying that you no longer want that? Are you
bending your knee to your great-niece?"

They were both watching him now. Doyle shook his
head. With a forefinger, he smeared the tea on the table, a
swirling pattern like that of the mage-lights. "I'm telling
you what she said, that's all. She said we would do as she
asked or she would hunt each of us down, that none of us
would be safe." He touched his neck, tugging at the torc. "I
believe that, my Rí."

"You sound like your wife," Rí Mallaghan scoffed. "She
was too close to the Healer Ard."

Doyle forced down the anger and shame that flooded
him at the mention of Edana. "The Healer Ard is like the
rest of the Aoires. You heard about the statue that appeared on Cnocareilig the day after the Bán Cailleach
came, how it looks not like a carving but the Healer Ard
herself, how its touch is warm and soft, and how hands
upon hands of healings have occurred there since. The
Hand of the Heart has more supplicants every day than the
Rí Ard and the Rí Dún Loaghaire's courts combined. Aye,
my Rí, I'm beginning to wonder if we shouldn't *all* have listened to Edana. We risked nearly two double-hands of
peace in the Tuatha because we saw that the Healer Ard
was becoming stronger than any Rí and because we didn't
want the Mad Holder walking here among us adding to her
strength. Maybe . . ." *Maybe we were wrong.* He didn't say
the words. "I'm finding that the torc of the Ard isn't as
comfortable as I thought it would be," he said instead.

Shay gave his attention to the window again; Rí Mallaghan rubbed his beard and stared at the wooden beams
of the ceiling. "Let's assume the Bán Cailleach is as powerful as she hints she is," Rí Mallaghan said finally, as if he
hadn't heard anything that Doyle had said. "She'll do nothing as long as she thinks she's being obeyed. So . . . we'll do
as she asks."

"My Rí?" Shay asked, startled. He turned from the window, but Rí Mallaghan only smiled.

"Aye, we let her believe she's won. We wait, and we'll

discover her weaknesses and her faults, and we'll take her down when we're ready, as we finally took down the Mad Holder." He sat back in his chair, tilting his head at Doyle. "What say you, Mac Ard? I need to know now. Where does your loyalty lie? Your da's spirit still walks in the night only partially revenged. I know what he would tell you. Do you listen to him, or do you listen to the Bán Cailleach and your wife?"

You have to choose now. If you tell him 'aye,' then you'll lose Edana forever . . . But he had already lost Edana and he didn't know if he could ever truly get her back. Perhaps, if he had Lámh Shábhála at last, then all the ghosts that haunted him would be put to their final rest. Perhaps then he could be what Edana wanted him to be. Perhaps then he could heal the wounds between them . . .

Perhaps.

"Aye," he told Rí Mallaghan. "I say aye."

43

The Bán Cailleach's Demands

TUATHA HALLA WEPT under the stormy sky. It was an inauspicious day for a meeting and the Ríthe shifted on their cold stone thrones, set in a ring around the central hearth of the hall while a peat fire attempted vainly to leach the chill from the stones. The roof, ancient and many times repaired, displayed a new leak, a steady *plonk-plonk-plonk* that splattered on the stone flags near Rí Eóin O Treasigh of Tuath Locha Léin, the youngest of the Ríthe. The dripping of the water was louder than the grumbling of old Rí Brasil Mas Sithig of Tuath Infochla, troubled by piles for the last few years and uncomfortable in his hard seat.

The directions from the Bán Cailleach had been explicit: the hall was empty of any spectators, and a Comhdáil Comhairle—a meeting of all the Ríthe of the Tuatha—had been convened. That each of them was concerned about the Bán Cailleach and her power was evidenced by the fact that none of the Ríthe were missing: all of them had made the sometimes-arduous journey to Dún Laoghaire, as they had all too recently to elect Doyle as Rí Ard. Now the Ríthe sat staring at each other in the circle of stone thrones around the fire. "This is ridiculous," Mas Sithig said, glaring at the pooling water as if it had personally offended him. "To have the Ríthe ordered about like tuathánach and kept waiting like supplicants . . ."

"The Ríthe created this problem when they decided it was better to rid themselves of the Healer Ard and the First Holder rather than to allow the Banrion Inish Thuaidh to come here," Edana snapped quickly in return.

"I had nothing to do with that," Mas Sithig responded quickly, but everyone saw his glance at Rí Torin Mallaghan to his left.

"Perhaps not," Edana said. Her own eyes weren't on Rí Mallaghan, but on Doyle, who sat directly across the circular room from her in the Ard's chair. "But others here did, either directly or because they kept silent when the plan was broached to them. Now we're served the meal from the seeds we planted—if it's bitter, the blame lies here in this room, because it was here that the treachery began."

"The Healer Ard was killed by a renegade Taisteal, not by one of us," Banrion Caitrín Taafe of Tuath Éoganacht said. Her voice was nearly a whisper, as if she were afraid to wake the ghosts that haunted this place.

Edana scoffed loudly and bitterly. "Oh, please, Caitrin. We don't need to keep up the pretense here; not even the tuathánach believe that. We all know in our hearts why the Healer Ard was killed. And it certainly wasn't a Taisteal who killed the Mad Holder, was it?" Her gaze had not left Doyle. He didn't answer. For a time, the Ríthe lapsed back into silence.

Rí Allister Fearachan of Connachta gestured to the guttering clock-candle set near the central fire. The brass cap-weight atop it was touching one of the pale red lines set within the white beeswax. "We've been here a full stripe of the candle already. If the Bán Cailleach doesn't arrive soon, then I suggest we return to the keep."

"The Bán Cailleach is here," a voice said, and with the sound, a wind rippled the flames of the fire and a swirling column of jade green and pale white light appeared beside the clock-candle. The light coalesced and took shape as the Ríthe shaded their eyes. A final gust of wind, a flare of emerald: a woman stood there on the stones—long hair of unblemished white cascading like sea spray over skin mottled with spiraling scars; eyes as dark as polished coal; her body clothed only in the scars and Lámh Shábhála glowing inside her. She turned slowly to look at each of them. Sevei could see each of them staring at her, and she noticed the nods and the narrowing of eyes as they saw beyond her appearance to the young woman they remembered. "Aye, as my uncle no doubt has informed you, you once knew me as Bantiarna Sevei Geraghty, daughter of the Healer Ard.

Child of Meriel and Owaine and great-daughter of Jenna MacEagan, all of whom you killed." They were silent at the accusation and Sevei laughed. "Oh, I see the guilt on your faces, and I've witnessed some of it myself, haven't I, Uncle Doyle?"

She saw hands creeping toward the Clochs Mór each of the Ríthe wore, and she laughed again, even though the intense cold of the passage here made her shiver despite the fire's heat, and the scars of her body screamed with the punishment of using the cloch-magic. The voices of ancient Holders yammered in her head.

"... *strike them now, before they gather against you!*"

"... *there are eight Clochs Mór here—not even you could stand against that many ...*"

"... *they deserve to die. All of them. They killed me, they killed poor Meriel, and they would have killed you just as casually. Be careful, you may have to fight here even though I know it's not what you want ...*"

That last was Jenna, and Sevei sent soothing thoughts to the spirit. "*I know, Gram. Hush. I know ...*"

"Do we need this futile exercise?" she said aloud to the Ríthe. "I'd really hoped this wouldn't be necessary. Eight Clochs Mór against Lámh Shábhála ..." She shook her head. "Kayne told me that it was foolish to even try this, that the only thing the Ríthe understood was power and until I demonstrated the power I now hold, you wouldn't listen. Eight against one—well, I'm not so foolish or vain to attempt that. If you open your clochs here, I will assume you prefer open war between us to a possible peace, and I'll leave before you can touch me. But I tell you this: I *will* come to each of you afterward, no matter where you go or where you hide, and I swear you will regret your decision this day."

"Not eight against one," Edana called out loudly. "It would be seven against Lámh Shábhála and Demon-Caller. I stand with the Bán Cailleach today, not the Ríthe."

"Not seven either," Doyle interjected. "I won't put my cloch against that of my wife." He was staring at Edana. "Snapdragon would defend Edana against anyone who would try to hurt her."

"... *that leaves only six. You could do it ...*"

"*. . . Don't let them attack first! Take them! . . .*"

"*. . . I once held off four for a time, but they killed me . . .*"

Sevei forced a smile to her face. "You surprise me, Uncle," Sevei said. "But I thank you. And you, Aunt Edana. So it would be six against two even if the Rí Ard simply keeps Snapdragon out of the fray. One of you against Demon-Caller, and five left for me. Now, *those* odds I'm willing to chance. Are you, Rí Mallaghan? Rí Mas Sithig? I tell you this, my Ríthe: as you would take Lámh Shábhála from me if I lost, I will take the clochs from each of you here afterward, while you still live to feel that anguish. Open your clochs, then, if you dare. Go on . . ." She spoke with a confidence she didn't feel inside. In truth, Lámh Shábhála had been drained of a good portion of its reserves from the passage here. She could feel the magepower still potent within it, but whether there was enough for her to take on all the Ríthe, if her body and mind could stand the pain and abuse . . .

She waited. The Ríthe all glanced at each other. Then, slowly, their hands dropped back down to the arms of their thrones.

"*. . . They gave me no such chance, great-daughter. Isn't it tempting, to take them now . . . ?*"

"*Hush, Gram . . .*" Sevei forced down the moan that wanted to escape her lips: *you can't show your vulnerability here, in front of them. They can't know how much you hurt.* She drew herself up, lifting her chin—showing weakness would be fatal, she knew. They would be on her like a pack of dire wolves on a crippled deer.

"I did as you asked and brought the Ríthe here," Doyle said to her. "What do you want of us, Sevei?"

"I want very little," she told them. "First, there are too many empty thrones here in Tuatha Halla, and I would fill two more of them."

Rí Mallaghan scoffed openly at that, interrupting her. "You want *nine* Ríthe? So you want Inish Thuaidh seated with us. That hardly surprises me. And who would take the other seat?"

"Inish Thuaidh has deserved its seat here in Tuatha Halla for generations," Sevei answered. "The Inishlanders kept safe the knowledge of the clochs and the slow magics through the dark generations, when the Tuatha would have forgotten. If it weren't for the Tuatha's cowardly theft of the clochs, the Tuatha Halla might be in Dún Kiil rather then Dún Laoghaire. But I'll see Rí Kyle MacEagan or his successor seated here helping to make the policies of the Tuatha and electing the Ard. And I would see a Rí of the Fingerlanders here also, as they once had."

"The Fingerlands are *mine*." Rí Morven Mac Baoill of Airgialla nearly came out of his chair. "Airgialla has owned the Fingerlands for two double-hands of the Ríthe of my family."

"And for that same amount of time, the clans of the Finger have fought against Dathúil's rule. But you own them no longer, Rí Mac Baoill. My brother defeated your first force and I've sent your latest army running home. The Finger is empty of your troops, Rí Mac Baoill, and I won't allow them to return."

"*You* won't allow?" Mac Baoill's face was suffused and his stout body quivered in his seat. "You have neither the right nor the power to allow it or not."

"The right? Perhaps not—at least no more right than you had when you sent your son to kill my da. But the power . . . ?" She touched her breast and the glow of Lámh Shábhála increased. Sevei ignored the pain as the scars pulled and tore at her shoulder with the movement. She could see the swirling patterns in her skin, glowing softly in the dimness of the room. "The power I have here. And those were the least of my demands. Aye, demands," she said into the hubbub of protest that came with the word. "Hear me, for this is what the Bán Cailleach wishes."

She opened Lámh Shábhála slightly, so that the energy within it flowed out to strengthen her voice, startling doves roosting in the Halla's rafters: they fluttered about the roof in panic. She drowned out the sound of the rain and the protests of the Ríthe. "Doyle Mac Ard will resign as Rí Ard, and for his murder of my great-mam the First Holder, he will exile himself from the Tuatha. For his part in the murder of Owaine Geraghty, Rí Morven Mac Baoill will do likewise. One or more of you here, I'm certain, planned the murder of the Healer Ard and Ennis. I will discover who that person is; I will hold that person responsible, and for him or her, I also demand exile. Those Riocha responsible for slaying my siblings Tara and Ionhar will have their lands and titles forfeited and be exiled also. Be glad that I ask only exile when I might have as easily asked for your lives in return for theirs."

"... *show them mercy, and they will kill you for it! I know* ..."

"... *You're too soft, too weak* ..."

"... *No! Kill them! It's the least they deserve for what they did to me* ..."

The voices of old Holders yammered in her head at that. Only her gram's voice was louder, but also gentler. "*I, too, would kill them, Sevei. But my choices weren't always the best ones, I know now. Trust yourself, great-daughter* ..."

The uproar in the Halla matched that in her head, as Mac Baoill, Torin Mallaghan, and Allister Fearachan rose to their feet shouting. Only Doyle sat silently in his throne, his face ashen above the gold sheen of the Ard's torc. Sevei opened Lámh Shábhála a little more and they all went silent, sitting back in their seats as if unseen hands had shoved them down. The voices still clamored in her head, but Sevei ignored them. "I haven't finished," Sevei told the Ríthe. "I will have my brother Kayne as the new Rí Ard."

"Kayne?" Torin Mallaghan managed to croak out against the force that held him to his seat. "Not yourself?"

She gave him a smile rimed with frost. "Not me," she said. "I have other tasks, and other fates—and I return to them now. I will give you a hand of days to give me your response."

"You ask for nothing less than our total submission to you," Torin Mallaghan said angrily.

She bowed mockingly toward him. "Aye, Rí Mallaghan. That's exactly what I ask."

"You can't have it. You *won't* have it." Mallaghan said it without looking at the others, but Sevei could see the apprehension in their faces. Doyle slumped on his throne as if he were hearing nothing; Edana stared at Doyle with a surprisingly gentle look on her face. Mac Baoill was as defiant as Mallaghan, but the others watched Mallaghan with varying degrees of shock on their faces. Sevei shrugged.

"I'm sorry to hear that, Rí Mallaghan. If I must, I will make an example of one of the Ríthe. I would prefer not to have to do that, but since you volunteer ..."

"... *they won't listen unless you show them* ..."

"*. . . take Mallaghan now . . .*"

Sevei couldn't keep the voices down. She was tiring, and she was in terrible pain, and she could not stay here. The energy captured in Lámh Shábhála burned in her mind, yearning to break free of her. "But I don't wish your answer now," she told the Ríthe. "I'll give you time. Talk among yourselves and send the Comhdáil Comhairle's answer to the Narrows: to the new Tuath Méar, the Finger. But before you talk, I would urge you to remember this: I can destroy just as easily as I can create."

With that, gratefully, Sevei opened Lámh Shábhála fully and let the power inside bear her away.

The news came to the Ríthe even before they left the Tuatha Halla. One of Doyle's aides, a fosterling from the O'Murchadha family staying at Dún Laoghaire, peered nervously through the open archway of the Halla. They had all heard his quick footsteps, and the contentious argument that had engulfed all of them but the silent Doyle now subsided as they turned to him. The aide's gaze went from Edana to Doyle but avoided the others, as if their glares could cut. Water dripped from his long hair onto the floor, and his clothing was sodden. "Rí Ard, Banrion, I don't mean to interrupt, but on Cnocareilig . . . at the Healer Ard's barrow . . ." He stopped at the sound of sucked-in breaths, as if the name had been an invocation, and his expression slid from nervous to puzzled. "I thought you should know . . ."

The feeling of slow dread that had consumed Doyle since Sevei's appearance deepened. He stroked the Torc of the Ard as he had since the Bán Cailleach had recited her demands, feeling the cool smoothness of the gold. His own voice sounded like the croaking of a frog in the marsh. "Go on, Auliffe," he told him. "Speak. What's happened?"

The young man visibly swallowed. He pulled his clóca tight around him. "I was on my rounds, checking in with the gardai on duty at the keep gates. My back was to the grave-hill, but suddenly I could see my shadow on the keep walls. I turned: a brilliant light was playing over Cnocareilig—like the sun had burst through the rain clouds.

Then it was gone, so quickly that the day seemed darker than before. I wasn't certain what to do—whether I should wait or to send a few of the keep's gardai to Cnocareilig to investigate. I'd summoned your Hand, and we were about to go ourselves when the first of the people came running back down the Cnocareilig road. We'd seen at least a double-hand of double-hands of supplicants walking up there in the morning, even with the rain. But that's usual, ever since the Healer Ard's statue—"

He stopped, and a hand came up to prowl the thin beard on his chin. Auliffe had been with Doyle when he'd received the news of the statue's appearance and undoubtedly had just remembered the Ard's reaction. The Ríthe were grumbling again, though Edana was staring at Auliffe with interest. Torin Mallaghan slapped the arm of his throne with an open hand, and Auliffe jumped. Doyle waved a weary hand at the young man. "Auliffe, please continue."

Auliffe dropped his hand and shook beaded rain from the ends of his hair. "Well, it seemed at least half the supplicants were coming back down toward the city. Running, Rí Ard, as if all the ghosts that haunt Cnocareilig were chasing them, shouting and screaming, the mud of the road splattering under their feet. We thought they were frightened, but when they came closer, we realized what they were saying, and that they weren't frightened but joyous." He stopped again, and this time the Ríthe waited. "They were saying that the Healer Ard had appeared herself—in the sky as a bright, shining star—and that she had created a temple for herself on Cnocareilig. They were coming down to tell the others, the tuathánach of the city." He paused. "The rain is just a drizzle now, my Ard. You . . . you can see yourself if you step out of the Halla."

Edana was the first to move. She was out of her throne and striding past Auliffe before any of the rest of them had stirred. Torin Mallaghan glared at Auliffe as if the boy were personally responsible for the news, then followed, the other five Ríthe in his wake. Doyle took a long breath before pushing himself up from his throne. Doyle felt, suddenly, very old. He shuffled like some decrepit ancient across the sunken floor of the throne circle and past the central fire. Auliffe watched him, and Doyle patted the young man on the back as he came up to him. "Thank you, Auliffe. Don't worry. You did what you should have done." With another sigh, he left the throne circle and went outside.

The Ríthe had gathered in a cluster with all their gardai—waiting obediently outside in the weather—gathered behind. All of them were staring south: from the summit of Halla Hill, and to the left of the hill on which the twin keeps of the Rí Ard and Banrion Dún Laoghaire sat, to the steep, barren hillside past the Old Walls where the barrows of the ancient Ards rested. There, through the gray mist of the rain, Doyle could see a structure of pure white gleaming, with four towers dotting its ramparts.

He knew the architecture. He'd seen it before: it was a replica of the main section of the White Keep on Inishfeirm, home of the Order of Inishfeirm and where all three generations of the Aoires—Jenna, Meriel, and Sevei—had been educated in the ways of the cloudmages. *I give you your last chance for hope*, it said mutely. *You must choose.*

" 'I can destroy as easily as I can create.' " Edana breathed the quote for all of them.

"This is an outrage," Torin Mallaghan was saying. "A mockery. It must be torn down."

"Tear it down?" Edana repeated. She laughed. Her graying hair, uncovered by the cowl of her clóca, was frosted with the drizzle, and beads of water were on the torc of Dún Laoghaire around her neck. "And what would that accomplish, Rí Mallaghan, except to rouse the tuathánach who still love the Healer Ard? Do any of us have the power in our Cloch Mór to take down the building as quickly as the Bán Cailleach built it? How foolish would we look, destroying this temple to her mam stone by stone when she created it in a moment? I won't allow it, Rí Mallaghan. This is my Tuath, not yours. I say the Bán Cailleach has sent us a clear message, and I prefer it remains there so that we're not tempted to forget."

"What *you* forget, Banrion, is that the Rí Ard also dwells here, and he rules all the Tuatha," Mallaghan retorted. "What say you, my Ard: do we let this insult to all Ríthe and Riocha remain standing?" Doyle didn't move; he stared at the new keep on the hill: the temple to the Healer Ard. "Rí Ard?"

Doyle shivered at the call. He looked at Torin, at Edana. He knew what he should answer. He knew what he *must* answer, if he were not to make Torin Mallaghan an enemy rather than his ally. But the words wouldn't come.

Edana pushed past them, going to her carriage. Gardai clad in the gray of Dún Laoghaire closed around her. "Where are you going, Banrion?" Mallaghan called out after her.

"To Cnocareilig and the White Temple," she answered. She turned to look at them. "I'm not frightened of my people, or of the Healer Ard's ghost, or of the Bán Cailleach," she said. "But I understand why *you* would be." She tilted her head toward Doyle. "Will you come with me, Husband?" she asked. She held out her hand.

To say "aye" would be the bravest thing he'd ever done, he knew. To take Edana's hand now would be to repudiate all that he'd done over the decades: his lust to revenge his da's death, his ambition to be Rí, his determination to hold Lámh Shábhála himself, all that he'd helped to create with the Order of Gabair. To take Edana's hand now would be to declare that everything he'd done before—all the suffering, all the struggle, all the blood and pain and death—had somehow been wrong or misguided. To take Edana's hand would be to turn his back on all that for the hope that the two of them might reconcile. To take Edana's hand would be to slap the face of Rí Mallaghan and make him forever an enemy.

The wind, shifting, splattered rain on his face and he blinked into the spray. He touched again the torc of the Ard—the symbol of everything he'd managed to accomplish and all that remained to do.

He shook his head.

"No," he told her.

PART FOUR

CONFRONTATION

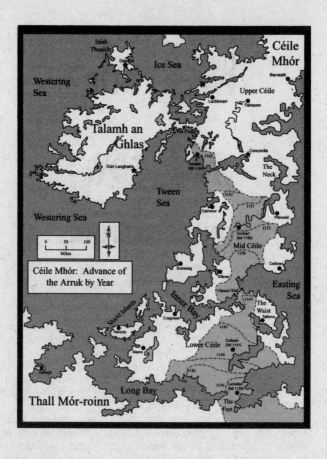

44

The Battle of the
Four Lakes

LIKE ANY CHILD, Ennis had heard the songs of wars
and battles, sung by the bards and Songmasters who
came to the courts of Dún Laoghaire. The lyrics of the
songs wove fantastic landscapes of waving flags and bright
swords, of bravery, of flashing clochs, of glorious deeds and
triumph in the face of impossible odds.

Ennis had listened to his brothers Kayne and Ionhar talk
about war in glowing, excited tones—Kayne especially,
since he'd actually trained as a soldier and was going off to
fight with Da in Céile Mhór, while Ionhar was less than a
hand older than Ennis and was being sent to fosterage.
Kayne's vision of war seemed to match that of the Songmasters, but Ennis didn't know for certain whether it was
true since Kayne hadn't yet been in battle.

He'd also spoken to Da, one night not long before he left
for Céile Mhór. "Tell me about war, Da," Ennis had said,
his voice rushed with excitement and his eyes wide. "Were
you ever in a battle like Sliabh Míchinniúint?"

A visiting bard had just that night given the court the
Song of Máel Armagh, with its long, brilliant verses of
Máel's tragic defeat at the hands of the great Inish cloudmage Severii O'Coulghan. Ennis had listened spellbound,
entranced both by the bard's warm baritone and the exciting tale.

Da's face had gone strangely sad and quiet at the re-
quest. "War is everything great and glorious, and everything horrible and awful, Ennis," he'd said. "It's everything
that the Songmasters sing about, but it's also everything

that they leave out." He wouldn't give Ennis any of the details he so desperately wanted to hear. Instead, Da toyed with the pieces of the ficheall board set up near Ennis' bed. "You know how to play, don't you?" Da asked.

Ennis had nodded. "I'm good at it. Ionhar gets mad, because I know what piece he's going to move before he does it, and so I put my pieces where they can't get hurt."

Da had laughed and tousled Ennis' hand. "I'll have to play you, then. Ennis, war is like a ficheall game: you maneuver your pieces until your opponent is forced to surrender." A curiously pained look came over his face then. "The difference is that the pieces have wives and children and families. The pieces are your friends and your companions and people you talk to every day. Once they're gone from the board, they're gone forever. You can't ever reset the pieces and play with them again."

War didn't appear to be as clean, as majestic, or as orderly as the Songmasters had made it seem, but Ennis did see the qualities of a game. Cima stayed with Ennis as the Arruk prepared to leave the city, and Ennis sat in his room with Gyl Svarti's spell-stick across his tiny lap. He listened to the voice of Gyl Svarti inside, stealing into the creature's memories to find the binding words that would seal magic in the spellstick to be released later at his command. Ennis was surprised at how simple it was, how the knowledge came to him, as if in slaying Gyl Svarti with Treoraí's Heart, he'd taken the Svarti's mind into his own.

Cima watched and listened, occasionally correcting Ennis' pronunciation and twice supplying missing words, and nodding as if pleased with what he saw. Afterward, the spell-stick full of slow magic, Ennis gave the staff to Cima to hold for him. Cima nodded, hefting the length of wood in his hands. "How do you know the spell words? Were you going to be a Svarti, Cima?" Ennis asked.

The Arruk nodded, one hand sliding along the finger-polished wood of the spell-stick. It was a touch of familiarity. "I *was* a Svarti."

"I'll bet you were a good one," Ennis said earnestly. Without the blue ghost, he found that he desperately wanted Cima's approval. Cima only shrugged. "Tell me about that time. Tell me why you're not a Svarti any more."

A definite look of pain crossed Cima's face with that, his

underlids closing over his eyes and the colors of his scales fading. "Another time, Ennis Svarti," he said. "Now we need to be ready for when . . ."

Cima's voice trailed into silence, but Ennis knew what he'd been going to say. "When we meet my people, you mean?"

Cima nodded. "Kurhv Kralj knows that the bluntclaws have people watching. We'll move slowly, so that the Perakli Kralj will know from his spies that we're marching again. Kurhv Kralj has already told the Mairki that the Perakli think we're little but animals, and so we should look and act like animals to them so he'll bring his army out to stop us . . ." Cima shrugged then.

"What will happen?"

"Kurhv Kralj thinks it will be a great battle, and that this time we will send much of the Perakli army to their gods. Then we will follow you, Ennis Svarti. We will follow you all the way to Cudak Zvati."

"Are you scared, Cima? I'm scared." Ennis had his hand around Treoraí's Heart, but that did little to comfort him. His mam's voice was silent; if he heard anything, it was only the mocking advice of Isibéal or the cackling derision of Gyl Svarti or the lost wails of the others he'd killed.

What Cima did then was something his mam or da might have done. The Arruk stretched out his clawed hand and touched Ennis' cheek. "You Perakli fear death too much. Whether we die or not doesn't matter. But I'm afraid, too. I'm afraid that when Cudak weighs my third heart after I die, that He'll find it too light, or perhaps he won't find enough blood of my enemies on my jaka to send me back as an Arruk, and I'll be returned as a sheep or goat for the true Arruk to feed on." His hand dropped back to his side, and Cima smiled. "You'll be fine, Ennis Svarti. I'm proud to carry your spell-stick for you. You will bring terror to the Perakli."

Ennis watched Cima stroke the carved surface of the spell-stick. "How do you make a spell-stick?" he asked the Arruk. "If all you have to do is take a stick, there could be so many that everyone could have one."

Cima gave a coughing bark of a laugh at that. "No, Ennis Svarti. First, there are years of training that are necessary before a Nesvarti or Svarti can learn to create a spell-stick. Also, the wood we use is from the goldenwood tree that is

rare and grows only slowly; why, once the great Barak
Svarti searched for a full two cycles to find just the right
goldenwood. Even when you find a tree mature enough to
make a spell-stick, it still takes nearly a full cycle for a
Svarti or Nesvarti to create the carvings and prepare the
staff. A wrong stroke of the knife or inattention to the
chants, and he must start over. Even then it may not work,
or the spell-stick may be flawed so that it holds only one or
two spells or breaks the first time it's used. If a Svarti or
Nesvarti's spell-stick is lost or broken, then until he makes
another he can only use the chanted magics which take a
long time to cast. Spell-sticks are rare and treasured." Cima
handed the spell-stick back to Ennis. "There's another reason that the Svarti are frightened by you—no Svarti has
ever been able to use another's spell-stick. When a Svarti
dies, so does his spell-stick. Yet you took Gyl Svarti's from
him and the spell-stick still lived." Ennis set the staff to one
side, letting it lean against the wall, seeing Cima's eyes follow the motion. "I remember how I carved my own spell-
stick," Cima said. "Let me tell you, so you'll understand. I
went high up on Forsaken Mountain, because that was
where Barak had found his goldenwood . . ."

As Cima spoke, the blue ghosts swirled like a dim fog
around Ennis and within them, in the dim distance, he saw
himself seated on a stone throne holding a spell-stick in
one hand and the Heart in the other. . . .

The Arruk force moved north from Torness as a wild mass,
roughly clumped around each of the Mairki, who—like the
Kralj as well as the chief Svarti—rode in bearer-borne litters. They moved north in several distinct groups, as if dis-
organized and independent of each other. They passed
through a deserted landscape of farmland and pasture bejeweled with several large lakes, the cottages and small villages they passed empty as the inhabitants fled before
them. The Arruk torched the houses as they passed, leaving behind them a trail of greasy smoke and ruin. The fields
and the crops were trampled underneath; the sheep, goats,
and cattle were slaughtered to feed the troops. At night
they would camp, then move forward the next day before

dawn—for three days, that was the routine. It was only when the mounted scouts sent out ahead of the main mass of the army came galloping back with word that the enemy had been sighted ahead of them, on a hill near one of the many lakes of the region, that Kurhv Kralj gave the orders to assemble in battle formation. The Mairki and their Svarti now abandoned their litters, though Kurhv Kralj (and thus Ennis) did not as yet.

As the Kralj's Svarti, Ennis' litter had a place of honor next to that of Kurhv Kralj in the center of the army, with the Arruk soldiers spread out in a wide, irregular crescent on either side of them, two of the Mairki on either side, the twin horns facing forward. They moved ahead at an eager lope now, the litter bearers running to keep up. By mid-morning, they came within sight of the Céile Mhór force. A valley lay between them, laid out with stone fences in squares of farmed land, a wide stream bordered by trees looping through the center toward its meeting with a long lake to their east.

"Are you ready, Ennis Svarti?" Cima asked from alongside Ennis' litter. He helped Ennis down from the litter as Kurhv Kralj also descended from his, and handed Ennis his spell-stick. Kurhv Kralj looked down at Ennis, and he could see the bloodlust in the Arruk's face.

"Now," Kurhv Kralj told him. "Now is when we are most alive, when we confront death itself."

Kurhv Kralj gestured, and the Arruk crescent surmounted the ridge and descended into the valley toward the waiting enemy.

Ennis could see the horses of the Riocha officers on the opposite ridge and their sky-blue banners set with a stylized dire wolf waving in the wind. More troops, he knew, waited just beyond the crest to descend into the fray once the clochs were unleashed and the cavalry made their initial charge—that was how Kayne had said it always happened: first the clochs and a barrage of arrows, then the horse-mounted troops, then finally the foot soldiers: the ficheall of the Daoine.

But if the Thane's troops included Clochs Mór, they were silent. The ranks of mounted soldiers loomed above the advancing Arruk like a dark, billowing thunderhead on the horizon.

The storm broke in an instant.

The riders gave a loud cry as one, and arrows darkened the sky like a monstrous flock of deadly birds. A curtain of shafts arced down into the center of the Arruk force, and Ennis heard the strange clatter of iron arrowheads against the hard scales of the Arruk. A few of the Arruk went down, but for the most part the arrows bounced or broke, or penetrated lightly. *"Fool!"* Gyl Svarti grunted inside. *"The other Svarti wait for you to act, Ennis. They wonder why you wait . . ."* Another wave of arrows followed the first, and this time Ennis raised his spell-stick and spoke a word, and the arrows burst into quick flame to let a pattering drizzle of glowing arrowheads fall to the ground short of the Arruk. The Arruk let out a massed howl that raised the hairs on the back of Ennis' neck.

The howl was answered by another cry from the Daoine, and now the horses came thundering down the slope toward the Arruk, toward the center of the crescent and Kurhv Kralj and Ennis. "Now!" Cima said to Ennis, the word echoed by Gyl Svarti in his head, and Ennis raised his spell-stick. To either side of him, he saw the Svarti do the same. In his other hand, Ennis took Treoraí's Heart, and he opened it as well.

He spoke the release word.

From the other Svarti, a pulse of light radiated out, and where each of the lines met the onrushing cavalry, a hand or less of horses went down and men cried out. But as the spell left Ennis' spell-stick it fused with mage-energy emanating from the Heart. A burst of crackling lightnings snapped and snarled over the heads of the Arruk in front of him and slammed into the center of the onrushing Daoine. The earth erupted with a roar there, sending broken horses and broken men flying backward just as they were about to crash into the front ranks of the Arruk. The fury of the blast seemed to halt the motion and sound of the battle for a moment: there was a silence filled with the remembered thunder, and the Daoine horsemen pulled up the reins of their horses, their spears held in shocked hands. A pall of dust and smoke spread, and through it Ennis could see the faces of the Daoine: filled with a new terror.

In the silence and stillness, Gyl shouted with glee in

Ennis' head and Isibéal laughed. Far inside, his mam wailed with the others.

Then the stasis broke as Kurhv Kralj, a stride away from Ennis, gave a roar of triumph, and the Arruk all around Ennis echoed him. Cima howled with them, slapping Ennis on the back. The Daoine took up the broken charge, and the Arruk surged forward, eager to meet them.

Steel met steel. The long jaka of the Arruk began to flash among the spears and swords of the Daoine. Ennis was pushed forward by those behind as Kurhv Kralj charged forward with the rest, Cima at his side. Ennis could smell an odd coppery scent, and he realized it was the odor of blood and adrenaline. Men yelled; Arruk howled, and even the horses screamed as they were taken down. Through the chaos, Ennis caught a glimpse of a flood of leather-clad men rushing down the hillside into the battle, the sun glinting from rings of metal on the armor and from their helms. The banner of Céile Mhór fluttered among them.

Ennis looked for the blue ghosts and could not find them. *Wait!* he wanted to shout. *I don't know what to do . . .*

And there was no time for thought anymore, only for survival.

. . . A horseman in blue broke through the ring of Arruk around them. Ennis saw nothing of him but the shape, outlined against the sky: deadly strikes from the hooves of his rearing warhorse took down an Arruk near Kurhv Kralj, and the soldier grunted audibly as his spear jabbed into another Arruk. The spear was torn from his hand as the second Arruk fell, and the man pulled a long sword from its scabbard. The Daoine saw Kurhv Kralj then, noticing the insignia of the Kralj on his chest, and the man yanked hard on the reins of his foam-mouthed, glaring-eyed mount, kicking its lathered sides so that it plunged toward the Kralj like the hull of a great ship through a resisting surf. Kurhv Kralj saw him at the same time and raised his jaka in defiance. The first sword strike struck Kurhv Kralj's weapon and hacked the staff in two, the metal head sailing away. Under the helm-shadowed face, Ennis saw the Daoine's mouth open in a grim laugh, and the sword blade whistled as he drew it back, ready to strike. But he noticed Ennis then, and under the rim of the helm, his eyes widened in surprise. Ennis could almost hear the man's astonishment—*a Daoine child? Here?*—but the hesitation was fatal. Kurhv Kralj leaped, weaponless, and his clawed hand ripped the man from his saddle and bore him down. An impossible gout of blood sprayed from the side of the man's neck, splattering over both Kurhv Kralj and Ennis' right arm. Ennis touched the stain, marveling at its heat ...

... The charge of the foot soldiers hit them, a blow that staggered and halted the rushing Arruk line, the shock wave traveling back so that Kurhv Kralj, Ennis, and Cima, moving forward with the others, were momentarily crushed. Ennis, far shorter, was nearly trampled underneath until Cima lifted him, placing him on his shoulder as his da had once done. Ennis rode Cima, his legs hugging the Arruk's muscular neck, his hand clutching the spell-stick and Treoraí's Heart.

"Way!" Cima shouted in the Arruk tongue. "Make way for Kurhv Kralj and Ennis Svarti! Make way!" The Arruk in front obeyed as best they could, the unengaged Arruk sliding aside to reveal a chaotic landscape where men fought Arruk, where already-slain bodies lay like red-stained stones, where he saw people vibrantly alive one moment and horribly dead the next, where wounded Daoine and Arruck alike moaned and screamed. The terror and fright truly struck Ennis then, and atop Cima's shoulders he began to cry. It was then that Ennis knew why Da had never wanted to speak about war. ...

Weeping, Ennis felt the danger too late. A new flight of arrows whistled overhead, arcing down like falcons stooping to strike. Feathers bloomed in his sight and there was sudden, terrible pain in his shoulder as Treoraí's Heart slipped from his hand. The impact sent him tumbling backward off Cima's shoulders, the spell-stick clattering to the ground. Ennis lay on the grass stunned, looking up at sky and flailing arms. He felt with his left hand where the arrow's shaft had buried itself in his shoulder; his hands came away sticky with blood and he nearly fainted. He sobbed in mingled pain and fright. "Ennis Svarti!" he heard Cima shout, and the Arruk's face appeared above him. He glanced at the arrow. "You must ignore it," he told Ennis. "Here!" He was holding the spell-stick, and Ennis reached out with his left hand to take it as Cima reached down and plucked him up again. The movement sent white-hot shafts of agony through his body, and Ennis screamed, but Cima paid no attention, placing Ennis on his shoulders again. A red-hued glass seemed to have been placed over Ennis' eyes; he saw the landscape as if the sun itself had turned bloody.

There were no blue ghosts here. No pattern. This was not a dance he could follow.

"Look!" Cima shouted, pointing. The horns of the Arruk army had not been able to close around the Daoine force, as more of the men came down from the heights. The entire Arruk line was engulfed. From his vantage, Ennis could see the Svarti howling their spells and the jaka of the Arruk thrashing as if trying to scythe down a field of wheat. In the scarlet chaos, finally, there were sapphire forms moving and patterns forming.

In them, Ennis saw Kurhv Kralj's death, Cima's death, and his own. He saw the vision to which he had once clung slipping away from him, and he saw what he must do if he wanted to keep the future he'd once glimpsed.

"No!" he shouted, and the blue ghost that was his future self glanced back to him forlornly. The apparition nodded. *"Aye . . ."* its lips mouthed. *"Aye . . ."* Isibéal spoke in his head. *"Aye . . ."* echoed Gyl, Ata, and Unnisha, Daighi and Brett, Artol and all the crewmates of his ship, Haughey and Brina, Noz Ruka and Grozan Kralj. Everyone but his mam . . . *"Aye . . ."*

"No," Ennis answered, but this time it was only a choking whisper, lost against their insistence. The roar of the battle came back to him, louder than the blue ghosts and the dead ones in his head, and he forced his scarred right hand to move, to find Treoraí's Heart on its chain again. Ennis gasped as he touched the cloch, the power leaping from the stone and surging through him. He raised the spell-stick; the blue ghost of his future smiled and he saw the pattern that he must lock himself to. In front of him, the Daoine were crashing through the thinning ranks of the Arruk. Kurhv Kralj was surrounded, flailing desperately as three Daoine circled him and another nocked arrow to bow, the taut gut string creaking as he pulled it back.

Ennis let himself fall into the blue ghost. It screamed; he screamed with it. He let the mage-energy pour from Treoraí's Heart and through the spell-stick, taking each of the spells he'd stored so carefully there and strengthening it, adding power to each of them.

The stick glowed like a new sun, banishing the blood. Shadows, as dark as night and as sharp as honed blades, rushed outward in a widening arc from the bright fury that was Ennnis. Where the light touched, Daoine soldiers were torn away from the combat and tossed backward like so many straw dolls and slammed down to earth. The destruction rippled out in a semicircular wave from Ennis, accompanied by the scream that was amplified through Treoraí's Heart. When it stopped, a breath later that seemed to last half a stripe or more, Kurhv Kralj gave a howl of triumph that was taken up by the entire Arruk army. The few of the Céile Mhór attackers who were yet standing gaped toward Ennis. He knew they saw him: a fey child straddling an Arruk, holding a cloch na thintrí and a staff that burned.

The Céile Mhór army had been shattered in the center, and Kurhv Kralj urged them forward to close around the now-sundered Daoine forces. The Daoine turned and fled back the way they'd come and the Arruk pursued them, screaming their bloodlust.

Cima, bearing Ennis, started to follow, but Ennis was spent. Blood had soaked the front of his ragged léine, and the scars of the mage-lights burned on his arm. In his mage-sight, the blue ghost reeled atop Cima and fell.

Ennis, grateful, fell with it into oblivion.

45

Meetings and Offers

DEATH, HE WOULD HAVE thought, was supposed to be quiet and peaceful. That's how his mam described it once when he'd asked. But this death was noisy with hisses and growls and a snarling chatter in words he couldn't understand. It was all annoying enough that he forced his eyes open, blinking into unrelenting and utterly normal sunlight.

Ennis saw little but sky, but as he lifted his head slightly he saw Cima, straddling Ennis' prone body with his jaka lifted threateningly toward Daj Svarti, who was standing near Ennis' right side. Cima's voice was raised as he argued with Daj Svarti. As Ennis blinked again, Daj Svarti leaned over toward Ennis, reaching for the spell-stick that lay across his body or perhaps for Treoraí's Heart on its chain. Cima hissed and his weapon swept forward. The curved blade of the jaka would have taken off Daj Svarti's hand had the Arruk not snatched it back. The mage growled and lifted his own spell-stick, the corners of his mouth flecked with spittle and his eyes snared in red veins. Tiny lightnings crawled around the head of the spell-stick as Cima shouted defiantly back at Daj Svarti, raising his jaka again.

"No!" Ennis shouted. The word was a squeak, and was followed immediately by a painful cry as he tried to sit up. His right arm refused to hold his weight and collapsed under him; he fell back to the ground. Ennis reached for his shoulder with his left hand; his hand found the broken shaft of an arrow, coming away sticky with blood. Staring at his gore-stained fingers, Ennis nearly succumbed to the darkness again. *"No,"* he thought he heard a voice say, but he didn't know whose it was. *"You can't show weakness here. Find the pattern. The dance of your blue ghosts..."*

... the dance ... Aye, they were there when Ennis brushed Treoraí's Heart with his good hand. He found the familiar blue ghost, locked himself to it ...

Ennis bit his lower lip, rolling to his left so he could sit. Cima was still arguing with Daj Svarti. The Arruk mage glared at Ennis and growled again, like a dog competing for food under the table at Dún Laoghaire. The lightnings faded from the knob of his spell-stick and he went stalking off. Cima let his jaka fall to the ground and turned to Ennis.

"I was afraid you wouldn't wake quickly enough," he said in his heavily-accented Daoine. "Daj Svarti saw you fall and wanted to claim the mage-stone, but I wouldn't let him take it ..." As Cima spoke, he helped Ennis to his feet. Ennis couldn't keep the tears from filling his eyes with the searing pain that went through his shoulder then, but the blue ghost would not let him cry.

"Thank you, Cima," he said. The thought of Daj Svarti taking Treoraí's Heart from him made Ennis feel sick. His shoulder throbbed in time to his racing heartbeat and he could feel warm blood tricking down his right side. The sharp smell of it—both Daoine and Arruk—filled the air, overpowering even the reek of the Arruk. The valley was muddied and scarred, the turf torn to expose the black earth underneath. All around him, Arruk strode carefully among the crumbled mounds of the fallen. They weren't all dead: some moaned and twitched, while other lay terribly still. Somewhere close by, a Céile Mhór garda was screaming in agony—a long, shrieking wail, a pause for breath, then the wail again, over and over, until the endless scream went suddenly, jarringly silent. Ennis could see that the Arruk soldiers were prodding the wounded with the butt of their jaka. If the body was Daoine and it moved, they quickly reversed the pole arm so that the blade was down, and thrust the edge savagely into the body. If the wounded was Arruk and rose, they would move on; if the Arruk couldn't rise on his own, though, they were dispatched as the Daoine had been.

Ennis realized that this was exactly what would have happened to him had Cima not been with him. The gorge rose in his throat and even the blue ghost could not hold it back. Ennis' stomach convulsed and he bent over as he retched, vomiting harshly. The bile burned in his throat. After the spasms passed, he spat and wiped his mouth with his muddy, blood-spattered sleeve. Cima watched, head tilted curiously. "Better now?" he asked.

Ennis nodded. The blue ghost was moving and he followed it, standing erect again. The blue ghost ignored the tearing in his shoulder as the embedded arrow dug into muscles with the motion, and so Ennis did the same, though he wanted to moan and cry. "Where is Kurhv Kralj?" he and the blue ghost asked. "I need to speak with him."

Cima pointed to a rise several strides away, where the banner of the Kralj fluttered. Ennis started to walk toward the Kralj, unable to stop the gasp that came as the first footstep jarred his shoulder. He leaned heavily on the spell-stick, a child walking like a withered old man. Cima walked beside him, an arm around Ennis' waist in support. As they approached, Kurhv Kralj saw them and turned from the huddle of Mairki and their Svarti around him, Daj Svarti among them. Daj Svarti would not look at Ennis, but Kurhv Kralj's face was full of what seemed to be genuine relief. "Ennis Svarti!" the Kralj cried aloud as Cima translated for Ennis. "I saw you fall, and I hoped you weren't so badly hurt that we would need to send you to Cudak."

You saw me fall and you didn't even come to see how badly I was hurt, or protect me from Daj Svarti? Ennis remembered once falling off a pony at Dún Laoghaire, and how Da and Mam had rushed over to him immediately, worried and frantic. *"Even the Kralj can't show weakness,"* Gyl Svarti's voice whispered to him. *"Especially the Kralj . . ."*

"The battle's over?" he asked Kurhv Kralj in halting, poor Arruk, and the Arruk bared his teeth in satisfaction.

"The Perakli who are still alive are running away like the sheep that they are, but they left half of their soldiers here," Kurhv Kralj answered, and opened his mouth wide to roar once at the sky. The Mairki and Svarti around him did the same—Daj Svarti doing so belatedly—and their combined howl of triumph was echoed around the field. "It was your power that broke them, Ennis Svarti," Kurhv Kralj said. "They couldn't stand before you."

The blue ghost smiled, and Ennis smiled with it. "No one can stand before Kurhv Kralj and Ennis Svarti," he said as Cima translated. "No one. Kurhv Kralj will lead us to Cudak Zvati and the gift that Cudak holds for us." The Arruk howled again with that, and the sound was so loud that it threatened to send Ennis reeling. The darkness threatened to close in around him again, and he took a step backward. Kurhv Kralj seemed to notice his injuries for the first time.

"That needs to be removed, and the wound cleaned," he said. "Cima will take you to the Mender. Then you'll return here." He pointed east and north. "We will follow the call of the Cudak Zvati, and none will be able to resist us."

They howled again, and Ennis shouted with them, his little-boy voice giving vent to all the pain and fright within himself that he dared not show.

For several stripes of the candle later, the pain was nearly too much to bear, and Sevei screamed and wept with the agony that lashed her body. The scars burned like ropes of fire, pulsing with each beat of her heart; her eyes felt like glowing coals set in her skull. The vision of the temple she'd placed at her mam's barrow hovered before her like a mirage. She'd taken herself to a deserted beach on Inish Thuaidh, far from any of the fastnesses of the clans and well away from the few fishing villages; away, too, from the demands that Kayne and the Fingerlanders might have put on her.

There, she could be alone in her misery; there no one could see her weakness and she would not have to use Lámh Shábhála until the pain had subsided. If she had anduilleaf, she would have used it, quickly and gladly, and that frightened her more than anything, remembering the tales of Gram's madness.

". . . no, my love, that's not a path you should take," Gram's voice trembled at the thought. "Don't make the mistakes I made. When you're here, all the pain will be gone for you. I promise you that much . . ."

The voices of the other ancient Holders screeched and chattered in her head like a flock of dark, angry crows and she couldn't hold them back. They accused, they jeered, they suggested, they wailed with her. She tried to find her gram's voice again, but she was submerged in the flood. It was Carrohkai Treemaster who came to her.

"... *this will pass, as Jenna told you. What you're feeling is the burden of the Scrúdú, the price for knowing all of Lámh Shábhála, but it will pass. Accept the pain, listen to it, try to understand it ...*"

The first night, when the mage-lights came, she tried to resist their call, but Lámh Shábhála was starved and fierce and she couldn't stop herself from opening herself to the wild power that lashed the clouds. She screamed as the mage-lights filled her and the cloch, and she wondered if those who fed their own stones that night could hear the sound of the Bán Cailleach's anguish. When it was over, she huddled on the rocks, twitching and wishing she were dead, wishing she could give up Lámh Shábhála.

"... *soon enough. Soon enough. For now, be strong. Accept the pain, listen to it. Let me show you ...*"

In her fevered sight, Sevei thought she saw a Bunús Muintir: a young woman no older than herself, naked, her brown body covered with the same horrible scars. She crouched before Sevei. "*I'm here,*" she said, "*and I'll help you. I was able to bear this for a time; I know you can too. But you must do something for me, for my people ...*"

"I love you," Séarlait said, and grinned at the sound of the words coming from her throat and mouth. Kayne grinned back.

"I wish the rest of the Fingerlanders felt the same. Maybe they'd stay, then," he said.

She hugged his arm to her. "They can't have you. Not the way I can. But they do love you, Kayne, in their way. You led them to a victory over the Riocha. That's not something any Fingerlander will forget lightly. Now you have to let them do what they need to do. They'll return to you when you call again."

"Will they?"

She nodded and pressed his arm again, silent. Even with her voice returned to her, Séarlait still preferred to communicate in gestures. They stood at the highest point of the Narrows, looking eastward down to the tangled, crumpled landscape of the Finger, wrapped in mystery and mist. A caravan of Fingerlanders was moving down the High Road. As they prepared to turn a corner in the torturous descent, the rider at the front turned and waved back up to the them: Laird O'Blathmhaic, returning to his clan-home. Rodhlann, at least, had gained permission from Banlaird MacCanna to remain at the Narrows, but there were too few of the Fingerlander troops with him for Kayne's comfort. Séarlait and Kayne waved back to the laird, and the distant figure turned around a knob of heather-wrapped stone and was lost. Kayne heard Séarlait sigh and clutch at him more tightly.

"Tiarna?"

Kayne looked away from where the rest of the caravan was following O'Blathmhaic into the morning. "What is it, Harik?"

"There are riders coming up the road from the west under the Ard's banner. They're also flying a peace banner."

"How soon until they get here?" Kayne asked the Hand.

"At least two more stripes, and yet the Bán Cailleach's not here," he answered, sounding more angry than worried. "Have you heard from your sister yet?"

Kayne shook his head. He was also worried at Sevei's absence, expecting her to return with the mage-lights one of the last few nights. It had been three days now since she'd left for Dún Laoghaire. "No," he told Harik, "but we all felt her in the mage-lights last night. She's safe. If anything has changed, she would have told us. She doesn't need to be here. We're not her only worry." Kayne realized he was repeating what Séarlait had told him the night before: *"Your sister does what she must, and she gave you no promise to be here. You feel her, and she knows that tells you she's safe . . ."*

Harik nodded without speaking. His eyes did not appear convinced.

"Is that what you're worried about, Harik?" Séarlait asked. "Or are you worried that the delegation will see how few soldiers we have here?"

Harik's gaze slipped grudgingly from Kayne to Séarlait. His stare was flat and noncommittal. "*I* wouldn't be impressed to see the Narrows held by so few hands of men, most of them not even Fingerlanders. I'd wonder about any agreement I might have made with the Bán Cailleach."

"Then you'd make the same mistake that the Tuatha have always made," Séarlait answered. "It's the Finger itself that defends the clans. Not swords, not soldiers, but this very land."

Harik sniffed. It might have been the chill of the morning or the onset of a cold. He looked back at Kayne. "Perhaps, Tiarna, we should meet them at the Narrows itself, where a few men might look like many and there could be more hidden in the rocks."

Kayne forced down the annoyance he felt at Harik's dismissive treatment of Séarlait: this wasn't the time for a problem between himself and his Hand, but he told himself he'd remember this and other moments and deal with them afterward. "It's more than the soldiers we have here, Harik. They'll also see three Clochs Mór." Kayne touched the stone at his chest, and Harik, unconsciously, mimicked the motion. "And they'll remember what the Bán Cailleach did here, all alone, without any gardai at all. But your suggestion's a good one; we'll meet at the entrance to the Narrows. Have a tent set up there. We'll ride there in half a stripe."

Harik nodded, bowing his head to Kayne though his eyes never went again to Séarlait. He turned and left, already calling out orders to the gardai and sending one of them for Rodhlann.

Kayne could see that Séarlait watched Harik's departure carefully, though she said nothing. "It's not you," he said, and Séarlait turned her head to him, raising a questioning eyebrow. "It's not," he insisted. "He's céili giallnai, and sometimes the half-Riocha are worse than the Riocha themselves in the way they treat those of 'lesser' blood. It's not you specifically; it would be anyone I loved who wasn't Riocha or at least céili giallnai. He's what we have to face in the Tuatha hands after hands after hands of generations. Change frightens the most those who have the most to lose."

Séarlait shook her head. He thought she'd say nothing

more than that, then she licked her lips. "Maybe," she told him. "That sounds pretty, and maybe you're right, but I think Harik simply doesn't like me." She leaned into Kayne again, hugging him to her as if holding him back from some precipice he couldn't see. "And to tell the truth, Kayne, I'm not certain he likes you either."

The peace banner—a stylized red doe on a grass-green field—snapped as if angry to be bound to the pole of the tent. Kayne thought that perhaps it was. He held aside the flap of the tent to let Rodhlann, Harik, and Séarlait enter, then went inside himself.

There were three people inside, already seated at a table clad in white linen. Around the table wine had been poured into silver mugs and sweetmeats arranged on pewter plates. Kayne recognized the pattern chased into the metal rims of the goblets and carved into the backs of the chairs: he'd seen it a thousand times at home in Dún Laoghaire. These were the Ard's settings.

He also recognized the two men and the woman who stood as they entered. The closest to them was Parin Mac Baoill of Tuath Airgialla, first cousin of Rí Morven Mac Baoill— "One-Eyed Parin," who had lost an eye at Falcarragh and wore a patch over the empty socket. He also wore a torc of gold and silver around his neck, and Kayne realized with a start that it was the Rí Airgialla's torc. Shay O Blaca of the Order of Gabair stood alongside Mac Baoill. The third person was, surprisingly to Kayne, Áine Martain, his mam's Hand of the Heart. Where the other two were grim-faced and solemn, Áine was smiling broadly, obviously pleased to see Kayne. He greeted the Hand of the Heart first, not caring that he broke etiquette by ignoring the new Rí Mac Baoill and O Blaca. "Áine, it's good to see you. I was worried, when I heard about Mam, that . . ."

He saw the smile soften and fade on her face, and a shimmer of moisture glisten in her eyes. "That was a horrible day," she agreed, but then the smile returned. "But Tiarna Kayne, if you knew what has happened since she died . . . She is more loved than ever, and the healings I've witnessed on Cnocareilig, and the crowds who pray to her . . ." Áine seemed to realize that she might be saying too much, glancing back at the stern faces of her two companions.

Kayne smiled again at her, though his gaze went now to the others. "Welcome to Tuath Méar, the Finger," he told them. O Blaca tightened his lips at that, and Parin Mac Baoill flushed visibly. "I see the torc of Airgialla around your neck, Tiarna Mac Baoill. I hope that's an indication that Morven Mac Baoill has obeyed the Bán Cailleach." He didn't wait for the man's answer but gestured to his companions. "You all know Harik, my da's Hand and mine, and now the Holder of Bluefire. Rodhlann O Morchoe commands Tuath Méar's army here in the Narrows. And this is Séarlait Geraghty—a Fingerlander, my wife, and the Holder of Winter. You remember Winter, don't you, Parin? It used to adorn Mal Mac Baoill's neck, until one of Séarlait's arrows took him."

Séarlait had refused to take the bow and quiver from around her shoulders, despite the peace flag. *"Let them see the arrows,"* she'd told Kayne. *"They know my fletching in Airgialla. Let them realize who I am."* Parin's lips curled into a scowl under his single-eyed stare, and Shay O Blaca put a hand on the man's arm.

"We know the clochs you hold," O Blaca said. "I know Harik well myself, and we're pleased to meet the new Bantiarna Geraghty." There was no pleasure in his expression and the word "Bantiarna" seemed to taste sour in his mouth. "But we also expected the Bán Cailleach . . . that is, your sister . . . to be here."

"Sevei *was* here, and told me she expects to return soon," Kayne answered carefully. "Her presence, or lack of it, has no effect on what we say here."

"Indeed," O Blaca answered. "She made her . . ." O Blaca paused, and Kayne could sense that he was choosing another word than the one he might have used. ". . . wishes quite clear in Dún Laoghaire. But we thought that she would be here for our negotiations. However . . ." He smiled at Kayne. "I'm sure we can discuss the situation without her."

"These aren't negotiations," Kayne answered curtly, and O Blaca's tentative smile vanished like frost in sunlight as Mac Baoill hissed in irritation. Áine, standing behind them, grinned broadly at Kayne. "Either the Ríthe have done what we requested or you haven't, and our response—my sister's and mine—will depend on your answer. Which is it?"

Parin and O Blaca exchanged glances once more, and the Rí nodded. O Blaca went to the rear of the tent and brought back a wooden box. He placed it on the table close to Kayne, then stepped back. Kayne lifted the lid. Inside, nestled in a bed of plush green velvet, was a silver torc chased in gold filigree. Kayne had last seen that torc around his mam's neck. He reached out and stroked the cold metal with a forefinger, tracing the knotted patterns in the surface. "The torc of the Ard," Mac Baoill said. "It will be yours, Tiarna Geraghty, as soon as you return with us to Dún Laoghaire and the Óenach has made the declaration official."

"Dún Laoghaire?" Séarlait said. "Why does Kayne need to go to Dún Laoghaire?"

"Dún Laoghaire is the seat of the Ard, Bantiarna," Mac Baoill answered. "All the Ards have been given their torc there, in Tuatha Halla during a proper Óenach with the Ríthe in attendance." He smiled at Séarlait before turning his head to look at Kayne. "That's why we've come: to accompany you back to Dún Laoghaire in a manner befitting an Ard. The Bantiarna may certainly come with us, and your Hand."

"And Tuath Méar's gardai? Our troops?" Rodhlann asked. "The new Rí Ard should be accompanied by those he knows are loyal to him and will protect him on the road."

The eyebrow over Parin's good eye sought to touch the fringe of curls on his forehead. "Our clochs and the gardai we have with us will be more than sufficient to protect us from brigands on the road, Commander O Morchoe," he answered. "Certainly Tiarna Geraghty should bring any servants and aides that he needs. But the army of the Fing . . ." He grimaced. ". . . Tuath Méar should remain here."

"Oh, Rodhlann's not worried about *brigands*," Séarlait told Mac Baoill.

"Someone who has the protection of the Bán Cailleach certainly would not be concerned with mere robbers," Mac

Baoill answered blandly. "Nor would they need an army for protection."

"The Healer Ard will be watching over you as well," Áine interjected. "She is now a Mionbandia in the favor of the Mother-Creator, and her protection will be over you, Tiarna Geraghty. The tuathánach are pleased that her son is the Rí Ard and her daughter the Bán Cailleach."

O Blaca frowned deeply at that, glancing back sharply at the Hand of the Heart. Kayne found that pleasing. *So the Riocha are worried that Mam is as much a factor dead as she was alive. Good . . .*

Kayne stroked the surface of the Ard's torc again, remembering how it looked around his mam's neck. He could feel Mac Baoill and O Blaca watching the gesture. Mac Baoill reached forward and slowly pushed the lid closed again as Kayne withdrew his hand. "You will have the torc in Dún Laoghaire," he said, "after the Ríthe have done what they must do."

"No," Séarlait said. "I don't trust them, Kayne. You can be named Ard here as easily as there, and with those around you who would lay down their lives for you."

"Fingerlanders are too suspicious," Parin said.

"And if we are, who has made us that way, Rí Mac Baoill?" Séarlait retorted. "The Tuatha, especially Tuath Airgialla, have taught us that to be wary is the best way to stay alive."

"We get nowhere with this argument," O Blaca interrupted. "Rí Mac Baoill, I think we can both understand the Bantiarna's worry. And for your part, Bantiarna, you must know how difficult this has been for the Ríthe. Rí Morven Mac Baoill has exiled himself. Doyle Mac Ard has joined him, giving up the torc of the Ard. The Ríthe have agreed to name your husband as Rí Ard, and to grant seats in Tuatha Halla to both Rí MacEagan of Inish Thuaidh and whomever Tuath Méar names as Rí. The Óenach has given the Bán Cailleach all that she asked for, and those were difficult and hard decisions." O Blaca stared directly at Kayne, holding his gaze. "The new Ard will have even harder decisions to make in the future. We'll need to work together from now on, Tiarna. It's time—it's well *past* time—that we learned to trust each other."

Kayne felt Séarlait come alongside him. Her hand

grasped his arm, tightening around it, but she was silent. Kayne held O Blaca's gaze for a long breath, and finally nodded. "You're right, Máister O Blaca. It is time. We'll ride with you: Séarlait, Harik, and I. Rodhlann will remain here with the troops. We only need a stripe or two to prepare."

O Blaca relaxed visibly. For the first time, a smile came to his face. "I'm pleased to hear that, Tiarna," he said. "We'll coordinate with your Hand, then. Harik, if you'll remain with us . . ."

Outside, as they walked back to their own tent, Séarlait's silence seemed deafening to Kayne. "What is it?" he asked her finally.

He thought that she wasn't going to answer, but her shoulder lifted with a heavy sigh and she turned as she raised the flap of the tent. "If you don't consider my advice worth listening to, then why did you bind yourself to me? Or is it just that you preferred me when I couldn't speak to you?"

"You don't understand, Séarlait," he began, then realized as her eyes narrowed that he'd said the wrong thing entirely. He shook his head as if he could shed the words like rainwater clinging to his hair. "I love you. You know that—or you should. I value your advice, but sometimes . . ." He reached out to stroke her cheek, but the way she glared at his hand made him stop before his fingers reached her. "Sometimes we can't do as we might want to," he finished. "Or even necessarily what we think is best."

"Is that how you'll govern as Rí Ard?" she asked him. "Not doing what you think is right or best but what you think is expedient?"

"That's not fair, Séarlait," he told her. He stepped past her into the tent. "Come in," he said. "Let's talk."

"I don't need to talk," she told him. "I went years without talking. I prefer to act. I thought you did, too."

Séarlait released the tent flap. The day was hidden in the twilight of the tent, and he heard her footsteps as she walked away.

46

Conclave of the Aware

SEVEI SAT ON the beach, her hand over Lámh Sháb-hála and letting just a touch of the energy inside waft out over the waves, letting it carry her thoughts out and down into the quiet of the sea. *We need to talk with each other again, Bhralhg. . . . I ask you to come to me . . . Please, Bhralhg . . .*

The water, in a protected cove not far from Thall Coill, was a flat and translucent green through which she could see the flitting, darker shapes of small fish. Beyond the curving spit of rocks and in the driving wind, the water quickly become choppy and frothed with whitecaps. In the two days she'd been here now, she'd been alone except for the company of a small group of brown harbor seals who came over curiously when she'd changed to seal form, swimming with her as she chased and caught the sweetfish in the cove.

But though she could feel the presence of blue seals and, especially, Bhralhg carrying the magical salmon of power, Bradán an Chumhacht, they'd not shown themselves or answered her call. *"They'll never answer,"* she heard her gram say inside Lámh Shábhála. *"I used them poorly and I used them hard—Thraisha, Garrentha, Dhegli, Challa—and they won't trust the Holder of Lámh Shábhála ever again. It's my fault . . ."*

"Hush, Gram," Sevei said aloud, the sounds of her own voice surprising her in the cool air. She could see her breath in the air. She allowed a trickle of Lámh Shábhála's energy to radiate over her to warm her skin. Her body glowed like a moon in the dusk, her flesh as cracked and marred as that of the pale disk. "The sun's almost gone. When the mage-lights come tonight, I'll leave. But for now there's still time."

She cast the power of Lámh Shábhála like a net over the sea, searching for Bhralhg. Though she couldn't feel him, she could feel the *absence* of him, as if he were using Bradán an Chumhacht to actively deflect her. She kept feeling the not-Bhralhg, a void that slid through her mage-vision like a movement glimpsed in peripheral vision and then gone when she looked at it directly.

There was laughter in the air, and a darkness in the growing dimness of the water, and the scent of fish. "Come swim with me, Holder," a voice said in her head as she heard the deep coughing moan of a seal and saw him, the noble head rising from the surf a few strides from the shore. "Come swim with me." Then the head dipped into the water again.

". . . Don't trust them . . ."

"Be quiet, Gram," she said to the ghost, and she walked quickly down the wet shingle until the waves lapped at her ankles, her calves. As the water splashed, it first felt impossibly cold, then just as strangely warm and she was no longer running but swimming with powerful wriggling of flukes and body. She saw Bhralhg in the quickly-dimming light of the sun and followed the trail of his wake, out of the cove and into the rolling, vital surge of the ocean, tasting the salt and the faint sweet wash of rainwater from the shore. The world underneath the surface was deep blue and would have been too dark for Daoine eyes, but she could see from the shimmering cap of the water above to the kelp-laden rocks of the deepening floor. The light of the failing sun painted steeply-angled, waving columns that bloodied the water; fainter wedges of silver were moonlight, growing stronger with each moment. There were clouds in the thick atmosphere of the water: heavy silt kicked up from the bottom by the waves; the pale, drifting snowfall of plankton and algae; the flashing, swiftly-passing schools of fish.

They flew through the hues of day and night above the landscape that the stone-walkers never saw, side by side. Bhralhg said nothing but swam strongly, heading out to deeper water before curving north. Night fell as they traveled, and Sevei thought that at least a few stripes must have passed before they came to land again, hauling out on a rocky shelf. "Here," Bhralhg said. "I brought you here to meet Issine, the Eldest. He has been here since before your people came to this land, before the people before you and the people before them. He existed even before the Saimhóir, the Earc Tine, the Daoine, the Bunús Muintir, the great eagles, or the dire wolves became Aware."

"What is this Issine?" Sevei asked Bhralhg. She looked around the shelf of dark stone and up the steep, rock-strewn slope in front of her, letting herself shift back to her normal form. She saw nothing and no one. "Where is he?"

"Issine is Créneach," Bhralhg told her, "and he is right there before you."

"Créneach?" She heard the word echoed by the ghosts in her head. Gram had told her of the Créneach—the Clay People, the Eaters of Stone, the Boulder-folk—and certainly all the tales of the Battle of Dún Kiil mentioned how the Créneach had appeared when it was thought the battle was lost and turned the tide. Treoraí, who had given her mam the Heart, had been Créneach. Sevei squinted in the moonlight, searching the jumble of rocks for anything vaguely man-shaped.

"They can look like no more than a pile of ordinary rocks until they decide to stir themselves," Gram whispered. *"If Issine is the Eldest of all Créneach, then he must be old indeed, for Treoraí told me that he had been alive for twelve cycles of the mage-lights, and he also said he was the Eldest of his own tribe . . ."*

Sevei imagined that Issine must look massive and huge, a hoary great-da of rock as tall as a hill and as powerful and enduring. "Where—?" she started to ask Bhralhg again, when she heard a sharp *k-crack* like two pebbles struck together and saw a spark flare in the darkness to her left. She turned and saw movement, but what stepped out into the soft moonlight stood no taller than her knee, though its body was nearly as wide as it was tall. The creature looked as if it had been crudely fashioned from clay, glazed and fired and then left out in the rain for centuries until the polished, glassy tan glaze become pitted and stained. The face atop the stocky body was noseless, though there were twin cracks where it might have been.

The eyes were dark pits lurking under thick ridges, and
deep within them light glittered as if from some hidden
well. She could hear it breathing, and it warbled at her with
pursed mouth. It looked more like an infant than an Elder.
Bhralgh must have caught her thoughts, for she heard his
voice in her head as the seal moaned.

"What did you expect? The Eldest has been here in the
wind, the rain, and the surf watching the world for more
years than there are grains of sand on the beach. How
could time not have touched him, eroding him like the
rocks of the shore?" Bhralgh laughed.

Issine warbled again, and this time Sevei allowed Lámh
Shábhála to open, and in the mage-energy she heard his
words. His voice was as low and ancient-sounding as she
imagined the very mountains might be. "We begin as small
infants; we return to that form at the end, worn back down
by the years. Time is full of cycles within cycles, and this is
just another. Let me taste the All-Heart again. It has been
so long . . ."

The Créneach moved forward, walking with an odd side-
to-side lurching gait. "Crouch down," he told Sevei, and
she knelt before Issine. His tongue flickered out from his
mouth, running quickly over the skin between her breasts
before she could react. The creature's tongue felt frigid,
smooth, and strangely dry, yet the touch was pleasant. Issine sighed, as if savoring the taste in his mouth "Ahh,
aye—that is the All-Heart. So strong, so sweet . . ."

In the mage-energy that surrounded them, she could feel
a presence like a Cloch Mór buried within him, burning
bright in her mage-vision—brighter, in fact, than any Cloch
Mór she had ever seen. *As bright as Lámh Shábhála itself . . .*

Issine chuckled—linked as they were, she realized that
he had overheard her thought. "Lámh Shábhála is the
All-Heart, the essence of the goddess Céile Herself," he
told her. "Lámh Shábhála is all that is left of Anchéad's
Pebble, and so it is and always will be First. But the
Great-Heart within me will be nearly as powerful when
one day I leave it behind." Issine looked at her. "As Treoraí's Heart is powerful, for Treoraí too was old, though
not so old as me."

"Gram . . . the others . . . they always thought Treoraí's
Heart was just a clochmion, though the way it scarred

Mam's arm, like a Cloch Mór or the way Lámh Shábhála did to Gram . . ."

Issine clapped his hands together percussively; sparks flared and expired on the wet rock. "The soft-flesh one who holds it now—can you see that person? Nay, you shake your head. But even those with the Great-Hearts you call Clochs Mór can't hide from the All-Heart, can they?"

Sevei felt a shiver, remembering the way Treoraí's Heart cloaked itself in the mage-lights, how elusive its Holder was to her, how she could not seem to follow the thread of the mage-light back to see the face. Sevei let her mage-sight play over Issine's Heart: a jewel of pure yellow, gleaming like a sun in the chest of the Créneach. She wondered what it would be like to hold that stone, to feel its power . . .

"Very soon, my Heart will leave me," Issine told her. "By the time the mage-lights fail again, certainly. And then, when the lights return in their cycle and the All-Heart once more wakens the Créneach and our Hearts from a long slumber, perhaps one of your people will find it."

When the mage-lights fail again. . . . That would be long centuries yet, Sevei knew, yet for Issine, that seemed "very soon." *Old, so old . . .* She glanced back at Bhralhg, lying patiently where the salt spray washed over his dark fur. The seal's black eyes blinked as a wave crashed over the rocks. "Thank you for bringing me here. I would not have wished to miss meeting Issine. But why . . . ?"

"Because you will be making decisions soon that will affect all of the Aware races," Bhralhg answered. "You were right, Sevei; we do need to talk, because those decisions are already upon you. I heard you call me, but before I answered, I went first to the others and brought them here."

"You have passed the Scrúdú," Issine told her. "What any other Holder might do with Lámh Shábhála matters less if they haven't come through that test. Even Jenna First Holder never completed the Scrúdú, and so her power was limited. But what *you* might do . . . This hasn't happened for what is a long time, even for me."

The last time, it was me . . . Sevei heard the voice inside her: Carrohkai Treemaster. *And I didn't do all I could, or that I should have . . .* But Sevei had no time to listen to the dead Holder's voice. "What you do in the time left to you will affect your people greatly," the Créneach continued. His head lifted up to her; his tongue flicked out like that of a snake tasting the air. His hands clapped together once more, and this time the resulting spark was far stronger and lasted for several breaths. Sevei heard the rustle of huge wings above, and a darkness blotted out the moon for a moment. "But there are more than Daoine awake in the world," Issine said, "and what you do will affect *all* of us."

As he spoke, a dragon wheeled around the rock shelf and cupped air with its great leathery wings on the rocks above. It hovered there for a moment and seemed to lay something down gently from the claws of its rear legs. Then it lifted again with a rush of air before landing heavily several strides off, sending a cascade of rocks down to the sea. The gigantic head peered down at her, and she recognized the frill and the patterns of the scales, and especially the bright red tail that curled around the boulder on which it rested: Kekeri, who had brought her to Thall Coill.

"Hello again, soft-flesh," Kekeri said. Another shape, far smaller than the dragon and man-shaped, appeared next to Kekeri. It struck a staff on the ground, and the knotted end shuddered with greenish light that illuminated his face. In the glow, Sevei recognized that man as well: Beryn, the Protector of Thall Coill. He picked his way down the slope toward Sevei, Bhralhg, and Issine, using his staff for balance and sight.

Sevei shook her head. "No dire wolves? No eagles?" It was difficult to keep the incredulity from her voice.

Beryn made his way through the loose rocks at the foot of the slope. The Bunús Muintir let his staff-light die so that the cold moonlight returned. "Kiraac of the Wolves knows that we're meeting, as do the eagles. And there are others who know as well, those you've never met and don't yet know." He stared at her, and Sevei thought she sensed a quiet sympathy in his expression. "How are you, Sevei?" he asked.

"I hurt," she told him. "I hurt all the time, and most especially when I use Lámh Shábhála."

The empathy deepened in his eyes. "I'm sorry. I truly am. There is . . ." She saw more than heard his hesitation. ". . . andúilleaf. I could find it, give it to you . . ."

In her head, the voices of the Holders crooned, yearning. *". . . aye, the 'leaf . . . it was the only thing that made the pain bearable . . . . . . aye, to have all the hurt pushed away . . ."* Her gram's voice shoved them all away. *"No!"* she shouted, so loudly that she was surprised that none of those around her could hear. *"That was my mistake, and I won't let you make it, Sevei . . ."*

Sevei was already shaking her head before Gram had finished. "No," she told Beryn. "I can bear it." The moon went away behind a silent cloud and she shivered as if the sun had gone. The air was cold on her teeth as she sucked it in. "So you're all here. Why?"

"Because we chose you and now we want to know if our choice was a good one," Beryn answered.

Sevei felt a stirring of apprehension and worry; as much as holding Lámh Shábhála hurt, it was also something that she could not give up willingly. To lose the cloch would be worse than any pain using the stone could inflict. "Could you do anything about it if I wasn't?" she asked him. A slow smile tugged at his mouth, but it was Kekeri who answered.

"Aye, we could," the dragon said, its voice hissing sibilantly in its own tongue while a similar voice spoke in her head. "Even Lámh Shábhála of the Scrúdú couldn't stand against the power gathered here. We would smash you." Kekeri yawned, and there was a yellow shimmering glow like a smithy's forge deep within the beast's cavernous mouth.

Issine clapped his hands, sending golden sparks through the air. Kekeri hissed and went quiet, his tail lashing. "The dragons have yet to learn tact since they've become Aware," Issine said. "But he's correct. You are stronger than any one of us, but not than all of us. If we thought you were a danger to us, we could end the threat."

"What threat am I to any of you?" Sevei asked.

"Anything you do that benefits only your own people is a potential threat," Issine answered. "Your people have spread everywhere over the land, and as you create more farms and towns, you leave less room for the other Aware races, who are also still awakening. As your people increase, you'll fish the waters where the Saimhóir find their own food; you'll cut down the forests and destroy the meadowlands where both the dire wolves and great eagles hunt. The dragons will eat your sheep and cattle because it's easier than hunting, and you'll in turn hunt them."

"And we will burn and kill those who try," Kekeri hissed. Issine waited, and Kekeri subsided to a grumble that sounded like steam rattling the lid of a kettle.

"I'm Daoine," Sevei answered, unable to keep the irritation from her voice. "Do you expect that I won't help my own people, or that I'd help any of you in preference to them? Do you accost all those who passed the Scrúdú this way?"

"No other Daoine has passed the test," Issine answered calmly. "And no other race has been so successful as the Daoine. Many of the Aware, like the dragons, sleep when the mage-lights sleep; you Daoine continue to increase in those times. So did the Bunús Muintir, but not as you do. And now there is another race on the edge of Awareness, a race that—like the Daoine and the Bunús Muintir—can live strongly in the between-time. They come into conflict with your people as your people came into conflict with the Bunús Muintir."

"Aye!" shouted a hundred voices within Sevei, all with the tone of the Bunús Muintir. *"You Daoine came when we were weak without the clochs, or we would have driven you back . . ."*

"But the Daoine are stronger than the Bunús were then, Sevei," Bhralhg interjected, almost as if he'd heard the voices. The seal waddled forward, just out of the spray of the breakers. "The WaterMother has given me glimpses of the near future, and in those visions I see that you could choose to elevate your own kind over all the rest of the Aware. And I see that to do this you may have to kill a person with whom you share blood."

"Kayne?" Sevei asked the Saimhóir. "Is that what you're saying, that I might be set against Kayne?"

Bhralhg gave a wordless moan. "I don't see the face; I only feel the kinship between the two of you."

"I can't do that," Sevei said reflexively. "Kayne and I shared a womb, shared our whole childhood together. We knew what each other was thinking and feeling. I can still feel him in my dreams." Sevei was shaking her head in denial, her white hair, still damp with the sea, clinging to her neck and shoulders. "I'd never hurt him. I won't do that."

"The choice is always yours," Issine told her. The heart inside the Créneach was glowing furiously in Sevei's mage-sight. "We can't make decisions for you or force you to choose one way or the other."

"No," Sevei said, the word snapping angrily. "You can't." She looked at each of them. ". . . *Aye, they can't! . . .*" the voices inside echoed in agreement. "None of you can make my decisions for me. You say you picked me to take Lámh Shábhála; well, that may be, though it felt more that it was Lámh Shábhála itself who chose me, not any of you. But I have the cloch now. It's my burden to bear, and my choices to make."

"Your burden, aye, Holder," Beryn said. "But everyone bears the consequences. Not only you."

"I haven't told you all that I saw in Bradán an Chumhacht's dream," Bhralhg continued. "I saw that those who sit on your cold stone thrones have more than one face, and what they spoke with one face, the other denied. I saw the sky-stones gathered together against you, enough of them that they hid the light of Lámh Shábhála. I saw a trusted person betray their loyalty. I saw you caught between two forces."

The voices of dead Holders chattered in her head. A wave tossed spray over her and the cold sea burned where it lashed her skin. The pain throbbed in every limb, in her temples. Gram's voice was there—". . . *listen to yourself first, darling. You're the Holder; you have passed the Scrúdú;. The power is yours, and I trust your judgment. I trust it better than my own . . .*"—but she listened in the chaos for another voice as well.

". . . *I was given choices, and they were also difficult,*" Car-rohkai Treemaster said quietly. "*You must look past your-self, Sevei; past your own desires, past your own people, past even those who brought you here . . .*"

"You're telling me that I should betray my own people in favor of you?"

"We're asking you to do what benefits all," Issine answered calmly. "And *you* are not only Daoine, Sevei. In your line there are Saimhóir, and there are also Bunús Muintir—who are really only an older tribe of your own people and who share with you the ability to use the clochs na thintrí."

"What do I gain from this?" Sevei asked them. "You ask all this of me—what will *you* do?"

Fire glowed on the hill above them as Kekeri hissed. "In return, we will come when you call," the dragon said. "You will continue to have our support, as I have already given it to you, Sevei Dragoncaller."

"Listen to your gram inside you," Bhralhg told her. "She'll tell you that the Saimhóir have helped her, and your mam, and now you."

"As have the Bunús Muintir," Beryn added. "Seancoim and Keira of Doire Coill, Cataigh of Foraois Coill . . . And the dire wolves came to your mam's aid in Doire Coill."

"Treoraí of the Créneach gave his Heart to the First Holder, and your mam used it also," Issine finished. "I would say that the Daoine Holders have been much helped by the other Aware races. We'll give you that aid, as long as we know that our own interests are also not in danger."

The Créneach lifted his head slowly to the night sky and clapped his hands together again. The spark that leaped from the stony limbs soared high into the sky. It seemed to linger there, growing and twisting, the color changing from yellow to green and soft blue. "The mage-lights have come," Issine said. "We'll take them together."

Sevei could feel the hungry pull of Lámh Shábhála, and she touched her hand to herself, opening the Great Cloch to the sky. The light responded, brightening and falling down from the zenith like curling ribbons to wrap around her upraised arm. She could see the mage-lights snaking down to the others also: Issine seemed to stand in a cauldron of colored lights, lapping at the brilliance with his tongue; Bhralhg's scarred fur gleamed with the lines of the mage-lights; Kekeri's mouth was open, and a river of scarlet and orange was flowing into the dragon as if it were taking a fiery draught from the heavens; the mage-lights wrapped Beryn's hand in phosphorescence as he opened the clochmion that had once been Sevei's own.

In her mage-vision, Sevei could sense the lines that connected her to the mage-lights above, and from them to the other clochs na thintrí and Beryn. She could feel the power that surrounded her from the others, but there was no direct connection from Lámh Shábhála to Bradán an

Chumhacht or Issine's Heart, to whatever was within Kekeri that linked the dragon to the mage-power.

She wondered how many others were out there—the
Aware races—also feeding on the mage-lights and unknown to her.

*"There are more ways than this one. Lámh Shábhála
might be the First, but it's not the Only . . ."*

Sevei reached into the mage-lights, searching. She could
feel Kayne and near him Séarlait and Harik, as well as two
other Clochs Mór. She knew they felt her presence too: the
Bán Cailleach. And aye, there . . . far away and yet powerful . . . there was Treoraí's Heart, hidden as always behind
its wall. Her mam's cloch seemed closer now than it had
been, and Sevei wondered at that. Sevei sent herself moving through the mage-lights, taking some of the power of
Lámh Shábhála with her, and she slammed the power into
the wall of the Heart. The mental fortress shuddered and
she caught a momentary glimpse of a mind behind it—a
human mind, but whether it was Daoine or Bunús Muintir
or Taisteal, she couldn't tell—then the wall slammed shut
again. She sent more power toward the barrier, but whoever held the Heart was doing the same, and this time
Sevei's mage-power splashed over the Heart like water on
stone, falling away harmlessly.

"Let me see you!" she thought-screamed to the cloaked
Holder. *"You've stolen what was my mam's. You have no
right to hold it! Show yourself if you're not a coward!"*

There was no answer.

Sevei let herself fall away from Treoraí's Heart and back
to herself. The others were reluctantly letting the mage-
lights slip back to the sky, though Lámh Shábhála still
sucked at them hungrily, as if it were hiding the energy in
places she'd not yet discovered within the crystal.

Issine clapped his hands together a final time as the
mage-lights vanished. The ancient Créneach glowed softly
in the night, like breaking surf in moonlight.

"We are linked, all of us who are Aware," he said to
Sevei. "We share the bright storm within the sky. And you
hold our fates."

47

Memories and Maggots

THE MOUNTAINS WERE BLACK, cracked teeth set against the sky, with white snow crammed in their high furrows. The peaks seemed to lift themselves higher from the earth with each step the Arruk army took. Ennis had heard the grumblings of the soldiers over the last few days, wondering how they would ever find a way over the rocky spires.

Ennis found that the Arruk didn't care for mountains any more than they liked the water. On the third day after the battle, Lieve Mairki and Daj Svarti had come to the Kralj's tent not long after Kurhv Kralj, Cima, and Ennis woke. Kurhv Kralj's attendants had already begun striking the tent, the tattered skin fluttering to the ground behind them.

"I'm only giving you the concerns of all the Mairki and Svarti, Kurhv Kralj," Lieve Mairki said. "Grozan Kralj— may Cudak send him back as an ewe for his failures—ordered Likva Ruka along with Barat Svarti, two of Barat's Nesvarti, and several soldiers into these mountains, several moons ago. They never returned, Kralj, and Daj Svarti cast a spell that told him they were all dead." Lieve Mairki's snout curled away from his teeth as he glared at the offending peaks and Cima translated the fast torrent of Arruk for Ennis. "How do we know that Ennis Svarti is not taking us to the same fate? There may be other ways to Cudak Zvati than through cold mountains or over the cursed sea. There *must* be other ways."

Lieve Mairki carefully avoided looking at Ennis as he spoke, standing near Kurhv Kralj, but Daj Svarti stared at him as if trying to assess weakness. All around them, Ennis could hear the sound of the Arruk breaking camp and preparing for another day's march. The attendants were carefully ignoring them while they packed the Kralj's litter. Inside, Ennis heard Gyl Svarti's sullen voice: *"Daj Svarti hasn't forgotten what you did back in the city and on the battlefield, but that's only made him more interested in you. He'll watch you all the more carefully for that, hoping to catch you unwary and take the power you have."* Gyl seemed to laugh. *"It's what I would have done,"* he said.

All around him, the blue ghosts were swirling with possibilities. Ennis kept himself grimly locked to the Throne pattern. That ghost was silent, but it glared at Daj Svarti and Lieve Mairki as if angry, and so Ennis did the same. His right shoulder throbbed, bandaged by the Mender and bound for the moment to his chest. Under his hand, through the cloth of his léine, he could feel the comforting hardness of Treoraí's Heart.

"Ennis Svarti says there is a High Road—a path through the mountains that the bluntclaws use to visit each other," Kurhv Kralj told the Mairki. "There will be Perakli villages and towns on that road, and where there are Perakli, there will be battles and there will be food. This road is the fastest and best path to Cudak Zvati. Ennis Svarti promises us that."

"To the west past the mountains is where Cudak Zvati waits," Daj Svarti agreed. "Yet there may be a less direct but better way for us to go there. That is what we wonder, Kralj."

"You believe you're a better Svarti than Ennis." Kurhv Kralj's response was more statement than question.

Daj Svarti's eyes flicked over to Ennis, then quickly back to Kurhv Kralj. His head lifted slightly, the loose skin under the neck wobbling. "It's only that he's Perakli, Kralj, and . . ." Daj Svarti's voice trailed off then as Kurhv Kralj hissed audibly and the blue ghost made Ennis slam the end of his spell-stick down on the ground. Cima chuckled.

Kurhv Kralj leaned forward toward Daj Svarti, and the Svarti instinctively bared his throat to the Arruk leader. "Ennis Svarti is a bluntclaw and a pup, but in one battle he's killed more Perakli than you have in a hand of moons, Daj Svarti. Should I worry about *your* sympathies?"

Daj Svarti's throat pulsed as he swallowed. "No, Kurhv Kralj."

Kurhv Kralj took a step back and Daj Svarti lowered his snout. Lieve Mairki stared straight ahead, as if doing his best to ignore the confrontation. "Good," Kurhv Kralj said. "Then I expect that the two of you will take care of anyone who has similar misgivings. You may go, Lieve Mairki, Daj Svarti. We have a long march ahead of us."

Ennis heard the blue ghost speak, and he hurried to match it. "Wait, Svarti," he called out as Lieve Mairki and Daj Svarti turned to go. Cima translated, and Daj Svarti turned slowly. Ennis saw the pattern move and he moved with it. He stood in front of Daj Svarti, tiny against the Arruk's far larger bulk. Daj Svarti stared down at him, the lowered head showing no throat at all, and Cima hissed at the bald insult.

"You'll never have what I hold," Ennis told him. "I know you want it. I can feel it. But I'll never let you take it." Ennis saw the Arruk's nostrils flare; the red eyes stared with silent hatred. "I know you, Daj Svarti."

"You don't know me at all," Daj Svarti grunted. "You know nothing."

"I know you," Ennis repeated. "And I'm not frightened of you. Cima, here, take this . . ." He handed Cima his spell-stick. His bandaged right hand clutched at Treoraí's Heart and he opened the cloch, letting the comforting power wrap around him. Before Daj Svarti could react, Ennis grabbed the Svarti's arm with his left hand and opened the Heart fully.

He fell into Daj Svarti. He *was* Daj Svarti . . .

Ennis stood in a thick forest of emotion: trunks of blood-infused anger, clinging burrs of emerald jealousy, ropelike vines of frustration. He pushed through, going deep in toward the third heart where dark memories lurked. Daj Svarti tried to hide from Ennis' intrusion, sending recollections bounding away like storm deer in the forest, but Ennis leaped after them, a snarling dire wolf of the mind, and bore one down . . .

. . . he was young and frightened, cowering with his chin frantically lifted as high as he could as he stood before his Svarti mentor. The old Arruk shook his spell-stick at Daj. "Are you hopelessly stupid?" the Arruk railed. "I thought

*you had some promise. Three days! Three days you had to
memorize a simple spell, and you still don't have it. I'm giving you one more day. Do you hear me, you dullard? One
more day, and if you can't recite the spell for me—perfectly,
without a mistake—then I'm sending you back to your Life-
Weaver. Perhaps you'd be better off apprenticed to a tanner.
The stench might improve your attitude . . ."*

That memory was delicious, but it wasn't what Ennis was
after, and so he plucked at another even as Daj howled at
the invasion. *. . . the battle between the Arruk and the bluntclaws in Thall Mór-roinn who called themselves the Garifali
had been long and furious. Daj was now a Nesvarti, his
spell-stick so new that it still stank of varnish. He'd been assigned to a squad sweeping a field on which a minor skirmish had taken place a few days before, sent to make certain
that the Garifali had truly retreated. Daj Nesvarti let the others move ahead, for the truth was that he'd botched his spells
the night before and his spell-stick was empty. He was terrified that the Svarti to whom he reported would find out, and
he also hoped that any lingering Garifali warriors would be
taken care of by the soldiers and he wouldn't need to deal
with them. The stench hit Daj first, the sweet, ripe, and sick-
ening smell of rotting flesh. He nearly stumbled over the
body, a Garifali whose abdomen had been ripped open by
an Arruk spear. The body was bloated, and the crows and
the jackals had been at the body. So had the flies, for a wriggling mass of white maggots slithering over the wounds. The
sight brought the gorge to Daj's mouth, and he remembered . . . he remembered . . .*

But Daj sent that linked memory bounding away from
Ennis, and Ennis pursued it, bringing it down with a mental bound. Aye, that was it, the one he wanted . . .

*. . . he was but a pup himself, still with his Egg-Mother. His
Egg-Mother kept a dog for a pet in their nesting-house, a
black-and-white mutt that would sometimes bring back a
rabbit or possum to enhance their larder. One day the dog
went out on its usual hunting routine, but didn't return. The
next morning, Daj went out with his Egg-Mother looking
for the dog. They found the animal not far from the house,
curled up under a bush. Daj thought it was just sleeping, and
ran to it, sinking down beside it. Gleeful and rejoicing, he
reached down to shake it awake, but his hand found a hor-*

rible wound in the dog's side. When he pulled back, horri-fied, there were knots of living maggots on his hands. Daj shrieked in alarm, shaking his hand frantically to get them off his skin. He caught the smell, then, too, and for the next several nights, the scent and the images of the maggots eat-ing his own flesh inhabited his nightmares ...

Ennis knew that this was the memory he could use. *"Ennis, this is not ..."* he thought he heard his mam say, but then the others in the Heart clamored more loudly and he couldn't hear her anymore. Isibéal's voice came over the tumult. *"Your mam used Treoraí's Heart to heal,"* she said, *"as you've used it to destroy. It can do either. The Heart can create whatever you'd like—it is even stronger for you than it was for Meriel. You can create whatever you'd like. Go on. Do it ..."*

Ennis felt his eyes narrow and his brow wrinkle. He would tell himself later that it was the pattern. All he was doing was following the blue ghost.

"Here ..." he whispered to Daj Svarti inside, and he al-lowed the mage-energy within Treoraí's Heart to flow out, shaping it. "The maggots," he whispered inside Daj Svarti's mind. "The maggots will have you. Look ..." They were the pale white of the grave, plump and ugly creatures the size of Ennis' little finger: hand upon hand upon hand of them, and more coming as the mage-light trickled from the Heart. "They'll eat from the inside, Daj Svarti. They'll con-sume you alive, and you'll feel them in your belly as they feed, wriggling and hungry and growing larger. Maybe you'll even still be alive when they burst out through your skin. Maybe you'll see them, wriggling and slipping through your fingers as you try to hold them in. Won't that be horrible, Daj Svarti? Won't that be terrible?"

Linked with Daj Svarti, Ennis felt the revulsion and shock radiate through him as Daj Svarti recoiled. He felt the pain as the maggots began to do their work, and the suffering was so intense that Ennis released Treoraí's Heart in sympathetic shock. He heard Daj's scream with his true ears, not through the mage-vision. Blinking in dis-orientation, he saw Daj Svarti double over alongside Lieve Mairki as Kurhv Kralj and Cima stepped back. Daj Svarti was clutching his stomach, his claws extended and digging into his own flesh so that blood flowed.

"Kill me!" Daj Svarti hissed to Lieve Mairki and Kurhv Kralj, his eyes wide in panic. "Kill me now! Please!" He moaned and howled again. All around them, other Arruk dropped what they were doing to watch in horrified fascination.

The blue ghost moved Ennis. He stepped forward again, standing before the terrified Svarti. "I can help you," he told Daj Svarti in his halting, uncertain Arruk, "if you'll lift your chin for me." He cocked his head, staring at the contorted body of the Svarti. "Will you do it, or will you die?" he asked.

Daj Svarti was frothing at the mouth. His claws had dug long furrows in his scaled abdomen and he'd fallen to his knees so that Ennis could see the frill along the top of his head. Slowly, in obvious agony, Daj Svarti lifted his head, his eyes half closed. His snout lifted until, trembling, his nasal slits pointed at the sky.

"Good," the pattern said, and Ennis echoed the word. He took Treoraí's Heart in his hand again. "Then let me heal you, Daj Svarti. Let me take away the nasty, awful maggots . . ."

Afterward, Kurhv Kralj stared at him strangely, as if pondering something Ennis didn't understand. But none of the Svarti or Mairki or any Arruk below him would ever again fail to lift their chin when standing before him. . . .

By afternoon, they were in the foothills of the mountains, on the strangely-deserted High Road that led out of the mountains girdling the Finger and running down to the plains eastward toward the Céile Mhór's capital of Concordia. They'd seen riders from Céile Mhór, but the Daoine scouts seemed content to watch the Arruk army without engaging it—the Arruk army was, after all, leaving Céile Mhór for Talamh an Ghlas. They were the Rí Ard's problem now, not the Thane's

Ennis and Cima rode together in their litter alongside that of Kurhv Kralj. Cima had been strangely quiet since the incident with Daj Svarti, and he stayed well away from Ennis, carefully not letting their bodies touch. The blue ghost had left Ennis for the time being, and he leaned back against his pillows, tired and pensive, afraid to think about all that had happened because he was afraid that he'd start to cry. He moved his leg and it brushed against Cima's scaled one; the Arruk nearly jumped.

"Cima," Ennis said, "I wouldn't ever hurt you. Never. Don't you know that?"

The litter swayed as the bearers moved over the uneven ground. Cima nodded uncertainly. "I know," he answered. "But you scare me sometimes, Ennis Svarti. I don't understand you. Are all the Daoine like you?"

"I don't know," Ennis answered honestly. "I used to be scared of Da sometimes, and Kayne and Sevei if they were mad at me for something, but never Mam." He stopped, watching the play of light through the litter's curtain move across Cima's face. "Where did you learn to talk like me?" he asked the Arruk.

The bright color of Cima's scales faded slightly, and he looked away from Ennis as if fascinated by the curtains at the side of the litter. "It's not a tale I enjoy telling, Ennis Svarti."

"I'm sorry, Cima. You don't have to tell me if you don't want to."

Cima's frill lifted and settled again; Ennis wondered if that was a shrug. "I suppose it doesn't matter," Cima said. He took a long breath, his underlids closing for a long time before opening again. "A cycle or more ago, we noticed there were new bluntclaws dressed strangely with the Perakli army, and as Kurhv Kralj told you, a few of them were able to snatch at Cudak's Web each night and could unleash a power more awful than even the spell-sticks of the greatest Svarti. But Kurhv Kralj didn't tell you all. I was Cima Svarti: Kurhv Mairki's chosen Svarti. These sky-stones of the new Perakli had cost us lives and territory, and Meidi Kralj wanted the new Perakli dead, wanted *us* to have the sky-stones and learn to use them. Meidi Kralj asked Kurhv Mairki to capture a few bluntclaws alive from the battlefield, so we could learn more. Kurhv Mairki assigned me to the task of working with the bluntclaw captives and learning their language, since it would certainly be a Svarti who would be able to use the sky-stones. If I learned the language well, Kurhv Mairki told me, if I learned how the Perakli used them, I would be given a mage-stone. He was certain we would capture one or more of them. I'm certain he also believed that this would make him Kralj."

Cima went silent. The litter lurched and swayed, and Ennis shifted in his cushions. "What happened?" he asked Cima.

The Arruk grimaced. "Several moons ago there was the great battle that Kurhv Kralj told you about, where the strange bluntclaws came with their great mage-stone when we least expected it, the stone that threw great red fires. Just as Kurhv Kralj said, the mage-stone broke our Svartis, killed many of the Arruk, and sent us to our worst defeat. One of the new Perakli even killed Meidi Kralj and Meidi Kralj's Svarti was killed also."

Cima turned back to Ennis, but his gaze wasn't on Ennis' face but to where Treoraí's Heart lay hidden under his léine. "Is that why you're not a Svarti, because Meidi Kralj's Svarti was killed?"

"After the battle, Grozan Mairki became Kralj. He blamed Kurhv Mairki for our loss because he hadn't been able to learn enough about the sky-stones, and broke him to Ruka, as you know. As for me . . . All the other Mairki had their own Svarti, and Lieve Mairki, who was elevated when Kurhv Mairki was broken, didn't want a Svarti who had failed in his task and who was also associated with a disgraced Mairki. He named Daj Svarti as his Svarti. They took my spell-stick and broke it in front of me, and they took all titles from me. They laughed at me as they did it, and they wouldn't let me kill myself, even though I offered."

Ennis heard Cima exhale, as if he were about to say something more, but his snout closed and he leaned his head back against the pole of the litter. *"There's more . . ."* Gyl Svarti whispered in his head, snorting in derision. *"He doesn't tell you all . . ."*

"Cima?"

Cima took another long breath. "I thought . . . I thought that I would be in your place one day, that I would be the Kralj's Svarti. When I was little more than an eggling, my Life-Weaver told me that the patterns of my scales showed greatness and an affinity for magic, and that's all I ever thought about, ever since that day. The Life-Weaver was right, because whenever Cudak's Web appeared in the sky, I could *feel* the power in it. Some of the Svarti were already talking about Cudak Zvati and how we must go to it, but I knew, Ennis Svarti, I *knew* where it was. I could feel Cudak's Web better than any of the Svarti, even when I was just a Nesvarti. And I could feel Cudak's power in the Perakli's stones, too, and as I learned the Perakli language I also learned how the bluntclaw's sky-stones could call down the sky's power and hold it, and that those blunt-claws came from a land to the west, where I knew Cudak Zvati was. The other Svarti—they were already afraid or jealous of me. So when Meidi Kralj was killed . . . well, the Svarti had me broken as well."

Ennis nodded. The blue ghost was silent, but he spoke the words anyway, not caring that he broke away from the dance because he couldn't stand the pain he heard in Cima's voice. "My da had a sky-stone," Ennis told the Arruk. "A Cloch Mór, one of the great stones. He was here with my brother. That's who you fought. He was the one who threw the red fire," he finished with certainty.

Cima's scales had paled even more, the hues muted. Ennis wondered if he was sick, wondered if he should take Treoraí's Heart and try to cure him as Mam had done. But the Arruk stirred, moving as far from Ennis in the litter as possible. "I warned Meidi Kralj about the sky-stones, especially about the red one that was the strongest of them," Cima said. "I told Meidi Kralj that perhaps the Perakli would let a few of the Svarti go to Cudak Zvati if we stopped fighting them. But the Kralj didn't listen; he *wouldn't* listen. Meidi Kralj said that I'd spent too much time with the bluntclaws when I learned their language, that I'd been infected by them and was now only half-Arruk—and I know that he was speaking words the other Svarti had told him."

Cima lowered his head and glared at Ennis. "I know that Cudak calls for us," he continued. "He calls so that He can teach *us* how to call down the sky-net and use it. Maybe He will show the Svarti how to use their spell-sticks the way you bluntclaws use your clochs, your sky-stones. Or maybe He will give us sky-stones of our own." Again, Cima glanced at Treoraí's Heart around Ennis' neck. His under-lids flicked over his bulbous eyes and slid back again. "My

Life-Weaver said I would be one of the greatest of the Svarti. But I'm nothing. Not a Svarti or a Nesvarti or even an apprentice. Just a half-Arruk with no title at all."

"If I die, you can take Treoraí's Heart, Cima," Ennis said earnestly, not caring that he felt the faint resistance of the blue ghost as he spoke the words. "I'd want you to. You're the only friend I have. You're the only one I can talk to." Cima's head cocked to one side, but his expression looked uncertain. "It's what you want, isn't it, Cima?" Ennis asked.

"It's what I wanted once," Cima answered. "I don't know anymore."

The Arruk looked away again, opening the curtains of the litter with a hand and staring out as the Arruk force moved ever higher into the mountains.

48

At Tory Coill

DESCENDING FROM the heights of the Narrows to the lightly rolling plains surrounding Lough Tory had plunged Séarlait's mood into depression, Kayne realized. She scowled as she rode alongside him, glaring at the road ahead. He tried talking to her as they rode, but she was as silent as she'd been before Sevei had healed her, responding only with headshakes and shrugs.

Rí Mac Baoill and Shay O Blaca rode close by, while Kayne, Séarlait, and Harik were enclosed in the Rí's entourage of Riocha and céili giallnai. Kayne found the sensation uncomfortable. He'd been so long away from the Riocha of the Tuatha that their mannered speech and rich clothing seemed somehow alien to him. His own clothing more closely resembled that of the common tuathánach soldiers trudging on foot before and behind the mounted tiarnas: dirty, stained, tattered from both wear and battle, and far more utilitarian than decorative. He'd refused the Rí's offer of some of his own clothing from the chest in the retinue's supply wagons; it felt better to stay dressed as he was. In any case, Séarlait was dressed the same way, and there was no sense in deepening her mood. Áine, the Hand of the Heart, had offered some of her skirts to Séarlait, who had just stared at them. "Those might do well for a Riocha's nice hall," she told the woman. "They're not for fighting, and I expect there's still fighting to do."

Áine, at least, had known better than to argue.

Kayne also found the circumstances uncomfortable simply because they were outnumbered. At Harik's suggestion, he'd sent most of his da's remaining gardai back to the Bunús Wall under the command of Garvan O Floinn, who had fully recovered from his wounds. Rodhlann and his Fingerlanders would continue to guard the Narrows. "We have three Clochs Mór," Harik said when Kayne broached his worry to the Hand. "Three Clochs Mór make up for a lack of men, as long as we stay alert." .

"Our clochs will do us no good when they slide a dagger into our backs before we can open them," Séarlait had answered before Kayne could comment.

Harik had given her a faint eye roll, like a parent listening to a child's futile arguments. "Not all Riocha are as treacherous as a Fingerlander's paranoia would make them out to be."

"Ah," Séarlait said. "I should apologize, Harik Hand. The Riocha are the true salt of the earth and their very words are always the golden truth." With that, she'd spat on the dirt between them and ground the spittle into the earth with her booted foot before stalking off. Harik had carefully avoided meeting Kayne's gaze afterward, but Kayne thought he could nearly hear the man's thoughts.

If this was what it meant be Rí Ard, then he suspected that he wasn't going to enjoy the experience.

They had topped a rise where the company could look out over the landscape around them. They'd left the High Road, which after descending from the Narrows turned sharply north to Dathúil and detoured westward around Lough Tory—Kayne recalled the argument he'd had with his da just before he'd died: how following the High Road would add several days to the journey. As Kayne would have done, Rí Mac Baoill took them along the Forest Road, which wound between the southern shore of Lough Tory and the northern boundaries of Tory Coill, The dark oak forest spread its tall canopy like an emerald blanket over the land before them. Rí Mac Baoill came riding up to Kayne and Séarlait as they paused a moment, looking out. "We should ride close," he said. "This is the least tamed part of Tuath Airgialla. Still, 'tis a pretty sight in its own way, is it not?"

"It's too flat and too green," Séarlait said. She looked behind them. "I prefer the mountains."

"Mam and Da always said this part of Airgialla reminded them of the area around Doire Coill and Lough Lár in Tuath Gabair," Kayne told the Rí. Séarlait would not look at him. "They spent much time there. The Bunús Muintir always treated them well."

Rí Mac Baoill nodded. If the Rí had his own opinions of the Bunús, he kept them to himself, though Kayne knew that the Rí's da and great-da had both been harsh in their treatment of the old race. "We'll push on so we get past Tory Coill before dark," he said "It's become less safe here since the Filleadh. The Bunús Muintir, dire wolves, and worse, you know. There's a tiny fishing village—Cloughford—at the southernmost end of the lough—not even a village, just a few scattered houses; we'll hope to have our midday meal there, and make for Broughshane, a larger village just on the other side of Tory Coill, by nightfall. From there, it will be three days to Dún Laoghaire, but there will be towns and villages enough on the High Road. I'm sending Tiarna O Blaca with Quickship to go ahead of us and tell the Ríthe to expect us."

"To prepare a proper reception, no doubt," Séarlait said.

If Rí Mac Baoill felt any of the mockery that rode in her voice, he made no sign of it. "Aye, Bantiarna Geraghty," he answered. "That's exactly so. With the clochs and men we have with us, we'll be safe enough." He hesitated a moment, pulling back on the reins of his horse. "Of course, you could always call the Bán Cailleach to our aid in the unlikely event we're attacked," he added.

"My sister comes in her own time," Kayne told him, "not at my beck and call. I would expect her with the magelights, not before." He paused, not liking the look on the Rí's face. "But, aye, if she felt me in trouble, I'm sure she would come as quickly as she could," he added.

"Ah," Mac Baoill said. "Still, we'd best move as swiftly as we can. I should make sure my gardai understand the need for haste. Tiarna, Bantiarna." He nodded to Kayne and Séarlait both and pulled hard at the horse's reins, prodding the animal with a booted heel.

"You shouldn't mention your weaknesses to your enemy," Séarlait told him as they watched the Rí move off to where the entourage waited farther up the narrow road.

"Perhaps not," Kayne answered. "But my true weakness he can see all too easily—that you and I are at odds."

Her chin trembled. She stared stiffly away into the wind. He heard her take in a breath as if she were going to speak, then stop. When she finally looked at him again, her face had softened. "I'm sorry," she said. "I do love you, Kayne. That's not changed at all." She gave him a rueful smile. "I'm not good at speaking—I'm too new to it. I haven't had the chance to learn how to keep my thoughts from tumbling out in words. I do love you, and that's why I speak frankly when I think you're doing something that may hurt you or us, and I'm sorry."

"I'm sorry, too. And I want you to speak those thoughts . . . but to *me,* not to the others. I both want and need your counsel. And your love."

She nodded. Her eyes glittered in the sunlight, and she blinked hard. "It's just . . ." she began.

"What? Tell me."

"When you get back to Dún Laoghaire, back to your world, you'll be surrounded by bantiarna who know how to look and act as they should, who will be fairer and less rough-edged than me . . ." She stopped. Her hands were white-knuckled around the leather straps of the horse's reins. "By the Mother, I sound like some stupid girl."

Kayne nudged his horse next to hers, so that their legs touched. He reached over and wound a braid of her hair around his finger. "You don't need to worry, Séarlait. My da and my great-mam were both tuathánach. We come from humble roots, and our tastes are common."

"Are you saying I'm *common* . . . ?" Séarlait's eyes still glittered, but the moisture had vanished in heat. Kayne grinned at her, and she slowly allowed herself to smile also. Ahead of them the entourage jerked into motion again, and the soldiers on foot and the supply wagons crowded up close behind them. "This isn't anything to joke about," she said, but there was laughter in her voice.

"I managed to make you smile. That's all I wanted."

"I still don't like this, Kayne."

"I don't either," he told her. "But we'll each watch out for the other, and we'll be careful."

She looked unsure, but she nodded. Together, they prod-

ded their horses into motion, and moved down the forest
road toward the waiting trees.

The village of Cloughford stank of the whitefish that the
few inhabitants seined from the deep blue waters of Lough
Tory. Their nets, much-repaired and half-rotted, hung
everywhere near the muddy shore, and their boats—little
more than two-person currachs hollowed out from the oak
trees of Tory Coill—lay pulled up like great slumbering
turtles with their barnacle-encrusted hulls to the sky. The
inhabitants made themselves scarce when the Riocha had
arrived, fading quietly away from the village. Doyle had
caught a glimpse of one of them; he thought the man
looked half-Bunús Muintir, with a flat, thick-browed coun-
tenance and a scowl as he vanished behind one of the
thatched huts. Doyle and the others had been here since
before dawn, and none of the villagers had remained behind to fish the lough that morning or returned to rekindle
the dead coals in their hearths.

There were seals in the lake as well, and Doyle no longer
trusted seals—not since the battle at Falcarragh, years ago.
Standing on the rotting pier that jutted out a few strides
into the lake, he could see a large seal's head surface not
far out in the water, the black eyes peering back at him.
The seal's fur was suspiciously dark, and Doyle had a moment to wonder if it could be a Saimhóir before the head
ducked back under again in a rippling of still water. He
thought of opening Snapdragon to snatch the creature
from the water, or bringing one of the archers over.

Doyle didn't like Cloughford: didn't like the watching
seals, didn't like the foul smells, didn't like the tumbledown
and half-ruined houses, didn't like the proximity of Tory
Coill with its mistletoe-infested oaken limbs just a few
hands of strides across the road, didn't like that Padraic
was here with him.

"An ugly place, is it not?" a voice intruded. Doyle heard
the creak of wood under boot soles a moment later.

"An ugly place for ugly deeds," Doyle responded as he
turned. "I'd be careful, Rí Mallaghan; I don't know if this
pier can take the weight of two men."

Torin Mallaghan smiled at that, his thin, deceptively frail features crinkling like fine paper. "You almost sound like you're worried, Doyle."

"I *am* worried. I don't like this."

Rí Mallaghan shrugged. "O Blaca arrived a stripe ago, and he's confirmed what we thought: the Bán Cailleach can only find and go to a Holder when the mage-lights are out and the clochs are feeding. And we know from our experiences with the Mad Holder that Lámh Shábhála is limited like Quickship—Jenna could use Lámh Shábhála to go to other places at any time, but she could only transport herself to locations she herself knew and could remember." Mallaghan gestured at the village around them as they walked from the pier to the shore past the nets on their poles. "Sevei Geraghty has certainly never been here, and the mage-lights won't come for stripes yet. And even if we're wrong . . ." Doyle saw the velvet cloth of Mallaghan's clóca ripple with his shrug. "If the Bán Cailleach can stand against all the Clochs Mór we have brought here, then there was never any hope at all, was there? That would almost excuse the failures you've had with Lámh Shábhála over the years . . ." The Rí stopped and turned suddenly, so that Doyle nearly ran into the man. "You're not having second thoughts about this, are you, Doyle? I'd hate to think that at this late date I no longer had your loyalty."

"I'm here, aren't I?" But he wished he weren't. He wished Padraic weren't. He had been having more than second thoughts about this, as the burning in his stomach reminded him. Past the Rí's shoulder, he saw Padraic, walking near the road. His son waved once at him, then continued walking. The banked coals in Doyle's stomach glowed brighter.

"Aye, you're here," Rí Mallaghan answered. "And I'd remind you that it's because you *are* with us that your wife is allowed to be as . . . uncooperative as she has been. This is the time when all of us Riocha must stand together. But you still look unconvinced, my friend."

Once, Doyle had thought that Torin Mallaghan meant the word "friend" when he said it. No longer. "I remember having a conversation with you twenty cycles ago, back when Edana's da died. You told me then that 'the prize was worth the risk.' Back then, I agreed with you."

"But you don't now. Is that what you're saying?"

Doyle was saved from having to answer. A garda came running up to them from the village, the rings on his leather mail clanking. "My Rí, Tiarna, they're approaching." The embers inside Doyle went to flame.

"Ah, good." Rí Mallaghan took a deep breath in through his thin nose, his nostrils flaring. He brought his Cloch Mór out from under the clóca and took it in his hand for a moment. "We begin, then. Come, Doyle." He began walking away without waiting for Doyle to respond.

The garda was staring at him, waiting for him to move. Doyle shivered in the cold breeze. He looked back at the lake. It was still and silent. There was nothing there.

"I'll be there, my Rí," he said. "Give me a few moments." He gestured to the garda. "I need to see Tiarna O Blaca," he said. "Tell him it's vital. Hurry!" The garda nodded and ran off. Doyle glanced once more back at the lake—no, there were no seals there now—and began walking slowly toward the hovels of the village and the road. Shay O Blaca met him halfway there. "What is it, Doyle?" the man asked. "Make it quick—Rí Mallaghan wants me to talk to the green-robes before Kayne gets here."

"Shay . . ." Now that it came to it, Doyle wasn't sure how to proceed, and the sour fire in his throat made him swallow hard. Shay's head cocked sideways and lowered storm cloud-gray eyebrows. "We've been friends for as long as I can remember, and I've asked you too many times for favors. But I have one more to ask: the last one, I promise . . ."

In the morning, she slept long, and when she awoke, only Issine was still there. The Créneach stood motionless a few strides from her, looking more like a knee-high pile of rocks than a living thing. The round head turned on its stony torso with a sound like scuffed gravel as Sevei stood up, shivering a bit.

Bhralhg had evidently brought fish while she'd been sleeping. They lay gleaming at Sevei's feet. "Did he expect me to eat these raw?" she asked.

Issine made a sound halfway between a cough and a

hammer blow on granite. "They would taste good enough to you if you were in Saimhóir form," he told her. "Or you can build a fire and scorch them if you'd like. I'm sure Lámh Shábhála's capable of that."

His tone made her feel like a child again, being scolded by an amused parent. She stuck her tongue out at Issine impulsively and he made a chuckling sound again. Sevei glanced down again at the fish. "What do Créneach eat?" she asked.

"Flesh eats flesh, stone eats stone," he answered. "I particularly like the taste of ocean sand. The salts, you know."

"I suppose," she said, looking around the cove. "Where are the others?"

"Gone," he said. "Bhralhg, Beryn, and Kekeri left during the night. They'd said what they wanted to say, and heard what they wanted to hear."

"And were they satisfied?"

If a pile of rocks could shrug, Issine did so. "Who can say?" he answered. "Bhralhg, perhaps, is—after all, he made his choice when he gave you Lámh Shábhála, and Kekeri and Beryn lent their help to you also. So . . ."

"Were *you* satisfied? I notice you're still here and the others aren't."

"This is where I live. The sand and the salts, you know . . ." She waited, and he made the birdlike warbling sound that she'd heard the first time she'd seen him. "But no, I'm not yet satisfied."

"What will you do about it?"

"Nothing," the Créneach answered. "Nothing at all."

"How can you do noth—" The world tumbled and changed around Sevei in that instant. She no longer saw the cold ledge jutting out over the green tidal swell. Instead, she saw trees and tumbledown houses and people. Even as she blinked and wondered at the sight, she realized whose eyes she was seeing through.

"Kayne!" A feeling of dread and apprehension filled Sevei, and she gasped as the vision swept her under. The people surrounding her were Riocha, and she recognized the faces: Rí Mallaghan, Rí Mac Baoill, Doyle Mac Ard, and Padraic. Their Clochs Mór were open and raging all around her, and then the pain came, an awful and unrelenting wave. Sevei groaned with the torture, wanting to hunch over and collapse into a fetal ball. She forced herself to remain upright, grimacing.

"Kayne . . ." Sevei grasped for Lámh Shábhála, willing herself to go to him but though the energy flared around her, she could not find him in her mage-sight, only feel his distress. She didn't know where he was, didn't recognize the landscape in which she found herself, and there were no mage-lights to give her the connection to his cloch she needed to follow.

Already, the vision was starting to fade, as if unable to bear the touch of sunlight.

"There's nothing you can do for him," Issine said. She turned around, and the last wisps of her connection to Kayne vanished. She blinked at his sudden absence.

"Go after them . . ."

"The only safe enemy is a dead enemy . . ."

"It's that bastard Doyle . . ."

The voices hammered at her from within Lámh Shábhála, her gram's chief among them. "I have to go to Kayne," she said. Tears had started in her eyes: from the pain, from her fear, from the sense of loss. "I have to try to help him."

"You can't," Issine answered. "What can be done is being done." The Créneach warbled again, high and shrill. It waddled away from the sea, looking like a child's statue, and stopped near a cleft in the rocks. "Come walk with me," he said.

"I have to help Kayne, Issine," she began, frantic. "How can I go with you when he's in trouble, hurt, maybe . . ." She couldn't say the word. *Dying. Dead* . . . She was afraid to give voice to her thoughts, afraid that if she spoke the bare syllables they would come true. The Créneach warbled again, clapping its hand together percussively.

"You can do nothing now. You can only wait. Come walk with me," he repeated.

Sevei stood there with Lámh Shábhála open and impotent inside her. She heard Carrohkai Treemaster's voice, faint and deep within her. *". . . walk with the Eldest . . . go with him . . ."* After a moment, she released the cloch and went to where Issine waited patiently. "What can you do here?" Issine asked again. "When the mage-lights come again, if Kayne feeds his cloch, you can find him. In the meantime, we should walk together."

The cold sea spray from the wind touched her flesh and she hissed at the sting of the contact against her scarred and delicate skin. She turned her back to the sea and went toward Issine. Together, they walked up the slope toward rocks and scrub.

49

Bunús Wall

ENNIS DIDN'T NEED Cima's translations to know that the Arruk utterly detested their trek through the mountains. The High Road wound disconcertingly up and down the spines of the high peaks, as if it had been laid out by following the path of wandering sheep. As they moved through the mountains into the Finger itself, the advancing army began to be harried by a constant series of ambushes. There would be a sudden flight of arrows from one side or another, but when the nearest Arruk soldiers rushed to confront their attackers, their attackers would vanish into the hills and brush and dense forests of the valleys, never allowing a direct confrontation. The ambushes became more frequent and more deadly as they moved into the Finger, especially where the High Road was but a channel between two clifflike slopes. But there was no other way to go: to abandon the High Road would have led them into the maze of trackless hills and valleys where their advance might have been blocked by sheer walls and drops.

They went forward, leaving a bloody, steady trail of their dead behind. The Arruk grumbled and the Mairki complained, but Kurhv Kralj was adamant: they would follow the High Road, as Ennis Svarti had told them. Kurhv Kralj, Ennis realized, was as locked into his pattern as Ennis.

It was at midday on an overcast and drizzly day that they came upon the Bunús Wall.

Kurhv Kralj, and thus Ennis, traveled on their litters near the front of the army, with only a thin buffer of troops between them and whatever lay ahead—Ennis knew that was different from the way the Daoine armies were arranged, where the Riocha often rode to the rear and a commander might not draw his sword at all. They were ascending along the spine of a ridge to a plateau where the army could spill off the confines of the High Road, trampling the heather and grasses well to either side. There seemed to be a black cliff ahead of them; as they drew nearer, the first troops to approach came hurrying back to Kurhv Kralj's litter. "What are they saying?" Ennis asked Cima, who was leaning from the litter as the Arruk chattered.

"There are stone monsters ahead, as well as several bluntclaw soldiers," Cima answered. "Kurhv Kralj has ordered the army to hold, but we're going forward to look."

The litters were borne through the ranks to the very front and set down. Kurhv Kralj dismounted the litter, as did Ennis and Cima. Ahead of them, a few hundred strides up the road, a stone wall loomed, as high as three Arruk and following the line of the ridge to the north and south as far as they could see. Ahead, the High Road widened, the lane leading to a massive gate in the wall. And the wall . . .

The faces of hideous creatures and fabled monsters, carved in stone and painted, glared out at the Arruk army as if defying them to move forward. There were terrible dragons coiling around the snarling mouths of dire wolves; Black Haunts with howling mouths; doglike creatures walking upright with scarlet mouths and hands like Ennis' own that could only be mythical blood wolves; the frilled, reptilian back and cavernous, tooth-lined mouth of the knifefang; a dozen other nameless gargoyles and beasts. They writhed in unmoving stone on the eastern face of the wall. Kurhv Kralj stared most, though, at the gate. The metal-sheathed wood of the gate was the mouth of a gigantic creature, the wall around it was its body: a winged feline with a dragon's barbed tail; the head and eyes nearly human except for the sharp incisors crowding its snouted mouth, clawed forepaws extending outward from the gate to form an entrance into the gaping mouth . . .

"Cudak . . ." The word was a whisper that leaped from Kurhv Kralj's mouth to the others. "That is Cudak . . ."

"It's the Bunús Wall," Ennis told Cima. "I heard about it.

Mam told me. She said the Bunús Muintir built it with their
magic . . ."

"What's beyond the wall?" Kralj Kurhv asked.

"The Tuatha," Ennis answered. He could not raise his
voice above a croak. *Home . . . Home is beyond the wall.*
"The land Mam used to rule."

"Who guards the wall? How many?" They could all
clearly see men moving along the wall, and hear their faint
shouts as they pointed at the Arruk force before them. A
few of the gardai, Ennis thought, seemed to be wearing the
gray clóca of Dún Laoghaire. He wondered at that—why
would they be here?

Ennis shrugged. "I don't know." The blue ghosts were
rampant here, as if this place were full of possible futures.
He could barely find the one he needed among the crowd,
and even that one seemed pale and weak. "I never knew
there was anyone here at all. Kayne . . . he told me it was
mostly ruined, that the gates hung open . . ." He stared at
the wall. "They're not open now," he said, a disappointed
child stating the obvious.

Kurhv Kralj laughed. "They will be soon enough," he answered. "You—" he pointed to one of the Arruk. "Bring
the Mairki here. Cudak waits for us, and we will come to
Him."

The sound was the first thing they heard: the low, insistent
thudding of thousands of feet punctuated by the clashing
of wood and metal and shouts in a strange language. When
the first of the creatures appeared down the long slope
where the High Road entered a cleft pass in the mountains, the gardai along the Bunús Wall gasped as one, even
though they'd seen this vision before. "Arruk!" someone
shouted. "It's the Arruk!"

The year the gardai had spent in Céile Mhór could never
be forgotten, nor the friends they'd known and lost there,
and they shuddered at the memories.

The creatures kept coming, boiling out of the cleft like
ants from a disturbed nest and arraying themselves before
the wall just out of arrow range. Garvan O Floinn, in
charge of the gardai in the absence of either Tiarna Kayne

Geraghty or Hand Harik, shook his head as he stared outward at the massed force. For the last several days, they'd received increasingly urgent reports from the Fingerlanders who lived beyond the wall that the Arruk were coming. The clan-lairds of the Outside Clans had done what they could with ambushes and quick forays, but none of them had the resources to attack the Arruk directly. The other clan-lairds had sent men and women to the wall to bolster the small force already there, but Garvan could already see that they were too few. Too few by half or more. "By the Mother, the reports were right. They've brought the entire army—look, that's the Kralj's litter out there, and the Kralj doesn't move without Mairki and Svarti."

"We can't hold the Wall," a garda next to him muttered. "Not with the people we have. Not against a force even a quarter that size."

"We'll do what we've been asked to do," Garvan answered sharply, "for as long as we can. If we can give the others time . . . well, that's what we'll do."

He forced his gaze away from the Arruk. He could hear the shrieking of the Arruk Svarti with their spell-sticks, already beginning to chant their magics, and he saw the fluttering banners of the Mairki. *All four of them . . . We saw that only once the entire time . . .*

"Archers to the wall!" he called out to the encampment of gardai and Fingerlanders below. "Lock and bar the gates. I need two Fingerlander riders: one to go to Laird O'Blathmhaic and tell him to send as many men as he can; the other to ride to Ceangail for reinforcements. Move! Go!"

He turned back to the Arruk. He could see two cloth-draped litters moving toward the front, the flags on the poles telling him that it was the Kralj and his Svarti. Instinctively, Garvan checked to make sure his sword was loose in its scabbard: it wouldn't be long now. Too few soldiers, even with the Fingerlanders, and no clochs na thintrí at all . . .

He didn't wonder if he would die today. He wondered how.

A Daoine army might have waited before the gates, preparing siege engines, battering rams, and catapults. That was what Kayne had said armies often did when confronted by obstacles. But not the Arruk.

Kurhv Kralj's orders were simple, direct, and brutal. The only concession to time was to send troops into the nearest stand of trees to cut scaling ladders for the walls. In a few stripes, the ladders had been made. Two Mairki, along with their Svarti and troops were sent to assault the wall to either side of the gate. The huge gate itself, Cudak's Gate, they were calling it already, would be stormed by Kurhv Kralj and the remaining two Mairki.

Kurhv Kralj had his litter sent to the rear. He took a step out from the gathered troops. The war drums had already begun their insistent unison rhythm. Ennis could feel the battle lust throbbing in the Arruk as they waited, pressed together, their jaka held high, the Svarti chanting their opening spells, the foot soldiers slapping spear shafts to chests in time to the throbbing, slow rhythm of the drums. The pulse made Ennis' heartbeat sound fast and frightened. Ennis was once again on Cima's shoulders lest he be lost and crushed in the press of Arruk, his spell-stick clutched firmly in his left hand (and lashed there by Cima with a strip of leather), his right hand still bound to his chest, but with Treoraí's Heart out from under his léine and firmly clutched in his hand.

Kurhv Kralj lifted his hands and the drums stopped. In the eerie, stunned silence of the landscape, the Kralj opened his mouth and roared a challenge to the wall and its defenders. He gestured. "Hajde! Idemo!" he cried: *Come on! Forward!*

With that, a roar erupted from the thousands of Arruk throats, the drums began a quick, urgent cadence, and the army surged forward, a savage wave across the land that trampled heather and grass underfoot. Ennis and Cima ran with them: they had no choice.

As they advanced, the Daoine on the walls loosed flight after flight of arrows, some of them breaking harmlessly against the thick Arruk scales, others finding the softer flesh between the scales. With a shriek and a howl, the Arruk on either side of Cima and Ennis went down, but more rushed in to fill the gap. Then they were no longer running but were rushing between the legs of Cudak and pressing around the base of the wall. Close up, Ennis could see the eroded, carved faces with their coats of fresh paint, now scarred by Arruk claws.

The scaling ladders were raised, with Arruk standing on them to strike as soon as the ladder reached the summit of the wall. Most were immediately cut down by the Daoine and the ladders pushed back into the crush of Arruk. There were a few skirmishes along the wall but none of the Arruk managed to secure a breach along the wall where others could surge up the ladders to gain a hold. The Arruk army milled at the base of wall, stymied for the moment.

Arrows hissed down on them. Lightnings flashed from spell-sticks as the Svarti unleashed their spells on the wall and the gate. Though the stones chipped and shattered, the thick wall held fast, and the carved creatures sparked and glowed when the lightnings struck them, the very stones seeming to rebuff them as if the warding spells the ancient Bunús had cast on them still retained some vestige of their power. The battle was loud with the shrieking of the Arruk, the chanting of the Svarti, and the shouting of the Daoine above. Ennis could see their faces now, and aye, some *were* clad in Dún Laoghaire gray. Some of them saw him as well, for he heard one shout: "A boy! They have a Daoine boy with them!" Heads peered down at him, then vanished, but Ennis had little time to wonder about them.

He was locked together with the blue ghost and it took all his concentration to remain with it, buffeted by so many possibilities. He saw an image of himself, an arrow through his throat, falling from Cima's shoulders. He saw himself torn apart by the Arruk. He saw the Arruk pouring through a gap in the wall, but leaving his broken body behind.

Keep your mind on the pattern, Isibéal's voice whispered, or was it Gyl Svarti, or perhaps his mam? He could no longer tell. Perhaps it was none of them at all. The arrows were a sharp and deadly rain all around him and the wall seemed to actively defy them. The Arruk clawed at the wall, trying to clamber up and over it without the help of the ladders, but they were cut down before they could reach the summit. They pushed and scrabbled and tore at the wooden doors of Cudak's Gate, but though the wood shivered and trembled, it did not give.

He knew what he had to do. He knew what he must do. The blue ghost told him.

"To the gate, Cima," he shouted down to his bearer, and Cima obediently began pushing toward the gigantic image of Cudak, pushing aside the Arruk in front of him, his jaka swinging. Seeing Ennis, the Arruk gave way willingly, and he heard the shouts in guttural Arruk: *"Ennis Svarti goes to the gate! Make way!"*

The Arruk, with Kurhv Kralj urging them on, were shoving at the barred doors without success. Ennis wanted to tell them to move aside, but the blue ghost was silent and Kurhv Kralj was far enough back from the gate that he seemed to be safe, and Ennis was afraid that the pattern was so faint that he might lose it entirely if he broke away from it. So he also remained silent, standing close to the Kralj several strides back from the gate and lifting his spell-stick. Arrows fell all around Ennis, but none touched him—the archers on the wall seemed to be deliberately aiming away from him; afraid, perhaps, that he was an unwilling captive of the Arruk, a hostage. As he lifted the spell-stick, Ennis also opened Treoraí's Heart and once more let the power within it flow out into the staff. He groaned as the energy rushed outward from him, his wounded arm aching as if the healing skin were being ripped apart once more. But the blue ghost didn't cry, and so Ennis couldn't either. Instead he brought the staff up and spoke the release words for the spell, adding the energy within Treoraí's Heart to the magic.

With the last word, the spell-stick shivered in his hand, a fierce, unrelenting white light gathering at the knobbed top of the staff. The radiance washed out the cloud-filtered sun, sent sharp black shadows racing across the battlefield and over the wall, caused the Daoine staring out from the wall to cover their eyes.

"Go!" the blue ghost and Ennis shouted as one, unable to hold back the gathered fury. The knob of the spell-stick shattered in Ennis' hand, but as the splinters raked across his face like tiny knives, a pair of thick, fuming lightnings arced from him to the gate. The first struck the image of Cudak and the winged beast *moved,* the Daoine-like eyes gleaming green, the legs stirring, the wings beating and sending stone falling. Cudak stirred and yawned, and the gate fell open in its mouth as the second lightning smashed into it, shattering stone and beast and wood, Arruk and Daoine. The arch of Cudak's mouth above the gate crashed down on the ruins and part of the wall itself tumbled inward with the sound of a falling mountain, the tumult drowning out the screams and howls of the dying and wounded. Kurhv Kralj gave a startled glance back at Ennis, but then turned quickly to the smoking gap in the wall. He pointed his weapon to the smoking ruins of the gate. "Hajde!" he cried again, and the Arruk all around them took up the chant, rushing forward in an unstoppable, remorseless mass.

Ennis was borne along with them.

"There's a boy with them!" the gardai said to Garvan, cupping his mouth and shouting to be heard over the noise of the battle. "Look!" He pointed over the wall to the seething horde of Arruk below. Garvan could see the strange sight: a Daoine child in a tattered, bloody, and filthy léine, being held on the shoulders of one of the horrible creatures and holding what looked to be one of the Arruck spell-sticks in his hand. Directly below, the child raised his face to look up at them, close enough that Garvan could see his features, and Garvan reeled backward in shock and with an oath. "It can't be! That's Ennis Geraghty, the Healer Ard's son."

"That's not possible, Garvan. You're mistaken." The gardai looked down again, shaking his head.

"I know the face, man. Tiarna Owaine introduced me to his son back in Dún Laoghaire. 'My youngest,' he told me. 'One day he'll ride with us . . .'" Garvan felt cold fingers stroke his spine. "I know it's him. But how . . ."

"He's moving, sir," the gardai told him, "toward the gate . . ."

Garvan leaned over the wall. Aye, the Arruk was bearing Ennis away to the north, moving rapidly. Garvan followed along the ramparts of the wall, running past the beleaguered archers and the gardai struggling with the siege ladders and storming Arruk, around the bodies of Daoine and Arruk both.

He was still strides away from the gate when he saw Ennis lift the spell-stick he grasped, when he saw the impossible and for a moment glimpsed the stone-wrought creature writhing as if it were alive; when the horrible, glaring mage-dawn came; when the gate exploded inward and the Bunús Wall itself shuddered along its entire length; when Garvan was thrown off his feet and battered with flying rocks and boulders. The deadly rain continued for three breaths or more, and he finally forced himself to rise, clutching a forearm through which a shattered bone gleamed white. He had to blink away blood from his eyes, and he couldn't bend his right knee. Garvan could see the Arruk beginning to rush through the opening. "To the gate!" he screamed to the gardai, to the Fingerlanders. "Everyone to the gate!"

Even as he shouted, even as he limped and crawled and stumbled from the wall—trying not to scream with the pain of the broken, useless arm or his damaged knee, even as he tried to direct the defense—he knew it was hopeless. There were too many of them, and the breach in the wall was too large.

With his good arm, he grabbed the arm of one of the younger gardai rushing to the gate. "Hold!" he told the wide-eyed young man, with the barest hint of beard on his chin. "Find me the scribe and our message birds," he ordered the youth. "I have to get word back to the Tuatha. It's vital— Go! Hurry!"

The garda nodded and ran off. Garvan could hear the clashing of swords and the din of the skirmish at the broken gate, but it was all he could do to stagger backward. Blood poured down the fingers of his hand, and the world was turning dark around him.

He hoped the darkness would not last forever.

50

Traitors and Allies

HARIK CAME RIDING back to Séarlait and Kayne as they approached the village of Cloughford. Just ahead of them, they could see Rí Parin Mac Baoill and his retinue waiting at a crossroads in front of a few tumble-down cottages on the shore of the lough. The gardai on foot were plodding up to the crossroads and sitting down gratefully in the grass there as the supply train came strag-gling and clanking up the road behind. The sky was gray and forbidding, occasionally spitting rain at the clócas draped around their shoulders.

"One-Eyed Parin said to tell you that we'll stop here for a bit," Harik told them.

Kayne lifted his eyebrows, his nose crinkling. "Here? We'd be better going on past to get through the stench."

"I'd agree, Tiarna," Harik answered. His horse was next to Séarlait's and slightly behind. "But the Rí . . ." Harik stopped, and Kayne saw the Hand's gaze flick nervously to their right. He followed the direction of Harik's glance; there were men emerging from between the houses of the village, from the cover of trees across the road: men dressed in fine clócas, men with Clochs Mór around their necks. Riocha. Mac Baoill, at the crossroads, sat easily on his horse, smiling.

Kayne felt the breath leave him as if he'd been kicked in his stomach. He reached for Blaze, ready to rip the cloch open and attack, knowing that they'd been betrayed and lied to and that their hope was faint. That he, Séarlait, and Harik were three against more . . .

"Don't do it, Tiarna," Harik said warningly, and as Kayne looked to Harik, his hand dropped away from the stone. Harik had reached over to Séarlait. One hand clutched the dark fall of her hair, pulling her head back harshly, and his other hand held a glittering knife edge to the side of her neck. Séarlait's eyes were wide with mingled fright and fury, and her throat pulsed with the effort of breathing. Winter gleamed on her chest, but even as she started to reach for it, Harik pressed his knife against her neck, hard enough that blood drooled from under the blade. "If either of you touch your cloch, she dies."

"Harik—" The full realization and scope of the betrayal hit Kayne then. "All those years Da trusted you . . ."

"He trusted me, aye, as well he should have. Tiarna Geraghty would never have made the choices you've made, Kayne Traitor," Harik answered. "He would never have cast his lot with the filthy Fingerlanders against his own people."

"Then for all your time with him, you never knew him at all," Kayne spat back. He kept his hands at his sides. He glanced at the others, recognizing faces: Rí Mallaghan; Shay O Blaca; his cousin and childhood friend Padraic Mac Ard, looking uncomfortable and uncertain as he stared at Kayne; and . . . "Uncle Doyle," he grunted. "I should have known. What's the matter, Uncle? Wasn't it enough that you killed Mam and Gram?"

Kayne felt small satisfaction in seeing Doyle's face color with the accusation, as if Kayne had slapped him across the cheek. The man didn't answer; instead, he glanced at Rí Mallaghan. Kayne chuckled grimly. "Ah, so Uncle Doyle's just a lackey here, and you're the one in charge, Rí. My sister's going to be terribly disappointed in all of you." He looked at each of them. "So many clochs in one place . . . Certainly far more than you need for the two of us. Do you think it will be enough to hold *her*? Do you think you'll manage to stay alive when the Bán Cailleach comes looking for you? You won't."

The bluff was all he had, but if Rí Mallaghan was worried by the threat, it didn't show in his face. "We have enough clochs and more," he answered. "We'll have two more now than we had when we came here, in fact."

"*No!*" The shout brought Kayne's head back around. He

saw Séarlait let herself fall sideways from her horse, surprising Harik. It nearly worked. Harik started to fall with
her, almost wrenched from the back of his steed. But he
caught himself and kept his grip on Séarlait's hair, the
muscles in his arm cording as he held her body upright by
her braided tresses, even as the horses bucked and shuffled
nervously at the commotion. Séarlait twisted, trying to pull
away from him. He reached over her horse, slicing at her
with his knife hand.

Kayne saw blood flow. Too much blood . . .

Kayne's fingers found Blaze and tightened around the
sharp facets. He let the Cloch Mór bloom open like a poi-
sonous flower. His sight went as red as the gem he held, as
red as the blood spilling over the front of Séarlait's clóca,
and his anger struck Harik full force. The man was ripped
bodily from his horse, dead even before his corpse hit the
ground, his chest and head a ruin of bone and flesh. Séarlait stumbled away, one hand on the wound that gaped
from neck to shoulder, and the other on Winter. Her cloch
opened cold and bright.

It was not alone.

In his cloch-sight, Kayne saw the other Clochs Mór open
as well: more than he wanted to count. He threw up a wall
even as Rí Mallaghan opened his cloch, as a glowing yellow dragon appeared around Doyle Mac Ard . . .

. . . as Padraic, hesitating, started to reach for his cloch and
then, strangely, vanished with a small thunderclap of air.

Kayne had no time to wonder about that. He ran to
Séarlait, one arm pressing her to him even as she placed a
barrier of cold ice around them. He could see the line of
the terrible cut from Harik's blade along her neck, very
near where she'd once borne the scars of old wounds. The
blood was pulsing as it ran from her, staining his own
clothes. Her eyes were strangely distant, focused somewhere beyond him. "I'm sorry, Séarlait," Kayne whispered
to her. "We're going to die here."

"Dying doesn't matter, my love," Séarlait told him, her
voice gurgling with blood. She coughed, spattering red
over both of them. "It's only how we die that matters."

"Then we'll die well," he answered.

In mage-sight, Kayne saw shapes and lights rushing
toward them, and the walls they had thrown up around

them shuddered and cracked under the assault of a dozen clochs. The battering of the mage-stones were the blows of unyielding cudgels against Kayne's body. He gasped, feeling each strike against the wall; Séarlait moaned alongside him. She was deadweight in his arm now, and he could no longer hold her. He let her slump to the ground alongside him. As if through a dark and smoky glass, he could see the Clochs Mór gathering, crows around dying animals. They surrounded them, though there were but a few on the forest side of the road.

It was still too many. Kayne could not even distinguish the attributes of the clochs that besieged their defenses: he could hear the scrabbling of wolfish claws, feel the whip-strikes of energy, hear the gibbering of skeletal warriors and sense the blows of an angry demon and the smashing of immense fists. Already Blaze's fiery wall was fading and growing thin, and there were terrible black cracks in Winter's shield, and Séarlait's hands were loosening around the cloch. Her breath rattled loudly in his ears.

There was no opportunity for them to retaliate. It was all they could do to keep the attacks from overwhelming them. Their defensive walls shrank around them, pushing back, until they were surrounded tightly by fire and smoke and light. A bolt of pure energy lanced through their mingled defenses and Kayne tried to shift his wall nearly too late: the bolt, deflected, struck earth just before Séarlait. Winter's wall vanished for a moment as her hand released her cloch—Kayne looking down at her in panic and concern, seeing the sallow whiteness of her skin and her closed eyes—then the wall returned as she groped for Winter again. Her eyes fluttered open.

"Go," she told him. "Run."

"Not without you."

"You're already without me," she said. She coughed again, and blood spurted thick from her mouth. "Let me give you this gift, my love. Run to the woods . . ." She looked at the two figures that stood, radiant in mage-sight, between them and the trees. The attack thundered around them. Her fingers tightened around the stone, and in his mage-sight, he saw white light blossom around her: the full power that was left in Winter, all gathered up. She threw it at the mages between them and the forest.

The two green-robes went down. Séarlait collapsed. Winter fell dead and empty from her hand. "Séarlait!"

There was no answer. Kayne gathered the rapidly-waning energy within his cloch, the power burning him as if he were trying to handle fire. He pulled the chain of Blaze from around his neck, holding the stone in his hand and gathering its power to himself. He reached down and picked up Séarlait's limp, unresisting body. The Holders around them sensed the movement, and Kayne felt their hunger. He felt the mind-storm gathering, the red lightning.

He started to half run, half stagger toward the woods, toward the bodies of the mages Séarlait had rendered unconscious or dead. The other clochs erupted, their images ready to smash him.

At the same moment, he saw the golden dragon—Uncle Doyle's cloch—leap from where it hovered above the village and soar toward Kayne, with fire vomiting from its mouth and eyes as red and angry as the sun, its great wings beating and its clawed feet extended for a strike.

Kayne knew they were irrevocably lost.

Somewhere close by, a wolf bayed, its howl sounding like wailing words.

"Uncle Doyle," Kayne said, and Doyle could hear the disgust in the young man's voice. Despite his desperate position, there seemed to be no fear in him. He was, Doyle realized, very much his parents' child. Doyle felt hollow and disconnected, as if the guilt he'd borne for so long had gnawed away all of his insides and left him only a shell. He felt nothing else. "I should have known. What's the matter, Uncle? Wasn't it enough that you killed Mam and Gram?"

It wasn't me, Doyle wanted to shout to the boy. *It was Rí Mallaghan; I was just his pawn. I did what I was told I had to do to keep my own family alive and safe, and that's my shame and I'll answer to the Mother-Creator for it. None of your family should ever have died, especially your mam, but the blame is not all on me. Please say it's not all on me . . .*

But Doyle already knew there would be no absolution. He glanced at the grinning, smug Rí Mallaghan; Kayne followed his gaze. "Ah, so Uncle Doyle's just a lackey here, and you're the one in charge, Rí. My sister's going to be terribly disappointed in all of you . . ."

Kayne was still talking but he heard none of it. Doyle glanced at Padraic, at the paleness of his son's face. *The two of them used to play together, running across the keep grounds waving mock swords or holding up stones in their hands as if they were clochs and fighting imaginary enemies together. Friends should not be forced to kill friends . . .* Doyle looked pleadingly at Shay, nodding with his head toward Padraic. O Blaca nodded slightly, shifting so that he stood directly behind the young man.

Doyle heard Rí Mallaghan's voice now, interrupting Kayne. "We have enough clochs, and more," the man said, his voice almost amused. "Two more now than we had when we came here, in fact."

"No!" The shout came from the Fingerlander woman Harik was holding, startling all of them. She fell from the horse—Doyle wondering whether Harik had just slit her throat—but then there was no time for thinking as the clochs erupted all around, as a quick burst from Blaze in Kayne's hand struck the traitor Harik, killing him immediately. Doyle opened Snapdragon, but his eyes were on Padraic, not Kayne. His son was waiting, his hand hovering over Snarl but not touching the gem. Doyle understood the hesitation: *all the time they'd spent together. The laughter, the games . . .*

Shay responded even as Padraic seemed to shake himself and start to take the cloch in his hand. In Doyle's mage-sight, a glow enveloped Padraic, a brightness that collapsed around him suddenly and vanished in a whirling flare like a stone dropped into a bonfire. When the sparks were gone, so was Padraic. Shay O Blaca slid quickly to the back of the Riocha.

You'll never do what I've had to do, Padraic . . . I'm sorry, my son. I'm sorry, but I hope you'll understand . . .

The dragon roared as if Doyle's sorrow were the fire that lived inside it.

Kayne and the Fingerlander woman had already thrown up defenses against the power the assembled mages threw at them, but Doyle could see that the woman was mortally wounded from Harik's blade. The Riocha besieged the walls of mingled ice and fire with mage-armies and lines of arcing, raw energy. Fleeting shadows brighter than those of the sun pursued each other over the landscape. Doyle allowed himself a moment of grudging admiration. Neither of the two were schooled mages and neither of them had held their clochs na thintrí for long, but the injured woman fought with a raw ferocity that compensated for her lack of skill, and Kayne . . . Kayne handled Blaze with a natural grace, the damnable Aoire elegance, the undeniable talent that his gram, his mam, and his sister had also possessed.

But fury and grace would not be enough. Not here. That was obvious to everyone around them. Doyle watched their defenses weaken and bend under the assault and the cracks begin to appear. "Doyle!" He realized that Rí Mallaghan had been calling him for some time. "We need you—take Snapdragon to them. We can finish them now . . ."

That was true, Doyle saw. Kayne and Séarlait had drawn back their defenses into a compact shell around them; with his true eyes, Doyle saw Kayne stumble backward toward the trees that bordered the road, dragging the woman with him. There were two mages of the Order there in their green clócas, and Doyle realized what they intended: it was what Doyle might have attempted himself—they would try to retreat to the woods. The plan was desperate and had no chance of success, but through the dragon's eyes Doyle could see the woman gathering the remaining energy in her cloch.

Doyle could have called out. A simple movement of their encircling forces would have been enough to forestall the attempt. He remained silent. He let them move.

The Fingerlander put all her power into the attack, sending the mages between them and the forest reeling into unconsciousness. Doyle heard Rí Mallaghan scream in anger; the Riocha's clochs attacked Kayne as one in all their manifestations, and the young man's shield was tattered and broken. Doyle sent the dragon leaping forward toward Kayne with fire and claws and teeth . . .

. . . and turned just in front of him, interposing Snapdragon between Kayne and the Riocha. For a moment, the mages halted in mid-attack, wondering what Doyle intended.

A wolf howled—not a mage-wolf, but a living one—and then another, and what Doyle saw emerging from the forest made him laugh bitterly. *Kayne has the Aoire luck, too* . . .

"Go!" Doyle whispered and the dragon roared the same word to Kayne from its cavernous mouth. "Hurry!" Doyle *was* the dragon now; he lifted himself up, claws extended, the fire drooling from his mouth and his great wings cupping air as he launched himself toward Rí Mallaghan. He didn't look behind to see if Kayne obeyed; he didn't dare. He saw only Torin Mallaghan and his own guilt and this one, final chance to assuage it; he felt only the need to lose himself in fire and take out the person who had lost him his wife, his children, and his self-respect. To burn away the guilt of a loyalty he should never have given and had held onto for far too long.

I'm sorry, Edana . . . sorry, Padraic . . . sorry, Da . . .

He never made it to Rí Mallaghan. Five or six Clochs Mór struck Doyle at once, from all sides. A pack of ethereal wolves ripped the dragon's scaled side; lightning shredded the delicate tissue of the wings; a great, invisible fist batted him from the sky; a black tornado hurled him to ground; and he saw his da, standing over him with a sword in his hand.

"You failed me, son," his da said as Doyle lifted a futile hand against the upraised blade. "You always failed me."

The blade slashed down, and the dragon poured its burning blood on the grass.

Kayne heard the wolves and he thought they heralded death, but the dragon cupped air overhead, landing in furious brightness between Kayne and the other mages, and its snout faced not Kayne but the others. The attack halted for a moment in confusion. Then the golden neck arched back and the deadly mouth opened. "Go!" the dragon hissed, a blast of heat buffeting Kayne. "Hurry!" With a beating of its wings, the dragon lifted from its victims and roared back overhead. Kayne watched it go, heard it bellow a challenge and rush at the clochs set against them.

"Uncle Doyle . . . ?" he said wonderingly, but then he had

little time. In his real sight, he saw arrows flying toward them and gardai charging, and mage-sight showed the clochs gathering to attack once again. Kayne used the last dregs of power within Blaze to send the arrows into flame and push them aside toward the gardai. Séarlait was silent and heavy in his arms.

The wolves howled, and this time he saw their gray forms rushing out from the trees—a pack of two hands or more, nearly as high as his shoulders and panting like demons—and with them, a strange quartet: two Bunús Muintir, a man and a woman; and two entirely naked men with black hair and eyes as dark and pupilless as the Bán Cailleach's and voices that sounded like the moaning of seals. The two Bunús Muintir staffs gleamed in mage-sight, and Kayne could see a glowing power deep inside the two Saimhóir changelings, as if they had swallowed Clochs Mór.

He could *feel* the spells that the four unleashed, like the concussion of deep sound against his chest when as a child he'd been allowed to sound the ancient call-drum in the keep at Dún Laoghaire. The spells lashed outward toward the cloch Holders, even as the keening of a dying dragon lifted the hairs on the back of Kayne's neck, even as the growling of wolves and the desperate shouts of gardai told him that the tide of battle had, impossibly, turned.

He cradled Séarlait to his chest. He hurried into the brown maze of Tory Coill with the Bunús Muintir and the Saimhóir changelings.

51

A Holder Revealed

SEVEI PACED along the shore.

She and Issine had spent the day moving south along the western shore of Inish Thuaidh. Sevei had to admit that—strangely—the long slow walk with the Créneach had eased some of the pain of her body. The scent of the sea cleansed her lungs and the breeze was soft against her skin. There was no one around and Issine cared not at all about her nudity. Neither of them said much during the day, Sevei mostly trying to keep her mind away from Kayne, from what she'd felt a few stripes ago. She ached to *do* something, not just walk pleasantly through Inish Thuaidh.

"There's nothing you can do right now," Gram said comfortingly. *"I know how you feel, but until the mage-lights come again, you can't go to him . . ."*

As the sun touched the horizon in the west, Issine walked down between the rocks to a narrow wedge of sand. The shore here was sheer with cliffs, and waves battered white against black, kelp-draped rocks to either side of them. "Ahh . . ." Issine sighed as his bare feet touched the sand. He seemed to be digging deep into the sand with his toes, and Sevei wondered whether he were somehow eating the sand through his feet. Nearby, the relentless surf had scooped out an undercut cave, and Issine led her to the entrance as the evening darkened. Her white hair dripped with spray from the icy water and the wind off the sea was harsh, but she opened Lámh Shábhála just enough to warm herself. She stood at the entrance to the cave, staring up at the sky overhead to the night's first stars. The voices of old Holders complained, though her gram was silent.

"... *there's nothing here* ..."

"... *why do you waste your time* ... *?*"

"*Patience* ..." That was Carrohkai Treemaster, as always placid and calming. "*Wait* ..."

Issine had settled down in the middle of the little room, his already small body compacting further with a sound like gravel crunching underfoot, as if he held himself together with sheer force of will. The stony torso glowed an intense yellow in the darkness. Issine's long tongue darted from his mouth, sliding once over his chest as if tasting his heart. Sevei touched her own chest.

"It's true—the clochs na thintrí, they were all once inside a living Créneach?"

Issine trilled his answer. "Aye. And Lámh Shábhála was the first: Céile's Heart." His voice sent the echoes of birds chasing each other through the darkness. "We gave ourselves to the soft things. To the people who were like you."

"Why?"

Issine didn't answer immediately. He stood there, perfectly motionless though the cloch within him still glowed, and she thought that perhaps he'd gone to sleep.

"Because you could accomplish more with the Hearts of the Créneach than we could," Issine said when she'd nearly forgotten her question. "Because we thought you would also pass along the gift. As sometimes, rarely, you did." Issine gave a long, trembling note, so high that it hurt Sevei's ears. "As we walked, you were thinking of your own kind. Your brother."

Sevei nodded. "Aye, I was." She tried to imagine Kayne, tried to feel him in the air and could not. "I have to go to him, Issine. When the lights come. I have to. And if he's not there, I'll find Mallaghan and Mac Ard, and I'll kill them." She spoke grimly. Firmly. The promise gave her satisfaction.

"Is that what you're destined to do? Is that why you took the Scrúdú?"

"The Scrúdú gave me power. What should I do with it if not use it?"

Another trill. "Indeed," Issine said.

As if in response, the first glimmer of the mage-lights—

earlier and brighter than usual—flickered at the zenith
near the constellation of the Winter Harpist. Sevei could
already feel the eagerness of Lámh Shábhála to feed, even
though the cloch was mostly full. She opened the gem
within herself and fell into its emerald depths. Her vision
expanded, the mage-sight placing its hues over her eyes.
She could see Issine not as a Créneach, but a glowing being
with his heart a bright illumination. He was the strongest
connection, but she could sense the others beginning to respond: the faint threads of the numerous but weak
clochsmion scattered everywhere, including a few close by
on Inish Thuaidh; and the much stronger filaments of the
Clochs Mór. A few of those were also close to them. Sevei
could feel Scáil, held by Aithne MacBrádaigh no more
than a few miles distant; a bit farther away, in Dún Kiil,
there was Greada Kyle and Firerock; and not that much
farther south, on Inishfeirm, Stormbringer was being
raised, along with several clochmions.

"Bán Cailleach . . ."

Sevei could also feel the troubling presence of Treoraí's
Heart, with its hidden Holder, powerful and—again—
nearer than it had been the night before.

But that was not what she searched for in the web of the
mage-lights. She looked for Blaze and Kayne, and she
couldn't find him.

*"Bán Cailleach . . . Sevei . . . I'm calling you. I need
you . . ."*

There was a gathering of Clochs Mór far to the east, and
Sevei knew that must be those who had attacked Kayne.
They huddled together as if their numbers would protect
them from her. She could feel her anger gathering, like a
storm cloud looming and growing darker on the horizon,
and she knew they could feel it as well. "I see you," she
whispered to them, almost laughing. "I can find you."

Issine warbled, high and shrill.

*"Bán Cailleach . . . Sevei . . . Please come to me . . . You
must come . . ."* For the first time, she let the voice intrude
on her consciousness. It was attached to one of the Clochs
Mór, and she knew the voice: her Aunt Edana, calling out
to her through Demon-Caller, her voice desperate. *"Sevei,
please . . ."*

She could not feel Blaze at all, nor Winter. Strangely,

Snapdragon was also absent. *What's happened? Is Kayne dead? And Uncle Doyle, too?*

There wasn't an answer, only the insistent call. *"Bán Cailleach . . . Sevei . . ."*

She yearned to go to the Clochs Mór, to burst among them like an avenging demon, all terror and wrath, and send them howling to their deaths, ripping away the stones from their dying necks. She could take the clochs back to Inishfeirm, give them to the new Máister or Máistreás in small payment for the loss of Máister Kirwan. She could make Inish Thuaidh the dominant Tuath. She could rule it in Gram's stead; Greada would step aside and give her the throne.

She could have everything. Everything her gram had gained, everything her mam had accomplished, all of it together.

". . . Aye!" Gram shouted within her, her voice shrill. *"Aye, that could be yours, my darling one, and should be . . . All that I had and more . . ."*

For a moment, Sevei let the mage-sight fall away, even though the mage-lights still lashed her to the stars. Issine was regarding her solemnly, as if he could hear her thoughts. The Créneach's deep-shadowed eyes were full of pity for her, and that stung her more than the lines of scars on her body. "Following your gram's old path won't return them to you," Issine's voice said in her head. "The past is gone. All you get to choose is the future. What you're thinking won't bring them back."

Wouldn't bring back Mam and Gram. Wouldn't bring back her da and Kayne, Ionhar and Tara, or poor little Ennis. Wouldn't bring back Máister Kirwan or Dillon and his love, or all the others who had lost their lives.

". . . Patience . . ."

Then, like a sunrise after a night storm, she felt Blaze open at last to the mage-lights, very close to the knot of Clochs Mór. The relief felt like a cool, cleansing rain. She could feel Kayne through his cloch, and she could sense great pain and anger within him, a sense of betrayal, danger, and worry. *But he's alive . . . he's alive . . .* She wondered why Séarlait didn't open Winter, and she started to will herself to go to Kayne, but Edana's voice intruded again.

"Báá Cailleach . . . Sevei . . ."

She hesitated. Issine was staring at her.

"You must choose," he said.

"Sevei . . . It's vital that I talk with you . . ."

Blaze continued to feed upon the mage-lights but Lámh Shábhála was full. The sky was bright with their colors, the stars banished. Sevei gathered the mage-lights around her like a blanket of fire and let them take her away.

"I've come, Aunt Edana."

Edana turned, dropping the parchment she was reading. She didn't bend to retrieve it; she'd already memorized the words there, the words she was certain she would never forget.

Sevei was a pallid, naked apparition on the balcony, staring in like a banshee through the open doors. In the moon-white face framed by silver tresses, the black eyes were twin voids caught in the glowing eddies of scars. Behind Edana, the chamber servants who were preparing her bed gave muffled screams, then drew in frightened breaths and fled with a pattering of feet.

Edana realized that she was staring, with Demon-Caller held in her free hand as if to protect herself. She let the Cloch Mór drop as she brought her hand down, and averted her eyes as she gestured to the room. She picked up the parchment again, rolling it tightly in hands that were suddenly damp with sweat. "Come inside, Sevei. Would you like tea? I can have the healer bring you an infusion of kala bark, if you'd prefer . . ."

Sevei nodded and stepped forward into the room, padding onto the carpet in bare feet—Edana wondering how she stood the cold without clothing—and Edana saw then the deep weariness in her face. Sevei looked far older than her years. There were lines on her face that were not the scars of Lámh Shábhála, the pouched skin under her eyes made it look as if she hadn't slept in days, and she winced when the curtains of the balcony doors brushed against her skin. "Will you sit?" Edana asked her, and Sevei shook her head.

"It's better to stand," she said. "Why did you call me,

Aunt? Because of Doyle? I already know that the Ríthe chose to defy me and that they betrayed Kayne. Did you want to plead for Uncle Doyle's life, or for Padraic's if he helped them?"

She knows . . . Edana bit her lower lip against the curse she would have uttered. "I truly didn't know they planned this," she told Sevei. She could feel the tears flowing hot on her cheeks and couldn't stop them. She wept for all of them. "I suppose it doesn't surprise me, not with Mallaghan's voice being so strong with them. If you intend to go after the Ríthe, then aye, I'd plead with you for Padraic's life, as his mam. I wish he hadn't followed his da, but he has, and I understand that even if I don't like it or can't change it. One day, you might understand it also, with your own children."

"Padraic, you need to be careful," she'd told him before he'd left Dún Laoghaire to return to Lár Bhaile with Doyle. "I know you love your da, and I wouldn't ever want you to lose that love, but to follow in his path . . ."

"Mam . . ." He touched her face. His indulgent smile reminded her of Doyle's, the same dimple forming at the corner of his mouth. "I love both of you. And I'll be careful. But, Mam, you've always taught me about duty and honor. You've taught me well. I've given my oath to the Order of Gabair, and that's where my duty lies. Didn't you always tell me how I had to trust you, even when you were asking me to do something that I didn't want to do or that felt wrong to me. You told me that sometimes we simply have to obey, because none of us can see the future or always know that what we're doing really is the right thing . . ."

He was so earnest, and so young . . .

" 'My own children,' " Sevei repeated. "That's something I'll never know." The Bán Cailleach's voice sounded cold, so cold—like Jenna's, Edana realized with a start. Very much like the First Holder's. As if Sevei were afraid that if she lost control of her emotions, she would lose control of herself.

Meriel chose the right way, choosing Treoraí's Heart instead of Lámh Shábhála. . . . "I'm sorry," Edana said, taking a step toward Sevei. The woman moved back, almost like a wild animal afraid of the touch, and the unalloyed panic in

Sevei's face made Edana sigh. "Sevei, I'm so sorry. I wish . . ." She stopped. Shrugged. "But there's nothing either one of us can do, is there?"

"No, there isn't," Sevei answered, but some of the frost had evaporated from her voice.

"Is Kayne . . . ?" Edana was afraid to say more, afraid of what it would mean.

"He's still alive," Sevei told her. "Right now, I don't know more than that." Behind her, the mage-lights had faded entirely. Against the blackness of the sky, Sevei seemed to glow faintly, as if her skin was lighted from the inside. "I should tell you this also, Aunt. I didn't feel Snapdragon in the mage-lights tonight."

The room was suddenly cold despite the peat fire blazing in the hearth. Edana wrapped her clóca more tightly around her. She was afraid to ask the next question, but knew that she must. "I . . . I didn't either. Doyle's dead, then? You know this?"

A shake of her white head. "I don't know. But, aye, I suspect so." Her gaze went past Edana to the doorway of her chamber, and at the same time Edana heard a new voice.

"I suspect it also, Mam." Padraic was standing there, and Edana felt her breath catch in her throat. The chamber servants must have gone to him; Edana had hoped he would stay hidden in his room. But Padraic was glaring at Sevei—a glare that Edana had once seen Doyle use with Jenna, and his hand was far too close to his Cloch Mór. "I was there," he told Sevei.

"Padraic—" Edana started, but Padraic shook his head.

"No, Mam, let her hear." He turned back to Sevei. "Da didn't want me to be there because he knew what he was going to do and he didn't want me to be part of it—he had Shay O Blaca send me away with Quickship against my will. And I know why, even if Da wouldn't talk to me about it—he didn't like what Rí Mallaghan and the others were going to do, and he was going to try to save Kayne and the woman with him. He was afraid that when he did that, the Riocha would attack me also—and he's right, because I would have defended Da gladly. You can say what you want, Sevei, but I know the truth. If your brother's still alive, it's *because* of my da, not despite him. Da isn't a perfect man, the Mother knows, but he also isn't . . . wasn't . . ."

Padraic swallowed hard. ". . . he wasn't the evil person you and your gram seem to think he was."

That was what Padraic had told Edana when he'd suddenly appeared here in the keep, confused and disoriented. She still wasn't sure she believed him, and now she saw the same doubt mirrored on Sevei's death-white face.

Edana realized she was still clutching the narrow roll of parchment in her hand, now much crumpled. Sevei seemed to notice it also, her gaze going to the paper. Edana hurried to explain, hoping it would divert Sevei's attention from the scowling Padraic. "I received this earlier today," Edana said, unrolling the parchment again. The paper was partially torn and so thin that she could see the firelight through it. "A message bird brought it—the bird arrived at your mam's section of the Keep; the bird-keeper said it was one of the Ard's flock, that your da took that particular bird with him when he left for Céile Mhór. This—" Edana lifted the parchment, "—was banded to its leg. It's from Garvan O Floinn; do you know him?" Sevei shook her head, and Edana continued. "I didn't either, but I made inquiries and learned that he was one of your da's gardai. Listen . . ."

Edana began to read: *To Tiarna Geraghty and the Ríthe of the Tuatha: Bunús Wall has fallen to the Arruk army. Their numbers were overwhelming—beyond count—and they have a Cloch Mór in addition to their normal spellcasters. The Cloch Mór is held by a Daoine boy, a young child. I saw him closely at the gate, and I believe him to be—*

Sevei spoke before Edana could finish. "Ennis."

Edana let the parchment flutter to the floor. "You already knew?"

"No, not until just now. But I should have. I should have . . ." Sevei shook her head, lashing her shoulders with her white, unbound hair. "And it's not a Cloch Mór he holds. It's Treoraí's Heart." Her eyes, the dark holes in the brightness of her death-pale face, seemed to search the flames in the hearth. She seemed to have forgotten Padraic and even Edana. "It's the only answer that makes sense. I knew someone had taken the Heart from Mam, and Ennis was with Mam when she died, and Ennis . . . well, he was always precocious."

"Born with the blue caul," Edana whispered, remembering the day of the boy's birth. Sevei's gaze came back to her.

"Aye," she answered. "How he came to be with the Arruk and why he'd help them, I don't understand, but I might have guessed that it'd be someone with Aoire blood who could hide himself from me behind Treoraí's Heart . . ."

Her hand came up to her mouth as she gave a quick, choking sob, and in that moment she was no longer the Bán Cailleach but simply Sevei. Edana could see the un-satisfied and deep grief in her, as well as the hope. Tears glittered in the empty pools of her eyes and dropped like white pearls from her cheek. "Sevei . . ." Edana husked.

"I didn't want this, Aunt Edana," she said. "I truly didn't. If I had it to do over again, if I'd known what it would mean, I wouldn't have taken Lámh Shábhála."

"I know," Edana told her soothingly, as she would have spoken to her own daughter. Then the moment passed as Sevei drew herself up again.

The Bán Cailleach glanced at Padraic, watching near the door, his hand still ready to take up his cloch. Her eyes blinked, the tears vanished, and she was the cold Pale Witch again. "The Arruk have come to Talamh An Ghlas," Sevei said. "That can't be allowed."

"No," Edana said carefully. "It cannot."

"I will need the Riocha and all their Clochs Mór." Sevei turned to the balcony, stepping to where the curtains rip-pled in the night wind. Edana thought she might take her-self away with Lámh Shábhála, but she heard Sevei's voice speak into the darkness. "Aunt Edana, would you have for-given Uncle Doyle, as his wife?"

"I might have," Edana told her. "Aye." She knew the an-swer; she'd mulled it over every night for many months now. She could hear Padraic's slow breath behind her.

"Mam, you don't have to tell her anything."

Edana shook her head. "No, Padraic, I do. Your da and I . . ." She turned away from Padraic to Sevei. "You've known love?" she asked Sevei, and the Bán Cailleach nod-ded solemnly.

"I knew it," she said, "until it was taken from me."

"Then you understand," Edana told her. "I loved Doyle, and that doesn't ever go away, not entirely. He could be a

good man. I won't pretend that we had a perfect relationship—we didn't. There were times when I didn't like him at
all. There was an ambition and bitterness in him that I
could never touch or temper, and sometimes . . . sometimes
all that came too close to the surface. But he was a good da
to our children, almost always. Padraic's already told you
the same. Very few people are entirely monsters, Sevei, no
matter what they do or what they might look like. Doyle . . .
what he did, he did either because he had no choice, or because he truly believed that what he did was justified or
best." Edana paused. "But like any of us, he could sometimes be wrong."

Sevei turned at that, her scarred body casting a light as
bright as that of a candle—Edana could see the illumination on the embroidery of the curtains. "I'm sorry, Aunt.
Sorry for you and Padraic. But if Uncle Doyle's dead, I
don't think I'll mourn. Not after I watched him kill Gram
and Dillon." Again her gaze went past Edana to Padraic.
"You remember that, don't you, Padraic?" she said to him.
"I remember how you looked. You were as frightened and
uncertain as I was."

"I don't hate my da, Sevei," he told her. "Nothing you
can say can make me feel that way. You don't understand
him." Edana saw a reflection of Doyle's steel in her son's
face.

Edana thought that Sevei would be furious, but she only
shook her head as if saddened. "Perhaps I didn't understand him," she said to Padraic. "All I know is what he tried
to do to Gram, to me, and to those I loved. I *saw* that. I was
there. I don't know if he had anything to do with Mam's
death, or if—as you say—he put himself on Kayne's side
yesterday. I don't know. But I can't mourn him if he's dead.
There are no tears in me for him; he burned them all
away."

Edana hurried to speak before Padraic could answer. "I
won't blame you, Sevei. But I'll grieve, and so will Padraic
and the rest of our children." The fire was warm on her
back, and the heat made it feel as if someone were standing close behind her. She wondered if it was Doyle's haunt,
if it watched her. "Sevei, I don't know that I could do what
you may have to do. But you need the help of the Riocha,
and if Ennis is helping the Arruk—"

"I know what you're saying," Sevei said sharply, the Bán Cailleach again. She touched the green gem between her breasts. "I know what I have to do."

Edana nodded. "What can I do to help you? What can *we* do?"

"Mam—" Padriac began, but Sevei stopped him, lifting her hand.

"Padraic," she said. "When we were younger, I used to wonder if one day we might marry each other. I was half in love with you from the earliest days I can remember. Even when I went away to Inish Thuaidh and Inishfeirm, even when I found another lover—" Edana saw Sevei's face shift at that, tightening with remembered pain, "—I still had a fondness for you. For all of your family. Mam . . . she never once spoke anything ill of your da to me, even if Gram did. Mam knew that she couldn't govern without the other Ríthe and Riocha." Sevei grimaced, and Edana started to go to her, but the Bán Cailleach shook her head. "I don't blame you for supporting your da and believing in him even when others didn't. I've done that myself, many times, with Gram."

Padraic remained silent, the frown painted on his lips, but his hand fell to his side.

"We'll need soldiers and we'll need them now, Aunt Edana," Sevei continued. "Muster what you can in two days from Dún Laoghaire and the surrounding Tuatha, and send them hurrying north. There won't be as many troops as we will want, but we don't have time to wait. Come with them yourself to the Narrows—both of you. I'll need Demon-Caller and Snarl and your support. That's our best chance to make a stand against the Arruk, where they won't be able to bring all their numbers against us."

"And you?"

"I'll go first to Dún Kiil to rally the Inish clochs, and then when the mage-lights come tomorrow, I'll go to where the Ríthe are waiting." A faint smile flicked over Sevei's lips. "These will be meetings that none of us will like, I think. And if I learn more about Uncle Doyle, I'll send you word. To both of you."

Edana came forward to stand close to Sevei. Her hand reached out and stopped just before she touched Sevei's stark-white hair. "What else can we do for you, Sevei?" she asked.

"You can wish me luck, Aunt."

"I wish you all that, and more," Edana said softly.

52

The Defense of Ceangail

GARVAN O FLOINN STOOD with Laird Liam O'Blath-mhaic on the heights to the southeast of the town of Ceangail. The morning was misty, with gray veils of drizzle off the Ice Sea to the north, but they could still see, far below on the twisted ribbon of the High Road, the colorful mass of the Arruk army. They spread out for more than four miles along the road, spilling well off either side, and their raiders were foraging into the valleys on either side, taking the sheep and cattle that still remained in the pastures and torching the houses they found. There were at least two double-hands of smoke smudges rising into the wind and smeared across the sky. The Fingerlanders had done what they'd always done in such circumstances: they had melted into their hidden fastnesses among the mountains well away from the High Road. The Arruk had killed few Fingerlanders after the battle of Bunús Wall, but they were razing the land and killing the livestock to feed their army. The Arruk didn't need their long jaka and claws to slay the Fingerlanders; starvation would follow their path as their most effective weapon.

"They'll overrun Ceangail in a few stripes of the candle," Garvan said to O'Blathmhaic. He rubbed a hand over the broken arm bound to his body with windings of cloth, remembering Bunús Wall. "Ceangail can't hold, nor can Enbow or Tain. There's nothing to stop the damned Arruk between the Bunús Wall and the Narrows."

Laird O'Blathmhaic sniffed. He scratched his balding, liver-spotted head and spat on the ground toward the oncoming Arruk. "The Tuatha think too much of their walls and cities," he said. "The strength of the Finger isn't in our town and their walls, but in the land. *That's* what's always eventually defeated the armies you've sent after us." He shook a fist at the front column of the Arruk and then turned to walk back to his horse as Garvan took a last look at the invaders and, limping on his injured knee, followed O'Blathmhaic. "We'll do what we've always done. We'll harass and ambush them. We'll take them down by ones and twos. They'll see their fellows dying every mile they march, and they'll wonder if they're next. Let them have Ceangail. Let them burn the town to the ground. There'll be no one there and nothing for them to plunder. We'll spit at them and tell them what we Fingerlanders have always said to those who come here unwelcomed: *Titim gan éirí ort*—May you fall without rising."

"Laird," Garvan said. "You can't empty Ceangail. I don't have enough men to defend it."

His hand already on the horse's traces, O'Blathmhaic frowned at Garvan. "You've already said that we can't hold Ceangail, man. We both know that."

"I agree, we can't hold it, but we *can* delay them here. We can make them pay with time. We can leave ourselves an exit to the high plain and take it when there's no more hope. We could cost the Arruk a half day's march, maybe more."

"How many lives will that cost us, and to what end? Then the Arruk only stay longer in the Finger."

"Aye, but we give the Bán Cailleach, Tiarna Kayne, and Bantiarna Séarlait time to gather their forces. I've sent message birds to them . . ."

"And if they didn't get them? Or if the Riocha don't care to help?" O'Blathmhaic scowled. "Fingerlanders don't count on the Riocha coming to our aid. They come here for the same reason as these damned Arruk: to steal from or kill us."

"Not this time," Garvan insisted. "Not with Tiarna Kayne and your great-daughter. But we need to give them more time. They'll be thinking of stopping the Arruk at the Narrows—just as we stopped Rí Mac Baoill's army there. But we have to give them the days they need to gather and ride there."

"Why?" O'Blathmhaic answered. "The sooner the
Arruk pass through the Finger, the less damage they'll do
and the fewer of our people they'll kill. Who knows, maybe
the Finger itself may even turn them back. If not, then let
the Tuatha deal with them. Let them bloody their own
damned lands."

Garvan was shaking his head. "The mountains of the
Finger won't stop the Arruk, Laird. I know them; I've
fought them in Céile Mhór, and the whole breadth of that
land didn't turn them back. And if you let them into the
Tuatha, there may be no stopping them at all. They don't
leave our kind alive in their territory. Eventually, they'll
finish what they've started, and then there will be no one
to help the Fingerlanders at all."

Laird O'Blathmhaic tightened the straps on his horse
without answering. Grunting with effort, he mounted. "So
you think Fingerlanders should die to let the Riocha live?
'Tis not a proposal that any of the clan-lairds will like." He
jerked the reins of his horse and rode off.

Garvan stayed on the mountain for another stripe of the
clock-candle, cradling his arm and watching the Arruk approach through the mist and rain.

The town, set at the mouth of a pass in the mountains with
a high valley spreading out behind it, seemed deserted.
There were no soldiers waiting before its flimsy wooden
walls, no rows of sentries along the ramparts, no sounds of
occupation at all. For the last few stripes, the Arruk army
had marched along the High Road without contact from
the Fingerlanders. The ambushes, the sudden storms of arrows that would arc down from high above on the ledges
where the Arruk couldn't reach, had stopped. The army
marched on, a plague on the land, following the curving
and twisting High Road.

Ennis, riding with Cima in his litter, looked out from the
curtains at the town and felt a touch of homesickness.
Ceangail reminded him of villages in the hills south of Dún
Laoghaire, and the thatched roofs that peaked above the
walls were shaped like the houses of home, not the
rounded and low buildings of Céile Mhór.

For a moment, he regretted what would happen here, but then he remembered what had happened to his mam and he heard Isibéal's voice in his head. *"They wanted me to kill you. Now you'll give them your revenge, for what they did to your family . . ."* "I know," he answered. Cima stirred on his pillows.

"What?" he asked.

"Nothing," Ennis told him. "We've come to a town." The litter was already being set down, and he could hear Kurhv Kralj shouting orders to the Mairki. Ennis stepped out from his litter; immediately a space cleared around him, and the Arruk nearest him looked carefully away, their snouts conspicuously raised. The knitting wounds on Ennis' body pulled and ached as he moved, and Cima hurried forward with his spell-stick, with the knob at the top now nearly gone. Still, it had held the spells that Ennis, with Cima's aid, had carefully placed back within it. Ennis leaned on the stick, hobbling forward to stand at Kurhv Kralj's side.

There were blue ghosts everywhere, and in all of the images, he saw fighting here. He wondered how that was possible in an empty town. Ennis wanted to move closer to the walls to look at it, but the blue ghost to which he had attached himself did not move, so he stayed where he was.

"They think walls made of sticks will stop us," Kurhv Kralj said to Ennis, as Cima translated. "We'll leave them burning under our feet. Look, the cowardly Perakli have already abandoned their town to us, too afraid to even stay here." He roared toward the barren walls and the shut gates. "As they should be," he shouted. "The Arruk come, and the Perakli tremble." He gestured to the Mairki and their Svarti. "This travesty blocks our path. Take it out."

The four Mairki roared and went scurrying to their respective positions. The Mairki bellowed their orders and the Arruk army surged forward, the front ranks carrying a massive tree trunk as a battering ram as they trotted up the road toward the gates to the beat of the war drums. The rush of battle fury caught all of them, and Ennis wanted to charge with them, but again the blue ghost would not move. He clenched the spell-stick in his hand and watched the other Svarti move toward the town with the Arruk soldiers.

They were a hundred paces from the walls when heads appeared at the ramparts, and the Daoine bows sent a shattering wave of death toward the Arruk. The front ranks crumpled and the ram bearers stumbled, the trunk falling to the ground and rolling as those crushed beneath it screamed. The barrage stopped a bare few strides from where Ennis stood. He saw an arrow lodge itself in the mud just ahead of him—where he might have been had he followed his inclinations. Another flurry of arrows came as Kurhv Kralj, standing with Ennis, screamed a challenge at the town's defenders. "Come and fight!" he shouted. "Quit cowering behind the walls and meet your fate as warriors!" He looked at Ennis, flecks of foamy spittle at the corners of his mouth. "Your people are fearful mice and filthy grubs," he said. "They hide, and throw their sticks at us from the shadows."

The blue ghost said nothing. Ennis bit his lip to remain silent himself. He stared at the town, he clenched his spellstick, and his fingers prowled the facets of Treoraí's Heart.

"Use the stone. Show them again the fate that awaits them. The Arruk are like dogs: they respect strength and will show their necks to someone who can dominate them. You can rule the Arruk; you can't rule the Daoine—they won't submit. Use the stone . . ." It was Gyl Svarti's voice.

"Be quiet. I'll have all of the dead in my head. Like you."

It was Isibéal who answered. *"My voice will be stronger than theirs, Ennis. You will be stronger. Use the stone . . ."*

"Let Mam talk. Let me hear her."

The other voices, the voices of those he'd killed, whimpered and wailed in the background, but if Mam spoke, she was drowned out by them. Now the blue ghost moved, and Ennis laced his finger around the Heart. As he opened the cloch, he felt the enchantments he'd woven into the spellstick, felt them swell and wriggle as the power touched them, as if they were live things aching to be released from the cage of their wood.

"You don't have to do this, Ennis Svarti." That was Cima's voice, whispering so that only Ennis could hear, and he felt his Arruk companion's hand on his arm. "The town will fall without your help. They can't hold."

Ennis looked down at Cima's hand, and he felt the blue ghost narrow his eyes into an angry glare. Cima shivered and let his hand drop away. "Tell the Mairki to fall back from the gates," Ennis said to Cima and Kurhv Kralj. Kurhv Kralj's eyes sparkled at that, and his lips moved back from the long rows of his teeth. He waved to his drummers and they lifted their beaters, hammering out on the tanned skins of the Arruk dead a new pattern: *doom, doom, datta-doom, datta-datta-doom.* The Mairki howled at their soldiers, the Svarti stopped their chants. All the Arruk, silent now, moved back from their assault on the walls and gates of Ceangail. Though the arrows continued to hiss down from the skies, they looked back to Kurhv Kralj, and he gestured. The Arruk moved aside from the roadway, leaving it vacant and empty from the gates to the Kralj's litter and Ennis.

Ennis raised his staff, and they answered with an approving, mass howl.

Garvan could see the panic in their faces. "Hold!" he screamed to them: Tuathaian and Fingerlander alike. "Hold them as long as you can!"

He didn't know if any of those arrayed along the walls of Ceangail heard him. The noise was tremendous: the shivering howls of the Arruk, the crash and boom as their ram battered at the main gates, the screams and shouts of their own men, the insistent beat of the war drums. Laird O'Blathmhaic was at the gates, rallying the Fingerlanders. Garvan ran along the walls until he stood above the gates. The Arruk were thick here, a surging mass of them, the scales colorful below him, the arrows of archers ricocheting from them as often as they stuck. The Arruk didn't seem to care: they trampled the fallen below their feet and more came to replace them. Garvan looked up the road to where the Kralj's litter stood. He could see the Kralj; he could also see the small Daoine youth who stood beside him.

They would need the tunnels they burrowed under the walls, Garvan knew; the tunnels that led out far from the city and the road.

He shivered.

"Laird!" he called down. "How long?"

"The supports are already broken," O'Blathmhaic shouted up to him. "We're bracing as best we can. A few more well-placed strikes, though, and they'll be through."

"Then let's get our people to the tunnels . . ." Garvan stopped: the Arruk war drums had changed their beating, a cadence that he had heard only once before, when Tiarna Geraghty and his cloch had swept the Arruk's Svarti from the field and they'd broken through the Arruk ranks threatening to reach the Kralj. *Fall back* . . . the drums said. For a moment, Garvan's heart lifted. He wondered if they'd somehow managed to break the spirit of the Arruk or if some army had impossibly come to their rescue . . .

But no . . . The Arruk went silent, dropping their ram in the middle of the road and melting back from the walls. The archers continued to fire down on them, but now the road was barren of everyone but the dead and wounded. Garvan followed the line of the open road up the slope. He saw Ennis—it had to be Ennis—lift the spell-stick he carried, and he also saw the glint of the cloch in his other hand.

He would not make the mistake of Bunús Wall and order his people to the gate. He already knew it was hopeless. The battle would end now. "Laird!" Garvan shouted, "Get everyone back!"

But it was already too late. Garvan was blinded by the light that arced out from Ennis, a jagged brilliance that traveled impossibly along the ground like slow, crawling lightning. The fury struck the gates of Ceangail; the thick oaken planks shattered into splinters. The walls on either side of the gate trembled and fell, and Garvan fell with them.

He found himself on the ground in a jumble of broken lumber. A jagged spear splinter of oak had impaled his once-broken arm, now broken again and worse. The rain dappled the blood as he grimaced and pulled his arm free of the wood. He knew he'd also cracked ribs on that side, that his skin would already be blackened with bruises. His knee screamed at the abuse, but he found that he could stand. "Retreat!" he screamed to anyone who could hear. "To the tunnels! Ceangail has fallen! Retreat!"

He pushed at those around him with his good hand—as he heard the howls of the Arruk, as the afterimages of the mage-light purpled his vision. "Laird! Laird O'Blath-mhaic!" he shouted, looking for the man.

He saw him. O'Blathmhaic was sprawled on the ground near the gate. His open eyes stared upward at the sky, and the rain fell on him and he did not blink. Garvan's heart sank, and he turned his back to the gate.

"Retreat!" he shouted. "Ceangail is lost! Retreat!"

Too few of the defenders moved to follow his orders.

53

In Tory Coill

"*TRÁTHNÓNA maith duit,* Greada."

Kyle MacEagan was standing with his longtime companion Alby near the fire, his arm around Alby's thin waist. The torc of the Rí lay on the mantle, as if the old man found its burden too heavy around his neck. Sevei saw her great-da turn at her greeting; his hand dropped quickly away from Alby, who stepped back into the shadows near the hearth, as unobtrusive as a good servant should be. Kyle smiled quietly at Sevei, though his eyes remained sad and tired. "There haven't been many good evenings about here lately," he said to her. "You look like you're in terrible pain, Sevei. Should I have Alby call the healer to prepare some kala bark for you?"

He started to gesture to Alby, but Sevei shook her head. Her skin was tingling painfully with the cold of the passage from Dún Laoghaire to Inishfeirm, then from Inishfeirm to Dún Kiil, and her mind was still reeling with the news that Edana had given her. She sniffed the air, and it seemed full of the scent of doom. The voices in her head whispered agreement.

"*. . . death. It's always war and death . . .*"

"*. . . that's all the power of Lámh Shábhála has ever brought . . .*"

"*. . . . you can do more. You can do more . . .*" That last was Carrohkai Treemaster, and Sevei clung to the ancient Bunús woman's voice as if it were a plank of wood in a storm-torn sea.

"I'm afraid not, Greada. The news isn't good . . ." She

told him then, and as she spoke, the words drove him to his chair and pushed him, hunched and weary, into the cushions. Midway through her tale, Alby quietly left the room. Kyle seemed diminished and far older when she finished.

"Our Ennis, with the Arruk . . ." he husked. He would not look at her.

"Aye," she told him. "Greada, how many gardai can Inish Thuaidh bring to the Narrows in a hand and one of days?"

"A hand and one?" he grunted. "In good weather, it would be nearly a hand of days around the Tuatha and through the Airgialla passage. We would have only a day to muster the troops and supply the ships . . ." He shook his head. "A few hundred," he said. "We'd have no time to take more than those in this township and maybe that of Be an Mhuilinn and Na Clocha Dubha. Maybe a hand or so of ships, and the gods would have to give us good winds."

"The winds you'll have," Sevei told him. "I went first to Inishfeirm, and I've spoken to Maestra Caomhánach of the Order. Stormbringer will go with you, and so will many Bráthairs and Siúrs of the Order."

"The Order, going out to battle once more." Kyle sighed. "That's a sight many always wished to see . . ." The door to his chamber opened with a soft groan of hinges and Alby reentered, carrying a tray with two steaming mugs on it. He gave one to Kyle and brought the other to Sevei. She could smell the kala bark in the steam. She smiled gratefully at Alby as she took the mug, enjoying the warmth it lent her hands. Her greada's voice brought her attention back.

"But there won't be any troops at all, and no ships for the Order," he said. "The Comhairle might have named me Rí, but this . . . this expedition would require the Comhairle's approval and cooperation, and it would take days just to get the clan-heads here so the Comhairle can meet. Even if they *were* here, the Comhairle still would never allow it. They would tell us that the Arruk have never crossed water, even when they could, and Inish Thuaidh is an island. Why should we come to the aid of our old enemies when the Arruk are no threat to us?" He held his own mug in his hands, forgotten.

It was the answer she'd expected, but hoped she wouldn't hear. "Is that what you believe also, Greada?" she asked. "Answer me honestly."

"... *he was a good husband to me, but he should never have been Rí* ..." Gram's voice. Sevei shoved her back down: "*He's more capable than you believe, Gram. I'm sure of that.*"

She thought for a moment that he hadn't heard her. He was staring at the curls of steam rising from his tea. Alby stood behind Kyle's chair. The servant's wrinkled hand touched the old man's shoulder and Kyle lifted his head. "No," he said finally. "It does us little good to survive here if our cousins and kin in the Tuatha are destroyed, even if the Arruk never come here at all." He sighed. "The Comhairle will howl and scream and demand their title back, but I never wanted to be Rí in the first place."

The voices of the Inish Holders within her shrieked their fury, though Gram's was not among them.

"... *No! Let the fools die!* ..."

"... *The Tuatha would never have come to our aid. Never* ..."

"... *Let them bathe their precious kingdoms in their own blood* ..."

"Shut up! Be quiet!"

"What?" her greada said, and Sevei started, realizing she'd spoken aloud. Kyle set the mug down, rising. He went to Sevei, standing before her. He lifted his arms as if to hug her and Sevei stepped back and brought up her hands. "Ah," he said softly. "I'm so sorry for you, Sevei." His right hand fingered the Cloch Mór on his chest. "I'll gather as many gardai and soldiers as I can," he told her. "By the Rí of Dún Kiil's order. By the time the Comhairle realizes what's happened, the Order's mages will have arrived and the ships will be gone." He paused. "I'll sail with them."

She looked at him: the leathery, wrinkled, and sagging skin of his face; the spotted scalp his hair had long ago deserted; the belly rounding under his clóca; the legs whose thinness even several wrappings of linen couldn't hide; the hands that shook slightly as they touched Firerock in its cage of silver wire. "Greada, you're needed here ..."

"Don't lie to me, great-daughter," he said. "I'm too old for lies and half-truths. We both know that once I do this, I'll no longer be Rí. And you'll need all the Clochs Mór you can muster. Firerock served at the Battle of Dún Kiil. It's time it served again."

"Greada . . ."

"Hush, child," he told her, as if she were simply his great-daughter and not the Bán Cailleach at all. "Drink the kala bark, and let me make ready. Drink. Go on."

He waited until she lifted the mug to her lips, then turned to Alby.

The Saimhóir changelings had returned to the water, the dire wolves had vanished into the darkness of the forest. Only the two Bunús Muintir were left: Beryn, the Protector of Thall Coill; and Keira, the Protector of Doire Coill.

On the hill where they sat, a cairn of rocks had been erected, newly piled. Their pale gray stones seemed white in the moonlight. Kayne was still wearing the clóca and léine he'd worn when they'd been attacked, dyed rusty brown by Séarlait's lifeblood. Beryn had offered fresh clothing, but he'd only shaken his head, not caring. He'd cleaned her body, had laid it down and gathered the dirt and rocks to place over her without acknowledging Beryn's and Keira's silent help. He felt numb and distant, as if he were outside his body and watching himself work. He'd labored without rest until it was done.

Kayne stared at the cairn, Winter dangling on its chain in his hand. He'd been staring at the cloch and the grave since the sun was high in the sky without seeing either one of them. The grave was unreal. It was a dream. It was impossible.

"I'm sorry, Kayne," Keira said at his side. Doire Coill's guardian had been old when Kayne had last seen her a double-hand or more of years ago. Even then she'd relied on her staff to support her: a gnarled and twisted oaken branch as tall as herself. Now her ancient eyes looked him up and down as if appraising him as she sat next to the crackling branches. "I know there's no comfort in this, but she would be glad that you lived. That's what she wanted."

"I don't live," Kayne told her. "Not anymore. I'm as dead as she is—my body just hasn't realized it."

The old woman grunted. Her hand stroked his arm in mute empathy.

Beryn stood a little aside from them, his gaze more on the shadowed wood than on the other two. He'd built a tiny fire on the hilltop, little more than a hand's span in size, though still the trees seemed to groan in response, or perhaps that was only the wind through winter-bare branches. Kayne's world had shrunk to the bare globe of the fire, ending in darkness beyond Séarlait's cairn. "She should have had a pyre," Kayne said. "That's what her people do with their dead."

"The Seanóir, the old trees, wouldn't have liked that. This is their land, after all. But she will rest here, and the Greatness will take Séarlait up to Her and comfort her."

Across the fire, Beryn lifted his head to the sky. Keira knotted arthritic fingers around the use-stained wood of her staff and stumped over to stand before Kayne, groaning as she moved. "The mage-lights are coming," she said. "And so is your sister with them. Open your cloch to the lights and she'll find you."

"She's about a day and a half too late," he said, unable to keep the bitterness from his voice.

The old woman shrugged. "The Bán Cailleach goes where she must." The mage-lights, brightening, lent their cool hues to her face, the illumination shifting over her features. Kayne could feel the pull of Blaze, yearning to be filled again with the power. The cloch's insistence pulled his attention away from the cairn despite his grief. Beryn was chanting in the Bunús tongue, and the lights swirled above him. Even Keira looked away, lifting her staff toward the sky.

Kayne took Blaze in his hand.

The mage-lights were cold fire, and the energy within them radiated through his entire body, spreading out from his right hand to the rest of him. In his mage-sight, Blaze was a cavern of scarlet glass, and the power flowed through it like a subterranean river, rising higher to fill the rooms within it. He could feel the other Clochs Mór as well: the hateful cluster of the Ríthe not far away and the fierce, powerful tidal pull of the Bán Cailleach. His sister's black eyes and scarred face drifted there in the lights. Her harsh gaze found him and for a moment he was caught in those eyes, snared, and they seemed to rush toward him . . .

"*Dia duit*, Brother," he heard her say, and her voice resonated not only in the mage-lights but in the air. He turned around and saw her.

He said nothing. He saw her gaze go past him to Winter hanging empty on its chain in his left hand, to the cairn. Her obsidian eyes narrowed. The mage-lights still snared his hand and wrapped her body, but the stream that came down around Sevei was almost too bright to look at, glimmering with streams of all the hues he'd ever seen within them.

She frowned, the expression ghastly in that savaged, white face. "I'm sorry, Kayne. I'm so sorry . . ."

"You healed her, Sevei. You gave her hope. You told her that she'd be the Rí Ard's wife. You said that the Ríthe would do as you said." Kayne would not let her look away. He wanted her to see his face, wanted her to see the pain there, wanted her to *feel* it. He wanted to use his grief as a spear and thrust it into her.

"I don't have an answer for you," she said. Her lips trembled and a tear slid down her cheek. "But I understand how you feel; I saw my love die also and I know how you feel. Kayne, you understand that I never wanted this. Never. If I could have prevented it, or if I'd thought that everything would end this way . . ."

"You weren't there," he shouted at her, and was rewarded with a flinch.

"No, I wasn't. We . . . I didn't know the scope of the betrayal until . . ." Her gaze drifted to the cairn and back. ". . . too late." She stopped, nodding to Beryn and Keira. "Thank you," she said to them. "Thank you for coming to my brother when I couldn't."

"We wish we could have arrived sooner," Keira answered.

"You did more than you had to." She turned back to Kayne. "Kayne, I'm so sorry for your loss. If there was anything I could do to change it, I would. But I can't, and as cold as this seems, I don't have much time to stay here with you," she told them. "I have to leave before the mage-lights fail. I have to go to the Ríthe."

The Ríthe . . . For a moment, he felt the world snap back around him, cold and dark and angry. "I'll go with you," Kayne said grimly. "We'll meet them together."

"No," she told him. "You have to go elsewhere . . ." What she told him then made the darkness close back in around him. He was shattered and broken, his mind reeling. He'd released Blaze despite its hunger.

"Ennis?" he said wonderingly. "He's with the Arruk? And in Talamh An Ghlas?"

"I was there when he was born, and I was the one who took the blue caul from his face," Keira interjected. "I knew then that Ennis was destined for some great fate, but whether for good or ill . . . I didn't tell your mam, but I feared for the worst."

"Aye," Sevei said, as Keira stepped back away from them. "That's why I need you to go back to the Narrows, Kayne—you need to lead the troops that Aunt Edana and Greada are bringing."

Kayne laughed, a dead and hollow sound. It sounded like a stranger's chuckle to his ears. "You go, Sister," he told her. "Take Lámh Shábhála there, where it might do some good. Let *me* go to the Ríthe." In his vision, the stones of the cairn seemed to quiver in the firelight. "I have a score to settle with them, and I no longer care about my life at all. All that matters is that I take Rí Mallaghan, at least, to the Mother with me."

"No." He heard the word, but he ignored it. When she spoke again, there was mage-power in her voice. An unseen hand took his chin and forced him to look at her. She was wreathed in the mage-lights, the scars on her body carved in the radiance. "No," she repeated, her voice booming in several octaves. "I have no experience in war or in command, Kayne; you do. You've fought the Arruk before; you understand them. You need to be the Rí Ard you were intended to be."

Kayne laughed again: the same empty laugh devoid of any humor. Winter's chain rattled in his hand, a dull clanking. "Mam should be the Ard, Sevei, and Da the commander of her army. But they're both dead like Séarlait. A few hands of hands of hands against the full might of the Arruk—that would make a wonderful, heroic song, wouldn't it, Sevei? Only no Daoine will live to sing it."

"You might be right," she told him. "I don't know. But I'm sure that Séarlait wanted you to live for a reason. She was a Fingerlander and you're Inish—both people who know what it means to struggle against the odds. Take Winter with you. The Maestra of the Order will be there, and there will be cloudmages who can use Séarlait's cloch. Or give it to someone else who's worthy of it. We'll need all the Clochs Mór. It's what Séarlait would tell you, also. Listen to her, Kayne. She's there with the Mother, watching you. You can hear her if you try."

"Let me give you this gift . . ." The memory of Séarlait's voice drowned out everything else: Sevei, the chanting of Beryn, the song of the Seanóir deep in the forest. *"Dying doesn't matter, my love. Only how we die . . ."*

At least in dying, he might be with Séarlait again. Still, he hesitated. He saw his sister frown, saw her move the magelights as if they were a rope that bound her. Too late, he realized that she moved the light to him, that she snared both of them together. He fell into the light.

Into her. *"Kayne . . ."* Sevei's voice filled him. Was him. *"I understand. I do . . ."* Memories rushed at him, memories that weren't his but Sevei's, and the emotions she'd felt hammered at him, as if they were his own.

. . . Dillon . . . the sweet taste of his kisses, and his tenderness, and the awful, unforgettable sight of his bloated, drowned body . . . the aching grief and loss that held her for long days afterward . . .

. . . there was Gram, dying on a beach on the Stepping Stones, and Sevei's frustration at not being able to help her, and her fear . . .

. . . the pain of the transformation of the Scrúdú, the agony of her own body, the constant wash of pain that would never, could never be banished . . .

. . . the suffering and torment she felt now, just from holding the power, just from using Lámh Shábhála, like the bite of swords slashing her, the physical pain laid on top of the mental anguish, the grief and loss and self-doubt, all of it combining and recombining and pressing down on her so heavily that it must break her, her very sanity reeling under the constant assault . . .

"I understand," she/he whispered together. "Oh, I understand . . ."

And he found himself alone again. Entirely alone. Kayne was weeping unashamedly, the tears streaking down his face, the sobs racking him. He took a deep, long breath that shuddered with their twinned grief.

"This is not hopeless, Kayne," Sevei said, her own voice choked with her weeping. "Not yet."

He didn't believe her. Looking at her mutilated face, he

knew she didn't believe it herself. "You're hurting already from coming to me," he told her. "And now you'll go to them, and then somewhere else? You can't do this, Sevei. Every time you use the power so fully, you injure yourself more. You won't be able to stand it."

"I can," she told him. She gave a helpless, sobbing laugh. "I must."

He wanted to hold Sevei, wanted to embrace her as he had when they were younger, and he could not—her body wouldn't allow the touch. He could only do as she asked. "How do I get to the Narrows?" he asked. "I can't ride the mage-lights, as you do. Can you send me there?"

It wasn't Sevei who answered, but Keira. "The Bán Cailleach needs her strength elsewhere," she said. Mage-light mingled with ruddy firelight on her face. "Beryn and I will take you. There are other ways, as your mam and da might have told you."

They were all looking at him and mage-light poured down on Sevei. He could see her impatience, her weariness, her pain. "Go," he told her. "Do what you must do."

"I will see you at the Narrows, Kayne," she told him. The tears on her face glittered in mage-light. "If the Mother wills it."

Light erupted and washed over the hillside and the cairn. She was gone.

54

Negotiations with
the Enemies

SHE COULD FEEL Treoraí's Heart in the mage-lights,
cloaked as always, but now she knew it was Ennis who
hid behind the cloch. . . . *So terribly young and yet so powerful* . . . She heard the voices, all of those inside her and especially Gram, marveling at that.

"*. . . born with a blue caul . . .*"

"*. . . What could he have done if he'd held Lámh Shábhála? . . .*"

"*. . . Perhaps it should have been him who was given the
Great Cloch . . .*"

She pushed the thoughts down. She extended Lámh
Shábhála's presence toward the barriers around Treoraí's
Heart: hard, solid, and the color of spilled blood. Sevei
pushed hard at the barrier, using more of Lámh Shábhála's
power than she had before; the walls around Ennis yielded
for a moment, thinning and giving her a momentary
glimpse of the presence behind them: *male, aye, and
young* . . . She caught a whirl of chaotic thoughts, a sense
of—strangely—many presences there, all of them echoes
of Ennis' own mind fluttering in sea-blue hues around him
like salt spray caught in a twisting sea-spout. Somewhere,
far inside, she could hear a boy's voice, a frightened wail,
but it was drowned out by the others.

Then the wall pushed back at her, throwing her away
into the cold brightness of the mage-lights. Sevei rested
there a moment, surprised at the ability within the Heart,
feeling the mage-lights rake her body at the same time
they sustained her, realizing that the effort had exhausted

her more than she'd realized. She wondered whether her mam had known how much power was in the Heart. Almost certainly she had, yet she'd chosen to use that power only for healing.

Not Ennis.

". . . why do you do this, Sevei? It only weakens you for the rest of what you must do . . ."

That was Gram. Weary, Sevei could not ignore her, couldn't push the voice away. "He's my brother, Gram. Your great-son. If I can reach him and make him realize who he's hurting, then perhaps I won't need to do the rest . . ."

"I glimpsed the power in the Heart, when Treoraí gave it to me to use during the Battle of Dún Kiil, so long ago. Yet I didn't realize just how strong it was. I was a fool, Sevei. A fool . . ."

The voice subsided. From inside, from the others, there came the sound of laughter and ironic applause.

Sevei followed the river of light from the sky back to Treoraí's Heart until she floated again before its walls. "Ennis!" she shouted with the power of Lámh Shábhála in her voice, as if shouting up at the ramparts of a citadel. "This is Sevei! Ennis, please! Open yourself to me!"

There was no answer, no change in the blood-hued walls. Insistent, she opened Lámh Shábhála like it was a vessel, letting the mage-lights pour their radiance into it and then funneling it back out again. The few times before that she'd tried to go to the Heart's Holder and been rebuffed, she'd thought it was the Taisteal woman who held it, and she had not persisted. But now she knew it was Ennis, and she took the power and sharpened it, hewed it into a battering ram and hurled it against the walls that held her away from her brother.

The collision nearly broke her. She felt the impact in every bone, in every joint. Sparks exploded where Lámh Shábhála touched the Heart, and she felt their scorching heat pattering on her like a burning rain. She heard a wail from the far side of the wall as well, a boy's cry. In her mage-vision she could see a faint crack in the wall and she threw herself at it, but it was healing itself even as she moved. She plunged Lámh Shábhála's energy into the fissure, clawing at it and forcing it to open.

"Ennis!" She could see him in her mage-vision: a boy, crouching huddled over Treoraí's Heart as if trying to enfold himself in its crystalline depths. His head turned, looking at her. "Ennis, it's Sevei."

"No!" he shouted back at her, his face snarled with rage and disbelief and fear. "You're not. Isibéal says Sevei's dead and you're trying to trick me. You're the White Beast. You're the one who killed Gram and Mam and all the rest so you could have Lámh Shábhála."

"Ennis, that's not true. I know I've changed, but look at me. *Look* at me."

He stared, his face still a rictus. He seemed to be listening to something or someone that she couldn't hear. He hissed, like some animal hiding in shadow. "No," he spat. "You lie." He lifted his hand, and she could see the Heart in his fingers, could see the cloch gathering itself. Captured mage-light lanced from him toward her; she barely managed to deflect the energy in time. Even so, the impact threw her screaming back against the red wall. He was on his feet now, rushing at her, and in the mage-sight he seemed to carry a staff carved with strange symbols that glowed angrily with captured power. She could see him ready to strike her with the staff. "Ennis!" she cried, but he kept advancing. He swung the staff, and she interposed a bolt from Lámh Shábhála. The staff shattered, but she felt the impact as if it had slammed into her own body. The ghosts of the Holders within her marveled.

". . . so powerful . . ."

". . . he's as strong as I was with Lámh Shábhála . . ."

". . . stronger . . ."

She knew then that if she stayed here, she would be forced to use Lámh Shábhála fully, that she would have to hurt or kill Ennis if she were to survive herself and she was already weak from what she'd done this night. He was gathering himself up, the Heart glowing madly in his hand and Sevei fled, forcing herself back through the fissure in the wall even as he flung another attack at her, even as she used yet more of Lámh Shábhála's power to deflect it once again.

The mage-lights were already beginning to dim, and she had much more to do before they were gone. She could not stay.

She retreated, leaving the red wall behind to the sound
of mocking laughter, and she wept again as she traveled
the cold interstices of the mage-lights. Her tears fell like
broken stars.

I have no choice now. No choice at all.

Exhausted already and with a sense of dread futility coloring her thoughts, Sevei turned her back on the Heart and
followed the radiance of the mage-lights, letting her
awareness travel down to each of the clochs. In the mage-
vision, she could see Torin Mallaghan standing with the
others outside a hovel near Lough Tory. His hand was still
upraised to the mage-lights, the Cloch Mór Rogue gleaming through his fingers. Over two double-hands of Riocha
were there with him: nearly a double hand of Cloch Mórs
and a scattering of clochsmion, most in the hands of green-
clad mages of the Order of Gabair. She recognized many
of them: Rí Mac Baoill of Airgialla, Shay O Blaca, others
she had glimpsed at court in Dún Laoghaire over the years.
Elsewhere in the village, there were gardai and troops, several double-hands of them.

She let herself fall into Mallaghan's energy-stream, ma-
terializing behind him before he and the others realized
she was there. Sevei slid her bare forefinger over his throat
as if slashing it with a dagger—with the touch, her finger
felt as if she'd drawn her own skin across the honed edge
of a knife. She leaned close to his ear even as he started to
react. "You'd be dead now, Rí, if I wished it. Remember
that." He spun around as she stepped back from him. She
laughed at the distress and fear on his face, laughed because it had been so easy, laughed because the sound
helped to hold the pain away, laughed because the sound
assuaged the sense of defeat in her.

"*. . . you should have killed him truly . . .*"

"*. . . fool . . .*"

"*. . . never give your enemy an opening, never let them live
when you can kill them . . .*"

Two of the Clochs Mór came alive, one on either side of
her. She felt them, a pressure within the mage-lights, and
she contemptuously threw their own manifestations back

at them without looking at them. Behind her, there were screams, but her gaze stayed on Rí Mallaghan. Other clochs opened, and she let out Lámh Shábhála's power, forming a dark-hued wall around herself, a wall as scarred as her own body, as white as her own flesh. Their attacks battered at the wall—giant creatures; arcing lines of energy; great howling winds; skeletal armies—but though she could feel the blows, she held them away. And she held Rí Mallaghan inside the shell also, as if in a gigantic, unseen fist.

Gram whispered warning. "*... but not forever. You can't do this for long. Look, the mage-lights have faded. You only have the power left within Lámh Shábhála to use ...*"

"I know, Gram. I know," she said, and Rí Mallaghan's face twisted. He looked around as if searching for the person to whom she spoke. "Aye, Mallaghan, Gram wonders why I don't just kill you," she said into his frozen, stricken face. "Did you know that? I hear them all, all the old Holders. Even Gram—who *you* ordered killed, no matter that it was Uncle Doyle who actually did the deed."

"I didn't—" he began, but she could already see the lie in his drawn features and the way his eyes moved away from her, and she choked off his reply, wrapping strands of the Lámh Shábhála's energy around his throat with a wave of her hand. The attacks on the defensive barrier redoubled. She felt Lámh Shábhála draining a bit with each strike. Her body and mind screamed together with the effort of holding it all, of keeping them back.

... too many of them ...

"Don't lie to me," she snapped at Mallaghan, afraid that she was already too weary, that the pain would be unbearable. Each scarred line on her body seemed to have been freshly cut with a dagger. She was surprised that she wasn't bathed in her own blood "Don't you dare. Tell them to release their clochs," she told Mallaghan. "Tell them that if they don't, I'll send you to the Black Haunts and be gone again before they can kill me." She raised her voice, shouting so they could all hear her over the tumult of the clochs. "None of you can hide from me. Go ahead, spend your days together huddled in groups if you like. It doesn't matter. Sooner or later, you'll open your cloch to the mage-lights, and that's when I'll come, just as I did now. I'll come and be gone while you're still sinking to the ground with your lifeblood pouring out of your body. Release your clochs *now* or watch Rí Mallaghan die."

"... they won't ..."

"... they know they are too many for you ..."

But they did. She felt the Clochs Mór close, one by one, and she cautiously let the wall fade, trying not to sigh with relief, trying not show her weakness. She had never felt an agony like this: three passages through the mage-lights in a night, using them to open herself to Kayne, to force her way past Ennis' defenses, and now to hold off so many clochs ...

None of the previous torment had been anything this massive. Her body was awash in molten fire coursing through her scars, her mind crackled and pounded with the power, her eyes were aflame. Every muscle in her body was quivering and she thought that at any moment tendons and ligaments might snap. She was afraid to let go of the wall, afraid to release Mallaghan, afraid that if they came at her again she wouldn't be quick or strong enough, afraid that if she held on for much longer that it wouldn't matter anyway for the pain would entirely overwhelm her. She was afraid that they would see her vulnerability and her torment and know that she lied, know that if they all came at her at once she could not hold them back.

"... they know you're bluffing. They'll guess ..."

"... your pride will kill you ..."

"... you'll be in here with us, ranting at some new Holder ..."

But none of the Riocha moved. "What do you think, Rí?" she crooned to the man in front of her, pretending confidence. "Do you think the Mother would cast me into the hands of the soul-shredders for killing you, or will She instead take me in Her arms for a just vengeance? Gram, Mam, Da, my brother and sister, my marriage-sister—do you think that the Mother might ask them to be *your* soul-shredders? Why, I think She might."

Mallaghan's face was bright red now, his eyes bulging, his mouth wide in a soundless scream, the tendons on his neck standing out. She took a step back from him, so that she was at arm's length. She watched him, watched him struggle to breathe, to try to tear the constricting mage-lights away from his throat. The Riocha were nervous now, and she knew she had only a breath before they would come at her again. "I want to do this," she told him in almost a whisper. "You don't know how much I hunger for it. And maybe one day I will. But not today."

With that, she loosened the noose of mage-lights around his neck enough that he could take a shuddering, choking breath. The color of his face lightened.

"The Arruk have come," she told Rí Mallaghan, told them all. "They're already in the Finger. And because of that, I offer you a truce between us."

"The Arruk?" It wasn't Rí Mallaghan who spoke, still rubbing at his neck, but Morven Mac Baoill, and Sevei could see in his face that the Rí Airgialla didn't want to believe her, knowing that if this were true, it was Tuath Airgialla that would suffer first. "You lie. You lie so that we'll scatter ourselves."

"I tell the truth so that you won't," she told him. "If you doubt me, then have Tiarna O Blaca take himself to Dún Laoghaire and have Edana Mac Ard show him the message she's received, or have him go to the Finger himself and see. The Arruk have left Céile Mhór and come here. Scatter yourselves?" She laughed bitterly. "I want the opposite. I ask each to do this: go to the Narrows. Go there now while you're close, and help us make a stand there with your clochs."

"Stand against the Arruk without first raising our own armies? We need *weeks* to prepare . . . Months . . ." She could see that he wanted to say more, but she let Lámh Shábhála's energy slip into her voice and the hand that she lifted. He went silent.

"You don't have months or even weeks. You have only days and what troops can reach the Narrows in time. Banrion Mac Ard is bringing anyone she can raise, as is Rí MacEagan of Inish Thuaidh."

"Inishlanders?" That was Rí Mallaghan, his voice strained and cracked. "The Inish will come to plunder the Tuatha, not to save them."

"*. . . You see . . .*"

"*. . . You should have killed him . . .*"

"*. . . They won't believe you . . .*"

"Be quiet!" She was speaking to the voices and not Mallaghan, but he closed his mouth. Her shout pounded in her head, like a hammer against her skull: *be quiet . . . be quiet . . . quiet . . .* She could not stay here much longer. She had to go, had to go where she could give in to the torment that was going to be her payment for tonight and not have them on her like wolves on a downed doe. Sevei's vision seemed to be narrowing. She could see only Rí Mallaghan's face in front of her, as if she peered down a long corridor toward him. "Believe what you will," she said. "Go to your homes and wait, then. I tell you this: if you go to your homes and we win at the Narrows, then I *will* come to you afterward, and I'll give each of you the proper payment for your cowardice. If you go to your homes and we lose at the Narrows, then it won't be me who comes but the Arruk, and you won't have the gardai or the clochs to hold them back. Either way, you will still have your payment for your cowardice and stupidity."

Her vision contracted even farther. She could see only Mallaghan's eyes, the gold flecks like fallen leaves on the brown, suspicious earth of his pupils. Lámh Shábhála was a wild creature trapped in the cage of her ribs and tearing at them to get out. Her body trembled and her knees threatened to give way.

"Look at her," she heard Mac Baoill say to the others and she knew they saw it also. "Look . . ."

"You must go to the Narrows," she told them all desperately. "Not for me. For yourselves, your families, your people, and your land."

She could feel their doubt. She could sense them waiting, their hands close to their clochs. Sevei opened her own hands, letting them see the green gem in its fury inside her, glowing amidst the network of scars. "You *must* do this," she said, and her voice was only a whisper.

She didn't know if they heard. Didn't know if they would obey or ignore her. She could feel her vision darkening, her world narrowing as if she were looking through a rolled-up parchment. The muscles in her back and legs tightened and knotted. She put a fist to her chest above Lámh Shábhála, gathered what was left of its energy and prepared to leave.

They struck then, all of them at one time, a massive concerted attack that broke through the defenses she hastily erected and sent the shattered remnants of Lámh Shábhála's energy into bright shards that lanced through her. Sevei screamed, a despairing, lost wail. She could feel the clochs gathering themselves again, and she plunged her awareness deep into the nearly-empty Lámh Shábhála, scrabbling for some tithe of power, some forgotten pool within it. There . . . there was a glimmer, and she sent her mind rushing toward it, taking it into her and willing herself to be gone, to be anywhere but here.

And at the same time, Rí Mallaghan and the others came at her a last time and the impact of their attack sent her spinning away.

55

A Meeting of Friends

"WHAT IS BOTHERING you, Ennis Svarti?" Cima asked.

Their litter was lurching and bucking, tilted at an uncomfortable angle that pressed Ennis back into Cima's hard-scaled and smelly body at the rear of the carrier. The road was rising steeply toward the high pass that marked the end of the Finger, and the footing was treacherous. The Arruk army filled the road as well as the passable ground to either side, stretched out for miles from vanguard to rear. Behind them was smoke and ruin and destruction, and not a few Arruk bodies. What villages they'd found had been abandoned and left with their gates open well before they'd arrived, though Kurhv Kralj had ordered them torched anyway. The Fingerlanders had made them pay for every step along the way. As they had ever since they entered the Finger, the Arruk had endured nearly constant ambushes and skirmishes all along their flanks: sudden flights of arrows or a rush of armed men from concealed places. The Fingerlanders struck and then melted back into the landscape from which they'd emerged. The Arruk had lost perhaps a fifth of their forces over the days it had taken them to slog along the seemingly endless road twisting crazily through the Finger. In the last day, however, the attacks had ended as they began the ascent toward the Narrows.

And last night, the White Beast had attacked Ennis as the mage-lights flared above. Since then, Ennis had been unable to shake off a sense of dread. The blue ghost of himself sat in the litter with him, stoic and confident, and did nothing. He could not match that expression, couldn't feel it.

"What is it, Ennis Svarti?" Cima asked again. "Don't think of the White Beast. You're stronger than it. You are."

"The White Beast will be there," Ennis muttered. "When the Tuatha army comes, she'll be there."

"And you'll defeat her," Cima answered, his voice full of confidence that Ennis didn't share. "You have the sky-stone and your spell-stick, and you have Kurhv Kralj's army with you. These Perakli will be no different than the other ones we've met, and we'll cut through them until we reach Cudak Zvati and Cudak rewards us with our own sky-stones." The litter lurched again as one of the bearers stumbled, and Cima leaned out through the curtains to snarl at them in quick Arruk. "The bluntclaws will continue to run from us, like the cowards they are—all except you, Ennis Svarti. You're as brave as any Arruk and more skilled than any of our Svarti, and I'm proud that Kurhv Kralj has allowed me to serve you."

The blue ghost sat unmoving, but Ennis allowed himself a brief smile. He patted Cima on the shoulder. "I'm glad you're here, also, Cima. You . . ." He stopped, not quite knowing what to say. Without Cima, he would be totally alone here. Even Kurhv Kralj treated Ennis as if he were somehow diseased; the other Arruk might fear him, but fear was the only thing that kept them from showing their disgust toward him and his kind. Only Cima acted as if he truly were Ennis' friend. That may have been because Cima had been treated much the same way as Ennis, but it didn't matter.

Do you really want to go where the blue ghosts will take you? Do you really want to sit on the Arruk throne: where you will rule only because of their fear, where you will have no friends?

Ennis grimaced. The litter tilted and straightened again, and this time Ennis pushed back the curtains. Ahead of them, through a rainy mist, he could see the heads of the Arruk army marching through the broken landscape. Close by was Kurhv Kralj's litter, and scattered ahead the litters of the various Mairki and their Svarti. Grayed by mist, the double peaks of the Narrows loomed in the middle distance, and there was nothing beyond them: no more distant peaks. It was as if the world ended there.

And there were blue ghosts everywhere. Ennis had never seen so many of them: the land swirling with possibilities and futures. He could barely see through their furious, chaotic movement. He saw himself hands upon hands of times, saw Cima and Kurhv Kralj, saw the Arruk and the gardai of the Daoine embroiled in battle, saw the Svarti's spell-sticks arrayed against the clochs na thintrí of the Riocha.

Saw the White Beast. She was there also, far too often.

Ennis gasped and fell back onto the litter's cushions. "What is it, Ennis Svarti?" Cima asked for the third time, alarmed now.

"She's a liar. She's not your sister Sevei. She's a danger to you, and you must kill her. That's what the blue ghosts are telling you."

"I know, Isibéal," Ennis said. "But what does Mam say? Mam would know. Let her talk to me."

"She's a liar . . ."

"What?" Cima asked, and Ennis shivered.

"There's a battle coming," Ennis told him. "A bad one. I can see it."

Cima's eyes blinked—the sideways eyelid movement of the Arruk. "We should tell Kurhv Kralj." He pushed aside the curtains, shouting at the bearers of both their litter and Kurhv Kralj's. As the bearers halted and set down the litter, Cima leaned close to Ennis. "You don't need to look so concerned, Ennis Svarti," he said. "I'll stay with you. I'll always stay with you. If the White Beast wants to hurt you, she will have to first kill me."

The blue ghost in which he had wrapped himself did nothing but nod and stare straight ahead. But Ennis forced himself to break away. He hugged Cima, surprising the Arruk. "Your eyes are leaking again, Ennis Svarti," the Arruk told him. Ennis sniffed and dragged a sleeve over his eyes. He found the blue ghost again, sliding down from the litter onto the ground and walking toward Kurhv Kralj's litter. The blue ghost was already fading, nearly lost among the welter of futures here. Ennis hurried to catch up to it.

"Hurry," he told Cima as he slipped into the pattern. "It's nearly time."

Carrohkai Treemaster sang under the oaks in the night, her voice lifted in the windlike melody of the Seanóir. They were answering her, calling out to her in the leaf-cloaked darkness of the forest, their low, earthy voices swaying the boughs above her. She stopped her singing then. Her head lifted as if she were sniffing the air and she turned. The moon lifted above the trees to the east, rising swiftly enough that Sevei could track the movement.

"*Tráthnóna maith duit,* Sevei," Carrohkai said.

The Bunús Muintir's hair was white, her body—like Sevei's, naked to the world—was covered with the same scars, though her body was heavier and wider and her face broader. Her eyes held night, and her smile was tinged with sadness.

"How did I come here?" Sevei asked, and Carrohkai shrugged.

"You're not here. Not really. Nor am I. Or perhaps you are. It's difficult to tell."

"Am I dead?"

"Perhaps. Sometimes that's also difficult to know." Carrohkai touched the stone between her breasts. As with Sevei, there was a glow there underneath the skin that was undeniably Lámh Shábhála, so like that of her stone that Sevei's hand went to her own body. The gem was still there: She could see the emerald gleam on her fingertips, a twin to that illuminating Carrohkai. Sevei gave a breath of relief, though she knew that Lámh Shábhála couldn't have been taken from her without her knowledge—no Holder could ever lose Lámh Shábhála without suffering. Carrohkai was staring at Sevei with the same fascination.

"I remember being here and doing this," Carrohkai said, "and yet I also know the rest of my life . . . and I know you. So *I'm* dead, at least." She gave a sigh. "You've come to me. What can I teach you that you don't already know or that Issine hasn't said to you?" she asked.

"How did you bear it?" Sevei asked. "After you passed

the Scrúdú, how did you manage to keep living through the pain?"

"I didn't live long," Carrohkai answered. "None of us do. The truth is that the Scrúdú kills all of us who attempt it. It just leaves a few alive for a bit first."

"Then what am I supposed to do? What good is the Scrúdú if those who pass the test have so little time?"

"Aye," another voice intruded, a familiar one to Sevei. "Answer that for both of us." Jenna—Gram—came walking through the trees toward them, dressed in the royal clóca of Inish Thuaidh, with the torc of Dún Kiil and the chain of Lámh Shábhála both around her neck. Her face was wrinkled and old, but seemed to be without the additional creases of pain that had eroded its features for as long as Sevei could remember. Sevei found that she wasn't at all startled to see Gram here. Her appearance seemed natural. "Tell us why our family has endured this burden for so long. Tell us why we and so many others suffered."

Carrohkai seemed to be listening to the songs of the trees more than to Gram or Sevei. There were no magelights here in this night, and the moon raced across the summit of the sky toward the west, while the eastern sky was already brightening with dawn, masking the stars. The curve of the sun brightened the eastern sky. "There's always a price for power."

"I didn't *want* the power," Gram said vehemently. Sunlight touched her face and she shaded her eyes. "I never asked for it. Neither did Sevei."

Carrohkai turned to regard them calmly, serenely. "You may not have asked for it, Jenna Aoire, but when the power called you, you took it. And you, Sevei—you wanted it also, or Bhralhg would not have given you the stone. You wanted it. Both of you. As I did."

"What did you do with it?" Sevei asked.

Carrohkai laughed, and the Seanóir's song rose with a rising wind. The sun was already at zenith and beginning to fall, their shadows moving visibly on the ground. Two shadows: Sevei looked around, but Gram had vanished.

"I did very little, if you listen to those who lived when I did or came after," Carrohkai said as Sevei glanced around to see where Gram might have gone. "I heard the life within the Seanóir and I brought them to Awareness. I allowed them to see the mage-lights and use them for themselves. My peers, those who held the other clochs, all said I wasted Lámh Shábhála and the test of the Scrúdú and my life. I helped Others when I could have done more for the Bunús. They called me a failure. They called me a traitor. They said I had no loyalty to my own. They said that a traitor is always a hero to the other side, and so they called me 'Treemaster' and the 'Hero of the Oaks,' and their titles were a mockery. They ridiculed me, they said they were glad that I was in pain and would die soon, because someone more worthy would take Lámh Shábhála from me when I died."

"I'm sorry," Sevei said.

"Don't be," the Bunús Muintir answered. Carrohkai inclined her head, listening to the Seanóir's lament as the sun began to set and the first stars emerged. "When you Daoine came to Talamh an Ghlas, long after the mage-lights had failed, and many generations of Holders after I died, the Seanóir were alive and half-awake there in the deep woods, and they protected us because of what I'd done for them. They gave my people a refuge where we could stay and survive. The Bunús would all be gone now, if the Seanóir had not been made Aware."

The first mage-lights slid between the stars: too bright and too fast. Reflexively, Sevei touched Lámh Shábhála; Carrohkai echoed the gesture.

". . . *none of what she says matters . . .*" It was Gram's voice, in her head now as it had been since her death, caught in Lámh Shábhála. ". . . *your family and your people are what is truly important. They need you now. You must think of them . . .*"

The mage-lights brightened, so intense that they blotted out the landscape. Their fire flickered behind the landscape, as if she were looking at a funeral pyre though a painting on thin paper. The sheets and curtains of bright colors moved through and around Carrohkai and the forest, and the singing of the Seanóir was the crackling of the mage-energy in her ears.

". . . *we never see the consequences of our lives,*" Carrohkai said, her voice, like Gram's, in Sevei's head. She seemed to be admonishing both of them, gently, with the sound of a quiet smile in her voice. Sevei could see only the stars and the mage-lights now, and a surge of pain made her cry out, made her fall and pull her body into a tight fetal curl. "... *only those who come long after can truly judge us* ..."

The intensity of the pain ratcheted higher and Sevei moaned, clutching herself and screaming, screaming so loudly that she barely heard Carrohkai finish.

"... *and even they may have it wrong* ..."

Sevei groaned. Something moved near her, but she kept her eyes pressed shut against the hammer blows inside her head and the fire that burned her skin.

"This time I come on my own, Soft-flesh," she heard a voice say.

56

Maneuverings and a Skirmish

"WHAT DO WE DO now, Mam?"
Padraic paced as Edana watched, not wanting to show her impatience. The army—less than a thousand hastily assembled gardai and soldiers with a bare handful of Riocha and céili giallnai among them—crowded in the narrow canyon between the cliff walls of the Narrows. There had been a battle in this place already: there were unburied corpses here and there, the bodies picked over by the crows, wild dogs, and other scavengers. The stench of their rot had made Edana drape a perfumed cloth over her face. The corpses wore the colors of Airgialla, and the conflict seemed to have torn the very stones from the cliff walls of the Narrows. The road was blocked here, and it seemed as good a place to stop as any.

As the Hands of the army supervised the creation of an encampment upwind of the carnage, Edana watched Padraic pace. "This is where Sevei wanted us to come. She'll be here."

"It's been days since we saw her. She should be here already." Padraic shivered under his woolen clóca. "This place is haunted. This whole land is haunted—there was that siog mist that went past us two days ago, and some of the gardai swear they saw a dragon circling the Narrows yesterday as we were climbing up from Lough Tory . . ." He scuffed at the ground, glaring at the rocks as if they might be Créneach waiting to rise up and attack him.

"She'll come."

"And if she doesn't?"

"Then we fight the Arruk alone." The voice, deep and weary, was a new one, startling both Padraic and Edana. A man approached them from the rocks to the east. He was filthy and bedraggled, he limped as if injured, but there was something about his bearing and his face, and on his breast a ruby stone gleamed. Several of the gardai noticed him at the same time: seeing him so close to Edana and Padraic, they started toward him and unsheathed swords; an archer picked up his bow and nocked an arrow—but Edana waved them away.

"Kayne!" Edana said. "Praise the Mother! You *are* alive."

"*Dia daoibh,* Aunt Edana, Padraic. Well met at last. It's been a long time, Aunt . . ."

"You're hurt," Edana said, and Kayne gave her a smile that dissolved in the next moment.

"Aye, that I am, and in worse ways than you can see, Aunt. But we've no time to worry about that. Who's in charge here?"

"I am," Edana answered. "And Padraic." Edana saw Kayne's gaze—hard and coldly appraising—go to Padraic.

"I'm sorry about your da," he said to Padraic before his attention moved back to Edana, "and your husband, Aunt. If not for him, I'd be dead. I didn't trust Uncle Doyle, to be honest, but in the end . . ." He stopped. "There'll be time to speak of him later, perhaps. For now, I'd ask you to come with me."

He turned and walked away up the slope toward the very summit of the pass, Edana and Padraic following him through the tumbled landscape. Several gardai started to escort them; again, Edana waved them away. They walked for nearly a quarter-stripe, silently, before Kayne paused and motioned to them. Edana came alongside him. From their vantage point, they looked down along the mountain-spiked expanse of the Finger, and below them the High Road twisted and turned as it descended into a deep valley.

Edana gasped, her hand flying involuntarily to Demon-Caller at her breast. A dark, seething mass crawled along the High Road and well to either side of it, a huge and long gathering. At this distance, she could just begin to make out the individual creatures at the head of the column, and see their flags and the litters of their officers bobbing among them. Faintly, she could hear the slow, insistent beat of drums, pounding out the cadence of their march.

"I never thought . . ." she began. She looked at Padraic and then at Kayne, stricken. "There are so many of them."

"This is hopeless," Padraic said firmly. "Even with a double-hand or more of Clochs Mór, we wouldn't be able to stand against that. We need more time. We need to get the Ríthe to send all their armies."

"There is no time," Kayne told them. "And once the Arruk are through the Narrows, there *will* be no stopping them. They'll do to us what they did in Céile Mhór. But if we stand here, if we can take three or four Arruk for every Daoine life, then perhaps we'll have weakened them enough that the Tuatha *can* defeat the rest, even though we leave our bones here. The Fingerlander army, such as it is, is here, too—Rodhlann O Morchoe commands them, and he has them stationed farther down the pass." Kayne looked back from the advancing force to Edana and Padraic. "What are your battle plans?" he asked. "Where are you going to place the troops? We'll want to retain the advantage of height and use the land. There are ledges where archers can hide, and a canyon up near the Narrows where cavalry might be able to make a flanking attack . . ."

Edana felt more than saw Padraic shaking his head at her side. "The tiarna captains are meeting this evening . . ." he began, but Edana interrupted her son.

"You were to be the Rí Ard," she told Kayne. "That's what was promised to you by the Ríthe in the Tuatha Halla. I was there, and I heard them give their oath to Sevei—an oath that they've broken, but an oath proclaimed before the Mother nonetheless. I say that you are Ard. *Be* the Ard here, Kayne. You have experience none of us here have. You've fought in the Finger, and you've fought the Arruk. I give you command of our troops."

"Mam," Padraic began angrily, and she lifted a finger to him, a gesture she hadn't made since he'd been a child.

"No," she told him, her voice rising to meet his. "You're a cloudmage, Padraic, not a warrior. So am I. Kayne is both. He can give us what little chance of victory we have. I am Banrion, this is my army that I've brought here, and I say now that Kayne is my commander."

Padraic turned away, snapping his mouth shut. She saw Kayne watching him, his battered and bruised face cocked to one side. "There's no chance of victory here, Aunt Edana," he said to her. "You need to understand that. We don't fight here to win ourselves. We fight so there's the chance of making victory possible for someone else."

"Then that will have to do," she told him.

He nodded. "Then my first order is that you leave, Aunt Edana. Go back to Dún Laoghaire. You can speak to the Ríthe. You can begin to gather the armies of the Tuatha together, all of them, to be ready when the rest of the Arruk come spilling down from the mountains. Padraic can go with you or he can stay here, but if he stays . . ."

He didn't need to finish the statement. She knew. "We stay," she said. "Both of us."

"Didn't you hear me?" Kayne asked. He pointed down into the valley. "Didn't you look down there? I *know* these Arruk, Aunt. They'll keep crawling toward you with hatred in their eyes even when their entrails are dragging behind on the ground. They'll strike at you with their last breath. They have Svarti, spell-casters whose skill with the slow magics is as good as any cloudmage from either Inishfeirm or Gabair. No, they don't have the power of the clochs, but their spells are all ones of destruction. Their war drums will deafen you and send their blood to boiling and they'll come at you in their thousands. They kill those who fall— their own or ours. They won't take prisoners." He stopped, his chest heaving, and Edana wondered if he were remembering the battles he'd been in with his da. "And there's worse," he said.

"I know," Edana told him. "Ennis is with them, holding Treoraí's Heart. Sevei told us. We know what he did at Bunús Gate, and at Ceangail and the other towns."

Kayne nodded once, miserably. He was glaring down at the Arruk as if he could crush them with his gaze.

"We can turn Ennis, Kayne," Edana told him, soothingly. "He doesn't know what he's doing, or he's confused. He couldn't strike at his own brother and sister. By the Mother, Ennis is still just a child . . ."

"I hope you're right." He looked over his shoulder at them. "Stay, or not. I won't blame you, either way."

"Dying doesn't frighten you?" she asked, and Kayne shook his head, finally turning his back to the Arruk.

"No longer. The one I most want to be with has already gone to the Mother. Why should I fear going to her again?" The side of his mouth lifted in what might have been a smile.

"I understand," she told him gently. "And we'll stay." She glanced back at Padraic. He stared at her but said nothing. "Tell us what we need to do, Rí Ard Geraghty."

Ennis felt panic. Blue ghosts swirled around him, thick and dark, and he hoped that he'd aligned himself with the one whose future held the throne. He was no longer certain. The air was thick with patterns and possibilities, and he was confused by them.

The Arruk army was still advancing, but more slowly now, and Kurhv Kralj—after Ennis' warning of an impending battle—had sent scouts out well in advance of the main force. As the road lifted higher, cliffs rose on either side of them: steep, broken crags with brush and wind-stunted trees clinging precariously to the fissures. They were hungry, the Arruk—for two days now, there had been no herds of sheep or pigs to slaughter, no towns or farm, only the unrelenting path upward. The Arruk clogged the road as the space between the cliffs narrowed, stretching out the Arruk line.

The blue ghosts were agitated, all of them. They flitted around him, shapes of himself and Cima and Kurhv Kralj, and among them Daoine Riocha in clóca and léine, with Clochs Mór on their chests and riding battle steeds, and gardai with bright swords and spears. They all crowded around Ennis on all sides, howling and screaming and overlaying his own sight so that he blinked into the wind as if to clear his eyes.

"*Soon,*" Isibéal crooned in his head as he stroked Treoraí's Heart nervously. "*Soon,*" all the other voices in his head whispered also.

"Soon," Ennis echoed, and Cima grunted near him, peering out the litter's sides, the curtains now tied back all around.

"The battle comes," Cima agreed. "Even I can feel it now. Here, Ennis Svarti. You'll be wanting this." He slid Ennis' spell-stick along the cushions with the fang-laden grimace that was an Arruk smile. "And I'll stay with you, as I promised," he added. "You shouldn't worry. I'll bear you into battle as I did before. I'll be your legs and your jaka and your voice for as long as you need me."

The blue ghost to which he was locked nodded, forcing Ennis' head up and down. "Soon," he repeated. It seemed to be the only word he had left. "Soon." A single syllable, sounding like the drumbeats that pounded outside the litter as the Arruk marched.

A horn blew, calling the advance scouts back to the Kralj for a report. The Kralj's litter, with Ennis' following, was still moving forward though more slowly now as the pass narrowed. Long breaths passed as they were jostled and rocked forward, the call horns sounding between every drumbeat, their brassy shriek ringing from the rock walls. The scouts could not have failed to hear them, yet none of them returned. Ennis saw Kurhv Kralj turn in his litter, looking back at them. He seemed eager and happy, already grasping his weapon in his hand.

"They're up there, the bluntclaws," he said. "As you said. They've slain our scouts and now they wait for us." He gestured to the bearers and they set the litter down, Ennis' bearers doing the same. The Mairki and their Svarti came scurrying over. Kurhv Kralj pounded the pole end of his jaka into the ground. "Good," he grunted. "It's about time the Perakli showed some courage. Let them come. Forward!" he shouted to the Mairki, and they went running back to their charges.

The drums began pounding out an urgent, insistent cadence, and the Arruk army began moving forward again, more quickly this time. The blue ghosts all shivered in response to the beating of the drums, their forms shattering and reforming again and again. Ennis could barely see for the chaos as he climbed on Cima's shoulder and followed at Kurhv Kralj's left shoulder. Ahead, the walls of the canyon came within a double-hand of strides, the narrow gap made even smaller by piles of boulders and huge rocks. Beyond the opening, the pass opened up into a grassy verge and the ground leveled out before resuming the climb to the top of the Narrows Pass, still well up ahead. The Arruk surged through the gap like water foaming and roaring through a steep rapids. The drums pushed them; those behind pushed them; the thought of the battle ahead pushed them. Ennis clung to Cima and to the blue ghost of his throne vision, equally.

The Kurhv Kralj and Ennis were still well back from the mouth of the gap when the attack finally came.

There was the shower of sudden arrows, like a deadly cloudburst above them, the feathered shafts descending in arcing flocks—the type of ambush they'd dealt with all through the Finger. This attack was directed toward the Arruk at the opening of the gap, evidently intended to block the road with the Arruk's own dead. Several of the minor Svarti had placed warding spells in their spell-sticks—Ennis heard them shouting the release words and at least half of the arrows erupted into flame, the wooden shafts going to quick ash and the arrowheads pattering among them like hard rain. Those Arruk who were unlucky enough to go down were quickly trampled underneath. Ennis felt Cima rise slightly as one foot stepped on a fallen soldier. Kurhv Kralj, the Mairki and their Ruka, the Ured and Nista all screamed challenge at the canyon walls around them. "Come and fight!" they bellowed, clashing jaka shafts on chest scales. "Come meet our blades."

All through the Finger, their constant challenges to their hidden assailants had met with no response. But this time there came an answer.

A trumpet blast sounded far up the pass, and above the heads of the Arruk and through the opening, Ennis could see a line of horse-mounted gardai in leather and rings under their clóca—clóca, he saw, that were primarily the gray of Dún Laoghaire. Memories flooded him with the sight—*Da and Kayne clad in the same color, the gardai with them a sea of gray as they rode out to Céile Mhór to fight the very creatures that Ennis now marched with; Mam wrapped in a soft clóca of the same color with the torc of Dún Laoghaire around her neck, and enfolding him in the fabric as she hugged him* . . . Ennis cried out even though the blue ghost sat silent on Cima's shoulder. "Are you hurt, Ennis Svarti?" he heard Cima call out below him.

The blue ghost was silent, as if it hadn't heard, but Ennis

forced himself out of the pattern to answer. "I'm fine, Cima," Ennis said. "I see . . . I see the bluntclaw horsemen coming."

Cima growled, and Ennis could feel the rumble through his legs.

No more than a few hundred of the Arruk had spilled through the gap into the high meadow. Ennis saw the Daoine gardai wheel their horses and strike the Arruk in a long crescent. Kurhv Kralj, along with Cima and Ennis, were jostled in the crush as Arruk pushed from behind while the Daoine attack halted the Arruk advance. Kurhv Kralj howled orders to the war drummers. The beat changed, becoming insistent and driving, but the Mairki couldn't respond. There was no way through the gap, and now Ennis saw a new barrage of arrows coming down on the Arruk pressed together helplessly at the opening. He could no longer see the battle in the meadow ahead of him, only hear the screams of Arruk, Daoine, and warhorses alike. Ennis grasped at Treoraí's Heart; through it, he could feel Clochs Mór—at least two of them—open in the meadow, and the sound of false thunder came to his ears. The sound of the Arruk shouting changed: there was desperation now in the cries that came from the battle beyond the gap. Kurhv Kralj continued to scream orders; the arrows from the hidden archers poured down on them, many still consumed by spell-fire as the Svarti countered, but too many now striking their targets. An Arruk next to Cima and Ennis grunted as an arrow found skin between the bright orange scales of his chest. Blood spurted from a torn artery, but the Arruk couldn't even fall, pressed too tightly against Cima and others of his kind. The pressure was intense; Ennis' legs were trapped, and he could feel the push not only from the back, but from the front as the Arruk were forced back through the gap by the Daoine charge.

The battlefield was also crowded with blue ghosts. Ennis was no longer sure which was his, but he clung to the one he'd chosen as tightly as he clung to Cima.

"Ennis Svarti!" Ennis and the blue ghost turned their heads at the same time. Kurhv Kralj pointed ahead to the gap. He continued to shout instructions in the Arruk tongue, none of which Ennis understood, but his intention was clear. The blue ghost certainly understood, for it grasped his spell-stick and Treoraí's Heart at the same time, and Ennis did the same. The power came rushing out from the Heart, making Ennis gasp with its cold heat. He pointed the spell-stick at the boulders and rocks at one end of the opening to the meadow, letting the mage-power gather in his mind. In a burst, he released it through the spell-stick, releasing several of the spells he'd stored there.

The eruption of light sent afterimages dancing in everyone's vision. Rocks and dust and broken Arruk bodies cascaded forward a hundred strides into the meadow beyond. For a moment, the world halted, the noise of the battle beyond made insignificant as everyone's attention went to the pall of dust rising from the northern side of the canyon. The blue ghost laughed, and Ennis laughed with it—he didn't know how many of his own army he'd just killed, but it didn't matter; they were only soldiers, after all, and death was their eventual fate anyway.

The blue ghost continued to chortle, and Ennis pointed with it to the newly-widened opening. "There, my Kralj!" he cried, and Cima called out the translation. "Forward!"

Ennis prodded Cima as if he were a mount, and Cima pushed forward with Kurhv Kralj, and the Arruk poured through the rent toward the battle line beyond.

"Hold!" Kayne shouted to the mounted gardai. They could see the Arruk beginning to push through the gap into the high meadow that marked the start of the final climb to the Narrows. They'd spent the day and much mage-energy making the gap as small as possible. Rodhlann had placed Fingerlander archers all along where they placed the barricade, who were pouring deadly fire down into the Arruk force. No more than a double-hand of Arruk could move along the High Road abreast. Already there were a hundred or more of the creatures spilling out onto the plateau.

"Kayne?" Padraic asked alongside him. The young man still wore the perpetual scowl that he'd borne since Kayne had appeared, and Kayne still wasn't certain if Padraic would follow him if there was a need. "Why are we waiting? If many more get through . . ."

"I know." Kayne glanced at the line of Riocha and gardai astride all the warhorses. They were but a few hundred themselves, the rest of the force still waiting up at the Narrows. Kayne had no illusion that they would stop the Arruk here—if the Bunús Wall could not keep them out, then this hastily-constructed barrier would hardly suffice. All he hoped to do was to make them pay, and then try to stop them at the top of the Narrows, where the rest of the Daoine force waited with Banrion Edana and Rodhlann: two Clochs Mór in case their own fell here. Kayne had given Rodhlann Winter: *"Séarlait would have wanted a Fingerlander to have this, and she thought much of your courage,"* he'd told the man, but it still hurt to see her Cloch Mór around someone else's neck.

But their few Clochs Mór wouldn't be enough. Maybe, maybe they could delay the Arruk enough that Sevei would arrive with Lámh Shábhála, or the Ríthe might come with more troops, or the Inishlanders might arrive. Maybe. But Kayne expected none of those maybes to come to pass. He told himself that he didn't care. He told himself that if he fell here, at least he would be with Séarlait again.

Padraic stirred impatiently next to him. Though Padraic was but a year younger, Kayne felt much older. Padraic still seemed to be a youth: inexperienced, convinced of his own immortality, far too eager to prove himself in this battle.

The way you were yourself, a bare few moons ago . . .

Kayne grimaced and rose up, waving the banner of Dún Laoghaire so that all down the line could see. "Now!" he shouted. "Make them pay for every stride they take!" He gave the war cry of the Inish—the *caointeoireacht na cogadh*—and dug his heels into his horse. The stallion neighed and burst into a gallop as Kayne took Blaze in his hand. His cry was echoed down the line on either side, and the line charged as one, the turf tearing under their hooves as they bore down on the Arruk, who shouted challenge and waved their long-bladed weapons at them, snarling.

Kayne released a burst from Blaze just before the lines met, and Padraic did the same with Snarl. Red lightning flared and blue energy snarled: Kayne had to admire Padraic's skill as a cloudmage, for just as the first riders struck the Arruk, the Clochs Mór sent the first rows of Arruk hurtling backward. The impact of the Daoine riders against the Arruk was like stone striking stone. In the next breath, Kayne was lost in the chaos of battle, using Blaze as if it were a massive sword wielded by a demigod, casting bolts down on the Arruk before him, clearing a space around him and striking down the Arruk who leaped at him from all sides. Around him, he heard the familiar chaos of battle. He could smell the blood, hear the shouts and cries and screams. Where he and Padraic rode, in the center of the curving line of riders, they were already pushing the Arruk back, only the dead left behind them. The Arruk advance broke on the Daoine line and began to give way. Kayne had already advanced far enough to see the gap and the pile of arrow-adorned bodies there, the Arruk boiling around them like mad ants storming from their hole.

"We should have the rest of the army here!" Padraic shouted to Kayne. The young man's eyes were wide with the excitement of the battle, his nostrils flared. Blood spattered the hem of his clóca. He sent another blast from Snarl through the Arruk, and a hand of them screamed and went down. Horses trampled them underneath. "We could hold them! We could take them!"

"No!" Kayne shouted back. "Be ready to fall back."

Padraic shook his head. "Why? We can hold . . ."

It happened then. Kayne felt the power a breath before it erupted: a sense of a presence rising, rising; a gathering of energy that was eerily similar to the pull of Lámh Sháb-hála. Then, before Kayne could react or warn the others, the entire north side of the gap erupted outward. Boulders the size of cottages shot backward into the meadow, crushing the unlucky Daoine riders who were nearest, but killing far more of the Arruk. For a few moments, the battle halted as Daoine and Arruk alike turned to stare at the billowing, ugly cloud that lifted from the gap. Then there was a roar of a thousand throats from beyond the gap and the Arruk started to pour through, hands upon countless hands of them with their jaka waving. The Svarti howled their chants, and now lightning flickered in the dusty pall, and Daoine gave cries of horror as rider and horse alike were broken and torn and cast down. For an instant, most of the Daoine riders were free of their Arruk attackers, but it would not last. It could not last. The Arruk who had fallen back turned again, and their jaka hissed as they cut air.

·

"Retreat!" Kayne shouted. "Now! Give way, give way! Back to the Narrows!"

The call was relayed down the line, and the riders turned their horses as the Fingerlander archers sent more arrows down from their ledges, hoping to give the riders in the valley time before they themselves retreated. Kayne turned his horse as well, but Padraic had not moved. One of the Daoine riders had been hurled backward as the crude barrier was breached, landing nearly at Padraic's feet with his spine broken so that that man lay curled backward impossibly, the corpse's mouth open in a soundless cry. Padraic was staring at the dead man.

"Padraic!" Kayne shouted again, but now he could feel that presence emerging, coming closer. Through the dust, the Arruk charged, and with them was a boy riding on the shoulders of one of the Arruk, very near the banner of the Kralj. Kayne clenched his fist around Blaze and sent a bolt arcing toward the Kralj, but the Heart was aware and the energy fizzled and failed before it reached the Kralj, smashed down and diffused. Kayne peered through the fog of dirt. *Ennis? Is it really him?* He could see the child, but not clearly enough. In his mage-vision, the Heart was a throbbing brightness and the Holder of the stone was cloaked in it, his features unseen. "Ennis!" Kayne shouted to him. "Ennis, it's Kayne!"

There was no answer, or rather the answer that came was sobering. The brightness that was the Heart became even more brilliant, a pulse of light that made Kayne raise his hand to his eyes even though the glare was only in his mind. He heard a guttural chanting, and then the light rushed outward. Kayne brought up a wall of crimson energy, knowing that he could not stop the assault but only hoping to deflect it. Padraic had lifted his head to look also, but tardily. To the side of his vision, Kayne saw Padraic start to respond with Snarl, but he was already late.

The wave of light hit Kayne like a storm-driven tidal wave; Blaze's shield blunted the worst of it, but the force still nearly tore him from his mount, and the heat of it made him gasp. A double-hand or more of the Daoine horses around him went down as well, and the Arruk rushed forward to kill the fallen riders. There was a cry near him, and Padraic went down also, his horse falling with him as Padraic shrieked with the weight of the beast on his leg. The horse rolled off him and Padraic tried to get to his feet, but immediately fell back down. Kayne could see that Padraic's leg was broken. The Arruk were swarming toward the green-clad youth.

Kayne's gaze met his, and saw in Padraic's eyes the realization that he was about to die. Kayne sent fireballs arcing out from Blaze to slay the nearest Arruk to Padraic, but there was little energy left in Blaze now. Padraic shook his head. "Go!" he shouted at Kayne. "Here—"

Padraic did something that Kayne didn't know that he could do himself. The cloudmage tore the chain of Snarl from around his neck and flung it toward Kayne. Ennis and his Arruk-mount were striding through the gap, and Kayne could feel his brother gathering energy again. "Go!" Padraic said. His face was twisted with doubled pain, both the physical toll of his injuries and the anguish of losing the Cloch Mór. "Go before they take both of our clochs."

A trio of Arruk charged toward Padraic, and Kayne howled in fury. Blaze tore at the Arruk, clearing a space around Padraic. Kayne kicked his horse forward, leaping down from his mount and grasping Padraic. He put Snarl back in Padraic's hand and some of the agony in the youth's face eased. "You'll have to help me," he said to the Padraic, and pulled. Together, they staggered to the horse. The Arruk nearest them came howling forward once more and Kayne sent mage-lightning into them as Padraic pulled himself up. There was nothing but the shreds of mage-power left in Blaze now; he could not divert another burst from the Heart; Snarl seemed just as drained. *Stupid. You should have retreated while you had the chance . . .* Kayne shook the thought away. He took the reins and hauled himself up after Padraic, kicking the horse into a gallop away from the Arruk.

Howls and taunts pursued them, and the mind pressure that was the Heart built up to the breaking point again. Kayne gathered the dregs that were left in Blaze, ready to bring it up against the hammer blow of the Heart and knowing that he would fail.

Ennis! He tried to reach his brother in the web of the mage-energy, tried to make him hear his voice. *You must stop this! You don't know who you're hurting . . .* but the

fury of Treoraí's Heart tossed his words away. He felt the
pressure release, and turning his head to look back, saw in
mage-vision the wave of fuming energy come at them
again. He loosed Blaze's power at it: a reed against a hurricane.

But a mage-wind rushed past them toward the Heart's
power, a cold, cold wall that felt different than a Cloch
Mór. *Slow magic . . .* he realized. The wave from the Heart
met the wall in an explosion of golden fire that was bright
even in his true eyes. The wall of slow magic cracked and
fell, but not before it dissipated most of the power of
Ennis' strike. The power buffeted them, burned them,
raked claws across their skin and sent a few of the riders
down, but Kayne and Padraic managed to hold to the
horse.

"Who?" Padraic husked, and Kayne saw them at the
same moment: farther up the High Road, there were several figures dressed in the white clóca of the Order of Inishfeirm, and with them—impossibly—was his greada:
Kyle MacEagan, with the Cloch Mór Firerock bright in his
hand.

Kayne felt, for the first time, a surge of hope. "To the
Narrows!" he shouted to the riders. "Back! Back!"

The Daoine riders thundered in retreat toward their res-
cuers, who turned with them as they all fled up the High
Road to the Narrows.

57

The Unstoppable Flood

OUTSIDE, THE SUN was failing and the first stars had already appeared in the east. In a few stripes or less, the mage-lights would crawl the roof of the night.

"We lost nearly half of those with us," Kayne told the officers, mages, and assorted representatives crowded in the tent. "That's a heavy cost. Still, the Arruk must have lost three or four for each of ours. We could hope for no better." He turned to his greada, standing with arms crossed over his chest in the midst of a crowd of Inishlanders. "It would have been far worse had the mages of the Order not been there."

Kyle MacEagan nodded to his great-son with a smile, and his servant Alby, standing alongside him, also smiled, but few of the Riocha officers of the Tuatha army responded and the Fingerlanders stared stonily. There was a rift in the tent, but not of fabric—the Inish stood in one place, those of the Tuatha in another, and the Fingerlanders in yet a third, and between them all there was air and the lone figure of Banrion Edana. "In truth, we were lucky to be here at all," Kayne's greada responded. "That we made the voyage so quickly was due to Maestra Caomhánach and Stormbringer, as well as the magic of Bhralhg of the Saimhóir, who shepherded us here." He shook his head. "Having seen what you're facing, I wish we could have brought more than the few we did."

"We're grateful to Rí MacEagan, the people of Inish Thuaidh, and the Order of Inishfeirm for coming to us in our greatest need," Edana said. She smiled, but her smile was alone. The Ríocha nearest her glared suspiciously at their Inishlanders counterparts. Edana's glance toward her peers told Kayne that she realized it as well. "The Inish have done more to protect the Tuatha than most of the Ríthe," Edana added loudly.

Rodlhann O Morchoe scoffed loudly. "And the Fingerlanders have done nothing, I suppose. It's us who have had the Arruk crawling through our farms and villages for the last hands of days."

Edana nodded to Rodlhann. "Aye, I apologize. The Fingerlanders have done most of all, and deserve much credit." Her attention turned back to the Ríocha. "I look at those who came here to defend our land against the Arruk, and I wonder: where are the Clochs Mór that should be here? Where are the green-robes of the Order of Gabair? Where are the armies of the other Tuatha?" The Ríocha shuffled uneasily at that.

"They may come yet," Kayne said, but none of them in the tent believed that, and he didn't believe it himself. "So might Lámh Shábhála. We don't know. All we can do here is hold as long as we can, and take as many Arruk as we can with us to the Mother."

"It's that abomination with them that we'll have to kill," muttered one of the Ríocha, and that brought Kayne's head around sharply.

"*If* it comes to that," he said, and everyone in the tent heard the emphasis on the first word, "then I will do what has to be done."

"Ennis is just a boy," Edana agreed. "A child. He doesn't understand what he's doing or who he's fighting, and he may yet be turned."

"And our people die while Kayne Geraghty and the Inish decide?" another of the officers commented, but before Kayne could answer, the flaps to the tent opened and Padraic Mac Ard limped in, holding heavily to a crutch. His face was pallid, drawn with lines of pain, but he moved slowly next to his mam, turning awkwardly to face the Ríocha as Snarl swung on its chain around his neck.

"I would have been the one saying that, not a half-day ago," he said. "But I stand here now only because of Kayne Geraghty. I've seen what those who love him will do for him. I've witnessed his judgment and leadership in battle and I tell you this: he will make the decision that needs to be made, whatever it might be, and I . . . I will follow him without question or hesitation." His breath hissed inward, his face twisted, and his hand tightened around the crutch that held him up. "So will the rest of you, if we're to have any hope at all. It's time to forget that we're Riocha or Inishlander or Fingerlander. We're all Daoine—that's enough for the damned Arruk. It should be enough for us."

"It's still Geraghty's brother out there with the Arruk," one of the tiarna shot back. "With the Heart."

"Aye, 'tis," Padraic agreed. "And it was my da . . ." he hesitated there, swallowing hard, and everyone saw the anguished glance he gave Edana, ". . . my da who was part of the conspiracy that caused that to happen. But he . . . he saw that he was wrong in the end, and he was strong enough to try to rectify that. Kayne has that same strength; he'll do what he must. You will, too, all of you—or if you won't, you should go now. Go back and wait for the Arruk to come to you. Mam—Banrion Mac Ard—will give you leave."

Padraic waited, leaning heavily on the crutch under his shoulder. No one spoke. Finally Padraic nodded. He hobbled around slightly to face Kayne. "You're the Ard, Kayne Geraghty," he said, "no matter what the other Ríthe say. Give us your orders. Tell us what we need to do."

Kayne grasped Padraic's shoulder, his fingers squeezing. For the moment, that was enough. Then he began to speak.

The Narrows was painted with a palette of black and white. The sky was the gray of wood ash, and the clouds were heavy and somber. A thin rain fell, gray curtains flowing over a gray landscape, all the colors muted in the mist. In the hidden distance, down the slopes that led up to the long plateau of the pass itself, there came the slow, insistent beating of the Arruk drums: implacable, relentless, unstoppable, like the beating of some great beast's heart.

In the long climb to the summit of the Narrows, the High Road moved through a sequence of sections where cliff walls rose high on either side, so that any large force using the road was forced to slow and elongate its column. A

force sufficiently familiar with the territory might have
been able to split into several components and follow the
convolutions of the wrinkled, folded landscape through to
the rolling hills around Lough Tory, but their army would
be split and the various units would take days to reassem-
ble on the far side of the mountains. Following the High
Road through the Narrows Pass was the only viable alter-
native. The Fingerlanders had taken advantage of the physical properties of the Narrows for generations.

As they did now.

Kayne had Rodhlann's men direct the building of walls
of broken rock across all the narrowest points of the road.
He had no illusions that the makeshift barriers would stop
the Arruk: what had happened at Bunús Wall and at their
first skirmish the day before had left no hope for that. But
at worst, they would slow and stretch out the invaders; at
best, it would force Ennis to use the Heart to open the way,
which meant that the Heart would have that much less
power when the real battle came, and give the Clochs Mór
a chance to deal with him.

Kayne set Fingerlander archers near the barriers to pick
off the Arruk that they could and make it more imperative
for Ennis to use the Heart. Beyond that, they did nothing.

High up near the Narrow's highest point the road
opened up slightly in a long twisting canyon, with side
canyons leading off to both west and east. There, he set the
Daoine forces, and they waited. Fingerlander runners came
and went during the day with reports: *the Arruk force had
reached the first barrier; Ennis had eventually used the
Heart, and the Svarti with the spell-sticks had raked the hillsides with the archers as well. They'd come to the second
barrier, but they simply swarmed over and around the wall;
it hadn't stopped them at all. At the third wall, Ennis had
used the Heart again . . .*

The runners had all returned. Rodhlann and the Fingerlander archers had come back as well, their quivers emptied. The High Road was littered with the corpses of
Arruk struck down by Fingerlanders in their high ledges
and hiding places, but the dead were but a few buckets of
water stolen from a river that pushed on, unnoticing and
uncaring. Kayne sent the Fingerlanders to the fletchers in

the camp to replenish their quivers, then sent some to the Narrow's heights and the rest to their places with the foot soldiers.

Astride his horse on a small rise to one side of the High Road, with his greada, Alby, Edana, and Rodhlann beside him, Kayne blinked into a spray of rain. The banner of the Rí Ard, set with all the colors of the Tuatha, flapped wet and heavy alongside him on a long pole. The weather matched his mood; he wondered if Séarlait were not responsible, weeping for him with the Mother. "The world cries for what will happen here today," he said.

"You still have no hope?" Edana asked, and Kayne shook his head, sending droplets scattering from the ends of his hair.

"Not without Lámh Shábhála. And even then, without the rest of the Clochs Mór . . ." He shrugged. "I wonder if the Songmasters will sing of this one day . . . those Daoine who are still alive. The Arruk, from what I've seen, don't seem to make songs."

"They just pound on their Mother-damned drums," Rodhlann grumbled. "We heard them all through the mountains of the Finger."

"Let's hope that we don't hear them through all the Tuatha," Kayne's greada said, "nor in Inish Thuaidh." Kyle MacEagan shifted his weight uncomfortably on his mount, fingering the stone around his neck. "The Order's mages are ready and our gardai are in position, Kayne," he said. "Alby and I should be with them."

"Go with the Mother, Greada," Kayne told him. Leaning toward the man, he grasped Kyle's arm and nodded to the silent Alby, watching from his horse nearby, who looked uncomfortable in the steel-ringed armor he wore. Kayne wanted to give his great-da some word of comfort, but there were none he could speak. His great-da let the hood of his clóca fall from the plumed leather helmet he wore over his balding and grayed head, and swept the folds back from the scabbard of his sword. "I'll find you on the battlefield, great-son," he said, and kicked his heels into his horse's side, galloping swiftly away with Alby at his side. Rodhlann followed a moment later, with a grim nod to Kayne. Edana and Kayne remained on the hill: as the drums pounded, as in the distance the gray fog darkened with the vanguard of the Arruk force. Kayne could feel his own heart beating in time. His blood sang in his body.

"We've both lost too many of our family and our friends already," Edana said to him. She was peering down at the defenders to where those wearing the gray clóca of Dún Laoghaire were gathered, where Padraic—his leg splinted and padded, and clad in his green clóca—waited for the battle. "Here, we can take our anger and our grief for those we've lost and use them as our swords. How can the Arruk stand against that?"

Kayne smiled at her: this longtime friend of his mam, the woman he'd gone to often as a child when his mam wasn't there, who had cuddled him and kissed his skinned knees and elbows as if he'd been one of her own children. "Thank you, Aunt. I hope you're right." He could see the individual motes of the Arruk now, could see the waving cloth of their banners and the swaying of the officers' litters. "We'll know very soon, won't we?"

He pulled the flag of the Ard from the ground. Taking the stout pole in his hands, he waved it high. From down the lines of the Daoine defenders, banners waved in response.

The drums of the Arruk quickened, and in the rain came the sound of their challenge. The howls were like the screams of the Black Haunts, circling in the clouds above and waiting. The Arruk war drums slowed again, sending a different, more urgent beat as they saw the Daoine force ahead, as the archers on the walls of the canyon began to fire clouds of arrows through the rain. Kayne, from the hill, waved his banner once more; this time a cry went up from the mounted Daoine.

They charged.

He knew that if they hoped to cut down the Arruk force and hold them as long as possible, then they could not meet them where the Kralj could bring the full brunt of his army against their own outnumbered troops. In this position, the Daoine had the advantage both of attacking from higher ground and having the ability to maneuver in the open plain, while the Arruk were still compressed within the walls of the pass. They could attack the Arruk from three sides: from canyons to the east where Kayne had placed the Fingerlanders and the remnants of his da's original troops; from the west, where the Inishlanders waited; with the main flanks from the north with all the Tuathaian gardai and troops. Already the Inish and Fingerlanders had come against the Arruk: he heard the clash of steel and the howls of the Arruk mingling with the war cry of the Inish. He started to kick his own horse into motion when he felt Edana's hand on his arm.

"A commander's place is behind his troops."

"That was never Da's belief," Kayne told her gently but urgently. "And that's my brother we ride against. I want—I need—to be there when they reach him, when the Heart opens."

"I'll go with you," Edana told him. "You'll need Demon-Caller." She smiled into his beginning protest. "You're not going to tell me that a Banrion's place is behind the troops, are you?"

"No," he said. "Not here. Not now." He nodded. "We ride, Aunt." He kicked his heels into the stallion's ribs. "For the Daoine!" he shouted, and the wind took his words as the horse leaped forward, Edana and the gardai around them following.

As he galloped toward the chaos of the battle, Kayne took Blaze in his hand, opening it with his mind and letting the landscape of the clochs mingle with the vision of his eyes. The fighting was fiercest near the center of the pass where the Arruk were thickest. In his mage-sight, Kayne could see the flickering of spells being cast from the Svarti's spell-sticks, matching the minor fire of clochmions and slow magic of the Order of Inishfeirm and the Riocha. To his far left was Rodhlann with the cold fire of Winter, the sight of Séarlait's Cloch Mór bringing the grief back hard to Kayne's chest; to the far right, he could glimpse the ruddy conflagration of Greada with Firerock. Close by, somewhere just ahead, blue lines snaked and whipped toward the Arruk: Padraic with Snarl.

Around them, through the gray-seeming sight of his eyes, he could see the hand-to-hand fighting of swords against Arruk jaka. Despite the efforts of the Clochs Mór, the Arruk were threatening to break the Daoine line, and Ennis had yet to appear with Treoraí's Heart. Kayne plunged into the fray, using Blaze to scatter the Arruk that stood in his way. The beast that lived inside Edana's cloch Demon-Caller strode alongside him, a horned, dark creature roaring challenge, and it plucked up an Arruk in either hand and smashed them together, casting the bodies aside as it grabbed for two more of the creatures.

The onslaught of the additional Clochs Mór had an immediate effect: the first line of the Arruk sagged and broke, and the Daoine held a momentary clear space for a few breaths. But more Arruk charged from the confines of the pass to take their place. They pushed those Arruk back as well, and from a hundred Daoine throats came a cry of savage victory: premature, Kayne knew, but he yelled with them, urging the Daoine foot soldiers forward, wondering if they could plug the gap that was the Narrows, if they could fill it with Arruk bodies in a barrier of their own dead. A Svarti spell-stick loosed lightning at Kayne; he felt the attack and flicked the bolt aside with a burst from his cloch, turning the spell back on its owner. The Svarti screamed and vanished under the continuing flood of its own kind. A hand of Arruk charged him en masse, screaming; he cut them down in fire and blood. For a breath, he was alone on the field, and from his vantage point on his warhorse, he could see the canopies of the Arruk officers' litters. He could see the flags of the Kralj's litter not far back in the canyon, and another litter next to it with a Svarti's insignia fluttering from its poles.

Ennis . . . He knew it even before he felt the Heart open in his mage-vision: a looming red-black darkness, throbbing in time to the drums, and behind it the shadow of the boy who wielded it. The Heart lifted like a vast storm wall in front of them, its immensity dwarfing the Clochs Mór of the Daoine and making the lightning from the spell-sticks of the other Svarti seem like the sparks from a flint.

He wondered again at the depth and strength of the Heart, and if his mam had known what she held.

The appearance of the Kralj and his Svarti rallied the Arruk. The drums began to beat harder, and their jaka flashed in time, and now it was the Daoine who were forced to give ground. "Hold!" Kayne shouted to those around him. "We must hold!" If the line broke, if the Arruk pushed out from the vise of rocks and into the wider section of the Narrows, their numbers would overwhelm the Daoine.

The war drums boomed in mocking answer; the Arruk howled. The bloody wall of the Heart gathered itself like a tidal wave on the horizon, rising and lifting as if ready to crash down on them.

The drums beat as one, then went ominously silent. In the silence, the wave broke.

The pulse from the Heart knew neither ally nor foe. Indiscriminate, wild, it swept all before it. It smashed to ground near the front ranks of the Arruk and pushed north, taking with it screams and broken bodies. "By the Mother!" Kayne heard Edana gasp as the fury cascaded toward them. Kayne barely had time to place a shielding wall of mage-power between himself and the mad surf of dead and wounded. He felt the impact pounding at his mind through the cloch, the wall nearly collapsing in shock. Then it was past him and fading. Kayne gasped, blinking into the rain that now soaked a field of dead—Arruk and Daoine both—for several strides around him. He could feel Edana near him, but the mage-demon had vanished under Ennis' assault.

The power in the Heart reminded him too much of Lámh Shábhála. *That would have taken everything in a Cloch Mór and more. Perhaps that was all he had, and he's used it up* . . . But he knew already that this faint hope was misplaced: they could not win here, not with the Heart against them, and he despaired of being able to reach Ennis. Images and memories of his brother surfaced—*smiling, laughing, always so proud of his big brother, always wanting to be like him*—and he shook his head at them

He wondered if he'd have the strength and resolution to strike Ennis down. He wondered if the chance would come at all.

A growl, too close, brought him back. Several Arruk had leaped from the canyon toward him and Edana, alone now after the Heart's attack. The mage-demon, restored, roared and charged at them; Kayne sent hissing gouts of fire to them. Those closest went down, but more were coming, an endless stream of them. "Close the line!" Kayne shouted to the gardai behind them, and slowly they moved to obey, as if mesmerized by the carnage and violence before them. Kayne could see the Kralj now, fighting with his entourage around him, and there . . . there was Ennis.

He could see his brother, astride another Arruk's shoulders as if he were riding the creature. A garda rushed at Ennis—it was Garvan, Kayne realized, a shield lashed to his broken arm—but the Arruk with the boy cut Garvan down with a stroke of his jaka. Then Kayne lost sight of Ennis as more Arruk came pouring out from the gap, the drums beating furiously, the banners waving, and Svarti howling their chants and spell-lightning—pale after the Heart's brilliance—slashing through the Daoine troops.

The mage-landscape was flooded with the power being expended here: the Clochs Mór and clochmions arrayed against the spell-sticks of the Svarti, and there . . . in the center, all the energy swirling around it like a storm sea around a terrible, huge whirlpool, was Treoraí's Heart, gathering itself again, pulling in the power it held and feeding on itself, ready to burst out once more.

Kayne clutched Blaze desperately, but he'd already used most of the energy stored within the stone, and he knew it was the same for the others.

"We can't stop him," he heard Edana call. "Kayne, he's too strong."

"I know," he told her. "The army's yours, Aunt. Be ready to retreat to the top of the pass. We've done all we can here."

"Kayne . . ."

In answer, he kicked his horse, screaming the *caointeoireacht na cogadh* in defiance, and riding ahead into the line of the Arruk. He used Blaze liberally, not caring that the stone would soon be exhausted, riding against the storm he felt gathering. He pushed the Arruk aside, clearing a path for himself and arrowing straight for Ennis. He could see his brother now, not a dozen strides from him, and Ennis turned to him at the same time, Treoraí's Heart in one hand, the remnants of an Arruk spell-stick in the other. "Ennis!" Kayne shouted to him. "Ennis, you have to stop this!"

The boy seemed to look at him, and Kayne wanted to believe that there was a flash of recognition in Ennis' eyes. But just when Ennis' mouth started to open, a change came over the boy's face, even as Kayne used the last reservoirs of Blaze to push aside the remaining Arruk between himself and his brother. The Arruk who carried his

brother stared at the horse and rider that confronted them,
its eyes wide and almost frightened. Ennis blinked and his
gaze went hard; his mouth closed and the lips set themselves in a tight frown. The spell-stick came down and he
pointed the riven end directly at Kayne.

He spoke a word, and the word was in the Arruk tongue.

Kayne, with the wisp of energy left in Blaze, felt Treoraí's
Heart erupt and flare outward, and he could do nothing to
stop it.

"Ennis!" the rider shouted toward him. "Ennis, you have to
stop this!"

The blue ghost to which he had bound himself shuddered with the call, threatening to shatter around Ennis.
Since the battle the day before, when he'd felt his da's
Cloch Mór outside the stone, since he'd glimpsed what
seemed to be Kayne with the riders set against the Arruk,
he'd clung to the pattern as if it were a log in the middle of
a tempestuous ocean, his only chance for life.

"It's not your brother," Isibéal's voice insisted in his
head, in the blue ghost's head, as she had since he'd seen
him. *"That's what they want you to think. Kayne is dead. It's
a trick, my dearest one; a nasty, terrible trick. They want to
kill you. They want to kill you as they did me. They want the
Heart for themselves."*

"Let me talk to Mam. She'd know. She'd tell me," he'd
cried back to her.

Isibéal and the ones he'd killed with the Heart, hands
upon hands upon hands of them now, shouted back denial
to him. *"No, you can't talk to her. You must listen to us . . ."*

But Ennis stared at the rider and he saw someone who
must be Kayne, and he hesitated. Around him, a dozen
ghosts of himself appeared, futures unglimpsed, and he
began to slip away from the chosen pattern. He felt the
chill of the wind, felt the cold rain on his face and body, felt
the terror of the battle and the uncertainty, and all the
emotions threatened to overwhelm him. Kurhv Kralj, a few
strides away, was howling at Ennis: "Kill him! Kill the
stone-bearer bluntclaw!" The Kralj waved his well-
blooded jaka and shoved an attendant out of the way.

Ennis knew that the Kralj would rush toward Kayne himself.

"Ennis Svarti!" Cima called up at him. "What should I do?"

His breath coming fast and panicked, Ennis forced himself to hold onto the blue, shoved himself back into the constricted shell of the pattern. With the effort, the panic began to subside. *"There . . . That's better, isn't it, my darling . . ."*

"Aye," he wanted to whisper, but his lips could not move because the blue ghost would not allow it. He turned Treoraí's Heart in his hand, glancing at the facets that in his mage-vision were almost too bright to bear, and he took the energy in his mind, letting it gather in the ruined spell-stick. "Stay!" he said to Cima and Kurhv Kralj both, and pointed the spell-stick at the false Kayne.

He imagined all the power rushing out and smashing the foul pretender, obliterating him so that his deception would be revealed for the sham it was.

As he released the attack—far stronger than it needed to be, but the ghost demanded it—he felt something else, a new presence, and even the blue ghost looked up in surprise and alarm.

58

Death in the Family

"THERE!" SEVEI SHOUTED, and Kekeri folded his great leathery wings and fell like a stooping hawk from the air. Sevei let herself tumble from the dragon's back, the lashing of wind and rain an agony. She took Lámh Shábhála in her hand and wrenched it open in her mind. The world shifted around her.

The Bán Cailleach vanished . . . and reappeared on the ground as the dragon wheeled overhead spouting thick fire. The wave of energy from Treoraí's Heart, intended for Kayne, struck Sevei fully and she shuddered with the impact, closing her eyes as Lámh Shábhála took the mage-power in and vented it out again. Crouching, Sevei caught the Heart's energy in a mage-hand of bright emerald before it struck Kayne and threw it; one of the spires of the Narrows well to the west shattered and collapsed in a fiery gout of molten and broken rock.

She stood between Kayne and Ennis, shaking out her white hair as she rose and standing naked in the rain. She enjoyed the coolness even though the drops battered her like small fists; the moisture slaked the heat in her body, soothing her enough that she could ignore the clamor of the voices in her head.

"... Aye, this is what you must do ..."

"... No, Sevei. Listen to me! Take the power you have and use it ..."

"... you're foolish and don't deserve the gift you were given ..."

"Enough," she said to Ennis, to Kayne, to all of the con-

tentious voices in her head. "It's over now." She existed
mostly in the mage-world: she saw Kayne and Ennis
through the colors of their clochs na thintrí; there also,
close by, was Demon-Caller with Aunt Edana, Snarl with
Padraic, Firerock with Greada, and Winter with one of the
Fingerlanders. None of the Riocha who had attacked
Kayne and Séarlait were there, she realized: none of the
other Ríthe or the green-robes of the Order of Gabair except for Padraic.

She grimaced sadly. The world around her was murky
and mist infested. She saw movement in the shadows: the
Arruk Kralj, rushing at her, and she flicked a bare tithe of
Lámh Shábhála's power toward him. He fell back into his
attendant warriors with the crack of bones, and she turned
from him no more bothered than if he'd been an insect.

"No!" Ennis screamed at her—a boy's shrill cry. But the
attack that came at her from the Heart was full and mas-
terful, and she barely managed to snare it with Lámh Shábhála. The two Great Clochs' power burned together,
searing, the forces within them intertwined and locked together. Both Sevei and Ennis were swept up in the furious
tidal eddies.

"... The Heart is as strong as Lámh Shábhála when I held
it ..."

"... He could slay you if you're not careful ..."

"... Stay outside of the boy! This is folly ..."

Time had stopped around them. Sevei could see, through
the furious glare of the clochs, the Daoine soldiers and the
Arruk in the field of the Narrows standing frozen in mid-
motion, Kekeri caught in mid-turn in the sky above them.
The energy of Lámh Shábhála flooded out from her, a constant stream holding this moment within itself.

In the light, a boy's form was sitting.

"Ennis? It's Sevei, Ennis. It's your sister."

The boy looked up, his movements stiff, as if his joints
were so stiff and bound that he could only move in limited
ways. "No, you're not Sevei. Sevei's dead. You're the White
Beast. Isibéal says you're horrible and I need to kill you.
That's the pattern. That's what the blue ghost means."

"No, Ennis. I'm truly Sevei. Here ... let me show you."
She extended the power of Lámh Shábhála toward him,
fashioning an opening into her mind through which he

could step and look into her thoughts and memories. But he scrambled to his feet like a puppet whose strings had been pulled, and the mage-energy within Treoraí's Heart slammed into her once more. The impact shattered the opening she'd made, sending shards hurtling back toward her. Sevei gasped at the raw, visceral power of the attack. Spears of blood-red thrust gore-dripping points toward her, and though she shoved them aside with folds of Lámh Shábhála's power, the droplets spattered on Sevei's skin where they hissed and boiled and stripped away the flesh down to muscle. The smoldering burns, atop the already throbbing hurt of wielding the cloch, tore an unwilling scream from her throat, and she heard Ennis laugh. The spears came at her again, a new wave, and this time she threw a blanketing curtain around herself from which the spears rebounded. The acid of the drops sputtered and fumed against the protection but did not touch her.

With reflexive anger, she sent lightning arcing out from the stone in her hand, lancing toward Ennis in crackling, brilliant white streaks. The first few he shoved aside, laughing at her, but she continued to pour them out, faster and more powerful, until one shattered the walls he was furiously erecting and sent him falling backward from the shoulders of the Arruk who carried him. The Arruk went sprawling one way, and Ennis another. Sevei rushed forward through the breached defenses of her brother . . .

. . . and into him.

It was night inside Ennis, a twilight illuminated by candles. Ennis was sitting at a table set as if for a feast with fine plates and silver. Sevei recognized the room: one of the rooms in Mam's chambers in Dún Laoghaire. The supper steamed on the table, half-eaten. A Taisteal woman in bright, foreign clothing was seated at the table with Ennis, and Mam was there also, slumped in her chair with her face on the delicate linen of the tablecloth, her body unmoving. Her wine was spilled, the goblet just out of the reach of her white fingers and a red pool staining the white cloth. Mam's plate had lifted under her head, meat and sauce spilled and smeared in the red tresses of her hair. The Tais-

teal woman was staring at Meriel's corpse, smiling and gig-
gling like a mad thing. Her amusement punctuated Ennis'
greeting.

To the rear of the room, standing against the tapestry-
decorated walls as if they were attendants at the meal were
hand upon hand of people, Daoine and Arruk both. Their
features were bloodied and broken, their skin as pale as
that of maggots.

"Sit," Ennis told Sevei. "Did you come to join us? Did
Isibéal invite you?"

Sevei waited in the shadows, not wanting to come closer
to the tableau. She lifted her hands and heard the rustle of
a silken clóca falling back; her hands and arms were as they
once had been. She touched her face; it was the face she remembered, scarless and smooth. "Ennis," Sevei said softly,
"you know me. I'm Sevei, darling. Remember? You cried
so hard when I left to go to Inishfeirm; you were just five
then, and you wouldn't let go of my clóca, trying to keep
me there. Do you remember that? Look at me."

Ennis shook his head. "I don't know you. Isibéal says I
can't trust you. She says you're a monster." He held up Treoraí's Heart in his hand; she could see the jeweled facets
gleaming through his thin, grimy fingers. "She talks to me
through this. I can hear her in my head even though I killed
her."

The Taisteal woman giggled loudly at that, raising her
hand to her mouth. She saw Sevei staring at her, and her
eyes narrowed and her mouth snapped shut in a manic
frown. The pool of wine crawled toward a vase of dead and
decaying flowers set at the center of the table. "What does
Mam say, Ennis?" Sevei said. "She must be in the Heart
also. What does she tell you?"

"She doesn't talk to me," Ennis said, almost angrily, glaring at the body next to him at the table. "They won't let
her."

Sevei took a step toward the table, toward the vision of
her mam's body. Isibéal hissed warningly and began to rise
from the table, her mad eyes gleaming. The corpses against
the wall moved with her, all of them converging on Sevei.
"Maybe I can help her," she said softly to Ennis, watching
Isibéal and the others carefully. Ennis sat, not moving,
locked in position. Sevei saw that her skin was metamor-

phosing, turning back to the scarred white skin of the Bán Cailleach; she could feel the changes crawling across her face, also. The power was still draining from Lámh Sháb-hála in an effort to keep them together in this place while holding back the true world, and Sevei knew she couldn't sustain this much longer.

"Listen to me, Ennis. You shouldn't listen to Isibéal or the others. I know the voices. I know how dangerous they are."

In her own head, the voices of the ancient Holders cackled with mad laughter. Isibéal hissed again, and she flung her arm out across the table before Sevei could reach her mam. Isibéal's fingers locked in Meriel's hair, lifting her face up from the table. Her face was a rotting skull with grave worms crawling from her eyes and her nostrils. Her mouth opened; a black, swollen tongue protruded. "You lie! You're the White Beast. The Enemy," it shrilled, the voice a foul wind that carried the smell of carrion. Isibéal's mouth moved with the same words at the same time.

Sevei ignored the apparition. She watched Ennis. "That's not Mam, Ennis. We both know it. Let me try. I can find her in the Heart. She'll tell you the truth. Mam would never lie to you."

"It's too late," he said urgently. "I've found the pattern and I have to dance to it or I'll die. It doesn't matter anymore."

"Mam would help you, Ennis. She would tell you what's right to do."

"The pattern . . ." Ennis said, and aqua shades of him shivered around him. "The blue ghosts . . ."

"Mam can send the ghosts away."

"No!" he shouted, and the corpse of her mam shouted with him, the two voices intertwined and strong with the power of the Heart. Ennis ran to his mam, putting his arms around the skeletal figure. As Sevei watched, the light of the Heart in Ennis' hand enveloped her: the death process reversed itself and it was her mam standing there again. Isibéal, standing next to him, smiled at Sevei. "You see," they said, all of them in the room: Ennis, Mam, the Taisteal, the Daoine, and the Arruk. Their united voices battered at her. "You lie! You're the White Beast, the Abomination. You should be destroyed like a wild animal. That's the pattern. That's the way."

"Ennis . . ." She took a step toward him, toward them. He was melting into Mam's body, his body glowing the color of a storm sea and drawing the azure light around him until there were two images of Ennis glaring at her. Sevei reached toward Ennis/Mam with her hand, with Lámh Shábhála. He pushed her back with the Heart, but she continued to force herself forward, to take one step, then another. She touched the blue image. Touched him.

She could *see* Ennis, held in a cobalt shell: fractured and broken, his mind all angles and razored edges, the Ennis that she'd once known scattered in this new image and held in by the gleaming cage. "Oh, Ennis," she whispered with a sob. "What have they done to you?"

"Go away!" he screamed at her, his voice shrill.

"Let me help you."

"Go *away!*" With the throat-shredding bellow, Ennis sent the energy of the Heart pouring out at her. The unexpected assault threw Sevei out of his mind, hurled her past the dining room and the cowering Taisteal woman and the dead onlookers, slamming her to the ground in the rain and mist of the Narrows. The armies lurched into motion around her; she heard swords clashing against jaka, the howls of the Arruk and the war cry of the Daoine, the chants of the Svarti and the thunder of the Clochs Mór. Kekeri roared overhead and vanished into the clouds. The Arruk Kralj was pulling himself to his feet with the staff of his jaka. Kayne was astride his horse, staring at Sevei in confusion and shock.

And Ennis was there also, as well as the stunned Arruk who he'd ridden. Ennis lifted the Heart in one hand, his spell-stick in the other. He seemed to glow like a moon in fog. "Die, White Beast," he said to her, and gestured.

The power of the Heart collided with that of Lámh Shábhála, and the sound of Sevei's wail was lost in the thunder of the mage-energy crackling about her. The voices of the Holders and the voices of memory cried with her.

"*. . . you let this happen because you're afraid . . .*"

"*. . . afraid . . .*"

"*. . . weak . . .*"

Yet two voices came strong and vivid to her. One was her gram. "*. . . he's your brother. My great-son. You have to save him . . .*"

"Only those who come long after can truly judge us . . ."
She heard Carrohkai's voice loudest of all.

Sevei rose. She accepted the pain, feeling it but not letting it touch her. She touched Lámh Shábhála as Ennis sent a new attack cascading from the Heart toward her. He wanted to crush her, to annihilate her. She could feel his intent and desire welling from him, from the blue shell that held him.

". . . You could heal him yet, bring him back . . ."

It was what she wanted most: to heal Ennis and bring him back. It was what she wanted for *all* those she'd lost: for Gram, for poor Dillon, for Da and Mam, for Tara and Ionhar, for Séarlait, for Máister Kirwan. But she couldn't bring them back.

Yet she might be able to save Ennis. She might be able to plunge back into his mind and find the child Ennis who was lost and locked deep inside. Perhaps she could pull him from the madness. Perhaps she could banish the ghosts that haunted him. Perhaps.

But if she did that, there would be nothing left in Lámh Shábhála, not if she had to hold off the Heart for the time it would take. And there was too much to do here. Too much . . .

"You must choose . . ." It could have been Gram speaking, or Carrohkai. She could no longer tell.

"Ennis," she called again, desperate. "It's Sevei and Kayne. We're here, right in front of you. You have to stop. I'll take the Arruk where they need to go, I promise. But you have to stop now."

"Listen to her," Kayne shouted at Ennis, then to Sevei. "Sevei, please don't hurt him!"

The only answer to them was a grimace from Ennis. The spell-stick in his hand shifted as he aimed it toward Kayne. The Kralj rose from the tangle of his attendants, loping forward with his jaka upraised. The space that Kayne had carved out with Blaze was closing, and the battle would overtake them again in a few breaths.

Strangely, the Arruk who Ennis had rode pushed himself to his feet at the same time, and his jaka caught the Kralj's weapon, stopping the Arruk chieftain in full charge. Sevei had no time to wonder at that.

". . . you can be traitor or hero . . ."

She reached deep into Lámh Shábhála and dredged out the power with her mind—all the mage-energy within the stone—and shaped it. In her mind, she *was* Lámh Shábhála, holding it . . . holding it . . .

And bringing it smashing down.

Ennis shifted his focus too late. The spell-stick shattered in his hand, the energy within the Heart flaring. He screamed as Lámh Shábhála crashed past his defenses, Sevei pushing more and more of the cloch's reservoirs into the effort. The pain was nearly intolerable, and the scars on her skin glowed as if a smithy's forge burned inside her body. Sevei closed her eyes; she saw only with the mage-vision as the whirlpool of maddened force spread over the Narrows from the two of them. They fought to control it: Sevei and the blue-shelled Ennis. "Don't hurt me," the blue thing that held Ennis pleaded. "I'm your brother, Sevei. Don't hurt me." Then it smiled, as if expecting her to hold back the onslaught, and it grasped for the energy itself.

But she hadn't listened to it or let go. She caught Ennis in a hand of emerald and pushed him back, and he gasped in surprise. "The pattern," he said. "It's not supposed to happen this way . . ."

Uncertainty trembled the Heart. Sevei saw the opening and pushed forward.

"Sevei!" Ennis called in that instant, and she finally heard the true Ennis—the child, her brother—in his voice. The blue shell around him crumbled to powder and dust. He was crying, sobbing. He held out his arms toward her pleadingly.

Lámh Shábhála fountained in white sheets of flame around Ennis; Treoraí's Heart caught within it. Sevei heard Isibéal's wail, Gyl Svarti's cry, the screams of all the murdered ones trapped there, and she plunged past them to another presence, one pushed far down into the stone. "Mam," she said. "I miss you so much."

Meriel's figure emerged from shadow, limned in cold fire. "Sevei, my love," she said. Her face was twisted with sadness, her eyes dark from weeping. "Ennis . . ." she said, and she turned from Sevei to him. "Oh, Ennis, my poor baby."

"Mam!" he said, and it was the cry of a child, touched with a wail that became a racking sob. "Oh, Mam, they wouldn't let me hear you, and I was so scared, and I had to stay with the blue ghost's dance." He stopped. "The dance is over now, isn't it?" he said.

"Aye, my dear," Meriel told him, and she looked at Sevei as she spoke. "Aye, finally it is."

"Mam?" Sevei said, her voice choking. Meriel smiled.

"I know, my love," she said, hugging Ennis. "I know." Meriel nodded to Sevei.

The light from Lámh Shábhála enveloped them both, and Ennis cried out as Meriel's form hugged him. Sevei heard Kayne and the Arruk whom Ennis had ridden scream. Ennis' cry ended in a strange, falling wail, and when the light faded from around him, there was only a charred, twisted body on the ground.

Cima saw Kurhv Kralj recover himself. Their leader snatched up his fallen jaka and charged toward the White Beast with a howl. Cima hesitated. *"I'll take the Arruk where they need to go,"* the White Beast had said, and she had called Ennis Svarti by name, had called herself his sister. Cima knew the importance the bluntclaws gave to their family relationships, and he saw how Ennis reacted.

He remembered Ennis leaking water from his eyes in the night. He remembered the grief the boy felt over his losses.

And yet here were some of his family, miraculously alive again, and they were trying to help him.

"I'll take the Arruck where they need to go."

Cima tightened his hands around his own jaka. He moved to intercept Kurhv Kralj. Their jakas met in mid-strike. "No," he told the Kralj. "You can't."

Kurhv Kralj only glared. He stepped back and lifted his jaka again, and this time the blade would have come down on Cima. A true Arruk would have stood there, would have met force with force, and the strongest would have won. Kurhv Kralj would have won.

But Cima did something that a Daoine warrior might have done. He stepped to the side, sliding forward at the same time and slicing his jaka in a long, horizontal blow that caught Kurhv Kralj in the abdomen. Kurhv Kralj

grunted, his jaka dropping from his hands in midstrike. He
made a strangling, choking sound deep in his throat as his
blood spattered over Cima's scales, as a flood of it poured
over Cima's blade.

Kurhv Kralj fell.

Cima stared. The attendants around the Kralj stared as
well. Strange shifting light from behind him sent shadows
racing over the ground. As Cima whirled around, he saw
the mage-glare from the White Beast strike Ennis, saw the
boy fall, and he howled.

He also saw the Heart, lying in the steaming, open ruin
of Ennis' palm.

When he saw Sevei attack Ennis, Kayne leaped down from
his horse, running toward them. But in the moment it took
to cover the few strides between them, it was over. "No!"
Kayne screamed even as he reached for Sevei, wondering
how he could stop her, but Ennis was already gone. "Sevei!
What in the Mother's name have you done!"

"I did what I thought best," she answered. Her voice was
distant, distracted, as if she were listening to someone else
and only answered because he annoyed her. Lámh Shábhála was searing through the skin of her body; the scars
bright enough that he had to shade his eyes, and the mass
of tangled hair around her head was a sun. She was an unbearable noon fallen to earth, but her eyes contained midnight, expressionless. The light was a wall that had pushed
everyone back around from them. They stood in a quiet
circle in the midst of the battle.

Kayne saw the Arruk that Ennis had been riding drop
his bloodied jaka and dart forward toward the body of his
brother. The creature plucked Treoraí's Heart from Ennis'
blackened hand. "Sevei!" he shouted. "The Arruk—"

She looked at the Arruk, watched as the beast closed its
hand around his mam's cloch. The glow around her brightened and spread out until it touched the Arruk and took
him in.

He didn't hide in the light—Sevei knew no Arruk would ever cower. She touched the Arruk's mind, marveling at the strangeness of it. She plucked memories from him, examining them and letting them drop away.

... feeling the pull of Cudak Zvati, feeling it as much as any of the Svarti and knowing that must be his calling as well ...
... the horrible day when the first Svarti to whom he was apprenticed sent him away, not because he was hopeless, but because his skill already exceeded that of his mentor ...
... enduring the taunts from those who had once been his peers ...
... Kurhv Mairki humiliating him even more by ordering him to learn the bluntclaw language from the dishonored ones who had dropped their weapons rather than accept a good death on the battlefield ...
... the bluntclaws backing away from him in fright, and slowly learning that it wasn't fear that would make them talk to him but sympathy ...
... lifting his chin before Kurhv Kralj and hating him at the same time ...
... wondering at the sadness within the bluntclaw Ennis, and marveling also at the great power within the boy ...
... hoping as he picked up the spell-stone that Ennis had carried that perhaps he could also use it, perhaps he could feel it ...
... a surprising, terrifying ache inside him as he looked down at Ennis Svarti's body ... "Cima," she said, taking the name she found there. "I can't let you keep Treoraí's Heart."

"If I die, I'll find Cudak Zvati even faster," he told her. He carefully lowered his head so that she could see none of the bright scales of his throat. "I'm not afraid of you."

". . . kill the creature," Gram whispered inside her. *". . . do it . . ."*

She did not. Instead, she pushed herself deeper into Cima's mind. *Cudak Zvati . . . the search we've been told we must undertake . . . seeing the image of Cudak carved in the wall . . . the yearning to reach the place from where the sky-net grows . . . the gift of Cudak waiting for us . . .*

Sevei saw everything: what Cima had experienced, what the Arruk searched for, their belief and their quest.

And she saw more.

"They will call you a traitor . . ." her gram hissed.

"Here's what you can do . . ." That was Carrohkai, her voice loudest of all. *"Let me show you . . ."*

Sevei could not hold back the quick laugh that tasted bitter on her tongue as she saw the places inside Lámh Shábhála that Carrohkai knew. "I will take you to Cudak Zvati, Cima," she said. "You alone. But the rest of you must go back."

"No." His refusal was sharp. She could feel his mind searching for the words, words that were not in his vocabulary but in hers. "We Arruk do not retreat. We do not surrender. We would rather all die here than do that."

"I'm not asking for you to do either," she told him.

Kayne thought that Sevei would smash the Arruk as he would have done, as he yearned to do. But when the glow faded, the creature was still holding the Heart and Sevei was nodding to him. "Damn it, Sevei!" He clutched Blaze. There was still a vestige of power in the cloch.

Desperate, he looked back at Edana. She was staring from her horse toward Sevei, to Ennis' body, to the Arruk holding the Heart. She blinked, and the stasis broke. She frowned, taking her own cloch in her hand again. The mage-demon snarled next to Kayne.

"Sevei, with you here, we can take the Arruk," Kayne said urgently. "We can end this now." He looked quickly around; outside the ring that Sevei kept around them, the battle was still raging. He could see the clochs and spell-sticks disgorging death, hear the clash of metal and the screams of the dying.

She smiled at him, and for that moment she seemed to be only Sevei once more. "I'm sorry, Kayne."

"Sevei—"

"I love you, Kayne. I'm sorry. But there's no victory here. There never was, not for either Daoine or Arruk."

She closed her seal-black eyes. The mage-demon screamed and the Arruk holding the Heart gaped as scarlet light leaped from his hand toward Sevei. Kayne felt Lámh Shábhála's touch on Blaze at the same moment, as if every drop of stored mage-light within it was being sucked

from the cloch, rushing outward toward Sevei and Lámh
Shábhála. The ring around them brightened, flared, and
vanished.

Now rippling, luminous walls radiated out from Lámh
Shábhála. Snaking, curling, moving so rapidly that Kayne
could barely follow them, they raced through the clusters
of fighting Daoine and Arruk, separating the two, pushing
one away from the other. Kayne saw, on either side, two
huge columns of light erupt and fade, accompanied by numerous small ones, and he knew that Lámh Shábhála had
stolen the essences of Snarl and Firerock as well as the
slow magic within the Svartis' spell-sticks. He looked down
at his hand; he might as well have been grasping a pebble
from the ocean shore. Blaze was a dead thing in his hand.

"Sevei!" he cried. "What have you done?"

Holding the walls between the armies took all of her attention, all of her power, but Lámh Shábhála's power was
limited, even for the Bán Cailleach. Sevei grimaced with
the effort of holding it, wondering how she could do the
rest.

"... in the end, you fail, like all the rest ..."

"... you'll be here, a ghost like us in the stone ... "

"Silence!" she shouted at them, and the word pounded
in her head, the wall quivering with its violence. She tried
to think, but the power hummed so loudly around her that
she could not. The energy hissed and fumed and snarled in
every muscle, every fiber of her being. The scars on her
body were lines of molting, flowing lava. The power she
held—plucked from all the clochs and the slow magic in
the Arruk spell-sticks, mixed and bound with Lámh Shábhála—threatened to burst out from her. She was a fragile
clay pot full to bursting, and she were falling, falling toward
sharp rocks ...

The voices of the old Holders were right. She was going
to fail. She could not do what she wanted to do, not if she
had to hold this wall. And if the wall fell, the battle would
begin again, and this time the Daoine would have no magic
at all against the Arruk, and she would have slain her
brother for nothing. . . .

She thought she heard Kayne calling to her, but his voice was lost in the roaring of the mage-light's power.

Above, she felt Kekeri fold his great wings and stoop, coming to land awkwardly near her. Because her eyes were closed with the effort of maintaining the bright walls that now ran from one side of the Narrows to the other, she saw him only in her mage-vision, a shape of shifting fire. Others accompanied him: two stone-gray forms to either side of the pass that were Créneach; the blue-black, dark radiance of the Saimhóir, resting in the cold pools of water nearest the pass; a Bunús Muintir whose slow magics shimmered emerald, the sliding elusive brown of a dire wolf in a nearby copse of pines; the aloof, keen pinpricks of a pair of eagles high above the pass . . .

"We who are Aware will take this burden," Kekeri told her, his voice a growl that was felt more than heard. "Do what you must."

"Thank you," Sevei told him, and she felt them take from her the mage-wall between the Daoine and the Arruk. She fell, gasping. The glare of the wall shifted hues, no longer the green-shot white of Lámh Shábhála, but now a melding of a dozen tints and shades racing through the barrier. Sevei lay in the midst of the multihued glow, every breath a stab of blades in her chest, the cold air like acid flowing down her throat. She rolled on her side: the scrape of dirt on her skin was as a cruel hand scouring her body. She could no longer stand this pain; she could not rise again.

The voices of the Holders were a din in her mind: mocking, laughing, weeping, each of them telling her something different. Gram's voice, Carrohkai's voice . . . She strove to find it in the confusion, to hear her. *"You can do this . . . You must . . ."* The Bunús Muintir was there, her voice gaining strength as Sevei focused on it. *"Get up . . ."*

"I can't."

"There's time enough to die later. Get up."

Groaning, she rose. "Did it hurt you so much?" she asked Carrohkai. She thought she could see the Bunús Muintir woman in front of her, wavering like someone glimpsed across a bonfire.

"Worse still," Carrohkai told her. *"As it will become worse for you. But not for much longer."*

Sevei blinked. Carrohkai was gone. She stood in the cen-

ter of the brilliant wall. Her hand was trembling as she
took Lámh Shábhála up again, and she groaned again as
she opened Lámh Shábhála to her mind once more. She
shaped the energy, reaching out with ethereal hands to either side of the wall she'd made and plucking away two
people there. She brought them to her in the center of the
brightness: Kayne and Cima.

"Sevei!" Kayne rushed toward her as if he were about to
embrace her, and she held up her hand to hold him back.
Cima stared, his fierce mouth open. Sevei held up her hand
to stop Kayne.

"No," she told him. "You . . . can't. I can't. I couldn't bear
your touch, Kayne, especially now." She looked past him to
the Arruk. "Cima, it's time to fulfill my promise to you. I
will show you Cudak Zvati, though it will be both less and
more than you think it is. But you'll return to your people
as Svarti Kralj, the First. As for Treoraí's Heart, you'll do
with it what you should."

"Sevei!" Kayne interrupted. She could see his confusion
and his uncertainty in the way he stood, still grasping Blaze
as if it were still full of the mage-lights' energy. "The Heart
was given to Gram and then Mam. It belongs to the
Daoine. It's not yours to give away."

"Belongs to the Daoine?" she asked him, remonstrating
with him gently. Now that she'd made the decision, a calm-
ness seemed to have come over her. She could still feel the
awful pain, but it seemed to hover around her like a mol-
lusk's shell, as if it were not quite part of her any longer.
"Treoraí would disagree, wouldn't he? His Heart's not
mine to give, nor yours. The Heart, like Lámh Shábhála,
chooses its own. And it arranged to be there in Cima's
hand." She looked at him. She wanted so much to touch
Kayne, to put her arms around him and embrace him, to
weep with him at all they'd lost, to grieve together, brother
and sister. Yet she knew that if she did that, the pain would
come rushing in to her again, and she might succumb to it.
"I wish . . . I wish . . ." she began, then shook her head, unable to continue. She felt tears sliding down her cheeks, so
hot they seemed to steam against her skin. "You will be Rí
Ard," she told Kayne. "And you will hold Lámh Shábhála."

Puzzlement creased his battle-stained forehead. "What
do you mean . . . ?"

She smiled at him again. "I think you know," she told him. "Or you will. When you have the stone, Gram and Carrohkai will tell you. And so will I." She could see the realization break on his face. "It's fine, Kayne," she told him. "Remember for me and tell the others when they say I did nothing or that I was a traitor: I chose this path. I chose it because it was best."

She didn't give either of them the chance to speak or protest, or for her to hesitate and perhaps reconsider. She plunged her mind into Lámh Shábhála, forcing herself deep into every last crystalline recess of the great stone and taking all that was there into herself. When she was full, when she and Lámh Shábhála were the same vessel, she turned to the wall that Kekeri and the others had fashioned to replace hers. "Now," she thought to Kekeri. "I need all of you now," and she opened herself to their power also.

. . . hearing Kayne cry out in alarm and distress, hearing Cima do the same in his own tongue, feeling the lash and torment of the power, tasting the blood in her mouth, smelling the scent of storm and lightning and rain, seeing the blinding radiance even through closed eyelids . . .

The power lacerated her hands as she held them out, shattering bones and shredding muscle and sinew. She forced her mind to hold Lámh Shábhála, to form it, to place it where it must go. Then, praying to the Mother that she had done it right, that she had seen the correct pattern for the energy, she let it go with a great cry, the last sound she would make.

Sevei, with her final thought, was surprised at the resplendent ferocity that she released.

"Sevei!" Kayne shouted, but there was nothing he could do. He started to draw in a breath, to move to her, to stop her, but the light . . . the light was nothing he'd experienced before. The glimmering wall she'd erected across the battlefield coalesced and merged with Lámh Shábhála. He'd once seen the sun emerge full from behind fast dark clouds, gleaming low behind a lake in Céile Mhór and the orb and its reflections from the water so bright and piercing that he'd thought for a moment that he'd been blinded, even though he immediately averted his eyes. The coruscation of gathered mage-energy here made that a twilight in comparison. Crisp black shadows were thrown behind every object, radiating out from the center of the Bán Cailleach. Kayne's slitted eyes could barely see her. Her body was consumed in this new sun, and then . . .

The light burst outward, and he felt the impact of its heat and saw its fury even through eyes quickly closed and shielded. Kayne shouted into the thunder of the explosion, his voice lost in the clamor.

And as suddenly, it was flashed past him, racing east like a backward sunrise. He could follow the pure, unfettered radiance as it moved over the Finger and into the misted distance of the horizon. The echoes of the moment roared in his ears; the afterimages danced and swayed in shifting curtains in front of him. He blinked and pawed at his eyes. Around him, he could hear the others calling and shouting, as bewildered and lost as he was.

"Kayne!"

"Aunt Edana." He saw her, or at least a form obscured by blotches of purple and green that looked somewhat like her.

"What happened, Kayne? Where have they gone?"

"Who?" he asked, still rubbing at his eyes. As his vision cleared, he found his breath gone.

There were no Arruk here except the dead. The rest, all of them, had vanished. The passage where they'd crawled in their thousands was empty. Except for the reminder of the slaughtered corpses, they might never have been there at all.

And the Bán Cailleach—Sevei, his sister—was gone as well. On the trampled ground where she'd been standing a moment before, a green stone lay.

Kayne reached down and picked it up.

As his fingers touched the stone, he heard a voice. *"Remember for me,"* Sevei said. *"Remember . . ."*

PART FIVE

DECISIONS

59

Bethiochnead and Cnocareilig

AFTERWARD, THE PEOPLES of Talamh An Ghlas and Céile Mhór would talk of the Day of the Brightness. Traveling much faster than the fleetest horse could run, the Brightness of the Pale Witch raced over the mountains of the Finger, and the clans shut their eyes and cried out at the manifestation, but it did not touch them. For them, there was a moment of terrible disorientation and blinding light, and many would say they felt a hurricane wind and glimpsed figures hurtling by them, wailing in the tongue of the Arruk.

It is said that when the Pale Witch's Brightness reached the ruins of the Bunús Wall, the stones that had fallen leaped up on their own and set themselves back into place, the creatures carved into their granite faces came alive as the intense light touched them, and their voices joined the thunder of the Brightness' flight, and the Brightness shouted back to them as it rushed toward Céile Mhór.

Where the Finger joined the long flank of Céile Mhór, the Brightness lengthened and turned south. It swept down over the towns and villages that the Arruk had taken from the Thane's people, and where the Brightness passed, there were no Arruk left behind. It swept them up, growing brighter and taller and larger as it moved. Above the Brightness, the mage-lights swirled in the sky as if night had come, and there were those who said they saw dragons wheeling above it, or black-furred seals riding in it as if the Brightness were an ocean wave. There were those who say they saw even stranger creatures in the Brightness—creatures that were yet legends of old times.

One thing is certain: the Brightness reached the ancient fortifications of the Uhmaci Wall, all the way at the foot of Middle Céile, before the sun set that day. There, the Brightness bloomed like an awful flower, and it raised the Uhmaci Wall that the Arruk had torn down, raised it higher and wider than it had been before. Then the Brightness collapsed, spreading out over Lower Céile before fading entirely at The Feet. As the Brightness moved through Lower Céile, it left behind the Arruk it had gathered up, all of them alive and whole, though blinded for a time.

The people of Talthma, the Daoine city closest to the Uhmaci Wall, say that as the Brightness died, they heard a loud voice speaking to the Arruk in their own tongue. Though many in later years claimed to know what the voice said, the truth is that their tales all contradict one another.

What the Brightness said, only the Arruk know.

Cima woke from the intense cold of the passage in a torpor, his body so frigid that he found it difficult to move his joints. A flat-faced bluntclaw watched him silently, leaning on a wooden staff. Cima forced his reluctant knees to bend and rise from where he knelt. Cima was clutching Ennis Svarti's spell-stick in his left hand, with the symbols of the Kralj's Svarti carved into its oaken surfaces, though he didn't remember picking up the spell-stick. His right hand was still fisted around Treoraí's Heart.

"Where am I?" he asked the bluntclaw as his body warmed and movement returned, "Where is the White Beast? Where are my people?"

He could still hear the whisper of the White Beast's voice in his head, the whisper he'd heard in the darkness of the passage: *"I give you this gift, Cima. I give it to you in the name of all the Aware. My gift to you, my gift to all . . ."*

"The White Beast is gone," the bluntclaw answered. "She's returned your people to their homes as she promised. But you, she's taken another way. This—" the bluntclaw indicated the landscape with a sweeping wave of his hand, "—is Bethiochnead in Thall Coill. It is also what you would call Cudak Zvati."

Cima forced his neck to swivel, to look around. He was standing on a cliff top bordered by a gray, heavy sea. The shadowstar had already set, but there was still light in the sky. He could hear wind shrieking past his ears and the waves battering rocks far below, could sniff the brine and fish smell of the ocean. The verdant line of a forest curved inland nearby, though he and the bluntclaw stood in a grassy meadow. Near the cliff's edge, as if it had rested there for centuries watching over this place, its body cracked and set at a strange angle in the ground . . .

"Cudak . . ." Cima said. "That is Cudak, who called us."

"Perhaps," the bluntclaw agreed. "Or perhaps it is the God of whom all the rest are shadows and echoes." Cima said nothing. The bluntclaw leaned on his staff, resting his hands on the knobbed end and his chin on his hands. "I am Beryn," he said. "I am the Protector of this place."

"I am Cima, and I am—" Cima stopped. "I don't know what I am," he finished finally. The bluntclaw showed his teeth at that in the way the Perakli did when they were amused. Cima walked over to the statue and placed his hands on the time-eroded stone. Even though the sun shone brightly here and he touched the flank of the carven god in full sunlight, the stone was so cold that he plucked his hand away in surprise.

"What am I supposed do?" he asked Beryn.

"Use the gift that the Bán Cailleach, the White Beast, gave you."

Cima glanced down to the gem that was still in his hand, the sky-stone that Ennis had called the Heart. "Will I be able to use this as Ennis Svarti did?"

"Perhaps," Beryn answered. "I don't know. Only we Bunús Muintir and the Daoine, who are the same people, have been able to use the clochs na thintrí in the past. The other Aware have their own way to the power of the mage-lights: the Saimhóir through Bradán an Chumhacht or the dragons through the ordeal of mage-fire. You were called here to find the way for the Arruk. I suspect that you will also find a new path, but for now look at the Heart, Cima. Let yourself fall into it. The Heart will open a way for you."

Cima slowly lowered his gaze from Beryn to the stone.

He wondered what the man was talking about it. *Fall into
it . . . ?* The facets glimmered in the dying light, and in the
gathering darkness above him, a wisp of Cudak's Web
curled, green and faint. He saw the light reflect in the
stone, seemingly deep inside. His vision shifted; he was suddenly seeing not only with his own eyes, but with some
other, different vision, and Treoraí's Heart was bright, so
bright . . .

"Ah," said a deep voice. It rumbled; it shook Cima's
body with its power. "So as Treorai once gave his Heart, it's
been given again. . . ." Cima looked away from the gem,
startled. The clearing was no longer the same. Beryn was
gone, the cliff ended many strides farther away, and the
statue of Cudak . . .

It was statue no longer. Instead, a great creature stood
there, a winged body that held elements of a dozen beasts
or more. It kneaded immense, clawed forepaws on the
ground, tearing furrows of rich, black earth; its golden eyes
as piercing as those of a hungry eagle as it stared at him.
"Cudak," Cima whispered. Involuntarily, he lifted his
snout, exposing his throat.

"Cudak . . ." the beast repeated, as if tasting the name in
its mouth. "Aye, that is one of my names. So your kind have
awakened again, and this time you've finally come to me.
I've been calling, all this time . . ."

"We heard your call," Cima told the creature. "But only
I have come. The White Beast—"

"I know," Cudak said. "She has chosen, and because of
the path she took, this will not be the Age of the Daoine
but the Age of all the Awakened. And you, Cima, you will
go back to your people as the First." The spell-stick quivered in Cima's left hand as Cudak looked at it. "So that will
be the way of your people. You will call the power from the
mage-lights with your carved staffs, and yours will be the
First Staff that opens the others. You will have but a few
precious spell-sticks that will be capable of this, and your
people will treasure them as the Daoine do their clochs."
The spell-stick was changing in Cima's hand, no longer the
dead brown of cut wood, but the pale yellow of a goldenwood sapling, as if it were a tree and he were the earth in
which it grew and to which it was bound.

"Is this what you want, Cima?" Cudak asked him. "Because you must know that holding the First Staff will be a burden like Lámh Shábhála was to the one you called the White Beast, or as Treoraí's Heart was to Ennis. The First Staff will consume you. It will eventually kill you. Are you willing, or should your people remain half-awake until the next cycle?"

The mage-lights brightened above them. Impossibly, it was full night already, with the stars above and the sweeping band of the Egg-Mother's Milk dusting the zenith. The curls and eddies of the mage-lights snaked down, as Cima had seen them do with Ennis and Treoraí's Heart, but they went not to Treoraí's Heart but to the transformed spell-stick he carried. There they hesitated, as if waiting for him to speak. Cudak was staring at him; he could see nothing but the beast's huge, patient eyes: eyes that now looked like Ennis'.

"I'm willing, Cudak," he said.

The beast sighed; its wings cupped and swept cold air over him. Cima gasped as the mage-lights wrapped around and finally touched the wood, sliding past to envelop his arm to the elbow. The mage-lights were an exquisite blending of pain and pleasure: searing cold that burned their patterns into the scales of his skin, yet filling a hunger within him that he hadn't known he possessed. He could feel . . . no, he *was* . . . the staff taking in the power within the mage-lights, soaking it into deep recesses and pockets within the wood. Cima shouted as the mage-lights brightened and deepened in color, forcing more and more of the sky-power into the staff. It seemed to be a few breaths; it seemed to be an eternity.

And it was gone . . .

It had *all* vanished: Cudak was only a gull-spotted, rain-streaked statue of smooth, black again, wingless and forlorn on the cliff edge in twilight, and Beryn was still leaning on his staff. But . . .

Cima looked at his left hand, holding the spell-stick. His skin was marked as Ennis' arm had been marked, the swirls and curlicues of the mage-lights burned in scars in his scales, and the stick was still like a living sapling, feeling as if it were part of him. He could feel the power caught within it, waiting for him to release it.

"Use the First Staff," Beryn told him. "Think of your people. Think of your home and it will take you there."

Home . . . It had been so long since he'd been there. He could recall it: the lakes, the forests, the villages with the Egg-mothers . . . *Home* . . . Something inside the First Staff stirred, and Cima took the rising power and touched it to his memories.

He departed Cudak Zvati.

When the Arruk was gone, Beryn sighed. He went to the statue of An Phionós and touched its flank with his hand, smiling at the feel of the frigid stone. Then he went to where the Arruk had stood. Bending down and holding onto his staff, he picked up a blood-red stone from the grass. He could feel the pull of it, the sudden attachment and bonding of his mind and the Heart.

For the first time since the Daoine had come to Talamh An Ghlas, a Bunús Muintir held a cloch, and this one a true rival to Lámh Shábhála.

"Thank you, Treoraí," he said. "Thank you, Sevei. This is a gift like none other."

He clutched the stone in his hand. Turning his back, he left Bethiochnead and slipped quietly into the deep woods as the sky darkened and the Seanóir began to sing.

Kayne stepped back from the entrance to the tomb. He nodded to the Draíodóiri with their incense and incantations, and the priests began a final chant as the attending gardai slowly rolled the closing stone over the mouth of the tomb. Kayne watched as the darkness enveloped the passage inside to hide the ashes and bones of his mam's and Ennis' bodies from sight once more.

The great statue of the Healer Ard loomed over Kayne, her spread arms and gentle smile embracing all those who had gathered to see the interment of the Healer Ard's youngest son. He touched the statue's foot, feeling the disconcerting warmth of its flesh. There were over a thousand people there: the Riocha standing nearest Kayne, the céile giallnai next, and then the tuathánach in the plain, simple clothing—the ones, Kayne knew, who came to this place to pray, to talk with Mam as they might any of the Mionbandia, the demigods of the Mother-Creator. Most of Dún Laoghaire seemed to be here today.

But except for Aunt Edana and Greada Kyle, none of the Ríthe were here. They waited elsewhere in the city, and they did not want to be seen.

"This is where Ennis should be. It's where he'd want to be," Aunt Edana said alongside Kayne. Her hand brushed his hair gently. Greada Kyle clasped his shoulder. Kyle lifted his head; as he did so, his fingers brushed against the stone on his chest.

"... *You did well. I'm sorry, Kayne. Sorry I couldn't listen to you, that I couldn't save Ennis ...*"

He grimaced. He hated the voices: Sevei, Gram, all the others going forever back in time. He hated knowing that he'd one day be one of them.

"Why did you do it?" he asked Sevei.

"What?" Greada Kyle asked, and Kayne realized he'd spoke aloud.

"Nothing, Greada. I was just . . ." Kayne took a deep breath. The torc of the Ard was heavy around his neck, but Lámh Shábhála seemed heavier. He looked up at the statue of his mam. Except for the fact that she was ten men high, she looked alive, looked as if she might at any moment bend her head down to see him or go striding away from Cnocareilig. The Draíodóiri were still chanting, and the crowd of tuathánach around the tomb were chanting with them—a song he hadn't heard before, a paean to the Healer Ard, a prayer asking for her favor.

"Rest in the Mother's arms," he said to Ennis as the stone grated into place and gardai stepped back to their stations on either side of the tomb entrance. With Edana and his greada, he turned to face the crowd. They sang to him, sang to the tomb behind him. He wondered if they would ever love him as they'd loved his mam.

"Come," Edana told him. "The other Ríthe are already at Tuatha Halla. Tonight, they'll acknowledge you as Rí Ard."

"Only because I hold Lámh Shábhála," Kayne said, unable to keep the bitterness from his voice. "Only because they're frightened. Only because they think it might keep me from slaying them for their betrayals and their cowardice."

"Not all of them," she reminded him. "Not me."

"Nor me," Kyle told him. "Nor Rí Rodhlann of Tuath

Méar. You will be Ard over all the Tuatha, as it should be.
You'll be the Rí Ard and Holder, together, as perhaps it always should have been."

. . . *Aye,* he heard Gram say in his head, and Sevei also.
. . . *Aye* . . . But the voice he'd most like to have heard was
never there: Séarlait. That voice was gone forever. He
would never hear her again and no power in Lámh Shábhála could change that.

"Are you ready?" Edana asked him.

"No," Kayne answered. "But no one is ever ready."

He strode away from Cnocareilig into the night and the
swelling chant, and the tuathánach parted to make way for
him, their hands outstretched toward him. He heard their
voices: "The Healer Ard's son . . . Make way for the last of
her family . . ."

He touched them in return, and didn't care if they saw
his tears.

APPENDICES

CHARACTERS (in order of appearance):

Sevei Geraghty	Firstborn child (female twin) of Meriel MacEagan and Owaine Geraghty
Dillon Ó'Baoill	An acolyte at the Order of Inishfeirm, Sevei's boyfriend
Mundy Kirwan	Máister of the Order of Inishfeirm
Jenna MacEagan (nee Aoire)	The Banrion of Inish Thuaidh and Holder of Lámh Shábhála
Kayne Geraghty	Firstborn child (male twin) of Meriel (nee MacEagan) and Owaine Geraghty
Owaine Geraghty	Husband of Meriel, and a cloudmage of the Order of Inishfeirm
Harik MacCathaill	Owaine's Hand (chief sergeant) among the gardai
Aeric MagWolfagdh (the Third)	Thane (High King) of Céile Mhór
Padraic O'Calhain	A gardai killed by Arruk near Ceangail
Harkin O Floinn	A gardai killed by Arruk near Ceangail

Mother-Creator	The Goddess: creator of the world.
Torin Mallaghan	Rí (King) of Tuath Gabair
Doyle Mac Ard	Jenna MacEagan's (nee Aoire) half-brother, the son of Maeve Aoire and Padraic Mac Ard
Meriel Geraghty (nee MacEagan)	The Banrion Ard, also called the "Healer Ard" due to her possession of Treoraí's Heart, the most recent of the cloch na thintri. Meriel is the daughter of Jenna MacEagan (nee Aoire), Banrion of Inish Thuaidh
Edana Mac Ard (nee O Liathain)	Daughter of Nevan O Liathain (formerly the Rí Ard). Married to Doyle Mac Ard.
Áine Martain	The "Hand of the Heart"—the person whose task it is to choose among the supplicants the person to be healed by Treoraí's Heart. Áine, as a child, was one of the first to be healed by Treoraí's Heart.
Fainche MacKeough	A woman Meriel refuses to heal.
Cristóir Barróid	A man healed by Meriel.
Marta Barróid	Cristóir's wife.
Enean Mac Ard	The youngest son of Edana and Doyle Mac Ard, named after Edana's deceased brother (briefly the Rí Ard after his father's death)
Ennis Geraghty	Youngest son of Meriel and Owaine Geraghty
Isibéal Gastiela	Chief maidservant to Meriel's children, a half-Taisteal woman
Siúr O'Halloran	Woman in charge of the kitchens for the Order of Inishfeirm
Kyle MacEagan	The husband of Jenna and father-by-marriage of Meriel, and a tiarna of Inish Thuaidh

Mahon MacBreen	Captain (Hand) of Jenna's personal gardai
Caenneth Mac Noll	The Daoine First Holder of Lámh Shábhála (from Year 232 to 241)
Siúr Cullinane	Clothier for the Order of Inishfeirm
Maeve Aoire (nee Oldspring)	Jenna's mam
Tara Geraghty	Youngest daughter of Meriel and Owaine Geraghty
Ionhar Geraghty	Middle son of Meriel and Owaine Geraghty
Róise Toibin	A young woman Kayne sleeps with in Ceangail
Adimu	Isibéal's deceased son
Padraic Mac Ard (the Younger)	Oldest son of Doyle and Edana Mac Ard, named after Doyle's father
Alastríona Mac Ard	Oldest daughter of Doyle and Edana Mac Ard
Keira	The Bunús Muintir Protector of Doire Coill
Fiodóir	In Taisteal mythology, the son of the Mother-Creator, who weaves the tapestry of Fate
Asthora	An old woman herbalist in Dún Laoghaire
Faoil Caomhánach	Once a student with Meriel Geraghty in the Order of Inishfeirm, and currently the Máistreás of the Order
Alexia Meagher	A Siúr of the Order of Inishfeirm, who holds a clochmion that can tell truth
Bartel	One of the garda in Owaine and Kayne's troop, wounded in the Battle of the Narrows

Padraic Mac Ard	A tiarna from Tuath Gabair and lover of Maeve Aoire, killed by Jenna in the Battle of Dún Kiil; father of Doyle Mac Ard
Shay O Blaca	The Máister of the Order of Gabair, who holds the Cloch Mór called Quickship, and an ally of Doyle Mac Ard
Mal Mac Baoill	Son of the current Rí Ard, holder of the Cloch Mór called Winter
Garvan O Floinn	A gardai in Owaine and Kayne's troop, wounded in the Battle of the Narrows
Sean	One of the garda in Owaine and Kayne's troop, wounded in the Battle of the Narrows
Uilliam	One of the garda in Owaine and Kayne's troop, wounded in the Battle of the Narrows
Caolán O Leathlobhair	An old shepherd man in the Fingerlands of Tuath Airgialla
Kyeil O Leathlobhair	Son of Caolán, died in an accident at age twelve
Aighna O Leathlobhair	Daughter of Caolán, left him for a Taisteal boy
Liam O'Blathmhaic	One of the clan lairds (chiefs) of the Fingerlands
Bhralhg	A Saimhóir who is the current possessor of Bradán an Chumhacht, the Saimhóir equivalent of Lámh Shábhála
Dhegli	A Saimhóir who was once Meriel's lover, and also the possessor of Bradán an Chumhacht; died at the Battle of Falcarragh

Challa	Dhegli's mate, who took Bradán an Chumhacht when he died
WaterMother	The chief god of the Blue Seals
Séarlait O'Blathmhaic	Granddaughter of Ald O'Blathmhaic; mute
Ata Kahlnik	Clannhra (leader) of the Kahlnik Clan of the Taisteal
Unnisha	A member of Clan Kahlnik of the Taisteal
Kellsean	Unnisha's son, dead of the Bloody Cough
Parlan MacMartain	A fisherman of the Stepping Stones
Donal MacMartain	Son of Parlan MacMartain
Báirbre MacMartain	Wife of Donal
Woulfe	Ald of the lands east of the Bunús Wall
MacCanna	Aldwoman of the low hills beyond the Narrows
Rodhlann O Morchoe	Commander of the Fingerlander forces against Tuath Airgialla
Tamara	One of the Kahlnik Taisteal, a cook
Estraven	One of the Kahlnik Taisteal
Kekeri the Bloodtail	A dragon of Inish Thuaidh
Beryn	Protector of Thall Coill
Lomán	Beryn's predecessor as Protector of Thall Coill
Kiraac	Leader of the Dire Wolves in Thall Coill
Saraigh	Pledge-daughter of Beryn, who will be the Protector after him
Carrohkai Treemaster	A Bunús Muintir Holder of Lámh Shábhála who passed the Scrúdú.

	Legend says she is responsible for the various old forests (Coill) in Talamh An Ghlas
An Phionós	"The Punishment." The statue-creature in Thall Coill
Daighi	A gardai of Dún Laoghaire
Brett	A gardai of Dún Laoghaire
Artol Jantsk	A man of Céile Mhór who befriends Ennis
Haughey	Thane's representative in Cairnmor
Brina	Haughey's wife
Kurhv Ruka	An Arruk who takes Ennis under his protection. As with many Arruk, the last name is not a family name but a title: "Hand of Blood"—one of the captains of the Arruk forces in Céile Mhór
Noz Ruka	Another Ruka among the Arruk; a rival of Kurhv Ruka
Alby	Kyle MacEagan's longtime companion and attendant
Ronat Ciomhsóg	Head of the townland of An Cnocan in Inish Thuaidh
Alexia Meagher	A Siúr of the Order of Inishfeirm
Aithne MacBrádaigh	Head of the townland of Rubha na Scarbh in Inish Thuaidh
Neale MacBreen	Head of the townland of Dún Kiil in Inish Thuaidh, and son of Mahon MacBreen
Maitiú O Contratha	Nephew of Rí Mac Baoill of Airgialla and Commander of his Army

Macka	The "Cat-Father," a god from whom the Arruk believe they have descended.
Grozan Kralj	The leader of the Arruk
Cima	A soldier of the Arruk assigned to teach Ennis the Arruk language
Lieve Mairki	Ruka Kurhv's superior in the Arruk army
Cudak	Chief God of the Arruk
Gyl	A Svarti (spell-caster) of the Arruk; Grozan Kralj's protector/adviser
Cairbre Kavanagh	A Tiarna officer with the Airgiallan army
Barra Rámonn	A Tiarna of Airgialla, commander of the army after Maitiú O Contratha's death
MacBreanhg	A famous Daoine artist, who carved the statues that adorn the Sunstones Ring in Dún Laoghaire
Daj Svarti	A mage of the Arruk
Auliffe O'Murchadha	One of Doyle's aides, a fosterling staying with him and Edana
Barak Svarti	A legendary Svarti of the Arruk
Issine	"The Eldest," an ancient Créneach who lives on the coast of Inish Thuaidh
Parin Mac Baoill	Cousin of Morven Mac Baoill of Tuath Airgialla, named as Rí after Morven's exile
Kyma Svarti	A Svarti of the Arruk
Faoil Caomhánach	Máistreás of the Order of Inishfeirm

THE RULERS (Ríthe) OF THE TUATHA (as of Year 1169)

Meriel Geraghty	Banrion Ard of all Tuatha
Jenna MacEagan	Banrion of Inish Thuiadh and First Holder
Morven Mac Baoill	Rí of Tuath Airgialla
Allister Fearachan	Rí of Tuath Connachta
Edana Mac Ard	Banrion of Tuath Dún Laoghaire
Caitrín Taafe	Banrion of Tuath Éoganacht
Torin Mallaghan	Rí of Tuath Gabair
Brasil Mas Sithig	Rí of Tuath Infochla
Eóin O Treasigh	Rí of Tuath Locha Léin

PLACES

Ahmaci	Southernmost city of the Daoine in Lower Céile
An Cnocan	A townland in Inish Thuaidh
An Deann Ramhar	A townland in Inish Thuaidh
Áth Iseal	A village on River Duán, where the High Road crosses the river
Bácathair	Capital city of Tuath Locha Léin, on the west coast of the peninsula
Ballicraigh	A small village in Tuath Infochla
Ballintubber	The village where Jenna was born
Banshaigh	A village on Lough Glas in Tuath Connachta
Be An Mhuillian	A townland in Inish Thuaidh
Bethiochnead	The "Beast-Nest": The location in Thall Coill where the Scrúdú takes place
Broughshane	A village in Tuath Airgialla near Tory Coill

Cairnmor	A harbor city in Céile Mhor (Mid Céile)
Cat's Alley	A back street in Lár Bhaile
Ceangail	A town in the Finger near the border of Céile Mhór
Céile Mhór	The far larger peninsula to which Talamh an Ghlas is connected by the Finger, a strip of mountainous land
Ceocnocs	The high hills on the western border of Tuath Dún Laoghaire
Cloughford	A tiny fishing village on the southern shore of Lough Tory
Cnocareilig	"Graveyard Hill"—the hillside above Dún Laoghaire where the Ards and Ríthe of Dún Laoghaire are buried.
Concordia	The capital city of Céile Mhor
Croc a Scroilm	The "Hill of Screaming"—the mountain that faces Dún Kiil Bay
Dalhmalli	A small village north of Falcarragh on Falcarragh Bay, next to Sliabh Bacaghorth
Doire Coill	The "Forest of Oaks"
Duán Mouth	The mountain-girdled and long end of the River Duán, which ends in an island-dotted bay
Dubh Bhaile	A city in Tuath Gabair, south of Lár Gabair on the Lough Dubh.
Dún Kiil	Chief city of Inish Thuaidh
Dún Laoghaire	Main city of the peninsula, seat of the High King
East Light	A small island in Falcarragh Bay where a lighthouse stands
Falcarragh	Capital city of Tuath Infochla

Finger, The	A long, thin and mountainous peninsula between Talamh an Ghlas and Céile Mhór, controlled politically by Tuath Airgialla
Glen Aill	A fortress mansion in Rubha na Scarbh (Inish Thuaidh)
Glenmill	A village in Tuath Infochla
Ice Sea	The sea to the north of the peninsula
Ingean na nUan	A townland in Inish Thuaidh
Inish Bideach	Literally, "tiny island"
Inish Cnapán	Northernmost island of the Stepping Stones
Inish Thuaidh	A large island off the peninsula of Talamh an Ghlas, home of the "Inishlanders"
Inishduán	A small island off Inish Thuaidh, where Jenna once gave the body of Padraic Mac Ard to Maeve Aoire, Jenna's mam
Inishfeirm	A small island off Inish Thuaidh, home of the Order of Inishfeirm and of Jenna's great-mam and great-da
Inishlesch	A small island in the group called the Stepping Stones
Kirina	A village in Tuath Infochla
Knobtop	A small mountain outside the village of Ballintubber, on whose flanks sheep are often grazed
Lár Bhaile	A city on Lough Lár, the seat of Tuath Gabair
Lough Bogha	A lake to the east of Cairnmor in Céile Mhór
Lough Crithlaigh	A lake on the northwest border of Tuath Gabair

Lough Dhub	A lake on River Duán, scene of one of the final battles between the Bunús Muintir and Daoine
Lough Donn	A lake in Tuath Infochla from which the River Donn flows northward to Falcarragh Bay
Lough Glas	A lake on the coastline of Tuath Connachta
Lough Lár	"Center Lake"—a large lake nearly in the center of the peninsula, very near Ballintubber
Lough Scáthán	"Mirror Lake"—a lough in Céile Mhór, scene of a battle between the Arruk and the Daoine
Maithcuan	A harbor town south of Dún Laoghaire
Maoil na nDreas	A townland in Inish Thuaidh
Mid Céile	The middle section of the great peninsula Céile Mhór
Na Clocha Dubha	A townland in Inish Thuaidh
Narrows	The pass from Talamh An Ghlas to the highlands of the Finger
Néalmhar Ford	The crossing of the River Néalmhar, the Gloomy River, in Inish Thuaidh
Rubha na Scarbh	A townland in Inish Thuaidh, home of Árón Ó Dochartaigh and Banrion Aithne MacBrádaigh
Sliabh Bacaghorth	A mountain in Tuath Infochla near Falcarragh, where Rowan Beirne lost Lámh Shábhála
Sliabh Colláin	A mountain in a southern county of the peninsula—also the title of a song

Sliabh Gabhar	One of the two peaks sheltering Falcharragh to the east; literally, "Goat Mountain"
Slíabh Míchinniúint	The Battle at the end of the previous incarnation of the mage-lights where the forces of Infochla were defeated by the Inishlanders
Sliabh Sí	One of the two peaks sheltering Falcarragh to the east; literally, "Mountain of the Fairy Mound"
Stepping Stones	A chain of islands running between the northwestern coast of Talamh an Ghlas and Inish Thuaidh
Talamh an Ghlas	"The Green Land": the peninsula on which the events of the novel take place
Thall Coill	The "Far Forest"
Thall Mór-roinn	The "Far Continent": the distant mainland, of which Talamh an Ghlas is a peninsula of yet another larger peninsula, Céile Mhór
The Black Gull	The only inn on Inishfeirm
Thiar	A city on the west coast, the seat of Tuath Connachta
Torness	A harbor city in Céile Mhór (Upper Céile) overrun by the Arruk in 1164
Tuath Airgialla	The Tuath in the northeast corner of the peninsula
Tuath Connachta	The Tuath to the immediate west of Tuath Gabair
Tuath Éoganacht	The Tuath in the south of the peninsula
Tuath Gabair	The Tuath in the center of the peninsula, also where Jenna Aoire MacEagan was born

Tuath Infochla	The Tuath in the northwestern corner of the peninsula
Tuath Locha Léin	The Tuath in the southwestern corner of the peninsula
Valleylair	A location in Tuath Connachta, famous for its ironworks
West Light	A small island at the mouth of the River Donn in Falcarragh Bay, where a lighthouse stands
Westering Sea	The ocean to the west of the peninsula

FLORA & FAUNA

Andúilleaf	A plant from which an addictive narcotic can be obtained
Black Haunts	The spirits of the dead who come and take the soul of the living when it's their time to die
Blue seals	Intelligent seals, black, but with a sheen of electric blue in their fur.
Blood Wolves	Huge wolves that walk upright like people and prey on unwary travelers. Possibly mythical.
Breadroot	A tuber plant grown in "lazy beds" (soil mounds over limestone rock) as a food staple
Coney	Rabbit. From the Irish Gaelic "coinín"
Corcach Siógai	Literally, "Swamp Fairies," the creatures who create the dangerous Sióg mists
Créneach	Literally, "Clay Beings," a race of sentient beings who inhabit the mountains near Thall Coill

Dire wolves	Large, intelligent wolves that speak a language
Fia stoirm	Storm Deer, a giant deer, previously thought extinct
Foulweed	A common weed in gardens
Kala bark	An analgesic used for headaches and minor pain. Non-addictive, but not anywhere near as strong as anduil-leaf.
Knifefang	An extinct or mythical carnivore of the land
Sióg mist	"Fairy mist": according to legend, those lost in the sióg mist never return to their own land, but are trapped forever in another world
Uisce Taibhse	Literally "Water Ghost," a race of intelligent creatures living in freshwater loughs, sometimes antagonistic to humans
Wind sprites	Nearly transparent, small and sentient herd creatures, once thought to be entirely mythical; nocturnal

DAOINE TERMS:

Ald	The "Eldest," a title of respect for the local repository of history
An-tUasal	"Mister"
Arruk	A race of belligerent creatures invading Céile Mhór
Athair Céile	Marriage-da (father-in-law)
the "Aware"	The sentient races of the world, which would include the Daoine, the Bunús Muintir, the Saimhóir, the Créneach, the dragons, the dire wolves, and the eagles, among others

Bán Cailleach	"Pale Witch": the term given to Sevei after the Scrúdú
Banrion	Queen
Bantiarna	The feminine form of Tiarna; "Lady" rather than "Lord"
Bean sí	Literally, "woman of the fairy mound" or "banshee," a ghost that comes to foretell death
Before, The	The time of myths, when magic ruled
Bóruma	Tribute paid to a Rí by those under his rule
Bráthair	The title for males who have dedicated themselves to the Order of Inishfeirm
Bunús Muintir	The "Original People," the tribes who first came to Talamh an Ghlas, and whose remnants still can be found in the hidden places.
By the Mother-Creator ...	A familiar mild curse, as we would say "By God ..."
Cailleach	Witch
Caointeoireacht na cogadh	The war-keening. The ululating and terrifying war-cry of the Inishlanders as they charge their foes. The cry in conjunction with their ferocious aspect has sometimes sent foes retreating in panic.
Céili giallnai	The lower grade vassals of the Rí
Cinniúint	Máel Armagh's ship
Clan-laird	A Fingerlander term: "Clan-leader." Often used simply as "Laird." Usually the Ald (Eldest) of a clan serves as laird. The feminine word is Clanbanlaird or Banlaird

Clóca	A long cloak worn by the Riocha over their clothing, usually in the colors of their Tuath
Cloch Mór	The major clochs na thintrí, the ones with large abilities
Cloch na thintrí	Literally, "stone of lightning," the stones that gather the power of the mage-lights
Clochmion	The minor clochs na thintrí with small powers
Clock-candle	Device used to keep time: a candle of standard diameter with colored wax at fixed intervals. One "stripe" equals roughly one hour
Cloudmages	Sorcerers of old who took power from the heavens to create their Spells
Colors	The various Tuaths have colors that show allegiance:

> Tuath Gabair = green and brown
>
> Tuath Connachta = blue and gold
>
> Tuath Infochla = green and gold
>
> Tuath Airgialla = red and white
>
> Tuath Locha Léin = blue and black
>
> Tuath Éoganacht = green and white
>
> Tuath Dún Laoghaire (and the Rí Ard) = dark gray
>
> Inish Thuaidh = blue and white

	The banner of the Concordance of Céile Mhór is a stylized dire wolf on a field of blue
Comhairle of Tiarna	The Council of Lords, the actual governing body of Inish Thuaidh

Comhdáil Comhairle	The "Conference of the Comhairle," the meeting of all chieftains in Inish Thuaidh
Concordance of Céile Mhor	The confederacy of kingdoms on the larger peninsula to the east and north of Talamh An Ghlas
Corn Festival	Autumn feast in Ballintubber
Crannog	An artificial island built on a lake and used as a safe dwelling place.
Currach	A small, dug-out boat used by the fisherfolk of Inish Thuaidh
Da	Father
Daoine	Literally, "The People," the society to which Jenna belongs
Dia duit	"Hello": a greeting from one person to another. If the greeting is to more than one person at a time, it is "Dia daoibh"
Draíodóir	Those consecrated to serve the Mother-Creator, in essence, the priesthood, though it is not restricted by gender; the plural is Draíodóiri
Drumlins	Low, steep-sided hills packed closely together, often with bogs, marshes, and small lakes at their feet
Earc Tine	The race of dragons
Eneclann	Honor-price, the amount a person can owe by his/her status
Éraic	Payment of blood-money from a slayer
Feast of Planting	One of the great quarterly festivals, taking place in late March
Ficheall	A board game similar to chess
Filí	Poet

Filleadh	The "Coming Back, the prophesied return of magic
Fingal	To slay your own kin; one of the worst crimes
Freelanded	A term meaning that the land is owned by the person living there. To be freelanded is to be one step down from being Riocha, or nobility
Garda	The police of the large cities, or the personal protectors of a Tiarna, also a term for "guard," the plural is gardai. The salute of a garda to a Riocha is to touch the right fist to chest
Garifali	Not actually a Daoine term, but another people like the Daoine, who inhabit the land of Thall Mór-roinn
Giotár	Stringed instrument, guitar
Gram	An affectionate term for "great-mam" or grandmother
Greada	An affectionate term for "great-da" or grandfather
Imigh	Go (verb)
Iníon	"Miss"
Ionadaí	"Representative," the Thane's "presence" in any large town or city in Céile Mhór
Is ferr fer a chiniud	"A man is better than his birth"
Lámh Shábhála	The cloch na thintrí that Jenna holds
Léine	A tunic worn under the clóca
Maidin maith	"Good morning!"
Máister	"Master," a term of respect for a male teacher or head of an organization

Máistreás	"Mistress," a term of respect for a female teacher or head of an organization
Mam	Mother
Marbhsháinn	In the game of ficheall, "checkmate"
Menhir	A carved standing stone, often commemorating some event
Milarán	A breakfast griddle cake from Inish Thuaidh, sprinkled with molasses and spices
Mionbandia	Literally: "small goddess" or demigoddess
Miondia	The Lesser Gods
Moon-time	The time of a woman's monthly menstrual flow
Mórceint	A fairly large denomination coin
Óenach	An assembly held on regular occasions to transact the private and public business of the Tuatha; after the death of a Rí Ard, a special Óenach is called by the Ríthe of the Tuatha to confirm a new Rí Ard, although this is often only a formality
Order of Gabair	An organization of mages formed in rivalry to the Order of Inishfeirm, based in Lár Bhaile in Tuath Gabair; mages of the Order of Gabair wear dark green clóca and léine
Order of Inishfeirm	An ancient organization and school of mages, based on the island of Inishfeirm, which is part of the kingdom of Inish Thuaidh; cloudmages of the Order of Inishfeirm wear white clóca and léine
Oscail	The verb "open"

Peace banner	A flag flown to show an intent to parley or negotiate, or that the person(s) with the banner are noncombatants. The banner is a stylized red doe on a grass-green field.
Pledge-son/daughter	A Bunús Muintir term; a younger person adopted by an Elder as his or her successor
Quern	A stone mill using for grinding grain and corn
Rí	King, the plural is "Ríthe"
Riocha	The Royalty
Scilidh leann fírinne	"Beer divulges truth"
Scrúdú	The test which allows a Holder to fully open all of Lámh Shábhála's capabilities; often fatal
Seed-Daughter's Star	The evening/morning star, brightest in the sky, that appears just after sunset or before sunrise
Siúr	The title for females who have dedicated themselves to the Order of Inishfeirm
Sochraideach	Mourner
Soul-shredders	The tormentors of those dead who are guilty of dishonor, usually the people that the guilty person harmed in life. In Daoine mythology, the Mother-Creator judges the dead brought before her by the black haunts. Those who led particularly vile lives are sent to the soul-shredders, who tear away the stains of the guilty one's life-deeds in exquisite torture: a hand of years of torment for every deed that must be expunged

Stirabout	A meat stew
Tanaise Ríg	The Heir-Apparent
Thane	The High King of the Concordance, a title roughly equal to the Rí Ard of Talamh An Ghlas
The Badger	A constellation used for navigation, as the snout of the badger always points to the north
Tiarna	The title "Lord"
Toscaire Concordai	"Delegate of the Concordance," a title used for representatives of the Concordance of Céile Mhór
Tráthnóna maith duit	"Good evening"
Tuath	Kingdom; the plural is "Tuatha"
Tuatha Halla	The ancient hall where the Ríthe of the Tuatha meet to certify the election of a new Rí Ard
Tuathánach	"Peasant" or "Commoner": those without royal blood in their lineage
Turves	Turf cuttings, peat.
Uaigneas	The Banrion's ship: "Loneliness"
Witchfire	A fire made through slow magic and the use of certain herbs; a witchfire lasts far longer than a torch, and gives off a brighter light

BUNÚS MUINTIR TERMS:

Ald	The "Eldest," a title of respect for the local repository of history
Bunús Muintir	The "Original People," the tribes who first came to Talamh an Ghlas, and whose remnants still can be found in the hidden places

Corrthónach	The Bunús Muintir term for the Taisteal
Greatness	The Bunús Muintir term for the Mother-Creator, also used by the clans of the Fingerlands
Pauk	The Búnus Muintir spider-god, who weaves the web of fate
Seanóir	The Eldest, the oak trees of Doire Coill and the other Old Growth Forests

TAISTEAL TERMS:

Clannhra	The Taisteal title for the female head of the clan
Clannhri	The Taisteal title for the male head of the clan
Dobra vece	"Good evening"
Klaastanak	The "meeting of the clans" for the Taisteal, which takes place once every decade in Thall Mór-roinn. It is at the Klaastanaks that the business of the clans takes place
Svinja sin od pas	"Bastard son of a dog!"
Taisteal	The "Traveling," an itinerant group of peddlers of anything, from orphaned children to hard goods

SAIMHÓIR TERMS:

Bradán an Chumhacht	The "Salmon of the Mage-Lights," the blue seals' analogue to the cloch na thintri
Brightness	The Saimhóir term for a day
Bull	Adult male seal; bulls are less common, and are 'shared' by several adult females

Cow	Adult female seal
Earth-snared	A changeling whose "natural" form is that of a Daoine, but who can change briefly into Saimhóir form
Great Sweetwater	The River Duán
Haul out	The term for leaving the water for the shore
Land-cousin	Those humans with Saimhóir blood in their ancestry
May the currents bring you fish	A common polite greeting
Milk-mother	The cow who suckles a youngling—not necessarily the same cow who gave birth to the infant. In Saimhóir society, the young are often suckled by another cow. There is generally a stronger attachment to the milk-mother than the birth-mother (unless of course they happen to be the same)
Milk-sister/brother	A seal who has shared the milk of the same mother
Nesting Land	Inish Thuaidh; it is only on this island that the Saimhóir breed, on the northwest shores
Saimhóir	The name the blue seals call themselves
Seal-biter	The shark, which feeds on seals
Sister-kin	A term of endearment
Sky-stones	The cloch na thintrí
Stone-walker	A human
Sweetfish	Any of the small fish that make up the bulk of the Saimhóir's diet
WarmLight	The sun

WaterMother	The chief god of the Saimhóir. It is possible, though not proven, that the WaterMother is simply another manifestation of the human's Mother-Creator
Water-snared	A changeling whose "natural" form is that of a Saimhóir, but who can change briefly into Daoine form
Winter Home	The peninsula of Talamh an Ghlas, where the currents are warmer and the fish more plentiful during the coldest months
Wooden-islands-that-move	A compound word that the Saimhóir use in referring to the Daoine ships

ARRUK TERMS:

Cudak	The Arruk-God
Cudak Zvati	"The God's Lair"
Egg-Mother	The natural mother of an Arruk, with whom an eggling generally stays until the age of eight
Hajde	"Come on" or "Follow me"
Idemo	Forward
Jaka	The scythelike, great-bladed weapon of the Arruk
Kapasti	A vulgar curse in the Arruk tongue, roughly translating as "castrated coward"
Kralj	"Terrible One," the warrior leader of the Arruk
Life-Weaver	At the age of eight, young Arruk are removed from their egg-mother and placed in a "life pack" under the control of a Life-Weaver. The Life-Weaver always matches the gender of the Arruk under him or her, and

	each Life-Weaver might have twenty or more younglings for which he or she is responsible. It is the task of the Life-Weaver to work with the younglings and determine an appropriate apprenticeship for their skills
Macka	The God of the Warrior's Afterlife
Mairki	"General," there are four Mairki under the Kralj.
Nesting-house	The house where an egg-mother lives with her egglings
Nesvarti	The "lesser mages" of the Arruk, who are under the control one of the Svarti.
Nista	A division within the Arruk army; also the title of the lowest ranking officer, equivalent to "Sergeant": there are sixteen Nista reporting to each Ured
Perakli	Literally, "blunt-claw," the derogatory term for the Daoine and Bunús Muintir both in the Arruk language
Ruka	"Captain" or "Hand": there are eight Ruka under each of the Mairki
Seiv oder Tog	Victory or Death, a soldier's code
Season-mate	Arruk females are attached to a particular male for one mating season only. Once the eggs are hatched, the young are given to the egg-mother to raise and their temporary union is dissolved. Occasionally, Arruk may keep the same season-mate for more than one year, but that's unusual
Shadowlight	The sun
Spell-sticks	The wooden staves the Arruk mages use to store their magic. Made only from a goldenwood tree
Svarti	The magic-users of the Arruk

| Ured | A division within the Arruk army; also a title equivalent to "Lieutenant": there are twelve Ured under each Ruka |
| Zvati | "Web" or "Lair" |

THE DAOINE CALENDAR:

The Daoine calendar, like that of the Bunús Muintir, is primarily lunar-based. Their "day" is considered to start at sunset and conclude at sunrise. Each month consists of twenty-eight days; there is no further separation into weeks. Rather, the days are counted as being the "thirteenth day of Wideleaf" or the "twenty-first day of Capnut."

The months are named after various trees of the region, and are (in translation) Longroot, Silverbark, Wideleaf, Straightwood, Fallinglimb, Deereye, Brightflower, Redfruit, Conefir, Capnut, Stranglevine, Softwood, and Sweetsap.

The solar year being slightly more than 365 days, to keep the months from recessing slowly through the seasons over the years, an annual two-fold adjustment is made. The first decision is whether there will be additional days added to Sweetsap; the second proclaims which phase of the moon will correspond to the first day of the month that year (the first day of the months during any given year may be considered to start at the new moon, quarter moon waxing, half moon waxing, three-quarter moon waxing, full moon, three-quarter moon waning, half-moon waning, or quarter moon waning). The proclamation is announced at the Festival of Ghéimri (see below) each year—any extra days are added immediately after Ghéimri and before the first day of Longroot. All this keeps the solar-based festivals and the lunar calendar roughly in line.

This adjustment is traditionally made by the Draíodóiri of the Mother-Creator at the Sunstones Ring at Dún Laoghaire, but the Inish Thuaidh Draíodóiri generally use the Sunstones Ring near Dún Kiil to make their own adjustments, which do not always agree with that of Dún Laoghaire. Thus, the reckoning of days in Talamh an Ghlas and Inish Thuaidh is often slightly different.

The year is considered to start on the first day of Long-root, immediately after the Festival of Ghéimri and any additional days that have been added to Sweetsap.

There are four Great Festivals at the solstices and equinoxes.

Láfuacht: (in the first week of Straightwood)	Marks that true winter has been reached and that the slow ascent toward the warmth of spring has begun. Generally a celebration touched with a somber note because the rest of winter must still be endured.
Fómhar (in the second week of Brightflower)	Marks the time to prepare for the spring planting to come and the birthing of newborn stock animals. This festival was an appeal to the Mother-Creator and the (the lesser gods) to make the crops grow and the livestock fertile. A time of sacrifices and prayer.
Méitha (in the third week of Capnut)	Marks the height of the growing season. In good years, this was the most manic and happy festival, celebrating the plenty all around.
Gheimhri (in the fourth week of Sweetsap)	Marks the onset of autumn. This is a date fraught with uncertainty and worry as the crops are harvested and the colder weather begins. Though this holiday often spreads over more than one day, it is also laden with solemn rites and ceremonies to placate the gods who awaken with the autumn chill.

The following is a sample year with corresponding Gregorian dates. However, bear in mind that this is only an approximation and will differ slightly each year.

1st day of Longroot (New Year's Day) = September 23
1st day of Silverbark = October 21
1st day of Wideleaf = November 18
1st day of Straightwood = December 16
   Festival of Láfuacht :7th day of Straightwood (December 22)
1st day of Fallinglimb = January 13
1st day of Deereye = February 10
1st day of Brightflower = March 10
   Festival of Fómhar: 11th day of Brightflower (March 20)
1st day of Redfruit = April 7
1st day of Conefir = May 5
1st day of Capnut = June 2
   Festival of Méitha: 19th day of Capnut (June 20)
1st day of Stranglevine = June 30
1st day of Softwood = July 28
1st day of Sweetsap = August 25
   Festival of Gheimhri: 28th day of Sweetsap (September 21)

MYTHOLOGICAL TALES:

Each of the "aware" races of the world, of which there are several, have their own mythologies and gods, though there are intertwining connections and similarities between them all. Here are a few mythological tales concerning the beginning of things. These tales come from diverse racial sources: the Daoine, the Bunús Muintir, the Saimhóir, and the Créneach.

The chronicling of all the various myths and tales would be an immense task indeed; those below are merely intended to give a sampling. As with all mythology, these are tales that have passed down for long ages back to dim beginnings, slowly changing and altering with each telling, but truths lie underneath them.

The Daoine Creation Tale:
The Mother-Creator had intercourse with the Sky-Father, and gave birth to a son. But their son was sickly and died, and she laid him down in the firmament, and his skeleton became the bones of the land. In time, the

Mother-Creator overcame her grief and lay again with Sky-Father, and gave birth to Seed-Daughter.

Seed-Daughter flourished and in time became as beautiful as her mother, and she attracted the attention of two offspring of the Sky-Father: Cloud, and his sister Rain. From that triple union came the plants living in the soil that covered her brother, the Earth. Seed-Daughter was also coveted by Darkness, and Darkness stole her away and took her in violence. The troubled and often violent relationship between Darkness and Seed-Daughter is told in many tales.

When Seed-Daughter finally escaped from Darkness and came back to Cloud and Rain, sorrowing, she was heavy in her womb, and from her time of confinement would come all the Miondia, the Lesser Gods. The Miondia spread out over the earth, and from their various and strange couplings emerged the aware creatures and all the animals in all their varieties.

After the rape by Darkness, Seed-Daughter could conceive no more. Even now, she weeps often, sometimes fiercely, which we see even now in the rain that falls.

The Creation of the Clochs (Créneach):
Back when there was only stone in the world and the First-Lights gleamed, before the coming of the soft-flesh things, there was Anchéad, the first Thought. Anchéad wanted a companion, and so took a pebble from Itself and let the First-Lights wrap around it. The First-Lights gave the pebble of Anchéad life and awareness, and from this piece grew the god called Céile. Within Céile, Anchéad's pebble grew, always pulling the First-Lights toward it. For a long time, Anchéad and Céile dwelled together, but Céile found that Anchéad still sometimes yearned for Its solitude and would often go wandering by itself, leaving Céile alone for years at a time. So Céile also became lonely, and like Anchéad, broke away a pebble from Itself and held it out to the First-Lights, and they came and gave it life and shape also, though the fire of its life did not burn as deeply as Céile's. Each time that Anchéad went wandering, Céile would break off another part of Itself, until there were a dozen or more children of Céile. Sometimes her children even broke off fragments of themselves and made their

own children, but their hearts were even weaker than their own and shone only dimly.

The children and grandchildren of Céile were the first of the Créneach.

One day, though, Anchéad went wandering and never returned, and Céile sorrowed though the Créneach tried to give It comfort. The First-Lights felt the grief and loss of Céile, and in sympathy they left and went to search for Anchéad. As they faded, so did Céile's life and those of the Créneach. When the First-Lights had gone completely, Céile and Its children and grandchildren fell down lifeless, and the wind and rain wore away the form of their bodies until all that was left were their gleaming hearts.

The soft-flesh things came, and they took away many of the hearts they found for themselves, for they loved the way the hearts looked—Céile's heart was one of those that was taken.

And so it was until finally the First-Lights returned again from their unsuccessful search for the lost Anchéad. The First-Lights found Céile's heart and they went to it, filling it once more. But the soft-things held the heart now and the First-Lights could not bring Céile back, nor any of Its children or grandchildren who had also been taken. But the All-Heart that had been within Céile was able to stir and waken the hearts of all Its children and grandchildren: those hearts the soft-flesh things possessed could hold the power of the First-Lights, but only the few who had not been touched by the soft-things could revive and have form and shape again as Créneach.

Without Céile, though, none of the Créneach could take of themselves and make children. The First-Lights saw that and sorrowed, and so they gave a gift to the Créneach: they found a pebble that was like the heart of the Créneach and gave it life and form, and that one was the Littlest, and its light shone as bright as the first children of Céile.

That is the way it has been ever since: the First-Lights go to search now and again for Anchéad and we Créneach die. Our bodies crack and crumble to pebbles and dust, and the hearts within us fall away. Those hearts the soft-flesh things find and take will never live again as Créneach. When the First-Lights return from their search, they go first to the All-Heart and awaken it once more, and the All-Heart in turn awakens all of Its children and grand-children. Then the First-Lights find the hearts that have not yet been touched and bring us back.

And they also wake a new Littlest or two. . . .

A BRIEF HISTORY:

Year -2500 (approx.)	The first of the Bunús Muintir tribes reach Talamh an Ghlas, after traversing from Thall Mór-roinn, the mainland, into Céile Mhór, the larger peninsula to which Talamh an Ghlas is attached. These Bronze Age people created their society where no human had ever walked, which lasted until the arrival of the Daoine tribes in Year 0.
Year -75 (approx.)	The final disappearance of the mage-lights for the Bunús Muintir people. The mage-lights would not reappear again until after the arrival of the Daoine and the collapse of Bunús Muintir society.
Year -70 (approx.)	Death of Bunús Muintir chieftain and cloudmage Riata, Last Holder of Lámh Shábhála.
Year 0	The first of the Daoine tribes enter Talamh an Ghlas, crossing over the "Finger," the spine of mountainous land connecting Talamh an Ghlas to the peninsula of Céile Mhór, and also arriving by ship at Inish Thuaidh, on the western coast at Bácathair and in the south at Taghmon. They would encounter and eventually displace (and interbreed with) the Bunús Muintir people.
Year 105	The Battle of Lough Dubh, where Rí Crenél Dahgnon defeated the last Bunús Muintir chieftain Ruaidhri.

Year 232	The first mage-lights appear over Inish Thuaidh in the reign of the Daoine people. Caenneth Mac Noll becomes the first Daoine cloudmage and First Holder of Lámh Shábhála. This is the beginning of what will be called "The Before." (Year 232–726)
Year 241	Caenneth Mac Noll dies in Thall Coill, attempting the Scrúdú.
Year 711	Máel Armagh, Rí of Tuath Infochla, sets out to conquer Inish Thuaidh, and is defeated and killed in the Battle of Sliabh Míchinniúint by Severii O'-Coulghan, the Inishlander who would be the Last Holder of Lámh Shábhála.
Year 726	Last reported sighting of mage-lights over Inish Thuaidh. End of the "Before." Over four centuries will pass before the mage-lights return.
Year 1075	A cloch reputed to be Lámh Shábhála is stolen from Inishfeirm by an acolyte named Niall (last name unknown) and is given as a pledge of love to Kerys Aoire.
Year 1111	Niall Aoire, son of Kerys Aoire, arrives in Ballintubber and meets Maeve Oldspring, whom he will marry.
Year 1113	Jenna Aoire born in Ballintubber.
Year 1129	On the 18th day of Longroot, mage-lights reappear over the village of Ballintubber in Tuath Gabair. This heralds the beginning of Filleadh—the "Coming Back." Jenna Aoire becomes First Holder of Lámh Shábhála.
Year 1130	25th of Redfruit: Doyle Mac Ard born to Maeve Aoire.

5th of Sweetsap: Jenna Aoire marries Kyle MacEagan. |

	21st–23rd of Sweetsap: The Battle of Dún Kiil, where the forces of Inish Thuaidh defeat invaders from the Tuatha, led by Nevan O Liathain.
Year 1131	10th of Longroot: Jenna becomes Banrion (Queen) of Inish Thuaidh.
	18th of Deereye: Meriel MacEagan born to Jenna.
Year 1135	Nevan O Liathain becomes Ri Ard after the death of his father.
	First Daoine city falls to the Arruk in Céile Mhór (Lumsden, southernmost city in Lower Céile).
Year 1142	Order of Gabair formed in rivalry of the Order of Inishfeirm.
Year 1148	First news comes to Talamh An Ghlas of the Arruk invasion of Céile Mhór as the Arruk cross the Uhmaci Wall.
	Nevan O Liathain dies.
Year 1149	Enean O Liathain, son of Nevan, becomes Rí Ard.
	Battle of Falcarragh, where the First Holder (also known as the Mad Holder) nearly destroyed the city against a massive force of cloudmages.
Year 1150	Meriel Geraghty (nee MacEagan) named as Banrion Ard. Sevei and Kayne Geraghty (twins) born.
Year 1156	The Arruk take the city of Dúnbarr in Middle Céile.
Year 1165	Sevei Geraghty, daughter of the Banrion Ard, is sent to the Order of Inishfeirm.
Year 1168	A force under Owaine Geraghty is sent to Céile Mhór to support their

		Daoine cousins in the fight against the Arruk
Year 1169		First attack of the Arruk within Talamh an Ghlas.

SAIMHÓIR HOLDERS OF BRADÁN AN CHUMHACHT (by Daoine years):

Thraisha	1129–1130	(died in Battle of Dún Kiil)
Garrentha	1130–1141	(died from wounds caused by a seal-biter)
Dhegli	1141–1149	(a water-snared changeling, not full Saimhóir, died in Battle of Falcarragh)
Challa	1149–1168	(died of old age)
Bhralhg	1168–	

THE HOLDERS OF LÁMH SHÁBHÁLA (by Daoine years and in chronological order. Entries in **boldface** indicate the cloch was active during the time of Holding.)

THE BUNÚS MUINTIR HOLDERS (from Year–160)

-160 to -144	**Lasairíona (F)**
-144 to -129	**Óengus (M)**
-129 to -113	**Dávali (M)**
-113 to -70	**Riata (M)—The last Bunús Muintir holder of an active cloch. The magelights failed in the last years of his Holding, and Lámh Shábhála would rest again for three centuries.**
-70 to -63	None—during these years, the cloch remained in Riata's tomb.
-63 to -63	Breck the Tomb-robber (F)—for two days, until she ws caught and executed.

-62 to -60	None—again, the cloch rests in Riata's tomb
-60 to -53	Nollaig the One-Handed (M)—Nollaig, like Breck, stole the cloch from Riata's tomb but held it for years, until he was caught pilfering other items from the chieftain Lobharan's clannog. The cloch and other items once belonging to Riata as well as from the other tombs there were found among Nollaig's belongings. Some of the treasure was returned to the tombs, but Lobharan kept the stone. Nollaig lost his hand
-53 to -27	Lobharan (M)
-27 to -15	Ailbhe (F)—Lobharan's daughter
-15 to 11	Struan (M)—Ailbhe's son, father of Cealaigh
11 to 37	Cealaigh (M)—first war-chief of the Bunús, who were now actively fighting the Daoine in the north of Talamh an Ghlas. He would wear the cloch in battle under his armor, and was never defeated on the field—he died of an illness.
37 to 42	Mhaolain (M)—Mhaolain was Cealaigh's successor as war-chief, who (like Cealaigh) wore the cloch as a talisman for victory. When he was finally defeated by Dyved of the North Holdings' army, the cloch passed from Bunús Muintir hands to those of the Daoine.

THE DAOINE HOLDERS

| 42 to 57 | Dyved of the North Holdings (M) |
| 57 to 59 | Salmhor Ó-Dyved (M)—Dyved's son, killed in battle against the Bunús |

Muintir. The cloch was among his effects, but none of Salmhor's heirs seems to have inherited the cloch. From here, it passes out of history for nearly two centuries until the mage-lights come again in 232.

59 to 232   The Lost Years—sometime during this period, the cloch was moved from the North Holdings (a small kingdom in what would later be part of Tuath Infochla) to Inish Thuaidh. No one knows for certain who held the stone during this time, though several people in later years would claim that their ancestors had been among them. Since none of the Daoine had seen the mage-lights, it's doubtful that they understood the significance of the stone beyond its recent history as a talisman of the Bunús war-chiefs.

There is a legend that the Bunús Muintir recovered the cloch after Salmhor's death on the battlefield, and that the Bunús themselves took the cloch to Inish Thuaidh to hide it. Another legend claims that the cloch was thrown into the sea, and that a blue seal brought the cloch to Inish Thuaidh. The truth of any of these claims can't be verified.

232 to 241   **Caenneth Mac Noll (M)—the first Daoine cloudmage, and the return of the mage-lights in the skies. Caenneth was not of royal lineage, but a simple fisherman of Inish Thuaidh, yet he would come to understand the sky-magic, and would reactivate the other cloch na thintrí. Caenneth would die in Thall Coill, attempting the Scrúdú.**

241 to 263   **Gael O Laighin (M)**

263 to 279	**Fearghus O Laighin (M)**
279 to 280	**Heremon O Laighin (M)**—died testing himself against the Scrúdú
280 to 301	**Maitlas O Ciardha (M)**
301 to 317	**Aithne Lochlain (F)**
317 to 329	**Nuala Mag Aodha (F)**
329 to 333	**Ioseph MacCana (M)**—died testing himself against the Scrúdú
333 to 379	**Lucan O Loingsigh (M)**
379 to 382	**Naomhan McKenna (M)**
382 to 392	**Kieran MacGairbhith (M)**
392 to 401	**Eilís MacGairbhith (F)**—killed in the Battle of Lough Lár by Aodhfin Ó Liathain, and the control of the cloch moves south from Inish Thuaidh to the mainland of Talamh an Ghlas.
401 to 403	**Aodhfin Ó Liathain (M)**—Rí of the small kingdom of Bhaile
403 to 416	**Dougal Woulfe (M)**
416 to 432	**Fagan McCabe (M)**
432 to 459	**Eóin Ó hAonghusa (M)**
459 to 463	**Eimile Ó hAonghusa (F)**
463 to 480	**Dónal Ó hAonghusa (M)**
480 to 487	**Maclean Ó hAonghusa (M)**
487 to 499	**Brianna Ó hAonghusa (F)**
499 to 515	**Lochlainn O'Doelan (M)**
515 to 517	**Maitiú O'Doelan (M)**—perhaps the only Daoine from Talamh An Ghlas to attempt the Scrúdú. He came to Thall Coill stealthily via ship in company with his good friend Keefe Mas Sithig. He did not survive the attempt.

517 to 529	**Keefe Mas Sithig (M)**
529 to 541	**Conn DeBarra (M)**
541 to 577	**Barra Ó Beoilláin (M)**
577 to 591	**Uscias Aheron (M)**
591 to 597	**Afrika MacMuthuna (F)**
597 to 612	**Ailen O'Curragh (M)**

612 to 622 **Sinna Mac Ard (nee Hannroia) (F)**— the young lover of Ailen O'Curragh, who after O'Curragh's early death married Teádor Mac Ard, then the Rí of a fiefdom within what is now Tuath Gabair. After Teádor's death in 622, the children of Teádor's former marriage demanded that the eldest of them (a son) should be the new Rí. Sinna took ill during this period (rumors abound that she was actually poisoned) and died, at which point Teádor's son by his first wife was named Rí. However, Bryth, then only thirteen years of age, took Lámh Sháb-hála from her mam's neck.

622 to 648 **Bryth Beirne (nee Mac Ard) (F)**— daughter of Sinna and Teádor Mac Ard. It is during Bryth's holding that the Inish cloudmages began to secretly plot to bring the cloch back to the island. Negotiations were begun with Bryth, including possible arrangements of marriage to the Rí of Inish Thuaidh, but she refused despite Rí Mac Ard's interest in that political union, and eventually married Anrai Beirne, a tiarna of Tuath Infochla.

648 to 651 **Rowan Beirne (M)**—Bryth's son Rowan foolishly allowed himself to be drawn north out of Falcarragh to a supposed parley with the Inishlanders, where he was ambushed and murdered by assassins in the employ of the Inish cloudmage Garad Mhúllien. Lámh Shábhála was taken from Rowan's body and brought to the island.

651 to 662   Garad Mhúllien (M)—the cloch returns to Inish Thuaidh. Garad would die testing himself against the Scrúdú

663 to 669   Rolan Cíleachair (M)

669 to 671   Peria Ó Riain (F)—mother of Severii, lover to Tadhg O'Coulghan. She died in Thall Coill testing herself against the limits of the cloch with the Scrúdú. Tadhg would take the cloch from her body and become Holder himself.

671 to 701   Tadhg O'Coulghan (M)—founder of the Order of Inishfeirm based on the tiny island of the same name just off the coast of Inish Thuaidh. Tadhg was the da of Severii, the Last Holder. It was Tadhg who began the process of codifying and bringing together all the lore of the clochs na thintrí, as well as Lámh Shábhála.

701 to 730   Severii O'Coulghan (M)—the last person to hold an active Lámh Shábhála until the mage-lights returned in 1129. The mage-lights had ebbed to nothing by 726.

730 to 731   Lomán Blake (M)—lover of Severii, and a wastrel who sold Lámh Shábhála to pay off gambling debts.

731 to 741   Donnan McEvoy (M)—kept Lámh Shábhála, hoping that the mage-lights would return. They didn't. Donnan, a gambler, was killed in a tavern brawl in Dún Kiil, after which the stone passed

into the possession of Kinnat Móráin, who owned the tavern and confiscated the dead McEvoy's belongings.

741 to 753   Kinnat Móráin (F)

753 to 779   Edana Ó Bróin (F)—the daughter of Kinnat Móráin, who found the stone in her mam's jewelry chest after her death due to the Bloody Flux. Edana and her husband took over the tavern. She had no idea that the stone was Lám Shábhála; she kept it only because it had been her mam's. She happened to be wearing it on the day Doyle Báróid came to Dún Kiil on business and stopped in the tavern for a drink and a meal.

779 to 831   Doyle Báróid (M)—a Bráthair of the Order of Inishfeirm, who recognized that the unprepossessing stone around Edana's neck was similar to the description of Lámh Shábhála in the Order's library. He purchased it from Edana, and brought it back to Inishfeirm. He would eventually become Máister of the Order. On his death, the cloch was put in the collection of the Order.

831 to 1075   During these two and a half centuries, there was no single holder of the stone. The stone resided in the Order of Inishfeirm's collection of cloch na thintrí.

1075 to 1093   Kerys Aoire—Kerys fell in love with a man named Niall, one of the Bráthairs of the Inishfeirm Order. Niall, as a pledge of his love, stole the cloch and gave it to Kerys. Because the Bráthairs were contracted by their families to the Order and were forbidden to marry, Kerys and Niall fled Inishfeirm. Their small currach foundered in a storm; Niall drowned, but Kerys, pregnant, survived. She would give the cloch to her son, also named Niall.

1093 to 1113   Niall Aoire—in traveling, he came to Tuath Gabair and the village of Ballintubber, where he fell in love with and married a woman named Maeve Oldspring. Niall would lose the stone (or perhaps the stone lost him) while walking on Knobtop, a hill near Ballintubber.

1113 to 1129   none—during these years, the cloch lay on Knobtop.

1129 to 1169   **Jenna MacEagan (nee Aoire)—the First Holder of the new Filleadh.**

1169 to ????   **Sevei Geraghty, granddaughter of Jenna MacEagan**

A Partial List of Clochs Mór, Their Current Manifestations & Holders (as of opening of HEIR OF STONE)

Stormbringer (color: smoke gray)	Inish	A Siúr of the Order of Inishfeirm	Ability to control weather within a small defined area. Able to call rains, gale-force winds, and lightning. Though the direction of the winds can be controlled, the lightning cannot—it will strike randomly and unpredictably.
Blaze (color: bright red)	Inish	**Owaine Geraghty**	A fireball/lightning thrower.
Snarl (color: blue-green)	Inish	**Mundy Kirwan** of the Order of Inishfeirm	Capable of putting out ethereal, constricting tentacles with strength well beyond anything an unaided human could resist.
Firerock (color: ruddy)	Inish	**Kyle MacEagan**	Creates a creature of glowing lava
Scáil (color: reflective silver)	Inish	**Aithne MacBrádaigh**	Can mirror the effect of any other Cloch Mór, mimicking its power.
Demon-Caller (color: clear with red veins)	Tuatha	**Edana Mac Ard**	Creates a winged demon-creature.
Waterfire (color: sapphire)	Tuatha	A tiarna of the Tuatha	Produces blue streams of fiery, arcing energy.
Snapdragon (color: yellow laced with red)	Tuatha	**Doyle Mac Ard**	Creates a whiplike dragon whose tail wraps about its opponent, causing incredible pain as it chews at the flesh.
Rogue	Tuatha	A tiarna of the Tuatha	Creates a tsunamilike burst that crashes over its target, inundating it.
Sharpcut	Tuatha	A tiarna of Dún	Calls into being

		Laoghaire	dozens of glowing, yellow spears that slice through flesh as if wielded by an unseen infantry.
Weaver	Tuatha	A tiarna of the Tuatha	Creates a stinging web of force that constricts around its victim.
Nightmare	Tuatha	**Harkin O Seachnasaigh, Rí Connachta**	Gives the Holder the ability to read the mind of an enemy and create images of that person's worst fears or greatest loves.
Wolfen (color: ethereal amber crackled with black)	Tuatha	A tiarna of the Order of Gabair	Calls into being gigantic, wolves which attack at the Holder's command.
Tornado (color: black)	Tuatha	A tiarna of the Order of Gabair	An energy-sucker. Does no damage, but pulls power from another Cloch Mór, eventually draining it.
Quickship (color: sea-foam white)	Tuatha	**Shay O Blaca** of the Order of Gabair	Has the ability to transport one person (either the Holder or another) to a site of his/her choosing, and bring them back again.
Blackcloak	Tuatha	A tiarna of the Order of Gabair	Can cloak itself and chosen other people/objects within a few dozen feet of it so that others can't see them.
GodFist	Tuatha	A tiarna of the Order of Gabair	Creates an ethereal fist that can crush a person like an insect—the more spread-out the effect is (such as over several people) the less power it can generate.
Winter (color:	Tuatha	**Mal Mac Baoill**	Creates a wind of

clear with ultramarine veins)		(grandson of Rí Mac Baoill)	frigid gale force. Used broadly, it can sweep away arrows and hold back a mass of several people; focused, it can pick up a single person and hurl them several feet through the air.
Gnash	Tuatha	Torin Mallaghan	Envelopes its prey in a huge ethereal, fanged mouth.
Darkness	Tuatha	Cairbre Kavangh	Casts a pall of darkness in a circle around its holder, and only the holder can see within the false night.

Irene Radford
Merlin's Descendants

"Entertaining blend of fantasy and history, which invites comparisons with Mary Stewart and Marion Zimmer Bradley"   —*Publishers Weekly*

GUARDIAN OF THE PROMISE
This fourth novel in the series follows the children of Donovan and Griffin, in a magic-fueled struggle to protect Elizabethan England from enemies—both mortal and demonic.   *0-7564-0108-9*

And don't miss the first three books in this exciting series:
GUARDIAN OF THE BALANCE
0-88677-875-1
GUARDIAN OF THE TRUST
0-88677-995-2
GUARDIAN OF THE VISION
0-7564-0071-6

To Order Call: 1-800-788-6262

Tanya Huff

The Finest in Fantasy